One Thousand Poems for Children

One Thousand Poems for Children

BASED ON THE SELECTIONS OF ROGER INGPEN

Selected and arranged

by

Elizabeth (Hough) Sechrist , *1903 -*

WITH DECORATIVE DRAWINGS

by

Henry C. Pitz

Macrae-Smith-Company

Philadelphia

COPYRIGHT, 1946, MACRAE - SMITH - COMPANY

Thirteenth Printing

465

Manufactured in the United States of America

Acknowledgments

THE editor wishes to express her thanks and appreciation to the following publishers and authors for their kind permission to reprint their poems in this volume:

D. Appleton-Century Company, Inc. for " Jorridge and Porridge " by Louise Ayres Garnett from *St. Nicholas Magazine*, and the poems by William Cullen Bryant; The Bobbs-Merrill Company for the poems by James Whitcomb Riley from the Biographical Edition of his COMPLETE WORKS; Brandt & Brandt for " Tavern " by Edna St. Vincent Millay from RENASCENCE AND OTHER POEMS, published by Harper & Brothers, copyright, 1917, by Edna St. Vincent Millay; Bruce Humphries, Inc. for " Babushka—A Russian Legend " from CHILDREN OF CHRISTMAS by Edith M. Thomas, copyright, 1907, used by permission of Bruce Humphries, Inc.; Dodd, Mead & Company, Inc., for " Song of Summer " by Paul Laurence Dunbar from THE COMPLETE POEMS OF PAUL LAURENCE DUNBAR, reprinted by permission of Dodd, Mead & Company, Inc.; Doubleday & Company, Inc. for "The Animal Store " by Rachel Field from TAXIS AND TOADSTOOLS by Rachel Field, copyright, 1926, by Doubleday, Doran & Company, Inc.; " Fairies " and " Yesterday in Oxford Street " by Rose Fyleman from FAIRIES AND CHIMNEYS by Rose Fyleman, copyright, 1920, by Doubleday, Doran & Company, Inc.; E. P. Dutton & Company, Inc. for " O Little Town of Bethlehem " from CHRISTMAS SONGS AND EASTER CAROLS by Phillips Brooks, and " Pussy-Willows " from DEATH AND GENERAL PUTNAM by Arthur Guiterman; The Great-West Life Assurance Company and D. E. Kilgour for " In Flanders Fields " from IN FLANDERS FIELDS AND OTHER POEMS by John McCrae; Harcourt, Brace & Company, Inc. for " When Young Melissa Sweeps " from MAGPIE LANE by Nancy Byrd Turner, copyright, 1927, by Harcourt, Brace & Company, Inc., and " Questions at Night " by Louis Untermeyer from RAINBOW IN THE SKY edited by Louis Untermeyer, copyright, 1935, by Harcourt, Brace & Company, Inc.; George G. Harrap & Company, Ltd. for " Fairy Frilly," from THE LITTLE WHITE GATE by Florence Hoatson; Mrs. Katharine Tynan Hinkson for her poem " Chanticleer "; Henry Holt & Company, Inc., for " The Bee's Song " and " Martha " from PEACOCK PIE by Walter de la Mare, and " Wind in the Pine " from THE BOX OF GOD by Lew Sarett; Houghton Mifflin Company for " A Turkish Legend " by Thomas Bailey Aldrich from COMPLETE POEMS OF THOMAS BAILEY ALDRICH, " The Plaint of the Camel " and " Robinson Crusoe's Story " from DAVY AND THE GOBLIN by Charles E. Carryl, " The Chickadee " by Ralph Waldo Emerson, " The Reveille " by Bret Harte, " The Height of the Ridiculous " by Oliver Wendell Holmes, " March " by Lucy Larcom, " Yussouf " by James Russell Lowell, " Nikolina " from STORIES AND POEMS FOR CHILDREN by Celia Thaxter, " In School-Days " by John Greenleaf Whittier, also all selections included in this volume from the works of Henry Wadsworth Longfellow, Oliver Wendell Holmes, John Greenleaf Whittier, Lucy Larcom, Bayard Taylor, James Russell Lowell, John Townsend Trowbridge, Ralph Waldo Emerson, Christopher Pearse Cranch and

John Godfrey Saxe, by permission of and special arrangement with Houghton Mifflin Company, the authorized publishers of their works; J. B. Lippincott Company for "To England" by George Henry Boker, "Sheridan's Ride" by Thomas Buchanan Read and "Animal Crackers" from SONGS FOR A LITTLE HOUSE, copyright, 1917, by Christopher Morley, published by J. B. Lippincott Company; Little, Brown & Company for "How the Leaves Came Down" by Susan Coolidge, "The Grass" and "The Bee" by Emily Dickinson, "The Singing Lesson" by Jean Ingelow, "September" by Helen Hunt Jackson from COMPLETE POEMS OF HELEN HUNT JACKSON, and "At Easter Time" from IN MY NURSERY by Laura E. Richards; Robert M. McBride & Company for "Bells in the Country" from YOUTH GROWS OLD by Robert Nathan; The Macmillan Company for "My Dog" by John Kendrick Bangs from FOOTHILLS OF PARNASSUS, "The Old Woman of the Roads" by Padraic Colum from WILD EARTH AND OTHER POEMS, "An Explanation of the Grasshopper" by Vachel Lindsay, from COLLECTED POEMS, "Sea-Fever" by John Masefield from POEMS, "April" by Sara Teasdale from RIVERS TO THE SEA and "Barter" by Sara Teasdale from LOVE SONGS, all by permission of the Macmillan Company, publishers; Macrae-Smith-Company for "The Teapot Dragon," "P's and Q's," "Jack-in-the-Pulpit," "The Secrets of Our Garden," "Foolish Flowers," and "When I Grow Up" from ALL ROUND OUR HOUSE by Rupert Sargent Holland; Miss Juanita Joaquina Miller for "Columbus" by Joaquin Miller, by special permission; Milton Bradley Company for "The Five Little Fairies" from RHYMES FOR LITTLE HANDS by Maud Burnham; G. P. Putnam's Sons for "Bartholomew" by Norman Gale, "Rodney's Ride" by Elbridge Streeter Brooks, "What Am I?" from HOP! SKIP! AND JUMP! by Dorothy Aldis, courtesy of G. P. Putnam's Sons; Charles Scribner's Sons for "Jest 'Fore Christmas," "Seein' Things" and "Wynken, Blynken, and Nod" from POEMS OF CHILDHOOD by Eugene Field, "One, Two, Three" by H. C. Bunner, "The Sleepy Song" by Josephine Daskam Bacon from POEMS, 1903, "Snow-Flakes" by Mary Mapes Dodge from St. Nicholas Magazine, "Ducks' Ditty" by Kenneth Grahame from WIND IN THE WILLOWS, "Song of the Chattahoochee" by Sidney Lanier from POEMS, 1918, "The Vagabond" by Robert Louis Stevenson from COLLECTED POEMS and "America for Me" by Henry Van Dyke from THE TOILING OF FELIX; Yale University Press for "Prayer" from SONGS FOR PARENTS by John Farrar; and Mr. Virgil Markham for "A Prayer" from MAN WITH THE HOE by Edwin Markham and "Rules for the Road" from GATES OF PARADISE AND OTHER POEMS by Edwin Markham, reprinted by permission.

Acknowledgment is also made to D. Appleton-Century Company, Inc., for permission to reprint "The Elf and the Dormouse" by Oliver Herford from ARTFUL ANTICS; Brandt & Brandt for "Johnny Appleseed" by Rosemary Benét from A BOOK OF AMERICANS published by Rinehart & Company, Inc., copyright, 1933, by Rosemary and Stephen Vincent Benét; Jonathan Cape, Ltd. for "Happy Wind" by W. H. Davies from COLLECTED POEMS; Coward-McCann, Inc. for "The Mouse" by Elizabeth Coatsworth from COMPASS ROSE, copyright, 1929, by Coward-McCann, Inc.; Dodd, Mead & Company for "The Death of Robin Hood" by William Rose Benét, "Butterfly" by John Bannister Tabb, "A Vagabond Song" by Bliss Carmen, "The Soldier" by Rupert Brooke; Doubleday & Company, Inc. for "I'd Like to Be a Lighthouse" by Rachel Field from TAXIS AND TOADSTOOLS, copyright, 1926, Doubleday, Doran & Company, Inc., "Trees" by

Joyce Kilmer from TREES AND OTHER POEMS, copyright, 1914, by Doubleday, Doran & Company, Inc.; E. P. Dutton & Company, Inc. for " America the Beautiful " by Katherine Lee Bates from THE RETINUE AND OTHER POEMS; Rinehart & Company, Inc. for " The Swan " by John Gould Fletcher from SELECTED POEMS, copyright, 1938, by John Gould Fletcher; Follet Publishing Company for " The Airplane " by Rowena Bennett; Harcourt, Brace & Company, Inc. for " The Willow Cats " by Margaret Widdemer from LITTLE BOY AND GIRL LAND, copyright, 1924, by Harcourt, Brace & Company, Inc., " Evening Waterfall " by Carl Sandburg from SMOKE AND STEEL, copyright, 1920, by Harcourt, Brace & Company, Inc., " Leetla Giorgio Washeenton " by T. A. Daly from SELECTED POEMS; Harper & Brothers for " Mood from 3,000 B. C." by Genevieve Taggard from NOT MINE TO FINISH, " Trains " by James S. Tippett from I GO A-TRAVELING, " Near Dusk " by Joseph Auslander from NO TRAVELER RETURNS; Henry Holt & Company, Inc. for " Loveliest of Trees " by A. E. Housman from A SHROPSHIRE LAD, " A Prayer in Spring " and " Stopping by Woods on a Snowy Evening " by Robert Frost from COLLECTED POEMS; Houghton Mifflin Company for " The Fishing-Pole " by Mary Carolyn Davies from A LITTLE FRECKLED PERSON, " Trades " by Amy Lowell from PICTURES OF THE FLOATING WORLD, " The Brown Bear " by Mary Austin from CHILDREN SING IN THE FAR WEST, " The Waterfall " by Frank Dempster Sherman from LITTLE FOLK LYRICS; Doubleday & Company, Inc., The Macmillan Company of Canada, Ltd. and Mrs. George Bambridge for " If " by Rudyard Kipling from REWARDS AND FAIRIES, copyright, 1910, by Rudyard Kipling; Alfred A. Knopf, Inc. for " At the Aquarium " by Max Eastman, copyright, 1939, by Max Eastman, " Velvet Shoes " by Elinor Wylie from COLLECTED POEMS, copyright, 1932, by Alfred A. Knopf, Inc.; J. B. Lippincott Company for " Indian Children " by Annette Wynne from FOR DAYS AND DAYS, copyright, 1919, by J. B. Lippincott Company, " Sun and Wind " by Eleanor Farjeon from JOAN'S DOOR, copyright, 1926, by J. B. Lippincott Company, " Song of Sherwood " by Alfred Noyes from VOLUME I OF COLLECTED POEMS, copyright, 1906, by Alfred Noyes, " Prayer for a Pilot " by Cecil Roberts from POEMS, copyright, 1920, by J. B. Lippincott Company; Liveright Publishing Corp. for " Evening " by H. D. from COLLECTED POEMS; The Macmillan Company for " The Oxen " by Thomas Hardy from COLLECTED POEMS, " The Lake of Innisfree " by William Butler Yeats from EARLY POEMS AND STORIES," " The Rivals " by James Stephens from COLLECTED POEMS, " Frolic " by " AE " (G. W. Russell) from COLLECTED POEMS, " The Spider " by Robert P. Tristram Coffin from STRANGE HOLINESS and " Joy Meets Boy " from PRIMER FOR AMERICA; The Mosher Press for " A Christmas Folk-Song " and " The Lark " by Lizette Reese from A WAYSIDE LUTE; Random House, Inc. for " Evening Ebb " by Robinson Jeffers; Charles Scribner's Sons for " The Sugarplum Tree " and " The Duel " by Eugene Field from POEMS OF CHILDHOOD, " The Master " by Edward Arlington Robinson from THE TOWN DOWN BY THE RIVER; The Viking Press, Inc. for " Firefly " and " Milking Time " by Elizabeth Madox Roberts from UNDER THE TREE, copyright, 1922, 1930, by The Viking Press, Inc., New York; Miss Helen Wing for permission to reprint her poem " Other Children " and special permission from Jonathan Cape, The Housman Estate and the Society of Authors for the use of " Loveliest of Trees." Acknowledgment is also made to Punch, Methuen & Co., the Society of Authors and Miss Rose Fyleman for " Fairies " and " Yesterday in Oxford Street." The Macmillan Company for " Four-Leaf Clover " by Ella Higginson from WHEN THE BIRDS GO NORTH AGAIN.

Preface to the New Edition

POETRY, more than any other form of literature, has the quality of timelessness. It is that which makes it possible for the compiler of an anthology to delve into the writings of the past as well as those of the present for his material. And it is to the poetry of previous generations he is usually most indebted. Poems that have been read and reread and have become familiar and loved are the foundation of every anthology.

Since the original edition of ONE THOUSAND POEMS FOR CHILDREN was published fifty years ago, naturally there have been changes in standards and in the appeal of poetry to children. When the second edition was prepared some twenty-five years ago, many of the original poems were omitted and replaced with newer material. During the next quarter of a century other changes took place in the field of children's literature, these changes following a natural course in a rapidly altering world. It was the task of the editor of this new volume to omit that poetry which no longer appealed to the child of today. That task included the removal of certain didactic poems, poems whose subjects were no longer applicable to the life of the modern child, and poems whose authors have, with the passing years, become so little known as to have lost literary standing.

A glance at some of the poems of the earlier editions, now rejected, tell their own story.

> " Busy, curious, thirsty Fly,
> Drink with me, and drink as I;
> Freely welcome to my cup,
> Could'st thou sip, and sip it up."

The lines, " Observe, dear George, this nut so small, the acorn is its name "— and verses whose purpose is instruction have passed into oblivion, just as have those which deal with old-time customs that are no longer a part of the modern child's experience:

> " Joy to Philip! he this day
> Has his long coats cast away,
> And (the childish season gone)
> Puts the manly breeches on."

ix

However, in the selection of other poems to be discarded, the decision was not so easy. Some of the old poems of the earlier editions of this work are useful to librarians and teachers simply because it is difficult to find them in any other volume. And yet their usefulness is so limited that the editor felt their inclusion injudicious. In an age when children's poetry is alive and vigorous, and breathing with realism rather than coated with sweetness, it seemed unfair to the child-reader to include them.

The compiler of an anthology of poetry may be compared to a weaver. Each anthology must conform to a pattern, the threads carefully selected to form a design. Now, when an editor undertakes to reweave or rework that pattern, his is a difficult task. He wishes to retain the spirit of the original work, he hopes not to disturb too much the design woven there, and yet he must make strong the weak spots and use good materials in the reweaving.

In this new edition of ONE THOUSAND POEMS FOR CHILDREN, some four hundred poems have been replaced with others. Many are by modern poets, living and writing today. The arrangement has been changed to make a more thorough distinction in age groups. Part I includes poems for children from nursery age to sixth grade; Part II for children from seventh to tenth grades. In order that these two age groups should be more clearly defined it will be noticed that some of the subjects have been repeated. For instance, there are holiday poems in both sections, as well as humorous poems, poems of reverence, nature, and animal poetry. Parents, teachers, librarians and others working with poetry will recognize this change in plan upon glancing over the Table of Contents. It is hoped that the new arrangement will be helpful in using this volume, and that the users of the older book will recognize many old friends and be gladdened at the sight of new ones. Francis Bacon once said that old authors are best to read, but it was Samuel Johnson who declared: " I look upon every day to be lost in which I do not make a new acquaintance."

Within these pages the editor has endeavored to unite the new with the old. The old has endured and been proven over and over; the new will speak for itself in the years to come.

—*Elizabeth Hough Sechrist*

York, Pennsylvania
March, 1946

Contents

Poems for Younger Children

xi

Poems for Older Children

Contents

One Thousand Poems for Children

Part One

FOR THE NURSERY

Sing, sing, what shall I sing?
The cat has eaten the pudding-string!
Do, do, what shall I do?
The cat has bitten it quite in two.

>>><<<

Young lambs to sell!
Young lambs to sell!
If I'd as much money as I could tell,
I never would cry—Young lambs to
sell!

>>><<<

Pease-pudding hot,
Pease-pudding cold,
Pease-pudding in the pot,
Nine days old.
Some like it hot,
Some like it cold,
Some like it in the pot,
Nine days old.

>>><<<

A dillar, a dollar,
A ten o'clock scholar,
What makes you come so soon?
You used to come at ten o'clock
But now you come at noon.

Cross patch,
Draw the latch,
Sit by the fire and spin;
Take a cup,
And drink it up,
And call your neighbors in.

>>><<<

Hickory, dickory, dock,
The mouse ran up the clock;
The clock struck one,
The mouse ran down,
Hickory, dickory, dock.

>>><<<

Rowley Powley, pudding and pie,
Kissed the girls and made them cry;
When the girls came out to play,
Rowley Powley ran away.

>>><<<

Rub-a-dub-dub,
Three men in a tub,
And who do you think they be?
The butcher, the baker,
The candlestick-maker;
Turn 'em out, knaves all three!

3

As Tommy Snooks and Bessy Brooks
  Were walking out one Sunday,
Said Tommy Snooks to Bessy Brooks,
  "Tomorrow will be Monday."

-»)«(-

Mother, may I go in to swim?
  Yes, my darling daughter,
Hang your clothes on a hickory limb,
  But don't go near the water.

-»)«(-

Curly locks, curly locks! wilt thou be
  mine?
Thou shalt not wash dishes, nor yet
  feed the swine;
But sit on a cushion, and sew a fine
  seam,
And feed upon strawberries, sugar, and
  cream!

-»)«(-

See, saw, Margery Daw,
  Baby shall have a new master.
She can earn but a penny a day,
  Because she can't work any faster.

See, saw, Margery Daw,
  Sold her bed to lie upon straw.
Was not she a naughty puss,
  To sell her bed to lie on a truss?

-»)«(-

Polly, put the kettle on,
Polly, put the kettle on,
Polly, put the kettle on,
  And let's drink tea.

Sukey, take it off again,
Sukey, take it off again,
Sukey, take it off again,
  They're all gone away.

Mary, Mary, quite contrary,
  How does your garden grow?
With cockle-shells and silver bells
  And columbines all of a row.

-»)«(-

Little Miss Muffit,
  Sat on a tuffit,
Eating of curds and whey;
  There came a great spider
  That sat down beside her,
And frightened Miss Muffit away.

-»)«(-

Matthew, Mark, Luke and John,
Guard the bed that I lie on!
  Four corners to my bed,
  Four angels round my head—
One to watch, one to pray,
And two to bear my soul away.

-»)«(-

Little Polly Flinders,
  Sat among the cinders,
Warming her pretty little toes;
  Her mother came and caught her,
  And whipped her little daughter
For spoiling her nice new clothes.

-»)«(-

Come, let's to bed,
  Says Sleepy-head,
Tarry a while, says Slow,
  Put on the pan, says Greedy Nan,
Let's sup before we go.

-»)«(-

Hark, hark,
  The dogs do bark,
Beggars are coming to town;
  Some in jags
  Some in rags
And some in velvet gowns.

Barber, barber, shave a pig,
How many hairs will make a wig?
"Four and twenty, that's enough."
Give the barber a pinch of snuff.

->>><<<-

Oh where and oh where is my little
    wee dog?
Oh where and oh where is he?
With his ears cut short and his tail
    cut long,
Oh where and oh where can he be?

->>><<<-

Higglepy, Piggleby,
    My black hen,
She lays eggs
    For gentlemen;
Sometimes nine,
    And sometimes ten,
Higglepy, Piggleby,
    My black hen.

->>><<<-

"Come hither, little puppy-dog,
    I'll give you a new collar,
If you will learn to read your book,
    And be a clever scholar."
"No! no!" replied the puppy-dog,
    "I've other fish to fry;
For I must learn to guard your house,
    And bark when thieves come nigh."

->>><<<-

Ba, ba, black sheep,
    Have you any wool?
Yes, sir, no, sir,
    Three bags full.
One for my master,
    And one for my dame,
But none for the little boy
    Who cries in the lane.

Pussy sits beside the fire—
    How can she be fair?
In comes little puppy-dog:
    "Pussy, are you there?
So, so, Mistress Pussy,
    Pray how do you do?"
"Thank you, thank you, little dog,
    I'm very well just now."

->>><<<-

Goosey, goosey gander,
    Whither shall I wander?
Up stairs, down stairs,
    And in my lady's chamber:
There I met an old man
    That would not say his prayers,
I took him by the left leg,
    And threw him down stairs.

->>><<<-

Jack and Jill went up the hill,
    To fetch a pail of water;
Jack fell down and broke his crown
    And Jill came tumbling after.

Up Jack got and home did trot
    As fast as he could caper,
Dame Jill had the job, to plaster his
    knob,
    With vinegar and brown paper.

->>><<<-

Little Jack Horner sat in the corner
    eating a Christmas pie;
He put in his thumb, and he took out
    a plum,
And said, "What a good boy am I!"

->>><<<-

Bobby Shaftoe's gone to sea,
Silver buckles at his knee;
When he comes back, he'll marry
    me,
    Bonny Bobby Shaftoe.

Bobby Shaftoe's fat and fair,
Combing down his yellow hair;
He's my love for evermair,
   Bonny Bobby Shaftoe.

>>><<<

Is John Smith within?
Yes, that he is.
Can he set a shoe?
Ay, marry, two,
Here a nail, there a nail
Tick, tack, too.

>>><<<

Handy Spandy, Jack-a-dandy,
Loved plum-cake and sugar-candy;
He bought some at a grocer's shop,
And out he came, hop, hop, hop.

>>><<<

Hector Protector was dressed all in
   green;
Hector Protector was sent to the
   Queen.
The Queen did not like him, no more
   did the King;
So Hector Protector was sent back
   again.

>>><<<

Jack Spratt could eat no fat,
   His wife could eat no lean;
And so betwixt them both, you see,
   They lick'd the platter clean.

>>><<<

There were two blackbirds,
   Sitting on a hill,
The one named Jack,
   The other named Jill;
Fly away, Jack!
Fly away, Jill!
Come again, Jack!
Come again, Jill!

Little Tommy Tucker
Sings for his supper;
What shall he eat?
White bread and butter.
How shall he cut it
Without e'er a knife?
How will he be married
Without e'er a wife?

>>><<<

Little boy blue, come blow your horn,
The sheep's in the meadow, the cow's
   in the corn;
Where's the little boy that looks after
   the sheep?
He's under the hay-cock fast asleep.
Will you wake him? No, not I;
For if I do, he'll be sure to cry.

>>><<<

Tom, Tom, the piper's son,
Stole a pig and away he run!
The pig was eat, and Tom was beat,
And Tom went roaring down the
   street.

>>><<<

Peter White will ne'er go right:
   Would you know the reason why?
He follows his nose where'er he goes,
   And that stands all awry.

>>><<<

Tom he was the piper's son,
He learn'd to play when he was young,
But the only tune that he could play
Was, " Over the hills and far away."

>>><<<

Peter, Peter, pumpkin eater,
Had a wife and couldn't keep her;
He put her in a pumpkin shell
And there he kept her very well.

Hi! diddle diddle,
The cat and the fiddle,
The cow jumped over the moon;
The little dog laughed
To see such sport,
While the dish ran after the spoon.

BIRTHDAYS

Monday's child is fair of face,
Tuesday's child is full of grace,
Wednesday's child is full of woe,
Thursday's child has far to go,
Friday's child is loving and giving,
Saturday's child works hard for its living,
And a child that's born on the Sabbath day
Is fair and wise and good and gay.

Thirty days hath September,
April, June, and November;
February has twenty-eight alone.
All the rest have thirty-one,
Excepting leap-year, that's the time
When February's days are twenty-nine.

Multiplication is vexation,
Division is as bad;
The Rule of Three perplexes me
And Practice drives me mad.

He that would thrive
Must rise at five;
He that hath thriven
May lie till seven;
And he that by the plough would thrive,
Himself must either hold or drive.

They that wash on Monday
Have all the week to dry;
They that wash on Tuesday,
Are not so much awry;
They that wash on Wednesday
Are not so much to blame;
They that wash on Thursday,
Wash for shame;
They that wash on Friday,
Wash in need;
And they that wash on Saturday,
Oh, they are slovens, indeed.

For want of a nail, the shoe was lost;
For want of the shoe, the horse was lost;
For want of the horse, the rider was lost;
For want of the rider, the battle was lost;
For want of the battle, the kingdom was lost;
And all from the want of a horseshoe nail.

If wishes were horses,
Beggars would ride;
If turnips were watches,
I'd wear one by my side.

For every evil under the sun,
There is a remedy, or there is none.
If there be one, try and find it;
If there be none, never mind it.

I'll tell you a story
About Jack a Nory,—
And now my story's begun:
I'll tell you another
About Jack and his brother,—
And now my story's done.

Needles and pins, needles and pins,
When a man marries, his trouble
    begins.

➤➤❮❮❮

There was a crooked man, and he went
    a crooked mile.
He found a crooked sixpence against a
    crooked stile:
He bought a crooked cat, which caught
    a crooked mouse,
And they all lived together in a little
    crooked house.

➤➤❮❮❮

There was a man of Newington,
    And he was wondrous wise,
He jump'd into a quickset hedge,
    And scratch'd out both his eyes;
But when he saw his eyes were out,
    With all his might and main,
He jump'd into another hedge,
    And scratch'd 'em in again.

➤➤❮❮❮

There was a little man,
    And he had a little gun,
And his bullets were made of lead,
    lead, lead;
He shot Johnny King
Through the middle of his wig,
And knocked it right off his head,
    head, head.

➤➤❮❮❮

Solomon Grundy,
Born on a Monday,
Christened on Tuesday,
Married on Wednesday,
Took ill on Thursday,
Worse on Friday,
Died on Saturday,
Buried on Sunday.
This is the end of
Solomon Grundy.

There was an old man,
And he had a calf,
    And that's half;
He took him out of the stall,
And tied him to the wall,
    And that's all.

➤➤❮❮❮

The man in the moon
Came down too soon,
And asked his way to Norwich:
He went by the south,
And burnt his mouth
With eating cold plum-porridge.

➤➤❮❮❮

The man in the wilderness asked me,
How many strawberries grew in the
    sea?
I answered him as I thought good,
As many as red herrings grew in the
    wood.

➤➤❮❮❮

Three wise men of Gotham
Went to sea in a bowl:
And if the bowl had been stronger,
My song would have been longer.

➤➤❮❮❮

Mr. East gave a feast;
Mr. North laid the cloth;
Mr. West did his best;
Mr. South burnt his mouth
With eating a cold potato.

➤ ❮❮❮

Hot-cross buns!
Hot-cross buns!
One a penny, two a penny,
    Hot-cross buns!

Hot-cross buns!
Hot-cross buns!
If you have no daughters,
    Give them to your sons.

Poor old Robinson Crusoe!
Poor old Robinson Crusoe!
They made him a coat
Of an old nanny goat,
I wonder how they could do so!
With a ring a ting tang,
And a ring a ting tang,
Poor old Robinson Crusoe!

→»«←

Tweedle-dum and tweedle-dee
  Resolved to have a battle,
For tweedle-dum said tweedle-dee
  Had spoiled his nice new rattle.
Just then flew by a monstrous crow,
  As big as a tar barrel,
Which frightened both the heroes so,
  They quite forgot their quarrel.

→»«←

Robin Hood, Robin Hood,
Is in the mickle wood!
Little John, Little John,
He to the town is gone.

Robin Hood, Robin Hood,
  Is telling his beads,
All in the green wood,
  Among the green weeds.

Little John, Little John,
  If he comes no more,
Robin Hood, Robin Hood,
  He will fret full sore!

→»«←

Robin and Richard were two pretty
  men;
They lay in bed till the clock struck
  ten;
Then up starts Robin and looks at the
  sky;
Oh! brother Richard, the sun's very
  high:
You go on with bottle and bag,
And I'll follow after on jolly Jack Nag.

YANKEE DOODLE

Yankee Doodle went to town
  Upon a little pony;
He stuck a feather in his hat
  And called it Macaroni.

→»«←

Ding, dong, bell,
Pussy's in the well!
Who put her in?
Little Tommy Lin.
Who pulled her out?
Dog with long snout.
What a naughty boy was that
To drown poor pussy-cat,
Who never did any harm,
But kill'd the mice in his master's
  barn.

→»«←

I had a little pony,
  His mane was dapple gray,
I lent him to a lady,
  To ride a mile away.

She whipped him, she slashed him,
  She rode him through the mire;
I would not lend my pony now
  For the lady's hire.

→»«←

Pussy-cat, pussy-cat, where have you
  been?
I've been to London to look at the
  queen.
Pussy-cat, pussy-cat, what did you
  there?
I frighten'd a little mouse under the
  chair.

→»«←

Fiddle-de-dee, fiddle-de-dee,
The fly has married the bumble-bee;
They went to church, and married was
  she
The fly has married the bumble-bee.

The Lion and the Unicorn
  Were fighting for the crown;
The Lion beat the Unicorn
  All round about the town,
Some gave them white bread,
  And some gave them brown;
Some gave them plum-cake,
  And sent them out of town.

※

    Sneel, snaul,
Robbers are coming to pull down your
  wall;
    Sneel, snaul,
    Put out your horn,
Robbers are coming to steal your corn,
Coming at four o'clock in the morn.

※

    Pussycat Mole
    Jumped over a coal,
And in her best petticoat burnt a great
  hole.
Poor Pussy's weeping, she'll have no
  more milk,
Until her best petticoat's mended with
  silk.

※

Hey, my kitten, my kitten,
  And hey, my kitten, my deary,
Such a sweet pet as this
  Was neither fat nor weary.

※

To market, to market, to buy a fat pig.
  Home again, home again, dancing a
    jig;
To market, to market, to buy a fat hog,
  Home again, home again, jiggety-jog.

※

    Bye, baby bunting,
    Daddy's gone a hunting
    To get a little rabbit-skin
    To wrap a baby bunting in.

    Hush thee, my babby,
    Lie still with thy daddy,
Thy mammy has gone to the mill,
    To grind thee some wheat
    To make thee some meat,
And so, my dear babby, lie still.

※

Ride a cock-horse to Banbury Cross,
To see an old lady upon a white horse,
Rings on her fingers, and bells on her
  toes,
And so she makes music wherever she
  goes.

※

Dance, little baby, dance up high,
Never mind, baby, mother is by;
Crow and caper, caper and crow,
There, little baby, there you go;

Up to the ceiling, down to the ground,
Backwards and forwards, round and
  round;
Dance, little baby, and mother will
  sing,
With the merry chorus, ding, ding,
  ding!

※

There was an old woman toss'd up
  in a basket
  Nineteen times as high as the
    moon;
Where she was going I couldn't but
  ask it,
  For in her hand she carried a
    broom.
"Old woman, old woman, old
  woman," quoth I,
  "O whither, O whither, O
    whither so high?"
"To brush the cobwebs off the sky!"
  "Shall I go with thee?" "Ay, by-
    and-by."

Here we go up, up, up,
   And here we go down, down, downy
And here we go backwards and for-
   wards
     And here we go round, round,
     roundy.

-»)«(-

There was an old woman, and what do
   you think?
She lived upon nothing but victuals
   and drink:
Victuals and drink were the chief of
   her diet:
This tiresome old woman could never
   be quiet.

She went to the baker to buy her some
   bread,
And when she came home her old husband was dead;
She went to the clerk to toll the bell,
And when she came back her old husband was well.

-»)«(-

" Old woman, old woman, shall we go
   shearing? "
" Speak a little louder, sir, I am very
   thick of hearing."
" Old woman, old woman, shall I love
   you dearly? "
" Thank you, kind sir, I hear you very
   clearly."

-»)«(-

Doctor Faustus was a good man,
He whipt his scholars now and then;
When he whipp'd them he made them
   dance
Out of Scotland into France,
Out of France into Spain,
And then he whipp'd them back
   again!

There was an old woman who lived in
   a shoe,
She had so many children she didn't
   know what to do;
She gave them some broth without any
   bread,
She whipped them all round, and put
   them to bed.

-»)«(-

See-saw sacradown,
Which is the way to London town?
One foot up, the other foot down,
That is the way to London town.

-»)«(-

There was an old woman
   Lived under a hill;
And if she's not gone,
   She lives there still.

-»)«(-

Blow, wind, blow! and go, mill, go!
   That the miller may grind his corn;
That the baker may take it and into
   rolls make it,
   And send us some hot in the morn.

-»)«(-

If all the world were apple pie,
   And all the sea were ink,
And all the trees were bread and
   cheese,
   What should we have to drink?

-»)«(-

Bat, bat, come under my hat,
And I'll give you a slice of bacon;
   And when I bake,
   I'll give you a cake,
If I am not mistaken.

-»)«(-

Sing a song of sixpence,
   A pocket full of rye;

Four and twenty blackbirds
  Baked in a pie;

When the pie was opened
  The birds began to sing;
Was not that a dainty dish
  To set before the king?

The king was in his counting-
    house
  Counting out his money;
The queen was in the parlor
  Eating bread and honey;

The maid was in the garden
  Hanging out the clothes,
There came a little blackbird
  And snapt off her nose.

->»)«<-

Old King Cole
Was a merry old soul,
And a merry old soul was he;
He called for his pipe,
And he called for his bowl,
And he called for his fiddlers three.
Every fiddler, he had a fiddle,
And a very fine fiddle had he;
Twee tweedle dee, tweedle dee,
Went the fiddlers.
Oh, there's none so rare,
As can compare
With King Cole and his fiddlers
  three!

->»)«<-

A cat came fiddling out of a barn,
With a pair of bagpipes under her arm;
She could sing nothing but fiddle cum
  fee,
The mouse has married the bumble-
  bee.
Pipe, cat—dance, mouse,
We'll have a wedding at our good
  house.

Six little mice sat down to spin,
Pussy passed by, and she peeped in.
" What are you at, my little men? "
" Making coats for gentlemen."

" Shall I come in and bite off your
  threads? "
" No, no, Miss Pussy, you'll snip off
  our heads."
" Oh, no, I'll not, I'll help you to
  spin."
" That may be so, but you don't come
  in! "

->»)«<-

Pretty maid,
Pretty maid,
Where have you been?
  Gathering a posie
To give to the queen.

Pretty maid,
Pretty maid,
What gave she you?
  She gave me a diamond
As big as my shoe.

->»)«<-

Cock a doodle doo!
My dame has lost her shoe;
My master's lost his fiddling stick,
And don't know what to do.

Cock a doodle doo!
What is my dame to do?
Till master finds his fiddling stick,
She'll dance without her shoe.

Cock a doodle doo!
My dame has found her shoe,
And master's found his fiddling stick,
Sing doodle doodle do!

Cock a doodle doo!
My dame will dance with you,
While master fiddles his fiddling stick,
For dame and doodle doo.

Where are you going, my pretty maid?
I am going a-milking, sir, she said.
May I go with you, my pretty maid?
You're kindly welcome, sir, she said.
What is your father, my pretty maid?
My father's a farmer, sir, she said.
Say, will you marry me, my pretty
  maid?
Yes, if you please, kind sir, she said.
Will you be constant, my pretty maid?
That I can't promise you, sir, she said.
Then I won't marry you, my pretty
  maid!
Nobody asked you, sir! she said.

THERE WAS A PIPER

There was a piper had a cow,
  And he'd no hay to give her.
He took his pipe, and played a tune,—
  " Consider, cow, consider."

The cow considered very well,
  For she gave the piper a penny,
That he might play the tune again
  Of " Corn rigs are bonnie."

    The Queen of Hearts
    She made some tarts,
All on a summer's day;
    The Knave of Hearts
    He stole those tarts,
And with them ran away.

    The King of Hearts
    Called for the tarts,
And beat the Knave full sore;
    The Knave of Hearts
    Brought back the tarts,
And vowed he'd steal no more!

Taffy was a Welshman, Taffy was a
  thief,

Taffy came to my house, and stole a
  piece of beef;
I went to Taffy's house, Taffy was not
  at home;
Taffy came to my house, and stole a
  marrow-bone;
I went to Taffy's house, Taffy was not
  in;
Taffy came to my house, and stole a
  silver pin;
I went to Taffy's house, Taffy was in
  bed;
I took up a poker and flung it at his
  head.

Simple Simon met a pieman
  Going to the fair;
Says Simple Simon to the pieman,
  " Let me taste your ware."

Says the pieman to Simple Simon,
  " Show me first your penny,"
Says Simple Simon to the pieman,
  " Indeed I have not any."

Simple Simon went a-fishing
  For to catch a whale;
All the water he had got
  Was in his mother's pail.

What are little boys made of, made of,
What are little boys made of?
Snaps and snails, and puppy-dogs' tails;
And that's what little boys are made of,
  made of.

What are little girls made of, made of,
What are little girls made of?
Sugar and spice, and all that's nice;
And that's what little girls are made of,
  made of.

THIS IS THE HOUSE THAT JACK BUILT

This is the house that Jack built.

This is the malt that lay in the house
that Jack built.

This is the rat that ate the malt, etc.

This is the cat that killed the rat, etc.

This is the dog that worried the cat,
etc.

This is the cow with the crumpled
horn
That tossed the dog, etc.

This is the maiden all forlorn
That milk'd the cow with the crumpled horn, etc.

This is the man all tatter'd and torn
That kiss'd the maiden all forlorn, etc.

This is the priest all shaven and shorn,
That married the man all tatter'd and
torn, etc.

This is the cock that crowed in the
morn,
That waked the priest all shaven and
shorn, etc.

This is the farmer sowing his corn,
That kept the cock that crow'd in the
morn,
That waked the priest all shaven and
shorn,
That married the man all tatter'd and
torn,
That kissed the maiden all forlorn,
That milk'd the cow with the crum-
pled horn,
That tossed the dog,
   That worried the cat,

That kill'd the rat,
   That ate the malt,
That lay in the house that Jack built.

→》《←

I had a little husband
   No bigger than my thumb;
I put him in a pint pot,
   And there I bid him drum.

I bought him a little horse,
   That galloped up and down.
I bridled him and saddled him,
   And sent him out of town.

I gave him some garters,
   To garter up his hose,
And a little handkerchief,
   To wipe his pretty nose.

→》《←

Little Bo-peep has lost her sheep,
   And can't tell where to find them;
Leave them alone, and they'll come
   home,
   And bring their tails behind them.

Little Bo-peep fell fast asleep,
   And dreamt she heard them bleat-
   ing;
And when she awoke, she found it a
   joke,
   For they still were all fleeting.

Then up she took her little crook,
   Determin'd for to find them;
She found them indeed, but it made
   her heart bleed,
   For they'd left all their tails behind
   'em.

→》《←

I had a little nut tree,
   Nothing would it bear,
But a silver nutmeg,
   And a golden pear,

The King of Spain's daughter
  Came to visit me,
And all was because of
  My little nut tree.
I skipped over water,
  I danced over sea,
And all the birds in the air
  Could not catch me.

>><<<

Johnny shall have a new bonnet,
  And Johnny shall go to the fair,
And Johnny shall have a blue ribbon
  To tie up his bonny brown hair.

And why may I not love Johnny?
  And why may not Johnny love me?
And why may I not love Johnny,
  As well as another body?

And here's a leg for a stocking,
  And here's a leg for a shoe,
And he has a kiss for his daddy,
  And two for his mammy, I trow.

And why may I not love Johnny?
  And why may not Johnny love me?
And why may I not love Johnny,
  As well as another body?

OH! DEAR! WHAT CAN THE MATTER BE?

Oh! dear! what can the matter be?
Dear! dear! what can the matter be?
Oh! dear! what can the matter be?
Johnny's so long at the fair.

He promis'd he'd buy me a fairing
  should please me,
And then for a kiss, oh! he vow'd he
  would teaze me;
He promis'd he'd bring me a bunch
  of blue ribbons
To tie up my bonny brown hair.

Oh! dear! what can the matter be?
Dear! dear! what can the matter be?
Oh! dear! what can the matter be?
Johnny's so long at the fair.

He promis'd he'd bring me a basket
  of posies,
A garland of lilies, a garland of roses,
A little straw hat, to set off the blue
  ribbons
That tie up my bonny brown hair.

And it's oh dear! what can the matter
  be?
Dear! dear! what can the matter be?
Oh! dear! what can the matter be?
Johnny's so long at the fair.

>><<<

When good King Arthur ruled this
  land,
  He was a goodly king;
He stole three pecks of barley meal,
  To make a bag-pudding.

A bag-pudding the king did make,
  And stuff'd it well with plums;
And in it put great lumps of fat,
  As big as my two thumbs.

The king and queen did eat thereof,
  And noblemen beside;
And what they could not eat that
  night,
  The queen next morning fried.

ALL AROUND THE MULBERRY BUSH

All around the mulberry bush,
        mulberry bush,
        mulberry bush,
All around the mulberry bush,
All on a Monday morning.

This is the way we wash our clothes,
      wash our clothes,
      wash our clothes,
This is the way we wash our clothes,
All on a Monday morning.

This is the way we hang our clothes,
      hang our clothes,
      hang our clothes,
This is the way we hang our clothes,
All on a Tuesday morning.

This is the way we sprinkle our clothes,
      sprinkle our clothes,
      sprinkle our clothes,
This is the way we sprinkle our clothes,
All on a Wednesday morning.

This is the way we iron our clothes,
      iron our clothes,
      iron our clothes,
This is the way we iron our clothes,
All on a Thursday morning.

This is the way we sweep our house,
      sweep our house,
      sweep our house,
This is the way we sweep our house,
All on a Friday morning.

This is the way we take a walk,
      take a walk,
      take a walk,
This is the way we take a walk,
All on a Saturday morning.

This is the way we go to church,
      go to church,
      go to church,
This is the way we go to church,
All on a Sunday morning.

All around the mulberry bush,
      mulberry bush,
      mulberry bush,
All around the mulberry bush,
All on a Sunday morning!

I saw a ship a-sailing,
    A-sailing on the sea;
And, oh! it was all laden
    With pretty things for thee!

There were comfits in the cabin,
    And apples in the hold;
The sails were made of silk,
    And the masts were made of gold,

The four-and-twenty sailors
    That stood between the decks,
Were four-and-twenty white mice,
    With chains about their necks,

The captain was a duck,
    With a packet on his back,
And when the ship began to move,
    The captain said, " Quack, quack! "

->>><<<-

I love sixpence, pretty little sixpence,
    I love sixpence, better than my life;
I spent a penny of it, I gave a penny
    of it,
    And I took fourpence home to my
    wife.

Oh! my little fourpence, pretty little
    fourpence,
    I love fourpence better than my life;
I spent a penny of it, I gave a penny
    of it,
    And I took twopence home to my
    wife.

Oh! my little twopence, pretty little
    twopence,
    I love twopence better than my life;
I spent a penny of it, I gave a penny
    of it,
    And I took nothing home to my
    wife.

Oh! my little nothing, pretty little
    nothing,

What will nothing buy for my wife;
I have nothing, I spend nothing,
   I love nothing better than my wife.

TO THE LADY-BIRD

Lady-bird! Lady-bird! fly away home;
   The field-mouse is gone to her nest,
The daisies have shut up their sleepy
     red eyes,
   And the birds and the bees are at
     rest.

Lady-bird! Lady-bird! fly away home;
   The glow-worm is lighting her lamp,
The dew's falling fast, and your fine
     speckled wings
   Will flag with the close-clinging
     damp.

Lady-bird! Lady-bird! fly away home;
   The fairy-bells tinkle afar;
Make haste, or they'll catch you and
     harness you fast
   With a cobweb to Oberon's car.

→»«←

Upon a great black horse-ily
A man came riding cross-ily;
A lady out did come-ily,
Said she, "No one's at home-ily,

"But only little people-y,
  Who've gone to bed sleep-ily."
The rider on his horse-ily
Said to the lady, cross-ily,

"But are they bad or good-ily?
  I want it understood-ily."
"Oh, they act bad and bold-ily,
  And don't do what they're told-ily."

"Good-by!" said he, "dear Ma-am-
  ily,
I've nothing for your family."
And scampered off like mouse-ily
Away, way from the house-ily.

Old Mother Hubbard
  Went to the cupboard,
To get her poor dog a bone:
  But when she came there
  The cupboard was bare,
And so the poor dog had none.

She went to the baker's
  To buy him some bread,
But when she came back
  The poor dog was dead.

She went to the joiner's
  To buy him a coffin,
When she came back
  The dog was laughing.

She took a clean dish
  To get him some tripe,
But when she came back
  He was smoking his pipe.

She went to the fishmonger's
  To buy him some fish,
And when she came back
  He was licking the dish.

She went to the ale-house
  To get him some beer,
But when she came back
  The dog sat in a chair.

She went to the tavern
  For white wine and red,
But when she came back
  The dog stood on his head.

She went to the hatter's
  To buy him a hat,
And when she came back
  He was feeding the cat.

She went to the barber's
  To buy him a wig,
But when she came back
  He was dancing a jig.

She went to the fruiterer's
  To buy him some fruit,
But when she came back
  He was playing the flute.

She went to the tailor's
  To buy him a coat,
But when she came back
  He was riding a goat.

She went to the cobbler's
  To buy him some shoes,
But when she came back
  He was reading the news.

She went to the sempstress
  To buy him some linen,
But when she came back
  The dog was spinning.

She went to the hosier's
  To buy him some hose,
But when she came back
  He was dress'd in his clothes.

The dame made a curtsey,
  The dog made a bow,
The dame said, " your servant,"
  The dog said, " bow-wow."

I HAD A LITTLE DOGGY

I had a little Doggy that used to sit
  and beg;
But Doggy tumbled down the stairs
  and broke his little leg.
Oh! Doggy, I will nurse you, and try
  to make you well,
And you shall have a collar with a little silver bell.

Ah! Doggy, don't you think that you
  should very faithful be,
For having such a loving friend to

comfort you as me?
And when your leg is better, and you
  can run and play,
We'll have a scamper in the fields and
  see them making hay.

But, Doggy, you must promise (and
  mind your word you keep)
Not once to tease the little lambs, or
  run among the sheep;
And then the little yellow chicks that
  play upon the grass,
You must not even wag your tail to
  scare them as you pass.

WHEN I WAS A BACHELOR

When I was a bachelor
  I lived by myself;
And all the bread and cheese I got
  I put upon the shelf.

The rats and the mice
  They made such a strife,
I was forced to go to London
  To buy me a wife.

The streets were so bad,
  And the lanes were so narrow,
I was forced to bring my wife home
  In a wheelbarrow.

The wheelbarrow broke,
  And my wife had a fall,
Down came wheelbarrow,
  Little wife and all.

TREE ON THE HILL

On yonder hill there stands a tree;
Tree on the hill, and the hill stood
  still.

And on the tree there was a branch;
Branch on the tree, tree on the hill,
  and the hill stood still.

And on the branch there was a nest;
Nest on the branch, branch on the tree, tree on the hill, and the hill stood still.

And in the nest there was an egg;
Egg in the nest, nest on the branch, branch on the tree, tree on the hill, and the hill stood still.

And in the egg there was a bird;
Bird in the egg, egg in the nest, nest on the branch, branch on the tree, tree on the hill, and the hill stood still.

And on the bird there was a feather;
Feather on the bird, bird in the egg, egg in the nest, nest on the branch, branch on the tree, tree on the hill, and the hill stood still.

ROBIN REDBREAST

Little Robin Redbreast sat upon a tree,
Up went pussy-cat, and down went he;
Down came pussy-cat, and away Robin ran;
Said little Robin Redbreast, " Catch me if you can."

Little Robin Redbreast jumped upon a wall,
Pussy cat jumped after him, and almost got a fall;
Little Robin chirped and sang, and what did pussy say?
Pussy-cat said naught but " Mew," and Robin flew away.

THERE WAS A JOLLY MILLER

There was a jolly miller once,
  Lived on the river Dee;

He worked and sung from morn till night,
  No lark more blithe than he.

And this the burthen of his song
  Forever used to be—
I care for nobody, not I,
  If no one cares for me.

Isaac Bickerstaffe

A FARMER WENT TROTTING

A farmer went trotting upon his gray mare;
Bumpety, bumpety, bump!
With his daughter behind him, so rosy and fair;
Lumpety, lumpety, lump!

A raven cried croak! and they all tumbled down;
Bumpety, bumpety, bump!
The mare broke her knees, and the farmer his crown;
Lumpety, lumpety, lump!

The mischievous raven flew laughing away;
Bumpety, bumpety, bump!
And vowed he would serve them the same the next day;
Lumpety, lumpety, lump!

BALLAD OF THE FOX

The Fox jumped up on a moonlight night,
The stars were shining and all things bright;
" Oh, oh! " said the Fox, " it's a very fine night
For me to go through the town, e'oh! "

The Fox when he came to yonder
stile,
He lifted his ears and he listened a
while;
" Oh, oh! " said the Fox, " it is but a
short mile
From this to yonder town, e'oh! "

The Fox, when he came to the
Farmer's gate,
Who should he see but the Farmer's
Drake,
" I love you well for your master's
sake,
And I long to be picking your bones
e'oh! "

The grey Goose, she ran round the
haystack,
" Oh, oh! " said the Fox, " you are
very fat,
And you'll do very well to ride on
my back
From this to yonder town, e'oh! "

The Farmer's wife she jumped out
of bed,
And out of the window she popped
her head,
" Oh husband! oh husband! the Geese
are all dead,
For the Fox has been through the
town, e'oh! "

The Farmer he loaded his pistol
with lead,
And shot the old rogue of a Fox
through the head,
" Ah, ah! " said the Farmer, " I think
you're quite dead,
And no more you'll trouble the
town, e'oh! "

POOR COCK ROBIN

Who killed Cock Robin?
  I, said the Sparrow,
  With my bow and arrow,
I killed Cock Robin.

Who saw him die?
  I, said the Magpie,
  With my little eye,
I saw him die.

Who caught his blood?
  I, said the Fish,
  With my little dish,
I caught his blood.

Who made his shroud?
  I, said the Eagle,
  With my thread and needle,
I made his shroud.

Who'll dig his grave?
  The Owl, with aid
  Of mattock and spade
Will dig Robin's grave.

Who'll be the parson?
  I, said the Rook,
  With my little book,
I'll be the parson.

Who'll be the clerk?
  I, said the Lark,
  If not in the dark,
I'll be the clerk.

Who'll carry him to the grave?
  I, said the Kite,
  If not in the night,
I'll carry him to his grave.

Who'll be chief mourner?
  I, said the Swan,
  I'm sorry he's gone,
I'll be chief mourner.

Who'll bear his pall?
    We, said the Wren,
    Both the cock and the hen,
We'll bear the pall.

Who'll toll the bell?
    I, said the Bull,
    Because I can pull,
And I'll pull the bell.

Who'll lead the way?
    I, said the Martin,
    When ready for starting,
And I'll lead the way.

All the birds in the air
    Began sighing and sobbing,
When they heard the bell toll
    For poor Cock Robin.

To all it concerns,
    This notice apprises,
The sparrow's for trial
    At next bird assizes.

->>><<<-

Here comes a candle to light you to
    bed,
And here comes a chopper to chop off
    your head.

LONDON BRIDGE

London bridge is broken down,
    Dance o'er my lady lee;
London bridge is broken down,
    With a gay lady.

How shall we build it up again?
    Dance o'er my lady lee;
How shall we build it up again?
    With a gay lady.

Silver and gold will be stole away,
    Dance o'er my lady lee;
Silver and gold will be stole away,
    With a gay lady.

Build it up again with iron and steel,
    Dance o'er my lady lee;
Build it up again with iron and steel,
    With a gay lady.

Iron and steel will bend and bow,
    Dance o'er my lady lee;
Iron and steel will bend and bow,
    With a gay lady.

Build it up with wood and clay,
    Dance o'er my lady lee;
Build it up with wood and clay,
    With a gay lady.

Wood and clay will wash away,
    Dance o'er my lady lee;
Wood and clay will wash away,
    With a gay lady.

Build it up with stone so strong,
    Dance o'er my lady lee;
Huzza! 'twill last for ages long,
    With a gay lady.

PETER PIPER

Peter Piper picked a peck of pickled
    peppers;
A peck of pickled peppers Peter Piper
    picked;
If Peter Piper picked a peck of pickled
    peppers,
Where's the peck of pickled peppers
    Peter Piper picked?

->>><<<-

When a Twister a twisting will twist
    him a twist;

For the twisting of his twist, he three
times doth intwist;
But if one of the twines of the twist
do untwist,
The twine that untwisteth, untwisteth
the twine.

Untwirling the twine that untwisteth
between,
He twirls, with the twister, the two in
a twine.
Then twice having twisted the twines
of the twine
He twisteth the twine he had twined
in twain.

The twain that in twining, before in
the twine,
As twines were intwisted; he now doth
untwine;
'Twixt the twain inter-twisting a twine
more between,
He twirling his twister, makes a twist
of the twine.

>>)(<<

A Frog he would a-wooing go,
    Sing heigho says Rowley,
Whether his mother would let him or
no,
    *With a rowley powley gammon
    and spinach,*
    Heigho says Anthony Rowley.

So off he marched with his opera hat,
    Heigho says Rowley,
And on the way he met with a rat,
    With a rowley powley, etc.

And when they came to the mouse's
hall,
    Heigho says Rowley,
They gave a loud knock, and they gave
a loud call,
    With a rowley powley, etc.

Pray, Mrs. Mouse, are you within?
    Heigho says Rowley,
Yes, kind sir, I am sitting to spin,
    With a rowley powley, etc.

Pray, Mrs. Mouse, will you give us
some beer?
    Heigho says Rowley,
For Froggy and I are fond of good
cheer,
    With a rowley powley, etc.

Now while they were all a merry-
making,
    Heigho says Rowley,
The cat and her kittens came tumbling in,
    With a rowley powley, etc.

The cat she seized the rat by the
crown,
    Heigho says Rowley,
The kittens they pulled the little
mouse down,
    With a rowley powley, etc.

This put poor Frog in a terrible fright,
    Heigho says Rowley,
So he took up his hat, and he wished
them good-night,
    With a rowley powley, etc.

But as Froggy was crossing over a
brook,
    Heigho says Rowley,
A lily-white duck came and gobbled
him up,
    With a rowley powley, etc.

So there was an end of one, two and
three,
    Heigho says Rowley,
The rat, the mouse, and the little
Froggie!
    *With a rowley powley gammon
    and spinach,*
    Heigho says Anthony Rowley.

A was an apple-pie:
B bit it;
C cut it;
D dealt it;
E ate it;
F fought for it;
G got it;
H had it;
J joined it;
K kept it;
L longed for it;
M mourned for it;
N nodded at it;
O opened it;
P peeped in it;
Q quartered it;
R ran for it;
S stole it;
T took it;
V viewed it;
W wanted it;
X, Y, Z, and ampersand
All wish'd for a piece in hand.

TOM THUMB'S ALPHABET

A was an archer, who shot at a frog;
B was a butcher, he had a great dog;
C was a captain, all covered with lace;
D was a drunkard, and had a red face;
E was an esquire, with pride on his
brow;
F was a farmer, and followed the
plough;
G was a gamester, who had but ill
luck;
I was an innkeeper, who loved to
bouse;
J was a joiner, and built up a house;
K is King Edward, who governs Eng-
land;
L was a lady, who had a white hand;
M was a miser, and hoarded up gold;
N was a nobleman, gallant and bold;

O was an oyster girl, and went about
town;
P was a parson, and wore a black
gown;
Q was a queen, who wore a silk slip;
R was a robber, who wanted a whip;
S was a sailor, and spent all he got;
T was a tinker, and mended a pot;
U was an usurer, a miserable elf;
V was a vintner, who drank all him-
self;
W was a watchman, and guarded the
door;
X was expensive, and so became poor;
Y was a youth, that did not love
school;
Z was a zany, a poor harmless fool.

->>><<<-

Gay go up, and gay go down
To ring the bells of London town.

Bulls' eyes and targets,
Say the bells of St. Marg'ret's.

Brickbats and tiles,
Say the bells of St. Giles's.

Halfpence and farthings,
Say the bells of St. Martin's.

Oranges and lemons,
Say the bells of St. Clement's.

Pancakes and fritters,
Say the bells of St. Peter's.

Two sticks and an apple,
Say the bells of Whitechapel.

Old Father Baldpate,
Say the slow bells at Aldgate.

You owe me ten shillings,
Say the bells of St. Helen's.

Pokers and tongs,
Say the bells at St. John's.

Kettles and pans,
Say the bells at St. Ann's.

When will you pay me?
Say the bells at Old Bailey.

When I grow rich,
Say the bells at Shoreditch.

Pray when will that be?
Say the bells at Stepney.

I'm sure I don't know,
Says the great bell at Bow.

PEMMY WAS A PRETTY GIRL

Pemmy was a pretty girl,
  But Fanny was a better;
Pemmy look'd like any churl,
  When little Fanny let her.

Pemmy had a pretty nose,
  But Fanny had a better;
Pemmy oft would come to blows,
  But Fanny would not let her.

Pemmy had a pretty doll,
  But Fanny had a better;
Pemmy chatter'd like a poll,
  When little Fanny let her.

Pemmy had a pretty song,
  But Fanny had a better;
Pemmy would sing all day long,
  But Fanny would not let her.

Pemmy loved a pretty lad,
  And Fanny loved a better;
And Pemmy wanted for to wed,
  But Fanny would not let her.

THE DREAM OF A GIRL WHO LIVED AT SEVEN-OAKS

Seven sweet singing birds up in a tree;
Seven swift sailing-ships white upon
  the sea;
Seven bright weather-cocks shining in
  the sun;
Seven slim race-horses ready for a run;
Seven gold butterflies, flitting over-
  head;
Seven red roses blowing in a garden
  bed;
Seven white lilies, with honey bees in-
  side them;
Seven round rainbows with clouds to
  divide them;
Seven pretty little girls with sugar on
  their lips;
Seven witty little boys, whom every-
  body tips;
Seven nice fathers, to call little maids
  joys;
Seven nice mothers, to kiss the little
  boys;
Seven nights running I dreamt it all
  plain;
With bread and jam for supper I could
  dream it all again!
              William Brighty Rands

THE LITTLE STAR

Twinkle, twinkle, little star,
How I wonder what you are;
Up above the world, so bright,
Like a diamond in the night.

When the blazing sun is gone,
When he nothing shines upon,
Then you show your little light,
Twinkle, twinkle, all the night.

Then the traveller in the dark,
Thanks you for your tiny spark;

He could not tell which way to go
If you did not twinkle so.

In the dark blue sky you keep,
And often through my curtains peep;
For you never shut your eye
Till the sun is in the sky.

As your bright and tiny spark
Lights the traveller in the dark,
Though I know not what you are,
Twinkle, twinkle, little star.

Jane Taylor

THERE WAS A LITTLE GIRL

There was a little girl, who had a little
    curl
    Right in the middle of her forehead,
And when she was good, she was very,
    very good,
    But when she was bad she was
    horrid.

She stood on her head, on her little
    trundle-bed,
    With nobody by for to hinder;
She screamed and she squalled, she
    yelled and she bawled,
    And drummed her little heels
    against the winder.

Her mother heard the noise, and
    thought it was the boys
    Playing in the empty attic,
She rushed upstairs, and caught her
    unawares,
    And spanked her, most emphatic.

MARVELS

If all the seas were one sea,
What a *great* sea that would be!
If all the trees were one tree,

What a *great* tree that would be!
And if all the axes were one axe,
What a *great* axe that would be!
And if all the men were one man,
What a *great* man that would be!
And if the *great* man took the *great*
    axe,
And cut down the *great* tree
And let it fall into the *great* sea,
What a splish-splash *that* would be!

GRAMMAR IN RHYME

Three little words, you often see,
Are articles A, An, and The.
A Noun is the name of anything,
As School, or Garden, Hoop, or Swing.
Adjectives tell the kind of Noun,
As Great, Small, Pretty, White, or
    Brown.
Instead of Nouns the Pronouns stand,
Her head, His face, Your arm, My
    hand.
Verbs tell of something being done—
To Read, Count, Laugh, Sing, Jump,
    or Run.
How things are done the Adverbs tell,
As Slowly, Quickly, Ill, or Well.
Conjunctions join the words together—
As men And women, wind And
    weather.
The Preposition stands before
A noun, as In or Through a door,
The Interjection shows surprise,
As Oh! how pretty! Ah! how wise!
The Whole are called nine parts of
    speech,
Which reading, writing, speaking
    teach.

THIS IS THE KEY

This is the Key of the Kingdom:
    In that Kingdom is a city;
    In that city is a town;

In that town there is a street;
In that street there winds a lane;
In that lane there is a yard;
In that yard there is a house;
In that house there waits a room;
In that room an empty bed;
And on that bed a basket—
A Basket of Sweet Flowers:
  Of Flowers, of Flowers;
  A Basket of Sweet Flowers.

Flowers in a Basket;
Basket on the bed;
Bed in the chamber;
Chamber in the house;
House in the weedy yard;
Yard in the winding lane;
Lane in the broad street;
Street in the high town;
Town in the city;
City in the Kingdom—
This is the Key of the Kingdom;
  Of the Kingdom this is the Key.

I'M GLAD

I'm glad the sky is painted blue,
And earth is painted green,
With such a lot of nice fresh air
All sandwiched in between.

BABY SEEDS

In a milkweed cradle,
  Snug and warm,
Baby seeds are hiding,
  Safe from harm.
Open wide the cradle,
  Hold it high!
Come, Mr. Wind,
  Help them to fly.

RAIN

The rain is raining all around,
  It falls on field and tree,

It rains on the umbrellas here,
  And on the ships at sea.
Robert Louis Stevenson

HOBBLEDY HOPS

Hobbledy Hops,
He made some tops
  Out of the morning-glory;
He used the seed,—
He did indeed,
  And that's the end of my story.

A LITTLE COCK SPARROW

A little cock-sparrow sat on a green tree,
And he cherruped, he cherruped, so merry was he;
A naughty boy came with his wee bow and arrow,
Determined to shoot this little cock-sparrow.
This little cock-sparrow shall make me a stew,
And his giblets shall make me a little pie, too;
Oh, no! said the sparrow, I won't make a stew,
So he flapped his wings and away he flew!

THE COCK'S ON THE HOUSETOP

The cock's on the housetop blowing his horn,
The men are in the barn threshing the corn,
The maids are in the meadow making the hay,
The ducks are in the river swimming away.

MOTHER

Birdies with broken wings
Hide from each other,
But babies in trouble
Run home to mother.

THE CLOCKING HEN

" Will you take a walk with me,
My little wife, today?
There's barley in the barley-fields,
And hay-seed in the hay."

" Thank you," said the clocking hen;
" I've something else to do;
I'm busy sitting on my eggs,
I cannot walk with you."

" Clock, clock, clock, clock,"
Said the clocking hen;
" My little chicks will soon be hatch'd,
I'll think about it then."

The clocking hen sat on her nest,
She made it in the hay;
And warm and snug beneath her
breast
A dozen white eggs lay.

Crack, crack, went all the eggs;
Out dropp'd the chickens small!
" Clock," said the clocking hen,
" Now I have you all.

" Come along, my little chick,
I'll take a walk with you."
" Hallo! " said the barn-door cock,
" Cock-a-doodle-doo."

Ann Hawkshawe

ONE MISTY, MOISTY
MORNING

One misty, moisty morning,
When cloudy was the weather,

There I met an old man
Clothed all in leather;
Clothed all in leather,
With cap under his chin,—
How do you do, and how do you do,
And how do you do again?

STITCHING

A pocket handkerchief to hem—
Oh dear, oh dear, oh dear!
How many stitches it will take
Before it's done, I fear.

Yet set a stitch and then a stitch,
And stitch and stitch away,
Till stitch by stitch the hem is
done—
And after work is play!

Christina Rossetti

THE MUFFIN-MAN'S BELL

" Tinkle, tinkle, tinkle ": 'tis the
muffin-man you see:
" Tinkle, tinkle," says the muffin-
man's bell;
" Any crumpets, any muffins, any
cakes for your tea:
There are plenty here to sell."

" Tinkle," says the little bell, clear
and bright;
" Tinkle, tinkle," says the muffin-
man's bell;
We have had bread and milk for
supper tonight,
And some nice plum-cake as well.

" Tinkle, tinkle, tinkle," says the lit-
tle bell again,
But it sounds quite far away;
" If you don't buy my muffins and
my cakes, it is plain
I must take them home today."

Ann Hawkshawe

MIX A PANCAKE

Mix a pancake,
Stir a pancake,
   Pop it in the pan.

Fry a pancake,
Toss a pancake,
   Catch it if you can.

Christina Rossetti

THE CLOCK

Tick, tock, tick, tock,
Merrily sings the clock;
It's time for work,
It's time for play,
So it sings throughout the day.
Tick, tock, tick, tock,
Merrily sings the clock.

TIME TO RISE

A birdie with a yellow bill
Hopped upon my windowsill,
Cocked his shining eye and said:
" Ain't you 'shamed, you sleepy-
   head! "

Robert Louis Stevenson

HERE WE COME A-PIPING

Here we come a-piping,
In Springtime and in May;
Green fruit a-ripening,
And Winter fled away.
The Queen she sits upon the strand,
Fair as lily, white as wand;
Seven billows on the sea,
Horses riding fast and free,
And bells beyond the sand.

MERRY ARE THE BELLS

Merry are the bells, and merry would
   they ring,
Merry was myself, and merry could I
   sing;
With a merry ding-dong, happy, gay,
   and free,
And a merry sing-song, happy let us be!

Merry have we met, and merry have
   we been;
Merry let us part, and merry meet
   again;
With our merry sing-song, happy, gay,
   and free;
With a merry ding-dong, happy let us
   be!

WATER JEWELS

A million little diamonds
   Twinkled on the trees;
And all the little maidens said,
   " A jewel, if you please! "

But when they held their hands
   outstretched
   To catch the diamonds gay,
A million little sunbeams came,
   And stole them all away.

Mary F. Butts

GIRLS AND BOYS COME OUT TO PLAY

Girls and boys come out to play,
The moon doth shine as bright as day;
Leave your supper, and leave your
   sleep,
And come with your playfellows into
   the street.
Come with a whoop, come with a call,
Come with a goodwill or not at all.
Up the ladder and down the wall,
A half-penny roll will serve us all.
You find milk, and I'll find flour,
And we'll have a pudding in half-an-
   hour.

HEARTS, LIKE DOORS

Hearts, like doors, will ope with ease
To very, very little keys,
And don't forget that two of these
Are "Thank you, sir" and "If you
    please."

OLD CHAIRS TO MEND

If I had as much money as I could
    spend,
I never would cry old chairs to mend;
Old chairs to mend, old chairs to
    mend;
I never would cry old chairs to mend.

If I had as much money as I could tell,
I never would cry old clothes to sell;
Old clothes to sell, old clothes to sell!
I never would cry old clothes to sell.

THE TWO DOGS

Two little dogs
Sat by the fire,
Beside a scuttle of coal-dust;
Said one little dog
To the other little dog,
"If you don't talk, why, I must."

JENNY WREN

Jenny Wren fell sick
    Upon a merry time;
In came Robin Redbreast,
    And brought her sops and wine.

Eat well of the sop, Jenny,
    Drink well of the wine;
Thank you, Robin, kindly,
    You shall be mine.

Jenny, she got well,
    And stood upon her feet,
And told Robin plainly,
    She lov'd him not a bit.

Robin being angry,
    Hopped upon a twig,
Saying, Out upon you, Jenny!
    Fie upon you, bold faced jig!

THE CHORUS OF FROGS

"Yaup, yaup, yaup!"
Said the croaking voice of a frog:
    "A rainy day
    In the month of May,
And plenty of room in the bog."

"Yaup, yaup, yaup!"
Said the frog, as it hopped away:
    "The insects feed
    On the floating weed,
And I'm hungry for dinner today."

"Yaup, yaup, yaup!"
Said the frog as it splashed about:
    "Good neighbors all,
    When you hear me call,
It is odd that you do not come out."

"Yaup, yaup, yaup!"
Said the frogs; "it is charming
    weather;
    We'll come and sup
    When the moon is up,
And we'll all of us croak together."
                Ann Hawkshawe

TWENTY FROGGIES

Twenty froggies went to school
Down beside a rushy pool.
Twenty little coats of green,
Twenty vests all white and clean.

"We must be in time," said they,
"First we study, then we play;
    That is how we keep the rule,
    When we froggies go to school."

Master Bull-frog, brave and stern,
Called his classes in their turn,
Taught them how to nobly strive,
Also how to leap and dive;

Taught them how to dodge a blow,
From the sticks that bad boys throw.
Twenty froggies grew up fast,
Bull-frogs they became at last;

Polished in a high degree,
As each froggie ought to be,
Now they sit on other logs,
Teaching other little frogs.

George Cooper

A LITTLE HOBBY-HORSE

There was a little hobby-horse,
  Whose name I do not know,—
An idle little hobby-horse,
  That said he wouldn't go.

But his master said, " If it be so
  That you will only play,
You idle rogue, you shall not eat
  My nice sweet clover-hay! "

Then Hobby shook his saucy head,
  And said, " If that's the case,
Rather than go without my hay,
  I'll try and mend my pace."

Eliza Grove

I LOVE LITTLE PUSSY

I love little Pussy.
  Her coat is so warm,
And if I don't hurt her,
  She'll do me no harm.
So I'll not pull her tail,
  Or drive her away,
But Pussy and I
  Very gently will play,

She will sit by my side,
  And I'll give her her food,
And she'll like me because
  I am gentle and good.

I'll pat little Pussy,
  And then she will purr,
And thus show her thanks
  For my kindness to her;
I'll not pinch her ears,
  Nor tread on her paw,
Lest I should provoke her
  To use her sharp claw;
I never will vex her,
  Nor make her displeased,
For Pussy can't bear
  To be worried or teased.

Jane Taylor

THE THREE LITTLE KITTENS

Three little kittens lost their mittens;
  And they began to cry,
  " Oh, mother dear,
    We very much fear
That we have lost our mittens."
  " Lost your mittens!
    You naughty kittens!
Then you shall have no pie."

The three little kittens found their
    mittens;
  And they began to cry,
  " Oh, mother dear,
    See here, see here!
See, we have found our mittens! "
  " Put on your mittens,
    You silly kittens,
And you may have some pie."
  " Purr-r, purr-r, purr-r,
Oh, let us have some pie!
    Purr-r, purr-r, purr-r."

The three little kittens put on their
    mittens,

And soon ate up the pie.
"Oh, mother dear,
  We greatly fear
That we have soiled our mittens!"
"Soiled your mittens!
  You naughty kittens!"
Then they began to sigh,
"Mee-ow, mee-ow, mee-ow."

The three little kittens washed their
    mittens,
  And hung them out to dry;
"Oh, mother dear,
  Do you not hear
That we have washed our mittens?"
"Washed your mittens!
  Oh, you're good kittens!
But I smell a rat close by;
  Hush, hush! mee-ow, mee-ow."
"We smell a rat close by,
  Mee-ow, mee-ow, mee-ow."

THE CATS HAVE COME
TO TEA

What did she see,—oh, what did she
    see,
As she stood leaning against the tree?
Why, all the cats had come to tea.

What a fine turn-out from round
    about!
All the houses had let them out,
And here they were with scamper
    and shout.

"Mew, mew, mew!" was all they
    could say,
And, "We hope we find you well
    today."

Oh, what would she do—oh, what
    should she do?
What a lot of milk they would get
    through;

For here they were with. "Mew,
    mew, mew!"

She did not know—oh, she did not
    know,
If bread and butter they'd like or no;
They might want little mice, oh! oh!
    oh!

Dear me—oh, dear me,
All the cats had come to tea.

Kate Greenaway

ROMANCE

I saw a ship a-sailing,
  A-sailing on the sea;
Her masts were of the shining gold,
  Her deck of ivory;
And sails of silk, as soft as milk,
  And silvern shrouds had she.

And round about her sailing,
  The sea was sparkling white,
The waves all clapped their hands and
    sang
  To see so fair a sight.
They kissed her twice, they kissed her
    thrice,
  And murmured with delight.

Then came the gallant captain,
  And stood upon the deck;
In velvet coat, and ruffles white,
  Without a spot or speck;
And diamond rings, and triple strings
  Of pearls around his neck.

And four-and-twenty sailors
  Were round him bowing low;
On every jacket three times three
  Gold buttons in a row;
And cutlasses down to their knees;
  They made a goodly show.

And then the ship went sailing,
  A-sailing o'er the sea;
She dived beyond the setting sun,
  But never back came she,
For she found the lands of the golden
    sands,
  Where the pearls and diamonds be.

Gabriel Setoun

THE MEN OF GOTHAM

Seamen three! What men be ye?
Gotham's three wise men we be.
Whither in your bowls so free?
To rake the moon from out the sea.
The bowl goes trim. The moon doth
    shine.
And our ballast is old wine—
And your ballast is old wine.

Who art thou, so fast adrift?
I am he they call Old Care.
Here on board we will thee lift.
No: I may not enter there.
Wherefore so? 'Tis Jove's decree,
In a bowl Care may not be—
In a bowl Care may not be.

Fear ye not the waves that roll?
No; in charmèd bowl we swim.
What the charm that floats the bowl?
Water may not pass the brim.
The bowl goes trim. The moon doth
    shine.
And our ballast is old wine—
And your ballast is old wine.

Thomas Love Peacock

LADY MOON

Lady Moon, Lady Moon, where are
  you roving?
    " Over the sea."
Lady Moon, Lady Moon, whom are
  you loving?
    " All that love me."

Are you not tired with rolling, and
  never
    Resting to sleep?
Why look so pale and so sad, as forever
    Wishing to weep?

" Ask me not this, little child, if you
  love me:
    You are too bold:
I must obey my dear Father above
  me,
    And do as I'm told."

Lady Moon, Lady Moon, where are
  you roving?
    " Over the sea."
Lady Moon, Lady Moon, whom are
  you loving?
    " All that love me."

Lord Houghton

MOON, SO ROUND AND YELLOW

Moon, so round and yellow,
  Looking from on high,
How I love to see you
  Shining in the sky.
Oft and oft I wonder,
  When I see you there,
How they get to light you,
  Hanging in the air:

Where you go at morning,
  When the night is past,
And the sun comes peeping
  O'er the hills at last.
Sometime I will watch you
  Slyly overhead,
When you think I'm sleeping
  Snugly in my bed.

Matthias Barr

OH! LOOK AT THE MOON

Oh! look at the moon,
  She is shining up there;
Oh! mother, she looks
  Like a lamp in the air.

Last week she was smaller,
  And shaped like a bow;
But now she's grown bigger,
  And round as an O.

Pretty moon, pretty moon,
  How you shine on the door,
And make it all bright
  On my nursery floor!

You shine on my playthings,
  And show me their place,
And I love to look up
  At your pretty bright face.

And there is a star
  Close by you, and may be
That small, twinkling star
  Is your little baby.

  Eliza Lee Follen

LITTLE WHITE LILY

Little White Lily sat by a stone,
Drooping and waiting till the sun
  shone.
Little White Lily sunshine has fed;
Little White Lily is lifting her head.

Little White Lily said: "It is good,
Little White Lily's clothing and food."
Little White Lily dressed like a bride!
Shining with whiteness, and crownèd
  beside!

Little White Lily drooping with pain,
Waiting and waiting for the wet rain,
Little White Lily holdeth her cup;
Rain is fast falling and filling it up.

Little White Lily said: "Good again,
When I am thirsty to have the nice
  rain.
Now I am stronger, now I am cool;
Heat cannot burn me, my veins are so
  full."

Little White Lily smells very sweet;
On her head sunshine, rain at her feet.
Thanks to the sunshine, thanks to the
  rain,
Little White Lily is happy again.

  George Macdonald

HOW THE LITTLE KITE
LEARNED TO FLY

" I never can do it," the little kite said,
  As he looked at the others high over
    his head;
" I know I should fall if I tried to fly."
" Try," said the big kite; " only try!
  Or I fear you never will learn at all."
  But the little kite said, " I'm afraid
    I'll fall."

The big kite nodded: "Ah, well,
  good-by;
I'm off;" and he rose toward the
  tranquil sky.
Then the little kite's paper stirred
  at the sight,
And trembling he shook himself free
  for flight.
First whirling and frightened, then
  braver grown,
Up, up he rose through the air alone,
Till the big kite looking down could
  see
The little one rising steadily.

Then how the little kite thrilled
  with pride,
As he sailed with the big kite side
  by side!

While far below he could see the
   ground,
And the boys like small spots moving round.
They rested high in the quiet air,
And only the birds and the clouds
   were there.
"Oh, how happy I am!" the little
   kite cried,
"And all because I was brave, and
   tried."

CHARLIE IS MY DARLING

'Twas on a Monday morning,
   Right early in the year,
That Charlie came to our town,
   The young Chevalier.
     And Charlie he's my darling,
      My darling, my darling,
     Charlie he's my darling,
      The young Chevalier.

As Charlie he came up the gate,
   His face shone like the day;
I grat to see the lad come back
   That had been lang away.
     And Charlie he's my darling,
      My darling, my darling,
     Charlie he's my darling,
      The young Chevalier.

And ilka bonnie lassie sang,
   As to the door she ran,
"Our king shall hae his ain again,
   And Charlie is the man ":
     And Charlie he's my darling,
      My darling, my darling,
     Charlie he's my darling,
      The young Chevalier.

Out-owre yon moory mountain,
   And down the craigy glen,
Of naething else our lassies sing
   But Charlie and his men.

And Charlie he's my darling,
   My darling, my darling,
Charlie he's my darling,
   The young Chevalier.

Our Highland hearts are true and
   leal,
   And glow without a stain;
Our Highland swords are metal keen,
   And Charlie he's our ain.
     And Charlie he's my darling,
      My darling, my darling,
     Charlie he's my darling,
      The young Chevalier.

James Hogg

THE BABES IN THE WOOD

My dear, do you know
How, a long time ago,
   Two poor little children,
Whose names I don't know,
Were stolen away
On a fine summer's day,
   And left in a wood,
As I've heard people say?

And when it was night,
So sad was their plight,
   The sun it went down,
And the moon gave no light!
They sobbed and they sighed,
And they bitterly cried,
   And the poor little things
They lay down and died.

And when they were dead,
The robins so red
   Brought strawberry leaves
And over them spread;
And all the day long
They sang them this song:
"Poor babes in the wood!
Poor babes in the wood!
   And don't you remember
The babes in the wood?"

A LEGEND OF THE NORTHLAND

Away, away in the Northland,
  Where the hours of the day are
    few,
And the nights are so long in winter
  That they cannot sleep them
    through;

Where they harness the swift rein-
    deer
  To the sledges, when it snows;
And the children look like bear's
    cubs
  In their funny, furry clothes:

They tell them a curious story—
  I don't believe 'tis true;
And yet you may learn a lesson
  If I tell the tale to you.

Once, when the good Saint Peter
  Lived in the world below,
And walked about it, preaching,
  Just as he did, you know,

He came to the door of a cottage,
  In traveling round the earth,
Where a little woman was making
    cakes,
  And baking them on the hearth;

And being faint with fasting,
  For the day was almost done,
He asked her, from her store of
    cakes,
  To give him a single one.

So she made a very little cake,
  But as it baking lay,
She looked at it, and thought it
    seemed
  Too large to give away.

Therefore she kneaded another,
  And still a smaller one;

But it looked, when she turned it
    over,
  As large as the first had done.

Then she took a tiny scrap of dough,
  And rolled and rolled it flat;
And baked it thin as a wafer—
  But she couldn't part with that.

For she said, "My cakes that seem
    too small
  When I eat of them myself
Are yet too large to give away."
  So she put them on the shelf.

Then good Saint Peter grew angry,
  For he was hungry and faint;
And surely such a woman
  Was enough to provoke a saint.

And he said, "You are far too selfish
  To dwell in a human form,
To have both food and shelter,
  And fire to keep you warm.

"Now, you shall build as the birds do,
  And shall get your scanty food
By boring, and boring, and boring,
  All day in the hard, dry wood."

Then up she went through the chim-
    ney,
  Never speaking a word,
And out of the top flew a wood-
    pecker,
  For she was changed to a bird.

She had a scarlet cap on her head,
  And that was left the same,
But all the rest of her clothes were
    burned
  Black as a coal in the flame.

And every country schoolboy
  Has seen her in the wood,
Where she lives in the trees till this
    very day,
  Boring and boring for food.
                    Phoebe Cary

THE SINGING LESSON

A nightingale made a mistake;
   She sang a few notes out of tune;
Her heart was ready to break,
   And she hid away from the moon.
She wrung her claws, poor thing,
   But was far too proud to weep;
She tucked her head under her wing,
   And pretended to be asleep.

A lark, arm-in-arm with a thrush,
   Came sauntering up to the place;
The nightingale felt herself blush,
   Though feathers hid her face;
She knew they had heard her song,
   She felt them snicker and sneer;
She thought that life was too long,
   And wished she could skip a year.

" O nightingale! " cooed a dove,
   " O nightingale! what's the use;
You bird of beauty and love,
   Why behave like a goose?
Don't skulk away from our sight,
   Like a common contemptible fowl;
You bird of joy and delight,
   Why behave like an owl?

" Only think of all you have done;
   Only think of all you can do;
A false note is really fun
   From such a bird as you!
Lift up your proud little crest;
   Open your musical beak;
Other birds have to do their best—
   You need only to speak."

The nightingale shyly took
   Her head from under her wing
And, giving the dove a look,
   Straightway began to sing.
There was never a bird could pass;
   The night was divinely calm;
And the people stood on the grass
   To hear that wonderful psalm!

The nightingale did not care,
   She only sang to the skies;
Her song ascended there,
   And there she fixed her eyes.
The people that stood below
   She knew but little about;
And this tale has a moral, I know,
   If you'll try to find it out!

                   Jean Ingelow

THE WIND AND THE MOON

Said the Wind to the Moon, " I will
   blow you out;
      You stare
      In the air
      Like a ghost in a chair,
Always looking what I am about—
I hate to be watched; I'll blow you
   out."

The Wind blew hard, and out went
   the Moon.
      So, deep
      On a heap
      Of clouds to sleep,
Down lay the Wind, and slumbered
   soon,
Muttering low, " I've done for that
   Moon."

He turned in his bed; she was there
   again!
      On high
      In the sky,
      With her one ghost eye,
The Moon shone white and alive
   and plain.
Said the Wind, " I will blow you
   out again."

The Wind blew hard, and the Moon
   grew dim.

" With my sledge,
     And my wedge,
         I have knocked off her edge!
If only I blow right fierce and grim,
The creature will soon be dimmer
     than dim."

He blew and he blew, and she
     thinned to a thread.
     " One puff
         More's enough
             To blow her to snuff!
One good puff more where the last
     was bred,
And glimmer, glimmer, glum will go
     the thread."

He blew a great blast, and the thread
     was gone.
         In the air
         Nowhere
             Was a moonbeam bare;
Far off and harmless the shy stars
     shone—
Sure and certain the Moon was gone!

The Wind he took to his revels once
     more;
         On down,
         In town,
             Like a merry-mad clown,
He leaped and hallooed with whistle
     and roar—
" What's that? " The glimmering
     thread once more!

He flew in a rage—he danced and
     blew;
         But in vain
         Was the pain
             Of his bursting brain;
For still the broader the Moon-scrap
     grew,
The broader he swelled his big
     cheeks and blew.

Slowly she grew—till she filled the
     night,
         And shone
         On her throne
             In the sky alone,
A matchless, wonderful silvery light,
Radiant and lovely, the queen of the
     night.

Said the Wind: " What a marvel of
     power am I!
         With my breath,
         Good faith!
             I blew her to death—
First blew her away right out of the
     sky—
Then blew her in; what strength
     have I! "

But the Moon she knew nothing
     about the affair;
         For high
         In the sky,
             With her one white eye,
Motionless, miles above the air,
She had never heard the great Wind
     blare.

                    George Macdonald

THE SPIDER AND THE FLY

" Will you walk into my parlor? " said
     the Spider to the Fly,
" 'Tis the prettiest little parlor that
     ever you did spy;
The way into my parlor is up a
     winding stair,
And I have many curious things to
     show when you are there."
" Oh, no, no," said the little Fly; " to
     ask me is in vain;
For who goes up your winding stair
     can ne'er come down again."
" I'm sure you must be weary, dear,
     with soaring up so high;

Will you rest upon my little bed? "
　　said the Spider to the Fly.
" There are pretty curtains drawn
　　around; the sheets are fine and
　　thin,
And if you like to rest a while, I'll
　　snugly tuck you in! "
" Oh, no, no," said the little Fly,
　　" for I've often heard it said,
They never, never wake again, who
　　sleep upon your bed! "
Said the cunning Spider to the Fly:
　　" Dear friend, what can I do,
To prove the warm affection I've
　　always felt for you?
I have within my pantry good store
　　of all that's nice;
I'm sure you're very welcome—will
　　you please to take a slice? "
" Oh, no, no," said the little Fly,
　　" kind sir, that cannot be,
I've heard what's in your pantry,
　　and I do not wish to see! "
" Sweet creature! " said the Spider,
　　" you're witty and you're wise,
How handsome are your gauzy
　　wings, how brilliant are your eyes;
I have a little looking-glass upon my
　　parlor shelf,
If you'll step in one moment, dear,
　　you shall behold yourself."
" I thank you, gentle sir," she said,
　　" for what you're pleased to say,
And bidding you good morning now,
　　I'll call another day."
The Spider turned him round about,
　　and went into his den,
For well he knew the silly Fly would
　　soon come back again:
So he wove a subtle web in a little
　　corner sly,
And set his table ready to dine upon
　　the Fly.

Then he came out to his door again,
　　and merrily did sing,
" Come hither, hither, pretty Fly,
　　with the pearl and silver wing;
Your robes are green and purple—
　　there's a crest upon your head;
Your eyes are like the diamond
　　bright, but mine are dull as lead! "
Alas, alas! how very soon this silly
　　little Fly,
Hearing his wily, flattering words,
　　came slowly flitting by;
With buzzing wings she hung aloft,
　　then near and nearer drew,
Thinking only of her brilliant eyes,
　　and green and purple hue—
Thinking only of her crested head—
　　poor foolish thing!—at last
Up jump'd the cunning Spider, and
　　fiercely held her fast.
He dragg'd her up his winding stair,
　　into his dismal den,
Within his little parlor—but she
　　ne'er came out again!

And now, dear little children, who
　　may this story read,
To idle, silly, flattering words, I
　　pray you ne'er give heed:
Unto an evil counsellor close heart
　　and ear and eye,
And take a lesson from this tale, of
　　the Spider and the Fly.

　　　　　　　　　　Mary Howitt

THE BLUE BOY IN LONDON

All in the morning early
　　The Little Boy in Blue
(The grass with rain is pearly)
　　Has thought of something new.

He saddled dear old Dobbin;
　　He had but half a crown;

And jogging, cantering, bobbing,
  He came to London town.

The sheep were in the meadows,
  The cows were in the corn,
Beneath the city shadow
  At last he stood forlorn.

He stood beneath Bow steeple,
  That is in London town;
And tried to count the people
  As they went up and down.

Oh! there was not a daisy,
  And not a buttercup;
The air was thick and hazy,
  And Blue Boy gave it up.

The houses, next, in London,
  He thought that he would count;
But still the sum was undone,
  So great was the amount.

He could not think of robbing—
  He had but half a crown;
And so he mounted Dobbin,
  And rode back from the town.

The sheep were in the meadows,
  And the cows were in the corn;
Amid the evening shadows
  He stood where he was born.

William Brighty Rands

JACK HORNER

Jack Horner was a pretty lad,
  Near London he did dwell;
His father's heart he made full glad,
  His mother loved him well.

While little Jack was sweet and
    young,
  If he by chance should cry,
His mother pretty sonnets sung,
  With a lul-la-lul-la-by,

With such a dainty curious tone,
  As Jack sat on her knee,
That soon, ere he could go alone,
  He sang as well as she.

A pretty boy of curious wit,
  All people spoke his praise,
And in the corner he would sit
  In Christmas holidays.

When friends they did together meet,
  To pass away the time—
Why, little Jack, be sure, would eat
  His Christmas pie in rhyme.

He said, " Jack Horner, in the corner,
  Eats good Christmas pie,
And with his thumbs pulls out the
    plums,
  And says, ' Good boy am I! ' "

DICKY OF BALLYMAN

On New Year's Day, as I heard say,
Dicky he saddled his dapple grey;
He put on his Sunday clothes,
His scarlet vest, and his new made
    hose.
    Diddle dum di, diddle dum do,
    Diddle dum di, diddle dum do!

He rode till he came to Wilson Hall,
There he rapped, and loud did call;
Mistress Ann came down straight-
    way,
And asked him what he had to say.

" Don't you know me, Mistress Ann?
I am Dicky of Ballyman;
An honest lad, though I am poor,—
I never was in love before.

" I have an uncle, the best of friends,
Sometimes to me a fat rabbit he
  sends;

And many other dainty fowl,
To please my life, my joy, my soul.

" Sometimes I reap, sometimes I mow,
And to the market I do go,
To sell my father's corn and hay,—
I earn my sixpence every day! "

" Oh, Dickey! you go beneath your
mark,—
You only wander in the dark;
Sixpence will never do,
I must have silks, and satins, too!

" Besides, Dicky, I must have tea
For my breakfast, every day;
And after dinner a bottle of wine,—
For without it I cannot dine."

" If on fine clothes our money is
spent,
Pray how shall my lord be paid his
rent?
He'll expect it when 'tis due,—
Believe me, what I say is true.

" As for tea, good stirabout
Will do far better, I make no doubt;
And spring water, when you dine,
Is far wholesomer than wine.

" Potatoes, too, are very nice food,—
I don't know any half so good:
You may have them boiled or roast,
Whichever way you like them
most."

This gave the company much delight,
And made them all to laugh outright;
So Dicky had no more to say,
But saddled his dapple and rode
away.
    Diddle dum di, diddle dum do,
    Diddle dum di, diddle dum do!

THE COURTSHIP AND MERRY MARRIAGE OF COCK ROBIN AND JENNY WREN

It was a merry time
    When Jenny Wren was young,
So neatly as she danced,
    And so sweetly as she sung,
Robin Redbreast lost his heart:
    He was a gallant bird;
He doffed his hat to Jenny,
    And thus to her he said:—

" My dearest Jenny Wren,
    If you will but be mine,
You shall dine on cherry pie,
    And drink nice currant wine.
I'll dress you like a Goldfinch,
    Or like a Peacock gay;
So if you'll have me, Jenny,
    Let us appoint the day."

Jenny blushed behind her fan,
    And thus declared her mind:
" Then let it be tomorrow, Bob,
    I take your offer kind—
Cherry pie is very good!
    So is currant wine!
But I will wear my brown gown,
    And never dress too fine."

Robin rose up early
    At the break of day;
He flew to Jenny Wren's house,
    To sing a roundelay.
He met the Cock and Hen,
    And bid the Cock declare,
This was his wedding-day
    With Jenny Wren the fair.

The Cock then blew his horn,
    To let the neighbors know,
This was Robin's wedding-day,
    And they might see the show.
And first came Parson Rook,
    With his spectacles and band,

And one of Mother Hubbard's books
    He held within his hand.

Then followed him the Lark,
    For he could sweetly sing,
And he was to be clerk
    At Cock Robin's wedding.
He sang of Robin's love
    For little Jenny Wren;
And when he came unto the end,
    Then he began again.

Then came the bride and bride-
    groom;
Quite plainly was she dressed,
And blushed so much, her cheeks
    were
As red as Robin's breast.
But Robin cheered her up;
    " My pretty Jen," said he,
" We're going to be married
    And happy shall we be."

The Goldfinch came on next,
    To give away the bride;
The Linnet, being bride's maid,
    Walked by Jenny's side;
And, as she was a-walking,
    She said, " Upon my word,
I think that your Cock Robin
    Is a very pretty bird."

The Bullfinch walked by Robin
    And thus to him did say,
" Pray, mark, friend Robin Redbreast,
    That Goldfinch dressed so gay;
What though her gay apparel
    Becomes her very well,
Yet Jenny's modest dress and look
    Must bear away the bell."

The Blackbird and the Thrush,
    And charming Nightingale,

Whose sweet jug sweetly echoes
    Through every grove and dell;
The Sparrow and Tom Tit,
    And many more, were there:
All came to see the wedding
    Of Jenny Wren, the fair.

" O then," says Parson Rook,
    " Who gives this maid away? "
" I do," says the Goldfinch,
    " And her fortune I will pay:
Here's a bag of grain of many sorts,
    And other things beside;
Now happy be the bridegroom,
    And happy be the bride! "

" And will you have her, Robin,
    To be your wedded wife? "
" Yes, I will," says Robin,
    " And love her all my life."
" And will you have him, Jenny,
    Your husband now to be? "
" Yes, I will," says Jenny,
    " And love him heartily."

Then on her finger fair
    Cock Robin put the ring;
" You're married now," says Parson
    Rook,
    While the Lark aloud did sing:
" Happy be the bridegroom,
    And happy be the bride!
And may not man, nor bird, nor
    beast,
    This happy pair divide."

The birds were asked to dine;
    Not Jenny's friends alone,
But every pretty songster
    That had Cock Robin known.
They had a cherry pie,
    Beside some currant wine,
And every guest brought something.
    That sumptuous they might dine.

Part Two

CRADLE SONGS

BABY, SLEEP

Lie a-bed,
Sleepy head,
Shut up eyes, bo-peep;
Till daybreak
Never wake:—
Baby, sleep.

Christina Rossetti

THE SLEEPY SONG

As soon as the fire burns red and low,
And the house upstairs is still,
She sings me a queer little sleepy song,
Of sheep that go over a hill.

The good little sheep run quick and
soft,
Their colors are gray and white:
They follow their leader nose to tail,
For they must be home by night.

And one slips over and one comes
next,
And one runs after behind,
The gray one's nose at the white one's
tail,
The top of the hill they find.

And when they get to the top of the
hill

They quietly slip away,
But one runs over and one comes
next—
Their colors are white and gray.

And over they go, and over they go,
And over the top of the hill,
The good little sheep run quick and
soft,
And the house upstairs is still.

And one slips over and one comes
next,
The good little, gray little sheep!
I watch how the fire burns red and
low,
And she says that I fall asleep.

Josephine Daskam Bacon

WYNKEN, BLYNKEN, AND
NOD

Wynken, Blynken, and Nod onc
night
Sailed off in a wooden shoe,—
Sailed on a river of crystal light
Into a sea of dew.
" Where are you going, and what do
you wish? "
The old moon asked the three.
" We have come to fish for the her-
ring fish

45

That live in this beautiful sea;
Nets of silver and gold have we! "
     Said Wynken,
     Blynken,
     And Nod.

The old moon laughed and sang a
     song,
     As they rocked in the wooden
     shoe;
And the wind that sped them all
     night long
Ruffled the waves of dew.
The little stars were the herring fish
     That lived in that beautiful sea—
" Now cast your nets wherever you
     wish,—
     Never afeard are we! "
So cried the stars to the fishermen
     three,
     Wynken,
     Blynken,
     And Nod.

All night long their nets they threw
     To the stars in the twinkling
     foam,—
Then down from the skies came the
     wooden shoe,
     Bringing the fishermen home:
'Twas all so pretty a sail, it seemed
     As if it could not be;
And some folk thought 'twas a
     dream they'd dreamed
     Of sailing that beautiful sea;
     But I shall name you the fisher-
     men three:
     Wynken,
     Blynken,
     And Nod.
Wynken and Blynken are two little
     eyes,
     And Nod is a little head,
And the wooden shoe that sailed the
     skies

Is a wee one's trundle-bed;
So shut your eyes while Mother sings
     Of wonderful sights that be,
And you shall see the beautiful
     things
     As you rock in the misty sea
Where the old shoe rocked the
     fishermen three:—
     Wynken,
     Blynken,
     And Nod.

              Eugene Field

ROCK-A-BYE, BABY

Rock-a-bye, baby, thy cradle is green;
Father's a nobleman, mother's a
     Queen;
Betty's a lady, and wears a gold ring;
And Johnny's a drummer, and drums
     for the King.

Hush-a-bye, baby, on the tree top,
When the wind blows, the cradle will
     rock;
When the bough bends, the cradle will
     fall,
Down will come baby, bough, cradle
     and all.

LULLABY, O LULLABY

Lullaby, O lullaby!
Baby, hush that little cry!
     Light is dying,
     Bats are flying,
Bees today with work have done;
So, till comes the morrow's sun,
Let sleep kiss those bright eyes dry!
     Lullaby! O lullaby!

Lullaby! O lullaby!
Hush'd are all things far and nigh;
     Flowers are closing,
     Birds reposing,

All sweet things with life are done.
Sweet, till dawns the morning sun,
Sleep then kiss those blue eyes dry!
Lullaby! O lullaby!

William Cox Bennett

CHINESE LULLABY

Chinese Sandmen,
Wise and creepy,
Croon dream-songs
To make us sleepy.
A Chinese maid with slanting eyes
Is queen of all their lullabies.
On her ancient moon-guitar
She strums a sleep-song to a star;
And when big China-shadows fall
Snow-white lilies hear her call.
Chinese Sandmen,
Wise and creepy,
Croon dream-songs
To make us sleepy.

Unknown

LULLABY OF AN INFANT CHIEF

Oh, hush thee, my baby! thy sire was a
knight,
Thy mother a lady, both lovely and
bright;
The woods and the glens, from the
towers which we see,
They all are belonging, dear baby, to
thee.

Oh, fear not the bugle, though loudly
it blows!
It calls but the warders that guard thy
repose;
Their bows would be bended, their
blades would be red,
Ere the step of a foeman draws near
to thy bed.

Oh, hush thee, my baby! the time will
soon come
When thy sleep shall be broken by
trumpet and drum;
Then hush thee, my darling! take rest
while you may;
For strife comes with manhood, and
waking with day.

Walter Scott

SLEEP, BABY, SLEEP!

Sleep, baby, sleep!
Thy father watches the sheep;
Thy mother is shaking the dream-land
tree,
And down falls a little dream on thee:
Sleep, baby, sleep!

Sleep, baby, sleep!
The large stars are the sheep,
The wee stars are the lambs, I guess,
The fair moon is the shepherdess:
Sleep, baby, sleep!

From the German

BY THE CRADLE

Close her eyes; she must not peep!
Let her little puds go slack;
Slide away far into sleep:
Sis will watch till she comes back.

Mother's knitting at the door,
Waiting till the kettle sings;
When the kettle's song is o'er
She will set the bright tea things.

Father's busy making hay
In the meadow by the brook,
Not so very far away—
Close its peeps, it needn't look!

God is round us everywhere—
Sees the scythe glitter and rip;

Watches baby gone somewhere;
  Sees how mother's fingers skip!

Sleep, dear baby; sleep outright:
  Mother's sitting just behind;
Father's only out of sight;
  God is round us like the wind.

George Macdonald

BABY DEAR

In thy hammock gently sleeping,
Dearest baby, have no fear;
While thy mother watch is keeping
  Danger never can come near.
  I am here,
  Baby dear,
  Mother's eyes
  Watch her prize;
Pois'nous wing
Nor noisome sting
Shall harm thy sleep,
Tho' I may weep,
Weep for one that's far from me
Far across the stormy sea.
Let me dash the tear away!—
Better far to hope and pray;
  Oh, solace rare!

A tear may mingle with a pray'r,
A prayer for thee, my baby dear,
And one, alas! that is not here,—
  Baby dear, baby dear,
In thy hammock gently swinging,
Gently is thy mother singing
  Lullaby to thee.

Samuel Lover

LULLABY

Golden slumbers kiss your eyes,
Smiles awake you when you rise.
Sleep, pretty wantons, do not cry,
And I will sing a lullaby.
Rock them, rock them, lullaby.

Care is heavy, therefore sleep you,
You are care, and care must keep you.
Sleep, pretty wantons, do not cry,
And I will sing a lullaby.
Rock them, rock them, lullaby.

Thomas Dekker

A CRADLE SONG
(Selected Stanzas)

Hush! my dear, lie still and slumber;
  Holy angels guard thy bed!
Heavenly blessings without number
  Gently falling on thy head.

How much better thou'rt attended
  Than the Son of God could be,
When from Heaven He descended,
  And became a child like thee!

Soft and easy is thy cradle:
  Coarse and hard thy Saviour lay:
When His birthplace was a stable,
  And His softest bed was hay.

Lo, He slumbers in His manger,
  Where the hornèd oxen fed;—
Peace, my darling! here's no danger!
  Here's no ox a-near thy bed!—

May'st thou live to know and fear
  Him,
  Trust and love Him all thy days:
Then go dwell for ever near Him;
  See His face, and sing His praise.

Isaac Watts

MY DEAREST BABY, GO
TO SLEEP

My dearest baby, go to sleep,
For now the bright round moon doth
  peep
On thy little snow-white bed,
And upon thy pretty head.

The silver stars are shining bright,
And bid my baby dear good-night;
And every bird has gone to rest
Long since in its little nest.

The lambs no longer run and leap,
But by the daisies lie asleep;
The flowers have closed their pretty
  eyes
Until the sun again shall rise.

All things are wrapp'd in sweet repose,
The dew falls noiseless on the rose;
So thou must like an angel lie
'Till golden morning streaks the sky.

Soon will I gently steal to bed,
  And rest beside thy pretty head,
And all night keep thee snug and
  warm,
Nestling fondly on my arm.

Then, dearest baby, go to sleep,
While the moon doth on thee peep,
Shining on thy little bed,
And around thy pretty head.

Thomas Miller

WHAT DOES LITTLE BIRDIE SAY?

What does little birdie say
In her nest at peep of day?
Let me fly, says little birdie,
Mother, let me fly away.
Birdie, rest a little longer,
Till the little wings are stronger.
So she rests a little longer,
Then she flies away.

What does little baby say,
In her bed at peep of day?
Baby says, like little birdie,
Let me rise and fly away.

Baby, sleep a little longer,
Till the little limbs are stronger,
If she sleeps a little longer,
Baby too shall fly away.

Alfred Tennyson

LULLABY

Lullaby, oh, lullaby!
Flowers are closed and lambs are sleep-
    ing;
  Lullaby, oh, lullaby!
Stars are up, the moon is peeping;
  Lullaby, oh, lullaby!
While the birds are silence keeping,
  Lullaby, oh, lullaby!
Sleep, my baby, fall a-sleeping,
  Lullaby, oh, lullaby!

Christina Rossetti

GOOD NIGHT

Baby, baby, lay your head
On your pretty cradle bed;
Shut your eye-peeps, now the day
And the light are gone away;
All the clothes are tuck'd in tight;
Little baby, dear, good night.

Yes, my darling, well I know
How the bitter wind doth blow;
And the winter's snow and rain
Patter on the window-pane;
But they cannot come in here,
To my little baby dear.

For the window shutteth fast,
Till the stormy night is past,
And the curtains warm are spread
Roundabout her cradle bed;
So till morning shineth bright,
Little baby, dear, good night.

Jane Taylor

WHEN LITTLE BIRDIE BYE-BYE GOES

When little Birdie bye-bye goes,
  Quiet as mice in churches,
He puts his head where no one knows,
  On one leg he perches.

When little Babie bye-bye goes,
  On Mother's arm reposing,
Soon he lies beneath the clothes,
  Safe in the cradle dozing.

When pretty Pussy goes to sleep,
  Tail and nose together,
Then little mice around her creep,
  Lightly as a feather.

When little Babie goes to sleep,
  And he is very near us,
Then on tiptoe softly creep,
  That Babie may not hear us.
Lullaby! Lullaby! Lulla, Lulla, Lullaby!
Unknown

SWEET DREAMS FORM A SHADE

Sweet dreams, form a shade
O'er my lovely infant's head;
Sweet dreams of pleasant streams
By happy, silent, moony beams.

Sweet sleep, with soft down
Weave thy brows an infant crown.
Sweet sleep, angel mild,
Hover o'er my happy child.

Sweet smiles in the night
Hover o'er my delight;
Sweet smiles, mother's smiles,
All the live-long night beguiles.

Sweet moans, dove-like sighs,
Chase not slumbers from thy eyes.
Sweet moans, sweeter smiles,
All the dove-like moans beguiles.

Sleep, sleep, happy child,
All creation slept and smiled;
Sleep, sleep, happy sleep,
While o'er thee thy mother weep.

Sweet babe, in thy face
Holy image I can trace.
Sweet babe, once like thee,
Thy Maker lay and wept for me.

Wept for me, for thee, for all,
When He was an infant small;
Thou His image ever see,
Heavenly face that smiles on thee.

Smiles on thee, on me, on all;
Who became an infant small;
Infant smiles are His own smiles;
Heaven and earth to peace beguiles.
William Blake

SLEEP, SLEEP, BEAUTY BRIGHT

Sleep, sleep, beauty bright,
Dreaming in the joys of night;
Sleep, sleep; in thy sleep
Little sorrows sit and weep.

Sweet babe, in thy face
Soft desires I can trace,
Secret joys and secret smiles,
Little pretty infant wiles.

As thy softest limbs I feel,
Smiles as of the morning steal
O'er thy cheek, and o'er thy breast
Where thy little heart doth rest.

Oh, the cunning wiles that creep
In thy little heart asleep!
When thy little heart doth wake
Then the dreadful night shall break.
William Blake

STRANGE LANDS

Where do you come from, Mr. Jay?
" From the land of Play, from the
    land of Play."
And where can that be, Mr. Jay?
  " Far away—far away."

Where do you come from, Mrs.
    Dove?
" From the land of Love, from the
    land of Love."
And how do you get there, Mrs.
    Dove?
  " Look above—look above."

Where do you come from, Baby
    Miss?
" From the land of Bliss, from the
    land of Bliss."
And what is the way there, Baby
    Miss?
  " Mother's kiss—mother's kiss."
                    Lawrence Alma-Tadema

BABY

Where did you come from, baby dear?
Out of the everywhere into the here.

Where did you get those eyes so blue?
Out of the sky as I came through.

What makes the light in them sparkle
  and spin?
Some of the starry spikes left in.

Where did you get that little tear?
I found it waiting when I got here.

What makes your forehead so smooth
  and high?
A soft hand stroked it as I went by.

What makes your cheek like a warm
  white rose?

I saw something better than anyone
  knows.

Whence that three-cornered smile of
  bliss?
Three angels gave me at once a kiss.

Where did you get this pearly ear?
God spoke, and it came out to hear.

Where did you get those arms and
  hands?
Love made itself into bonds and bands.

Feet, whence did you come, you darling things?
From the same box as the cherubs'
  wings.

How did they all just come to be you?
God thought about me, and so I grew.

But how did you come to us, you dear?
God thought about you, and so I am
  here.
                    George Macdonald

BARTHOLOMEW

Bartholomew is very sweet,
From sandy hair to rosy feet.

Bartholomew is six months old,
And dearer far than pearls or gold.

Bartholomew has deep blue eyes,
Round pieces dropped from out the
  skies.

Bartholomew is hugged and kissed:
He loves a flower in either fist.

Bartholomew's my saucy son:
No mother has a sweeter one!
                    Norman Gale

INFANT JOY

I have no name,
I am but two days old.
What shall I call thee?
I happy am,
Joy is my name—
Sweet joy befall thee.

Pretty joy!
Sweet joy but two days old;
Sweet joy I call thee.
Thou dost smile,
I sing the while,
Sweet joy befall thee!

William Blake

A MOTHER'S SONG

Love me,—I love you,
  Love me, my baby;
Sing it high, sing it low,
  Sing it as it may be.

Mother's arms under you,
  Her eyes above you;
Sing it high, sing it low,
  Love me,—I love you.

Christina Rossetti

BABY-LAND

"Which is the way to Baby-land?"
  "Anyone can tell;
    Up one flight,
    To your right;
  Please to ring the bell."

"What can you see in Baby-land?"
  "Little folks in white—
    Downy heads,
    Cradle-beds,
  Faces pure and bright!

"What do they do in Baby-land?"
  "Dream and wake and play,
    Laugh and crow,
    Shout and grow;
  Jolly times have they!"

"What do they say in Baby-land?"
  "Why, the oddest things;
    Might as well
    Try to tell
  What a birdie sings!"

"Who is the Queen of Baby-land?"
  "Mother, kind and sweet;
    And her love,
    Born above,
  Guides the little feet."

George Cooper

THE BIRD

"Birdie, Birdie, will you pet?
  Summer-time is far away yet,
  You'll have silken quilts and a velvet bed,
  And a pillow of satin for your head!"

"I'd rather sleep in the ivy wall;
  No rain comes through, tho' I hear it fall;
  The sun peeps gay at dawn of day,
  And I sing, and wing away, away!"

"Oh, Birdie, Birdie, will you pet?
  Diamond-stones and amber and jet
  We'll string for a necklace fair and fine,
  To please this pretty bird of mine!"

"O thanks for diamonds, and thanks for jet,
  But here is something daintier yet—
  A feather-necklace round and round,
  That I wouldn't sell for a thousand pound!"

"Oh, Birdie, Birdie, won't you pet?
We'll buy you a dish of silver fret,
A golden cup and an ivory seat,
And carpets soft beneath your feet."

"Can running water be drunk from gold?
Can a silver dish the forest hold?
A rocking twig is the finest chair,
And the softest paths lie through the air—
Good-bye, good-bye to my lady fair!"

William Allingham

NIGHT

The snow is white, the wind is cold—
The king has sent for my three-year-old.
Bring the pony and shoe him fast
With silver shoes that were made to last.
Bring the saddle trimmed with gold;
Put foot in stirrup, my three-year-old;
Jump in the saddle, away, away!
And hurry back by the break of day;
By break of day, through dale and down,
And bring me the news from Slumber-town.

Mary F. Butts

Part Three

RIDDLES AND FINGER PLAYS

A CLOCK

Twelve little figures around me,
  One pale face to guard,
Two hands crossed on my fair white
    breast;
  Can you guess me? I am not hard.

AN EGG

In marble walls as white as milk,
Lined with a skin as soft as silk,
Within a fountain crystal clear,
A golden apple doth appear.
No doors there are to this stronghold,
Yet thieves break in and steal the gold.

GUESSING SONG

Oh ho! oh ho! Pray, who can I be?
I sweep o'er the land, I scour o'er the
    sea;
I cuff the tall trees till they bow down
    their heads,
And I rock the wee birdies asleep in
    their beds.
Oh ho! oh ho! And who can I be,
That sweep o'er the land and scour o'er
    the sea?

I swing all the weather-cocks this way
    and that,

I play hare-and-hounds with a runaway
    hat;
But however I wander, I never can
    stray,
For go where I will, I've a free right
    of way!
Oh ho! oh ho! And who can I be,
That sweep o'er the land and scour o'er
    the sea?

THE WIND

Henry Johnstone

WHAT AM I?

They chose me from my brothers:
  "That's the
Nicest one," they said,
And they carved me out a face and
    put a
Candle in my head;

And they set me on the doorstep. Oh,
    the
Night was dark and wild;
But when they lit the candle, then I
Smiled!

JACK-O'-LANTERN

Dorothy Aldis

FOUR ARMS HAVE I

Four arms I have, with which to wing
    my way,
And round large circles in the sun-
    beams play,
Chasing each other as the wheels of a
    coach,
Which though they speed, each other
    ne'er approach.
Within my house, arrayed in robes of
    white,
My helpmates work from morning un-
    til night.
Much food I take, which goes my body
    through,
And then is rendered fit for food for
    you.

A WINDMILL

AS THE WORLD TURNS

I'm up and down and round about,
Yet all the world can't find me out.
Though hundreds have employed their
    leisure,
They never yet could take my measure.
I'm found in almost every garden,
Nay, in the compass of a farthing;
There's not a chariot, coach, nor mill,
Can move an inch except I will.

A CIRCLE

Jonathan Swift

AN AUTUMN RIDDLE

I know a little creature
    In a green bed,
With the softest wrappings
    All around her head.
When she grows old
    She is old and cannot feel,
So they take her to the mill
    To grind her into meal.

WHEAT

THE WONDERFUL WEAVER

There's a wonderful weaver
    High up in the air,
And he weaves a white mantle
    For cold earth to wear,
With the wind for his shuttle,
    The cloud for his loom,
How he weaves! how he weaves!
    In the light, in the gloom.

Oh, with finest of laces
    He decks bush and tree,
On the bare flinty meadows
    A cover lays he.
Then a quaint cap he places
    On a pillar and post,
And he changes the pump
    To a grim, silent ghost.

But this wonderful weaver
    Grows weary at last,
And the shuttle lies idle
    That once flew so fast;
Then the sun peeps abroad
    On the work that is done;
And he smiles: " I'll unravel
    It all just for fun! "

SNOW

George Cooper

A RIDDLE

'Twas whispered in Heaven, 'twas mut-
    tered in hell,
Our echo caught faintly the sound as
    it fell;
On the confines of earth, 'twas per-
    mitted to rest,
And the depths of the ocean its pres-
    ence confess'd;
'Twill be found in the sphere when
    'tis riven asunder,
Be seen in the lightning, and heard
    in the thunder;

'Twas allotted to man, with his earliest
breath,
Attends him at birth and awaits him
in death,
Presides o'er his happiness, honor and
health,
Is the prop of his house, and the end
of his wealth,
In the heaps of the miser 'tis hoarded
with care,
But is sure to be lost on his prodigal
heir;
It begins every hope, every wish it
must bound,
With the husbandman toils, and with
monarchs is crowned;
Without it the soldier and seaman
may roam,
But woe to the wretch who expels it
from home!
In the whispers of conscience its voice
will be found,
Nor e'er in the whirlwind of passion
be drowned;
'Twill soften the heart; but though
deaf be the ear,
It will make it actuely and instantly
hear.
Set in shade, let it rest like a delicate
flower;
Ah! breathe on it softly, it dies in an
hour.

THE LETTER " H "

Catherine Maria Fanshawe

DO YOU GUESS IT IS I?

I am a little thing;
    I am not very high;
I laugh, dance and sing,
    And sometimes I cry.

I have a little head
    All covered o'er with hair,

And I hear what is said
    With my two ears there.

On my two feet I walk;
    I run too with ease;
With my little tongue I talk
    Just as much as I please.

I have ten fingers too,
    And just so many toes;
Two eyes to see through,
    And but one little nose.

I've a mouth full of teeth,
    Where my bread and milk go in;
And close by, underneath,
    Is my little round chin.

What is this little thing,
    Not very, very high,
That can laugh, dance and sing?
    Do you guess it is I?

A BABY

Eliza Lee Follen

AS I WAS GOING TO ST. IVES

As I was going to St. Ives,
I met a man with seven wives;
Every wife had seven sacks,
Every sack had seven cats,
Every cat had seven kits—
Kits, cats, sacks, and wives,
How many were going to St. Ives?

ONE

TWO LEGS SAT UPON
THREE LEGS

Two legs sat upon three legs,
With one leg in his lap;
In comes four legs
And runs away with one leg;

Up jumps two legs,
Catches up three legs,
Throws it after four legs,
And makes him drop one leg.

A MAN, A STOOL, A LEG OF MUTTON,
AND A DOG

A RIDDLE

We are little airy creatures,
All of different voice and features;
One of us in glass is set,
One of us you'll find in jet.
T'other you may see in tin,
And the fourth a box within.
If the fifth you should pursue,
It can never fly from you.

THE VOWELS

Jonathan Swift

RIDDLES

There was a girl in our town,
Silk an' satin was her gown,
Silk an' satin, gold an' velvet,
Guess her name—three times I've tell'd
  it!

ANN

➤➤➤《《《

As I was going o'er Westminster
  bridge,
I met with a Westminster scholar;
He pulled off his cap, *an' drew* off his
  glove,
    And wished me a very good morrow.
    What is his name?

ANDREW

➤➤➤《《《

There's a flower in the garden,
  It's just like a cup;

It's yellow, as yellow as butter,
  And they call it ———.

A BUTTERCUP

➤➤➤《《《

Black within and red without,
With four corners round about.

A CHIMNEY

➤➤➤《《《

First it was a pretty flower, dressed in
  pink and white,
Then it was a tiny ball, almost hid
  from sight.
Round and green and large it grew—
  then it turned to red.
It will make a splendid pie for your
  Thanksgiving Spread.

AN APPLE

➤➤➤《《《

Black we are but much admired,
Men seek for us till they are tired.
We tire horse, but comfort man.
Tell me this riddle, if you can.

COAL

➤➤➤《《《

As soft as silk, as white as milk,
As bitter as gall, a thick green wall,
And a brown coat covers me all.

A WALNUT

➤➤➤《《《

I have a little sister. They call her
  Peep-peep;
She wades the waters deep, deep, deep;
She climbs the mountains high, high,
  high;
Poor little creature, she has but one
  eye.

A STAR

➤➤➤《《《

Riddle me, riddle me, what is that,
Over the head, and under the hat?

HAIR

First they dress in green,
    Then they change to brown;
And some will even wear
    A red or golden gown!

LEAVES

➤➤)《《←

There is one that has a head without
    an eye,
    And there's one that has an eye
    without a head:
You may find the answer if you try;
    And when all is said
Half the answer hangs upon a thread!

NEEDLE AND THREAD

Christina Rossetti

➤➤)《《←

Riddle-me, riddle-me, riddle-me-ree,
Perhaps you can tell what this riddle
    may be!
As deep as a house, as round as a cup,
And all the King's horses can't draw it
    up.

A WELL

➤➤)《《←

From house to house he goes
A messenger small and slight;
And whether it rains or snows
He sleeps outside in the night.

A LANE

➤➤)《《←

Humpty Dumpty sat on a wall,
Humpty Dumpty had a great fall;
All the king's horses and all the king's
    men
Cannot put Humpty Dumpty together
    again.

AN EGG

A BOOK

I'm a strange contradiction; I'm new
    and I'm old,
I'm often in tatters, and oft deck'd in
    gold:
Though I never could read, yet let-
    ter'd I'm found;
Though blind, I enlighten; though
    loose, I am bound—
I am always in black, and I'm always
    in white;
I am grave and I'm gay, I am heavy
    and light.
In form too I differ—I'm thick and
    I'm thin,
I've no flesh, and no bones, yet I'm
    cover'd with skin;
I've more points than the compass,
    more stops than the flute—
I sing without voice, without speak-
    ing confute;
I'm English, I'm German, I'm French
    and I'm Dutch;
Some love me too fondly; some slight
    me too much;
I often die soon, though I sometimes
    live ages,
And no monarch alive has so many
    pages.

Hannah More

ONE GIRL

Elizabeth, Lizzy, Betsy and Bess,
All went together to seek a bird's nest;
They found a nest with five eggs in it;
They each took one and left four in it.

THE TEETH

Thirty white horses upon a red hill,
Now they tramp, now they champ,
    now they stand still.

CATKIN

I have a little pussy,
  And her coat is silver gray;
She lives in a great wide meadow
  And she never runs away.
She always is a pussy,
  She'll never be a cat
Because—she's a pussy willow!
  Now what do you think of that!

THE RAINBOW—A RIDDLE

A bridge weaves its arch with pearls
  High over the tranquil sea;
In a moment it unfurls
  Its span, unbounded, free.
The tallest ship with swelling sail
  May pass beneath its arch with ease;
It carries no burden, 'tis too frail,
  And with your quick approach it
    flees.
With the flood it comes, with the rain
  it goes;
  What it is made of nobody knows.
                    Friedrich Schiller

THE YEAR

There is a tree of praise and dower
That beareth much of fruit and flower;
Twelve branches has it, spreading wide,
Where two-and-fifty nests abide,
In every nest the birds are seven:
Thankèd be the King of heaven.

TWO T'S

Thomas a Tattamus took two T's,
To tie two tups to two tall trees,
To frighten the terrible Thomas a
  Tattamus!
Tell me how many T's there are in all
  THAT!

CLOUDS

White sheep, white sheep,
On a blue hill,
When the wind stops
You all stand still.
When the wind blows
You walk away slow.
White sheep, white sheep,
Where do you go?
                    Christina Rossetti

A CANDLE

Little Nanny Etticoat,
In a white petticoat,
And a red nose;
The longer she stands
The shorter she grows.

A NEEDLE AND THREAD

Old Mother Twitchett had but one
  eye,
And a long tail which she let fly;
And every time she went over a gap,
She left a bit of her tail in a trap.

PARADOXES

A pin has a head, but has no hair;
A clock has a face, but no mouth there;
Needles have eyes, but they cannot see;
A fly has a trunk without lock or key;
A timepiece may lose, but cannot win;
A cornfield dimples without a chin;
A hill has no leg, but has a foot;
A winde-glass a stem, but not a root;
Rivers run, though they have no feet;
A saw has teeth, but it does not eat;
Ash-trees have keys, yet never a lock;
And baby crows, without being a cock.
                    Christina Rossetti

A BED

Formed long ago, yet made today,
Employed while others sleep;
What few would like to give away,
Nor any wish to keep.

A CHERRY

As I went through a garden gap,
Who should I meet but Dick Red-
Cap!
A stick in his hand, a stone in his
throat,

If you'll tell me this riddle, I'll give
you a groat.

A PAIR OF TONGS

Long legs, crooked thighs,
Little head and no eyes.

A PLUM PUDDING

Flour of England, fruit of Spain,
Met together in a shower of rain;
Put in a bag tied round with a string,
If you'll tell me this riddle, I'll give
you a ring.

Finger Plays

THE FIVE LITTLE FAIRIES

Said this little fairy,
" I'm as thirsty as can be! "

Said this little fairy,
" I'm hungry, too! dear me! "

Said this little fairy,
" Who'll tell us where to go? "

Said this little fairy,
" I'm sure that I don't know! "

Said this little fairy,
" Let's brew some Dew-drop Tea! "
So they sipped it and ate honey
Beneath the maple tree.
Maud Burnham

BABY AT PLAY

Brow bender, Eye peeper,
Nose smeller, Mouth eater,
Chin chopper,
Knock at the door—peep in,
Lift up the latch—walk in.

Ring the bell! (pull hair)
Knock at the door! (tap forehead)
Lift up the latch! (nose)
Walk in! (open mouth)

—»>«<—

How many days has the baby to play?
Saturday, Sunday, Monday,
Tuesday, Wednesday, Thursday,
Friday,
Saturday, Sunday, Monday.
Here sits the Lord Mayor, (forehead)
Here sit his two men, (eyes)
Here sits the cock, (right cheek)
And here sits the hen; (left cheek)
Here sit the chickens, (tip of nose)
And here they go in, (mouth, open)
Chippety, chippety, chippety chin!
(chin)

A SONG SET TO FIVE FINGERS

1. This little pig went to market.
2. This little pig stayed at home.
3. This little pig got roast beef.

4. This little pig got none.
5. This little pig cried wee, wee, all the
    way home.

-»)«<-

Pat-a-cake, pat-a-cake, baker's man!
So I will, master, as fast as I can:
Pat it and prick it and mark it with T,
Put in the oven for Tommy and me.

COUNTING OUT

Intery, mintery, cutery-corn,
Apple seed and apple thorn;
Wire, brier, limber-lock,
Five geese in a flock,
Sit and sing by a spring,
O-u-t, and in again.

-»)«<-

Here's a poor widow from Babylon
With six poor children all alone:
One can bake and one can brew,
One can shape, and one can sew,
One can sit at the fire and spin,
One can bake a cake for the king.
Come choose you east, come choose
    you west,
Come choose you the one that you
    love the best.

ONE, TWO, BUCKLE MY SHOE

One, two,
Buckle my shoe;
Three, four,
Shut the door;
Five, six,
Pick up sticks;
Seven, eight,
Lay them straight;
Nine, ten,
A good fat hen;
Eleven, twelve,
Who will delve?
Thirteen, fourteen,
Maids a courting;
Fifteen, sixteen,
Maids a kissing;
Seventeen, eighteen,
Maids a waiting;
Nineteen, twenty,
My stomach's empty.

SONG TO FIVE TOES

" Let us go to the wood," said this pig.
" What to do there? " says that pig.
" To look for my mother," says this
    pig.
" What to do with her? " says that
    pig.
" To give her a kiss," says this pig.

Part Four

FROM MORNING TO NIGHT

HAPPY THOUGHT

The world is so full of a number of
things,
I'm sure we should all be as happy as
kings.

Robert Louis Stevenson

THE WORLD'S MUSIC

The world's a very happy place,
  Where every child should dance and
    sing,
And always have a smiling face,
  And never sulk for anything.

I waken when the morning's come,
  And feel the air and light alive
With strange sweet music like the hum
  Of bees about their busy hive.

The linnets play among the leaves
  At hide-and-seek, and chirp and
    sing;
While, flashing to and from the eaves,
  The swallows twitter on the wing.

The twigs that shake, and boughs that
  sway;
  And tall old trees you could not
    climb;
And winds that come, but cannot stay,
  Are gaily singing all the time.

From dawn to dark the old mill-wheel
  Makes music, going round and
    round;
And dusty-white with flour and meal,
  The miller whistles to its sound.

And if you listen to the rain
  When leaves and birds and bees
    are dumb,
You hear it pattering on the pane
  Like Andrew beating on his drum.

The coals beneath the kettle croon,
  And clap their hands and dance in
    glee;
And even the kettle hums a tune
  To tell you when it's time for tea.

The world is such a happy place,
  That children, whether big or small,
Should always have a smiling face,
  And never, never sulk at all.

Gabriel Setoun

MY GARDEN

When I've hoed and dug my garden
All the day,
When I've put my spade and barrow
Safe away,
When I've said good-night to my
  garden,

When all my prayers are said,
I know that God will watch my garden,
When I am safe in bed.

When I wake and find my happy
    garden
Fresh and sweet,
When the diamond dew is shining
Round my feet,
When all the buds of yesterday
Are blossoms blooming bright,
I know that God has watched my
    garden
And blessed it all the night.

Frederick E. Weatherly

THE SECRETS OF OUR GARDEN

You think it's only a garden,
    With roses along the wall;
I'll tell you the truth about it—
    It isn't a garden at all!

It's really Robin Hood's forest,
    And over by that big tree
Is the very place where fat Friar Tuck
    Fought with the Miller of Dee.

And back of the barn is the cavern
    Where Rob Roy really hid;
On the other side is a treasure chest
    That belonged to Captain Kidd.

That isn't the pond you see there,
    It's an ocean deep and wide,
Where six-masted ships are waiting
    To sail on the rising tide.

Of course it looks like a garden,
    It's all so sunny and clear—
You'd be surprised if you really knew
    The things that have happened here!

Rupert Sargent Holland

THE GARDENER

The gardener does not love to talk,
He makes me keep the gravel walk;
And when he puts his tools away,
He locks the door and takes the key.

Away behind the currant row
Where no one else but cook may go,
Far in the plots, I see him dig,
Old and serious, brown and big.

He digs the flowers, green, red, and
    blue,
Nor wishes to be spoken to.
He digs the flowers and cuts the hay,
And never seems to want to play.

Silly gardener! summer goes
And winter comes with pinching toes,
When in the garden bare and brown
You must lay your barrow down.

Well now, and while the summer stays
To profit by these garden days
Oh, how much wiser you would be
To play at Indian wars with me!

Robert Louis Stevenson

SEVEN TIMES ONE

There's no dew left on the daisies and
    clover,
    There's no rain left in heaven;
I've said my " seven times " over and
    over—
    Seven times one are seven.

I am old! so old I can write a letter;
    My birthday lessons are done:
The lambs play always, they know no
    better;
    They are only one times one.

O Moon! in the night I have seen you
    sailing,
  And shining so round and low;
You were bright! ah, bright! but your
    light is failing;
  You are nothing now but a bow.

You Moon! have you done something
    wrong in heaven,
  That God has hidden your face?
I hope, if you have, you will soon be
    forgiven,
  And shine again in your place.

O velvet Bee! you're a dusty fellow,
  You've powdered your legs with
    gold;
O brave marsh Mary-buds, rich and
    yellow!
  Give me your money to hold.

O Columbine! open your folded
    wrapper
  Where two twin turtle-doves dwell;
O Cuckoo-pint! toll me the purple
    clapper,
  That hangs in your clear, green bell,

And show me your nest with the
    young ones in it—
  I will not steal them away,
I am old! you may trust me, Linnet,
    Linnet,—
  I am seven times one today.

Jean Ingelow

A BOY'S SONG

Where the pools are bright and deep,
Where the gray trout lies asleep,
Up the river and o'er the lea,
That's the way for Billy and me.

Where the blackbird sings the latest,
Where the hawthorn blooms the
  sweetest,

Where the nestlings chirp and flee,
That's the way for Billy and me.

Where the mowers mow the cleanest,
Where the hay lies thick and greenest,
There to trace the homeward bee,
That's the way for Billy and me.

Where the hazel bank is steepest,
Where the shadow falls the deepest,
Where the clustering nuts fall free,
That's the way for Billy and me.

Why the boys should drive away
Little sweet maidens from the play,
Or love to banter and fight so well,
That's the thing I never could tell.

But this I know, I love to play,
Through the meadow, among the hay;
Up the water and o'er the lea,
That's the way for Billy and me.

James Hogg

MILKING TIME

When supper time is almost come,
But not quite here, I cannot wait,
And so I take my china mug
And go down by the milking gate.

The cow is always eating shucks
And spilling off the little silk.
Her purple eyes are big and soft—
She always smells like milk.

And father takes my mug from me,
And then he makes the stream come
  out.
I see it going in my mug
And foaming all about.

And when it's piling very high,
And when some little streams com-
  mence
To run and drip along the sides,
He hands it to me through the fence.

Elizabeth Madox Roberts

FAREWELL TO THE FARM

The coach is at the door at last;
The eager children, mounting fast
And kissing hands, in chorus sing:
Good-bye, good-bye, to everything!

To house and garden, field and lawn,
The meadow-gates we swang upon,
To pump and stable, tree and swing,
Good-bye, good-bye, to everything!

And fare you well for evermore,
O ladder at the hayloft door,
O hayloft where the cobwebs cling,
Good-bye, good-bye, to everything!

Crack goes the whip, and off we go;
The trees and houses smaller grow;
Last, round the woody turn we swing:
Good-bye, good-bye, to everything!

Robert Louis Stevenson

AT THE SEASIDE

When I was down beside the sea
A wooden spade they gave to me
To dig the sandy shore.
My holes were empty like a cup,
In every hole the sea came up,
 Till it could come no more.

Robert Louis Stevenson

I'D LIKE TO BE A LIGHTHOUSE

I'd like to be a lighthouse
 All scrubbed and painted white.
I'd like to be a lighthouse
 And stay awake all night
To keep my eye on everything
 That sails my patch of sea;
I'd like to be a lighthouse
 With the ships all watching me.

Rachel Lyman Field

MY SHADOW

I have a little shadow that goes in and
 out with me,
And what can be the use of him is
 more than I can see.
He is very, very like me from the heels
 up to the head;
And I see him jump before me, when
 I jump into my bed.

The funniest thing about him is the
 way he likes to grow—
Not at all like proper children, which
 is always very slow;
For he sometimes shoots up taller like
 an India-rubber ball,
And he sometimes gets so little that
 there's none of him at all.

He hasn't got a notion of how children
 ought to play,
And can only make a fool of me in
 every sort of way.
He stays so close beside me, he's a
 coward you can see;
I'd think shame to stick to nursie as
 that shadow sticks to me!

One morning very early, before the
 sun was up,
I rose and found the shining dew on
 every buttercup;
But my lazy little shadow, like an
 arrant sleepy-head,
Had stayed at home behind me and
 was fast asleep in bed.

Robert Louis Stevenson

P'S AND Q'S

It takes a lot of letters to make up
 the alphabet,
And two or three of them are very
 easy to forget;

There's K—a funny letter—and X
and Y and Z—
There's hardly any use at all for any
of those three!
The vowels are the busy ones, A, E,
I, O, U—
They've twice the work that all the
other letters have to do;
I don't know why it is that grown-up
people always choose
To tell us children to be sure and
mind our P's and Q's.

They're funny-looking letters, par-
ticularly Q,
It never goes around except in com-
pany with U;
P is much more important, it starts
off pie and play,
It's not hard to remember if you
think of it that way;
But lots of words begin with F and
H and S and T,
They're just as worth remembering
as any, seems to me;
Yet when we've strangers in the
house, my parents always say,
" Be sure you don't forget to mind
your P's and Q's today! "

Rupert Sargent Holland

THE TEAPOT DRAGON

There's a dragon on our teapot,
With a long and crinkly tail,
His claws are like a pincer-bug,
His wings are like a sail;

His tongue is always sticking out,
And so I used to think
He must be very hungry, or
He wanted tea to drink.

But once when Mother wasn't round
I dipped my fingers in,

And when I pulled them out I found
I'd blistered all the skin.

Now when I see the dragon crawl
Around our china pot,
I know he's burned his tongue be-
cause
The water is so hot.

Rupert Sargent Holland

SUSAN BLUE

Oh, Susan Blue,
How do you do?
Please may I go a walk with you?
Where shall we go?
Oh, I know—
Down in the meadow where the cow-
slips grow!

Kate Greenaway

A TEA-PARTY

You see, merry Phillis, that dear little
maid,
Has invited Belinda to tea;
Her nice little garden is shaded by
trees,—
What pleasanter place could there
be?

There's a cake full of plums, there are
strawberries too,
And the table is set on the green;
I'm fond of a carpet all daisies and
grass,—
Could a prettier picture be seen?

A blackbird (yes, blackbirds delight
in warm weather),
Is flitting from yonder high spray;
He sees the two little ones talking to-
gether,—
No wonder the blackbird is gay.

Kate Greenaway

WHOLE DUTY OF CHILDREN

A child should always say what's true
And speak when he is spoken to,
And behave mannerly at table;
At least as far as he is able.

Robert Louis Stevenson

AROUND THE WORLD

In go-cart so tiny
  My sister I drew;
And I've promised to draw her
  The wide world through.

We have not yet started—
  I own it with sorrow—
Because our trip's always
  Put off till tomorrow.

Kate Greenaway

THE LOST DOLL

I once had a sweet little doll, dears,
  The prettiest doll in the world;
Her cheeks were so red and white,
    dears,
  And her hair was so charmingly
    curled.
But I lost my poor little doll, dears,
  As I played on the heath one day;
And I cried for her more than a week,
    dears,
  But I never could find where she lay.

I found my poor little doll, dears,
  As I played on the heath one day;
Folks say she is terribly changed, dears,
  For her paint is all washed away,
And her arms trodden off by the cows,
    dears,
  And her hair not the least bit curled;
Yet for old sake's sake, she is still,
    dears,
  The prettiest doll in the world.

Charles Kingsley

DOLL'S SONG

Matilda Jane, you never look
At any toy or picture book:
I show you pretty things in vain—
You must be blind, Matilda Jane.

I ask you riddles, tell you tales,
But *all* our conversation fails;
You *never* answer me again—
I fear you're dumb, Matilda Jane:

Matilda darling, when I call,
You never seem to hear at all;
I shout with all my might and main—
But you're so deaf, Matilda Jane!

Matilda Jane, you needn't mind:
For though you're deaf and dumb and
    blind,
There's someone loves you, it is plain—
And that is me, Matilda Jane!

Lewis Carroll

A GOOD PLAY

We built a ship upon the stairs
All made of the back-bedroom chairs,
And filled it full of sofa pillows
To go a-sailing on the billows.

We took a saw and several nails,
And water in the nursery pails;
And Tom said, " Let us also take
An apple and a slice of cake; "—
Which was enough for Tom and me
To go a-sailing on, till tea.

We sailed along for days and days,
And had the very best of plays;
But Tom fell out and hurt his knee,
So there was no one left but me.

Robert Louis Stevenson

A HAPPY CHILD

My house is red—a little house,
  A happy child am I,
I laugh and play the livelong day,
  I hardly ever cry.

I have a tree, a green, green tree,
  To shade me from the sun;
And under it I often sit,
  When all my work is done.

My little basket I will take,
  And trip into the town;
When next I'm there I'll buy some
    cake,
  And spend my bright half-crown.
    Kate Greenaway

THE SWING

How do you like to go up in a swing,
  Up in the air so blue?
Oh, I do think it the pleasantest thing
  Ever a child can do!

Up in the air and over the wall,
  Till I can see so wide,
Rivers and trees and cattle and all
  Over the countryside—

Till I look down on the garden green,
  Down on the roof so brown—
Up in the air I go flying again,
  Up in the air and down!
    Robert Louis Stevenson

THE LAND OF COUNTERPANE

When I was sick and lay a-bed,
I had two pillows at my head,
And all my toys beside me lay
To keep me happy all the day.

And sometimes for an hour or so
I watched my leaden soldiers go,
With different uniforms and drills,
Among the bed-clothes, through the
    hills;

And sometimes sent my ships in fleets
All up and down among the sheets;
Or brought my trees and houses out,
And planted cities all about.

I was the giant great and still
That sits upon the pillow-hill,
And sees before him, dale and plain,
The pleasant land of counterpane.
    Robert Louis Stevenson

PLAYGROUNDS

In summer I am very glad
  We children are so small,
For we can a see a thousand things
  That men can't see at all.

They don't know much about the moss
  And all the stones they pass:
They never lie and play among
  The forests in the grass:

They walk about a long way off;
  And, when we're at the sea,
Let father stoop as best he can
  He can't find things like me.

But, when the snow is on the ground
  And all the puddles freeze,
I wish that I were very tall,
  High up above the trees.
    Lawrence Alma-Tadema

MY BED IS A BOAT

My bed is like a little boat;
  Nurse helps me in when I embark;
She girds me in my sailor's coat
  And starts me in the dark.

At night, I go on board and say
  Good night to all my friends on
    shore;
I shut my eyes and sail away
  And see and hear no more.

And sometimes things to bed I take,
  As prudent sailors have to do;
Perhaps a slice of wedding-cake,
  Perhaps a toy or two.

All night across the dark we steer;
  But when the day returns at last,
Safe in my room, beside the pier,
  I find my vessel fast.

       Robert Louis Stevenson

A SWING SONG

  Swing, swing,
  Sing, sing,
Here! my throne and I am a King!
  Swing, sing,
  Swing, sing,
Farewell, earth, for I'm on the wing!

  Low, high,
  Here I fly,
Like a bird through sunny sky;
  Free, free,
  Over the lea,
Over the mountain, over the sea!

  Up, down,
  Up and down,
Which is the way to London Town?
  Where? Where?
  Up in the air,
Close your eyes, and now you are
    there!

  Soon, soon,
  Afternoon,
Over the sunset, over the moon;

  Far, far;
  Over all bar,
Sweeping on from star to star!

  No, no,
  Low, low,
Sweeping daisies with my toe.
  Slow, slow,
  To and fro,
Slow—
    slow—
       slow—
         slow.

       William Allingham

PIRATE STORY

Three of us afloat in the meadow by
  the swing,
  Three of us aboard in the basket on
    the lea.
Winds are in the air, they are blowing
  in the spring,
  And waves are on the meadow like
    the waves there are at sea.

Where shall we adventure, today that
  we're afloat,
  Wary of the weather and steering
    by a star?
Shall it be to Africa, a-steering of the
  boat,
  To Providence, or Babylon, or off
    to Malabar?

Hi! but here's a squadron a-rowing on
  the sea—
  Cattle on the meadow a-charging
    with a roar!
Quick, and we'll escape them, they're
  as mad as they can be,
  The wicket is the harbor and the
    garden is the shore.

       Robert Louis Stevenson

MARCHING SONG

Bring the comb and play upon it!
  Marching, here we come!
Willie cocks his highland bonnet,
  Johnnie beats the drum.
Mary Jane commands the party,
  Peter leads the rear;
Feet in time, alert and hearty,
  Each a Grenadier!

All in the most martial manner
  Marching double-quick;
While the napkin like a banner
  Waves upon the stick!

Here's enough of fame and pillage,
  Great commander Jane!
Now that we've been round the
  village,
  Let's go home again.

Robert Louis Stevenson

WHEN MOTHER READS ALOUD

When Mother reads aloud, the past
  Seems real as every day;
I hear the tramp of armies vast,
I see the spears and lances cast,
  I join the thrilling fray.
Brave knights and ladies fair and proud
I meet when Mother reads aloud.

When Mother reads aloud, far lands
  Seem very near and true;
I cross the deserts' gleaming sands,
Or hunt the jungle's prowling bands,
  Or sail the ocean blue.
Far heights, whose peaks the cold mists
  shroud,
I scale, when Mother reads aloud.

When Mother reads aloud, I long
  For noble deeds to do—

To help the right, redress the wrong;
It seems so easy to be strong,
  So simple to be true.
Oh, thick and fast the visions crowd
My eyes, when Mother reads aloud.

Unknown

KEEPING STORE

We have bags and bags of whitest
  down
  Out of the milkweed pods;
We have purple asters in lovely heaps,
  And stacks of golden-rods.

We have needles out of sweet pine
  woods,
  And spools of cobweb thread;
We have bachelors' buttons for dolly's
  dress,
  And hollyhock caps for her head.

Mary F. Butts

MARTHA

" Once . . . once upon a time . . ."
  Over and over again,
  Martha would tell us her stories,
  In the hazel glen.

Hers were those clear grey eyes
  You watch, and the story seems
  Told by their beautifulness
  Tranquil as dreams.

She would sit with her two slim
  hands
  Clasped round her bended knees;
While we on our elbows lolled,
  And stared at ease.

Her voice and her narrow chin,
  Her grave small lovely head,
  Seemed half the meaning
  Of the words she said.

" Once . . . once upon a time . . ."
Like a dream you dream in the
    night,
Fairies and gnomes stole out
In the leaf-green light.

And her beauty far away
Would fade, as her voice ran on,
Till hazel and summer sun
And all were gone;—

All fordone and forgot;
And like clouds in the height of the
    sky,
Our hearts stood still in the hush
Of an age gone by.

Walter de la Mare

WISHING

Ring-ting! I wish I were a Primrose,
A bright yellow Primrose blowing in
    the Spring!
  The stooping boughs above me,
  The wandering bee to love me,
The fern and moss to keep across,
    And the Elm-tree, for our King!

Nay—nay! I wish I were an Elm-tree,
A great lofty Elm-tree, with green
    leaves gay!
  The winds would set them danc-
    ing,
  The sun and moonshine glance in,
The Birds would house among the
    boughs,
    And sweetly sing!

O—no! I wish I were a Robin,
A Robin or a little Wren, everywhere
    to go;
  Through forest, field or garden,
  And ask no leave or pardon,
Till Winter comes with icy thumbs
    To ruffle up our wing.

Well—tell! Where should I fly to,
Where go to sleep in the dark wood or
    dell?
  Before a day was over,
  Home comes the rover,
For Mother's kiss—sweeter this
    Than any other thing!

William Allingham

UNDER THE SUN

Under the sun
  There's nothing new;
Poem or pun,
Under the sun,
Said Solomon
  And he said true.
Under the sun
  There's nothing new.

Henry Charles Beeching

THE PEDDLER'S CARAVAN

I wish I lived in a caravan,
With a horse to drive, like a peddler-
    man!
Where he comes from nobody knows,
Or where he goes to, but on he goes!

His caravan has windows two,
And a chimney of tin, that the smoke
    comes through;
He has a wife, with a baby brown,
And they go riding from town to town.

Chairs to mend, and delf to sell!
He clashes the basins like a bell;
Tea-trays, baskets ranged in order,
Plates, with alphabets round the
    border!

The roads are brown, and the sea is
    green,

But his house is like a bathing-machine;
The world is round, and he can ride,
Rumble and slash, to the other side!

With the peddler-man I should like to roam,
And write a book when I came home;
All the people would read my book,
Just like the Travels of Captain Cook!

William Brighty Rands

TRAINS

Over the mountains,
Over the plains,
Over the rivers,
Here come the trains.

Carrying passengers,
Carrying mail,
Bringing their precious loads
In without fail.

Thousands of freight cars
All rushing on
Through day and darkness,
Through dusk and dawn.

Over the mountains,
Over the plains,
Over the rivers,
Here come the trains.

James S. Tippett

THE AIRPLANE

An airplane has gigantic wings
But not a feather on her breast;
She only mutters when she sings
And builds a hangar for a nest.
I love to see her stop and start;
She has a little motor heart
That beats and throbs and then is still.
She wears a fan upon her bill.

No eagle flies through sun and rain
So swiftly as an airplane.
I wish she would come swooping down
Between the steeples of the town
And lift me right up off my feet
And take me high above the street,
That all the other boys might see
The little speck that would be me.

Rowena Bastin Bennett

BUNCHES OF GRAPES

" Bunches of grapes," says Timothy;
" Pomegranates pink," says Elaine;
" A junket of cream and a cranberry
tart
For me," says Jane.

" Love-in-a-mist," says Timothy;
" Primroses pale," says Elaine;
" A nosegay of pinks and mignonette
For me," says Jane.

" Chariots of gold," says Timothy;
" Silvery wings," says Elaine;
" A bumpity ride in a waggon of hay
For me," says Jane.

Walter Ramal

WHEN I GROW UP

When I grow up I mean to go
Where all the biggest rivers flow,
And take a ship and sail around
The Seven Seas until I've found
Robinson Crusoe's famous isle,
And there I'll land and stay a while,
And see how it would feel to be
Lord of an island in the sea.

When I grow up I mean to rove
Through orange and palmetto grove,
To drive a sledge across the snow
Where great explorers like to go,

To hunt for treasures hid of old
By buccaneers and pirates bold,
And see if somewhere there may be
A mountain no one's climbed but me.

When I grow up I mean to do
The things I've always wanted to;
I don't see why grown people stay
At home, when they could be away.

Rupert Sargent Holland

IF NO ONE EVER
MARRIES ME

If no one ever marries me
    I shan't mind very much;
I shall buy a squirrel in a cage
    And a little rabbit-hutch:

I shall have a cottage near a wood,
    And a pony all my own,
And a little lamb quite clean and
    tame
    That I can take to town:

And when I'm getting really old,
    —At twenty-eight or nine—
I shall buy a little orphan-girl
    And bring her up as mine.

Lawrence Alma-Tadema

TRADES

I want to be a carpenter,
To work all day long in clean wood,
Shaving it into little thin slivers
Which screw up into curls behind my
    plane;
Pounding square, black nails into white
    boards,
With the claws of my hammer glisten-
    ing
Like the tongue of a snake.

I want to shingle a house,
Sitting on the ridge-pole in a bright
    breeze.
I want to put the shingles on neatly,
Taking great care that each is directly
    between two others.
I want my hands to have the tang of
    wood:
Spruce, Cedar, Cypress.
I want to draw a line on a board with
    a flat pencil,
And then saw along that line,
With the sweet-smelling sawdust pil-
    ing up in a yellow heap at my feet.

That is the life!
Heigh-ho!
It is much easier than to write this
    poem.

Amy Lowell

LOOKING FORWARD

When I am grown to man's estate
I shall be very proud and great,
And tell the other girls and boys
Not to meddle with my toys.

Robert Louis Stevenson

FOREIGN LANDS

Up into the cherry tree
Who should climb but little me?
I held the trunk with both my hands
And looked abroad on foreign lands.

I saw the next door garden lie,
Adorned with flowers, before my eye,
And many pleasant places more
That I had never seen before.

I saw the dimpling river pass
And be the sky's blue looking-glass;
The dusty roads go up and down
With people tramping in to town.

If I could find a higher tree
Farther and farther I should see,
To where the grown-up river slips
Into the sea among the ships,

To where the roads on either hand
Lead onward into fairy land,
Where all the children dine at five,
And all the playthings come alive.

Robert Louis Stevenson

NIKOLINA

Oh, tell me, little children, have you
  seen her—
The tiny maid from Norway, Nikolina?
Oh, her eyes are blue as corn flowers
  'mid the corn,
And her cheeks are rosy red as skies of
  morn!

Oh, buy the baby's blossoms if you
  meet her,
And stay with gentle words and looks
  to greet her;
She'll gaze at you and smile and clasp
  your hand,
But no word of your speech can understand.

Nikolina! Swift she turns if any call
  her,
As she stands among the poppies
  hardly taller,
Breaking off their flaming scarlet cups
  for you,
With spikes of slender larkspur,
  brightly blue.

In her little garden many a flower is
  growing—
Red, gold, and purple in the soft wind
  blowing;
But the child that stands amid the
  blossoms gay

Is sweeter, quainter, brighter even than
  they.

Oh, tell me, little children, have you
  seen her—
This baby girl from Norway, Nikolina?
Slowly she's learning English words, to
  try
And thank you if her flowers you come
  to buy.

Celia Thaxter

THE KAYAK

Over the briny wave I go,
In spite of the weather, in spite of the
  snow:
What cares the hardy Eskimo?
In my little skiff, with paddle and
  lance,
I glide where the foaming billows
  dance.

Round me the sea-birds slip and soar;
Like me, they love the ocean's roar.
Sometimes a floating iceberg gleams
Above me with its melting streams;
Sometimes a rushing wave will fall
Down on my skiff and cover it all.

But what care I for a wave's attack?
With my paddle I right my little
  kayak,
And then its weight I speedily trim,
And over the water away I skim.

Unknown

INDIAN CHILDREN

Where we walk to school each day,
Indian children used to play—
All about our native land,
Where the shops and houses stand.

And the trees were very tall,
And there were no streets at all,

Not a church and not a steeple—
Only woods and Indian people.

Only wigwams on the ground,
And at night bears prowling round—
What a different place today
Where we live and work and play!

Annette Wynne

THE LITTLE TOY LAND
OF THE DUTCH

Away, 'way off 'cross the seas and such
Lies the little flat land of the Dutch,
　Dutch, Dutch!

Where the green toy meadows stretch
　off to the sea,
With a little canal where a fence ought
　to be!

Where the windmills' arms go round,
　round, round,
And sing to the cows with a creaky
　sound.

Where storks live up in the chimney
　top,
And wooden shoes pound, plop, plop,
　plop!

Where little toy houses stand in a row,
And dogcarts clattering past them go!

Where milk cans shine in the shiniest
　way,
And the housemaids scrub, scrub,
　scrub all day.

Where dikes keep out the raging sea,
And shut in the land as cozy as can be.

Oh, that little toy land, I like it much,
That prim little, trim little, land of the
　Dutch!

Unknown

A LITTLE DUTCH GARDEN

I passed by a garden, a little Dutch
　garden,
Where useful and pretty things grew,—
Heartsease and tomatoes and pinks and
　potatoes,
And lilies and onions and rue.

I saw in that garden, that little Dutch
　garden,
A chubby Dutch man with a spade,
And a rosy frau with a shoe like a scow,
And a flaxen-haired little Dutch maid.

There grew in that garden, that little
　Dutch garden,
Blue flag flowers lovely and tall,
And early blush roses, and little pink
　posies,
And Gretchen was fairer than all.

My heart's in that garden, that little
　Dutch garden,—
It tumbled right in as I passed,
'Mid wildering mazes of spinach and
　daisies,
And Gretchen is holding it fast.

Harriet Whitney Durbin

FOREIGN CHILDREN

Little Indian, Sioux or Crow,
Little frosty Eskimo,
Little Turk or Japanee,
O! don't you wish that you were me?

You have seen the scarlet trees
And the lions over seas;
You have eaten ostrich eggs,
And turned the turtles off their legs.

Such a life is very fine,
But it's not so nice as mine:
You must often, as you trod,
Have wearied *not* to be abroad.

You have curious things to eat,
I am fed on proper meat;
You must dwell beyond the foam,
But I am safe and live at home.

Little Indian, Sioux or Crow,
Little frosty Eskimo,
Little Turk or Japanee,
O! don't you wish that you were me?

Robert Louis Stevenson

ANIMAL CRACKERS

Animal crackers, and cocoa to drink,
That is the finest of suppers, I think;
When I'm grown up and can have
what I please
I think I shall always insist upon these.

What do you choose when you're offered a treat?
When Mother says, " What would you
like best to eat? "
Is it waffles and syrup, or cinnamon
toast?
It's cocoa and animals that I love the
most!

The kitchen's the cosiest place that I
know:
The kettle is singing, the stove is
aglow,
And there in the twilight, how jolly
to see
The cocoa and animals waiting for me.

Daddy and Mother dine later in state,
With Mary to cook for them, Susan to
wait;
But they don't have nearly as much
fun as I
Who eat in the kitchen with Nurse
standing by;

And Daddy once said, he would like
to be me
Having cocoa and animals once more
for tea!

Christopher Morley

THE LAMPLIGHTER

My tea is nearly ready and the sun has
left the sky;
It's time to take the window to see
Leerie going by;
For every night at teatime and before
you take your seat,
With lantern and with ladder he
comes posting up the street.

Now Tom would be a driver and
Maria go to sea,
And my papa's a banker and as rich
as he can be;
But I, when I am stronger and can
choose what I'm to do,
O Leerie, I'll go round at night and
light the lamps with you!

For we are very lucky, with a lamp
before the door,
And Leerie stops to light it as he
lights so many more;
And O! before you hurry by with
ladder and with light,
O Leerie, see a little child and nod to
him tonight!

Robert Louis Stevenson

ESCAPE AT BEDTIME

The lights from the parlor and kitchen
shone out
Through the blinds and the windows
and bars;
And high overhead and all moving
about,

There were thousands of millions of
   stars.
There ne'er were such thousands of
   leaves on a tree,
Nor of people in church or the Park,
As the crowds of the stars that looked
   down upon me,
And that glittered and winked in the
   dark.

The Dog, and the Plough, and the
   Hunter, and all
And the Star of the Sailor, and Mars,
These shone in the sky, and the pail by
   the wall
Would be half full of water and stars.
They saw me at last, and they chased
   me with cries,
And they soon had me packed into
   bed;
But the glory kept shining and bright
   in my eyes,
And the stars going round in my head.
             Robert Louis Stevenson

THE LAND OF STORY-BOOKS

At evening when the lamp is lit,
Around the fire my parents sit;
They sit at home and talk and sing,
And do not play at anything.

Now, with my little gun, I crawl
All in the dark along the wall,
And follow round the forest track
Away behind the sofa back.

There, in the night, where none can
   spy,
All in my hunter's camp I lie,
And play at books that I have read
Till it is time to go to bed.

These are the hills, these are the
   woods,

These are my starry solitudes;
And there the river by whose brink
The roaring lions come to drink.

I see the others far away
As if in firelit camp they lay,
And I, like to an Indian scout,
Around their party prowled about.

So, when my nurse comes in for me,
Home I return across the sea,
And go to bed with backward looks
At my dear land of Story-books.
             Robert Louis Stevenson

BED IN SUMMER

In winter I get up at night
And dress by yellow candle-light.
In summer, quite the other way,
I have to go to bed by day.

I have to go to bed and see
The birds still hopping on the tree,
Or hear the grown-up people's feet
Still going past me in the street.

And does it not seem hard to you,
When all the sky is clear and blue,
And I should like so much to play,
To have to go to bed by day?
             Robert Louis Stevenson

GOOD NIGHT AND GOOD MORNING

A fair little girl sat under a tree,
Sewing as long as her eyes could see,
Then smoothed her work, and folded
   it right,
And said, " Dear work, good night!
   good night! "

Such a number of rooks came over
   her head,

Crying " Caw! caw! " on their way
to bed;
She said as she watched their curious
flight,
" Little black things, good night!
good night! "

The horses neighed, and the oxen
lowed;
The sheep's " bleat! bleat! " came
over the road;
All seeming to say, with a quiet delight,
" Good little girl, good night! good
night! "

She did not say to the sun " Good
night! "
Though she saw him there like a ball
of light,
For she knew he had God's time to
keep
All over the world and never could
sleep.

The tall pink foxglove bowed his
head,
The violets curtsied and went to bed;
And good little Lucy tied up her
hair,
And said, on her knees, her favorite
prayer.

And while on her pillow she softly
lay,
She knew nothing more till again it
was day:
And all things said to the beautiful
sun,
" Good morning, good morning! our
work is begun."

Lord Houghton

THE DUSTMAN

When the toys are growing weary
And the twilight gathers in;
When the nursery still echoes
With the children's merry din;

Then unseen, unheard, unnoticed
Comes an old man up the stair,
Lightly to the children passes,
Lays his hand upon their hair.

Softly smiles the good old Dustman;
In their eyes the dust he throws,
Till their little heads are falling,
And their weary eyes must close.

Then the Dustman very gently
Takes each little dimpled hand,
Leads them through the sweet green
shadows,
Far away in slumberland.

Frederick E. Weatherly

BED-TIME

The evening is coming,
The sun sinks to rest,
The rooks are all flying
Straight home to the nest.
" Caw! " says the rook, as he flies over-
head.
" It's time little people were going to
bed! "

The flowers are closing;
The daisy's asleep,
The primrose is buried
In slumber so deep.
Shut up for the night is the pim-
pernel red;
It's time little people were going to
bed!

Here comes the pony,
　His work is all done,
Down through the meadow
　He takes a good run,
Up go his heels, and down his head,
It's time little people were going to
　　bed!

Good night, little people,
　Good night and good night;
Sweet dreams to your eyelids
　Till dawning of light.
The evening has come, there's no
　　more to be said;
It's time little people were going to
　　bed!

Thomas Hood

QUESTIONS AT NIGHT

Why
Is the sky?

What starts the thunder overhead?
Who makes the crashing noise?
Are the angels falling out of bed?
Are they breaking all their toys?

Why does the sun go down so soon?
Why do the night-clouds crawl
Hungrily up to the new-laid moon
And swallow it, shell and all?

If there's a Bear among the stars,
As all the people say,
Won't he jump over those Pasture-bars
And drink up the Milky Way?

Does every star that happens to fall
Turn into a fire-fly?
Can't it ever get back to Heaven at all?
And why
Is the sky?

Louis Untermeyer

THE RIVALS

I heard a bird at dawn
Singing sweetly on a tree,
That the dew was on the lawn,
And the wind was on the lea;
But I didn't listen to him,
For he didn't sing to me.

I didn't listen to him,
For he didn't sing to me
That the dew was on the lawn
And the wind was on the lea!
I was singing at the time,
Just as prettily as he!

I was singing all the time,
Just as prettily as he,
About the dew upon the lawn,
And the wind upon the lea!
So I didn't listen to him,
As he sang upon a tree!

James Stephens

THE FISHING-POLE

A fishing-pole's a curious thing;
It's made of just a stick and string;
A boy at one end and a wish,
And on the other end a fish.

Mary Carolyn Davies

OTHER CHILDREN

Some children live in palaces
Behind an iron gate
And go to sleep in beds of gold
Whenever it gets late.

Some other children live in tents
With feathers all around
And take their naps in blankets
That are spread upon the ground.

And way up north the children live
In houses built of ice

And think that beds made out of fur
Are really very nice.

In countries where the nights are hot,
Without a single breeze,
The children sleep on bamboo beds
That fasten in the trees.

Some day I think I'll travel 'round
And visit every land
And learn to speak the language that
Each child can understand.

They'll teach me how to play their
  games
And, if they want me to,
I'll show them different kinds of tricks
That I know how to do.

They'll want to ask me questions then
And I will ask them others,
Until at last we understand
Like sisters and like brothers.

Helen Wing

Part Five

FAIRIES AND ALL!

AN EXPLANATION OF THE GRASSHOPPER

The Grasshopper, the Grasshopper,
  I will explain to you:—
He is the Brownies' racehorse,
  The Fairies' Kangaroo.

Vachel Lindsay

THE ELVES' DANCE

Round about, round about
In a fairy ring-a,
Thus we dance, thus we dance
And thus we sing-a,
Trip and go, to and fro
Over this green-a,
All about, in and out,
For our brave Queen-a.

Unknown

THE FAIRY-BOOK

In summer, when the grass is thick, if
  Mother has the time,
She shows me with her pencil how a
  poet makes a rhyme,
And often she is sweet enough to
  choose a leafy nook,
Where I cuddle up so closely when
  she reads the Fairy-book.

In winter when the corn's asleep, and
  birds are not in song,
And crocuses and violets have been
  away too long,
Dear Mother puts her thimble by in
  answer to my look,
And I cuddle up so closely when she
  reads the Fairy-book.

And Mother tells the servants that of
  course they must contrive
To manage all the household things
  from four till half-past five,
For we really cannot suffer interrup-
  tion from the cook,
When we cuddle close together with
  the happy Fairy-book.

Norman Gale

THE LIGHT-HEARTED FAIRY

Oh, who is so merry, so merry, heigh
  ho!
As the light-hearted fairy? heigh ho,
  Heigh ho!
    He dances and sings
    To the sound of his wings
With a hey and a heigh and a ho!

Oh, who is so merry, so airy, heigh ho!
As the light-headed fairy? heigh ho,
  Heigh ho!

89

His nectar he sips
From the primroses' lips
With a hey and a heigh and a ho!

Oh, who is so merry, so merry, heigh
   ho!
As the light-footed fairy? heigh ho!
   Heigh ho!
   The night is his noon
   And his sun is the moon,
With a hey and a heigh and a ho!
                  Unknown

FAIRIES

There are fairies at the bottom of our
   garden!
   It's not so very, very far away;
You pass the gardener's shed and you
   just keep straight ahead—
   I do so hope they've really come to
   stay.
There's a little wood, with moss in it
   and beetles,
   And a little stream that quietly runs
   through;
You wouldn't think they'd dare to
   come merry-making there—
      Well, they do.

There are fairies at the bottom of our
   garden!
   They often have a dance on summer
   nights;
The butterflies and bees make a lovely
   little breeze,
   And the rabbits stand about and
   hold the lights.
Did you know that they could sit upon
   the moonbeams
  And pick a little star to make a fan,
And dance away up there in the middle of the air?
      Well, they can.

There are fairies at the bottom of our
   garden!
   You cannot think how beautiful they
   are;
They all stand up and sing when the
   Fairy Queen and King
   Come gently floating down upon
   their car.
The King is very proud and very hand-
   some;
   The Queen—now can you guess who
   that could be
(She's a little girl all day, but at night
   she steals away)?
      Well, it's Me!
              Rose Fyleman

YESTERDAY IN OXFORD
STREET

Yesterday in Oxford Street, oh, what
   d' you think, my dears?
I had the most exciting time I've had
   for years and years;
The buildings looked so straight and
   tall, the sky was blue between,
And, riding on a motor-bus, I saw the
   fairy queen!

Sitting there upon the rail and bobbing
   up and down,
The sun was shining on her wings and
   on her golden crown;
And looking at the shops she was, the
   pretty silks and lace—
She seemed to think that Oxford
   Street was quite a lovely place.

And once she turned and looked at
   me, and waved her little hand;
But I could only stare and stare—oh,
   would she understand?
I simply couldn't speak at all, I simply
   couldn't stir,

And all the rest of Oxford Street was
  just a shining blur.

Then suddenly she shook her wings—
  a bird had fluttered by—
And down into the street she looked
  and up into the sky;
And perching on the railing on a tiny
  fairy toe,
She flashed away so quickly that I
  hardly saw her go.

I never saw her any more, altho' I
  looked all day;
Perhaps she only came to peep, and
  never meant to stay:
But oh, my dears, just think of it, just
  think what luck for me,
That she should come to Oxford
  Street, and I be there to see!

Rose Fyleman

FAIRY FRILLY

Fairy Frilly for half an hour
Went to sleep in a poppy flower—
Went to sleep in her little green frock,
And the time of the ball was ten
  o'clock.
Quarter to ten and five to ten
Ticked from the dandelion clock again,
But Fairy Frilly was deaf to all,
And ten was the time of the fairy ball!
Little West Wind came by that way,
And he pulled off the petal where
  Frilly lay,
Pulled it off with the fairy on it,
And blew with a great big breath upon
  it.
Off sailed the petal, Frilly and all—
And *that's* how she managed to get to
  the ball.

Florence Hoatson

THE CHILD AND THE FAIRIES

The woods are full of fairies!
  The trees are all alive;
The river overflows with them,
  See how they dip and dive!
What funny little fellows!
  What dainty little dears!
They dance and leap, and prance
    and peep,
  And utter fairy cheers!

I'd like to tame a fairy,
  To keep it on a shelf,
To see it wash its little face,
  And dress its little self.
I'd teach it pretty manners,
  It always should say " Please ";
And then you know I'd make it sew,
  And curtsey with its knees!

Unknown

A FAIRY SONG

Buttercups in the sunshine look
  Like little cups of gold.
Perhaps the fairies come to drink
  The raindrops that they hold.

The daisies with their golden hearts ·
  Fringed all about with white,
Are little plates for fairy folk
  To sup from every night.

Soft moss a downy pillow makes,
  And green leaves spread a tent,
Where fairy folk may rest and sleep
  Until their night is spent.

The bluebird sings a lullaby,
  The firefly gives a light:
The twinkling stars are candles
    bright,
  Sleep, fairies all, good night.

Elizabeth T. Dillingham

A FAIRY VOYAGE

If I were just a fairy small,
  I'd take a leaf and sail away,
I'd sit astride the stem and guide
  It straight to Fairyland and stay.

Unknown

TO MOTHER FAIRIE

Good old Mother Fairie,
  Sitting by your fire,
Have you any little folk
  You would like to hire?

I want no chubby drudges
  To milk, and churn, and spin,
Nor old and wrinkled Brownies,
  With grisly beards, and thin;

But patient little people,
  With hands of busy care,
And gentle speech, and loving hearts,
  Now, have you such to spare?

Alice Cary

SONG

A lake and a fairy boat
To sail in the moonlight clear,—
And merrily we would float
From the dragons that watch us here!

Thy gown should be snow-white silk,
And strings of orient pearls,
Like gossamers dipped in milk,
Should twine with thy raven curls!

Red rubies should deck thy hands,
And diamonds should be thy dower—
But fairies have broke their wands
And wishing has lost its power!

Thomas Hood

FAIRY DAYS

Beside the old hall-fire—upon my
    nurse's knee,
Of happy fairy days, what tales were
    told to me!
I thought the world was once all
    peopled with princesses,
And my heart would beat to hear
    their loves and their distresses;
And many a quiet night, in slumber
    sweet and deep,
The pretty fairy people would visit
    me in sleep.

I saw them in my dreams—come fly-
    ing east and west,
With wondrous fairy gifts the new-
    born babe they blessed:
One has brought a jewel and one a
    crown of gold,
And one has brought a curse—but
    she is wrinkled and old.
The gentle queen turns pale to hear
    those words of sin,
But the king he only laughs and bids
    the dance begin.

The babe has grown to be the fairest
    of the land,
And rides the forest green, a hawk
    upon her hand,
An ambling palfrey white, a golden
    robe and crown;
I've seen her in my dreams, riding
    up and down,
And heard the ogre laugh, as she fell
    into his snare,
At the little tender creature who
    wept and tore her hair!

But ever when it seemed her need
    was at the sorest,
A prince in shining mail comes
    prancing through the forest,

A waving ostrich plume—a buckler
  burnished bright;
I've seen him in my dreams—good
  sooth! a gallant knight.
His lips are coral red beneath his
  dark moustache;
See how he waves his hand, and how
  his blue eyes flash!

"Come forth, thou Paynim knight!"
  he shouts in accents clear.
The giant and the maid both tremble his voice to hear.
Saint Mary guard him well!—he
  draws his falchion keen,
The giant and the knight are fighting on the green.
I see them in my dreams—his blade
  gives stroke for stroke,
The giant pants and reels—and tum-
  bles like an oak!

With what a blushing grace he falls
  upon his knee,
And takes the lady's hand and whispers, "You are free!"
Ah! happy childish tales, of knight
  and faërie!
I waken from my dreams—but
  there's ne'er a knight for me.
I waken from my dreams and wish
  that I could be
A child by the old hall-fire—upon
  my nurse's knee!

William Makepeace Thackeray

FAIRY SONG

Shed no tear! O, shed no tear!
The flower will bloom another year.
Weep no more! O, weep no more!
Young buds sleep in the root's white
  core.
Dry your eyes! Oh! dry your eyes!

For I was taught in Paradise
To ease my breast of melodies—
        Shed no tear.
Overhead! look overhead!
'Mong the blossoms white and red—
Look up, look up. I flutter now
On this flush pomegranate bough.
See me! 'tis this silvery bell
Ever cures the good man's ill.
Shed no tear! O, shed no tear!
The flowers will bloom another year.
Adieu, adieu—I fly, adieu,
I vanish in the heaven's blue—
        Adieu, adieu!

John Keats

WHERE THE BEE SUCKS

Where the bee sucks, there suck I;
In a cowslip's bell I lie:
There I couch, when owls do cry.
On the bat's back I do fly,
After summer, merrily:
Merrily, merrily, shall I live now
Under the blossom that hangs on the
  bough.

William Shakespeare

THE LIFE OF A FAIRY

Come follow, follow me,
You fairy elves that be,
Which circle on the green;
Come, follow Mab your queen:
Hand in hand, let's dance around,
For this place is fairy ground.

Upon a mushroom's head
Our table-cloth we spread;
A grain of rye or wheat,
Is manchet, which we eat;
Pearly drops of dew we drink
In acorn-cups fill'd to the brink.

The grasshopper, gnat, and fly
Serve for our minstrelsy;
Grace said, we dance a while,
And so the time beguile;
And if the moon doth hide her head,
The glow-worm lights us home to bed.

On the tops of dewy grass
So nimbly do we pass,
The young and tender stalk
Ne'er bends when we do walk;
Yet in the morning may be seen
Where we the night before have been.

Unknown

FAIRY BREAD

Come up here, O dusty feet!
Here is fairy bread to eat.
Here in my retiring room,
    Children, you may dine
On the golden smell of broom
    And the shade of pine;
And when you have eaten well,
Fairy stories hear and tell.

Robert Louis Stevenson

SONG OF THE ELFIN MILLER

Full merrily rings the millstone round,
    Full merrily rings the wheel,
Full merrily gushes out the grist—
    Come, taste my fragrant meal!
As sends the lift its snowy drift,
    So the meal comes in a shower;
Work, fairies, fast, for time flies past—
    I borrowed the mill an hour.

The miller he's a worldly man,
    And maun hae double fee;
So draw the sluice of the chur'l dam,
    And let the stream come free.
Shout, fairies, shout! see, gushing out,
    The meal comes like a river:

The top of the grain on hill and plain
    Is ours, and shall be ever.

One elf goes chasing the wild bat's
    wing,
    And one the white owl's horn;
One hunts the fox for the white o' his
    tail,
    And we winna hae him till morn;
One idle fay, with the glow-worm's ray,
    Runs glimmering 'mong the mosses;
Another goes tramp wi' the will-o'-
    wisp's lamp,
    To light a lad to the lasses.

O haste, my brown elf, bring me corn
    From Bonnie Blackwood plains;
Go, gentle fairy, bring me grain
    From green Dalgonar mains;
But, pride of a' at Closeburn ha',
    Fair is the corn and fatter;
Taste, fairies, taste, a gallanter grist
    Has never been wet with water.

Hillah! my hopper is heapèd high;
    Hark to the well-hung wheels!
They sing for joy; the dusty roof
    It clatters and it reels.
Haste, elves, and turn yon mountain
    burn—
    Bring streams that shine like siller;
The dam is down, the moon sinks
    soon,
    And I maun grind my meller.

Ha! bravely done, my wanton elves,
    That is a foaming stream:
See how the dust from the mill-ee flies,
    And chokes the cold moonbeam.
Haste, fairies! fleet come baptized feet,
    Come sack and sweep up clean,
And meet me soon ere sinks the moon,
    In thy green vale, Dalveen.

Allan Cunningham

THE MERMAID

I

Who would be
A mermaid fair,
Singing alone,
Combing her hair
Under the sea,
In a golden curl
With a comb of pearl,
On a throne?

II

I would be a mermaid fair;
I would sing to myself the whole of
the day;
With a comb of pearl I would comb
my hair;
And still as I comb'd I would sing
and say,
"Who is it loves me? who loves not
me?"
I would comb my hair till my ring-
lets would fall,
Low adown, low adown,
And I should look like a fountain of
gold
Springing alone
With a shrill inner sound,
Over the throne
In the midst of the hall.
Alfred Tennyson

THE MERMAN

I

Who would be
A merman bold,
Sitting alone,
Singing alone
Under the sea,
With a crown of gold,
On a throne?

II

I would be a merman bold;
I would sit and sing the whole of the
day;
I would fill the sea-halls with a voice
of power
But at night I would roam abroad and
play
With the mermaids in and out of the
rocks,
Dressing their hair with the white sea-
flower;
And holding them back by their flow-
ing locks
I would kiss them often under the sea,
And kiss them again till they kiss'd me
Laughingly, laughingly;
And then we would wander away,
away,
To the pale sea-groves straight and
high
Chasing each other merrily.
Alfred Tennyson

THE FAIRIES

Up the airy mountain,
Down the rushy glen,
We daren't go a-hunting,
For fear of little men;
Wee folk, good folk,
Trooping all together;
Green jacket, red cap,
And white owl's feather!

Down along the rocky shore
Some make their home,
They live on crispy pancakes
Of yellow tide-foam;
Some in the reeds
Of the black mountain-lake,
With frogs for their watch-dogs,
All night awake.

High on the hill-top
  The old King sits;
He is now so old and gray,
  He's nigh lost his wits.
With a bridge of white mist
  Columbkill he crosses,
On his stately journeys
  From Slieveleague to Rosses;
Or going up with music
  On cold starry nights,
To sup with the Queen
  Of the gay Northern Lights.

They stole little Bridget
  For seven years long;
When she came down again,
  Her friends were all gone.
They took her lightly back,
  Between the night and morrow,
They thought that she was fast
    asleep,
But she was dead with sorrow.
They have kept her ever since
  Deep within the lake,
On a bed of flag-leaves,
  Watching till she wake.

By the craggy hill-side,
  Through the mosses bare,
They have planted thorn-trees
  For pleasure here and there.
Is any man so daring
  As dig them up in spite,
He shall find their sharpest thorns
  In his bed at night.

Up the airy mountain,
  Down the rushy glen,
We daren't go a-hunting,
  For fear of little men;
Wee folk, good folk,
  Trooping all together;
Green jacket, red cap,
  And white owl's feather!

        William Allingham

FAIRIES' RECALL

While the blue is richest
  In the starry sky,
While the softest shadows
  On the greensward lie,
While the moonlight slumbers
  In the lily's urn,
Bright elves of the wild wood!
  Oh! return, return!

Round the forest fountains,
  On the river shore,
Let your silvery laughter
  Echo yet once more,
While the joyous bounding
  Of your dewy feet
Rings to that old chorus:
  " The daisy is so sweet! "

Oberon, Titania,
  Did your starlight mirth
With the song of Avon
  Quit this work-day earth?
Yet while green leaves glisten
  And while bright stars burn,
By that magic memory,
  Oh! return, return!
      Felicia Dorothea Hemans

A FAIRY IN ARMOR

He put his acorn helmet on;
It was plumed of the silk of the thistle
    down;
The corslet plate that guarded his
    breast
Was once the wild bee's golden vest;
His cloak, of a thousand mingled dyes,
Was formed of the wings of butter-
    flies;
His shield was the shell of a lady-bug
    green,
Studs of gold on a ground of green;

And the quivering lance which he
brandished bright,
Was the sting of a wasp he had slain
in fight.
Swift he bestrode his fire-fly steed;
He bared his blade of the bent-grass
blue;
He drove his spurs of the cockle-seed,
And away like a glance of thought
he flew,
To skim the heavens, and follow far
The fiery trail of the rocket-star.

Joseph Rodman Drake

THE ARMING OF PIGWIGGEN

He quickly arms him for the field—
A little cockle-shell his shield,
Which he could very bravely wield,
Yet could it not be piercèd;
His spear a bent both stiff and strong,
And well near of two inches long;
The pile was of a horse-fly's tongue,
Whose sharpness naught reversèd:

And put him on a coat of mail,
Which was of a fish's scale,
That when his foe should him assail,
No point should be prevailing.
His rapier was a hornet's sting,
It was a very dangerous thing;
For if he chanced to hurt the king,
It would be long in healing.

His helmet was a beetle's head,
Most horrible and full of dread,
That able was to strike one dead,
Yet it did well become him:
And for a plume a horse's hair,
Which being tossed up by the air,
Had force to strike his foe with fear,
And turn his weapon from him.

Himself he on an earwig set,
Yet scarce he on his back could get,

So oft and high he did curvet
Ere he himself could settle:
He made him turn, and stop, and
bound,
To gallop and to trot the round,
He scarce could stand on any ground
He was so full of mettle.

Michael Drayton

WATER-LILIES

Come away, elves, while the dew is
sweet,
Come to the dingles where fairies
meet;
Know that the lilies have spread their
bells
O'er all the pools in our forest dells;
Stilly and lightly their vases rest
On the quivering sleep of the water's
breast,
Catching the sunshine through leaves
that throw
To their scented bosoms an emerald
glow;
And a star from the depth of each
pearly cup,
A golden star unto heaven looks up,
As if seeking its kindred where bright
they lie,
Set in the blue of the summer sky.
—Come away! under arching boughs
we'll float,
Making those urns each a fairy boat;
We'll row them with reeds o'er the
fountains free,
And a tall flag-leaf shall our streamer
be,
And we'll send out wild music so
sweet and low,
It shall seem from the bright flower's
heart to flow,
As if 'twere breeze with a flute's low
sigh,

Or water drops train'd into melody.
—Come away! for the midsummer sun
    grows strong,
And the life of the lily may not be
    long.

Felicia Dorothea Hemans

THE LITTLE ELFMAN

I met a little elfman once,
    Down where the lilies blow.
I asked him why he was so small,
    And why he didn't grow.

He slightly frowned, and with his
        eye
    He looked me through and
        through—
" I'm just as big for me," said he,
    " As you are big for you! "

John Kendrick Bangs

THE DOOR AT THE END OF
OUR GARDEN

There's a door at the end of our
    garden,
Covered with dust and weeds,
The key is lost and the door is locked,
And I don't know where it leads.
But every day I go there
When shadows roll in from the sea,
And a dear little gold-haired Fairy
Comes through the door to me.

She tells me such lovely stories
That nobody seems to know,
Of mountains and seas and caverns
Where some day I may go;
Stories of beautiful ladies
And knights in armour of gold,
And all the wonderful gallant deeds
They did in the days of old.

I never doubt what she tells me,
I listen and long for more,
I never ask where she comes from,
Or how she gets through the door.
But you don't believe what I tell you,
And that very well may be,
For you have not seen the Fairy
Who comes through the door to me!

Frederick E. Weatherly

THE FAIRY TEMPTER

A fair girl was sitting in the green-
    wood shade,
List'ning to the music the spring
    birds made;
When sweeter by far than the birds
    on the tree,
A voice murmured near her, " Oh,
    come, love, with me—
        In earth or air,
        A thing so fair
    I have not seen as thee!
    Then come, love, with me."

" With a star for thy home, in a palace
    of light,
Thou wilt add a fresh grace to the
    beauty of night;
Or, if wealth be thy wish, thine are
    treasures untold,
I will show thee the birthplace of
    jewels and gold—
        And pearly caves
        Beneath the waves,
    All these, all these are thine,
    If thou wilt be mine."

Thus whispered a fairy to tempt the
    fair girl,
But vain was the promise of gold and
    of pearl;
For she said, " Tho' thy gifts to a
    poor girl were dear,

My father, my mother, my sisters are
    here:
      Oh! what would be
      Thy gifts to me
      Of earth, and sea, and air
    If my heart were not there? "

                Samuel Lover

THE FAIRIES

If ye will with Mab find grace,
Set each platter in his place;
Rake the fire up, and get
Water in, ere sun be set.
Wash your pails and cleanse your
    dairies,
Sluts are loathsome to the fairies;
Sweep your house: Who doth not so,
Mab will pinch her by the toe.

                Robert Herrick

QUEEN MAB

(*Selected Stanzas*)

A little fairy comes at night;
    Her eyes are blue, her hair is brown,
With silver spots upon her wings,
    And from the moon she flutters
    down.

She has a little silver wand,
    And when a good child goes to bed,
She waves her wand from right to left,
    And makes a circle round its head.

And then it dreams of pleasant
    things—
    Of fountains filled with fairy fish,
And trees that bear delicious fruit,
    And bow their branches at a wish;

Of arbors filled with dainty scents
    From lovely flowers that never fade,
Bright flies that glitter in the sun,
    And glow-worms shining in the
    shade;

And talking birds with gifted tongues
    For singing songs and telling tales,
And pretty dwarfs to show the way
    Through fairy hills and fairy dales.

                Thomas Hood

QUEEN MAB'S CHARIOT

Her chariot ready straight is made,
Each thing therein is fitting laid,
That she by nothing might be stayed,
    For naught must be her letting.
Four nimble gnats the horses were
Their harnesses of gossamer,
Fly, Cranion, her charioteer,
    Upon the coach-box getting.

Her chariot of a snail's fine shell,
Which for the colors did excel,
The fair queen Mab becoming well—
    So lively was the limning;
The seat the soft wool of the bee,
The cover (gallantly to see)
The wing of a pied butterflee:
    I trow, 'twas simple trimming.

The wheels composed of crickets'
    bones,
And daintily made for the nonce.
For fear of rattling on the stones,
    With thistle-down they shot it;
For all her maidens much did fear,
If Oberon had chanced to hear
That Mab his queen should have been
    there,
    He would not have abode it.

She mounts her chariot with a trice,
Nor would she stay for no advice,
Until her maids that were so nice
    To wait on her were fitted,
But ran herself away alone;
Which when they heard, there was not
    one

But hastened after to be gone,
　　As she had been diswitted.

Hop, and Mop, and Drap so clear,
Pip, and Trip, and Skip, that were
To Mab their sovereign dear,
　　Her special maids of honor;
Fib, and Tib, and Pink, and Pin,
Pick, and Quick, and Jill, and Jin—
Tip, and Nit, and Wap, and Wim—
　　The train that wait upon her.

Upon a grasshopper they got,
And what with amble and with trot,
For hedge nor ditch they sparèd not,
　　But after her they hie them.
A cobweb over them they throw,
To shield the wind if it should blow;
Themselves they wisely could bestow
　　Lest any should espy them.

Michael Drayton

QUEEN MAB

Oh then, I see, Queen Mab hath been
　　with you.
She is the fairies' midwife, and she
　　comes
In shape no bigger than an agate stone
On the forefinger of an alderman;
Drawn with a team of little atomies
Athwart men's noses as they lie asleep:
Her wagon spokes made of long spin-
　　ner's legs:
The cover, of the wings of grasshop-
　　pers;
The traces, of the smallest spider's
　　web;
The collars of the moonshine's watery
　　beams;
Her whip of cricket's bone, the lash,
　　of film;
Her wagoner, a small grey-coated gnat,
Not half so big as a round little worm,

Pricked from the lazy finger of a maid:
Her chariot is an empty hazel nut,
Made by the joiner squirrel, or old
　　grub,
Time out of mind the fairies' coach-
　　makers,
And in this state she gallops night by
　　night,
Through lovers' brains, and then they
　　dream of love;
On courtier's knees that dream on
　　court'sies straight;
O'er lawyers' fingers, who straight
　　dream on fees;
O'er ladies' lips, who straight on kisses
　　dream.

William Shakespeare

BY THE MOON WE SPORT AND PLAY

By the moon we sport and play,
With the night begins our day;
As we dance the dew doth fall;
Trip it, little urchins all!
Two by two, and three by three,
And about go we, and about go we!

John Lyly

THE FOUNTAIN OF THE FAIRIES

There is a fountain in the forest called
The Fountain of the Fairies: when a
　　child
What a delight of wonder I have heard
Tales of the elfin tribe who on its
　　banks
Hold midnight revelry. An ancient oak,
The goodliest of the forest, grows be-
　　side;
Alone it stands, upon a green grass
　　plat,

By the woods bounded like some little
  isle.
It ever hath been deem'd their favorite
  tree,
They love to lie and rock upon its
  leaves
And bask in moonshine. Here the
  woodman leads
His boy, and showing him the green
  sward mark'd
With darker circlets, says the midnight
  dance
Hath traced the rings, and bids him
  spare the tree.
Fancy had cast a spell upon the place
Which made it holy; and the villagers
Would say that never evil things ap-
  proached
Unpunished there. The strange and
  fearful pleasure
Which filled me by that solitary
  spring,
Ceased not in riper years; and now it
  wakes
Deeper delight, and more mysterious
  awe.

Robert Southey

OH! WHERE DO FAIRIES HIDE
THEIR HEADS?

Oh! where do fairies hide their heads,
  When snow lies on the hills,
When frost has spoiled their mossy
  beds,
  And crystallized their rills?
Beneath the moon they cannot trip
  In circles o'er the plain;
And draughts of dew they cannot sip,
  Till green leaves come again.

Perhaps, in small, blue diving-bells
  They plunge beneath the waves,

Inhabiting the wreathèd shells
  That lie in coral caves.
Perhaps, in red Vesuvius
  Carousals they maintain;
And cheer their little spirits thus,
  Till green leaves come again.

When they return, there will be mirth
  And music in the air,
And fairy wings upon the earth,
  And mischief everywhere.
The maids, to keep the elves aloof,
  Will bar the doors in vain;
No keyhole will be fairy-proof,
  When green leaves come again.

Thomas Haynes Bayly

THE FAIRY FOLK

Come cuddle close in daddy's coat
  Beside the fire so bright,
And hear about the fairy folk
  That wander in the night.
For when the stars are shining clear
  And all the world is still,
They float across the silver moon
  From hill to cloudy hill.

Their caps of red, their cloaks of green,
  Are hung with silver bells,
And when they're shaken with the
  wind
  Their merry ringing swells.
And riding on the crimson moth,
  With black spots on his wings,
They guide them down the purple sky
  With golden bridle rings.

They love to visit girls and boys
  To see how sweet they sleep,
To stand beside their cosy cots
  And at their faces peep.
For in the whole of fairy land
  They have no finer sight

Than little children sleeping sound
  With faces rosy bright.

On tiptoe crowding round their heads,
  When bright the moonlight beams,
They whisper little tender words
  That fill their minds with dreams;
And when they see a sunny smile,
  With lightest finger tips
They lay a hundred kisses sweet
  Upon the ruddy lips.

And then the little spotted moths
  Spread out their crimson wings,
And bear away the fairy crowd
  With shaking bridle rings.
Come bairnies, hide in daddy's coat,
  Beside the fire so bright—
Perhaps the little fairy folk
  Will visit you tonight.

      Robert Montgomery Bird

FAIRY LAND

Dim vales, and shadowy floods,
And cloudy-looking woods;
Whose forms we can't discover
For the tears that drip all over;
Huge moons there wax and wane—
Again, again, again—
Every moment of the night,
For ever changing places;
And they put out the star-light
With the breath from their pale faces.
About twelve by the moon-dial,
One more filmy than the rest
(A kind which, upon trial,
They have found to be the best)
Comes down—still down—and down
With its centre on the crown
Of a mountain's eminence
In easy drapery falls
Over hamlets, over halls,
Wherever they may be—

O'er the strange woods, o'er the sea,
Over spirits on the wing,
Over every drowsy thing—
And buries them up quite
In a labyrinth of light;
And then, how deep!—O deep,
Is the passion of their sleep!
In the morning they arise,
And their moony covering
Is roaring in the skies,
With the tempest as they toss,
Like—almost anything,
Or a yellow albatross.
They use that moon no more
For the same end as before—
Videlicet a tent—
Which I think extravagant:
Its atomies, however,
Into a shower dissever
Of which those butterflies
Of earth who seek the skies,
And so come down again
(Never contented things!),
Have brought a specimen
Upon their quivering wings.

      Edgar Allan Poe

THE FAIRIES OF THE CALDON-LOW

" And where have you been, my Mary,
  And where have you been from
  me? "
" I've been to the top of Caldon-Low,
  The midsummer night to see! "

" And what did you see, my Mary,
  All up on the Caldon-Low? "
" I saw the glad sunshine come down,
  And I saw the merry winds blow."

" And what did you hear, my Mary,
  All up on the Caldon-Hill? "
" I heard the drops of the water made,
  And I heard the green corn fill."

" Oh, tell me all, my Mary—
    All—all that ever you know;
For you must have seen the fairies
    Last night on the Caldon-Low! "

" Then take me on your knee, mother,
    And listen, mother of mine:
A hundred fairies danced last night,
    And the harpers they were nine.

" And the harp-strings rang so merrily
    To their dancing feet so small;
But, oh! the sound of their talking
    Was merrier far than all! "

" And what were the words, my Mary,
    That you did hear them say? "
" I'll tell you all, my mother,
    But let me have my way.

" And some they played with the
    water,
And rolled it down the hill;
' And this,' they said, ' shall speedily
    turn
The poor old miller's mill.

" ' For there has been no water
    Ever since the first of May;
And a busy man will the miller be
    At the dawning of the day!

" ' Oh! the miller, how he will laugh,
    When he sees the mill-dam rise!
The jolly old miller, how he will
    laugh,
Till the tears fill both his eyes! '

" And some they seized the little
    winds,
That sounded over the hill,
And each put a horn into his mouth,
    And blew both sharp and shrill:

" ' And there,' said they, ' the merry
    winds go
Away from every horn;

And these shall clear the mildew
    dank
From the blind old widow's corn:

" ' Oh, the poor blind widow—
    Though she has been blind so
    long,
She'll be merry enough when the
    mildew's gone,
And the corn stands stiff and
    strong! '

" And some they brought the brown
    linseed
And flung it down the Low:
' And this,' said they, ' by the sunrise
    In the weaver's croft shall grow!

" ' Oh, the poor lame weaver!
    How will he laugh outright
When he sees his dwindling flax-
    field
All full of flowers by night! '

" And then outspoke a brownie,
    With a long beard on his chin:
' I have spun up all the tow,' said he,
    ' And I want some more to spin.

" ' I've spun a piece of hempen cloth
    And I want to spin another—
A little sheet for Mary's bed,
    And an apron for her mother! '

" And with that I could not help but
    laugh,
And I laughed out loud and free;
And then on the top of Caldon-Low
    There was no one left but me.

" And all on the top of Caldon-Low
    The mists were cold and gray,
And nothing I saw but the mossy
    stones
That round about me lay.

"But, as I came down from the hill-
    top,
    I heard, afar below,
How busy the jolly miller was,
    And how merry the wheels did
      go!

"And I peeped into the widow's field,
    And, sure enough, was seen
The yellow ears of the mildew corn
    All standing stiff and green.

"And down the weaver's croft I
    stole,
    To see if the flax were high;
But I saw the weaver at his gate
    With the good news in his eye!

"Now, this is all I heard, mother,
    And all that I did see;
So, prithee, make my bed, mother,
    For I'm tired as I can be!"

                Mary Howitt

THE ELF AND THE DORMOUSE

Under a toadstool
    Crept a wee Elf,
Out of the rain
    To shelter himself.

Under a toadstool,
    Sound asleep,
Sat a big Dormouse
    All in a heap.

Trembled the wee Elf,
    Frightened, and yet
Fearing to fly away
    Lest he get wet.

To the next shelter—
    Maybe a mile!
Sudden the wee Elf
    Smiled a wee smile.

Tugged till the toadstool
    Toppled in two.
Holding it over him,
    Gaily he flew.

Soon he was safe home,
    Dry as could be.
Soon woke the Dormouse—
    "Good gracious me!

"Where is my toadstool?"
    Loud he lamented.
And that's how umbrellas
    First were invented.

                Oliver Herford

Part Six

CREATURES GREAT AND SMALL

SIR ROBIN

Rollicking Robin is here again,
What does he care for the April rain?
Care for it? Glad of it. Doesn't he
    know
That April rain carries off the snow,
And coaxes out leaves to shadow his
    nest,
And washes his pretty, red Easter vest,
And makes the juice of the cherry
    sweet,
For his hungry little robins to eat?
  " Ha! ha! ha! " hear the jolly bird
    laugh.
  " That isn't the best of the story, by
    half! "

Gentleman Robin, he walks up and
    down,
Dressed in orange-tawney and black
    and brown.
Though his eye is so proud and his
    step so firm,
He can always stoop to pick up a
    worm.
With a twist of his head, and a strut
    and a hop,
To his Robin-wife, in the peach-tree
    top,
Chirping her heart out, he calls: " My
    dear,

You don't earn your living! Come
    here! Come here!
  Ha! ha! ha! Life is lovely and sweet:
  But what would it be if we'd noth-
    ing to eat? "

Robin, Sir Robin, gay, red-vested
    knight,
Now you have come to us, summer's
    in sight.
You never dream of the wonders you
    bring,—
Visions that follow the flash of your
    wing.
How all the beautiful By-and-By
Around you and after you seems to fly.
Sing or eat on, as pleases your mind!
Well have you earned every morsel you
    find.
  " Aye! Ha! ha! ha! " whistles Robin.
    " My dear,
  Let us all take our own choice of
    good cheer! "

Lucy Larcom

THE ROBIN

When father takes his spade to dig
Then Robin comes along;
He sits upon a little twig
And sings a little song.

Or, if the trees are rather far
He does not stay alone,
But comes up close to where we are
And bobs upon a stone.

Laurence Alma-Tadema

THE SECRET

We have a secret, just we three,
The robin, and I, and the sweet cherry-
tree;
The bird told the tree, and the tree
told me,
And nobody knows it but just us three.

But of course the robin knows it best,
Because he built the—I shan't tell the
rest;
And laid the four little—something in
it—
I'm afraid I shall tell it every minute.

But if the tree and the robin don't
peep,
I'll try my best the secret to keep;
Though I know when the little birds
fly about
Then the whole secret will be out.

Unknown

ROBIN REDBREAST

Good-by, good-by to Summer!
  For Summer's nearly done;
The garden smiling faintly,
  Cool breezes in the sun;
Our thrushes now are silent,
  Our swallows flown away,—
But Robin's here in coat of brown,
  And scarlet breast-knot gay.
    Robin, Robin Redbreast,
      O Robin dear!
    Robin sings so sweetly
      In the falling of the year.

Bright yellow, red, and orange,
  The leaves come down in hosts;
The trees are Indian princes,
  But soon they'll turn to ghosts;
The scanty pears and apples
  Hang russet on the bough;
It's Autumn, Autumn, Autumn late,
  'Twill soon be Winter now.
    Robin, Robin Redbreast,
      O Robin dear!
    And what will this poor Robin do?
      For pinching days are near.

The fireside for the cricket,
  The wheat-stack for the mouse,
When trembling night-winds whistle
  And moan all round the house.
The frosty ways like iron,
  The branches plumed with snow,—
Alas! in Winter dead and dark,
  Where can poor Robin go?
    Robin, Robin Redbreast,
      O Robin dear!
    And a crumb of bread for Robin,
      His little heart to cheer!

William Allingham

BOB WHITE

There's a plump little chap in a speck-
led coat,
And he sings on the zigzag rails re-
mote,
Where he whistles at breezy, bracing
morn,
When the buckwheat is ripe, and
stacked is the corn,
  "Bob White! Bob White! Bob
White!"

Is he hailing some comrade as blithe
as he?
Now I wonder where Robert White
can be!

O'er the billows of gold and amber
grain
There is no one in sight—but, hark
again:

Ah! I see why he calls; in the stubble
there
Hide his plump little wife and babies
fair!
So contented is he, and so proud of
the same,
That he wants all the world to know
his name:
  "Bob White! Bob White! Bob
  White!"

George Cooper

THE NORTH WIND DOTH BLOW

The north wind doth blow,
And we shall have snow,
And what will poor Robin do then?
      Poor thing!
He'll sit in a barn,
And to keep himself warm,
Will hide his head under his wing.
      Poor thing!

Unknown

THE BROWN THRUSH

There's a merry brown thrush sitting
up in the tree.
He's singing to me! He's singing to
me!
  And what does he say, little girl,
  little boy?
"Oh, the world's running over with
joy!
      Don't you hear? Don't you see?
      Hush! Look! In my tree,
      I'm as happy as happy can be!"

And the brown thrush keeps singing,
  "A nest do you see
And five eggs, hid by me in the juniper
tree?
  Don't meddle! Don't touch! little
  girl, little boy,
  Or the world will lose some of its
  joy!
      Now I'm glad! now I'm free!
      And always shall be,
      If you never bring sorrow to
      me."

So the merry brown thrush sings away
in the tree,
To you and to me, to you and to me;
  And he sings all the day, little girl,
  little boy,
"Oh, the world's running over with
joy!
      But long it won't be,
      Don't you know? Don't you
      see?
      Unless we're as good as can be."

Lucy Larcom

SONG OF THE CHICKADEE

List to the song of the chickadee,
Perched on the top of the leafless
tree;
Keen winds ruffling his breast of
down,
Coat of gray with its trimmings
brown,
Tilting aloft his black-capped head,
Giving a lift to his wings outspread,
Chickadee chirps: "Chickadee-dee-
dee!
Got any crumbs to bestow on me?
Winter and summer I bring you
cheer;
There's never a day in all the year
You may not hear me. I'm small,
you see.

But I'm bright and active and full
of glee! "
From limb to limb then he hies
away,
Out on the branches you see him
sway,
Black cap bobbing about as he sings:
Chick-chick, chicka, chickadee-dee! "

Unknown

LITTLE BELL

(Selected Stanzas)

Piped the blackbird on the beech-
wood spray:
" Pretty maid, slow wandering this
way,
What's your name? " quoth he—
" What's your name? Oh, stop and
straight unfold,
Pretty maid with showery curls of
gold,"—
" Little Bell," said she.

Little Bell sat down beneath the
rocks—
Tossed aside her gleaming golden
locks—
" Bonny bird," quoth she,
" Sing me your best song before I go."
" Here's the very finest song I know,
Little Bell," said he.

And the blackbird piped; you never
heard
Half so gay a song from any bird;—
Full of quips and wiles,
Now so round and rich, now soft
and slow,
All for love of that sweet face below,
Dimpled o'er with smiles.

And the while the bonny bird did
pour

His full heart out freely o'er and
o'er,
'Neath the morning skies,
In the little childish heart below,
All the sweetness seemed to grow
and grow,
And shine forth in happy overflow
From the blue, bright eyes.

*   *   *

Little Bell sat down amid the fern:
" Squirrel, squirrel, to your task re-
turn;
Bring me nuts! " quoth she.
Up, away, the frisky squirrel hies,
Golden wood lights glancing in his
eyes;
And adown the tree,
Great ripe nuts, kissed brown by July
sun,
In the little lap drop, one by one:
Hark, how blackbird pipes to see the
fun!
" Happy Bell! " pipes he.

Little Bell looked up and down the
glade:
" Squirrel, squirrel, if you're not afraid,
Come and share with me! "
Down came squirrel, eager for his
fare,
Down came bonny blackbird, I de-
clare.
Little Bell gave each his honest
share,
Ah, the merry three!

*   *   *

By her snow-white cot at close of
day,
Knelt sweet Bell, with folded palms
to pray:
Very calm and clear
Rose the praying voice to where,
unseen,

In blue heaven, an angel shape
   serene
   Paused a while to hear.

"What good child is this," the angel
   said,
"That, with happy heart, beside her
   bed
   Prays so lovingly?"
Low and soft, oh! very low and soft,
Crooned the blackbird in the or-
   chard croft,
   "Bell, *dear* Bell!" crooned he.

"Whom God's creatures love," the
   angel fair
Murmured, "God doth bless with
   angels' care;
   Child, thy bed shall be
Folded safe from harm. Love deep,
   and kind,
Shall watch around, and leave good
   gifts behind,
   Little Bell, for thee."

          Thomas Westwood

THE BLUEBIRD

I know the song that the bluebird is
   singing,
Out in the apple-tree where he is
   swinging.
Brave little fellow! the skies may be
   dreary,
Nothing cares he while his heart is
   so cheery.

Hark! how the music leaps out from
   his throat!
Hark! was there ever so merry a
   note?
Listen awhile, and you'll hear what
   he's saying,
Up in the apple-tree, swinging and
   swaying:

"Dear little blossoms, down under
   the snow,
You must be weary of winter, I
   know;
Hark! while I sing you a message of
   cheer,
Summer is coming and spring-time
   is here!

"Little white snowdrop, I pray you
   arise;
Bright yellow crocus, come, open
   your eyes;
Sweet little violets hid from the cold,
Put on your mantles of purple and
   gold;
Daffodils, daffodils! say, do you hear?
Summer is coming, and spring-time
   is here!"

        Emily Huntington Miller

THE HUMMING-BIRD

The Humming-bird! the Humming-
   bird!
   So fairy-like and bright;
It lives among the sunny flowers,
   A creature of delight!

In the radiant islands of the East,
   Where fragrant spices grow,
A thousand, thousand Humming-birds
   Go glancing to and fro.

Like living fires they flit about,
   Scarce larger than a bee,
Among the broad palmetto leaves,
   And through the fan-palm tree.

And in those wild and verdant woods,
   Where stately moras tower,
Where hangs from branching tree to
   tree
   The scarlet passion-flower;

Where on the mighty river banks,
  La Plate and Amazon,
The cayman, like an old tree trunk,
  Lies basking in the sun;

There builds her nest the Humming-
    bird,
  Within the ancient wood—
Her nest of silky cotton down,
  And rears her tiny brood.

She hangs it to a slender twig,
  Where waves it light and free,
As the campanero tolls his song,
  And rocks the mighty tree.

All crimson is her shining breast,
  Like to the red, red rose;
Her wing is the changeful green and
    blue
  That the neck of the peacock shows.

Thou, happy, happy Humming-bird,
  No winter round thee lours;
Thou never saw'st a leafless tree,
  Nor land without sweet flowers.

A reign of summer joyfulness
  To thee for life is given;
Thy food, the honey from the flower,
  Thy drink, the dew from heaven!
                    Mary Howitt

THE YOUNG LINNETS

Did you ever see the nest
  Of chaffinch or of linnet,
When the little downy birds
  Are lying snugly in it?

Gaping wide their yellow mouths
  For something nice to eat?
Caterpillar, worm, or grub,
  They reckon dainty meat.

When the mother bird returns,
  And finds them still and good,
She will give them each by turns
  A proper share of food.

She has hopped from spray to spray,
  And peeped with knowing eye
Into all the folded leaves
  Where caterpillars lie.

She has searched among the grass,
  And flown from tree to tree,
Catching gnats, and flies, to feed
  Her little family.

I have seen the linnets chirp,
  And shake their downy wings;
They are pleased to see her come,
  And pleased with what she brings.
                    Ann Hawkshawe

THE SWALLOW

Fly away, fly away over the sea,
  Sun-loving swallow, for summer is
    done;
Come again, come again, come back
    to me,
  Bringing the summer and bringing
    the sun.
                    Christina Rossetti

THE CROW

Old crow, upon the tall tree-top
  I see you sitting at your ease,
You hang upon the highest bough,
  And balance in the breeze.

How many miles you've been today
  Upon your wings so strong and
    black,
And steered across the dark grey sky
  Without a guide or track;

Above the city wrapped in smoke,
 Green fields and rivers flowing clear;
Now tell me, as you passed them o'er
 What did you see and hear?

The old crow shakes his sooty wing,
 And answers hoarsely, " Caw, caw,
 caw,"
And that is all the crow can tell
 Of what he heard and saw.

Mrs. Alexander

I HAD A DOVE

I had a dove, and the sweet dove died;
 And I have thought it died of griev-
 ing;
O, what could it grieve for? Its feet
 were tied
 With a ribbon thread of my own
 hand's weaving.
Sweet little red feet! why should you
 die?
Why would you leave me, sweet bird!
 why?
You lived alone in the forest tree:
Why, pretty thing! would you not live
 with me?
I kissed you oft and gave you white
 peas;
Why not live sweetly, as in the green
 trees?

John Keats

THE OWL

When cats run home and light is
 come,
 And dew is cold upon the ground,
And the far off stream is dumb,
 And the whirring sail goes round,
 And the whirring sail goes round;
 Alone and warming his five wits,
 The white owl in the belfry sits.

When merry milkmaids click the latch,
 And rarely smells the new-mown
 hay,
And the cock hath sung beneath the
 thatch
 Twice or thrice his roundelay,
 Twice or thrice his roundelay;
 Alone and warming his five wits,
 The white owl in the belfry sits.

Alfred Tennyson

SIR LARK AND KING SUN

" Good-morrow, my lord! " in the sky
 alone,
 Sang the lark, as the sun ascended
 his throne.
" Shine on me, my lord; I only am
 come,
 Of all your servants, to welcome you
 home.
 I have flown right up, a whole hour,
 I swear,
 To catch the first shine of your
 golden hair."

" Must I thank you, then," said the
 king, " Sir Lark,
 For flying so high and hating the
 dark?
 You ask a full cup for half a thirst:
 Half was love of me, and half love
 to be first.
 There's many a bird makes no such
 haste,
 But waits till I come: that's as much
 to my taste."

And King Sun hid his head in a
 turban of cloud,
And Sir Lark stopped singing, quite
 vexed and cowed.
But he flew up higher, and thought,
 " Anon

The wrath of the king will be over
and gone;
And his crown, shining out of its
cloudy fold,
Will change my brown feathers to
a glory of gold."

So he flew—with the strength of a
lark he flew;
But, as he rose, the cloud rose too;
And not one gleam of the golden
hair
Came through the depths of the
misty air;
Till, weary with flying, with sighing
sore,
The strong sun-seeker could do no
more.

His wings had had no chrism of
gold:
And his feathers felt withered and
worn and old;
He faltered, and sank, and dropped
like a stone.
And there on her nest, where he left
her, alone
Sat his little wife on her little eggs,
Keeping them warm with wings and
legs.

Did I say alone? Ah, no such thing!
Full in her face was shining the
king.
"Welcome, Sir Lark! You look tired,"
said he;
"Up is not always the best way to
me.
While you have been singing so high
and away,
I've been shining to your little wife
all day."

He had set his crown all about the
nest,

And out of the midst shone her
little brown breast;
And so glorious was she in russet
gold,
That for wonder and awe Sir Lark
grew cold.
He popped his head under her wing,
and lay
As still as a stone, till King Sun was
away.

George Macdonald

ANSWER TO A CHILD'S QUESTION

Do you ask what the birds say? The
sparrow, the dove,
The linnet, and thrush say, "I love,
and I love!"
In the winter they're silent, the wind
is so strong;
What it says I don't know, but it
sings a loud song.
But green leaves, and blossoms, and
sunny warm weather,
And singing and loving—all come
back together.
But the lark is so brimful of gladness and love,
The green fields below him, the blue
sky above,
That he sings, and he sings, and for
ever sings he,
"I love my Love, and my Love loves
me."

Samuel Taylor Coleridge

THE ORPHAN'S SONG

I had a little bird,
I took it from the nest;
I prest it and blest it,
And nurst it in my breast.

I set it on the ground,
I danced round and round,
And sang about it so cheerly,
  With "Hey, my little bird, and ho!
    my little bird,
  And oh! but I love thee dearly!"

I make a little feast
  Of food soft and sweet,
I hold it in my breast,
  And coax it to eat;

I pit, and I pat,
I call this and that,
And I sing about so cheerly,
  With "Hey, my little bird, and ho!
    my little bird,
  And ho! but I love thee dearly."
                              Sydney Dobell

THREE THINGS TO REMEMBER

A Robin Redbreast in a cage
Puts all Heaven in a rage.

A skylark wounded on the wing
Doth make a cherub cease to sing.

He who shall hurt the little wren
Shall never be beloved by men.
                              William Blake

CRUMBS TO THE BIRDS

A bird appears a thoughtless thing,
He's ever living on the wing,
And keeps up such a carolling,
That little else to do but sing
  A man would guess had he.

No doubt he has his little cares,
And very hard he often fares,
The which so patiently he bears,

That listening to those cheerful airs,
  Who knows but he may be

In want of his next meal of seeds?
I think for *that* his sweet song pleads.
If so, his pretty art succeeds,
I'll scatter there among the weeds
  All the small crumbs I have.
                        Charles and Mary Lamb

A RULE FOR BIRDS' NESTERS

The robin and the red-breast,
  The robin and the wren;
If ye take out o' their nest,
  Ye'll never thrive agen!

The robin and the red-breast,
  The martin and the swallow;
If ye touch one o' their eggs,
  Bad luck will surely follow!
                              Unknown

WHO STOLE THE BIRD'S NEST?

"To-whit! to-whit! to-whee!
  Will you listen to me?
Who stole four eggs I laid,
  And the nice nest I made?"

"Not I," said the cow, "Moo-oo!
Such a thing I'd never do.
I gave you a wisp of hay,
But didn't take your nest away.
Not I," said the cow, "Moo-oo!
Such a thing I'd never do."

"To-whit! to-whit! to-whee!
  Will you listen to me?
Who stole four eggs I laid,
  And the nice nest I made?"

" Bob-o-link! Bob-o-link!
  Now what do you think?
  Who stole a nest away
  From the plum-tree, today? "

" Not I," said the dog, " Bow-wow!
  I wouldn't be so mean, anyhow!
  I gave hairs the nest to make,
  But the nest I did not take.
  Not I," said the dog, " Bow-wow!
  I'm not so mean, anyhow."

" To-whit! to-whit! to-whee!
  Will you listen to me?
  Who stole four eggs I laid,
  And the nice nest I made? "

" Bob-o-link! Bob-o-link!
  Now what do you think?
  Who stole a nest away
  From the plum-tree, today?"

" Coo-coo! Coo-coo! Coo-coo!
  Let me speak a word, too!
  Who stole that pretty nest
  From little yellow-breast? "

" Not I," said the sheep; " Oh, no!
  I wouldn't treat a poor bird so.
  I gave wool the nest to line,
  But the nest was none of mine.
  Baa! Baa! " said the sheep, " Oh, no,
  I wouldn't treat a poor bird so."

" To-whit! to-whit! to-whee!
  Will you listen to me?
  Who stole four eggs I laid,
  And the nice nest I made? "

" Bob-o-link! Bob-o-link!
  Now what do you think?
  Who stole a nest away
  From the plum-tree, today? "

" Coo-coo! Coo-coo! Coo-coo!
  Let me speak a word, too!
  Who stole that pretty nest
  From little yellow-breast? "

" Caw! Caw! " cried the crow;
" I should like to know
  What thief took away
  A bird's nest, today? "

" Cluck! Cluck! " said the hen;
" Don't ask me again,
  Why, I haven't a chick
  Would do such a trick.
  We all gave her a feather,
  And she wove them together.
  I'd scorn to intrude
  On her and her brood.
  Cluck! Cluck! " said the hen,
" Don't ask me again."

" Chirr-a-whirr! Chirr-a-whirr!
  All the birds make a stir!
  Let us find out his name,
  And all cry ' For shame! ' "

" I would not rob a bird,"
  Said little Mary Green;
" I think I never heard
  Of anything so mean."

" It is very cruel, too,"
  Said little Alice Neal;
" I wonder if he knew
  How sad the bird would feel? "

A little boy hung down his head,
And went and hid behind the bed,
For he stole that pretty nest
From poor little yellow-breast;
And he felt so full of shame,
He didn't like to tell his name.

Lydia Maria Child

FIVE LITTLE CHICKENS

Said the first little chicken,
With a queer little squirm,
" Oh, I wish I could find
A fat little worm! "

Said the next little chicken,
With an odd little shrug,
" Oh, I wish I could find
A fat little bug! "

Said the third little chicken,
With a sharp little squeal,
" Oh, I wish I could find
Some nice yellow meal! "

Said the fourth little chicken,
With a small sigh of grief,
" Oh, I wish I could find
A green little leaf! "

Said the fifth little chicken,
With a faint little moan,
" Oh, I wish I could find
A wee gravel-stone! "

" Now, see here," said the mother,
From the green garden-patch,
" If you want any breakfast,
You must come and scratch."

Unknown

DUCKS' DITTY

All along the backwater,
Through the rushes tall,
Ducks are a-dabbling,
Up tails all!

Ducks' tails, drakes' tails,
Yellow feet a-quiver,
Yellow bills all out of sight
Busy in the river!

Slushy green undergrowth
Where the roach swim—
Here we keep our larder
Cool and full and dim!

Everyone for what he likes!
We like to be
Heads down, tails up,
Dabbling free!

High in the blue above
Swifts whirl and call—
We are down a-dabbling
Up tails all!

Kenneth Grahame

FIREFLY

A little light is going by,
Is going up to see the sky,
A little light with wings.

I never could have thought of it,
To have a little bug all lit
And made to go on wings.

Elizabeth Madox Roberts

THE BUTTERFLY'S FIRST
FLIGHT

Thou hast burst from thy prison,
Bright child of the air,
Like a spirit just risen
From its mansion of care.

Thou art joyously winging
Thy first ardent flight,
Where the gay lark is singing
Her notes of delight:

Where the sunbeams are throwing
Their glories on thine,
Till thy colors are glowing
With tints more divine.

Then tasting new pleasure
  In summer's green bowers,
Reposing at leisure
  On fresh-open'd flowers.

Or delighted to hover
  Around them, to see
Whose charms, airy rover,
  Bloom sweetest for thee;

And fondly inhaling
  Their fragrance, till day
From thy bright eye is failing
  And fading away.

Then seeking some blossom
  Which looks to the west,
Thou dost find in its bosom
  Sweet shelter and rest.

And there dost betake thee
  Till darkness is o'er,
And the sunbeams awake thee
  To pleasure once more.

Unknown

WHITE BUTTERFLIES

Fly, white butterflies, out to sea,
Frail, pale wings for the wind to try,
Small white wings that we scarce can
    see,
      Fly!

Some fly light as a laugh of glee,
Some fly soft as a long, low sigh;
All to the haven where each would be,
      Fly!

Algernon Charles Swinburne

THE HAPPY WORLD

The bee is a rover;
  The brown bee is gay;
To feed on the clover,
  He passes this way.

Brown bee, humming over,
  What is it you say?
"The world is so happy—so happy
    today!"

William Brighty Rands

HOW DOTH THE LITTLE
BUSY BEE

How doth the little busy bee
  Improve each shining hour,
And gather honey all the day
  From every opening flow'r!

How skillfully she builds her cell!
  How neat she spreads the wax!
And labors hard to store it well
  With the sweet food she makes.

In works of labor or of skill,
  I would be busy too;
For Satan finds some mischief still
  For idle hands to do.

In books, or work, or healthful play,
  Let my first years be past,
That I may give for ev'ry day
  Some good account at last.

Isaac Watts

GRASSHOPPER GREEN

Grasshopper Green is a comical chap;
He lives on the best of fare.
Bright little trousers, jacket and cap,
These are his summer wear.
Out in the meadows he loves to go,
Playing away in the sun;
It's hopperty, skipperty, high and low—
Summer's the time for fun.

Grasshopper Green has a dozen wee
  boys,
And soon as their legs grow strong,

Each of them joins in his frolicsome
  joys,
Singing his merry song.
Under the hedge in a happy row
Soon as the day has begun,
It's hopperty, skipperty, high and low—
Summer's the time for fun.

Grasshopper Green has a quaint little
  house.
It's under the hedge so gay.
Grandmother Spider, as still as a
  mouse,
Watches him over the way.
Gladly he's calling the children, I
  know,
Out in the beautiful sun;
It's hopperty, skipperty, high and low—
Summer's the time for fun.

Unknown

OVER IN THE MEADOW

Over in the meadow,
  In the sand, in the sun,
Lived an old mother toad
  And her little toadie one.
"Wink!" said the mother;
  "I wink," said the one:
So she winked and she blinked
  In the sand, in the sun.

Over in the meadow,
  Where the stream runs blue,
Lived an old mother fish
  And her little fishes two.
"Swim!" said the mother;
  "We swim," said the two.
So they swam and they leaped
  Where the stream runs blue.

Over in the meadow,
  In a hole in a tree,
Lived a mother bluebird

And her little birdies three;
"Sing!" said the mother;
  "We sing," said the three:
So they sang, and were glad,
  In the hole in the tree.

Olive A. Wadsworth

A FRIEND IN THE GARDEN

He is not John the gardener,
  And yet the whole day long
Employs himself most usefully
  The flower-beds among.

He is not Tom the pussy-cat;
  And yet the other day,
With stealthy stride and glistening eye,
  He crept upon his prey.

He is not Dash, the dear old dog,
  And yet, perhaps, if you
Took pains with him and petted him,
  You'd come to love him, too.

He's not a blackbird, though he chirps,
  And though he once was black;
But now he wears a loose, grey coat,
  All wrinkled on the back.

He's got a very dirty face,
  And very shining eyes!
He sometimes comes and sits indoors;
  He looks—and p'r'aps is—wise.

But in a sunny flower-bed
  He has his fixed abode;
He eats the things that eat my plants—
  He is a friendly TOAD.

Juliana Horatia Ewing

THE CATERPILLAR

Brown and furry
Caterpillar, in a hurry

Take your walk
To the shady leaf or stalk
Or what not,
Which may be the chosen spot.
No toad spy you,
Hovering bird of prey pass by you;
Spin and die,
To live again a butterfly.

Christina Rossetti

THE SNAIL

The Snail he lives in his hard round
  house,
  In the orchard, under the tree:
Says he, " I have but a single room;
  But it's large enough for me."

The Snail in his little house doth dwell
  All the week from end to end,
You're at home, Master Snail; that's
  all very well,
  But you never receive a friend.

Unknown

DINAH

Our Dinah is a Persian cat
  Too beautiful for words!
She wears about her neck a bell
  To warn the garden-birds.

Her eyes are blue as thrushes' eggs,
  Her coat is brown as cloves,
And when she's wakeful, in my lap
  She kneads her little loaves.

If you could see how diligent
  Her paws are when they knead,
You'd think she had at least a score
  Of kittycats to feed.

And often, lying in my lap,
  So velvety and still,

With steadiness she grinds and
  grinds
  A little coffee-mill.

To hear the lovely miller grind,
  To watch her knead, is sweet;
It makes me want to pick her up
  To kiss her face and feet.

I love her sleeping in the sun,
  A hot and silky bale;
I love her when she tries to pounce
  Upon her shadow's tail.

I'd rather have her for my pet
  Than guinea-pigs or birds;
For Dinah is a Persian cat
  Too beautiful for words!

Norman Gale

THE CITY MOUSE AND THE
GARDEN MOUSE

The city mouse lives in a house;—
  The garden mouse lives in a bower,
He's friendly with the frogs and toads,
  And sees the pretty plants in flower.

The city mouse eats bread and
  cheese;—
  The garden mouse eats what he can;
We will not grudge him seeds and
  stocks,
  Poor little timid furry man.

Christina Rossetti

WHISKY FRISKY

Whisky Frisky,
Hippity hop,
Up he goes
To the tree top!

Whirly, twirly,
Round and round,

Down he scampers
To the ground.

Furly, curly,
What a tail!
Tall as a feather,
Broad as a sail!

Where's his supper?
In the shell,
Snap, cracky,
Out it fell.

                    Unknown

THE KITTEN AT PLAY

See the kitten on the wall,
Sporting with the leaves that fall,
Withered leaves, one, two, and three
Falling from the elder-tree,
Through the calm and frosty air
Of the morning bright and fair.

See the kitten, how she starts,
Crouches, stretches, paws and darts;
With a tiger-leap half way
Now she meets her coming prey.
Lets it go as fast and then
Has it in her power again.

Now she works with three and four,
Like an Indian conjurer;
Quick as he in feats of art,
Gracefully she plays her part;
Yet were gazing thousands there,
What would little Tabby care?

                    William Wordsworth

MY DOG

I have no dog, but it must be
Somewhere there's one belongs to
   me—

A little chap with wagging tail,
And dark brown eyes that never quail,
But look you through, and through,
   and through,
With love unspeakable, but true.

Somewhere it must be, I opine,
There is a little dog of mine
With cold black nose that sniffs
   around
In search of what things may be found
In pocket, or some nook hard by
Where I have hid them from his eye.

Somewhere my doggie pulls and tugs
The fringes of rebellious rugs,
Or with the mischief of the pup
Chews all my shoes and slippers up,
And when he's done it to the core
With eyes all eager pleads for more.

Somewhere upon his hinder legs
My little doggie sits and begs,
And in a wistful minor tone
Pleads for the pleasure of the bone—
I pray it be his owner's whim
To yield, and grant the same to him.

Somewhere a little dog doth wait,
It may be by some garden-gate,
With eyes alert and tail attent—
You know the kind of tail that's
   meant—
With stores of yelps of glad delight
To bid me welcome home at night.

Somewhere a little dog is seen,
His nose two shaggy paws between,
Flat on his stomach, one eye shut
Held fast in slumber, but
The other open, ready for
His master coming through the door.

                    John Kendrick Bangs

THE SHEEP

Lazy sheep, pray tell me why
In the grassy fields you lie,
Eating grass and daisies white,
From the morning till the night?
Every thing can something do,
But what kind of use are you?

Nay, my little master, nay,
Do not serve me so, I pray;
Don't you see the wool that grows
On my back to make you clothes?
Cold, and very cold you'd get,
If I did not give you it.

Sure it seems a pleasant thing
To nip the daisies in the spring,
But many chilly nights I pass
On the cold and dewy grass,
Or pick a scanty dinner where
All the common's brown and bare.

Then the farmer comes at last,
When the merry spring is past,
And cuts my woolly coat away
To warm you in the winter's day;
Little master, this is why
In the grassy fields I lie.

Ann Taylor

MARY'S LAMB

Mary had a little lamb,
  Its fleece was white as snow;
And everywhere that Mary went,
  The lamb was sure to go.

He followed her to school one day,
  Which was against the rule;
It made the children laugh and play
  To see a lamb at school.

And so the teacher turned him out,
  But still he lingered near,

And waited patiently about
  Till Mary did appear.

Then he ran to her, and laid
  His head upon her arm,
As if he said, " I'm not afraid—
  You'll keep me from all harm."

" What makes the lamb love Mary
  so? "
  The eager children cried.
" Oh, Mary loves the lamb, you
  know,"
  The teacher quick replied.

And you each gentle animal
  In confidence may bind,
And make them follow at your will,
  If you are only kind.

Sara J. Hale

THE COW

The friendly cow all red and white,
  I love her with all my heart:
She gives me cream with all her might,
  To eat with apple-tart.

She wanders lowing here and there,
  And yet she cannot stray,
All in the pleasant open air,
  The pleasant light of day;

And blown by all the winds that pass
  And wet with all the showers,
She walks among the meadow grass
  And eats the meadow flowers.

Robert Louis Stevenson

WHEN THE COWS COME HOME

When the cows come home the milk
is coming,

Honey's made while the bees are hum-
ming;
Duck and drake on the rushy lake,
And the deer live safe in the breezy
brake;
And timid, funny, brisk little bunny
Winks his nose and sits all sunny.

Christina Rossetti

THE COW

Thank you, pretty cow, that made
Pleasant milk to soak my bread,
Every day, and every night,
Warm, and fresh, and sweet, and
white.

Do not chew the hemlock rank,
Growing on the weedy bank;
But the yellow cowslip eat,
That will make it very sweet.

Where the purple violet grows,
Where the bubbling water flows,
Where the grass is fresh and fine,
Pretty cow, go there and dine.

Jane Taylor

THE CAVALIER'S ESCAPE

Trample! trample! went the roan,
Trap! trap! went the gray;
But pad! *pad!* PAD! like a thing that
was mad,
My chestnut broke away.
It was just five miles from Salisbury
town,
And but one hour to day.

Thud! THUD! came on the heavy roan,
Rap! RAP! the mettled gray;
But my chestnut mare was of blood
so rare,
That she showed them all the way.

Spur on! spur on!—I doffed my hat,
And wished them all good-day.

They splashed through miry rut and
pool,—
Splintered through fence and rail;
But chestnut Kate switched over the
gate,—
I saw them droop and tail.
To Salisbury town—but a mile of
down,
Once over this brook and rail.

Trap! trap! I heard their echoing hoofs
Past the walls of mossy stone;
The roan flew on at a staggering pace,
But blood is better than bone.
I patted old Kate, and gave her the
spur,
For I knew it was all my own.

But trample! trample! came their
steeds,
And I saw their wolf's eyes burn;
I felt like a royal hart at bay,
And made me ready to turn.
I looked where highest grew the May,
And deepest arched the fern.

I flew at the first knave's sallow throat;
One blow, and he was down.
The second rogue fired twice, and
missed;
I sliced the villain's crown,—
Clove through the rest, and flogged
brave Kate,
Fast, fast to Salisbury town!

Pad! pad! they came on the level
sward,
Thud! thud! upon the sand,—
With a gleam of swords and a burn-
ing match,
And a shaking of flag and hand;

But one long bound, and I passed the
　　gate,
　　Safe from the canting band.

Walter Thornbury

BUTTERFLY

Butterfly, Butterfly, sipping the sand,
Have you forgotten the flowers of the
　　land?
Or are you so sated with honey and
　　dew
That sand-filtered water tastes better
　　to you?

John Bannister Tabb

KINDNESS TO ANIMALS

Little children, never give
Pain to things that feel and live;
Let the gentle robin come
For the crumbs you save at home,—
As his meat you throw along
He'll repay you with a song;
Never hurt the timid hare
Peeping from her green grass lair,
Let her come and sport and play
On the lawn at close of day;
The little lark goes soaring high
To the bright windows of the sky,
Singing as if 'twere always spring,
And fluttering on an untired wing,—
Oh! let him sing his happy song,
Nor do these gentle creatures wrong.

Unknown

THE ANIMAL STORE

If I had a hundred dollars to spend,
　　Or maybe a little more,
I'd hurry as fast as my legs would go
　　Straight to the animal store.

I wouldn't say, " How much for this or
　　that? "—

" What kind of dog is he? "
I'd buy as many as rolled an eye,
　　Or wagged a tail at me!

I'd take the hound with the drooping
　　ears
　　That sits by himself alone;
Cockers and Cairns and wobbly pups
　　For to be my very own.

I might buy a parrot all red and green,
　　And the monkey I saw before,
If I had a hundred dollars to spend,
　　Or maybe a little more.

Rachel Field

THE MOUSE

I heard a mouse
Bitterly complaining
In a crack of moonlight
Aslant on the floor—

" Little I ask
And that little is not granted.
There are few crumbs
In this world any more.

" The bread-box is tin
And I cannot get in.

" The jam's in a jar
My teeth cannot mar.

" The cheese sits by itself
On the pantry shelf—

" All night I run
Searching and seeking,
All night I run
About on the floor.

" Moonlight is there
And a bare place for dancing,
But no little feast
Is spread any more."

Elizabeth Coatsworth

Part Seven

THE GREAT OUTDOORS

THE LITTLE PLANT

In the heart of a seed
  Buried deep, so deep,
A dear little plant
  Lay fast asleep.

" Wake! " said the sunshine
  " And creep to the light,"
" Wake! " said the voice
  Of the raindrops bright.

The little plant heard,
  And it rose to see
What the wonderful
  Outside world might be.
Kate Louise Brown

GREEN THINGS GROWING

Oh, the green things growing, the
green things growing,
The faint sweet smell of the green
things growing!
I should like to live, whether I smile
or grieve,
Just to watch the happy life of my
green things growing.

Oh, the fluttering and the pattering of
those green things growing!

How they talk each to each, when none
  of us are knowing;
In the wonderful white of the weird
  moonlight
Of the dim dreamy dawn when the
  cocks are crowing.

I love, I love them so,—my green
  things growing!
And I think that they love me, without false showing;
For by many a tender touch, they
  comfort me so much,
With the soft mute comfort of green
  things growing.
Dinah M. Mulock Craik

THE PROCESSION OF THE
FLOWERS

First came the primrose,
  On the bank high,
Like a maiden looking forth
From the window of a tower
When the battle rolls below,
  So look'd she,
And saw the storms go by.

Then came the wind-flower
In the valley left behind,
As a wounded maiden, pale

127

With purple streaks of woe,
When the battle has roll'd by
Wanders to and fro,
  So totter'd she,
Dishevell'd in the wind.

Then came the daisies,
On the first of May,
Like a banner'd show's advance
While the crowd runs by the way,
With ten thousand flowers about them
They came trooping through the fields.

As a happy people come,
  So came they,
As a happy people come
When the war has roll'd away,
With dance and tabor, pipe and drum,
And all make holiday.

Then came the cowslip,
Like a dancer in the fair,
She spread her little mat of green,
And on it danced she.
With a fillet bound about her brow,
A fillet round her happy brow,
A golden fillet round her brow,
And rubies in her hair.

Sydney Dobell

SNOWDROPS

Great King Sun is out in the cold,
  His babies are sleeping, he misses
    the fun;
So he knocks at their door with
    fingers of gold:
  "Time to get up," says Great
    King Sun.
Though the garden beds are
    sprinkled with snow,
It's time to get up in the earth
    below.

Who wakes first? A pale little maid
  All in her nightgown opens the
    door,
Peering round as if half afraid
  Before she steps out on the wintry
    floor.
All in their nightgowns, snowdrops
    stand,
White little waifs in a lonely land.

Great King Sun with a smile looks
    down,—
  "Where are your sisters? I want
    them, too!"
Each baby is hurrying into her
    gown,
  Purple and saffron, orange and
    blue,
Great King Sun gives a louder
    call,—
"Good morning, Papa!" cry the ba-
    bies all.

W. Graham Robertson

THE LILAC

Who thought of the lilac?
"I," dew said.
"I made up the lilac
out of my head."

"She made up the lilac!
Pooh!" thrilled a linnet,
And each dew-note had a
lilac in it.

Humbert Wolfe

BABY SEED SONG

Little brown brother, oh! little
    brown brother,
Are you awake in the dark?
Here we lie cosily, close to each
    other:

Hark to the song of the lark—
" Waken! " the lark says, " waken and
　　dress you;
　Put on your green coats and gay,
Blue sky will shine on you, sunshine
　　caress you—
　Waken! 'tis morning—'tis May! "

Little brown brother, oh! little
　　brown brother,
　What kind of flower will you be?
I'll be a poppy—all white, like my
　　mother;
　Do be a poppy like me.
What! you're a sun-flower? How I
　　shall miss you
　When you've grown golden and
　　high!
But I shall send all the bees up to
　　kiss you;
　Little brown brother, good-bye.
　　　　　　　　Edith Nesbit

THE VIOLET

Down in a green and shady bed,
　A modest violet grew,
Its stalk was bent, it hung its head,
　As if to hide from view.

And yet it was a lovely flower,
　Its color bright and fair;
It might have graced a rosy bower,
　Instead of hiding there.

Yet there it was content to bloom,
　In modest tints arrayed;
And there diffused its sweet perfume,
　Within the silent shade.

Then let me to the valley go,
　This pretty flower to see;
That I may also learn to grow
　In sweet humility.
　　　　　　　　Jane Taylor

TO DAFFODILS

Fair daffodils, we weep to see
　You haste away so soon;
As yet the early rising sun
　Has not attained his noon:
　　　　Stay, stay
Until the hastening day
　　　　Has run
But to the evensong;
And having prayed together, we
　Will go with you along!

We have short time to stay, as you,
　We have as short a spring,
As quick a growth to meet decay,
　As you or anything.
　　　　We die
As your hours do; and dry
　　　　Away,
Like to the summer's rain,
Or as the pearls of morning dew,
　Ne'er to be found again.
　　　　　　　　Robert Herrick

THE CROCUS

The golden crocus reaches up
To catch a sunbeam in her cup.
　　　　　　　　Walter Crane

DAFFY-DOWN-DILLY

Daffy-down-dilly
　Came up in the cold,
　Through the brown mould,
Although the March breezes
　Blew keen on her face,
Although the white snow
　Lay on many a place.

Daffy-down-dilly
　Had heard under ground,
　The sweet rushing sound

Of the streams, as they broke
　From their white winter chains
Of the whistling spring winds,
　And the pattering rains.

"Now then," thought Daffy,
　Deep down in her heart,
"It's time I should start."
So she pushed her soft leaves
　Through the hard frozen ground,
Quite up to the surface,
　And then she looked round.

There was snow all about her,
　Gray clouds overhead;
The trees all looked dead:
Then how do you think
　Poor Daffy-down felt,
When the sun would not shine,
　And the ice would not melt?

"Cold weather!" thought Daffy,
　Still working away;
"The earth's hard today!
There's but a half inch
　Of my leaves to be seen,
And two-thirds of that
　Is more yellow than green.

"I can't do much yet,
　But I'll do what I can:
It's well I began!
For, unless I can manage
　To lift up my head,
The people will think
　That the Spring herself's dead."

So, little by little,
　She brought her leaves out,
All clustered about;
And then her bright flowers
　Began to unfold,
Till Daffy stood robed
　In her spring green and gold.

O Daffy-down-dilly,
　So brave and so true!
I wish all were like you!—
So ready for duty
　In all sorts of weather,
And loyal to courage
　And duty together.

Anna R. Warner

APPLE BLOSSOM

Lady Apple Blossom
　Just arrived in town,
Wears a light green bonnet
　And a snowy gown.

The pretty dress is—
　What do you think?
Five white petals
　Just touched with pink.

Kate Louise Brown

BUTTERCUPS AND DAISIES

Buttercups and daisies,
　Oh, the pretty flowers;
Coming ere the spring time,
　To tell of sunny hours.
While the trees are leafless,
　While the fields are bare,
Buttercups and daisies
　Spring up here and there.

Ere the snow-drop peepeth,
　Ere the crocus bold,
Ere the early primrose
　Opes its paly gold,—
Somewhere on the sunny bank
　Buttercups are bright;
Somewhere 'mong the frozen grass
　Peeps the daisy white.

Little hardy flowers,
　Like to children poor,

Playing in their sturdy health
   By their mother's door.
Purple with the north-wind,
   Yet alert and bold;
Fearing not, and caring not,
   Though they be a-cold!

What to them is winter!
   What are stormy showers!
Buttercups and daisies
   Are these human flowers!
He who gave them hardships
   And a life of care,
Gave them likewise hardy strength
   And patient hearts to bear.

Mary Howitt

JACK-IN-THE-PULPIT

Four of us went to the woods one day,
Keeping the trail in the Indian way,
   Creeping, crawling,
   Sometimes sprawling,
Pushing through bushes; and there we
  found
A little green pulpit stuck in the
  ground
And in the pulpit a brown man stood,
Preaching to all the folk in the wood.

We lay as quiet as Indians do,
Because each one of the four of us
  knew,
   At any sound,
   The creatures 'round,
The squirrels and chipmunks, birds
  and bees,
Would fly away through the ring of
  trees,
And Jack-in-the-Pulpit would stop his
  speech
If he knew we four were in easy reach.

We listened as hard as ever we could,

But not a one of us understood,
   Or even heard,
   A single word,
Though I saw a chipmunk nod his
  head
As if he knew what the preacher said,
And a big gray squirrel clapped his
  paws
When he thought it was time for some
  applause.

Many and many a Jack we've found,
But none of us ever heard a sound;
   So I suppose
   That Jackie knows
When children try to hear him preach,
And talks in some peculiar speech;
I wonder if we could find a way
To hear what Jacks-in-the-Pulpit say?

Rupert Sargent Holland

THE POPPY

High on a bright and sunny bed
   A scarlet poppy grew;
And up it held its staring head,
   And thrust it full in view.

Yet no attention did it win,
   By all these efforts made,
And less unwelcome had it been
   In some retired shade.

For though within its scarlet breast,
   No sweet perfume was found,
It seemed to think itself the best
   Of all the flowers around.

From this I may a hint obtain,
   And take great care indeed,
Lest I appear as pert and vain
   As does this gaudy weed.

Jane Taylor

THE WILLOW CATS

They call them pussy-willows,
  But there's no cat to see
Except the little furry toes
  That stick out on the tree.

I think that very long ago,
  When I was just born new,
There must have been whole pussy-
  cats
    Where just the toes stick
    through—

And every spring it worries me,
  I cannot ever find
Those willow-cats that ran away
  And left their toes behind!

            Margaret Widdemer

THE CITY CHILD

Dainty little maiden, whither would
  you wander?
Whither from this pretty home, the
  home where mother dwells?
" Far and far away," said the dainty
  little maiden,
" All among the gardens, auriculas,
  anemones,
Roses and lilies and Canterbury
  bells."

Dainty little maiden, whither would
  you wander?
Whither from this pretty house, this
  city-house of ours?
" Far and far away," said the dainty
  little maiden,
" All among the meadows, the clover
  and the clematis,
Daisies and kingcups and honey-
  suckle-flowers."

            Alfred Tennyson

DEEDS OF KINDNESS

Suppose the little Cowslip
  Should hang its golden cup
And say, " I'm such a little flower
  I'd better not grow up! "
How many a weary traveller
  Would miss its fragrant smell,
How many a little child would grieve
  To lose it from the dell!

Suppose the glistening Dewdrop
  Upon the grass should say,
" What can a little dewdrop do?
  I'd better roll away! "
The blade on which it rested,
  Before the day was done,
Without a drop to moisten it,
  Would wither in the sun.

Suppose the little Breezes,
  Upon a summer's day,
Should think themselves too small to
  cool
  The traveller on his way:
Who would not miss the smallest
  And softest ones that blow,
And think they made a great mistake
  If they were acting so?

How many deeds of kindness
  A little child can do,
Although it has but little strength
  And little wisdom too!
It wants a loving spirit
  Much more than strength, to prove
How many things a child may do
  For others by its love.

            Unknown

THE TREE

The Tree's early leaf-buds were
  bursting their brown;
" Shall I take them away? " said the
  Frost sweeping down.

"No, leave them alone
Till the blossoms have grown,"
Prayed the Tree, while he trembled
from rootlet to crown.

The tree bore his blossoms, and all
the birds sung.
˟Shall I take them away? said the
Wind, as he swung.
"No, leave them alone
Till the berries have grown,"
Said the Tree, while his leaflets
quivering hung.

The Tree bore his fruit in the mid-
summer glow:
Said the girl, "May I gather thy
berries now?"
"Yes, all thou canst see:
Take them, all are for thee,"
Said the Tree, while he bent down
his laden boughs low.

Björnstjerne Björnson

OH, FAIR TO SEE

Oh, fair to see
Bloom-laden cherry tree,
    Arrayed in sunny white:
    An April's delight,
Oh, fair to see!

Oh, fair to see
Fruit-laden cherry tree,
    With balls of shining red
    Decking a leafy head,
Oh, fair to see!

Christina Rossetti

THE OAK AND THE BEECH

For the tender beech and the sapling
oak,
That grew by the shadowy rill,

You may cut down both at a single
stroke,
You may cut down which you will.

But this you must know, that as long
as they grow,
Whatever change may be,
You can never teach either oak or
beech
To be aught but a greenwood tree.

Thomas Love Peacock

COME, LITTLE LEAVES

"Come, little leaves," said the wind
one day.
"Come over the meadows with me
and play;
Put on your dresses of red and gold,
For summer is gone and the days
grow cold."

Soon as the leaves heard the wind's
loud call,
Down they came fluttering, one and
all;
Over the brown fields they danced
and flew,
Singing the sweet little song they
knew.

"Cricket, good-by, we've been friends
so long,
Little brook, sing us your farewell
song;
Say you are sorry to see us go;
Ah, you will miss us, right well we
know.

"Dear little lambs in your fleecy
fold,
Mother will keep you from harm
and cold;
Fondly we watched you in vale and
glade,

Say, will you dream of our loving
    shade? "

Dancing and whirling, the little
    leaves went,
Winter had called them, and they
    were content;
Soon, fast asleep in their earthy
    beds,
The snow laid a coverlid over their
    heads.

George Cooper

HOW THE LEAVES CAME DOWN

I'll tell you how the leaves came
    down.
    The great Tree to his children
        said:
" You're getting sleepy, Yellow and
    Brown,
    Yes, very sleepy, little Red.
    It is quite time to go to bed."

" Ah! " begged each silly, pouting
    leaf,
    " Let us a little longer stay;
Dear Father Tree, behold our grief!
    'Tis such a very pleasant day,
    We do not want to go away."

So, just for one more merry day
    To the great Tree the leaflets
        clung,
Frolicked and danced, and had
    their way,
    Upon the autumn breezes swung,
    Whispering all their sports
        among—

" Perhaps the great Tree will forget,
    And let us stay until the spring,
If we all beg, and coax, and fret."

But the great Tree did no such
    thing;
    He smiled to hear them whisper-
        ing.

" Come, children, all to bed," he
    cried;
    And ere the leaves could urge
        their prayer,
He shook his head, and far and
    wide,
    Fluttering and rustling every-
        where,
    Down sped the leaflets through
        the air.

I saw them; on the ground they lay,
    Golden and red, a huddled
        swarm,
Waiting till one from far away,
    White bedclothes heaped upon
        her arm,
    Should come to wrap them safe
        and warm.

The great bare Tree looked down
    and smiled.
    " Good-night, dear little leaves,"
        he said.
And from below each sleepy child
    Replied, "Good-night," and mur-
        mured,
    " It is so nice to go to bed! "

Susan Coolidge

FRIENDS

North Wind came whistling through
    the wood,
Where the tender, sweet things
    grew.
The tall fair ferns and the maiden's
    hair,
And the gentle gentians blue.

" It is very cold; are we growing old? "
They sighed, " What shall we do? "

The sigh went up to the loving
  leaves,—
" We must help," they whispered low.
" They are frightened and weak, O
  brave old trees!
But we love you well, you know."
And the trees said, " We are strong—
  make haste!
Down to the darlings go."

So the leaves went floating, floating
  down,
All yellow and brown and red,
And the frail little trembling, thank-
  ful things
Lay still and were comforted.
And the blue sky smiled through the
  bare old trees
Down on their safe warm bed.

L. G. Warner

SEWING

If Mother Nature patches
  The leaves of trees and vines,
I'm sure she does her darning
  With the needles of the pines;
They are so long and slender,
  And somewhere in full view,
She has her threads of cobweb,
  And a thimbleful of dew.

Unknown

THE WIND'S SONG

O winds that blow across the sea,
  What is the story that you bring?
Leaves clap their hands on every tree

And birds about their branches
  sing.
You sing to flowers and trees and
  birds
Your sea-songs over all the land.
Could you not stay and whisper words
  A little child might understand?

The roses nod to hear you sing;
  But though I listen all the day,
You never tell me anything
  Of father's ship so far away.

Its masts are taller than the trees;
  Its sails are silver in the sun;
There's not a ship upon the seas
  So beautiful as father's one.

With wings spread out it flies so fast
  It leaves the waves all white with
  foam.
Just whisper to me, blowing past,
  If you have seen it sailing home.

I feel your breath upon my cheek,
  And in my hair, and on my brow.
Dear winds, if you could only speak,
  I know that you would tell me now.

My father's coming home, you'd say,
  With precious presents, one, two,
  three;
A shawl for mother, beads for May,
  And eggs and shells for Rob and
  me.

The winds sing songs, where'er they
  roam;
  The leaves all clap their little
  hands;
For father's ship is coming home
  With wondrous things from foreign
  lands.

Gabriel Setoun

THE WIND

I saw you toss the kites on high
And blow the birds about the sky;
And all around I heard you pass,
Like ladies' skirts across the grass—
  O wind, a-blowing all day long,
  O wind, that sings so loud a song!

I saw the different things you did,
But always you yourself you hid.
I felt you push, I heard you call,
I could not see yourself at all—
  O wind, a-blowing all day long,
  O wind, that sings so loud a song!

O you that are so strong and cold,
O blower, are you young or old?
Are you a beast of field and tree,
Or just a stronger child than me?
  O wind, a-blowing all day long,
  O wind, that sings so loud a song!

                    Robert Louis Stevenson

WINTER NIGHT

Blow, wind, blow!
Drift the flying snow!
Send it twirling, whirling overhead!
  There's a bedroom in a tree
  Where, snug as snug can be,
The squirrel nests in his cosy bed.

Shriek, wind, shriek!
Make the branches creak!
Battle with the boughs till break o'
    day!
  In a snow-cave warm and tight,
  Through the icy winter night
The rabbit sleeps the peaceful hours
    away.

Call, wind, call,
In entry and in hall,
Straight from off the mountain white
    and wild!

Soft purrs the pussy-cat,
On her little fluffy mat,
And beside her nestles close her furry
    child.

Scold, wind, scold,
So bitter and so bold!
Shake the windows with your tap,
    tap, tap!
  With half-shut, dreamy eyes
  The drowsy baby lies
Cuddled closely in his mother's lap.

                    Mary Frances Butts

THE WIND IN A FROLIC

The wind one morning sprang up
    from sleep,
Saying, "Now for a frolic! now for a
    leap!
Now for a mad-cap galloping chase!
I'll make a commotion in every
    place!"

So it swept with a bustle right
    through a great town,
Cracking the signs and scattering
    down
Shutters; and whisking, with merci-
    less squalls,
Old women's bonnets and gingerbread
    stalls.
There never was heard a much lustier
    shout,
As the apples and oranges trundled
    about;
And the urchins that stand with their
    thievish eyes
For ever on watch, ran off each with a
    prize.

Then away to the field it went bluster-
    ing and humming.
And the cattle all wonder'd whatever
    was coming;

It pluck'd by the tails the grave
  matronly cows,
And toss'd the colts' manes all over
  their brows;
Till, offended at such an unusual
  salute,
They all turn'd their backs, and stood
  sulky and mute.

So on it went capering and playing its
  pranks,
Whistling with reeds on the broad
  river's banks,
Puffing the birds as they sat on the
  spray,
Or the traveller grave on the king's
  highway.
It was not too nice to hustle the bags
Of the beggar, and flutter his dirty
  rags;
'Twas so bold, that it feared not to
  play its joke
With the doctor's wig or the gentleman's cloak.
Through the forest it roar'd, and cried
  gaily, " Now,
You sturdy old oaks, I'll make you
  bow! "

And it made them bow without much
  ado,
Or it crack'd their great branches
  through and through.
Then it rush'd like a monster on cottage and farm,
Striking their dwellings with sudden
  alarm;
And they ran out like bees in a midsummer swarm.
There were dames with their kerchiefs
  tied over their caps,
To see if their poultry were free from
  mishaps;

The turkeys they gobbled, the geese
  scream'd aloud,
And the hens crept to roost in a terri-
  fied crowd;
There was rearing of ladders, and logs
  laying on,
Where the thatch from the roof
  threaten'd soon to be gone.
But the wind had swept on, and had
  met in a lane
With a schoolboy, who panted and
  struggled in vain;
For it toss'd him, and twirl'd him,
  then pass'd, and he stood
With his hat in a pool, and his shoes
  in the mud.

Then away went the wind in its holi-
  day glee,
And now it was far on the billowy sea,
And the lordly ships felt its stagger-
  ing blow,
And the little boats darted to and fro.
But lo! it was night, and it sank to
  rest
On the sea-bird's rock in the gleaming
  west,
Laughing to think, in its fearful fun,
How little of mischief it had done.

William Howitt

WHO HAS SEEN THE WIND

Who has seen the wind?
  Neither I nor you:
But when the leaves hang trembling,
  The wind is passing through.

Who has seen the wind?
  Neither you nor I:
But when the trees bow down their
  heads,
  The wind is passing by.

Christina Rossetti

WILD WINDS

Oh, oh, how the wild winds blow!
    Blow high,
    Blow low,
    And whirlwinds go,
To chase the little leaves that fly—
    Fly low and high,
To hollow and to steep hillside;
They shiver in the dreary weather,
And creep in little heaps together,
And nestle close and try to hide.
Oh, oh, how the wild winds blow!
    Blow low,
    Blow high,
    And whirlwinds try
To find a crevice—to find a crack,
They whirl to the front; they whirl to
    the back.
But Tommy and Will and the baby
    together
Are snug and safe from the wintry
    weather.
        All the winds that blow
        Cannot touch a toe—
        Cannot twist or twirl
        One silken curl.
They may rattle the doors in a noisy
    pack,
But the blazing fires will drive them
    back.

            Mary Frances Butts

BLOW, BLOW, THOU WINTER WIND

Blow, blow, thou winter wind,
Thou art not so unkind
    As man's ingratitude;
Thy tooth is not so keen,
Because thou art not seen,
    Although thy breath be rude.

Heigh, ho! sing, heigh, ho! unto the
    green holly;

Most friendship is feigning, most lov-
    ing mere folly:
    Then, heigh, ho, the holly!
This life is most jolly.

Freeze, thou bitter sky,
That dost not bite so nigh
    As benefits forgot:
Though thou the waters warp,
Thy sting is not so sharp
    As friends remember'd not.

Heigh, ho! sing, heigh, ho! etc.
            William Shakespeare

WHICH WAY DOES THE WIND BLOW?

Which way does the wind blow,
    Which way does he go?
He rides over the water,
    He rides over snow;

O'er wood and o'er valley,
    And o'er rocky height,
Which the great cannot traverse,
    He taketh his flight.

He rages and tosses
    In every bare tree,
As, if you look upwards,
    You plainly may see.

But whence he both cometh
    And whither he goes,
There's never a scholar
    In England that knows.
            Lucy Aikin

WHO LIKES THE RAIN?

"I," said the duck, "I call it fun,
For I have my little red rubbers on;
They make a cunning three-toed
    track

In the soft, cool mud. Quack!
Quack! Quack! "

" I," cried the dandelion, " I.
My roots are thirsty and dry ":
And she lifted a towsled head
Out of her green and grassy bed.

" I hope 'twill pour! I hope 'twill
pour! "
Purred the tree-toad at his gray back
door,
" For, with a broad leaf for a roof,
I am perfectly weatherproof."

Sang the brook: " I laugh at every
drop,
And wish they never need stop
Till a big, big river I grew to be,
And could find my way out to the
sea."

" I," shouted Ted, " for I can run,
With my high-top boots and my
raincoat on,
Through every puddle and runlet
and pool
That I find on my way to school."

Clara Doty Bates

THE RAINBOW FAIRIES

Two little clouds one summer's day
Went flying through the sky.
They went so fast they bumped their
heads,
And both began to cry.

Old Father Sun looked out and said,
" Oh, never mind, my dears,
I'll send my little fairy folk
To dry your falling tears."

One fairy came in violet,
And one in indigo,

In blue, green, yellow, orange, red,—
They made a pretty row.

They wiped the cloud tears all away,
And then, from out the sky,
Upon a line the sunbeams made,
They hung their gowns to dry.

Lizzie M. Hadley

SNOW-FLAKES

Whenever a snow-flake leaves the
sky,
It turns and turns to say " Good-
bye!
Good-bye, dear cloud, so cool and
gray! "
Then lightly travels on its way.

And when a snow-flake finds a tree,
" Good-day! " it says—" Good-day to
thee!
Thou art so bare and lonely, dear,
I'il rest and call my comrades here."

But when a snow-flake, brave and
meek,
Lights on a rosy maiden's cheek,
It starts—" How warm and soft the
day!
'Tis summer! "—and it melts away.

Mary Mapes Dodge

JACK FROST

The door was shut, as doors should be
Before you went to bed last night;
Yet Jack Frost has got in, you see,
And left your window silver white.

He must have waited till you slept;
And not a single word he spoke,
But pencilled o'er the panes and crept
Away again before you woke.

And now you cannot see the hills
  Nor fields that stretch beyond the
    lane;
But there are fairer things than these
  His fingers traced on every pane.

Rocks and castles towering high;
  Hills and dales, and streams and
    fields;
And knights in armour riding by,
  With nodding plumes and shining
    shields.

And here are little boats, and there
  Big ships with sails spread to the
    breeze;
And yonder, palm trees waving fair
  On islands set in silver seas.

And butterflies with gauzy wings;
  And herds of cows and flocks of
    sheep;
And fruit and flowers and all the
    things
  You see when you are sound asleep.

For creeping softly underneath
  The door when all the lights are out,
Jack Frost takes every breath you
    breathe,
  And knows the things you think
    about.

He paints them on the window pane
  In fairy lines with frozen steam;
And when you wake you see again
  The lovely things you saw in dream.

Gabriel Setoun

THE FROST

The frost looked forth, one still clear
    night,
And whispered, " Now I shall be out
    of sight;

So through the valley and over the
    height,
  In silence I'll take my way:
I will not go on like that blustering
    train,
The wind and the snow, the hail and
    the rain,
Who make so much bustle and noise
    in vain,
  But I'll be as busy as they."

Then he flew to the mountain and
    powdered its crest;
He lit on the trees, and their boughs
    he dressed
In diamond beads—and over the
    breast
  Of the quivering lake he spread
A coat of mail, that it need not fear
The downward point of many a spear
That hung on its margin far and near,
  Where a rock could rear its head.

He went to the windows of those who
    slept,
And over each pane, like a fairy, crept;
Wherever he breathed, wherever he
    slept,
  By the light of the moon were seen
Most beautiful things—there were
    flowers and trees;
There were bevies of birds and swarms
    of bees;
There were cities with temples and
    towers, and these
  All pictured in silver sheen!

But he did one thing that was hardly
    fair;
He peeped in the cupboard, and find-
    ing there
That all had forgotten for him to
    prepare—
  " Now just to set them a-thinking,

I'll **bite this basket of fruit,**" said he,
"This costly pitcher I'll burst in three,
And the glass of water they've left
    for me
Shall '*tchich!*' **to tell** them I'm
    drinking."

        Hannah Flagg Gould

THE TIDE

Sometimes we peep beneath the
    blinds,
And through the window bars.
We see the dew like silver clouds;
We see the lighted stars:

And down among the sea-weed pools
Where little fishes hide,
Swift coming through the dark we hear
The footsteps of the tide.

We know, when night is tucked away,
Tomorrow there will be
Across the flat and shining sand,
The footprints of the sea.

        Marjorie Wilson

MINNIE AND WINNIE

Minnie and Winnie slept in a shell.
Sleep, little ladies! And they slept
    well.

Pink was the shell within, silver
    without;
Sounds of the great sea wandered
    about.

Sleep, little ladies! Wake not soon!
Echo on echo dies to the moon.

Two bright stars peeped into the
    shell.

"What are they dreaming of? Who
    can tell?"

Started a green linnet out of the
    croft;
Wake, little ladies! The sun is
    aloft.

        Alfred Tennyson

BOATS SAIL ON THE RIVERS

Boats sail on the rivers,
    And ships sail on the seas;
But clouds that sail across the sky
    Are prettier far than these.

There are bridges on the rivers,
    As pretty as you please;
But the bow that bridges heaven,
    And overtops the trees,
And builds a road from earth to sky,
    Is prettier far than these.

        Christina Rossetti

PIPPA'S SONG

The year's at the spring
And day's at the morn;
Morning's at seven;
The hillside's dew-pearled;
The lark's on the wing;
The snail's on the thorn;
God's in his heaven—
All's right with the world.

        Robert Browning

SPRING

The alder by the river
    Shakes out her powdery curls;
The willow buds in silver
    For little boys and girls.

The little birds fly over,
    And oh, how sweet they sing!

To tell the happy children
   That once again 'tis spring.

The gay green grass comes creeping
   So soft beneath their feet;
The frogs begin to ripple
   A music clear and sweet.

And buttercups are coming,
   And scarlet columbine,
And in the sunny meadows
   The dandelions shine.

And just as many daisies
   As their soft hands can hold
The little ones may gather,
   All fair in white and gold.

Here blooms the warm red clover,
   There peeps the violet blue;
O happy little children!
   God made them all for you.

Celia Thaxter

SPRING

Sound the flute!
Now it's mute.
Birds delight
Day and night;
Nightingale
In the dale,
Lark in sky
Merrily
Merrily, merrily to welcome in the
   year.

Little boy,
Full of joy;
Little girl,
Sweet and small;
Cock does crow,
So do you.
Merry voice,
Infant noise,

Merrily, merrily, to welcome in the
   year.

Little lamb,
Here I am;
Come and lick
My white neck;
Let me pull
Your soft wool;
Let me kiss
Your soft face:
Merrily, merrily, we welcome in the
   year.

William Blake

A SPRING LILT

Through the silver mist
   Of the blossom-spray
Trill the orioles: list
   To their joyous lay!
"What in all the world, in all the
   world," they say,
"Is half so sweet, so sweet, is half so
   sweet as May?"

"June! June! June!"
   Low croon
The brown bees in the clover.
   "Sweet! sweet! sweet!"
   Repeat
The robins, nested over.

Unknown

SPRING

Spring, the sweet Spring, is the year's
   pleasant king;
Then blooms each thing, then maids
   dance in a ring;
Cold doth not sting, the pretty birds
   do sing,
Cuckoo, jug-jug, pu-we, to-witta-woo!

The palm and the may make country
   houses gay,
Lambs frisk and play, the shepherds
   pipe all day,
And we hear aye birds tune this merry
   lay,
Cuckoo, jug-jug, pu-we, to-witta-woo!

The fields breathe sweet, the daisies
   kiss our feet,
Young lovers meet, old wives a-sun-
   ning sit;
In every street these tunes our ears do
   greet,
Cuckoo, jug-jug, pu-we, to-witta-woo!
   Spring! the sweet Spring!
         Thomas Nash

THE ECHOING GREEN

The sun doth arise
And make happy the skies;
The merry bells ring
To welcome the spring;
The skylark and thrush,
The birds of the bush,
Sing louder around
To the bells' cheerful sound,
While our sports shall be seen
On the echoing green.

Old John with white hair
Does laugh away care,
Sitting under the oak
Among the old folk.
They laugh at our play
And soon they all say:
" Such, such, were the joys
When we, all girls and boys,
In our youth-time were seen
On the echoing green."

Till, the little ones, weary,
No more can be merry;

The sun doth descend,
And our sports have an end.
Round the laps of their mothers,
Many sisters and brothers,
Like birds in their nest,
Are ready for rest;
And sport no more seen
On the echoing green.
         William Blake

SUMMER DAYS

Winter is cold-hearted;
   Spring is yea and nay;
Autumn is a weathercock,
   Blown every way:
Summer days for me,
When every leaf is on its tree,

When Robin's not a beggar,
   And Jenny Wren's a bride,
And larks hang, singing, singing,
   singing,
   Over the wheat-fields wide,
   And anchored lilies ride,
And the pendulum spider
   Swings from side to side,

And blue-black beetles transact busi-
   ness,
   And gnats fly in a host,
And furry caterpillars hasten
   That no time be lost,
And moths grow fat and thrive,
And ladybirds arrive.

Before green apples blush,
   Before green nuts embrown,
Why, one day in the country
   Is worth a month in town—
   Is worth a day and a year
Of the dusty, musty, lag-last fashion
   That days drone elsewhere.
         Christina Rossetti

THE THROSTLE

"Summer is coming, summer is com-
 ing,
 I know it, I know it, I know it.
Light again, leaf again, life again,
 love again,"
Yes, my wild little Poet.

Sing the new year in under the blue.
 Last year you sang it as gladly.
"New, new, new, new!" Is it then
 so new
 That you should carol so madly?

"Love again, song again, nest again,
 young again,"
Never a prophet so crazy!
And hardly a daisy as yet, little
 friend,
 See, there is hardly a daisy.

"Here again, here, here, here, happy
 year!"
O warble unchidden, unbidden!
Summer is coming, is coming, my
 dear,
 And all the winters are hidden.

Alfred Tennyson

A MIDSUMMER SONG

Oh, father's gone to market-town: he
 was up before the day,
And Jamie's after robins, and the man
 is making hay,
And whistling down the hollow goes
 the boy that minds the mill,
While mother from the kitchen-door
 is calling with a will,
 "Polly!—Polly!—The cows are in
 the corn!
 Oh, where's Polly?"

From all the misty morning air there
 comes a summer sound,

A murmur as of waters, from skies and
 trees and ground.
The birds they sing upon the wing, the
 pigeons bill and coo;
And over hill and hollow rings again
 the loud halloo:
 "Polly!—Polly!—The cows are in
 the corn!
 Oh, where's Polly?"

Above the trees, the honey-bees swarm
 by with buzz and boom,
And in the field and garden a thousand
 blossoms bloom.
Within the farmer's meadow a brown-
 eyed daisy blows,
And down at the edge of the hollow
 a red and thorny rose.
 But, "Polly!—Polly!—The cows are
 in the corn!
 Oh, where's Polly?"

How strange at such a time of day the
 mill should stop its clatter!
The farmer's wife is listening now, and
 wonders what's the matter.
Oh, wild the birds are singing in the
 wood and on the hill,
While whistling up the hollow goes
 the boy that minds the mill.
 But, "Polly!—Polly!—The cows are
 in the corn!
 Oh, where's Polly!"

Richard Watson Gilder

JOY OF LIFE

The sun is careering in glory and
 might,
'Mid the deep blue sky and the clouds
 so bright;
The billow is tossing its foam on high,
And the summer breezes go lightly
 by;

The air and the water dance, glitter,
    and play—
And why should not I be as merry as
    they?

The linnet is singing the wild wood
    through,
The fawn's bounding footsteps skim
    over the dew,
The butterfly flits round the blossom-
    ing tree,
And the cowslip and blue-bell are bent
    by the bee:
All the creatures that dwell in the
    forest are gay,
And why should not I be as merry as
    they?

Mary Russell Mitford

THE MONTHS

January brings the snow,
Makes our feet and fingers glow.

February brings the rain,
Thaws the frozen lake again.

March brings breezes sharp and chill,
Shakes the dancing daffodil.

April brings the primrose sweet,
Scatters daisies at our feet.

May brings flocks of pretty lambs,
Sporting round their fleecy dams.

June brings tulips, lilies, roses,
Fills the children's hands with posies.

Hot July brings thunder-showers,
Apricots, and gilly-flowers.

August brings the sheaves of corn;
Then the harvest home is borne.

Warm September brings the fruit;
Sportsmen then begin to shoot.

Brown October brings the pheasant,
Then to gather nuts is pleasant.

Dull November brings the blast—
Hark! the leaves are whirling fast.

Cold December brings the sleet,
Blazing fire, and Christmas treat.

Sara Coleridge

WEATHER SIGNS

If the evening's red and the morning
    gray,
It is the sign of a bonny day;
If the evening's gray and the morn-
    ing's red,
The lamb and the ewe will go wet to
    bed.

⟫⟪

A swarm of bees in May
Is worth a load of hay;
A swarm of bees in June
Is worth a silver spoon;
A swarm of bees in July
Is not worth a fly.

⟫⟪

A sunshiny shower
Won't last half an hour.

⟫⟪

Rain before seven,
Fair by eleven.

⟫⟪

March winds and April showers
Bring forth May flowers.

⟫⟪

When the wind is in the east,
'Tis good for neither man nor beast;

When the wind is in the north,
The skillful fisher goes not forth;
When the wind is in the south,
It blows the bait in the fishes' mouth;
When the wind is in the west,
Then 'tis at the very best.

※

Evening red and morning gray
Set the traveller on his way;
But evening gray and morning red,
Bring the rain upon his head.

※

Rainbow at night
Is the sailor's delight;
Rainbow at morning,
Sailors, take warning.

THE WORLD

Great, wide, beautiful, wonderful
    world,
With the wonderful water round
    you curled,
And the wonderful grass upon your
    breast—
World, you are beautifully drest.

The wonderful air is over me,
And the wonderful wind is shaking
    the tree,
It walks on the water and whirls
    the mills,
And talks to itself on the tops of
    the hills.

You friendly Earth! how far you go,
With the wheat-fields that nod and
    the rivers that flow,
With cities and gardens, and cliffs
    and isles,
And people upon you for thousands
    of miles?

Ah! you are so great, and I am so
    small,

I tremble to think of you, World, at
    all;
And yet when I said my prayers
    to-day,
A whisper inside me seemed to say,
"You are more than the Earth,
    though you are such a dot:
You can love and think, and the
    Earth cannot!"

    William Brighty Rands

SUN AND WIND

The old sun, the gold sun,
    With lovely May returning,
Went among the chestnut trees
    And set their candles burning.

The cold winds, the bold winds,
    Came down like Goths and Van-
    dals,
And went among the chestnut trees
    Blowing out their candles.

    Eleanor Farjeon

EVENING WATERFALL

What was the name you called me?—
And why did you go so soon?

The crows lift their caw on the wind,
And the wind changed and was lonely.

The warblers cry their sleepy-songs
Across the valley gloaming,
Across the cattle-horns of early stars.

Feathers and people in the crotch of
    a treetop
Throw an evening waterfall of sleepy-
    songs.

What was the name you called me?—
And why did you go so soon?

    Carl Sandburg

Part Eight

POEMS FOR FUN

JORRIDGE AND PORRIDGE

Jorridge and Porridge
Went out for a walk.
Said Porridge to Jorridge:
" I wish you would talk."

Said Jorridge to Porridge:
" I've nothing to say."
So, silent as ever,
They wended their way.

Louise Ayres Garnett

THE BEES' SONG

Thouzandz of thornz there be
On the Rozez where gozez
The Zebra of Zee:
Sleek, striped, and hairy,
The steed of the Fairy
Princess of Zee.

Heavy with blozzomz be
The Rozez that growzez
In the thickets of Zee,
Where grazez the Zebra,
Marked Abracadeebra
Of the Princess of Zee.

And he nozez the poziez
Of the Rozez that growzez
So luvez'm and free,

With an eye, dark and wary,
In search of a Fairy,
Whose Rozez he knowzez
Were not honeyed for he,
But to breathe a sweet incense
To solace the Princess
Of far-away Zee.

Walter de la Mare

TOM TWIST

Tom Twist was a wonderful fellow,
　No boy was so nimble and strong;
He could turn ten somersets back-
　　ward,
　　And stand on his head all day
　　long.
No wrestling, or leaping, or running
　This tough little urchin could tire;
His muscles were all gutta-percha,
　And his sinews bundles of wire.

Tom Twist liked the life of a sailor,
　So off, with a hop and a skip,
He went to a Nantucket captain,
　Who took him on board of his
　　ship.
The vessel was crowded with sea-
　　men,
　　Young, old, stout and slim, short
　　and tall,

149

But in climbing, swinging, and jumping,
  Tom Twist was ahead of them all.

He could scamper all through the
  rigging,
  As spry and as still as a cat,
While as to a leap from the maintop
  To deck, he thought nothing of
  that:
He danced at the end of the yard-
  arm,
  Slept sound in the bend of a sail,
And hung by his legs from the bow-
  sprit,
  When the wind was blowing a
  gale.

The vessel went down in a tempest,
  A thousand fathoms or more;
And Tom Twist dived under the
  breakers,
  And, swimming five miles, got
  ashore.
The shore was a cannibal island,
  The natives were hungry enough;
But they felt of Tommy all over,
  And found him entirely too tough.

So they put him into a boy-coop—
  Just to fatten him up, you see—
But Tommy crept out, very slowly,
  And climbed to the top of a tree.
The tree was the nest of a condor,
  A bird with prodigious big wings,
Which lived upon boa-constrictors
  And other digestible things.

The condor flew home in the evening,
  And there lay friend Tommy so
  snug,
She thought she had pounced on a
  very

Remarkable species of bug;
  She soon woke him up with her
  pecking,
  But Tommy gave one of his
  springs,
And leaped on the back of the condor,
  Between her long neck and her
  wings.

The condor tried plunging and
  pitching,
  But Tommy held on with firm
  hand,
Then off, with a scream, flew the
  condor,
  O'er forest and ocean and land.
By and by she got tired of her burden,
  And flying quite close to the
  ground,
Tom untwisted his legs from the
  creature,
  And quickly slipped off with a
  bound.

He landed all right, and feet fore-
  most,
  A little confused by his fall,
And then ascertained he had lighted
  On top of the great Chinese Wall.
He walked to the city of Pekin,
  Where he made the Chinamen
  grin;
He turned ten somersets backward,
  And they made him a Mandarin.

Then he sailed for his dear home
  and harbor.
  The house of his mother he knew;
He climbed up the lightning-rod
  quickly,
  And came down the chimney-flue.

His mother in slumber lay dream-
ing
That she never would see him
more,
When she opened her eyes, and
Tommy
Stood there on the bedroom floor!

Her nightcap flew off in amazement,
Her hair stood on end with sur-
prise.
" What kind of a ghost or a spirit
Is this that I see with my eyes? "
" I am your most dutiful Tommy."
" I will not believe it," she said,
" Till you turn ten somersets back-
ward,
And stand half an hour on your
head."

" That thing I will do, dearest
mother."
At once with a skip and a hop,
He turned ten somersets backward,
But then was unable to stop!
The tenth took him out of the win-
dow,
His mother jumped from her bed,
To see his twentieth somerset
Take him over the kitchen shed;

Thence, across the patch of potatoes,
And beyond the church on the
hill;
She saw him tumbling and turning,
Turning and tumbling still—
Till Tommy's body diminished
In size to the head of a pin,
Spinning away in the distance,
Where it still continues to spin!

W. A. Butler

THE LOBSTER QUADRILLE

" Will you walk a little faster? " said
a whiting to a snail,

" There's a porpoise close behind us,
and he's treading on my tail.
See how eagerly the lobsters and the
turtles all advance!
They are waiting on the shingle—
will you come and join the
dance?
Will you, won't you, will you,
won't you, will you join the
dance?
Will you, won't you, will you,
won't you, won't you join the
dance?

" You can really have no notion how
delightful it will be
When they take us up and throw us,
with the lobsters, out to sea! "
But the snail replied, " Too far! Too
far! " and gave a look askance—
Said he thanked the whiting kindly,
but he would not join the dance.
Would not, could not, would not,
could not, would not join the
dance.
Would not, could not, would not,
could not, could not join the
dance.

" What matters it how far we go? "
his scaly friend replied,
" There is another shore, you know,
upon the other side.
The further off from England the
nearer is to France—
Then turn not pale, belovèd snail,
but come and join the dance.
Will you, won't you, will you,
won't you, will you join the
dance?
Will you, won't you, will you,
won't you, won't you join the
dance? "

Lewis Carroll

THE MAN IN THE MOON

The Man in the Moon as he sails the
    sky
Is a very remarkable skipper.
But he made a mistake
When he tried to take
A drink of milk from the Dipper.
He dipped right into the Milky Way
And slowly and carefully filled it.
The Big Bear growled
And the Little Bear howled,
And frightened him so he spilled it.

Unknown

THE FASTIDIOUS SERPENT

There was a snake that dwelt in Skye,
    Over the misty sea, oh;
He lived upon nothing but gooseberry
    pie
For breakfast, dinner, and tea, oh.

Now gooseberry pie—as is very well
    known—
Over the misty sea, oh,
Is not to be found under every stone,
    Nor yet upon every tree, oh.

And being so ill to please with his
    meat,
Over the misty sea, oh,
The snake had sometimes nothing to
    eat,
And an angry snake was he, oh.

Then he'd flick his tongue and his
    head he'd shake,
Over the misty sea, oh,
Crying "Gooseberry pie! For goodness'
    sake,
Some gooseberry pie for me, oh!"

And if gooseberry pie was not to be
    had,

Over the misty sea, oh,
He'd twine and twist like an eel gone
    mad,
Or a worm just stung by a bee, oh.

But though he might shout and
    wriggle about,
Over the misty sea, oh,
The snake had often to go without
    His breakfast, dinner, and tea, oh.

Henry Johnstone

THE STORY OF AUGUSTUS

Augustus was a chubby lad;
Fat ruddy cheeks Augustus had;
And everbody saw with joy,
The plump and hearty healthy boy.
He ate and drank as he was told,
And never let his soup get cold.
But one day, one cold winter's day,
He scream'd out—"Take the soup
    away!
O take the nasty soup away!
I won't have any soup to-day!"

How lank and lean Augustus grows!
Next day he scarcely fills his clothes,
Yet, though he feels so weak and ill,
The naughty fellow cries out still—
"Not any soup for me, I say:
O take the nasty soup away!
I won't have any soup to-day!"

The third day comes; oh! what a sin!
To make himself so pale and thin.
Yet, when the soup is put on table,
He screams as loud as he is able,
"Not any soup for me, I say:
O take the nasty soup away!
I won't have any soup to-day!"

Look at him, now the fourth day's
    come!

He scarcely weighs a sugar-plum;
He's like a little bit of thread,
And on the fifth day he was—dead!

Heinrich Hoffmann

THE NAUGHTY BOY

There was a naughty boy,
And a naughty boy was he,
He ran away to Scotland
The people for to see—
Then he found
That the ground
Was as hard,
That a yard
Was as long,
That a song
Was as merry,
That a cherry
Was as red—
That lead
Was as weighty,
That fourscore
Was as eighty,
That a door
Was as wooden
As in England—
So he stood in his shoes
And he wondered,
He wondered.
He stood in his shoes
And he wondered.

John Keats

MEDDLESOME MATTY

One ugly trick has often spoiled
The sweetest and the best;
Matilda, though a pleasant child,
One ugly trick possessed,
Which, like a cloud before the skies,
Hid all her better qualities.

Sometimes she'd lift the tea-pot lid,
To peep at what was in it;

Or tilt the kettle, if you did
But turn your back a minute.
In vain you told her not to touch,
Her trick of meddling grew so much.

Her grandmamma went out one day,
And by mistake she laid
Her spectacles and snuff-box gay
Too near the little maid;
"Ah! well," thought she, "I'll try them on,
As soon as grandmamma is gone."

Forthwith she placed upon her nose
The glasses large and wide;
And looking round, as I suppose,
The snuff-box too she spied:
"Oh! what a pretty box was that;
I'll open it," said little Matt.

"I know that grandmamma would say,
'Don't meddle with it, dear;'
But then, she's far enough away,
And no one else is near:
Besides, what can there be amiss
In opening such a box as this?"

So thumb and finger went to work
To move the stubborn lid,
And presently a mighty jerk
The mighty mischief did;
For all at once, ah! woeful case,
The snuff came puffing in her face.

Poor eyes, and nose, and mouth, beside,
A dismal sight presented;
In vain, as bitterly she cried,
Her folly she repented.
In vain she ran about for ease;
She could do nothing now but sneeze.

She dashed the spectacles away,
To wipe her tingling eyes,

And as in twenty bits they lay,
  Her grandmamma she spies.
" Heyday! and what's the matter
    now? "
Says grandmamma, with lifted brow.

Matilda, smarting with the pain,
  And tingling still, and sore,
Made many a promise to refrain
  From meddling evermore.
And 'tis a fact, as I have heard,
She ever since has kept her word.

Ann Taylor

MR. NOBODY

I know a funny little man,
  As quiet as a mouse,
Who does the mischief that is done
  In everybody's house!
There's no one ever sees his face,
  And yet we all agree
That every plate we break was cracked
  By Mr. Nobody.

'Tis he who always tears our books,
  Who leaves the door ajar,
He pulls the buttons from our shirts,
  And scatters pins afar;
That squeaking door will always
    squeak
  For, prithee, don't you see,
We leave the oiling to be done
  By Mr. Nobody.

He puts damp wood upon the fire,
  That kettles cannot boil;
His are the feet that bring in mud,
  And all the carpets soil.
The papers always are mislaid,
  Who had them last but he?
There's no one tosses them about
  But Mr. Nobody.

The finger-marks upon the door
  By none of us are made;
We never leave the blinds unclosed,
  To let the curtains fade.
The ink we never spill, the boots
  That lying round you see
Are not our boots; they all belong
  To Mr. Nobody.

Unknown

THE TABLE AND THE CHAIR

I

Said the Table to the Chair,
" You can hardly be aware
How I suffer from the heat
And from chilblains on my feet.
If we took a little walk,
We might have a little talk;
Pray let us take the air,"
Said the Table to the Chair.

II

Said the Chair unto the Table,
" Now, you *know* we are not able:
How foolishly you talk,
When you know we *cannot* walk! "
Said the Table with a sigh,
" It can do no harm to try.
I've as many legs as you:
Why can't we walk on two? "

III

So they both went slowly down,
And walked about the town
With a cheerful bumpy sound
As they toddled round and round;
And everybody cried,
As they hastened to their side,
" See! the Table and the Chair
Have come out to take the air! "

IV

But in going down an alley,
To a castle in a valley,

They completely lost their way,
And wandered all the day;
Till, to see them safely back,
They paid a Ducky-quack,
And a Beetle, and a Mouse,
Who took them to their house.

V

Then they whispered to each other,
" O delightful little brother,
What a lovely walk we've taken!
Let us dine on beans and bacon."
So the Ducky and the leetle
Browny-Mousy and the Beetle
Dined, and danced upon their heads
Till they toddled to their beds.

Edward Lear

THE DUCK AND THE
KANGAROO

I

Said the Duck to the Kangaroo,
" Good gracious! how you hop
Over the fields, and the water too,
As if you never would stop!
My life is a bore in this nasty pond;
And I long to go out in the world
beyond:
I wish I could hop like you,"
Said the Duck to the Kangaroo.

II

" Please give me a ride on your back,"
Said the Duck to the Kangaroo:
" I would sit quite still, and say noth-
ing but ' Quack '
The whole of the long day
through;
And we'd go to the Dee, and the
Jelly Bo Lee,
Over the land, and over the sea:
Please take me a ride! oh, do! "
Said the Duck to the Kangaroo.

III

Said the Kangaroo to the Duck,
" This requires some little reflec-
tion.
Perhaps, on the whole, it might
bring me luck:
And there seems but one objec-
tion;
Which is, if you'll let me speak so
bold,
Your feet are unpleasantly wet and
cold,
And would probably give me the
roo—
Matiz," said the Kangaroo.

IV

Said the Duck, " As I sat on the
rocks,
I have thought over that com-
pletely;
And I bought four pairs of worsted
socks,
Which fit my web-feet neatly;
And, to keep out the cold, I've
bought a cloak;
And every day a cigar I'll smoke;
All to follow my own dear true
Love of a Kangaroo."

V

Said the Kangaroo, " I'm ready,
All in the moonlight pale;
But to balance me well, dear Duck,
sit steady,
And quite at the end of my tail."
So away they went with a hop and a
bound;
And they hopped the whole world
three times round.
And who so happy, oh! who,
As the Duck and the Kangaroo?

Edward Lear

HOW DOTH THE LITTLE CROCODILE

How doth the little crocodile
  Improve his shining tail,
And pour the waters of the Nile
  On every golden scale!

How cheerfully he seems to grin,
  How neatly spreads his claws,
And welcomes little fishes in
  With gently smiling jaws!

Lewis Carroll

LAWKAMERCYME

There was an old woman, as I've
    heard tell,
She went to the market, her eggs to
    sell;
She went to the market all on a
    market day,
And she feel asleep on the King's
    highway.

There came by a pedlar, whose name
    was Stout,
He cut her petticoats all round
    about;
He cut her petticoats up to the
    knees,
Which made the old woman to
    shiver and freeze.

When the little woman first did
    wake,
She began to shiver and she began to
    shake,
She began to wonder and she began
    to cry,
"Lawkamercyme, this is none of I!

"But if it be I, as I do hope it be,
  I've a little dog at home and he'll
    know me;

If it be I, he'll wag his little tail,
  And if it be not I, he'll loudly bark
    and wail."

Home went the little woman all in
    the dark,
Up got the little dog, and he began
    to bark;
He began to bark, so she began to
    cry,
"Lawkamercyme, this is none of I!"

Unknown

CHILD'S SONG

The King and Queen were riding
  Upon a summer's day,
And a Blackbird flew above them,
  To hear what they did say.

The King said he liked apples,
  The Queen said she liked pears.
And what shall we do to the Blackbird
  Who listens unawares?

Kate Greenaway

THE RAGGEDY MAN

O The Raggedy Man! He works fer Pa;
An' he's the goodest man ever you saw!
He comes to our house every day,
An' waters the horses, and feeds 'em
    hay;
An' he opens the shed—an' we all ist
    laugh
When he drives out our little old wob-
    ble-ly calf;
An' nen—ef our hired girl says he
    can—
He milks the cow fer 'Lizabuth Ann.—
  Ain't he a' awful good Raggedy
    Man?
Raggedy! Raggedy! Raggedy Man!

W'y, The Raggedy Man—he's ist so
    good,
He splits the kindlin' an' chops the
    wood;
An' nen he spades in our garden, too,
An' does most things 'at boys can't
    do.—
He clumbed clean up in our big tree
An' shooked a' apple down fer me—
An' nother'n', too—fer 'Lizabuth
    Ann—
An' nother'n', too, fer The Raggedy
    Man.—
    Ain't he a' awful kind Raggedy
    Man?
Raggedy! Raggedy! Raggedy Man!

An' The Raggedy Man, he knows most
    rhymes,
An' tells 'em, ef I be good, sometimes:
Knows 'bout Giunts, an' Griffuns, an'
    Elves,
An' the Squidgicum-Squees 'at swal-
    lers the'rselves!
An', wite by the pump in our pasture-
    lot,
He showed me the hole 'at the Wunks
    is got,
'At lives 'way deep in the ground, an'
    can
Turn into me, er 'Lizabuth Ann!
Er Ma, er Pa, er The Raggedy Man!
    Ain't he a funny old Raggedy Man?
Raggedy! Raggedy! Raggedy Man!

The Raggedy Man—one time, when he
Was makin' a little bow-'n'-orry fer
    me,
Says, "When you're big like your
    Pa is,
Air you go' to keep a fine store likc
    his—
An' be a rich merchant—an' wear fine
    clothes?—

Er what *air* you go' to be, goodness
    knows? "
An' nen he laughed at 'Lizabuth Ann,
An' I says "'M go' to be a Raggedy
    Man!—
    I'm ist go' to be a nice Raggedy
    Man! "
Raggedy! Raggedy! Raggedy Man!

        James Whitcomb Riley

    This and the following poem by James
Whitcomb Riley are from the Biographical
Edition of his complete works, copyright
1913, and are used by special permission of
the publishers, The Bobbs-Merrill Company.

THE MAN IN THE MOON

Said The Raggedy Man, on a hot
    afternoon:
    My!
      Sakes!
        What a lot o' mistakes
Some little folks makes on The Man in
    the Moon!
But people that's b'en up to see him,
    like me,
And calls on him frequent and inti-
    muttly,
Might drop a few facts that would in-
    terest you
    Clean!
      Through!—
        If you wanted 'em to—
Some *actual* facts that might interest
    you!

O! The Man in the Moon has a crick
    in his back;
    Whee!
      Whimm!
        Ain't you sorry for him?
And a mole on his nose that is purple
    and black;

And his eyes are so weak that they
    water and run
If he dares to dream even he looks at
    the sun,—
So he jes' dreams of stars, as the doc-
    tors advise—
    My!
      Eyes!
        But isn't he wise—
To jes' dream of stars, as the doctors
    advise?

And The Man in the Moon has a boil
    on his ear,—
    Whee!
      Whing!
        What a singular thing!
I know! but these facts are authentic,
    my dear,—
There's a boil on his ear; and a corn
    on his chin,—
He calls it a dimple—but dimples
    stick in—
Yet it might be a dimple turned over,
    you know!
    Whang!
    Ho!
      Why, certainly so!—
It might be a dimple turned over,
    you know!

And The Man in the Moon has a
    rheumatic knee,—
    Gee!
      Whizz!
        What a pity that is!
And his toes have worked round where
    his heels ought to be.—
So whenever he wants to go North he
    goes South,
And comes back with porridge-crumbs
    all round his mouth,
And he brushes them off with a Jap-
    anese fan,

Whing!
Whann!
    What a marvelous man!
What a very remarkably marvelous
    man!

And The Man in the Moon, sighed
    The Raggedy Man,
    Gits!
    So!
      Sullonesome, you know,—
Up there by hisse'f sence creation be-
    gan!—
That when I call on him and then
    come away,
He grabs me and holds me and begs
    me to stay,—
Till—*Well!* if it wasn't fer *Jimmy-*
    cum-jim,
    Dadd!
      Limb!
        I'd go pardners with him—
Jes' jump my job here and be pard-
    ners with *him!*

                    James Whitcomb Riley

FOOLISH FLOWERS

We've Foxgloves in our garden;
    How careless they must be
To leave their gloves out hanging
    Where every one can see!

And Bachelors leave their Buttons
    In the same careless way,
If I should do the same with mine,
    What would my Mother say?

We've lots of Larkspurs in the yard—
    Larks only fly and sing—
Birds surely don't need spurs because
    They don't ride anything!

And as for Johnny-Jump-Ups—
    I saw a hornet light

On one of them the other day,
  He didn't jump a mite!
        Rupert Sargent Holland

THE MELANCHOLY PIG

There was a Pig that sat alone,
  Beside a ruined Pump.
By day and night he made his moan:
  It would have stirred a heart of stone
To see him wring his hoofs and groan,
  Because he could not jump.
        Lewis Carroll

THE CATS' TEA-PARTY

Five little pussy-cats, invited out to
    tea,
Cried: " Mother, let us go—Oh, do!
    for good we'll surely be.
We'll wear our bibs and hold our
    things as you have shown us
    how—
Spoons in right paws, cups in left—
    and make a pretty bow;
We'll always say, 'Yes, if you
    please,' and 'Only half of
    that.' "
" Then go, my darling children," said
    the happy Mother Cat.
The five little pussy-cats went out
    that night to tea,
Their heads were smooth and glossy,
    their tails were swinging free,
They held their things as they had
    learned, and tried to be polite,—
With snowy bibs beneath their chins
    they were a pretty sight.
But, alas, for manners beautiful, and
    coats as soft as silk!
The moment that the little kits were
    asked to take some milk,
They dropped their spoons, forgot
to bow, and—oh, what do you
    think?
They put their noses in their cups
    and all began to drink!
Yes, every naughty little kit set up a
    meow for more,
Then knocked their tea-cups over,
    and scampered through the
    door!
        Frederick E. Weatherly

BINGO

The miller's mill-dog lay at the mill-
    door,
And his name was little Bingo.
B with an I, I with an N, N with a G,
    G with an O,
And his name was little Bingo.

The miller he bought a cask of ale,
And he called it right good Stingo.
S with a T, T with an I, I with an N,
    N with a G, G with an O,
And he called it right good Stingo.

The miller he went to town one day,
And he bought a wedding Ring-o!
R with an I, I with an N, N with a
    G, G with an O,
And he bought a wedding Ring-o!
        Unknown

THE JOVIAL WELSHMEN

There were three jovial Welshmen,
  As I have heard them say,
And they would go a-hunting
  Upon St. David's day.

All the day they hunted,
  But nothing could they find;
But a ship a-sailing,
  A-sailing with the wind.

One said it was a ship,
  The other he said nay;
The third said it was a house,
  With the chimney blown away.

And all the night they hunted,
  And nothing could they find
But the moon a-gliding,
  A-gliding with the wind.

One said it was the moon,
  The other he said nay;
The other said it was a cheese,
  The half o't cut away.

And all the day they hunted,
  And nothing could they find
But a hedgehog in a bramble bush,
  And that they left behind.

The first said it was a hedgehog,
  The second he said nay;
The third it was a pin-cushion
  And the pins stuck in wrong way.

And all the night they hunted,
  And nothing could they find
But a hare in a turnip-field,
  And that they left behind.

The first said it was a hare,
  The second he said nay;
The third said it was a calf,
  And the cow had run away.

And all the day they hunted,
  And nothing could they find
But an owl in a holly-tree,
  And that they left behind.

One said it was an owl,
  The other he said nay;
The third said 'twas an old man,
  And his beard growing grey.
                    Unknown

THE OWL AND THE PUSSY-CAT

The Owl and the Pussy-cat went to
    sea
  In a beautiful pea-green boat:
They took some honey, and plenty
    of money
  Wrapped up in a five-pound note.
The Owl looked up to the stars
    above,
  And sang to a small guitar,
" O lovely Pussy, O Pussy, my love,
  What a beautiful Pussy you are,
      You are,
      You are!
  What a beautiful Pussy you are! "

Pussy said to the Owl, " You elegant
    fowl,
  How charmingly sweet you sing!
Oh! let us be married; too long we
    have tarried;
  But what shall we do for a ring? "
They sailed away, for a year and a
    day,
  To the land where the bong-tree
    grows;
And there in a wood a Piggy-wig
    stood,
  With a ring at the end of his nose,
      His nose,
      His nose,
  With a ring at the end of his nose.

" Dear Pig, are you willing to sell for
    one shilling
  Your ring? " Said the Piggy, " I
    will."
So they took it away, and were mar-
    ried next day
  By the Turkey who lives on the
    hill.

They dined on mince and slices of
    quince,

Which they ate with a runcible
  spoon;
And hand in hand, on the edge of
  the sand,
They danced by the light of the
  moon,
      The moon,
      The moon,
They danced by the light of the
  moon.

Edward Lear

THE JUMBLIES

They went to sea in a sieve, they did;
  In a sieve they went to sea:
In spite of all their friends could say,
On a winter's morn, on a stormy day,
  In a sieve they went to sea.
And when the sieve turned round and
  round,
And every one cried, "You'll all be
  drowned!"
They called aloud, "Our sieve ain't
  big;
But we don't care a button; we don't
  care a fig:
  In a sieve we'll go to sea!"
    Far and few, far and few,
      Are the lands where the Jum-
        blies live:
      Their heads are green, and their
        hands are blue;
      And they went to sea in a sieve.

They sailed away in a sieve, they did,
  In a sieve they sailed so fast,
With only a beautiful pea-green veil
Tied with a ribbon, by way of a sail,
  To a small tobacco-pipe mast.
And every one said who saw them go,
"Oh! won't they be soon upset, you
  know?

For the sky is dark, and the voyage is
  long;
And, happen what may, it's extremely
  wrong
  In a sieve to sail so fast."

The water it soon came in, it did;
  The water it soon came in:
So, to keep them dry, they wrapped
  their feet
In a pinky paper all folded neat:
  And they fastened it down with a
  pin.
And they passed the night in a crock-
  ery-jar;
And each of them said, "How wise we
  are!
Though the sky be dark, and the voy-
  age be long,
Yet we never can think we were rash
  or wrong,
  While round in our sieve we spin."

And all night long they sailed away;
  And, when the sun went down,
They whistled and warbled a moony
  song
To the echoing sound of a coppery
  gong,
  In the shade of the mountains
  brown,
"O Timballoo! How happy we are
When we live in a sieve and a crock-
  ery-jar!
And all night long, in the moonlight
  pale,
We sail away with a pea-green sail
  In the shade of the mountains
  brown."

They sailed to the Western Sea, they
  did,—
  To a land all covered with trees:
And they bought an owl, and a useful
  cart,

And a pound of rice, and a cranberry
tart,
And a hive of silvery bees;
And they bought a pig, and some
green jackdaws,
And a lovely monkey with lollipop
paws,
And forty bottles of ring-bo-ree,
And no end of Stilton cheese:

And in twenty years they all came
back,—
In twenty years or more;
And every one said, "How tall they've
grown!
For they've been to the Lakes, and the
Torrible Zone,
And the hills of the Chankly Bore."
And they drank their health, and gave
them a feast
Of dumplings made of beautiful yeast;
And every one said, " If we only live,
We, too, will go to sea in a sieve,
To the hills of the Chankly Bore."
Far and few, far and few,
Are the lands where the Jum-
blies live:
Their heads are green, and their
hands are blue;
And they went to sea in a sieve.

Edward Lear

THE POBBLE WHO HAS NO
TOES

The Pobble who has no toes
Had once as many as we;
When they said, " Some day you
may lose them all; "
He replied, " Fish fiddle-de-dee! "
And his Aunt Jobiska made him
drink
Lavender water tinged with pink,

For she said, " The World in general knows
There's nothing so good for a Pobble's toes! "

The Pobble who has no toes
Swam across the Bristol Channel;
But before he set out he wrapped his
nose
In a piece of scarlet flannel.
For his Aunt Jobiska said, " No
harm
Can come to his toes if his nose is
warm;
And it's perfectly known that a Pob-
ble's toes
Are safe,—provided he minds his
nose."

The Pobble swam fast and well,
And when boats or ships came
near him,
He tinkledy-blinkledy-winkled a bell,
So that all the world could hear
him.
And all the Sailors and Admirals
cried,
When they saw him nearing the fur-
ther side,—
" He has gone to fish, for his Aunt
Jobiska's
Runcible Cat with crimson whis-
kers! "

But before he touched the shore,—
The shore of the Bristol Chan-
nel,—
A sea-green Porpoise carried away
His wrapper of scarlet flannel.
And when he came to observe his
feet,
Formerly garnished with toes so
neat,
His face at once became forlorn

On perceiving that all his toes were
gone!

And nobody ever knew,
From that dark day to the present,
Whoso had taken the Pobble's toes
In a manner so far from pleasant.
Whether the shrimps or crawfish
gray,
Or crafty Mermaids stole them
away—
Nobody knew; and nobody knows
How the Pobble was robbed of his
twice five toes!

The Pobble who has no toes
Was placed in a friendly Bark,
And they rowed him back, and car-
ried him up
To his Aunt Jobiska's Park.
And she made him a feast, at his ear-
nest wish,
Of eggs and buttercups fried with
fish;
And she said, " It's a fact the whole
world knows,
That Pobbles are happier without
their toes."

Edward Lear

THE AUTHOR OF THE
" POBBLE "

How pleasant to know Mr. Lear!
Who has written such volumes of
stuff!
Some think him ill-tempered and
queer,
But a few think him pleasant
enough.

His mind is concrete and fastidious,
His nose is remarkably big;
His visage is more or less hideous,
His beard it resembles a wig.

He has ears, and two eyes, and ten
fingers,
Leastways if you reckon two thumbs;
Long ago he was one of the singers,
But now he is one of the dumbs.

He sits in a beautiful parlour,
With hundreds of books on the wall;
He drinks a great deal of Marsala,
But never gets tipsy at all.

He has many friends, laymen and
clerical,
Old Foss is the name of his cat:
His body is perfectly spherical,
He weareth a runcible hat.

When he walks in waterproof white,
The children run after him so!
Calling out, " He's come out in his
night-
Gown, that crazy old Englishman,
oh! "

He weeps by the side of the ocean,
He weeps on the top of the hill;
He purchases pancakes and lotion,
And chocolate shrimps from the
mill.

He reads but he cannot speak Spanish,
He cannot abide ginger-beer:
Ere the days of his pilgrimage vanish,
How pleasant to know Mr. Lear!

Edward Lear

THE REFORMATION OF
GODFREY GORE

Godfrey Gordon Gustavus Gore—
No doubt you have heard the name
before—
Was a boy who never would shut a
door!

The wind might whistle, the wind
    might roar,
And teeth be aching and throats be
    sore,
But still he never would shut the
    door.

His father would beg, his mother
    implore,
" Godfrey Gordon Gustavus Gore,
We really do wish you would shut
    the door! "

Their hands they wrung, their hair
    they tore;
But Godfrey Gordon Gustavus Gore
Was deaf as the buoy out at the
    Nore.

When he walked forth the folks
    would roar,
" Godfrey Gordon Gustavus Gore,
Why don't you think to shut the
    door? "

They rigged out a Shutter with sail
    and oar,
And threatened to pack off Gus-
    tavus Gore
On a voyage of penance to Singa-
    pore.
But he begged for mercy, and said,
    " No more!
Pray do not send me to Singapore
On a Shutter, and then I will shut
    the door! "

" You will? " said his parents; " then
    keep on shore!
But mind you do! For the plague
    is sore
Of a fellow that never will shut the
    door,
Godfrey Gordon Gustavus Gore! "
       William Brighty Rands

WHEN YOUNG MELISSA SWEEPS

When young Melissa sweeps a room
I vow she dances with the broom!

She curtsies in a corner brightly
And leads her partner forth politely.

Then up and down in jigs and reels,
With gold dust flying at their heels,

They caper. With a whirl or two
They make the wainscot shine like
    new;

They waltz beside the hearth, and
    quick
It brightens, shabby brick by brick.

A gay gavotte across the floor,
A Highland fling from door to door,

And every crack and corner's clean
Enough to suit a dainty queen.

If ever you are full of gloom,
Just watch Melissa sweep a room!
       Nancy Byrd Turner

THE WEE WEE MAN

As I was wa'kin' all alone,
    Between a water an a wa',
And there I spied a Wee Wee Man,
    And he was the least that e'er I
    saw.

His legs were scarce a shathmont's
    length
    And thick and timber was his
    thigh;
Between his brows there was a span,
    And between his shoulders there
    was three.

"O Wee Wee Man, but thou art
    strang!
  O tell me where thy dwelling
    be?"
"My dwelling's down at yon bonny
    bower;
  O will you go with me and see?"

On we lap, and awa' we rade,
  Till we came to yon bonny green;
We lighted down for to bait our
    horse,
  And out there came a lady fine.

Four-and-twenty at her back,
  And they were a' clad out in green;
Though the King of Scotland had
    been there,
    The warst o' them might hae been
    his queen.

On we lap, and awa' we rade,
  Till we came to yon bonny ha',
Whare the roof was o' the beaten
    gould,
  And the floor was o' the cristal a'.

When we came to the stair-foot,
  Ladies were dancing, jimp and
    sma,'
But in the twinkling of an eye,
  My Wee Wee Man was clean
    awa'.

Unknown

THE FARM YARD

The cock is crowing,
The cow is lowing,
The ducks are quacking,
The dogs are barking,
The ass is braying,
The horse is neighing;
Was there ever such a noise?

The birds are singing,
The bell is ringing,
The pigs are squeaking,
The barn door creaking,
The brook is babbling,
The geese are gabbling;
Mercy on us, what a noise!

The sheep are baa-ing,
The boys are ha-ha-ing,
The swallows twittering,
The girls are tittering,
Father is calling,
The cook is bawling;
I'm nigh crazy with the noise!

Nabby is churning,
The grindstone's turning,
John is sawing,
Charles hurrahing,
Old Dobson's preaching,
The peacock's screeching;
Who can live in such a noise?

Eliza Lee Follen

THE OSTRICH IS A SILLY BIRD

The ostrich is a silly bird,
  With scarcely any mind.
He often runs so very fast,
  He leaves himself behind.

And when he gets there, has to stand
  And hang about till night,
Without a blessed thing to do
  Until he comes in sight.

Mary E. Wilkins Freeman

TOPSY-TURVY WORLD

If the butterfly courted the bee,
  And the owl the porcupine;
If churches were built on the sea,
  And three times one was nine;

If the pony rode his master,
  If the buttercups ate the cows,
If the cats had the dire disaster
  To be worried, sir, by the mouse;
If Mamma, sir, sold the baby
  To a gypsy for half a crown;
If a gentleman, sir, was a lady,—
  The world would be Upside-down!
If any or all of these wonders
  Should ever come about,
I should not consider them blunders,
  For I should be Inside-out:

CHORUS

Baa-baa, black wool,
  Have you any sheep?
Yes, sir, a packful,
  Creep, mouse, creep!
Four-and-twenty little maids
  Hanging out the pie,
Out jumped the honey-pot,
  Guy Fawkes, Guy!
Cross latch, cross patch,
  Sit and spin the fire;
When the pie was opened,
  The bird was on the brier!

William Brighty Rands

THERE WAS A GUINEA-PIG

There was a little guinea-pig,
Who, being little, was not big;
He always walked upon his feet,
And never fasted when he eat.

When from a place he ran away,
He never at that place did stay;
When he ran, as I am told,
He ne'er stood still for young or old.

He often squeaked and sometimes
    vi'lent,
And when he squeaked he ne'er was
    silent;

Though ne'er instructed by a cat,
He knew a mouse was not a rat.

One day, as I am certified,
He took a whim and fairly died;
And, as I'm told by men of sense,
He never has been living since.

Unknown

TEN LITTLE INJUNS

Ten little Injuns standing in a line—
One went home, and then there were
    nine.

Nine little Injuns swinging on a gate—
One tumbled off, and then there were
    eight.

Eight little Injuns tried to get to
    Heaven—
One kicked the bucket, and then there
    were seven.

Seven little Injuns cutting up tricks—
One went to bed, and then there were
    six.

Six little Injuns learning how to dive—
One swam away, and then there were
    five.

Five little Injuns on a cellar door—
One jumped off, and then there were
    four.

Four little Injuns climbing up a tree—
One fell down, and then there were
    three.

Three little Injuns out in a canoe—
One fell overboard, and then there
    were two.

Two little Injuns fooling with a gun—
One shot the other, and then there was
    one.

One little Injun living all alone—
He got married, and then there was
    none!

Unknown

LIMERICKS FROM LEAR

There was an Old Man of the Isles,
Whose face was pervaded with smiles;
He sang "High dum diddle," and
    played on the fiddle,
That amiable Man of the Isles.

There was a Young Lady of Norway,
Who casually sat in a doorway;
When the door squeezed her flat, she
    exclaimed, "What of that?"
This courageous Young Lady of Nor-
    way.

There was a Young Lady of Bute,
Who played on a silver-gilt flute;
She played several jigs to her Uncle's
    white pigs:
That amusing Young Lady of Bute.

There was a Young Person of Crete,
Whose toilette was far from complete;
She dressed in a sack spickle-speckled
    with black,
That ombliferous Person of Crete.

There was an Old Man who said,
    "Well!
Will *nobody* answer this bell?
I have pulled day and night, till my
    hair has grown white,
But nobody answers this bell!"

There is a young lady whose nose

Continually prospers and grows;
When it grew out of sight, she ex-
    claimed in a fright,
"Oh! Farewell to the end of my
    nose!"

Edward Lear

THE DIVERTING HISTORY OF JOHN GILPIN

John Gilpin was a citizen
    Of credit and renown,
A train-band captain eke was he,
    Of famous London town.

John Gilpin's spouse said to her
    dear,
  "Though wedded we have been
These twice ten tedious years, yet we
    No holiday have seen.

"To-morrow is our wedding-day,
    And we will then repair
Unto the Bell at Edmonton,
    All in a chaise and pair.

"My sister, and my sister's child,
    Myself and children three
Will fill the chaise; so you must ride
    On horseback after we."

He soon replied, "I do admire
    Of womankind but one,
And you are she, my dearest dear,
    Therefore it shall be done.

"I am a linen-draper bold,
    As all the world doth know,
And my good friend the calender,
    Will lend his horse to go."

Quoth Mrs. Gilpin, "That's well
    said;
    And for that wine is dear,

We will be furnished with our own,
  Which is both bright and clear."

John Gilpin kiss'd his loving wife
  O'erjoyed was he to find,
That, though on pleasure she was
    bent,
  She had a frugal mind.

The morning came, the chaise was
    brought
  But yet was not allow'd
To drive up to the door, lest all
  Should say that she was proud.

So three doors off the chaise was
    stay'd,
  Where they did all get in;
Six precious souls, and all agog
  To dash through thick and thin.

Smack went the whip, round went
    the wheels,
  Were never folk so glad;
The stones did rattle underneath,
  As if Cheapside were mad.

John Gilpin at his horse's side
  Seized fast the flowing mane,
And up he got, in haste to ride,
  But soon came down again;

For saddle-tree scarce reach'd had he,
  His journey to begin,
When turning round his head he
    saw
  Three customers come in.

So down he came; for loss of time,
  Although it grieved him sore,
Yet loss of pence, full well he knew,
  Would trouble him much more.

'Twas long before the customers,

Were suited to their mind,
When Betty screaming came down
    stairs,
  "The wine is left behind!"

"Good lack!" quoth he; "yet bring
    it me,
  My leathern belt likewise,
In which I bear my trusty sword,
  When I do exercise."

Now, Mistress Gilpin (careful soul!)
  Had two stone bottles found,
To hold the liquor that she loved,
  And keep it safe and sound.

Each bottle had a curling ear,
  Through which the belt he drew,
And hung a bottle on each side
  To make his balance true.

Then over all, that he might be
  Equipp'd from top to toe,
His long red cloak, well brush'd and
    neat,
  He manfully did throw.

Now see him mounted once again
  Upon his nimble steed,
Full lowly pacing o'er the stones,
  With caution and good heed.

But finding soon a smoother road
  Beneath his well-shod feet,
The snorting beast began to trot,
  Which gall'd him in his seat.

So, "Fair and softly," John he cried,
  But John he cried in vain;
That trot became a gallop soon,
  In spite of curb and rein.

So stooping down, as needs he must,
  Who cannot sit upright,

He grasp'd the mane with both his
 hands,
 And eke with all his might.

His horse, who never in that sort
 Had handled been before,
What thing upon his back had got
 Did wonder more and more.

Away went Gilpin, neck or naught;
 Away went hat and wig;
He little dreamt, when he set out,
 Of running such a rig.

The wind did blow, the cloak did fly
 Like streamer long and gay,
Till, loop and button, failing both,
 At last it flew away.

Then might all people well discern
 The bottles he had slung;
A bottle swinging at each side,
 As hath been said or sung.

The dogs did bark, the children
 scream'd,
 Up flew the windows all;
And every soul cried out, "Well
 done!"
 As loud as he could bawl.

Away went Gilpin—who but he
 His fame soon spread around;
He carries weight; he rides a race
 'Tis for a thousand pound!

And still as fast as he drew near,
 'Twas wonderful to view,
How in a trice the turnpike men
 Their gates wide open threw.

And now as he went bowing down
 His reeking head full low,

The bottles twain behind his back
 Were shatter'd at a blow.

Down ran the wine into the road,
 Most piteous to be seen,
Which made his horse's flanks to
 smoke,
 As they had basted been.

But still he seem'd to carry weight
 With leathern girdle braced;
For all might see the bottle-necks,
 Still dangling at his waist.

Thus all through merry Islington
 Those gambols he did play,
Until he came unto the Wash
 Of Edmonton so gay;

And there he threw the wash about
 On both sides of the way,
Just like unto a trundling mop,
 Or a wild goose at play.

At Edmonton his loving wife
 From the balcony espied
Her tender husband, wondering
 much
 To see how he did ride.

"Stop, stop, John Gilpin! here's the
 house!"
 They all aloud did cry;
"The dinner waits, and we are tired";
 Said Gilpin, "So am I!"

But yet his horse was not a whit
 Inclined to tarry there;
For why? his owner had a house
 Full ten miles off, at Ware.

So, like an arrow swift he flew,
 Shot by an archer strong;

So did he fly—which brings me to
　　The middle of my song.

Away went Gilpin, out of breath,
　　And sore against his will,
Till at his friend the calender's,
　　His horse at last stood still.

The calender, amazed to see
　　His neighbour in such trim,
Laid down his pipe, flew to the gate,
　　And thus accosted him:

"What news? what news? your tid-
　　　ings tell!
Tell me you must and shall—
Say why bareheaded you are come,
　　Or why you come at all?"

Now Gilpin had a pleasant wit,
　　And loved a timely joke;
And thus unto the calender
　　In merry guise he spoke:

"I came because your horse would
　　　come,
And, if I well forbode,
My hat and wig will soon be here;
　　They are upon the road."

The calender, right glad to find
　　His friend in merry pin,
Return'd him not a single word,
　　But to the house went in.

When straight he came with hat and
　　　wig;
A wig that flowed behind;
A hat not much the worse for wear,
　　Each comely in its kind.

He held them up, and in his turn
　　Thus showed his ready wit:

"My head is twice as big as yours,
　　They therefore needs must fit.

"But let me scrape the dirt away
　　That hangs upon your face;
And stop and eat, for well you may
　　Be in a hungry case."

Said John, "It is my wedding-day,
　　And all the world would stare,
If wife should dine at Edmonton,
　　And I should dine at Ware."

So, turning to his horse, he said:
　　"I am in haste to dine;
'Twas for your pleasure you came
　　　here,
You shall go back for mine."

Ah! luckless speech, and bootless
　　　boast
For which he paid full dear;
For while he spake, a braying ass
　　Did ring most loud and clear;

Whereat his horse did snort, as he
　　Had heard a lion roar,
And gallop'd off with all his might,
　　As he had done before.

Away went Gilpin, and away
　　Went Gilpin's hat and wig!
He lost them sooner than the first;
　　For why?—they were too big.

Now, Mistress Gilpin, when she saw
　　Her husband posting down
Into the country far away,
　　She pull'd out half a crown;

And thus unto the youth she said,
　　That drove them to the Bell,
"This shall be yours, when you bring
　　　back,
My husband safe and well."

The youth did ride, and soon did
    meet
  John coming back amain;
Whom in a trice he tried to stop
  By catching at his rein;

But not performing what he meant,
  And gladly would have done,
The frighted steed he frighted more,
  And made him faster run.

Away went Gilpin, and away
  Went postboy at his heels;
The postboy's horse right glad to
  miss
  The lumbering of the wheels.

Six gentlemen upon the road,
  Thus seeing Gilpin fly,
With postboy scampering in the
  rear,
  They raised the hue and cry:

" Stop thief! stop thief! a highway-
  man! "
  Not one of them was mute;
And all and each that pass'd that
  way
  Did join in the pursuit.

And now the turnpike gates again
  Flew open in short space;
The toll-men thinking as before
  That Gilpin ran a race.

And so he did, and won it too,
  For he got first to town;
Nor stopp'd till where he had got up
  He did again get down.

Now let us sing, long live the King!
  And Gilpin, long live he!
And, when he next doth ride abroad,
  May I be there to see!

                William Cowper

THE SUGAR-PLUM TREE

Have you ever heard of the Sugar-Plum
  Tree?
  'Tis a marvel of great renown!
It blooms on the shore of the Lollypop
  sea
  In the garden of Shut-Eye Town;
The fruit that it bears is so wondrously
  sweet
  (As those who have tasted it say)
That good little children have only to
  eat
  Of that fruit to be happy next day.

When you've got to the tree, you
  would have a hard time
  To capture the fruit which I sing;
The tree is so tall that no person could
  climb
  To the boughs where the sugar-
  plums swing!
But up in that tree sits a chocolate cat,
  And a gingerbread dog prowls be-
  low—
And this is the way you contrive to get
  at
  Those sugar-plums tempting you so:

You say but the word to that ginger-
  bread dog
  And he barks with such terrible zest
That the chocolate cat is at once all
  agog,
  As her swelling proportions attest.
And the chocolate cat goes cavorting
  around
  From this leafy limb unto that,
And the sugar-plums tumble, of course,
  to the ground—
  Hurrah for that chocolate cat!

There are marshmallows, gumdrops,
  and peppermint canes,

With stripings of scarlet or gold,
And you carry away of the treasure
    that rains
    As much as your apron can hold!
So come, little child, cuddle closer to
    me
      In your dainty white nightcap and
       gown,
And I'll rock you away to that Sugar-
    Plum Tree
      In the garden of Shut-Eye Town.
              Eugene Field

THE DUEL

The gingham dog and the calico cat
Side by side on the table sat;
'Twas half-past twelve, and (what do
    you think!)
Nor one nor t' other had slept a wink!
    The old Dutch clock and the Chi-
      nese plate
Appeared to know as sure as fate
There was going to be a terrible spat.
      (*I wasn't there; I simply state*
      What was told to me by the Chi-
      nese plate!)

The gingham dog went "bow-wow-
      wow!"
And the calico cat replied "mee-ow!"
The air was littered, an hour or so,
With bits of gingham and calico,

While the old Dutch clock in the
    chimney-place
Up with its hands before its face,
For it always dreaded a family row!
      (*Now mind: I'm only telling you*
      What the old Dutch clock de-
      clares is true!)

The Chinese plate looked very blue,
And wailed, "Oh, dear! what shall we
    do!"
But the gingham dog and the calico
    cat
Wallowed this way and tumbled that,
    Employing every tooth and claw
    In the awfullest way you ever saw—
And, oh! how the gingham and calico
    flew!
      (*Don't fancy I exaggerate—*
      I got my news from the Chinese
      plate!)

Next morning, where the two had sat
They found no trace of dog or cat;
And some folks think unto this day
That burglars stole that pair away!
    But the truth about the cat and pup
    Is this: they ate each other up!
Now what do you really think of that!
      (*The old Dutch clock it told me*
      so,
      And that is how I came to know.)
              Eugene Field

Part Nine

POEMS FOR THE HOLIDAYS

Christmas

THE CHRIST CANDLE

Little taper set tonight,
Throw afar thy tiny light
Up and down the darksome street,
Guide the tender, wandering feet
Of the darling Christ-child sweet.

He is coming in the snow,
As He came so long ago,
When the stars set o'er the hill,
When the town is dark and still,
Comes to do the Father's will.

Little taper, spread thy ray,
Make His pathway light as day;
Let some door be open wide
For this guest of Christmastide,
Dearer than all else beside.

Little Christ-Child, come to me,
Let my heart Thy shelter be;
Such a home Thou wilt not scorn.
So the bells on Christmas morn,
Glad shall ring, "A Christ is born!"

Kate Louise Brown

MY GIFT

What can I give Him
Poor as I am;
If I were a shepherd,
I would give Him a lamb.
If I were a wise man,
I would do my part.
But what can I give Him?
I will give my heart.

Christina Rossetti

I SAW THREE SHIPS

(*Selected Stanzas*)

I saw three ships come sailing in,
  On Christmas day, on Christmas
    day,
I saw three ships come sailing in,
  On Christmas day, in the morning.

Pray whither sailed those ships all
    three
  On Christmas day, on Christmas
    day?
Pray whither sailed those ships all
    three
  On Christmas day, in the morning.

Oh, they sailed into Bethlehem
  On Christmas day, on Christmas
    day;
Oh, they sailed into Bethlehem
  On Christmas day, in the morning.

And all the bells on earth shall ring
  On Christmas day, on Christmas
    day;
And all the bells on earth shall ring
  On Christmas day, in the morning.

And all the angels in heaven shall
  sing,
  On Christmas day, on Christmas
    day;
And all the angels in heaven shall
  sing,
  On Christmas day, in the morning.

And all the souls on earth shall sing
  On Christmas day, on Christmas
    day;
And all the souls on earth shall sing
  On Christmas day, in the morning.

Unknown

SANTA CLAUS

Little fairy snowflakes
  Dancing in the flue;
Old Mr. Santa Claus,
  What is keeping you?
Twilight and firelight
  Shadows come and go;
Merry chime of sleigh-bells
  Twinkling through the snow.
Mother's knitting stockings,
  Pussy's got the ball.
Don't you think that Christmas
  Is pleasantest of all?

Unknown

CRADLE HYMN

Away in a manger, no crib for a bed,
The little Lord Jesus laid down His
  sweet head.

The stars in the bright sky looked
  down where He lay—
The little Lord Jesus asleep on the hay.

The cattle are lowing, the Baby awakes,
But the little Lord Jesus, no crying He
  makes.
I love Thee, Lord Jesus! look down
  from the sky,
And stay by my cradle till morning is
  nigh.

Be near me, Lord Jesus, I ask Thee to
  stay
Close by me forever and love me, I
  pray;
Bless all the dear children in Thy ten-
  der care,
And fit us for Heaven, to live with
  Thee there.

Martin Luther

A VISIT FROM ST. NICHOLAS

'Twas the night before Christmas,
  when all through the house
Not a creature was stirring, not even
  a mouse;
The stockings were hung by the
  chimney with care,
In hopes that St. Nicholas soon
  would be there;
The children were nestled all snug
  in their beds,
While visions of sugar-plums danced
  in their heads;
And mamma in her 'kerchief, and I
  in my cap,
Had just settled our brains for a long
  winter's nap,
When out on the lawn there arose
  such a clatter,
I sprang from the bed to see what
  was the matter.

Away to the window I flew like a flash,
Tore open the shutters and threw up the sash.
The moon on the breast of the new-fallen snow
Gave the lustre of mid-day to objects below,
When, what to my wondering eyes should appear,
But a miniature sleigh, and eight tiny reindeer,
With a little old driver, so lively and quick,
I knew in a moment it must be St. Nick.
More rapid than eagles his coursers they came,
And he whistled, and shouted, and called them by name:
"Now, *Dasher!* now, *Dancer!* now, *Prancer* and *Vixen!*
On, *Comet!* on, *Cupid!* on, *Donder* and *Blitzen!*
To the top of the porch! to the top of the wall!
Now dash away! dash away! dash away all!"
As dry leaves that before the wild hurricane fly,
When they meet with an obstacle, mount to the sky,
So up to the house-top the coursers they flew,
With the sleigh full of toys, and St. Nicholas too.
And then, in a twinkling, I heard on the roof
The prancing and pawing of each little hoof.
As I drew in my head, and was turning around,
Down the chimney St. Nicholas came with a bound.

He was dressed all in fur, from his head to his foot,
And his clothes were all tarnished with ashes and soot;
A bundle of toys he had flung on his back,
And he looked like a peddler just opening his pack.
His eyes—how they twinkled! his dimples how merry!
His cheeks were like roses, his nose like a cherry!
His droll little mouth was drawn up like a bow,
And the beard of his chin was as white as the snow;
The stump of a pipe he held tight in his teeth,
And the smoke it encircled his head like a wreath;
He had a broad face and a little round belly,
That shook, when he laughed, like a bowlful of jelly.
He was chubby and plump, a right jolly old elf,
And I laughed when I saw him, in spite of myself;
A wink of his eye and a twist of his head,
Soon gave me to know I had nothing to dread;
He spoke not a word, but went straight to his work,
And filled all the stockings; then turned with a jerk,
And laying his finger aside of his nose,
And giving a nod, up the chimney he rose;
He sprang to his sleigh, to his team gave a whistle,
And away they all flew like the down of a thistle.

But I heard him exclaim, ere he
    drove out of sight,
"Happy Christmas to all, and to all a
    good-night."
              Clement Clarke Moore

OLD CHRISTMAS
(Selected Stanzas)

Now, he who knows old Christmas,
    He knows a carle of worth;
For he is as good a fellow,
    As any upon the earth.

He comes warm-cloaked and coated,
    And buttoned up to the chin;
And soon as he comes a-nigh the door,
    We open and let him in.

And with sprigs of holly and ivy
    We make the house look gay,
Just out of an old regard to him,—
    For 'twas his ancient way.

He comes with a cordial voice,
    That does one good to hear;
He shakes one heartily by the hand,
    As he hath done many a year.

What a fine old fellow, in troth!
    Not one of your griping elves,
Who, with plenty of money to spare,
    Think only about themselves.

He must be a rich old fellow,—
    What money he gives away!
There is not a lord in England
    Could equal him any day!

Good luck unto old Christmas,
    And long life, let us sing,
For he doth more good unto the poor,
    Than many a crownèd king!
              Mary Howitt

BABUSHKA

Babushka sits before the fire
Upon a winter's night;
The driving winds heap up the snow,
Her hut is snug and tight;
The howling winds,—they only make
Babushka's fire more bright!

She hears a knocking at the door:
So late—who can it be?
She hastes to lift the wooden latch,
No thought of fear has she;
The wind-blown candle in her hand
Shines out on strangers three.

Their beards are white with age, and
    snow
That in the darkness flies;
Their floating locks are long and
    white,
But kindly are their eyes
That sparkle underneath their brows,
Like stars in frosty skies.

"Babushka, we have come from far,
We tarry but to say,
A little Prince is born this night,
Who all the world shall sway.
Come join the search; come, go with
    us,
Who go our gifts to pay."

Babushka shivers at the door;
"I would I might behold
The little Prince who shall be King
But ah! the night is cold,
The wind so fierce, the snow so
    deep,
And I, good sirs, am old."

The strangers three, no word they
    speak,
But fade in snowy space!
Babushka sits before her fire,

And dreams, with wistful face:
" I would that I had questioned them,
So I the way might trace!

" When morning comes with blessèd
  light,
I'll early be awake;
My staff in hand I'll go—perchance,
Those strangers I'll o'ertake;
And, for the Child some little toys
I'll carry, for His sake."

The morning came, and, staff in
  hand,
She wandered in the snow,
She asked the way of all she met,
But none the way could show.
" It must be farther yet," she sighed;
" Then farther will I go."

And still, 'tis said, on Christmas
  Eve,
When high the drifts are piled,
With staff, with basket on her arm,
Babushka seeks the Child:
At every door her face is seen,—
Her wistful face and mild!

Her gifts at every door she leaves;
She bends, and murmurs low,
Above each little face half-hid
By pillows white as snow:
" And is He here? " Then, softly sighs,
" Nay, farther must I go."

Edith M. Thomas

LITTLE GOTTLIEB

Across the German ocean,
  In a country far from our own,
Once a poor little boy, named Gott-
  lieb,
  Lived with his mother alone.

He was not large enough to work,
  And his mother could do no more
(Though she scarcely laid her knit-
  ting down)
  Than keep the wolf from the door.

She had to take their threadbare
  clothes,
  And turn, and patch, and darn;
For never any woman yet
  Grew rich by knitting yarn.

And oft at night, beside her chair,
  Would Gottlieb sit, and plan
The wonderful things he would do
  for her,
  When he grew to be a man.

One night she sat and knitted,
  And Gottlieb sat and dreamed,
When a happy fancy all at once
  Upon his vision beamed.

'Twas only a week till Christmas
  And Gottlieb knew that then
The Christ-Child, who was born
  that day,
  Sent down good gifts to men.

But he said, " He will never find us,
  Our home is so mean and small;
And we, who have most need of
  them,
  Will get no gifts at all."

When all at once a happy light
  Came into his eyes so blue,
And lighted up his face with smiles,
  As he thought what he could do.

Next day when the postman's letters
  Came from all over the land,
Came one for the Christ-Child, writ-
  ten
  In a child's poor trembling hand.

You may think the postman was
troubled
What in the world to do;
So he went to the Burgomaster,
As the wisest man he knew.

And when they opened the letter,
They stood almost dismayed
That such a little child should dare
To ask the Lord for aid.

Then the Burgomaster stammered
And scarce knew what to speak,
And hastily he brushed aside
A drop, like a tear, from his cheek.

Then up he spake right gruffly,
And turned himself about:
"This must be a very foolish boy,
And a small one, too, no doubt."

A wise and learned man was he,
Men called him good and just;
But his wisdom seemed like foolish-
ness
By that weak child's simple trust.

Now when the morn of Christmas
came
And the long, long week was
done,
Poor Gottlieb, who could scarcely
sleep,
Rose before the sun,

And hastened to his mother,
But he scarce might speak for fear,
When he saw her wondering look,
and saw
The Burgomaster near.

Amazed the poor child looked, to
find
The hearth was piled with wood,

And the table, never full before,
Was heaped with dainty food.

Then half to hide from himself the
truth
The Burgomaster said,
While the mother blessed him on
her knees,
And Gottlieb shook for dread:

"Nay, give no thanks, my worthy
dame,
To such as me for aid,
Be grateful to your little son,
And the Lord to whom he
prayed!"

Then turning round to Gottlieb,
"Your written prayer, you see,
Came not to whom it was addressed,
It only came to me!

"'Twas but a foolish thing you did,
As you must understand;
For though the gifts are yours, you
know,
You have them from my hand."

Then Gottlieb answered fearlessly
Where he humbly stood apart,
"But the Christ-Child sent them all
the same,
He put the thought in your
heart!"

Phoebe Cary

A CHRISTMAS FOLK-SONG

The little Jesus came to town;
The wind blew up, the wind blew
down;
Out in the street the wind was bold;
Now who would house Him from
the cold?

Then opened wide a stable door,
Fair were the rushes on the floor;
The Ox put forth a hornèd head:
"Come, Little Lord, here make Thy
　bed."

Up rose the Sheep were folded near:
"Thou Lamb of God, come, enter
　here."
He entered there to rush and reed,
Who was the Lamb of God indeed.

The Little Jesus came to town;
With Ox and Sheep He laid Him
　down;
Peace to the byre, peace to the fold,
For that they housed Him from the
　cold!

Lizette Woodworth Reese

New Year's Day

THE NEW YEAR

Who comes dancing over the snow,
His soft little feet all bare and rosy?
Open the door though the wild winds
　blow,
Take the child in and make him cozy.
Take him in and hold him dear,
He is the wonderful glad New Year.

Dinah M. Mulock Craik

Easter

AT EASTER TIME

The little flowers came through the
　ground,
　At Easter time, at Easter time;
They raised their heads and looked
　around,
　At happy Easter time.

And every pretty bud did say,
　"Good people, bless this holy day,
For Christ is risen, the angels say
　At happy Easter time!"

The pure white lily raised its cup
　At Easter time, at Easter time;
The crocus to the sky looked up
　At happy Easter time.
"We'll hear the song of Heaven!"
　they say,
　"Its glory shines on us today.
Oh! may it shine on us alway
　At holy Easter time!"

'Twas long and long and long ago,
　That Easter time, that Easter
　time;
But still the pure white lilies blow
　At happy Easter time,
And still each little flower doth say,
　"Good Christians, bless this holy
　day,
For Christ is risen, the angels say
　At blessed Easter time!"

Laura E. Richards

Arbor Day

CHILD'S SONG IN SPRING

The silver birch is a dainty lady,
　She wears a satin gown;
The elm tree makes the old church-
　yard shady,
　She will not live in town.

The English oak is a sturdy fellow,
　He gets his green coat late;
The willow is smart in a suit of yellow,
　While brown the beech trees wait.

Such a gay green gown God gives the
　larches—

As green as He is good!
The hazels hold up their arms for
    arches
    When Spring rides through the
    wood.

The chestnut's proud, and the lilac's
    pretty,
    The poplar's gentle and tall,
But the plane tree's kind to the poor
    dull city—
    I love him best of all!

Edith Nesbit

OCTOBER'S PARTY

October gave a party;
    The leaves by hundreds came—
The Chestnuts, Oaks, and Maples,
    And leaves of every name.
The Sunshine spread a carpet,
    And everything was grand,
Miss Weather led the dancing,
    Professor Wind the band.

The Chestnuts came in yellow,
    The Oaks in crimson dressed;
The lovely Misses Maple
    In scarlet looked their best;
All balanced to their partners,
    And gaily fluttered by;
The sight was like a rainbow
    New fallen from the sky.

Then, in the rustic hollow,
    At hide-and-seek they played.
The party closed at sundown,
    And everybody stayed.
Professor Wind played louder;
    They flew along the ground;
And then the party ended
    In jolly " hands around."

George Cooper

May Day

OXFORDSHIRE CHILDREN'S
MAY SONG

Spring is coming, spring is coming,
    Birdies, build your nest;
Weave together straw and feather,
    Doing each your best.

Spring is coming, spring is coming,
    Flowers are coming too:
Pansies, lilies, daffodillies,
    Now are coming through.

Spring is coming, spring is coming,
    All around is fair;
Shimmer and quiver on the river,
    Joy is everywhere.
We wish you a happy May.

Unknown

FOR GOOD LUCK

Little Kings and Queens of May,
If you want to be,
Every one of you, very good,
In this beautiful, beautiful, beautiful
    wood,
Where the little birds' heads get so
    turned with delight
That some of them sing all night:
Whatever you pluck,
Leave some for good luck!

Picked from the stalk or pulled by the
    root,
From overhead or under foot,
Water-wonders of pond or brook—
Wherever you look,
And whatever you find,
Leave something behind:
Some for the Naiads,
Some for the Dryads,
And a bit for the Nixies and Pixies!

Juliana Horatia Ewing

Memorial Day

REMEMBERING DAY

All the soldiers marching along;
All the children singing a song;
All the flowers dewy and sweet;
All the flags hung out in the street;
Hearts that throb in a grateful way—
For this is our Remembering Day.

Mary Wright Saunders

Mother's Day

OUR MOTHER

Hundreds of stars in the pretty sky,
  Hundreds of shells on the shore to-
    gether,
Hundreds of birds that go singing by,
  Hundreds of birds in the sunny
    weather,
Hundreds of dewdrops to greet the
    dawn,
  Hundreds of bees in the purple
    clover,
Hundreds of butterflies on the lawn,
  But only one mother the wide world
    over.

Unknown

A BOY'S MOTHER *

My mother she's so good to me,
Ef I was good as I could be,
I couldn't be as good—no, sir!—
Can't any boy be good as her.

She loves me when I'm glad er sad;
She loves me when I'm good er bad;
An', what's a funniest thing, she says
She loves me when she punishes,

I don't like her to punish me,—
That don't hurt—but it hurts to see
Her cryin'.—Nen I cry; an' nen
We both cry an' be good again.

She loves me when she cuts an' sews
My little cloak an' Sund'y clothes;
An' when my Pa comes home to tea,
She loves him most as much as me.

She laughs an' tells him all I said,
An' grabs me up an' pats my head;
An' I hug *her*, an' hug my Pa,
An' love him purt' nigh as much as
  Ma.

James Whitcomb Riley

* From the Biographical Edition of the
Complete Works of James Whitcomb Riley,
Copyright, 1913, by special permission of
the publishers, The Bobbs-Merrill Company.

Halloween

HALLOWE'EN

Heyhow for Hallowe'en,
When all the witches are to be seen,
Some in black and some in green,
Heyhow for Hallowe'en.

Unknown

THE FAIRIES

Have you ever heard the tapping of the
    fairy cobbler men,
When the moon is shining brightly
    thro' the branches in the glen?
Have you seen a crew of goblins in a
    water-lily boat,
Softly sliding, gently gliding,
'Mid the rushes tall afloat?

Have you seen the sleeping goblins
    'neath the mushrooms on the hills?

Have you heard the rippling music of
  the tiny fairy rills?
Have you seen the looms where spiders
  spin their sparkling silver threads?
Brightly shining and entwining
Round the nodding flower heads?

Have you seen the magic circles where
  the little fairies play,
From the last soft flush of sunset, till
  the first bright gleam of day?
Have you seen a band of fairies, with
  their pickaxes so bold,
Talking gravely, trudging bravely,
Off to seek for fairy gold?

If you want to see the fairies, you must
  visit them at night,
When the silvery stars are gleaming
  and the moon is shining bright.
If you make no sound to warn them,
  you will see the fairy-men
Laughing, singing, harebells ringing,
While the moonbeams light the glan.

       Sybil Morford

VERY NEARLY

I never *quite* saw fairy-folk
  A-dancing in the glade,
Where, just beyond the hollow oak,
  Their broad green rings are laid;
But, while behind that oak I hid,
One day I very nearly did!

I never *quite* saw mermaids rise
  Above the twilight sea,
When sands, left wet, 'neath sunset
  skies,
  Are blushing rosily:
But—all alone, those rock amid—
One day I very nearly did!

I never *quite* saw Goblin Grim,
  Who haunts our lumber room
And pops his head above the rim

Of that oak chest's deep gloom:
But once—when Mother raised the
  lid—
I very, very nearly did!
       Queenie Scott-Hopper

Thanksgiving

THANKSGIVING TIME

When all the leaves are off the
  boughs,
  And nuts and apples gathered in,
And cornstalks waiting for the cows,
  And pumpkins safe in barn and
  bin:

Then Mother says: "My children
  dear,
  The fields are brown and autumn
  flies;
Thanksgiving Day is very near,
  And we must make Thanksgiving
  pies!"

       Unknown

THANKSGIVING DAY

Over the river and through the wood,
  To grandfather's house we go;
    The horse knows the way
    To carry the sleigh
  Through the white and drifted
    snow.

Over the river and through the
  wood—
  Oh, how the wind does blow!
    It stings the toes
    And bites the nose,
  As over the ground we go.
Over the river and through the wood,
  To have a first-rate play.
    Hear the bells ring,
    "Ting-a-ling-ding!"
Hurrah for Thanksgiving Day!

Over the river and through the wood
  Trot fast, my dapple-gray!
    Spring over the ground,
    Like a hunting-hound!
  For this is Thanksgiving Day.

Over the river and through the wood,
  And straight through the barn-
      yard gate.
    We seem to go
    Extremely slow,—
  It is so hard to wait!
Over the river and through the
    wood—
  Now grandmother's cap I spy!
    Hurrah for the fun!
    Is the pudding done?
  Hurrah for the pumpkin-pie!
Lydia Maria Child

WE THANK THEE

For flowers so beautiful and sweet,
For friends and clothes and food to
  eat,
For precious hours, for work and play,
We thank Thee this Thanksgiving
  Day.

For Father's care and Mother's love,
For the blue sky and clouds above,
For springtime and autumn gay
We thank Thee this Thanksgiving
  Day.

For all Thy gifts so good and fair,
Bestowed so freely everywhere,
Give us grateful hearts we pray,
To thank Thee this Thanksgiving
  Day.
Mattie M. Renwick

Part Ten

POEMS OF PRAISE

A BOY'S PRAYER

God who created me
  Nimble and light of limb,
In three elements free,
  To run, to ride, to swim:
Not when the sense is dim,
  But now from the heart of joy,
I would remember Him:
  Take the thanks of a boy.

Henry Charles Beeching

THANKS

Thank you very much indeed,
River, for your waving reed;
Hollyhocks, for budding knobs;
Foxgloves, for your velvet fobs;
Pansies, for your silky cheeks;
Chaffinches, for singing beaks;
Spring, for wood anemones
Near the mossy toes of trees;
Summer, for the fruited pear,
Yellowing crab, and cherry fare;
Autumn, for the bearded load,
Hazelnuts along the road;
Winter, for the fairy-tale,
Spitting log and bouncing hail.

But, blest Father, high above,

All these joys are from Thy love;
And Your children, everywhere,
Born in palace, lane, or square,
Cry with voices all   agreed,
" Thank You very much indeed."

Norman Gale

FATHER, WE THANK THEE

Father, we thank Thee for the night
And for the pleasant morning light,
For rest and food and loving care,
And all that makes the world so fair.
Help us to do the thing we should,
To be to others kind and good;
In all we do, in all we say,
To grow more loving every day.

Unknown

WE THANK THEE

For mother-love and father-care,
For brothers strong and sisters fair,
For love at home and here each day,
For guidance lest we go astray,
  Father in Heaven, we thank Thee.

For this new morning with its light,
For rest and shelter of the night,

For health and food, for love and
   friends,
For everything His goodness sends,
   Father in Heaven, we thank Thee.

For flowers that bloom about our feet,
For tender grass, so fresh, so sweet,
For song of bird and hum of bee,
For all things fair we hear or see,
   Father in Heaven, we thank Thee.

For blue of stream and blue of sky,
For pleasant shade of branches high,
For fragrant air and cooling breeze,
For beauty of the blooming trees,
   Father in Heaven, we thank Thee.

Unknown

THE LAMB

Little lamb, who made thee?
Dost thou know who made thee?
Gave thee life and bid thee feed
By the stream and o'er the mead;
Gave thee clothing of delight,
Softest clothing, woolly, bright;
Gave thee such a tender voice
Making all the vales rejoice;
      Little lamb, who made thee?
      Dost thou know who made thee?

Little lamb, I'll tell thee,
Little lamb, I'll tell thee.
He is callèd by thy name,
For He calls Himself a Lamb;
He is meek and He is mild,
He became a little child
I a child and thou a lamb,
We are callèd by His Name
      Little lamb, God bless thee,
      Little lamb, God bless thee.

William Blake

I THINK WHEN I READ THAT SWEET STORY OF OLD

I think when I read that sweet story of
   old,
   When Jesus was here among men,
How He called little children as lambs
   to His fold,
   I should like to have been with them
   then.

I wish that His hands had been placed
   on my head,
   That His arm had been thrown
   around me,
And that I might have seen His kind
   look when He said,
   " Let the little ones come unto me."

Jemima Luke

GOD IS SO GOOD

God is so good that He will hear,
   Whenever children humbly pray;
He always lends a gracious ear
   To what the youngest child may say.

His own most holy Book declares
   He loves good little children still;
And that He listens to their prayers,
   Just as a tender father will.

Jane Taylor

A CHILD'S MORNING PRAYER

I thank Thee, Lord, for quiet rest,
   And for Thy care of me:
Oh! let me through this day be blest,
   And kept from harm by Thee.

Oh, let me love Thee! kind Thou art
   To children such as I;
Give me a gentle, holy heart,
   Be Thou my Friend on high.

Help me to please my parents dear,
  And do whate'er they tell;
Bless all my friends, both far and near,
  And keep them safe and well.
                    Mary Lundie Duncan

THE CREATION

All things bright and beautiful,
  All creatures, great and small,
All things wise and wonderful,
  The Lord God made them all.

Each little flower that opens,
  Each little bird that sings,
He made their glowing colors,
  He made their tiny wings;

The rich man in his castle,
  The poor man at his gate,
God made them, high or lowly,
  And order'd their estate.

The purple-headed mountain,
  The river running by,
The sunset and the morning
  That brightens up the sky;

The cold wind in the winter,
  The pleasant summer sun,
The ripe fruits in the garden—
  He made them every one.

The tall trees in the greenwood,
  The meadows where we play,
The rushes by the water
  We gather every day;—

He gave us eyes to see them,
  And lips that we might tell
How great is God Almighty
  Who has made all things well!
                    Cecil Frances Alexander

GENTLE JESUS, MEEK AND MILD

Gentle Jesus, meek and mild,
Look upon a little child,
Pity my simplicity,
Teach me, Lord, to come to Thee.

Fain would I to Thee be brought,
Lamb of God, forbid it not;
In the Kingdom of Thy grace
Give a little child a place.
                    Charles Wesley

A CHILD'S GRACE

Here a little child I stand
Heaving up my either hand.
Cold as Paddocks though they be,
Here I lift them up to Thee,
For a Benizon to fall
On our meat, and on us all.
                    Robert Herrick

A THOUGHT

It is very nice to think
The world is full of meat and drink,
With little children saying grace
In every Christian kind of place.
                    Robert Louis Stevenson

THE STARS

What do the stars do
  Up in the sky,
Higher than the wind can blow,
  Or the clouds can fly?

Each star in its own glory
  Circles, circles still;
As it was lit to shine and set,
  And do its Maker's will.
                    Christina Rossetti

A CHILD'S PRAYER

God make my life a little light,
  Within the world to glow—
A tiny flame that burneth bright,
  Wherever I may go.

God make my life a little flower,
  That bringeth joy to all,
Content to bloom in native bower,
  Although its place be small.

God make my life a little song,
  That comforteth the sad,
That helpeth others to be strong,
  And makes the singer glad.
            M. Betham Edwards

EVENING SONG

I hear no voice, I feel no touch,
  I see no glory bright;
But yet I know that God is near,
  In darkness as in light.

He watches ever by my side,
  And hears my whispered prayer:
The Father for His little child
  Both day and night doth care.
            Unknown

A CHILD'S EVENING PRAYER

Jesus, tender Shepherd, hear me,
  Bless Thy little lamb tonight;
Through the darkness be Thou near
  me,
  Watch my sleep till morning light.

All this day Thy hand has led me,
  And I thank Thee for Thy care;
Thou hast cloth'd and warm'd and fed
  me;
  Listen to my evening prayer.

Let my sins be all forgiven!
  Bless the friends I love so well!
Take me, when I die, to Heaven;
  Happy, there with Thee to dwell.
            Mary Lundie Duncan

AN EVENING HYMN FOR A LITTLE FAMILY

Now condescend, Almighty King,
  To bless this little throng;
And kindly listen while we sing
  Our pleasant evening song.

Before Thy sacred footstool, see
  We bend in humble prayer,
A happy little family,
  To ask Thy tender care.

May we in safety sleep tonight,
  From every danger free,
Because the darkness and the light,
  Are both alike to Thee.
            Ann and Jane Taylor

GOOD NIGHT

Good night! Good night!
Far flies the light;
But still God's love
Shall flame above,
Making all bright.
Good night! Good night!
            Victor Hugo

FATHER, NOW MY PRAYER IS SAID

Father, now my prayer is said,
Lay Your hand upon my head!
Pleasures pass from day to day,
But I know that love will stay.
            William Brighty Rands

TWENTY-THIRD PSALM

The Lord is my shepherd; I shall not want.

He maketh me to lie down in green pastures: he leadeth me beside the still waters.

He restoreth my soul: he leadeth me in the paths of righteousness for his name's sake.

Yea, though I walk through the valley of the shadow of death, I will fear no evil: for thou art with me; thy rod and thy staff they comfort me.

Thou preparest a table before me in the presence of mine enemies: thou anointest my head with oil; my cup runneth over.

Surely goodness and mercy shall follow me all the days of my life: and I will dwell in the house of the LORD for ever.

The Bible

Part One

POEMS THAT SING

BARTER

Life has loveliness to sell,
  All beautiful and splendid things,
Blue waves whitened on a cliff,
  Soaring fire that sways and sings,
And children's faces looking up
Holding wonder like a cup.

Life has loveliness to sell,
  Music like a curve of gold,
Scent of pine trees in the rain,
  Eyes that love you, arms that hold
And for your spirit's still delight,
Holy thoughts that star the night.

Spend all you have for loveliness,
  Buy it and never count the cost;
For one white singing hour of peace
  Count many a year of strife well lost,
And for a breath of ecstasy
Give all you have been, or could be.

Sara Teasdale

DREAMS TO SELL

If there were dreams to sell,
  What would you buy?
Some cost a passing bell;
  Some a light sigh,
That shakes from Life's fresh crown

Only a rose-leaf down.
If there were dreams to sell,
Merry and sad to tell,
And the crier rang the bell,
  What would you buy?

A cottage lone and still,
  With bowers nigh,
Shadowy, my woes to still,
  Until I die.
Such pearl from Life's fresh crown
Fain would I shake me down.
Were dreams to have at will,
This would best heal my ill,
  This would I buy.

T. L. Beddoes

THE BUGLES OF DREAMLAND

Swiftly the dews of the gloaming are
  falling:
Faintly the bugles of Dreamland are
  calling.
O hearken, my darling, the elf-flutes
  are blowing
The shining-eyed folk from the hillside are flowing,
In the moonshine the wild-apple
  blossoms are snowing

197

And louder and louder where the
white dews are falling,
The far-away bugles of Dreamland
are calling.

O what are the bugles of Dreamland
calling
There where the dews of the gloaming
are falling?
Come away from the weary old
world of tears,
Come away, come away to where
one never hears
The slow, weary drip of the slow
weary years,
But peace and deep rest where the
white dews are falling
And the blithe bugle-laughters
through Dreamland are calling.

Then bugle for us; where the cool dews
are falling,
O bugle for us, wild elf-flutes now
calling—
For Isla and I are too weary to wait
For the dim drowsy whisper that
cometh too late,
The dim muffled whisper of blind
empty fate—
O the world's well lost now the
dream-dews are falling,
And the bugles of Dreamland about
us are falling.

Fiona Macleod

THE SPLENDOUR FALLS ON
CASTLE WALLS

The splendour falls on castle walls
And snowy summits old in story:
The long light shakes across the
lakes
And the wild cataract leaps in
glory.

Blow, bugle, blow, set the wild echoes
flying,
Blow, bugle; answer, echoes, dying,
dying, dying.

O hark, O hear! how thin and clear,
And thinner, clearer, farther go-
ing!
O sweet and far from cliff and scar
The horns of Elfland faintly
blowing!
Blow, let us hear the purple glens
replying:
Blow, bugle; answer, echoes, dying,
dying, dying.

O love, they die in yon rich sky,
They faint on hill or field or river:
Our echoes roll from soul to soul,
And grow for ever and for ever.
Blow, bugle, blow, set the wild echoes
flying,
And answer, echoes, answer, dying,
dying, dying.

Alfred Tennyson

TO DIANA

Queen and huntress, chaste and fair,
Now the sun is laid to sleep,
Seated in thy silver chair,
State in wonted manner keep.
Hesperus entreats thy light,
Goddess, excellently bright.

Earth, let not thy envious shade
Dare itself to interpose;
Cynthia's shining orb was made
Heaven to clear, when day did close;
Bless us then with wishèd sight,
Goddess, excellently bright.

Lay thy bow of pearl apart,
And thy crystal-shining quiver;

Give unto the flying hart
  Space to breathe, how short soever:
Thou that mak'st a day of night
Goddess, excellently bright.

Ben Jonson

TO HELEN

Helen, thy beauty is to me
  Like those Nicæan barks of yore,
That gently, o'er a perfumed sea,
  The weary way-worn wanderer bore
  To his own native shore.

On desperate seas long wont to roam,
  Thy hyacinth hair, thy classic face,
Thy Naiad airs have brought me home
  To the glory that was Greece
And the grandeur that was Rome.

Lo! in your brilliant window-niche
  How statue-like I see thee stand
The agate lamp within thy hand,
Ah! Psyche, from the regions which
  Are Holy land.

Edgar Allan Poe

WHO IS SILVIA?

Who is Silvia? What is she,
  That all our swains commend her?
Holy, fair, and wise is she;
  The heaven such grace did lend
  her,
That she might admirèd be.

Is she kind as she is fair?
  For beauty lives with kindness:
Love doth to her eyes repair,
  To help him of his blindness;
And, being helped, inhabits there.

Then to Silvia let us sing,
  That Silvia is excelling;

She excels each mortal thing
  Upon the dull earth dwelling;
To her let us garlands bring.

William Shakespeare

O MALLY'S MEEK, MALLY'S SWEET

As I was walking up the street,
  A barefit maid I chanced to meet;
But O the road was very hard
  For that fair maiden's tender feet.
  O Mally's meek, Mally's sweet,
    Mally's modest and discreet,
  Mally's rare, Mally's fair,
    Mally's every way complete.

It were more meet that those fine feet
  Were weel laced up in silken shoon,
And 'twere more fit that she should sit
  Within yon chariot gilt aboon.

Her yellow hair, beyond compare,
  Comes trinkling down her swan-like
  neck,
And her two eyes, like stars in skies,
  Would keep a sinking ship frae
  wreck.
  O Mally's meek, Mally's sweet,
    Mally's modest and discreet,
  Mally's rare, Mally's fair,
    Mally's every way complete.

Robert Burns

JENNY KISSED ME

Jenny kissed me when we met,
  Jumping from the chair she sat in;
Time, you thief! who love to get
  Sweets into your list, put that in.
Say I'm weary, say I'm sad,
  Say that health and wealth have
  missed me,
Say I'm growing old, but add—
  Jenny kissed me!

Leigh Hunt

A PORTRAIT

I will paint her as I see her:
Ten times have the lilies blown,
Since she looked upon the sun.

And her face is lily-clear—
Lily-shaped, and drooped in duty
To the law of its own beauty.

Oval cheeks encolored faintly,
Which a trail of golden hair
Keeps from fading off to air:

And a forehead fair and saintly,
Which two blue eyes undershine,
Like meek prayers before a shrine.

Face and figure of a child—
Though too calm, you think, and
   tender,
For the childhood you would lend
   her.

Yet child—simple, undefiled,
Frank, obedient—waiting still
On the turnings of your will.

Moving light, as all young things—
As young birds, or early wheat
Where the wind blows over it.

Only free from flutterings
Of loud mirth that scorneth meas-
   ure—
Taking love for her chief pleasure.

Choosing pleasures (for the rest)
Which come softly—just as she,
When she nestles at your knee.

Quiet talk she likest best,
In a bower of gentle looks—
Watering flowers, or reading books.

And her voice, it murmurs lowly,
As a silver stream may run,
Which yet feels, you feel, the sun.

And her smile, it seems half holy,
As if drawn from thoughts more fair
Than our common jestings are.

And if any poet knew her,
He would sing of her with falls
Used in lovely madrigals.

And if any painter drew her,
He would paint her unaware
With a halo round her hair.

And if reader read the poem,
He would whisper, " You have done
   a
Consecrated little Una! "

And a dreamer (did you show him
That same picture) would exclaim,
" 'Tis my angel, with a name! "

And a stranger—when he sees her
In the street even—smileth stilly,
Just as you would at a lily.

And all voices that address her,
Soften, sleeken every word,
As if speaking to a bird.

And all fancies yearn to cover
The hard earth whereon she passes
With the thymy scented grasses.

And all hearts do pray, " God love
   her! "
Ay, and always, in good sooth,
We may all be sure He doth.
      Elizabeth Barrett Browning

PASSING BY

There is a lady sweet and kind,
Was never face so pleased my mind;
I did but see her passing by,
And yet I love her till I die.

Her gesture, motion, and her smiles,
Her wit, her voice, my heart beguiles,
Beguiles my heart, I know not why,
And yet I love her till I die. . . .

Cupid is wingèd and doth range,
Her country so my love doth change:
But change she earth, or change she
  sky,
Yet will I love her till I die.

Unknown

SHE WALKS IN BEAUTY

She walks in beauty, like the night
  Of cloudless climes and starry skies;
And all that's best of dark and bright
  Meet in her aspect and her eyes;
Thus mellowed to that tender light
  Which Heaven to gaudy day denies.

One shade the more, one ray the less
  Had half impaired the nameless
  grace,
Which waves in every raven tress,
  Or softly lightens o'er her face;
Where thoughts serenely sweet ex-
  press,
  How pure, how dear, their dwelling
  place.

And on that cheek, and o'er that brow,
  So soft, so calm, yet eloquent,
The smiles that win, the tints that
  glow,
  But tell of days in goodness spent,
A mind at peace with all below,
  A heart whose love is innocent.

George Gordon Byron

PHYLLIS

In petticoat of green,
  Her hair about her eyne,
    Phyllis beneath an oak
    Sat milking her fair flock;
'Mongst that sweet-strained moisture,
    rare delight,
  Her hand seemed milk, in milk it was
    so white.

William Drummond

SHE DWELT AMONG THE UNTRODDEN WAYS

She dwelt among the untrodden ways
  Beside the springs of Dove,
A maid whom there were none to
  praise,
  And very few to love:

A violet by a mossy stone
  Half hidden from the eye!—
Fair as a star, when only one
  Is shining in the sky.

She lived unknown, and few could
  know
  When Lucy ceased to be:
But she is in her grave, and, oh!
  The difference to me!

William Wordsworth

SHE WAS A PHANTOM OF DELIGHT

She was a Phantom of delight
When first she gleamed upon my
  sight;
A lovely Apparition, sent
To be a moment's ornament;
Her eyes as stars of Twilight fair;
Like Twilight's, too, her dusky hair:
But all things else about her drawn
From May-time and the cheerful
Dawn.

A dancing Shape, an Image gay,
To haunt, to startle, and waylay.
I saw her upon nearer view,
A Spirit, yet a Woman too!
Her household motions light and free,
And steps of virgin liberty;
A countenance in which did meet
Sweet records, promises as sweet;
A Creature not too bright or good
For human nature's daily food;
For transient sorrows, simple wiles,
Praise, blame, love, kisses, tears, and
    smiles.

And now I see with eye serene
The very pulse of the machine;
A Being breathing thoughtful breath,
A Traveller between life and death:
The reason firm, the temperate will,
Endurance, foresight, strength, and
    skill;
A perfect Woman, nobly planned,
To warn, to comfort, and command;
And yet a Spirit still, and bright,
With something of angelic light.

William Wordsworth

THE LINNET IN THE ROCKY DELLS

The linnet in the rocky dells,
    The moor-lark in the air,
The bee among the heather bells,
    That hide my lady fair:

The wild deer browse above her breast;
    The wild birds raise their brood;
And they, her smiles of love caressed,
    Have left her solitude!

I ween, that when the grave's dark wall
    Did first her form retain,
They thought their hearts could ne'er
    recall,
    The light of joy again.

They thought the tide of grief would
    flow,
    Unchecked through future years;
But where is all their anguish now,
    And where are all their tears?

Well, let them fight for honor's breath,
    Or pleasure's shade pursue—
The dweller in the land of Death,
    Is changed and careless too.

And if their eyes should watch and
    weep
    Till sorrow's source were dry,
She would not in her tranquil sleep
    Return a single sigh!

Blow, west wind, by the lonely mound,
    And murmur, summer streams—
There is no need of other sound
    To soothe my lady's dreams.

Emily Brontë

THE SOLITARY REAPER

Behold her, single in the field,
Yon solitary Highland lass!
Reaping and singing by herself;
    Stop here, or gently pass!
Alone she cuts, and binds the grain,
And sings a melancholy strain;
O listen! for the Vale profound
Is overflowing with the sound.

No nightingale did ever chant
More welcome notes to weary bands
Of travellers in some shady haunt,
    Among Arabian sands:
A voice so thrilling ne'er was heard,
In spring-time from the Cuckoo-bird,
Breaking the silence of the seas,
Amongst the farthest Hebrides.

Will no one tell me what she sings?
Perhaps the plaintive numbers flow

For old, unhappy, far-off things,
  And battles long ago:
Or is it some more humble lay,
Familiar matter of today?
Some natural sorrow, loss, or pain,
That has been, and may be again!

Whate'er the theme, the maiden sang
As if her song could have no ending:
I saw her singing at her work,
  And o'er the sickle bending;—
I listened, motionless and still;
And, as I mounted up the hill,
The music in my heart I bore,
Long after it was heard no more.

William Wordsworth

NIGHT

Night is a cavalier dauntless and bold;
Riding through clouds on a steed
  strapped with gold,
Sapphires flash from his cloak's sable
  folds
And each silken pocket a star-baby
  holds.

Christine Wood Bullwinkle

EVENING

Oh, Hesperus! thou bringest all good
  things—
  Home to the weary, to the hungry
  cheer,
To the young bird the parent's brooding wings,
  The welcome stall to the o'er-la-
  bored steer!
Whate'er of peace about our hearth-
  stone clings,
  Whate'er our household gods protect of dear,
Are gathered round us by thy look of
  rest;

Thou bring'st the child, too, to the
  mother's breast.

Soft hour! which wakes the wish and
  melts the heart
  Of those who sail the seas, on the
  first day
When they from their sweet friends
  are torn apart
  Or fills with love the pilgrim on his
  way,
As the far bell of vesper makes him
  start,
  Seeming to weep the dying day's
  decay;
Is this a fancy which our reason
  scorns?
Ah, surely nothing dies but something
  mourns!

George Gordon Byron

THE NIGHT HAS A THOUSAND EYES

The night has a thousand eyes,
  And the day but one;
Yet the light of the bright world dies
  With the dying sun.

The mind has a thousand eyes,
  And the heart but one;
Yet the light of a whole life dies
  When love is done.

Francis William Bourdillon

O FOR A MOON TO LIGHT ME HOME

O for a moon to light me home!
O for a lanthorn green!
For those sweet stars the Pleiades,
That glitter in the twilight trees;
  O for a lovelorn taper! O
  For a lanthorn green!

O for a frock of tartan!
    O for clear, wild, grey eyes!
For fingers light as violets,
'Neath branches that the blackbird
        frets;
    O for a thistly meadow! O
    For clear, wild grey eyes.

O for a heart like almond boughs!
    O for sweet thoughts like rain!
O for first-love like fields of grey,
Shut April—buds at break of day!
    O for sleep like music!
    For still dreams like rain!
                    " Walter Ramal "

THE NEW MOON
(Selected Stanzas)

When, as the garish day is done,
Heaven burns with the descended sun,
    'Tis passing sweet to mark,
Amid the flush of crimson light,
The new moon's modest bow grow
        bright,
    As earth and sky grow dark.

Few are the hearts too cold to feel
A thrill of gladness o'er them steal
    When first the wandering eye
Sees faintly, in the evening blaze,
That glimmering curve of tender rays
    Just planted in the sky.
                William Cullen Bryant

A FINE DAY

Clear had the day been from the dawn,
All checquer'd was the sky,
Thin clouds like scarfs of cobweb lawn
Veil'd heaven's most glorious eye.
The wind had no more strength than
    this,

That leisurely it blew,
To make one leaf the next to kiss
That closely by it grew.
                Michael Drayton

PACK, CLOUDS, AWAY

Pack, clouds, away! and welcome, day!
    With night we banish sorrow:
Sweet air, blow soft! mount, lark, aloft!
    To give my Love good-morrow;
Wings from the wind, to please her
        mind,
    Notes from the lark I'll borrow.
Bird, prune thy wing! nightingale, sing!
    To give my Love good-morrow.
    To give my Love good-morrow,
    Notes from them all I'll borrow.

Wake from thy nest, robin redbreast!
    Sing, birds, in every furrow!
And from each hill let music shrill
    Give my fair Love good-morrow.
Blackbird and thrush, in every bush—
    Stare, linnet, and cock-sparrow,
You pretty elves—amongst yourselves
    Sing my fair Love good-morrow!
    To give my Love good-morrow,
    Sing, birds, in every furrow!
                Thomas Heywood

TAVERN

I'll keep a little tavern
    Below the high hill's crest,
Wherein all grey-eyed people
    May set them down and rest.

There shall be plates a-plenty,
    And mugs to melt the chill
Of all the grey-eyed people
    Who happen up the hill.

There sound will sleep the traveller,
    And dream his journey's end,

But I will rouse at midnight
The falling fire to tend.

Aye, 'tis a curious fancy—
But all the good I know
Was taught me out of two grey eyes
A long time ago.
Edna St. Vincent Millay

THE OLD WOMAN OF THE ROADS

O, to have a little house!
To own the hearth and stool and all!
The heaped up sods upon the fire!
The pile of turf again' the wall!

To have a clock with weights and chains,
And pendulums swinging up and down!
A dresser filled with shining delph,
Speckled with white and blue and brown!

I could be busy all the day
Cleaning and sweeping hearth and floor,
And fixing on their shelf again
My white and blue and speckled store!

I could be quiet there at night
Beside the fire and by myself,
Sure of a bed, and loth to leave
The ticking clock and shining delph!

Och! but I'm weary of mist and dark,
And roads where there's never a house or bush,
And tired I am of bog and road,
And the crying wind and the lonesome hush!

And I am praying to God on high,
And I am praying Him night and day,
For a little house—a house of my own—
Out of the wind's and the rain's way.
Padraic Colum

I STOOD TIPTOE UPON A LITTLE HILL

I stood tiptoe upon a little hill;
The air was cooling and so very still,
That the sweet buds which with a modest pride
Pull droopingly, in slanting curve aside,
Their scanty-leaved, and finely-tapering stems,
Had not yet lost their starry diadems
Caught from the early sobbing of the morn.
The clouds were pure and white as flocks new-shorn,
And fresh from the clear brook; sweetly they slept
On the blue fields of heaven, and then there crept
A little noiseless noise among the leaves,
Born of the very sigh that silence heaves;
For not the faintest motion could be seen
Of all the shades that slanted o'er the green.
John Keats

RULES FOR THE ROAD

Stand straight:
Step firmly, throw your weight:
The heaven is high above your head,
The good gray road is faithful to your tread.

Be strong:
Sing to your heart a battle song:
Though hidden foemen lie in wait,
Something is in you that can smile at
　Fate.

Press through:
Nothing can harm you if you are true.
And when night comes, rest:
The earth is friendly as a mother's
　breast.

Edwin Markham

BELLS IN THE COUNTRY

Bells in the country,
　They sing the heart to rest
When night is on the high road
　And day is in the west.

And once they came to my house
　As soft as beggars shod,
And brought it nearer heaven,
　And maybe nearer God.

Robert Nathan

THE BELLS

I

Hear the sledges with the bells—
　　Silver bells!
What a world of merriment their
　melody foretells!
How they tinkle, tinkle, tinkle,
　　In the icy air of night!
While the stars that oversprinkle
All the heavens seem to twinkle
　　With a crystalline delight;
　　Keeping time, time, time,
　　In a sort of Runic rhyme,
To the tintinabulation that so mu-
　sically swells
　From the bells, bells, bells, bells,
　　　Bells, bells, bells—

From the jingling and the tinkling
　of the bells.

II

Hear the mellow wedding bells,
　　Golden bells!
What a world of happiness their
　harmony foretells!
Through the balmy air of night
How they ring out their delight!—
From the molten golden notes,
　　And all in tune,
　What a liquid ditty floats
To the turtle-dove that listens, while
　she gloats
　　On the moon!
Oh, from out the sounding cells,
What a gush of euphony volumi-
　nously wells!
　　　How it swells
　　　How it dwells
　On the Future; how it tells
　Of the rapture that impels
To the swinging and the ringing
　Of the bells, bells, bells,
　Of the bells, bells, bells, bells,
　　　Bells, bells, bells—
To the rhyming and the chiming of
　the bells!

III

Hear the loud alarum bells—
　　Brazen bells!
What a tale of terror now, their tur-
　bulency tells;
　In the startled air of night
　How they scream out their af-
　fright!
　　Too much horrified to speak
　　They can only shriek, shriek,
　　　Out of tune,
In a clamorous appealing to the mercy
　of the fire,

In a mad expostulation with the deaf
    and frantic fire
Leaping higher, higher, higher,
With a desperate desire,
    And a resolute endeavor
    Now—now to sit or never,
By the side of the pale-faced moon,
    Oh, the bells, bells, bells!
    What a tale their terror tells
        of Despair!
How they clang and crash and roar!
What a horror they outpour
On the bosom of the palpitating air!
    Yet the air it fully knows,
        By the twanging,
        And the clanging,
    How the danger ebbs and flows;
    Yet the air distinctly tells,
        In the jangling,
        And the wrangling,
    How the danger sinks and swells,
By the sinking or the swelling in the
    anger of the bells—
        Of the bells—
Of the bells, bells, bells, bells,
        Bells, bells, bells—
In the clamor and the clangor of the
    bells!

IV

Hear the tolling of the bells—
        Iron bells!
What a world of solemn thought their
    melody compels!
    In the silence of the night,
    How we shiver with affright
At the melancholy menace of their
    tone!
    For every sound that floats
    From the rust within their throats
        Is a groan.
And the people—ah, the people—
They that dwell up in the steeple,
        All alone.

And who tolling, tolling, tolling,
    In that muffled monotone,
    Feel a glory in the rolling
        On the human heart a stone—
They are neither man nor woman—
They are neither brute nor human—
        They are Ghouls:
    And their king it is who tolls;
    And he rolls, rolls, rolls,
        Rolls.
    A pæan from the bells!
    And his merry bosom swells
    With the pæan from the bells!
    And he dances and he yells;
        Keeping time, time, time,
        In a sort of Runic rhyme,
    To the throbbing of the bells—
    Of the bells, bells, bells—
    To the sobbing of the bells;
        Keeping time, time, time,
    As he knells, knells, knells,
    In a happy Runic rhyme,
    To the rolling of the bells—
    Of the bells, bells, bells—
    To the tolling of the bells,
Of the bells, bells, bells, bells—
        Bells, bells, bells—
To the moaning and the groaning of
    the bells.

Edgar Allan Poe

A MUSICAL INSTRUMENT

What was he doing, the great god
    Pan,
    Down in the reeds by the river?
Spreading ruin, and scattering ban,
Splashing and paddling with hoofs
    of a goat,
And breaking the golden lilies afloat
    With the dragon-fly on the river.

He tore out a reed, the great god
    Pan,

From the deep, cool bed of the
river,
The limpid water turbidly ran,
And the broken lilies a-dying lay,
And the dragon-fly had fled away,
Ere he brought it out of the river.

High on the shore sat the great god
Pan,
While turbidly flowed the river,
And hacked and hewed as a great
god can,
With his hard bleak steel at the pa-
tient reed,
Till there was not a sign of the leaf
indeed
To prove it fresh from the river.

He cut it short, did the great god
Pan,
(How tall it stood in the river!)
Then drew the pith, like the heart of
a man,
Steadily from the outside ring,
And notched the poor, dry, empty
thing
In holes as he sat by the river.

" This is the way," laughed the great
god Pan,
(Laughed while he sat by the
river),
" The only way, since gods began
To make sweet music, they could
succeed."
Then, dropping his mouth to a hole
in the reed,
He blew in power by the river.

Sweet, sweet, sweet, O Pan,
Piercing sweet by the river!
Blinding sweet, O great god Pan,
The sun on the hill forgot to die,
And the lilies revived, and the
dragon-fly
Came back to dream on the river.

Yet half a beast is the great god Pan,
To laugh as he sits by the river,
Making a poet out of a man:
The true gods sigh for the cost and
pain—
For the reed which grows nevermore
again
As a reed with the reeds in the
river.

Elizabeth Barrett Browning

MUSIC, WHEN SOFT VOICES DIE

Music, when soft voices die,
Vibrates in the memory;
Odors, when sweet violets sicken,
Live within the sense they quicken.

Rose leaves, when the rose is dead,
Are heaped for the belovèd's bed;
And so thy thoughts, when thou art
gone,
Love itself shall slumber on.

Percy Bysshe Shelley

ORPHEUS

Orpheus with his lute made trees,
And the mountain-tops, that freeze,
Bow themselves, when he did sing:
To his music, plants, and flowers,
Ever spring; as sun and showers,
There has been a lasting spring.

Everything that heard him play,
Even the billows of the sea,
Hung their heads, and then lay by.
In sweet music is such art;
Killing care and grief of heart,
Fall asleep, or, hearing die.

William Shakespeare

HUNTING SONG
(*Selected Stanzas*)

Waken, lords and ladies gay,
On the mountain dawns the day;
All the jolly chase is here,
With hawk and horse and hunting-
    spear!
Hounds are in their couples yelling,
Hawks are whistling, horns are knell-
    ing,
Merrily, merrily, mingle they.
" Waken, lords and ladies gay."

Waken, lords and ladies gay,
The mist has left the mountain gray,
Springlets in the dawn are steaming,
Diamonds on the brake are gleam-
    ing,
And foresters have busy been
To trace the buck in thicket green;
Now we come to chant our lay,
" Waken, lords and ladies gay."

Waken, lords and ladies gay,
To the greenwood haste away;
We can show you where he lies,
Fleet of foot and tall of size;
We can show the marks he made,
When 'gainst the oak his antlers
    fray'd;
You shall see him brought to bay.
" Waken, lords and ladies gay."

        Walter Scott

THE HUNTER'S SONG
(*Selected Stanzas*)

Rise! Sleep no more! 'Tis a noble
    morn!
The dews hang thick on the fringèd
    thorn,
And the frost shrinks back, like a
    beaten hound,
Under the steaming, steaming ground.

Behold where the billowy clouds flow
    by,
And leave us alone in the clear gray
    sky!
Our horses are ready and steady,—
    So, ho!
I'm gone like a dart from the Tartar's
    bow.
Hark, hark! who calleth the maiden
    morn
From her sleep in the woods and the
    stubble corn?
    The horn—the horn!
The merry sweet ring of the hunter's
    horn!

Sound, sound the horn! To the hunter
    good
What's the gully deep, or the roaring
    flood?
Right o'er he bounds, as the wild stag
    bounds,
At the heels of his swift, sure, silent
    hounds.
Oh! *what* delight can a mortal lack,
When he once is firm on his horse's
    back,
With his stirrups short, and his snaffle
    strong;
And the blast of the horn for his
    morning song!
Hark, hark! Now home! and dream
    till morn
Of the bold sweet sound of the hunt-
    er's horn!
    The horn—the horn!
Oh, the sound of all sounds is the
    hunter's horn!

        Barry Cornwall

HIE AWAY

Hie away, hie away!
Over bank and over brae,

Where the copsewood is the greenest,
Where the fountains glisten sheenest,
Where the lady ferns grow strongest,
Where the morning dew lies longest,
Where the blackcock sweetest sips it,
Where the fairy latest trips it:
Hie to haunts right seldom seen,
Lovely, lonesome, cool, and green;
Over bank and over brae,
Hie away, hie away!

Walter Scott

THE PIPER

Piping down the valleys wild,
  Piping songs of pleasant glee,
On a cloud I saw a child,
  And he laughing said to me:

" Pipe a song about a lamb."
  So I piped with merry cheer.
" Piper, pipe that song again; "
  So I piped; he wept to hear.

" Drop thy pipe, thy happy pipe,
  Sing thy songs of happy cheer: "
So I sang the same again,
  While he wept with joy to hear.

" Piper, sit thee down and write
  In a book that all may read—"
So he vanished from my sight;
  And I plucked a hollow reed,

And I made a rural pen,
  And I stain'd the water clear,
And I wrote my happy songs,
  Every child may joy to hear.

William Blake

THE INVITATION

Best and brightest, come away,—
Fairer far than this fair Day,
Which, like thee, to those in sorrow
Comes to bid a sweet good-morrow
To the rough year just awake
In its cradle on the brake.
The brightest hour of unborn Spring
Through the winter wandering,
Found, it seems, the halcyon morn
To hoar February born;
Bending from Heaven, in azure mirth,
It kiss'd the forehead of the earth,
And smiled upon the silent sea,
And bade the frozen streams be free,
And waked to music all their fountains,
And breathed upon the frozen mountains,
And like the prophetess of May
Strew'd flowers upon the barren way,
Making the wintry world appear
Like one on whom thou smilest, dear.

  Away, away, from men and towns,
To the wild wood and the downs—
To the silent wilderness
Where the soul need not repress
Its music, lest it should not find
An echo in another's mind,
While the touch of Nature's art
Harmonizes heart to heart.

  Radiant Sister of the Day
Awake! arise! and come away!
To the wild woods and the plains,
To the pools where winter rains
Image all their roofs of leaves,
Where the pine its garland weaves
Of sapless green, and ivy dun,
Round stems that never kiss the sun;
Where the lawns and pastures be
And the sandhills of the sea;
Where the melting hoar-frost wets
The daisy-star that never sets,
And wind-flowers and violets
Which yet join not scent to hue
Crown the pale year weak and new;

When the night is left behind
In the deep east, dim and blind,
And the blue moon is over us,
And the multitudinous
Billows murmur at our feet,
Where the earth and ocean meet,
And all things seem only one
In the universal Sun.

Percy Bysshe Shelley

THE FAIRY QUEEN

Over hill, over dale,
Through bush, through brier,
Over park, over pale,
Through flood, through fire,
I do wander everywhere,
Swifter than the moon's sphere;
And I serve the fairy queen,
To dew her orbs upon the green;
The cowslips tall her pensioners be;
In their gold coats spots you see;
Those be rubies, fairy favours,
In those freckles live their savours;
I must go seek some dewdrops here,
And hang a pearl in every cowslip's ear.

William Shakespeare

FOUR DUCKS ON A POND

Four ducks on a pond,
A grass-bank beyond,
A blue sky of spring,
White clouds on the wing—
What a little thing
To remember for years!
To remember with tears!

William Allingham

THE SONG MY PADDLE SINGS

West wind, blow from your prairie
nest,
Blow from the mountains, blow from
the west.

The sail is idle, the sailor too;
O wind of the west, we wait for you!
Blow, blow!
I have wooed you so,
But never a favor you bestow.
You rock your cradle the hills between,
But scorn to notice my white lateen.

I stow the sail and unship the mast:
I wooed you long, but my wooing's
past;
My paddle will lull you into rest:
O drowsy wind of the drowsy west,
Sleep, sleep!
By your mountains steep,
Or down where the prairie grasses
sweep,
Now fold in slumber your laggard
wings,
For soft is the song my paddle sings.

Be strong, O paddle! be brave, canoe!
The reckless waves you must plunge
into.
Reel, reel,
On your trembling keel,
But never a fear my craft will feel.

We've raced the rapids; we're far
ahead:
The river slips through its silent bed.
Sway, sway,
As the bubbles spray
And fall in tinkling tunes away.

And up on the hills against the sky,
A fir tree rocking its lullaby
Swings, swings,
Its emerald wings,
Swelling the song that my paddle
sings.

E. Pauline Johnson

THE VAGABOND

Give to me the life I love,
　　Let the lave go by me,
Give the jolly heaven above
　　And the byway nigh me.
Bed in the bush with stars to see,
　　Bread I dip in the river—
There's the life for a man like me,
　　There's the life for ever.

Or let autumn fall on me
　　Where afield I linger,
Silencing the bird on tree,
　　Biting the blue finger.
White as meal the frosty field—
　　Warm the fireside haven—
Not to autumn will I yield,
　　Not to winter even!

Let the blow fall soon or late,
　　Let what will be o'er me;
Give the face of earth around,
　　And the road before me,
Wealth I ask not, hope nor love,
　　Nor a friend to know me;
All I ask, the heaven above
　　And the road below me.

Robert Louis Stevenson

A SONG OF THE ROAD

The gauger walked with willing foot,
And aye the gauger played the flute;
But what should Master Gauger play
But *Over the hills and far away?*

Whene'er I buckle on my pack
And foot it gaily in the track,
O pleasant gauger, long since dead,
I hear you fluting on ahead.

You go with me the self-same way—
The self-same air for me you play;
For I do think and so do you
It is the tune to travel to.

For who would gravely set his face
To go to this or t' other place?
There's nothing under Heaven so blue
That's fairly worth the travelling to.

On every land the roads begin,
And people walk with zeal therein;
But wheresoe'er the highways tend,
Be sure there's nothing at the end.

Then follow you, wherever hie
The travelling mountains of the sky.
Or let the streams in civil mode
Direct your choice upon a road;

For one and all, or high or low,
Will lead you where you wish to go;
And one and all go night and day
Over the hills and far away!

Robert Louis Stevenson

SONG IN THE SONGLESS

They have no song, the sedges dry,
　　And still they sing.
It is within my breast they sing,
　　As I pass by.
Within my breast they touch a string,
　　They wake a sigh.
There is but sound of sedges dry;
　　In me they sing.

George Meredith

HYMN TO THE NORTH STAR

The sad and solemn Night
　　Has yet her multitude of cheerful
　　　fires;
The glorious host of light
　　Walk the dark hemisphere till she
　　　retires;
All through her silent watches, gliding
　　slow,
Her constellations come, and climb the
　　heavens, and go.

Day, too, hath many a star
    To grace his gorgeous reign, as
    bright as they:
Through the blue fields afar,
    Unseen, they follow in his flaming
    way;
Many a bright lingerer, as the eve
    grows dim,
Tells what a radiant troop arose and
    set with him.

And thou dost see them rise,
    Star of the Pole! and thou dost see
    them set.
Alone in thy cold skies,
    Thou keep'st thy old, unmoving
    station yet,
Nor join'st the dances of that glitter-
    ing train,
Nor dipp'st thy virgin orb in the blue
    western main.

There, at morn's rosy birth,
    Thou lookest meekly through the
    kindling air,
And eve, that round the earth
    Chases the day, beholds thee watch-
    ing there;
There noontide finds thee, and the
    hour that calls
The shapes of polar flame to scale
    heaven's azure walls.

Alike, beneath thine eye,
    The deeds of darkness and of light
    are done;
High towards the starlit sky
    Towns blaze—the smoke of battle
    blots the sun—
The nightstorm on a thousand hills is
    loud—
And the strong wind of day doth min-
    gle sea and cloud.

On thy unaltering blaze
    The half-wrecked mariner, his com-
    pass lost,
Fixes his steady gaze,
    And steers, undoubting, to the
    friendly coast:
And they who stray in perilous wastes
    by night,
Are glad when thou dost shine to guide
    their footsteps right.

And, therefore, bards of old,
    Sages, and hermits of the solemn
    wood,
Did in thy beams behold
    A beauteous type of that unchang-
    ing good,
That bright eternal beacon, by whose
    ray
The voyager of time should shape his
    heedful way.

William Cullen Bryant

BE LIKE THE BIRD

Be like the bird, who
Halting in his flight
On limb too slight
Feels it give way beneath him,
Yet sings
Knowing he hath wings.

Victor Hugo

SEA-FEVER

I must go down to the seas again, to
    the lonely sea and the sky,
And all I ask is a tall ship and a star
    to steer her by,
And the wheel's kick and the wind's
    song and the white sail's shaking,
And a grey mist on the sea's face and a
    grey dawn breaking.

I must go down to the seas again, for
    the call of the running tide
Is a wild call and a clear call that may
    not be denied;
And all I ask is a windy day with the
    white clouds flying,
And the flung spray and the blown
    spume, and the sea-gulls crying.

I must go down to the seas again, to
    the vagrant gypsy life,
To the gull's way and the whale's way
    where the wind's like a whetted
    knife;
And all I ask is a merry yarn from a
    laughing fellow-rover,
And quiet sleep and a sweet dream
    when the long trick's over.

John Masefield

WHERE LIES THE LAND?

Where lies the land to which the ship
    would go?
Far, far ahead is all her seamen know.
And where the land she travels from?
    Away,
Far, far behind, is all that they can say.

On sunny noons upon the deck's
    smooth face;
Linked arm in arm, how pleasant here
    to pace;
Or, o'er the stern reclining, watch
    below
The foaming wake far widening as we
    go.

On stormy nights when wild north-
    westers rave,
How proud a thing to fight with wind
    and wave!
The dripping sailor on the reeling mast
Exults to bear, and scorns to wish it
    past.

Where lies the land to which the ship
    would go?
Far, far ahead, is all her seamen know.
And where the land she travels from?
    Away;
Far, far behind, is all that they can say.

Arthur Hugh Clough

TWILIGHT AT SEA

The twilight hours, like birds, flew by,
    As lightly and as free,
Ten thousand stars were in the sky,
    Ten thousand on the sea;
For every wave, with dimpled face,
    That leaped upon the air,
Had caught a star in its embrace,
    And held it trembling there.

Amelia Coppuck Welby

DOVER BEACH

The sea is calm tonight.
The tide is full, the moon lies fair
Upon the straits; on the French coast
    the light
Gleams and is gone; the cliffs of Eng-
    land stand,
Glimmering and vast, out in the tran-
    quil bay.
Come to the window, sweet is the
    night-air!
Only, from the long line of spray
Where the sea meets the moon-
    blanch'd land,
Listen! you hear the grating roar
Of pebbles which the waves draw back,
    and fling
At their return, upon the high strand,
Begin, and cease, and then again begin,
With tremulous cadence slow, and
    bring
The eternal note of sadness in.

Sophocles long ago
Heard it on the Ægean, and it brought
Into his mind the turbid ebb and flow
Of human misery; we
Find also in the sound a thought,
Hearing it by this distant northern sea.
The Sea of Faith
Was once, too, at the full, and round
    earth's shore
Lay like the folds of a bright girdle
    furl'd.
But now I only hear
Its melancholy, long, withdrawing roar,
Retreating, to the breath
Of the night-wind, down the vast
    edges drear
And naked shingles of the world.

Ah, love, let us be true
To one another! for the world, which
    seems
To lie before us like a land of dreams,
So various, so beautiful, so new,
Hath really neither joy, nor love, nor
    light,
Nor certitude, nor peace, nor help for
    pain;
And we are here as on a darkling plain
Swept with confused alarms of struggle
    and flight,
Where ignorant armies clash by night.

Matthew Arnold

THE LIGHTHOUSE

Far in the bosom of the deep,
O'er these wild shelves my watch I
    keep;
A ruddy gem of changeful light,
Bound on the dusky brow of night,
The seaman bids my lustre hail,
And scorns to strike his timorous sail.

Sir Walter Scott

BESIDE THE SEA

Daily the fishers' sails drift out
    Upon the ocean's breast,
But nightly, like white courier doves
    They all come home to rest.

Ella Higginson

THE CATARACT OF LODORE

How does the water come down at
    Lodore?
    My little boy asked me thus, once
      on a time.
    Moreover, he task'd me to tell him
      in rhyme;
Anon at the word there first came one
    daughter,
    And then came another to second
      and third
The request of their brother, and hear
    how the water
Comes down at Lodore, with its rush
    and its roar,
As many a time they had seen it
    before.
So I told them in rhyme, for of rhymes
    I had store.
And 'twas in my vocation that thus I
    should sing,
Because I was laureate to them and
    the King.

    From its sources which well
    In the tarn on the fell,
    From its fountain in the moun-
      tain,
    Its rills and its gills,
    Through moss and through
      brake,
    It runs and it creeps,
    For a while till it sleeps,
    In its own little lake,
    And thence at departing,
    Awakening and starting,

It runs through the reeds,
And away it proceeds,
Through meadow and glade,
In sun and in shade,
And through the wood shelter,
Among crags in its flurry,
Helter-skelter—hurry-skurry.

How does the water come down at
   Lodore?
   Here it comes sparkling,
   And there it lies darkling;
   Here smoking and frothing,
   Its tumult and wrath in,
It hastens along, conflicting, and
   strong,
   Now striking and raging,
   As if a war waging,
Its caverns and rocks among.
   Rising and leaping,
   Sinking and creeping,
   Swelling and flinging,
   Showering and springing,
   Eddying and whisking,
   Spouting and frisking,
   Twining and twisting,
     Around and around,
   Collecting, disjecting,
     With endless rebound;
   Smiting and fighting,
   A sight to delight in;
   Confounding, astounding,
Dizzying and deafening the ear
   with its sound.

   Receding and speeding,
   And shocking and rocking,
   And darting and parting,
   And threading and spreading,
   And whizzing and hissing,
   And dripping and skipping,
   And whitening and brightening,
   And quivering and shivering,
   And hitting and splitting,

And shining and twining,
And rattling and battling,
And shaking and quaking,
And pouring and roaring,
And waving and raving,
And tossing and crossing,
And flowing and growing,
And running and stunning,
And hurrying and skurrying,
And glittering and frittering,
And gathering and feathering,
And dinning and spinning,
And foaming and roaming,
And dropping and hopping,
And working and jerking,
And heaving and cleaving,
And thundering and flounder-
   ing;

And falling and crawling and sprawl-
   ing,
And driving and riving and striving,
And sprinkling and twinkling and
   wrinkling,
And sounding and bounding and
   rounding,
And bubbling and troubling and
   doubling,
Dividing and gliding and sliding,
And grumbling and rumbling and
   tumbling,
And clattering and battering and
   shattering;
And gleaming and steaming and
   streaming and beaming,
And rushing and flushing and brush-
   ing and gushing,
And flapping and rapping and clap-
   ping and slapping,
And curling and whirling and purling
   and twirling,
Retreating and beating and meeting
   and sheeting,

Delaying and straying and playing and
spraying,
Advancing and prancing and glanc-
ing and dancing,
Recoiling, turmoiling and toiling and
boiling,
And thumping and flumping and
bumping and jumping,
And dashing and flashing and splash-
ing and clashing,—
And so never ending, but always
descending,
Sounds and motions for ever and ever
are blending,
All at once and all o'er, with a mighty
uproar—
And this way the water comes down at
Lodore.

Robert Southey

ODE TO THE WEST WIND

I

O wild West Wind, thou breath of
Autumn's being,
Thou from whose unseen presence the
leaves dead
Are driven, like ghosts from an en-
chanter fleeing,

Yellow, and black, and pale, and hectic
red,
Pestilence-stricken multitudes! O
thou
Who chariotest to their dark wintry
bed

The wingèd seeds, where they lie
cold and low,
Each like a corpse within its grave,
until
Thine azure sister of the Spring shall
blow

Her clarion o'er the dreaming earth,
and fill
(Driving buds like flocks to feed
in air)
With living hues and odours plain and
hill:

Wild Spirit, which art moving everywhere;
Destroyer and preserver; hear, O hear!

II

Thou on whose stream, 'mid the steep
sky's commotion,
Loose clouds like earth's decaying
leaves are shed,
Shook from the tangled boughs of
heaven and ocean,

Angels of rain and lightning! there
are spread
On the blue surface of thine airy surge,
Like the bright hair uplifted from
the head

Of some fierce Mænad, even from the
dim verge
Of the horizon to the zenith's
height,
The locks of the approaching storm.
Thou dirge

Of the dying year, to which this
closing night
Will be the dome of a vast sepulchre,
Vaulted with all thy congregated
might

Of vapours, from whose solid atmosphere
Black rain, and fire, and hail, will
burst: O hear!

III

Thou who didst waken from his summer dreams
  The blue Mediterranean, where he
  lay,
Lull'd by the coil of his crystalline
streams,

  Beside a pumice isle in Baiae's bay,
And saw in sleep old palaces and
  towers
  Quivering within the wave's intenser
  day,

All overgrown with azure moss, and
flowers
  So sweet, the sense faints picturing
  them! Thou
For whose path the Atlantic's level
  powers

  Cleave themselves into chasms,
  while far below
The sea-blooms and the oozy woods
  which wear
  The sapless foliage of the ocean,
  know

Thy voice, and suddenly grow grey
  with fear,
And tremble and despoil themselves:
  O hear!

IV

If I were a dead leaf thou mightest
  bear;
  If I were a swift cloud to fly with
  thee;
A wave to pant beneath thy power, and
  share
  The impulse of thy strength, only
  less free
Than thou, O uncontrollable! if even

I were as in my boyhood, and could
  be

The comrade of thy wanderings over
  heaven,
  As then, when to outstrip thy skiey
  speed
Scarce seem'd a vision—I would ne'er
  have striven

  As thus with thee in prayer in my
  sore need.
O! lift me as a wave, a leaf, a cloud!
  I fall upon the thorns of life! I
  bleed!

A heavy weight of years has chain'd
  and bow'd
One too like thee—tameless, and swift,
  and proud.

V

Make me thy lyre, even as the forest is:
  What if my leaves are falling like its
  own?
The tumult of thy mighty harmonies

  Will take from both a deep autum-
  nal tone,
Sweet though in sadness. Be thou,
  Spirit fierce,
  My spirit! Be thou me, impetuous
  one!

Drive my dead thoughts over the
  universe,
  Like wither'd leaves, to quicken a
  new birth;
And, by the incantation of this verse,

  Scatter, as from an unextinguish'd
  hearth
Ashes and sparks, my words among
  mankind!

Be through my lips to unawaken'd
  earth

The trumpet of a prophecy! O Wind,
If Winter comes, can Spring be far
  behind?

Percy Bysshe Shelley

LITTLE GARAINE

" Where do the stars grow, little
  Garaine?
  The garden of moons, is it far away?
The orchard of suns, my little Garaine,
  Will you take us there some day? "

" If you shut your eyes," quoth little
  Garaine,
  " I will show you the way to go
To the orchard of suns and the garden
  of moons
  And the field where the stars do
  grow.

" But you must speak soft," quoth little Garaine,
  " And still must your footsteps be,
For a great bear prowls in the field of
  stars,
  And the moons they have men to
  see.

" And the suns have the Children of
  Signs to guard,
  And they have no pity at all—
You must not stumble, you must not
  speak,
  When you come to the orchard wall.

" The gates are locked," quoth little
  Garaine,
  " But the way I am going to tell!
The key of your heart it will open
  them all

And there's where the darlings
  dwell! "

Sir Gilbert Parker

SYMPHONY IN YELLOW

An omnibus across the bridge
Crawls like a yellow butterfly,
And here and there, a passer-by
Shows like a little restless midge.

Big barges full of yellow hay
Are moored against a shadowy wharf,
And, like a yellow silken scarf,
The thick fog hangs along the quay.

The yellow leaves begin to fade
And flutter from the Temple elms,
And at my feet the pale green Thames
Lies like a rod of rippled jade.

Oscar Wilde

THE SONG OF THE WOOD

What are you singing of, soft and
  mild,
  Green leaves, waving your gentle
  hands?
Is it a song for a little child,
  Or a song of hope or fear—
A song of regret that you must die?

Is it a song of welcome cheer?
  Is it a song of a sad good-bye?
Is it some message that you bring?
  Hanging there 'mid the earth and
  sky?

Who taught you the song you sing?
  Or do you sing though you know
  not why?

Answered the green leaves, soft and
  mild,

Whispered the green leaves, soft and
    clear,
It is a song for every child,
It is a song God loves to hear,
It is the only song we know,

We never question how or why;
'Tis not a song of fear or woe—
A song of regret that we must die.
This is our song in the deep old wood.

" Earth is beautiful, Heaven is wide,
And we are happy, for God is good."
       Frederick Edward Weatherly

SONNET COMPOSED UPON WESTMINSTER BRIDGE SEPTEMBER 3, 1802

Earth has not anything to show more
    fair:
Dull would he be of soul who could
    pass by
A sight so touching in its majesty:
This City now doth, like a garment,
    wear
The beauty of the morning; silent,
    bare,
Ships, towers, domes, theaters, and
    temples lie
Open unto the fields, and to the sky;
All bright and glittering in the smoke-
    less air.
Never did sun more beautifully steep
In his first splendor, valley, rock, or
    hill;
Ne'er saw I, never felt, a calm so
    deep!
The river glideth at his own sweet
    will:
Dear God! the very houses seem
    asleep;
And all that mighty heart is lying
    still!

       William Wordsworth

THE HAUNTED PALACE

In the greenest of our valleys,
  By good angels tenanted,
Once a fair and stately palace—
  Radiant palace—reared its head.
In the monarch Thought's dominion—
  It stood there!
Never seraph spread a pinion
  Over fabric half so fair.

Banner yellow, glorious, golden,
  On its roof did float and flow;
(This—all this—was in the olden
  Time long ago)
And every gentle air that dallied,
  In that sweet day.
Along the ramparts plumed and pallid,
  A wingèd odour went away.

Wanderers in that happy valley
  Through two luminous windows saw
Spirits moving musically
  To the lute's well-tunèd law,
Round about a throne were sitting
  (Porphyrogene!)
In state his glory well befitting,
  The ruler of the realm was seen.

And all with pearl and ruby glowing
  Was the fair palace door,
Through which came flowing, flowing,
    flowing,
  And sparkling evermore,
A troup of Echoes whose sweet duty
  Was but to sing,
In voices of surpassing beauty,
  The wit and wisdom of their king.

But evil things in robes of sorrow,
  Assailed the monarch's high estate;
(Ah! let us mourn, for never morrow
  Shall dawn upon him desolate!)
And round about his home, the glory
  That blushed and bloomed

Is but a dim remembered story
  Of the old time entombed.

And travellers now within that valley,
  Through the red-litten windows, see
Vast forms that move fantistically
  To a discordant melody;
While like a rapid ghastly river,
  Through the pale door,
A hideous throng rush out forever,
  And laugh—but smile no more.

               Edgar Allan Poe

THE ERL-KING

Oh! who rides by night thro' the woodland so wild?
It is the fond father embracing his
  child;
And close the boy nestles within his
  loved arm,
To hold himself fast and to keep himself warm.

" O Father, see yonder! see yonder! "
  he says:
" My boy, upon what doest thou fear-
  fully gaze? "—
" Oh! 'tis the Erl-King with his crown
  and his shroud,"—
" No, my Son, it is but a dark wreath
  of the cloud."

     The Erl-King Speaks
" *Oh! come and go with me, thou
  lovliest child;
By many a gay sport shall thy time be
  beguiled;
My mother keeps for thee full many a
  fair toy,
And many a fine flower shall she pluck
  for my boy.*"

" O Father, my Father! and did you
  not hear

The Erl-King whisper so low in my
  ear? "—
" Be still, my heart's darling—my child,
  be at ease;
It was but the wild blast as it sung
  thro' the trees."

    The Erl-King Speaks Again
" *Oh! wilt thou go with me, thou
  loveliest boy?
My daughter shall tend thee with care
  and with joy;
She shall bear thee so lightly thro' wet
  and thro' wild,
And press thee and kiss thee and sing
  to my child.*"

" O Father, my Father, and saw you
  not plain,
The Erl-King's pale daughter glide past
  thro' the rain? "—
" Oh, yes, my loved treasure, I knew it
  full soon:
It was the grey willow that danced to
  the moon."

    The Erl-King Speaks Again
" *Oh! come and go with me, no longer
  delay,
Or else, silly child, I will drag thee
  away.*"—

" O Father! O Father! now, now keep
  your hold,
The Erl-King has seized me—his grasp
  is so cold! "

Sore trembled the father; he spurr'd
  thro' the wild,
Clasping close to his bosom his shud-
  dering child;
He reaches his dwelling in doubt and
  in dread,
But, clasped to his bosom, the infant
  was dead!

               Sir Walter Scott

OZYMANDIAS OF EGYPT

I met a traveller from an antique land
Who said: Two vast and trunkless legs
of stone
Stand in the desert. Near them on the
sand
Half sunk, a shatter'd visage lies, whose
frown
And wrinkled lip and sneer of cold
command
Tell that its sculptor well those pas-
sions read
Which yet survive, stamp'd on these
lifeless things,
The hand that mock'd them and the
heart that fled;
And on the pedestal these words appear:
"My name is Ozymandias, king of
kings:
Look on my works, ye Mighty and
despair!"
Nothing beside remains. Round the
decay
Of that colossal wreck, boundless and
bare,
The lone and level sands stretch far
away.

Percy Bysshe Shelley

ON FIRST LOOKING INTO CHAPMAN'S HOMER

Much have I traveled in the realms of
gold,
And many goodly states and king-
doms seen;
Round many western islands have
I been
Which bards in fealty to Apollo hold.
Oft of one wide expanse had I been
told
That deep-browed Homer ruled as
his demesne

Yet did I never breathe its pure
serene
Till I heard Chapman speak out loud
and bold;
Then felt I like some watcher of the
skies
When a new planet swings into his
ken;
Or like stout Cortez, when with eagle
eyes
He stared at the Pacific—and all
his men
Looked at each other with a wild
surmise—
Silent, upon a peak in Darien.

John Keats

ULYSSES

(Selected Stanzas)

There lies the port; the vessel puffs
her sail:
There gloom the dark, broad seas. My
mariners,
Souls that have toiled, and wrought,
and thought with me—
That ever with a frolic welcome took
The thunder and the sunshine, and
opposed
Free hearts, free foreheads—you and
I are old;
Old age hath yet his honor and his
toil;
Death closes all: but something ere
the end,
Some work of noble note, may yet be
done,
Not unbecoming men that strove with
gods.
The lights begin to twinkle from the
rocks:
The long day wanes: the slow moon
climbs: the deep

Moans round with many voices. Come,
    my friends,
'Tis not too late to seek a newer world.
Push off, and sitting well in order
    smite
The sounding furrows; for my purpose
    holds
To sail beyond the sunset, and the
    baths
Of all the western stars, until I die.
It may be that the gulfs will wash us
    down:
It may be we shall touch the Happy
    Isles,
And see the great Achilles, whom we
    knew.
Though much is taken, much abides;
    and though
We are not now that strength which
    in old days
Moved earth and heaven; that which
    we are, we are;—
One equal temper of heroic hearts,
Made weak by time and fate, but
    strong in will
To strive, to seek, to find, and not to
    yield.

Alfred Tennyson

A GOOD NAME

Good name in man and woman, dear
    my lord,
Is the immediate jewel of their souls:
Who steals my purse steals trash; 'tis
    something, nothing;
'Twas mine, 'tis his, and has been slave
    to thousands;
But he that filches from me my good
    name
Robs me of that which not enriches
    him,
And makes me poor indeed.

William Shakespeare

THE NOBLE NATURE

It is not growing like a tree
    In bulk, doth make man better be;
Or standing long an oak, three hun-
    dred year,
To fall a log at last, dry, bald, and sear:
    A lily of a day
    Is fairer far in May,
Although it fall and die that night,—
It was the plant and flower of Light.
In small proportions we just beauties
    see,
And in short measures life may perfect
    be.

Ben Jonson

FORBEARANCE

Hast thou named all the birds without
    a gun?
Loved the wood-rose, and left it on
    its stalk?
At rich men's tables eaten bread and
    pulse?
Unarmed, faced danger with a heart
    of trust?
And loved so well a high behavior,
In man or maid, that thou from speech
    refrained,
Nobility more nobly to repay?
O, be my friend, and teach me to be
    thine!

Ralph Waldo Emerson

FROLIC

The children were shouting together
And racing along the sands,
A glimmer of dancing shadows,
A dovelike flutter of hands.

The stars were shouting in heaven,
The sun was chasing the moon:

The game was the same as the children's,
They danced to the self-same tune.

The whole of the world was merry,
One joy from the vale to the height,
Where the blue woods of twilight encircled
The lovely lawns of the light.

A. E. (G. W. Russell)

LOVELIEST OF TREES

Loveliest of trees, the cherry now
Is hung with bloom along the bough,
And stands about the woodland ride
Wearing white for Eastertide.

Now, of my threescore years and ten,
Twenty will not come again,
And take from seventy springs a score,
It only leaves me fifty more.

And since to look at things in bloom
Fifty springs are little room,
About the woodlands I will go
To see the cherry hung with snow.

A. E. Housman

EVENING

The light passes
from ridge to ridge,
from flower to flower—
the hypaticas, wide-spread
under the light
grow faint—
the petals reach inward,
the blue tips bend
toward the bluer heart
and the flowers are lost.

The cornel-buds are still white,
the shadows dart
from the cornel-roots—
black creeps from root to root,
each leaf
cuts another leaf on the grass,
shadow seeks shadow,
then both leaf
and leaf-shadow are lost.

H. D. (Hilda Doolittle)

EVENING EBB

The ocean has not been so quiet for a
long while; five night-herons
Fly shorelong voiceless in the hush of
the air
Over the calm of an ebb that almost
mirrors their wings.
The sun has gone down, and the water
has gone down
From the weed-clad rock, but the distant cloud-wall rises. The ebb
whispers.
Great cloud-shadows float in the opal
water.
Through rifts in the screen of the
world pale gold gleams, and the
evening
Star suddenly glides like a flying torch.
As if we had not been meant to see her;
rehearsing behind
The screen of the world for another
audience.

Robinson Jeffers

MOOD FROM 3000 B. C.

The queen was sick for her hills.
She spread her long hands on her harp,
Plucking with fingers nimble and
sharp,
She sang of her queenly ills,
Alone. And the small twanging note
Touched the empty wave of the air
And put the air into tune.

A fisher in a painted boat
And a girl washing her midnight hair
In the shallow water of noon,
Listened as we listen to trills
Of little birds sheltered with green,
And they said: " Ah, the poor queen!
" She is sick again for her hills! "

Genevieve Taggard

THE LAKE ISLE OF INNISFREE

I will arise and go now, and go to
 Innisfree,
And a small cabin build there, of clay
 and wattles made;
Nine bean rows will I have there, a
 hive for the honey bee,
And live alone in the bee-loud glade.

And I shall have some peace there, for
 peace comes dropping slow,
Dropping from the veils of morning to
 where the cricket sings;
There midnight's all a glimmer, and
 noon a purple glow,
And evening full of the linnet's wings.

I will arise and go now, for always
 night and day
I hear lake water lapping with low
 sounds by the shore;
While I stand on the roadway, or on
 the pavement grey,
I hear it in the heart's deep core.

William Butler Yeats

A THING OF BEAUTY

A thing of beauty is a joy forever:
Its loveliness increases; it will never

Pass into nothingness; but still will
 keep
A bower quiet for us, and a sleep
Full of sweet dreams, and health, and
 quiet breathing.
Therefore, on every morrow, we are
 wreathing
A flowery band to bind us to the earth,
Spite of despondence, of the inhuman
 dearth
Of noble natures, of the gloomy days,
Of all the unhealthy and o'er-darken'd
 ways
Made for our searching: yea, in spite
 of all,
Some shape of beauty moves away the
 pall
From our dark spirits. Such the sun,
 the moon,
Trees old and young, sprouting a
 shady boon
For simple sheep; and such are daffo-
 dils
With the green world they live in; and
 clear rills
That for themselves a cooling covert
 make
'Gainst the hot season; the mid forest
 brake,
Rich with a sprinkling of fair musk-
 rose blooms:
And such too is the grandeur of the
 dooms
We have imagined for the mighty
 dead;
All lovely tales that we have heard or
 read:
An endless fountain of immortal drink,
Pouring into us from the heaven's
 brink.

John Keats

Part Two

STORIES IN VERSE

THE RAGGLE, TAGGLE GYPSIES

There were three gypsies a-come to my
   door,
  And downstairs ran this lady, O.
One sang high and another sang low,
  And the other sang " Bonnie, Bon-
   nie Biskay, O."

Then she pulled off her silken gown,
  And put on hose of leather, O.
With the ragged, ragged rags about
  her door
   She's off with the Raggle, Taggle
   Gypsies, O.

'Twas late last night when my lord
  came home,
  Inquiring for his lady, O.
The servants said on every hand,
  " She's gone with the Raggle, Tag-
   gle Gypsies, O."

" Oh, saddle for me my milk-white
  steed,
  Oh, saddle for me my pony, O.
That I may ride and seek my bride

Who's gone with the Raggle, Taggle
  Gypsies, O."
Oh, he rode high and he rode low,
  He rode through woods and copses,
   O,
Until he came to an open field,
  And there he espied his lady, O.

" What makes you leave your house
  and lands?
  What makes you leave your money,
   O?
What makes you leave your new-
  wedded lord
   To go with the Raggle, Taggle
   Gypsies, O? "

" What care I for my house and lands?
  What care I for my money, O,
What care I for my new-wedded lord?
  I'm off with the Raggle, Taggle
   Gypsies, O."

" Last night you slept on a goose-
  feather bed,
  With the sheet turned down so
  bravely, O.
Tonight you will sleep in the cold,
  open field,

Along with the Raggle, Taggle Gypsies, O."

"What care I for your goose-feather
  bed,
  With the sheet turned down so
    bravely, O?
For tonight I shall sleep in a cold,
  open field,
  Along with the Raggle, Taggle
    Gypsies, O."

Unknown

MEG MERRILIES

Old Meg she was a gipsy,
  And lived upon the moors:
Her bed it was the brown heath turf,
  And her house was out of doors.

Her apples were swart blackberries,
  Her currants, pods o' broom;
Her wine was dew o' the wild white
  rose,
  Her book a churchyard tomb.

Her Brothers were the craggy hills,
  Her Sisters larchen trees;
Alone with her great family,
  She lived as she did please.

No breakfast had she many a morn,
  No dinner many a noon,
And, 'stead of supper, she would stare
  Full hard against the Moon.

But every morn, of woodbine fresh,
  She made her garlanding,
And every night the dark glen Yew,
  She wove, and she would sing.

And with her fingers, old and brown,
  She plaited Mats of Rushes,

And gave them to the Cottagers
  She met among the Bushes.

Old Meg was brave as Margaret Queen,
  And tall as Amazon;
An old red blanket cloak she wore,
  A chip hat had she on.
God rest her aged bones somewhere:
  She died full long agone.

John Keats

ONE FRIDAY MORN

One Friday morn when we set sail,
  Not very far from land,
We there did espy a fair pretty maid
  With a comb and a glass in her
    hand, her hand,
  With a comb and a glass in her
    hand.
    While the raging seas did roar,
      And the stormy winds did blow,
    While we jolly sailor-boys were up
      into the top,
    And the land-lubbers lying down
      below, below,
    And the land-lubbers lying down
      below.

Then up starts the captain of our
  gallant ship,
  And a brave young man was he:
"I've a wife and a child in fair Bristol
  town,
  But a widow I fear she'll be."
    And the raging seas did roar,
      And the stormy winds did blow.

Then up starts the mate of our gallant
  ship,
  And a bold young man was he:
"Oh! I have a wife in fair Portsmouth
  town,

But a widow I fear she'll be."
   And the raging seas did roar,
     And the stormy winds did blow.

Then up starts the cook of our gallant
   ship,
   And a gruff old soul was he:
" Oh! I have a wife in fair Plymouth
   town,
   But a widow I fear she'll be."
   And the raging seas did roar,
     And the stormy winds did blow.

And then up spoke the little cabin-boy,
   And a pretty little boy was he;
" Oh! I am more grieved for my daddy
   and my mammy
   Than you for your wives all three."
   And the raging seas did roar,
     And the stormy winds did blow.

Then three times round went our gallant ship,
   And three times round went she;
And three times round went our gallant ship,
   And she sank to the bottom of the
   sea. . . .

   And the raging seas did roar,
     And the stormy winds did blow.
   While we jolly sailor-boys were up
   into the top,
     And the land-lubbers lying
     down below, below,
     And the land-lubbers lying
     down below.

          Unknown

BALLAD OF EARL HALDAN'S
DAUGHTER

It was Earl Haldan's daughter,
   She looked across the sea;

She looked across the water,
   And long and loud laughed she:
" The locks of six princesses
   Must be my marriage fee:
So, hey, bonny boat, and ho, bonny
   boat,
   Who comes a-wooing me! "

It was Earl Haldan's daughter,
   She walked along the sand,
When she was aware of a knight so
   fair,
   Come sailing to the land.
His sails were all of velvet,
   His mast of beaten gold,
And " Hey, bonny boat, and ho, bonny
   boat,
   Who saileth here so bold? "

" The locks of five princesses
   I won beyond the sea;
I shore their golden tresses
   To fringe a cloak for thee.
One handful yet is wanting,
   But one of all the tale;
So, hey, bonny boat, and ho, bonny
   boat,
   Furl up thy velvet sail! "

He leapt into the water,
   That rover young and bold;
He gript Earl Haldan's daughter,
   He shore her locks of gold:
" Go weep, go weep, proud maiden,
   The tale is full today.
Now, hey, bonny boat, and ho, bonny
   boat,
   Sail Westward ho, and away! "

          Charles Kingsley

BELL'S DREAM
(*Selected Stanzas*)

It was the little Isabel,
   Upon the sand she lay,

The summer sun struck hotly down,
    And she was tired of play;
And down she sank into the sea,
    Though how, she could not say.

She stood within a dreadful court,
    Beneath the rolling tide,
There sat a sturgeon as a judge,
    Two lobsters at her side;
She had a sort of vague idea
    That she was being tried.

And then the jurymen came in,
    And, as the clock struck ten,
Rose Sergeant Shark and hitched his
        gown,
    And trifled with a pen.
" Ahem! May't please your Lordship,
    And gentle jurymen!

" The counts against the prisoner
    Before you, are that she
Has eaten salmon once at least,
    And soles most constantly;
Likewise devoured one hundred
        shrimps
    At Margate with her tea."

" Call witnesses! "—An oyster rose,
    He spoke in plaintive tone:
" Last week her mother bought fish,"
    (He scarce could check a moan);
" He was a dear, dear friend of mine,
    His weight was half a stone! "

" ' No oysters, ma'am? ' the fishman
        said;
    ' No, not today! ' said she;
' My child is fond of salmon, but
    Oysters do not agree! '
The fishman wiped a salt, salt tear,
    And murmured, ' Certainly! ' "

" Ahem! but," interposed the judge,
    " How do you know," said he,

" That she did really eat the fish? "
    " My Lord, it so must be,
Because the oysters, I submit,
    With her did not agree! "

" Besides, besides," the oyster cried,
    Half in an injured way,
" The oysters in that fishman's shop
    My relatives were they:
They heard it all, they wrote to me,
    The letter came today! "

" ' Tis only hearsay evidence,"
    The judge remarked, and smiled;
" But it will do in such a case,
    With such a murd'rous child.
Call the next witness! " for he saw
    The jury getting wild.

And then up rose a little shrimp:
    " I am the last," said he,
" Of what was once, as you all know,
    A happy familee!
Without a care we leapt and danced
    All in the merry sea!

" Alack! the cruel fisherman,
    He caught them all but me,
The pris'ner clapped her hands and
        yelled—
    I heard her—' Shrimps for tea! '
And then went home and ate them
        all
    As fast as fast could be."

The foreman of the jury rose
    (All hope for Bell had fled),
" There is no further need, my Lord,
    Of witnesses," he said;
" The verdict of us one and all
    Is, Guilty on each head! "

" Guilty," his Lordship said, and
    sighed;

" A verdict sad but true:
To pass the sentence of the court
  Is all I have to do;
It is, that as you've fed on us,
  Why, we must feed on you! "

She tried to speak, she could not
    speak;
  She tried to run, but no!
The lobsters seized and hurried her
  Off to the cells below,
And each pulled out a carving-knife,
  And waved it to and fro.

But hark! there comes a voice she
    knows,
  And some one takes her hand;
She finds herself at home again
  Upon the yellow sand;
But how she got there safe and sound
  She cannot understand.

And many a morning afterwards,
  Whene'er she sees the tide,
She still retains that vague idea,
  That she is being tried,
And seems to see the sturgeon judge
  And the lobsters at her side.

   Frederick Edward Weatherly

THE LONG WHITE SEAM

As I came round the harbor buoy,
  The lights began to gleam,
No wave the land-locked harbor stirred,
  The crags were white as cream;
And I marked my love by candlelight
  Sewing her long white seam.
  It's aye sewing ashore, my dear,
   Watch and steer at sea,
  It's reef and furl, and haul the
   line,
    Set sail and think of thee.

I climbed to reach her cottage door;
  Oh sweetly my love sings!
Like a shaft of light her voice breaks
    forth,
  My soul to meet it springs,
As the shining water leaped of old
  When stirred by angel wings.
  Aye longing to list anew,
   Awake and in my dream,
  But never a song she sang like this,
   Sewing her long white seam.

Fair fall the lights, the harbor lights,
  That brought me in to thee,
And peace drop down on that low roof,
  For the sight that I did see,
And the voice, my dear, that rang so
    clear,
  All for the love of me.
  For O, for O, with brows bent
   low,
   By the flickering candle's gleam,
  Her wedding gown it was she
   wrought,
   Sewing the long white seam.

    Jean Ingelow

FAIR HELEN OF KIRCONNEL

I wish I were where Helen lies!
Night and day on me she cries;
O that I were where Helen lies,
  On fair Kirconnel Lee!

Curst be the heart that thought the
    thought
And curst the hand that fired the shot,
When in my arms burd Helen dropt,
  And died to succour me!

O think na ye my heart was sair,
When my love dropt down and spak
    nae mair!
There did she swoon wi' meikle care,
  On fair Kirconnel Lee.

As I went down the water side,
None but my foe to be my guide,
None but my foe to be my guide,
    On fair Kirconnel Lee.

I lighted down, my sword did draw,
I hackéd him in pieces sma',
I hackéd him in pieces sma',
    For her sake that died for me.

O Helen fair, beyond compare!
I'll make a garland for thy hair,
Shall bind my heart for evermair,
    Until the day I die.

O that I were where Helen lies,
Night and day on me she cries;
Out of my bed she bids me rise
    Says, " Haste, and come to me! "

O Helen fair! O Helen chaste!
If I were with thee, I were blest,
Where thou lies low, and takes thy rest
    On fair Kirconnel Lee.

I wish my grave were growing green,
A winding sheet drawn ower my een,
And I by my fair Helen lying,
    On fair Kirconnel Lee.

I wish I were where Helen lies!
Night and day on me she cries,
And I am weary of the skies,
    For her sake that died for me.

Unknown

JOCK OF HAZELDEAN

" Why weep ye by the tide, ladie?
  Why weep ye by the tide?
I'll wed ye to my youngest son,
  And ye sall be his bride:
And ye sall be his bride, ladie,
  Sae comely to be seen "—

But aye she loot the tears down fa'
  For Jock of Hazeldean.

" Now let this wilfu' grief be done,
  And dry that cheek so pale;
Young Frank is chief of Errington,
  And lord of Langley-Hale;
His step is first in peaceful ha',
  His sword in battle keen "—
But aye she loot the tears down fa'
  For Jock of Hazeldean.

" A chain of gold ye sall not lack,
  Nor braid to bind your hair;
Nor mettled hound, nor managed
  hawk,
  Nor palfrey fresh and fair;
And you, the foremost of them a'
  Shall ride our forest queen "—
But aye she loot the tears down fa'
  For Jock of Hazeldean.

The kirk was deck'd at morning-tide,
  The tapers glimmer'd fair;
The priest and bridegroom wait the
  bride,
  And dame and knight are there.
They sought her baith by bower and
  ha';
  The ladie was not seen!
She's o'er the Border, and awa'
  Wi' Jock of Hazeldean.

Walter Scott

ROSABELLE

O listen, listen, ladies gay!
  No haughty feat of arms I tell;
Soft is the note, and sad the lay,
  That mourns the lovely Rosabelle.

" Moor, moor the barge, ye gallant
  crew,
  And gentle lady, deign to stay!

Rest thee in Castle Ravensheuch,
  Nor tempt the stormy firth today.

" The blackening wave is edged with
    white;
  To inch and rock the sea-mews fly;
The fishers have heard the Water-
    Sprite,
  Whose screams forbode that wreck
    is nigh.

" Last night the gifted seer did view
  A wet shroud swathed round lady
    gay;
Then stay thee, Fair, in Ravensheuch?
  Why cross the gloomy firth today? "

" 'Tis not because Lord Lindesay's heir
  Tonight at Roslin leads the ball,
But that my lady-mother there
  Sits lonely in her castle hall.

" 'Tis not because the ring they ride,
  And Lindesay at the ring rides well,
But that my sire the wine will chide
  If 'tis not fill'd by Rosabelle."

—O'er Roslin all that dreary night
  A wondrous blaze was seen to
    gleam;
'Twas broader than the watch-fires'
    light
  And redder than the bright moon-
    beam.

It glared on Roslin's castled rock,
  It ruddied all the copse-wood glen;
'Twas seen from Dryden's groves of
    oak,
  And seen from cavern'd Hawthorn-
    den.

Seem'd all on fire that chapel proud
  Where Roslin's chiefs uncoffin'd lie,

Each Baron, for a sable shroud,
  Sheath'd in his iron panoply.

Seem'd all on fire within, around,
  Deep sacristy and altar's pale;
Shone every pillar foliage-bound,
  And glimmer'd all the dead men's
    mail.

Blazed battlement and pinnet high,
  Blazed every rose-carved buttress
    fair—
So still they blaze, when fate is nigh
  The lordly line of high St. Clair.

There are twenty of Roslin's barons
    bold
  Lie buried within that proud cha-
    pelle;
Each one the holy vault doth hold,
  But the sea holds lovely Rosabelle!

And each St. Clair was buried there,
  With candle, with book, and with
    knell;
But the sea-caves rung, and the wild
    wind sung,
  The dirge of lovely Rosabelle.
             Walter Scott

LORD LOVEL

Lord Lovel he stood at his castle gate,
  Combing his milk-white steed;
When up came Lady Nancy Belle
  To wish her lover good speed, speed,
  To wish her lover good speed.

" Where are you going, Lord Lovel? "
    she said,
  " Oh! where are you going? " said
    she;
" I'm going, my Lady Nancy Belle,
  Strange countries for to see, to see,
  Strange countries for to see! "

"When will you be back, Lord
Lovel?" said she,
"Oh! when will you come back?"
said she;
"In a year or two—or three at the
most,
I'll return to my fair Nancy—cy,
I'll return to my fair Nancy."

But he had not been gone a year and
a day,
Strange countries for to see,
When languishing thoughts came into
his head,
Lady Nancy Belle he would go see,
see,
Lady Nancy Belle he would go see.

So he rode, and he rode on his milk-
white steed,
Till he came to London-town;
And there he heard St. Pancras' bells,
And the people all mourning round,
round,
And the people all mourning round.

"Oh! what is the matter?" Lord Lovel
he said,
"Oh! what is the matter?" said he;
"A lord's lady is dead," a woman
replied,
"And some call her Lady Nancy—cy
And some call her Lady Nancy."

So he ordered the grave to be opened
wide,
And the shroud he turnèd down,
And there he kissed her clay-cold lips,
Till the tears came trickling down,
down,
Till the tears came trickling down.

Lady Nancy she died as it might be
today,

Lord Lovel he died as tomorrow;
Lady Nancy she died out of pure, pure
grief,
Lord Lovel he died out of sorrow,
sorrow,
Lord Lovel he died out of sorrow.

Lady Nancy was laid in Saint Pancras'
church,
Lord Lovel was laid in the chair;
And out of her bosom there grew a
red rose,
And out of her lover's a brier, brier,
And out of her lover's a brier.

They grew and they grew, to the
church steeple too,
And then they could grow no
higher;
So there they entwined in a true lover's
knot,
For all lovers true to admire—mire,
For all lovers true to admire.

Unknown

LADY CLARE

It was the time when lilies blow,
And clouds are highest up in air,
Lord Ronald brought a lily-white doe
To give his cousin, Lady Clare.

I trow they did not part in scorn;
Lovers long bethroth'd were they;
They two will wed the morrow morn;
God's blessing on the day!

"He does not love me for my birth,
Nor for my lands so broad and fair;
He loves me for my own true worth,
And that is well," said Lady Clare.

In there came old Alice the nurse,
Said, "Who was this that went from
thee?"

"It was my cousin," said Lady Clare,
 "Tomorrow he weds with me."

"O God be thank'd!" said Alice the
 nurse,
 "That all comes round so just and
 fair:
Lord Ronald is heir of all your lands,
 And you are not the Lady Clare."

"Are ye out of your mind, my nurse,
 my nurse,"
 Said Lady Clare, "that ye speak so
 wild?"
"As God's above," said Alice the
 nurse,
 "I speak the truth: you are my
 child.

"The old Earl's daughter died at my
 breast;
 I speak the truth, as I live by bread!
I buried her like my own sweet child,
 And put my child in her stead."

"Falsely, falsely have ye done,
 O mother," she said, "if this be true,
To keep the best man under the sun
 So many years from his due."

"Nay now, my child," said Alice the
 nurse,
 "But keep the secret for your life,
And all you have will be Lord Ron-
 ald's,
 When you are man and wife."

"If I'm a beggar born," she said,
 "I will speak out, for I dare not lie.
Pull off, pull off, the brooch of gold,
 And fling the diamond necklace by."

"Nay now, my child," said Alice the
 nurse,

"But keep the secret all ye can."
She said "Not so: but I will know
 If there be any faith in man."

"Nay now, what faith?" said Alice the
 nurse,
 "The man will cleave unto his
 right."
"And he shall have it," the lady replied,
 "Tho' I should die tonight."

"Yet give one kiss to your mother
 dear!
 Alas! my child, I sinn'd for thee."
"O mother, mother, mother," she said,
 "So strange it seems to me.

"Yet here's a kiss for my mother dear,
 My mother dear, if this be so,
And lay your hand upon my head,
 And bless me, mother, ere I go."

She clad herself in a russet gown,
 She was no longer Lady Clare:
She went by dale, and she went by
 down,
 With a single rose in her hair.

The lily-white doe Lord Ronald had
 brought
 Leapt up from where she lay,
Dropt her head in the maiden's hand,
 And follow'd her all the way.

Down stept Lord Ronald from his
 tower,
 "O Lady Clare, you shame your
 worth!
Why come you drest like a village
 maid,
 That are the flower of the earth?"

"If I come drest like a village maid,
 I am but as my fortunes are:

I am a beggar born," she said,
" And not the Lady Clare."

" Play me no tricks," said Lord
    Ronald,
    " For I am yours in words and in
    deed.
Play me no tricks," said Lord Ronald,
    " Your riddle is hard to read."

O and proudly stood she up!
    Her heart within her did not fail:
She look'd into Lord Ronald's eyes,
    And told him all her nurse's tale.

He laugh'd a laugh of merry scorn:
    He turn'd and kiss'd her where she
    stood.
" If you are not the heiress born,
    And I," said he, " the next in
    blood—

" If you are not the heiress born,
    And I," said he, " the lawful heir,
We two will wed tomorrow morn,
    And you shall still be Lady Clare."

Alfred Tennyson

LORD ULLIN'S DAUGHTER

A Chieftain to the Highlands bound
    Cries, " Boatman, do not tarry!
And I'll give thee a silver pound
    To row us o'er the ferry! "

—" Now, who be ye, would cross
    Lochgyle
    This dark and stormy water? "
—" O I'm the chief of Ulva's isle,
    And this, Lord Ullin's daughter.

" And fast before her father's men
    Three days we've fled together,
For should he find us in the glen,
    My blood would stain the heather.

" His horsemen hard behind us ride—
    Should they our steps discover,
Then who will cheer my bonny bride
    When they have slain her lover? "

Out spoke the hardy Highland wight,
    " I'll go, my chief, I'm ready:
It is not for your silver bright,
    But for your winsome lady:—

" And by my word! the bonny bird
    In danger shall not tarry;
So though the waves are raging white,
    I'll row you o'er the ferry."

By this the storm grew loud apace,
    The water-wraith was shrieking;
And in the scowl of heaven each face
    Grew dark as they were speaking.

But still as wilder blew the wind,
    And as the night grew drearer,
Adown the glen rode armèd men,
    Their trampling sounded nearer.

" O haste thee, haste! " the lady cries,
    " Though tempest round us gather;
I'll meet the raging of the skies,
    But not an angry father! "

The boat has left a stormy land,
    A stormy sea before her—
When, O! too strong for human hand
    The tempest gather'd o'er her.

And still they row'd amidst the roar
    Of waters fast prevailing:
Lord Ullin reach'd that fatal shore,—
    His wrath was changed to wailing.

For, sore dismayed, through storm and
    shade
    His child he did discover:—
One lovely hand she stretch'd for aid,
    And one was round her lover.

"Come back! come back!" he cried in
  grief,
  "Across this stormy water:
And I'll forgive your Highland chief:—
  My daughter!—O my daughter!"

'Twas vain: the loud waves lash'd the
  shore,
  Return or aid preventing;
The waters wild went o'er his child,
  And he was left lamenting.
                    Thomas Campbell

ALICE BRAND

I

Merry it is in the good greenwood,
  Where the mavis and merle are sing-
    ing,
When the deer sweeps by, and the
    hounds are in cry,
  And the hunter's horn is ringing.

"O Alice Brand, my native land
  Is lost for love of you;
And we must hold by wood and wold,
  As outlaws wont to do.

"O Alice, 'twas all for thy locks so
    bright,
  And 'twas all for thine eyes so blue,
That on the night of our luckless flight
  Thy brother bold I slew.

"Now must I teach to hew the beech
  The hand that held the glaive,
For leaves to spread our lowly bed,
  And stakes to fence our cave.

"All for vest of pall, thy fingers small
  That wont on harp to stray,
A cloak must shear from the slaugh-
    tered deer,
  To keep the cold away."—

"O Richard, if my brother died,
  'Twas but a fatal chance,
For darkling was the battle tried,
  And fortune sped the lance.

"If pall and vair no more I wear,
  Nor thou the crimson sheen,
As warm, we'll say, is the russet grey,
  As gay the forest green.

"And Richard, if our lot be hard,
  And lost thy native land,
Still Alice has her own Richard,
  And he his Alice Brand."

II

'Tis merry, 'tis merry, in good green-
    wood,
  So blithe Lady Alice is singing;
On the beech's pride, and the brown
    oak's side,
  Lord Richard's axe is ringing.

Up spoke the moody Elfin King,
  Who woned within the hill—
Like wind in the porch of a ruined
    church,
  His voice was ghostly shrill.

"Why sounds yon stroke on beech
    and oak,
  Our moonlight circle's screen?
Or who comes here to chase the deer,
  Beloved of our Elfin Queen?
Or who may dare on wold to wear
  The fairies' fatal green?

"Up, Urgan, up! to yon mortal hie,
  For thou wert christened man;
For cross or sign thou wilt not fly,
  For muttered word or ban.

"Lay on him the curse of the withered
    heart,

The curse of the sleepless eye;
Till he wish and pray that his life
    would part,
    Nor yet find leave to die."

III

'Tis merry, 'tis merry, in good green-
    wood,
    Though the birds have stilled their
      singing;
The evening blaze doth Alice raise,
    And Richard is fagots bringing.

Up Urgan starts, that hideous dwarf,
    Before Lord Richard stands,
And, as he crossed and blessed himself,
    " I fear not sign," quoth the grisly
      elf,
    " That is made with bloody hands."

But out then spoke she, Alice Brand,
    That woman void of fear—
" And if there's blood upon his hand,
    'Tis but the blood of deer."—

" Now loud thou liest, thou bold of
    mood!
    It cleaves unto his hand,
The stain of thine own kindly blood,
    The blood of Ethert Brand."

Then forward stepped she, Alice
    Brand,
    And made the holy sign—
" And if there's blood on Richard's
    hand,
    A spotless hand is mine.

" And I conjure thee, Demon elf,
    By Him whom Demons fear,
To show us whence thou art thyself,
    And what thine errand here? "

IV

" 'Tis merry, 'tis merry, in Fairyland,
    When fairy birds are singing,

When the court doth ride by their
    monarch's side,
    With bit and bridle ringing:

" And gaily shines the Fairyland—
    But all is glistening show,
Like the idle gleam that December's
    beam
    Can dart on ice and snow.

" And fading, like that varied gleam,
    Is our inconstant shape,
Who now like knight and lady seem,
    And now like dwarf and ape.

" It was between the night and day,
    When the Fairy King has power,
That I sunk down in a sinful fray,
And, 'twixt life and death, was
      snatched away
    To the joyless Elfin bower.

" But wist I of a woman bold,
    Who thrice my brow durst sign,
I might regain my mortal mould,
    As fair a form as thine."

She crossed him once—she crossed him
    twice—
    The lady was so brave;
The fouler grew his goblin hue,
    The darker grew the cave.

She crossed him thrice, that lady bold;
    He rose beneath her hand
The fairest knight on Scottish mould,
    Her brother, Ethert Brand!

Merry it is in good greenwood,
    When the mavis and merle are sing-
      ing,
But merrier were they in Dunfermline
    grey,
    When all the birds were ringing.
               Sir Walter Scott

THE SEVEN SISTERS, OR THE SOLITUDE OF BINNORIE

Seven daughters had Lord Archibald,
All children of one mother:
You could not say in one short day
What love they bore each other.
A garland, of seven lilies wrought!
Seven sisters that together dwell;
But he, bold knight as ever fought,
Their father took of them no thought,
He loved the wars so well.
Sing mournfully, oh! mournfully,
The solitude of Binnorie!

Fresh blows the wind, a western wind,
And from the shores of Erin,
Across the wave, a rover brave
To Binnorie is steering:
Right onward to the Scottish strand
The gallant ship is borne;
The warriors leap upon the land,
And hark! the leader of the band
Hath blown his bugle horn.
Sing mournfully, oh! mournfully,
The solitude of Binnorie!

Beside a grotto of their own,
With boughs above them closing,
The seven are laid, and in the shade
They lie like fawns reposing.
But now upstarting with affright
At noise of man and steed,
Away they fly, to left, to right—
Of your fair household, father-knight,
Methinks you take small heed!
Sing mournfully, oh! mournfully,
The solitude of Binnorie!

Away the seven fair Campbells fly;
And, over hill and hollow,
With menace proud, and insult loud,
The youthful rovers follow.
Cried they, "Your father loves to roam:

Enough for him to find
The empty house when he comes home;
For us your yellow ringlets comb,
For us be fair and kind!"
Sing mournfully, oh! mournfully,
The solitude of Binnorie!

Some close behind, some side by side,
Like clouds in stormy weather,
They run and cry, "Nay let us die,
And let us die together."
A lake was near; the shore was steep;
There foot had never been;
They ran, and with a desperate leap
Together plunged into the deep,
Nor ever more were seen.
Sing mournfully, oh! mournfully,
The solitude of Binnorie!

The stream that flows out of the lake,
As through the glen it rambles,
Repeats a moan o'er moss and stone
For those seven lovely Campbells.
Seven little islands, green and bare,
Have risen from out the deep:
The fishers say those sisters fair
By fairies are all buried there,
And there together sleep.
Sing mournfully, oh! mournfully,
The solitude of Binnorie!

William Wordsworth

LUCY GRAY

Oft I had heard of Lucy Gray:
    And, when I crossed the wild,
I chanced to see at break of day,
    The solitary child.

No mate, no comrade Lucy knew:
    She dwelt on a wide moor,—
The sweetest thing that ever grew
    Beside a human door!

You yet may spy the fawn at play,
    The hare upon the green;
But the sweet face of Lucy Gray
    Will never more be seen.

"Tonight will be a stormy night—
    You to the town must go;
And take a lantern, Child, to light
    Your mother through the snow."

"That, Father, will I gladly do:
    'Tis scarcely afternoon—
The minster-clock has just struck two,
    And yonder is the moon!"

At this the Father raised his hook,
    And snapped a faggot-brand;
He plied his work;—and Lucy took
    The lantern in her hand.

Not blither is the mountain roe;
    With many a wanton stroke
Her feet disperse the powdery snow,
    That rises up like smoke.

The storm came on before its time:
    She wandered up and down;
And many a hill did Lucy climb:
    But never reached the town.

The wretched parents all that night
    Went shouting far and wide;
But there was neither sound nor sight
    To serve them for a guide.

At daybreak on a hill they stood
    That overlooked the moor:
And thence they saw the bridge of
    wood
    A furlong from their door.

They wept—and, turning homeward,
    cried,
    "In heaven we all shall meet;"

When in the snow the mother spied
    The print of Lucy's feet.

Half breathless from the steep hill's
    edge
    They tracked the footmarks small;
And through the broken hawthorn
    hedge,
    And by the long stone wall.

And then an open field they crossed;
    The marks were still the same;
They tracked them on, nor ever lost;
    And to the bridge they came.

They followed from the snowy bank
    Those footmarks, one by one,
Into the middle of the plank;
    And farther there were none!—

Yet some maintain that to this day
    She is a living child:
That you may see sweet Lucy Gray
    Upon the lonesome wild.

O'er rough and smooth she trips along,
    And never looks behind;
And sings a solitary song
    That whistles in the wind.
               William Wordsworth

ALICE FELL

The post-boy drove with fierce career,
    For threatening clouds the moon
    had drowned:
When, as we hurried on, my ear
    Was smitten with a startling sound.

As if the wind blew many ways,
    I heard the sound,—and more and
    more;
It seemed to follow with the chaise,
    And still I heard it as before.

At length I to the boy called out;
  He stopped his horses at the word;
But neither cry, nor voice, nor shout,
  Nor aught else like it, could be
    heard.

The boy then smacked his whip, and
    fast
  The horses scampered through the
    rain;
And soon I heard upon the blast
  The cry, I bade him halt again.

Forthwith, alighting on the ground,
  "Whence comes," said I, "this
    piteous moan?"
And there a little Girl I found,
  Sitting behind the chaise, alone.

"My cloak!" no other word she spake,
  But loud and bitterly she wept,
As if her innocent heart would break;
  And down from off her seat she
    leapt.

"What ails you, child?"—she sobbed,
  "Look here!"
I saw it in the wheel entangled,
A weather-beaten rag as e'er
  From any garden scarecrow dangled.

'Twas twisted between nave and spoke:
  It hung, nor could at once be freed,
But our joint palms unloosed the cloak,
  A miserable rag indeed!

"And whither are you going, child,
  Tonight along these lonesome
    ways?"
"To Durham," answered she, half
    wild—
  "Then come with me into the
    chaise."

She sat like one past all relief;
  Sob after sob she forth did send
In wretchedness, as if her grief
  Could never, never have an end.

"My child, in Durham do you dwell?"
  She checked herself in her distress,
And said, "My name is Alice Fell;
  I'm fatherless and motherless.

"And I to Durham, sir, belong:"
  Again, as if the thought would choke
Her very heart, her grief grew strong:
  And all was for her tattered cloak!

The chaise drove on, our journey's end
  Was nigh; and sitting by my side,
As if she had lost her only friend,
  She wept, nor would be pacified.

Up to the tavern-door we post;
  Of Alice and her grief I told,
And I gave money to the host,
  To buy a new cloak for the old.

"And let it be of duffil gray,
  As warm a cloak as man can sell!"
Proud creature was she the next day,
  The little orphan, Alice Fell!
                    William Wordsworth

BETH GELERT

The spearman heard the bugle sound,
  And cheer'ly smiled the morn;
And many a brach, and many a hound,
  Attend Llewellyn's horn.

And still he blew a louder blast,
  And gave a louder cheer;
"Come, Gelert, why art thou the last
  Llewellyn's horn to hear?

"Oh, where does faithful Gelert roam,
  The flower of all his race.

So true, so brave—a lamb at home,
  A lion in the chase."

That day Llewellyn little loved
  The chase of hart or hare,
And scant and small the booty proved,
  For Gelert was not there.

Unpleased, Llewellyn homeward hied,
  When, near the portal seat,
His truant Gelert he espied,
  Bounding his lord to greet.

But when he gained the castle door,
  Aghast the chieftain stood;
The hound was smeared with gouts of
    gore,
  His lips and fangs ran blood!

Llewellyn gazed with wild surprise:
  Unused such looks to meet,
His favorite checked his joyful guise,
  And crouched, and licked his feet.

Onward in haste Llewellyn passed
  (And on went Gelert, too),
And still where'er his eyes were cast,
  Flesh blood-gouts shocked his view!

O'erturned his infant's bed he found,
  The bloodstained cover rent;
And all around the walls and ground
  With recent blood besprent.

He called his child—no voice replied;
  He searched with terror wild;
Blood! blood! he found on every side,
  But nowhere found his child!

"Hell-hound! by thee my child's de-
    voured!"
  The frantic father cried;
And to the hilt his vengeful sword
  He plunged in Gelert's side.

His suppliant, as to earth he fell,
  No pity could impart;
But still his Gelert's dying yell,
  Passed heavy o'er his heart.

Aroused by Gelert's dying yell,
  Some slumberer wakened nigh;
What words the parent's joy can tell,
  To hear his infant cry!

Concealed beneath a mangled heap,
  His hurried search had missed,
All glowing from his rosy sleep,
  His cherub-boy he kissed!

Nor scratch had he, nor harm, nor
    dread,
  But the same couch beneath
Lay a great wolf, all torn and dead,
  Tremendous still in death!

Ah! what was then Llewellyn's pain!
  For now the truth was clear:
The gallant hound the wolf had slain,
  To save Llewellyn's heir.

Vain, vain was all Llewellyn's woe;
  "Best of any kind, adieu!
The frantic deed which laid thee low
  This heart shall ever rue!"

And now a gallant tomb they raised,
  With costly sculpture decked;
And marbles storied with his praise
  Poor Gelert's bones protect.

Here never could the spearman pass,
  Or forester, unmoved,
Here oft the tear-besprinkled grass
  Llewellyn's sorrow proved.

And here he hung his horn and spear,
  And oft, as evening fell,
In fancy's piercing sounds would hear
  Poor Gelert's dying yell.
           William Robert Spencer

THE BAILIFF'S DAUGHTER OF ISLINGTON

There was a youth, a well-beloved youth,
  And he was a squire's son,
He loved the bayliffe's daughter dear,
  That lived in Islington.

Yet she was coy and would not believe
  That he did love her so,
No nor at any time would she
  Any countenance to him show.

But when his friends did understand
  His fond and foolish mind,
They sent him up to faire London
  An apprentice for to bind.

And when he had been seven long years,
  And never his love could see:
Many a tear have I shed for her sake,
  When she little thought of me.

Then all the maids of Islington
  Went forth to sport and play,
All but the bayliffe's daughter dear;
  She secretly stole away.

She pulled off her gown of green,
  And put on ragged attire,
And to faire London she would go
  Her true love to enquire.

And as she went along the high road,
  The weather being hot and dry,
She sat her down upon a green bank,
  And her true love came riding bye.

She started up, with a color so redd,
  Catching hold of his bridle-reine;
One penny, one penny, kind sir, she said,
  Will ease me of much pain.

Before I give you one penny, sweet-
    heart,
  Pray tell me where you were born.
At Islington, kind sir, said she,
  Where I have had many a scorn.

I prythe, sweetheart, then tell to n1
  O tell me, whether you know,
The bayliffe's daughter of Islington.
  She is dead, sir, long ago.

If she be dead, then take my horse,
  My saddle and bridle also;
For I will unto some far country,
  Where no man shall me know.

O stay, O stay, thou goodly youth,
  She standeth by thy side;
She is here alive, she is not dead,
  And ready to be thy bride.

O farewell grief, and welcome joy,
  Ten thousand times therefore;
For now I have found mine own true
    love,
  Whom I thought I should never see
    more.

Unknown

CAPTAIN REECE

Of all the ships upon the blue
No ship contained a better crew
Than that of worthy CAPTAIN REECE,
Commanding of *The Mantelpiece*.

He was adored by all his men,
For worthy CAPTAIN REECE, R. N.,
Did all that lay within him to
Promote the comfort of his crew.

If ever they were dull or sad
Their captain danced to them like
    mad,

Or told to make the time pass by
Droll legends of his infancy.

A feather bed had every man,
Warm slippers and hot-water can,
Brown windsor from the captain's
   store,
A valet, too, to every four.

Did they with thirst in summer burn
Lo! seltzogenes at every turn,
And all on very sultry days
Cream ices handed round on trays.

Then currant wine and ginger pops
Stood handily on all the "tops";
And also, with amusement rife,
A "Zoetrope, or Wheel of Life."

New volumes came across the sea,
From MISTER MUDIE's libraree;
The Times and *Saturday Review*
Beguiled the leisure of the crew.

Kind-hearted CAPTAIN REECE, R. N.,
Was quite devoted to his men;
In point of fact, good CAPTAIN REECE
Beatified *The Mantelpiece.*

One summer eve at half-past ten,
He said (addressing all his men):
"Come tell me, please, what I can do
To please and gratify my crew.

"By any reasonable plan
I'll make you happy if I can;
My own convenience count as *nil:*
It is my duty and I will."

Then up and answered WILLIAM LEE,
The kindly captain's coxswain he,
A nervous, shy, close-spoken man,
He cleared his throat and thus began:

"You have a daughter, CAPTAIN
   REECE,
Ten female cousins and a niece,
A ma, if what I'm told is true,
Six sisters, and an aunt or two.

"Now somehow, sir, it seems to me,
More friendly like we all should be,
If you united of 'em to
Unmarried members of the crew.

"If you'd ameliorate our life,
Let each select from them a wife;
And as for nervous me, old pal,
Give me your own enchanting gal!"

Good CAPTAIN REECE, that worthy
   man,
Debated on his coxswain's plan:
"I quite agree," he said. "Oh! Bill;
It is my duty, and I will.

"My daughter, that enchanting gurl,
Has just been promised to an earl,
And all my other familee
To peers of various degree.

"But what are dukes and viscounts to
The happiness of all my crew!
The word I gave you I'll fulfil;
It is my duty, and I will.

"As you desire it shall befall,
I'll settle thousands on you all,
And I shall be despite my hoard,
The only bachelor on board."

The boatswain of *The Mantelpiece,*
He blushed and spoke to CAPTAIN
   REECE:
"I beg your honour's leave," he said,
"If you should wish to go and wed,

"I have a widowed mother who
Would be the very thing for you—
She long has loved you from afar:
She washes for you, CAPTAIN R."

The Captain saw the dame that day—
Addressed her in his playful way:
"And did it want a wedding ring?
It was a tempting ickle sing!

"Well, well, the chaplain I will seek,
We'll all be married this day week,
At yonder church upon the hill;
It is my duty, and I will!"

The sisters, cousins, aunts, and niece,
And widowed ma of CAPTAIN REECE,
Attended there as they were bid;
It was their duty, and they did.

William Schwenck Gilbert

SIR PATRICK SPENS

The king sits in Dunfermline town,
  Drinking the blood-red wine:
"O where will I get a skeely skipper
  To sail this new ship of mine?"

O up and spake an eldern knight,
  Sate at the king's right knee—
"Sir Patrick Spens is the best sailor
  That ever sailed the sea."

Our king has written a broad letter,
  And sealed it with his hand,
And sent it to Sir Patrick Spens
  Was walking on the strand.

To Noroway, to Noroway
  To Noroway o'er the faem
The king's daughter of Noroway,
  'Tis thou must bring her hame.

The first word that Sir Patrick read,
  So loud, loud laughed he;
The next word that Sir Patrick read,
  The tear blinded his ee.

"O who is this has done this deed,
  And told the king o' me,
To send us out, at this time of the year,
  To sail upon the sea?

"Be it wind, be it weet, be it hail, be
    it sleet,
  Our ship must sail the faem;
The king's daughter of Noroway,
  'Tis we must fetch her hame."

They hoysed their sails on Monenday
    morn,
  With all the speed they may;
And they have landed in Noroway,
  Upon a Wodensday.

They had not been a week, a week,
  In Noroway but twae,
When that the lords of Noroway
  Began aloud to say:

"Ye Scottishmen spend all our king's
    goud,
  And a' our queenis fee."
"Ye lie, ye lie, ye liars loud!
  Full loud I hear ye lie!

"For I hae brought as much white
    money
  As gane my men and me—
And I hae brought a half fou o' good
    red goud
  Out o'er the sea with me.

"Make ready, make ready, my merry
    men all!
  Our good ship sails the morn."
"Now ever alack, my master dear,
  I fear a deadly storm!

"I saw the new moon, late yestreen,
  With the auld moon in her arm;
And if we gang to sea, master,
  I fear we'll come to harm."

They had not sailed a league, a league,
  A league but barely three,
When the lift grew dark, and the wind
    blew loud,
  And gurly grew the sea.

The anchors broke and the topmasts
    lap,
  It was such a deadly storm;
And the waves came o'er the broken
    ship
  Till all her sides were torn.

" O where will I get a good sailor,
  To take my helm in hand,
Till I get up to the tall topmast;
  To see if I can spy land? "

" O here am I, a sailor good,
  To take the helm in hand,
Till ye get up to the tall topmast:
  But I fear ye'll ne'er spy land."

He hadna gane a step, a step,
  A step but barely ane,
When a bolt flew out of our goodly
    ship,
  And the salt sea it came in.

" Go, fetch a web o' the silken cloth,
  Another o' the twine,
And wrap them into our ship's side,
  And let not the sea come in."

They fetched a web o' the silken cloth,
  Another o' the twine,
And they wrapped them round that
    good ship's side,
  But still the sea came in.

O loth, loth, were our good Scotch
    lords
  To wet their cor-heeled shoon!
But lang ere a' the play was play'd
  They wet their hats aboon.

And many was the featherbed
  That floated on the faem,
And many was the good lord's son
  That never more came hame.

The ladies wrang their fingers white—
  The maidens tore their hair,
All for the sake of their true loves—
  For them they'll see no mair.

O long, long may the ladies sit,
  With their fans into their hand,
Before they see Sir Patrick Spens
  Come sailing to the strand!

And long, long may the maidens sit,
  Wi' the goud combs in their hair,
All waiting for their own dear loves—
  For them they'll see no mair.

O forty miles off Aberdeen,
  'Tis fifty fathoms deep,
And there lies good Sir Patrick Spens,
  With the Scotch lords at his feet.

             Unknown

SKIPPER IRESON'S RIDE

Of all the rides since the birth of time,
Told in story or sung in rhyme,—
On Apuleius's Golden Ass,
Or one-eyed Calender's horse of brass,
Witch astride of a human back,
Islam's prophet on Al-Borák,—
The strangest ride that ever was sped
Was Ireson's out from Marblehead!

Body of turkey, head of fowl,
Wings a-droop like a rained-on fowl,
Feathered and ruffled in every part,
Skipper Ireson stood in the cart,
Scores of women, old and young,
Strong of muscle, and glib of tongue,
Pushed and pulled up the rocky lane,

Shouting and singing the shrill refrain:
"Here's Flud Oirson, fur his horrd
   horrt,
  Torr'd an' futherr' an' corr'd in
   a corrt
   By the women o' Morble'ead!"

Wrinkled scolds with hands on hips,
Girls in bloom of cheek and lips,
Wild-eyed, free-limbed, such as chase
Bacchus round some antique vase,
Brief of skirt, with ankles bare,
Loose of kerchief and loose of hair,
With conch-shells blowing and fish-
   horns' twang,
Over and over the Mænads sang:
  "Here's Flud Oirson, fur his horrd
   horrt,
  Torr'd an' futherr'd an' corr'd in a
   corrt
   By the women o' Morble'ead!"

Small pity for him!—He sailed away
From a leaking ship in Chaleur Bay,—
Sailed away from a sinking wreck,
With his own town's-people on her
   deck!
"Lay by! lay by!" they called to him.
Back he answered, "Sink or swim!
Brag of your catch of fish again!
And off he sailed through the fog and
   rain!
  Old Floyd Ireson, for his hard heart,
  Tarred and feathered and carried in
   a cart
   By the women o' Marblehead!

Fathoms deep in dark Chaleur
That wreck shall lie forevermore.
Mother and sister, wife and maid,
Looked from the rocks of Marblehead
Over the moaning and rainy sea,—
Looked for the coming that might not
   be!

What did the winds and the sea-birds
   say
Of the cruel captain who sailed away?—
  Old Floyd Ireson, for his hard heart,
  Tarred and feathered and carried in
   a cart
   By the women o' Marblehead!

Through the street, on either side,
Up flew windows, doors swung wide;
Sharp-tongued spinsters, old wives gray,
Treble lent the fish-horn's bray.
Sea-worn grandsires, cripple-bound,
Hulks of old sailors run aground,
Shook head, and fist, and hat, and
   cane,
And cracked with curses the hoarse
   refrain:
  "Here's Flud Oirson, fur his horrd
   horrt,
  Torr'd an' futherr'd an' corr'd in
   a corrt
   By the women o' Morble'ead!"

Sweetly along the Salem road
Bloom of orchard and lilac showed.
Little the wicked skipper knew
Of the fields so green and the sky so
   blue.
Riding there in his sorry trim,
Like an Indian idol glum and grim,
Scarcely he seemed the sound to hear
Of voices shouting, far and near:
  "Here's Flud Oirson, fur his horrd
   horrt,
  Torr'd an' futherr'd an' corr'd in a
   corrt
   By the women o' Morble'ead!"

"Hear me, neighbors!" at last he
   cried,—
"What to me is this noisy ride?
What is the shame that clothes the
   skin

To the nameless horror that lives
within?
Waking or sleeping, I see a wreck,
And hear a cry from a reeling deck!
Hate me and curse me,—I only dread
The hand of God and the face of the
dead! "
Said old Floyd Ireson, for his hard
heart,
Tarred and feathered and carried in
a cart
By the women of Marblehead!

Then the wife of the skipper lost at sea
Said, " God has touched him! why
should we! "
Said an old wife mourning her only
son,
" Cut the rogue's tether and let him
run! "
So with soft relentings and rude excuse,
Half scorn, half pity, they cut him
loose,
And gave him a cloak to hide him in,
And left him alone with his shame and
sin,
Poor Floyd Ireson, for his hard heart,
Tarred and feathered and carried in
a cart
By the women of Marblehead!
John Greenleaf Whittier

ROBIN HOOD AND
LITTLE JOHN

When Robin Hood was about twenty
years old,
He happened to meet Little John,
A jolly, brisk blade, right fit for the
trade,
For he was a lusty young man.

Though he was called Little, his limbs
they were large,
And his stature was seven foot high;

Wherever he came, they quaked at his
name,
For soon he would make them fly.

How they came acquainted, I'll tell you
in brief,
If you would but listen awhile;
For this very jest, among all the rest,
I think it may cause you to smile.

They happened to meet on a long,
narrow bridge,
And neither of them would give
way;
Quoth bold Robin Hood, and sturdily
stood,
" I'll show you right Nottingham
play."

" Thou talkest like a coward," the
stranger replied;
" Well armed with a long bow you
stand,
To shoot at my breast, while I, I
protest,
Have naught but a staff in my hand."

" The name of a coward," quoth
Robin, " I scorn,
Wherefore my long bow I'll lay by,
And now, for thy sake, a staff I will
take,
The truth of thy manhood to try."

Then Robin stept to a thicket of trees,
And chose him a staff of ground oak;
Now this being done, away he did run
To the stranger, and merrily spoke:

" Lo! see my staff is lusty and tough,
Now here on the bridge we will play;
Whoever falls in, the other shall win
The battle, and so we'll away."

"With all my whole heart," the
stranger replied,
"I scorn in the least to give out";
This said, they fell to't without more
dispute,
And their staffs they did flourish
about.

At first Robin he gave the stranger a
bang,
So hard that he made his bones ring:
The stranger he said, "This must be
repaid,
I'll give you as good as you bring.

"So long as I'm able to handle a staff,
To die in your debt, friend, I scorn."
Then to it each goes, and followed
their blows,
As though they'd been threshing of
corn.

The stranger gave Robin a crack on
the crown,
Which caused the blood to appear;
Then Robin, enraged, more fiercely
engaged,
And followed his blows more severe.

O then into fury the stranger he grew,
And gave him a furious look,
And with it a blow, that laid him full
low,
And tumbled him into the brook.

"I prithee, good fellow, where art thou
now?"
The stranger, in laughter, he cried.
Quoth bold Robin Hood, "Good faith,
in the flood,
And floating along with the tide.

"I needs must acknowledge thou art a
brave soul,
With thee I'll no longer contend;

For needs must I say, thou hast got the
day,
Our battle shall be at an end."

Then unto the bank he did presently
wade,
And pulled himself out by a thorn;
Which done, at the last he blew a loud
blast
Straightway on his fine bugle horn:

The echo of which through the valleys
did fly,
At which his stout bowmen appeared,
All clothed in green, most gay to be
seen,
So up to their master they steered.

"O, what is the matter?" quoth William Stutly,
"Good master, you are wet to the
skin."
"No matter," quoth he, "the lad
which you see
In fighting hath tumbled me in."

"He shall not go scot free," the others
replied.
So straightway they were seizing him
there,
To duck him likewise; but Robin Hood
cries,
"He is a stout fellow; forbear.

"There's no one shall wrong thee,
friend, be not afraid;
These bowmen upon me do wait;
There's three score and nine; if thou
wilt be mine,
Thou shalt have my livery straight,

"And other accouterments fit for a
man;

Speak up, jolly blade, never fear:
I'll teach you also the use of the bow,
  To shoot at the fat fallow deer."

"O, here is my hand," the stranger
  replied,
  "I'll serve you with all my whole
  heart;
My name is John Little, a man of
  good mettle;
  Ne'er doubt me, for I'll play my
  part."

"His name shall be altered," quoth
  William Stutly,
  "And I will his godfather be:
Prepare, then, a feast, and none of the
  least,
  For we will be merry," quoth he.

He was, I must tell you, but seven
  foot high,
  And may be, an ell in the waist;
A sweet pretty lad: much feasting they
  had;
  Bold Robin the christening graced,

With all his bowmen, which stood in
  a ring,
  And were of the Nottingham breed;
Brave Stutly came then, with seven
  yeomen,
  And did in this manner proceed:

"This infant was called John Little,"
  quoth he;
  "Which name shall be changed
  anon:
The words we'll transpose; so wherever
  he goes,
  His name shall be called Little
  John."

Then music and dancing did finish the
  day;

At length, when the sun waxed low,
Then all the whole train the grove did
  refrain,
  And unto their caves they did go.

And so, ever after, as long as he lived,
  Although he was proper and tall,
Yet, nevertheless, the truth to express,
  Still Little John they did him call.

Unknown

ROBIN HOOD

No, those days are gone away,
And their hours are old and gray,
And their minutes buried all
Under the downtrodden pall
Of the leaves of many years;
Many times have Winter's shears,
Frozen North, and chilling East,
Sounded tempests to the feast
Of the forest's whispering fleeces
Since men knew nor rents nor leases.

No! the bugle sounds no more,
And the twanging bow no more;
Silent is the ivory shrill,
Past the heath and up the hill;
There is no mid-forest laugh,
Whose lone echo gives the half
To some wight amazed to hear
Jesting, deep in forest drear.

On the fairest time of June
You may go, with sun or moon,
Or the seven stars to light you,
Or the polar ray to right you;
But you never may behold
Little John, or Robin bold—
Never one, of all the clan,
Thrumming on an empty can
Some old hunting ditty, while
He doth his green way beguile
To fair hostess Merriment

Down beside the pasture Trent;
For he left the merry tale,
Messenger for spicy ale.

Gone the merry morris din;
Gone the song of Gamelyn;
Gone the tough-belted outlaw
Idling in the " greené shawe "—
All are gone away and past;
And if Robin should be cast
Sudden from his tufted grave,
And if Marian should have
Once again her forest days,
She would weep, and he would craze;
He would swear, for all his oaks,
Fallen beneath the dock-yard strokes,
Have rotted on the briny seas;
She would weep that her wild bees
Sang not to her—Strange! that honey
Can't be got without hard money!

So it is! yet let us sing
Honor to the old bow-string!
Honor to the bugle-horn!
Honor to the woods unshorn!
Honor to the Lincoln green!
Honor to the archer keen!
Honor to tight Little John,
And the horse he rode upon!
Honor to bold Robin Hood,
Sleeping in the underwood!
Honor to Maid Marian
And to all the Sherwood clan!
Though their days have hurried by,
Let us two a burden try!

John Keats

SONG OF SHERWOOD

Sherwood in the twilight, is Robin
    Hood awake?
Gray and ghostly shadows are gliding
    through the brake,
Shadows of the dappled deer, dreaming
    of the morn,

Dreaming of a shadowy man that
    winds a shadowy horn.

Robin Hood is here again: all his
    merry thieves
Hear a ghostly bugle-note shivering
    through the leaves,
Calling as he used to call, faint and
    far away,
In Sherwood, in Sherwood, about the
    break of day.

Merry, merry England has kissed the
    lips of June:
All the wings of fairyland were here
    beneath the moon,
Like a flight of rose-leaves fluttering in
    a mist
Of opal and ruby and pearl and
    amethyst.

Merry, merry England is waking as of
    old,
With eyes of blither hazel and hair of
    brighter gold:
For Robin Hood is here again beneath
    the bursting spray
In Sherwood, in Sherwood, about the
    break of day.

Love is in the greenwood building him
    a house
Of wild rose and hawthorn and honey-
    suckle boughs;
Love is in the greenwood: dawn is in
    the skies;
And Marian is waiting with a glory in
    her eyes.

Hark! The dazzled laverock climbs the
    golden steep!
Marian is waiting: is Robin Hood
    asleep?
Round the fairy grass-rings frolic elf
    and fay,

In Sherwood, in Sherwood, about the
    break of day.

Oberon, Oberon, rake away the gold,
Rake away the red leaves, roll away
    the mould,
Rake away the gold leaves, roll away
    the red,
And wake Will Scarlett from his leafy
    forest bed.

Friar Tuck and Little John are riding
    down together
With quarter staff and drinking can
    and gray goose-feather.
The dead are coming back again; the
    years are rolled away
In Sherwood, in Sherwood, about the
    break of day.

Softly over Sherwood the south wind
    blows.
All the heart of England hid in every
    rose
Hears across the greenwood the sunny
    whisper leap,
Sherwood in the red dawn, is Robin
    Hood asleep?

Hark, the voice of England wakes him
    as of old
And, shattering the silence with a cry
    of brighter gold,
Bugles in the greenwood echo from
    the steep,
*Sherwood in the red dawn, is Robin
    Hood asleep?*

Where the deer are gliding down the
    shadowy glen
All across the glades of fern he calls
    his merry men—
Doublets of the Lincoln green glanc-
    ing through the May

In Sherwood, in Sherwood, about the
    break of day—

Calls them and they answer: from
    aisles of oak and ash
Ring the *Follow! Follow!* and the
    boughs begin to crash;
The ferns begin to flutter and the
    flowers begin to fly;
And through the crimson dawning the
    robber band goes by.

Robin! Robin! Robin! All his merry
    thieves
Answer as the bugle-note shivers
    through the leaves;
Calling as he used to call, faint and
    far away,
In Sherwood, in Sherwood, about the
    break of day.

Alfred Noyes

THE DEATH OF ROBIN HOOD

There hangs the long bow, the strong
    bow, once was bent
To cleave the clout, to split the willow
    wand;
Till the quiver's shafts were spent
The bow that wrought wild justice in
    this land.
The red deer, the roe deer knew that
    bow,
And king and clergy knew
How sure its clothyards flew
To right the poor and lay oppression
    low.

There grows our great oak, our girthed
    oak; over all
The shires of England may it branch
    and be
As once in Sherwood, tall
As truth, and honor's ever-living tree!

The hunted and the hounded knew its
  ground
For refuge, knew who stood
A stiff yew hedge in the wood
Around its bole, when that the horn
  was wound.

Merry men all, God spare you to the
  hunt;
Through time it stretches, down the
  centuries.
Outlawed, we bore the brunt
Of the hour's disfavor, and its penal-
  ties;
Freemen, forever we with free men ride
Whenever, by God in Heaven,
They gather to make odds even!
Our souls with them they shall not
  fail that tide.

Now lift me; I would see my forest
  walls
Badged with our colours, yea, till Time
  be done.
Where this last arrow falls
Sod me with turf the stag treads
  lightly on.
Go soft then, saying naught; but, hark
  ye! kneel
When the evil hour would awe—
Kneel and bend now and draw
And loose your shafts in a whistling
  sleet of steel!

William Rose Benét

JOHNNY APPLESEED

(1775–1847)

Of Jonathan Chapman
Two things are known
That he loved apples,
That he walked alone.

At seventy-odd
He was gnarled as could be,

But ruddy and sound
As a good apple tree.

For fifty years over
Of harvest and dew,
He planted his apples
Where no apples grew.

The winds of the prairie
Might blow through his rags,
But he carried his seeds
In the best deerskin bags.

From old Ashtabula
To frontier Fort Wayne,
He planted and pruned
And he planted again.

He had not a hat
To encumber his head.
He wore a tin pan
On his white hair instead.

He nested with owl,
And with bear cub and 'possum,
And knew all his orchards
Root, tendril, and blossom.

A fine old man,
As ripe as a pippin,
His heart still light,
And his step still skipping.

The stalking Indian,
The beast in its lair
Did no hurt
While he was there.

For they could tell,
As wild things can,
That Jonathan Chapman
Was God's own man.

Why did he do it?
We do not know.

He wishes that apples
Might root and grow.

He has no statue.
He has no tomb.
He has his apple trees
Still in bloom.

Consider, consider,
Think well upon
The marvelous story
Of Appleseed John.

Stephen Vincent Benét
and
Rosemary Carr Benét

ALLEN-A-DALE

Allen-a-Dale has no fagot for burning,
Allen-a-Dale has no furrow for turning,
Allen-a-Dale has no fleece for the
spinning,
Yet Allen-a-Dale has red gold for the
winning.
Come, read me my riddle! come,
hearken my tale!
And tell me the craft of bold Allen-a-
Dale.

The Baron of Ravensworth prances in
pride,
And he views his domains upon Arkin-
dale side,
The mere for his net, and the land for
his game,
The chase for the wild, and the park
for the tame;
Yet the fish of the lake, and the deer
of the vale,
Are less free to Lord Dacre than Allen-
a-Dale!

Allen-a-Dale was ne'er belted a knight,
Though his spur be as sharp, and his
blade be as bright:

Allen-a-Dale is no baron or lord,
Yet twenty tall yeomen will draw at
his word;
And the best of our nobles his bonnet
will vail
Who at Rere-cross on Stanmore meets
Allen-a-Dale!

Allen-a-Dale to his wooing is come;
The mother, she asked of his house-
hold and home:
"Though the castle of Richmond
stand fair on the hill,
My hall," quoth bold Allen, "shows
gallanter still;
'Tis the blue vault of heaven, with its
crescent so pale,
And with all its bright spangles!" said
Allen-a-Dale.

The father was steel, and the mother
was stone;
They lifted the latch, and they bade
him be gone;
But loud, on the morrow, their wail
and their cry:
He had laughed on the lass with his
bonny black eye,
And she fled to the forest to hear a
love tale,
And the youth it was told by was
Allen-a-Dale!

Sir Walter Scott

THE MOUNTAIN AND THE SQUIRREL

The mountain and the squirrel
Had a quarrel,
And the former called the latter "Lit-
tle prig;"
Bun replied,
"You are doubtless very big;
But all sorts of things and weather

Must be taken in together
To make up a year,
And a sphere.
And I think it no disgrace
To occupy my place.
If I'm not so large as you,
You are not so small as I,
And not half so spry:
I'll not deny you make
A very pretty squirrel track.
Talents differ; all is well and wisely put;
If I cannot carry forests on my back,
Neither can you crack a nut."

Ralph Waldo Emerson

THE DOG OF REFLECTION

A dog growing thinner, for want of a
dinner,
Once purloin'd a joint from a tray;
" How happy I am, with this shoulder
of lamb! "
Thought the cur, as he trotted away.

But the way that he took, lay just over
a brook,
Which he found it was needful to
cross,
So, without more ado, he plunged in to
go through,
Not dreaming of danger or loss.

But what should appear, in this rivulet
clear,
As he thought upon coolest reflec-
tion,
But a cur like himself, who with ill-
gotten pelf,
Had run off in that very direction.

Thought the dog, à propos! but that
instant let go
(As he snatched at this same water-
spaniel),

The piece he possess'd—so, with hunger distress'd,
He slowly walk'd home to his kennel.

Hence, when we are needy, don't let
us be greedy
(Excuse me this line of digression),
Lest in snatching at all, like the dog,
we let fall
The good that we have in possession.

Jeffreys Taylor

THE GOURD AND THE PALM

" How old art thou? " said the garru-
lous gourd,
As o'er the palm-tree's crest it poured
Its spreading leaves and tendrils fine,
And hung a bloom in the morning
shine.
" A hundred years! " the palm-tree
sighed:
" And I," the saucy gourd replied,
" Am at the most a hundred hours,
And overtop thee in the bowers! "

Through all the palm-tree's leaves
there went
A tremor as of self-content.
" I live my life," it whispering said,
" See what I see, and count the dead;
And every year, of all I've known,
A gourd above my head I've grown,
And made a boast, like thine today;
Yet here I stand—but where are *they?*"

Unknown

THE NIGHTINGALE AND GLOW-WORM

A nightingale, that all day long
Had cheered the village with his song,
Nor yet at eve his note suspended,

Nor yet when eventide was ended,
Began to feel, as well he might,
The keen demands of appetite;
When, looking eagerly around,
He spied far off, upon the ground,
A something shining in the dark,
And knew the glow-worm by his spark;
So, stooping down from hawthorn top,
He thought to put him in his crop.
The worm, aware of his intent,
Harangued him thus, right eloquent—
"Did you admire my lamp," quoth he,
" As much as I your minstrelsy,
You would abhor to do me wrong,
As much as I to spoil your song;
For 'twas the self-same power divine,
Taught you to sing, and me to shine;
That you with music, I with light,
Might beautify and cheer the night."
The songster heard his short oration,
And warbling out his approbation,
Released him, as my story tells,
And found a supper somewhere else.

William Cowper

THE LION AND THE MOUSE

A lion with the heat oppress'd,
One day composed himself to rest;
But whilst he dozed, as he intended,
A mouse his royal back ascended;
Nor thought of harm, as Æsop tells,
Mistaking him for some one else;
And travell'd over him, and round him,
And might have left him as he found
  him
Had he not—tremble when you hear—
Tried to explore the monarch's ear!
Who straightway woke, with wrath
  immense,
And shook his head to cast him thence.
" You rascal, what are you about? "
Said he, when he had turned him out.
" I'll teach you soon," the lion said,

" To make a mouse-hole in my head! "
So saying, he prepared his foot
To crush the trembling tiny brute;
But he (the mouse) with tearful eye,
Implored the lion's clemency,
Who thought it best at last to give
His little pris'ner a reprieve.

'Twas nearly twelve months after this,
The lion chanced his way to miss;
When pressing forward, heedless yet,
He got entangled in a net.
With dreadful rage, he stampt and
  tore,
And straight commenced a lordly roar;
When the poor mouse, who heard the
  noise,
Attended, for she knew his voice.
Then what the lion's utmost strength
Could not effect, she did at length;
With patient labor she applied
Her teeth, the network to divide;
And so at last forth issued he,
A *lion*, by a mouse set free.

Few are so small or weak, I guess,
But may assist us in distress,
Nor shall we ever, if we're wise,
The meanest, or the least despise.

Jeffreys Taylor

THE BLIND MEN AND THE ELEPHANT

It was six men of Indostan
  To learning much inclined,
Who went to see the Elephant
  (Though all of them were blind),
That each by observation
  Might satisfy his mind.

The *First* approached the Elephant,
  And happening to fall
Against his broad and sturdy side,
  At once began to bawl:

" God bless me! but the Elephant
Is very like a wall! "

The *Second*, feeling of the tusk,
Cried, " Ho! what have we here
So very round and smooth and sharp?
To me 'tis mighty clear
This wonder of an Elephant
Is very like a spear! "

The *Third* approached the animal,
And happening to take
The squirming trunk within his hands,
Thus boldly up and spake:
" I see," quoth he, " the Elephant
Is very like a snake! "

The *Fourth* reached out an eager hand,
And felt about the knee.
" What most this wondrous beast is
like
Is mighty plain," quoth he;
" 'Tis clear enough the Elephant
Is very like a tree! "

The *Fifth* who chanced to touch the
ear,
Said: " E'en the blindest man
Can tell what this resembles most;
Deny the fact who can,
This marvel of an Elephant
Is very like a fan! "

The *Sixth* no sooner had begun
About the beast to grope,
Than, seizing on the swinging tail
That fell within his scope,
" I see," quoth he, " the Elephant
Is very like a rope! "

And so these men of Indostan
Disputed loud and long,
Each in his own opinion
Exceeding stiff and strong,

Though each was partly in the right
And all were in the wrong!

MORAL

So oft in theologic wars,
The disputants, I ween,
Rail on in utter ignorance
Of what each other mean,
And *prate about an Elephant*
Not one of them has seen!

John Godfrey Saxe

THE GLOVE AND THE LIONS

King Francis was a hearty king, and
loved a royal sport,
And one day, as his lions fought, sat
looking on the court;
The nobles fill'd the benches, and the
ladies in their pride,
And 'mongst them sat the Count de
Lorge, with one for whom he
sigh'd;
And truly 'twas a gallant thing to see
that crowning show—
Valour and love, and a king above,
and the royal beasts below.

Ramped and roared the lions, with
horrid, laughing jaws;
They bit, they glared, gave blows like
beams, a wind went with their
paws;
With wallowing might and stifled roar
they rolled one on another,
Till all the pit, with sand and mane,
was in a thundrous smother;
The bloody foam above the bars came
whisking through the air;
Said Francis, then, " Faith, gentlemen,
we're better here than there! "

De Lorge's love o'erheard the King, a
beauteous, lively dame,

With smiling lips, and sharp, bright
    eyes, which always seemed the
    same:
She thought, " The Count my lover, is
    as brave as brave can be,
He surely would do wondrous things
    to show his love for me!
King, ladies, lovers, all look on, the
    occasion is divine;
I'll drop my glove to prove his love,
    great glory will be mine! "

She dropped her glove to prove his
    love, then looked at him and
    smiled;
He bowed, and in a moment leaped
    among the lions wild;
The leap was quick; return was quick;
    he has regained his place,
Then threw the glove, but not with
    love, right in the lady's face!
" In truth! " cried Francis, " rightly
    done! " and he rose from where
    he sat;
" No love," quoth he, " but vanity, sets
    love a task like that."

Leigh Hunt

THE BEGGAR MAID

(Selected Stanzas)

Her arms across her breast she laid;
    She was more fair than words can
    say:
Bare-footed came the beggar maid
    Before the king Cophetua.
In robe and crown the king stept
    down,
    To meet and greet her on her way;
" It is no wonder," said the lords,
    " She is more beautiful than day."

As shines the moon in clouded skies,
    She in her poor attire was seen:

One praised her ankles, one her eyes,
    One her dark hair and lonesome
    mien.
So sweet a face, such angel grace,
    In all that land had never been:
Cophetua sware a royal oath:
    " This beggar maid shall be my
    queen! "

Alfred Tennyson

BAUCIS AND PHILEMON

In ancient times, as story tells,
The saints would often leave their
    cells,
And stroll about, but hide their
    quality,
To try good people's hospitality.

    It happened on a winter night,
As authors of the legend write,
Two brother hermits, saints by trade,
Taking their tour in masquerade,
Disguised in tattered garments went
To a small village down in Kent;
Where, in the stroller's canting
    strain,
They begged from door to door in
    vain,
Tried every tone might pity win;
But not a soul would take them in.

    Our wandering saints, in woful
    state,
Treated at this ungodly rate,
Having through all the village
    passed,
To a small cottage came at last
Where dwelt a good old honest yeo-
    man,
Call'd in the neighborhood Phile-
    mon;
Who kindly did these saints invite
In his poor hut to pass the night;

And then the hospitable sire
Bid goody Baucis mend the fire;
While he from out the chimney took
A flitch of bacon off the hook,
And freely from the fattest side
Cut out large slices to be fried;
Then stepped aside to fetch them drink,
Filled a large jug up to the brink,
And saw it fairly twice go round;
Yet (what is wonderful!) they found
'Twas still replenished to the top,
As if they ne'er had touched a drop.
The good old couple were amazed,
And often on each other gazed;
For both were frightened to the heart,
And just began to cry, " What art! "
Then softly turned aside to view
Whether the lights were burning blue.

" Good folks, you need not be afraid,
We are but saints," the hermits said;
" No hurt shall come to you or yours:
But for that pack of churlish boors,
Not fit to live on Christian ground,
They and their houses shall be drowned;
Whilst you shall see your cottage rise,
And grow a church before your eyes."

They scarce had spoke, when fair and soft,
The roof began to mount aloft,
Aloft rose every beam and rafter,
The heavy wall climbed slowly after;
The chimney widened and grew higher,
Became a steeple with a spire.

The kettle to the top was hoist,
And there stood fastened to a joist;
Doomed ever in suspense to dwell,
'Tis now no kettle, but a bell.
A wooden jack which had almost
Lost by disuse the art to roast,
A sudden alteration feels,
Increased by new intestine wheels;
The jack and chimney, near allied,
Had never left each other's side:
The chimney to a steeple grown,
The jack would not be left alone;
But up against the steeple reared,
Became a clock, and still adhered.

The groaning chair began to crawl,
Like a huge snail along the wall;
There stuck aloft in public view,
And with small change a pulpit grew.
The cottage, by such feats as these,
Grown to a church by just degrees,
The hermits then desired the host
To ask for what he fancied most.
Philemon, having paused awhile,
Returned them thanks in homely style:
" I'm old, and fain would live at ease;
Make me the parson, if you please."

Thus happy in their change of life
Were several years this man and wife.
When on a day which proved their last,
Discoursing on old stories past,
They went by chance, amidst their talk,
To the churchyard to take a walk;
When Baucis hastily cried out,
" My dear, I see your forehead sprout! "
" But yes! Methinks I feel it true;
And really yours is budding too.

Nay—now I cannot stir my foot;
It feels as if 'twere taking root!"
Description would but tire my muse;
In short they both were turned to
    yews.

Jonathan Swift

KING JOHN AND THE ABBOT OF CANTERBURY

An ancient story I'll tell you anon
Of a notable prince, that was called
    King John;
And he ruled England with main
    and with might,
For he did great wrong and main-
    tained little right.

And I'll tell you a story, a story so
    merry,
Concerning the Abbot of Canter-
    bury;
How for his housekeeping and high
    renown,
They rode post for him to fair
    London town.

An hundred men, the King did hear
    say,
The Abbot kept in his house every
    day;
And fifty gold chains, without any
    doubt,
In velvet coats waited the Abbot
    about.

"How now, Father Abbot, I hear it
    of thee,
Thou keepest a far better house than
    me;
And for thy housekeeping and high
    renown,
I fear thou work'st treason against
    my crown."

"My liege," quo' the Abbot, "I would
    it were knowne,
I never spend nothing but what is
    my owne;
And I trust your Grace will not put
    me in fear,
For spending of my owne true-got-
    ten gear."

"Yes, yes, Father Abbot, thy fault is
    highe,
And now for the same thou needst
    must dye;
For except thou canst answer me
    questions three,
Thy head shall be smitten from thy
    bodie.

"And first," quo' the King, "when
    I'm in this stead,
With my crowns of gold so faire on
    my head,
Among all my liege-men, so noble of
    birthe,
Thou must tell to one penny what I
    am worthe.

"Secondlye, tell me, without any
    doubt,
How soon I may ride the whole
    world about,
And at the third question thou must
    not shrink,
But tell me here truly what I do
    think."

"Oh, these are hard questions for my
    shallow witt,
Nor can I answer your Grace as yet;
But if you will give me but three
    weeks space,
Ile do my endeavor to answer your
    Grace."

"Now three weeks' space to thee will
   I give,
And that is the longest time thou
   hast to live;
For if thou dost not answer my ques-
   tions three,
Thy land and thy livings are forfeit
   to me."

Away rode the Abbot all sad at that
   word,
And he rode to Cambridge and
   Oxenford;
But never a doctor there was so wise,
That could with his learning an an-
   swer devise.

Then home rode the Abbot of comfort so cold,
And he met his Shepherd a-going to
   fold:
"How now, my Lord Abbot, you are
   welcome home;
What news do you bring us from
   good King John?"

"Sad news, sad news, Shepherd, I
   must give,
That I have but three days more to
   live;
I must answer the King his questions
   three,
Or my head will be smitten from my
   bodie.

"The first is to tell him, there in that
   stead,
With his crown of gold so fair on his
   head,
Among all his liege-men so noble of
   birth
To within one penny of what he is
   worth.

"The seconde, to tell him, without
   any doubt,
How soone he may ride this whole
   world about:
And at the third question I must not
   shrinke,
But tell him truly what he does
   thinke."

"Now cheare up, Sire Abbot, did you
   never hear yet,
That a fool he may learne a wise
   man witt?
Lend me a horse, and serving-men,
   and your apparel,
And I'll ride to London to answere
   your quarrel.

"Nay, frowne not, if it hath bin told
   unto mee,
I am like your Lordship, as ever may
   bee:
And if you will but lend me your
   gowne,
There is none shall know us in fair
   London towne."

"Now horses and serving-men thou
   shalt have,
With sumptuous array most gallant
   and brave;
With crozier, and mitre, and rochet,
   and cope,
Fit to appear 'fore our Father the
   Pope."

"Now welcome, Sire Abbot," the
   King he did say,
"'Tis well thou'rt come back to keepe
   thy day;
For and if thou canst answer my
   questions three,
Thy living and thy life both saved
   shall bee.

" And first, when thou seest me, here
  in this stead,
  With my crown of golde so fair on
  my head,
  Among all my liege-men so noble of
  birthe,
  Tell me to one penny what I am
  worth."

" For thirty pence our Saviour was
  sold
  Among the false Jews, as I have bin
  told:
  And twenty-nine is the worth of
  thee,
  For I thinke, thou art one penny
  worse than he."

The King he laughed, and swore by
  St. Bittel,
" I did not think I had been worth so
  little!
  Now, secondly, tell me, without any
  doubt,
  How soon I may ride this whole
  world about."

" You must rise with the sun, and ride
  with the same,
  Until the next morning he riseth
  again;
  And then your Grace need not make
  any doubt
  But in twenty-four hours you'll ride
  it about."

The King he laughed, and swore by
  St. Jone,
" I did not think it could be done so
  soon.
  Now from the third question thou
  must not shrink,
  But tell me here truly what I do
  think."

" Yea, that I shall do and make your
  Grace merry;
  You think I'm the Abbot of Canter-
  bury;
  But I'm his poor shepherd, as plain
  you may see,
  That am come to beg pardon for
  him and for me."

The King he laughed, and swore by
  the mass,
" I'll make thee Lord Abbot this day
  in his place! "
" Nay, nay, my Liege, be not in such
  speed,
  For alack, I can neither write nor
  read."

" Four nobles a week, then, I will give
  thee,
  For this merry jest thou hast shown
  unto me;
  And tell the old Abbot, when thou
  gettest home,
  Thou hast brought him a pardon
  from good King John."

Unknown

THE ROMANCE OF THE SWAN'S NEST

Little Ellie sits alone
'Mid the beeches of a meadow,
By a stream-side on the grass;
And the trees are showering down
Doubles of their leaves in shadow
On the shining hair and face.

She has thrown her bonnet by;
And her feet she has been dipping
In the shallow waters' flow—
Now she holds them nakedly
In her hands, all sleek and dripping,
While she rocketh to and fro.

Little Ellie sits alone,
And the smile she softly useth
Fills the silence like a speech:
While she thinks what shall be
    done,
And the sweetest pleasure chooseth
For her future, within reach.

Little Ellie in her smile
Chooseth—" I will have a lover
Riding on a steed of steeds!
He shall love me without guile;
And to *him* I will discover
That swan's nest among the reeds.

" And the steed it shall be red-roan,
And the lover shall be noble,
With an eye that takes the breath;
And the lute he plays upon
Shall strike ladies into trouble,
As his sword strikes men to death.

" And the steed it shall be shod
All in silver, housed in azure,
And the mane shall swim the wind,
And the hoofs along the sod
Shall flash onward and keep measure,
Till the shepherds look behind.

" He will kiss me on the mouth
Then, and lead me as a lover
Through the crowds that praise his
    deeds;
And, when soul tied by one troth,
Unto *him* I will discover
That swan's nest among the reeds."

Little Ellie, with her smile
Not yet ended, rose up gaily—
Tied the bonnet, donn'd the shoe,
And went homeward round a mile,
Just to see, as she did daily,
What more eggs were with the two.

Pushing through the elm-tree copse,
Winding by the stream, light·
    hearted,
Where the osier pathway leads—
Past the boughs she stoops and
    stops:
So! the wild swan has deserted,
And a rat had gnaw'd the reeds.

Ellie went home sad and slow.
If she found the lover ever,
With his red-roan steed of steeds,
Sooth I know not! but I know
She could never show him—never—
That swan's nest among the reeds.

            Elizabeth Barrett Browning

EDWIN AND ANGELINA

" Turn, gentle Hermit of the dale,
    And guide my lonely way
To where yon taper cheers the vale
    With hospitable ray.

" For here forlorn and lost I tread,
    With fainting steps and slow,
Where wilds, immeasurably spread,
    Seem lengthening as I go."

—" Forbear, my son," the Hermit cries,
    " To tempt the dangerous gloom,
For yonder faithless phantom flies
    To lure thee to thy doom.

" Here to the houseless child of want
    My door is open still;
And though my portion is but scant
    I give it with goodwill.

" Then turn tonight, and freely share
    Whate'er my cell bestows;
My rushy couch and frugal fare,
    My blessing and repose.

"No flocks that range the valley free
    To slaughter I condemn;
Taught by that Power that pities me,
    I learn to pity them:

"But from the mountain's grassy side
    A guiltless feast I bring:
A scrip with herbs and fruits sup-
        plied,
    And water from the spring.

"Then, pilgrim! turn; thy cares forego;
    All earth-born cares are wrong:
Man wants but little here below,
    Nor wants that little long."

Soft as the dew from heaven de-
        scends
    His gentle accents fell:
The modest stranger lowly bends,
    And follows to the cell.

Far in the wilderness obscure
    The lonely mansion lay,
A refuge to the neighboring poor,
    And strangers led astray.

No stores beneath its humble thatch
    Required a master's care,
The wicket, opening with a latch,
    Received the harmless pair.

And now, when busy crowds retire
    To take their evening rest,
The hermit trimm'd his little fire,
    And cheer'd his pensive guest:

And spread his vegetable store,
    And gaily press'd and smiled:
And skill'd in legendary lore,
    The lingering hours beguiled.

Around, in sympathetic mirth,
    Its tricks the kitten tries;

The cricket chirrups on the hearth,
    The crackling fagot flies.

But nothing could a charm impart
    To soothe the stranger's woe;
For grief was heavy at his heart,
    And tears began to flow.

His rising cares the Hermit spied,
    With answering care oppress'd:
And "Whence, unhappy youth," he
        cried,
    "The sorrows of thy breast?

"From better habitations spurn'd
    Reluctant dost thou rove?
Or grieve for friendship unreturn'd,
    Or unregarded love?

"Alas! the joys that fortune brings
    Are trifling, and decay;
And those who prize the paltry
        things,
    More trifling still than they.

"And what is friendship but a name,
    A charm that lulls to sleep;
A shade that follows wealth or fame,
    But leaves the wretch to weep?

"And love is still an emptier sound,
    The modern fair-one's jest;
On earth unseen, or only found
    To warm the turtle's nest.

"For shame, fond youth! thy sorrows
        hush;
    And spurn the sex," he said;
But while he spoke, a rising blush
    His love-lorn guest betray'd!

Surprised he sees new beauties rise,
    Swift mantling to the view;
Like colors o'er the morning skies,
    As bright, as transient too.

The bashful look, the rising breast,
　Alternate spread alarms:
The lovely stranger stands confess'd,
　A maid in all her charms.

And " Ah! forgive a stranger rude,—
　A wretch forlorn," she cried;
" Whose feet, unhallow'd, thus intrude
　Where Heaven and you reside!

" But let a maid thy pity share,
　Whom love has taught to stray;
Who seeks for rest, but finds despair
　Companion of her way.

" My father lived beside the Tyne,
　A wealthy lord was he;
And all his wealth was mark'd as mine,
　He had but only me.

" To win me from his tender arms
　Unnumber'd suitors came,
Who praised me for imputed charms,
　And felt or feign'd a flame.

" Each hour a mercenary crowd
　With richest proffers strove:
Amongst the rest, young Edwin bow'd,
　But never talk'd of love.

" In humble, simple habit clad,
　No wealth, nor power had he:
Wisdom and worth were all he had,
　But these were all to me.

" And when, beside me in the dale,
　He caroll'd lays of love,
His breath lent fragrance to the gale,
　And music to the grove.

" The blossom opening to the day,
　The dews of heaven refined,

Could nought of purity display
　To emulate his mind.

" The dew, the blossom on the tree,
　With charms inconstant shine:
Their charms were his; but, woe to me!
　Their constancy was mine.

" For still I tried each fickle art,
　Importunate and vain;
And, while his passion touch'd my heart,
　I triumph'd in his pain:

" Till, quite dejected with my scorn,
　He left me to my pride;
And sought a solitude forlorn,
　In secret, where he died.

" But mine the sorrow, mine the fault!
　And well my life shall pay;
I'll seek the solitude he sought,
　And stretch me where he lay.

" And there, forlorn, despairing, hid,
　I'll lay me down and die;
'Twas so for me that Edwin did,
　And so for him will I."

—" Forbid it, Heaven! " the Hermit cried,
　And clasp'd her to his breast:
The wondering fair one turn'd to chide—
　'Twas Edwin's self that press'd!

" Turn, Angelina, ever dear,
　My charmer, turn to see
Thy own, thy long-lost Edwin here,
　Restored to love and thee.

" Thus let me hold thee to my heart,
　And every care resign:

And shall we never, never part,
  My life—my all that's mine?

" No, never from this hour to part,
  We'll live and love so true:
The sigh that rends thy constant
    heart
  Shall break thy Edwin's too."

                Oliver Goldsmith

THE SINGING LEAVES

I

" What fairings will ye that I bring? "
  Said the King to his daughters
    three;
" For I to Vanity Fair am bound,
  Now say what shall they be? "

Then up and spake the eldest daugh-
    ter,
  That lady tall and grand:
" Oh, bring me pearls and diamonds
    great,
  And gold rings for my hand."

Thereafter spake the second daugh-
    ter,
  That was both white and red:
" For me bring silks that will stand
    alone,
  And a gold comb for my head."

Then came the turn of the least
    daughter,
  That was whiter than thistle-down,
And among the gold of her blithe-
    some hair
  Dim shone the golden crown.

" There came a bird this morning,
  And sang 'neath my bower eaves,
Till I dreamed, as his music made
    me,

' Ask thou for the Singing
  Leaves.' "

Then the brow of the King swelled
    crimson
  With a flush of angry scorn:
" Well have ye spoken, my two eldest,
  And chosen as ye were born;

" But she, like a thing of peasant race,
  That is happy binding the
    sheaves; "
Then he saw her dear mother in her
    face,
  And said, " Thou shalt have thy
    leaves."

II

He mounted and rode three days
    and nights,
  Till he came to Vanity Fair,
And 'twas easy to buy the gems and
    the silk,
  But no Singing Leaves were there.

Then deep in the greenwood rode he,
  And asked of every tree,
" Oh, if you have ever a Singing Leaf,
  I pray you give it to me! "

But the trees all kept their counsel,
  And never a word said they,
Only there sighed from the pine-tops
  A music of seas far away.

Only the pattering aspen
  Made a sound of growing rain,
That fell ever faster and faster,
  Then faltered to silence again.

" Oh, where shall I find a little foot-
    page
  That would win both hose and
    shoon,

And will bring to me the Singing
    Leaves
  If they grow under the moon? "

Then lightly turned him Walter the
    page,
  By the stirrup as he ran:
" Now pledge you me the truesome
    word
  Of a king and gentleman,

" That you will give me the first, first
    thing
  You meet at your castle-gate,
And the Princess will get the Sing-
    ing Leaves,
  Or mine be a traitor's fate."

The King's head dropt upon his
    breast
  A moment, as it might be;
'Twill be my dog, he thought, and
    said,
  " My faith I plight to thee."

Then Walter took from next his
    heart
  A packet small and thin,
" Now give you this to the Princess
    Anne,
  The Singing Leaves are therein."

III

As the King rode in at his castle-
    gate,
  A maiden to meet him ran,
And " Welcome, father! " she
    laughed and cried
  Together, the Princess Anne.

" Lo, here the Singing Leaves," quoth
    he,
  " And woe, but they cost me
    dear! "

She took the packet, and the smile
  Deepened down beneath the tear.

It deepened down till it reached her
    heart,
  And then gushed up again,
And lighted her tears as the sudden
    sun
  Transfigures the summer rain.

And the first Leaf, when it was
    opened,
  Sang: " I am Walter the page,
And the songs I sing 'neath thy win-
    dow
  Are my only heritage."

And the second Leaf sang: " But in
    the land
  That is neither on earth nor sea,
My lute and I are lords of more
  Than thrice this kingdom's fee."

And the third Leaf sang, " Be mine!
    Be mine! "
  And ever it sang, " Be mine! "
Then sweeter it sang and ever
    sweeter,
  And said, " I am thine, thine,
    thine! "

At the first Leaf she grew pale
    enough,
  At the second she turned aside,
At the third, 'twas as if a lily flushed
  With a rose's red heart's tide.

" Good counsel gave the bird," said
    she,
  " I have my hope thrice o'er,
For they sing to my very heart," she
    said,
  " And it sings to them evermore."

She brought to him her beauty and
  truth,
But and broad earldoms three,
And he made her queen of the
  broader lands
He held of his lute in fee.

James Russell Lowell

THE WELL OF ST. KEYNE *

A well there is in the west-country,
  And a clearer one never was seen;
There is not a wife in the west-
  country
  But has heard of the well of St.
  Keyne.

An oak and an elm tree stand beside,
  And behind does an ash-tree grow,
And a willow from the bank above
  Droops to the water below.

A traveller came to the well of St.
  Keyne:
  Pleasant it was to his eye,
For from cock-crow he had been
  travelling
  And there was not a cloud in the
  sky.

He drank of the water so cool and
  clear,
  For thirsty and hot was he,
And he sat down upon the bank,
  Under the willow tree.

There came a man from the neighboring town

* I know not whether it be worth report-
ing that there is in Cornwall, near the parish
of St. Neots, a well, arched over with the
robes of four kinds of trees, withy, oak, elm
and ash, dedicated to St. Keyne. The re-
ported virtue of the water is this, that whether
husband or wife come first to drink thereof,
they get the mastery thereby.—*Thos. Fuller.*

At the well to fill his pail,
On the well-side he rested it,
  And bade the stranger hail.

" Now art thou a bachelor, stranger? "
  quoth he,
  " For an if thou hast a wife,
The happiest draught thou hast
  drank this day
  That ever thou didst in thy life.

" Or has your good woman, if one you
  have,
  In Cornwall ever been?
For an if she have, I'll venture my
  life
  She has drank of the well of St.
  Keyne."

" *I have left a good woman who never
  was here,*"
  The stranger he made reply;
" *But that my draught should be bet-
  ter for that,*
  I pray you answer me why."

" St. Keyne," quoth the countryman,
  " many a time
  Drank of this crystal well,
And before the angel summoned her
  She laid on the water a spell.

" If the husband of this gifted well
  Shall drink before his wife,
A happy man thenceforth is he,
  For he shall be master for life.

" But if the wife should drink of it
  first,
  God help the husband then! "
The stranger stoop'd to the well of
  St. Keyne,
  And drank of the waters again.

" *You drank of the well, I warrant,*
    betimes? "
He to the countryman said;
But the countryman smiled as the
    stranger spake,
And sheepishly shook his head.

" I hastened as soon as the wedding
    was done,
And left my wife in the porch,
But i' faith she had been wiser than
    me,
For she took a bottle to church."
                    Robert Southey

SIR HUMPHREY GILBERT

Southward with fleet of ice
    Sailed the corsair death;
Wild and fast blew the blast,
    And the east wind was his breath.

His lordly ships of ice
    Glistened in the sun,
On each side like pennons wide
    Flashing crystal streamlets run.

His sails of white sea-mist
    Dripped with a silver rain,
But where he passed there was cast
    Leaden shadows o'er the main.

Eastward from Campobello
    Sir Humphrey Gilbert sailed,
Three days or more eastward he bore,
    Then, alas! the land-wind failed.

Alas! the land-wind failed,
    And ice-cold grew the night,
And never more on sea or shore,
    Should Sir Humphrey see the light.

He sat upon the deck,
    The Book was in his hand,

" Do not fear! Heaven is as near,"
    He said, " by water as by land."

In the first watch of the night
    Without a signal's sound
Out of the sea mysteriously,
    The fleet of death rose all around.

The moon and the evening star
    Were hanging in the shrouds.
Every mast as it passed,
    Seemed to rake the passing clouds.

They grappled with their prize
    At midnight black and cold,
As of a rock was the shock,
    Heavily the ground-swell rolled.

Southward through day and dark,
    They drift in close embrace,
With mist and rain to the Spanish
    Main,
    Yet there seems no change of
    place.

Southward forever southward
    They drift through dark and day,
And like a dream, in the Gulf Stream,
    Sinking, vanish all away.
        Henry Wadsworth Longfellow

KING CANUTE

(Selected Stanzas)

King Canute was weary hearted; he
    had reigned for years a score,
Battling, struggling, pushing, fight-
    ing, killing much, and robbing
    more;
And he thought upon his actions,
    walking by the wild sea-shore.

'Twixt the Chancellor and the
    Bishop, walked the King with
    steps sedate,

Chamberlains and grooms came
after, silver-sticks and gold-sticks
great,
Chaplains, aides-de-camp and pages,
—all the officers of state.

Sliding after like his shadow, pausing
when he chose to pause,
If a frown his face contracted,
straight the courtiers dropped
their jaws;
If to laugh the King was minded,
out they burst in loud hee-haws.

But that day a something vexed him;
that was clear to old and young;
Thrice His Grace had yawned at table when his favorite gleemen
sung,
Once the Queen would have con-
soled him, but he bade her hold
her tongue.

" Something ails my gracious master! " cried the Keeper of the
Seal,
" Sure, my lord, it is the lampreys
served for dinner, or the veal? "
" Psha! " exclaimed the angry monarch, " Keeper, 'tis not that I feel.

" 'Tis the heart, and not the dinner,
fool, that doth my rest impair;
Can a king be great as I am, prithee,
and yet know no care?
Oh, I'm sick, and tired, and weary."
Someone cried: " The King's arm-
chair! "

Then toward the lackeys turning,
quick my Lord the Keeper nodded,
Straight the King's great chair was
brought him, by two footmen
able-bodied;

Languidly he sank into it; it was
comfortably wadded.

" Nay, I feel," replied King Canute,
" that my end is drawing near."
" Don't say so! " exclaimed the courtiers (striving each to squeeze a
tear).
" Sure your Grace is strong and lusty,
and may live this fifty year! "

" Live these fifty years! " the Bishop
roared, with actions made to suit.
" Are you mad, my good Lord Keeper,
thus to speak of King Canute!
Men have lived a thousand years,
and sure His Majesty will do 't.

" With his wondrous skill in healing
ne'er a doctor can compete,
Loathsome lepers, if he touch them,
start up clean upon their feet;
Surely he could raise the dead up,
did His Highness think it meet.

" Did not once the Jewish captain stay
the sun upon the hill,
And the while he slew the foemen,
bid the silver moon stand still?
So, no doubt, could gracious Canute,
if it were his sacred will."

" Might I stay the sun above us, good
Sir Bishop? " Canute cried,
" Could I bid the silver moon to pause
upon her heavenly ride?
If the moon obeys my orders, sure I
can command the tide!

" Will the advancing waves obey me,
Bishop, if I make the sign? "
Said the Bishop, bowing lowly:
" Land and sea, my Lord, are
thine."

Canute turned toward the ocean:
"Back!" he said, "thou foaming brine.

"From the sacred shore I stand on, I
command thee to retreat;
Venture not thou stormy rebel, to
approach thy master's seat;
Ocean, be thou still! I bid thee
come not nearer to my feet!"

But the sullen ocean answered with
a louder, deeper roar,
And the rapid waves drew nearer,
falling sounding on the shore;
Back the Keeper and the Bishop,
back the King and courtiers bore.

And he sternly bade them never
more to kneel to human clay,
But alone to praise and worship
That which earth and seas obey;
And his golden crown of empire
never wore he from that day.

William Makepeace Thackeray

SIR GALAHAD

My good blade carves the casques of
men,
My tough lance thrusteth sure;
My strength is as the strength of ten,
Because my heart is pure.
The shattering trumpet shrilleth
high,
The hard brands shiver on the
steel,
The splinter'd spear-shafts crack and
fly,
The horse and rider reel;
They reel, they roll in changing lists,
And when the tide of combat
stands,

Perfume and flowers fall in showers,
That lightly rain from ladies'
hands.

How sweet are looks that ladies bend
On whom their favours fall!
For them I battle till the end,
To save from shame and thrall:
But all my heart is drawn above,
My knees are bowed in crypt and
shrine:
I never felt the kiss of love,
Nor maiden's hand in mine.
More bounteous aspects on me
beam,
Me mightier transports move and
thrill;
So keep I fear thro' faith and prayer
A virgin heart in work and will.

When down the stormy crescent
goes,
A light before me swims,
Between dark stems the forest glows,
I hear a noise of hymns:
Then by some secret shrine I ride;
I hear a voice, but none are there;
The stalls are void, the doors are
wide,
The tapers burning fair.
Fair gleams the snowy altar-cloth,
The silver vessels sparkle clean,
The shrill bell rings, the censer
swings,
And solemn chants resound be-
tween.

Sometimes on lonely mountain-meres
I find a magic bark;
I leap on board: no helmsman steers:
I float till all is dark.
A gentle sound, an awful light!
Three angels bear the holy Grail:
With folded feet, in stoles of white,
On sleeping wings they sail.

Ah, blessed vision! blood of God!
  My spirit beats her mortal bars,
As down dark tides the glory slides,
  And star-like mingles with the
    stars.

When on my goodly charger borne
  Thro' dreaming towns I go,
The cock crows ere the Christmas
    morn,
  The streets are dumb with snow.
The tempest crackles on the leads,
  And, ringing, spins from brand
    and mail;
But o'er the dark a glory spreads,
  And gilds the driving hail.
I leave the plain, I climb the height;
  No branchy thicket shelter yields;
But blessed forms in whistling storms
  Fly o'er waste fens and windy
    fields.

A maiden knight—to me is given
  Such hope, I know not fear;
I yearn to breathe the airs of Heaven
  That often meet me here.
I muse on joy that will not cease,
  Pure spaces clothed in living
    beams,
Pure lilies of eternal peace,
  Whose odours haunt my dreams;
And, stricken by an angel's hand,
  This mortal armour that I wear,
This weight and size, this heart and
    eyes,
  Are touch'd, are turn'd to finest
    air.

The clouds are broken in the sky,
  And thro' the mountain-walls,
A rolling organ-harmony
  Swells up, and shakes and falls.
Then move the trees, the copses nod,
  Wings flutter, voices hover clear:

"O just and faithful knight of God!
  Ride on! the prize is near."
So pass I hostel, hall, and grange;
  By bridge and ford, by park and
    pale,
All-arm'd I ride, whate'er betide,
  Until I find the holy Grail.

                        Alfred Tennyson

THE LADY OF SHALOTT

Part I

On either side the river lie
Long fields of barley and of rye,
That clothe the wold and meet the
    sky;
And thro' the road runs by
        To many tower'd Camelot.
And up and down the people go,
Gazing where the lilies blow,
Round an island there below,
        The island of Shalott.

Willows whiten, aspens quiver,
Little breezes dusk and shiver
Thro' the wave that runs for ever.
By the island in the river,
        Flowing down to Camelot,
Four gray walls, and four gray towers,
Overlook a space of flowers,
And the silent isle embowers
        The Lady of Shalott.

By the margin, willow-veil'd,
Slide the heavy barges trail'd
By slow horses; and unhail'd
The shallop flitteth silken-sail'd
        Skimming down to Camelot:
But who hath seen her wave her
    hand?
Or at the casement seen her stand?
Or is she known in all the land,
        The Lady of Shalott?

Only reapers, reaping early
In among the bearded barley,
Hear a song that echoes cheerly
From the river winding clearly,
  Down to tower'd Camelot:
And by the moon the reaper weary,
Piling sheaves in uplands airy,
Listening, whispers " 'Tis the fairy
  Lady of Shalott."

PART II

There she weaves by night and day
A magic web with colours gay,
She has heard a whisper say
A curse is on her if she stay
  To look down to Camelot.
She knows not what the curse may be
And so she weaveth steadily,
And little other care hath she,
  The Lady of Shalott.

And moving thro' a mirror clear
That hangs before her all the year,
Shadows of the world appear.
There she sees the highway near
  Winding down to Camelot:
There the river eddy whirls,
And there the surly village-churls,
And the red cloaks of market girls,
  Pass onward from Shalott.

Sometimes a troop of damsels glad,
An abbot on an ambling pad,
Sometimes a curly shepherd-lad,
Or long-hair'd page in crimson clad,
  Goes by to tower'd Camelot:
And sometimes thro' the mirror blue
The knights come riding two and
  two:
She hath no loyal knight and true,
  The Lady of Shalott.

But in her web she still delights
To weave the mirror's magic sights,

For often thro' the silent nights
A funeral, with plumes and lights,
  And music, went to Camelot:
Or when the moon was overhead,
Came two young lovers lately wed.
" I am half sick of shadows," said
  The Lady of Shalott.

PART III

A bow-shot from her bower-eaves,
He rode between the barley-sheaves,
The sun came dazzling thro' the
  leaves,
And flamed upon the brazen greaves
  Of bold Sir Lancelot.
A red-cross knight for ever kneel'd
To a lady in his shield,
That sparkled on the yellow field,
  Beside remote Shalott.

The gemmy bridle glitter'd free,
Like to some branch of stars we see
Hung in the golden Galaxy.
The bridle bells rang merrily
  As he rode down to Camelot:
And from his blazon'd baldric slung
A mighty silver bugle hung,
And as he rode his armour rung,
  Beside remote Shalott.

All in the blue unclouded weather
Thick-jewell'd shone the saddle-
  leather.
The helmet and the helmet-feather
Burn'd like one burning flame to-
  gether
  As he rode down to Camelot.
As often thro' the purple night,
Below the starry clusters bright,
Some bearded meteor, trailing light,
  Moves over still Shalott.

His broad clear brow in sunlight
  glow'd;

On burnish'd hooves his war-horse
    trod;
From underneath his helmet flow'd
His coal-black curls as on he rode,
    As he rode down to Camelot.
From the bank and from the river
He flash'd into the crystal mirror,
"Tirra, lirra," by the river
    Sang Sir Lancelot.

She left the web, she left the loom,
She made three paces thro' the room,
She saw the water-lily bloom,
She saw the helmet and the plume,
    She looked down to Camelot.
Out flew the web and floated wide;
The mirror crack'd from side to side;
"The curse is come upon me," cried
    The Lady of Shalott.

PART IV

In the stormy east-wind straining,
The pale yellow woods were waning,
The broad stream in its banks com-
    plaining,
Heavily the low sky raining
    Over tower'd Camelot;
Down she came and found a boat
Beneath a willow left afloat,
And round about the prow she wrote
    The Lady of Shalott.

And down the river's dim expanse—
Like some bold seer in a trance,
Seeing all his own mischance—
With a glassy countenance
    Did she look to Camelot.
And at the closing of the day
She loosed the chain, and down she
    lay;
The broad stream bore her far away,
    The Lady of Shalott.

Lying, robed in snowy white
That loosely flew to left and right—

The leaves upon her falling light—
Thro' the noises of the night
    She floated down to Camelot;
And as the boat-head wound along
The willowy hills and fields among,
They heard her singing her last song,
    The Lady of Shalott.

Heard a carol, mournful, holy,
Chanted loudly, chanted lowly,
Till her blood was frozen slowly,
And her eyes were darken'd wholly,
    Turn'd to tower'd Camelot;
For ere she reach'd upon the tide
The first house by the water-side,
Singing in her song she died,
    The Lady of Shalott.

Under tower and balcony,
By garden-wall and gallery,
A gleaming shape she floated by,
Dead-pale between the houses high,
    Silent into Camelot;
Out upon the wharfs they came,
Knight and burgher, lord and dame,
And round the prow they read her
    name,
    The Lady of Shalott.

Who is this? and what is here?
And in the lighted palace near
Died the sound of royal cheer;
And they cross'd themselves for fear,
    All the knights at Camelot;
But Lancelot mused a little space;
He said, "She has a lovely face;
God in His mercy lend her grace,
    The Lady of Shalott."

Alfred Tennyson

SIR LAUNFAL AND THE LEPER

As Sir Launfal made morn through
    the darksome gate,

He was aware of a leper, crouched
by the same,
Who begged with his hand and
moaned as he sate;
And a loathing over Sir Launfal
came;
The sunshine went out of his soul
with a thrill,
The flesh 'neath his armor did
shrink and crawl,
And midway its leap his heart stood
still
Like a frozen waterfall;
For this man, so foul and bent of
stature,
Rasped harshly against his dainty
nature,
And seemed the one blot on the
summer morn,—
So he tossed him a piece of gold in
scorn.

The leper raised not the gold from
the dust:
" Better to me the poor man's crust,
Better the blessing of the poor,
Though I turn me empty from his
door;
That is no true alms which the hand
can hold:
He gives nothing but worthless gold
Who gives from a sense of duty;
But he who gives a slender mite,
And gives to that which is out of
sight,
That thread of the all-sustaining
Beauty
Which runs through all and doth all
unite,—
The hand cannot clasp the whole of
his alms,
The heart outstretches its eager
palms,

For a god goes with it and makes it
store
To the soul that was starving in
darkness before."

James Russell Lowell

LOCHINVAR

O, young Lochinvar is come out of
the west,
Through all the wide Border his
steed was the best,
And save his good broadsword he
weapons had none;
He rode all unarmed, and he rode
all alone.
So faithful in love, and so dauntless
in war,
There never was knight like the
young Lochinvar.

He stayed not for brake, and he
stopped not for stone,
He swam the Eske river where ford
there was none;
But, ere he alighted at Netherby
gate,
The bride had consented, the gallant
came late:
For a laggard in love, and a dastard
in war,
Was to wed the fair Ellen of brave
Lochinvar.

So boldly he entered the Netherby
hall,
Among bride's-men and kinsmen,
and brothers and all;
Then spoke the bride's father, his
hand on his sword
(For the poor craven bridegroom
said never a word),
" O come ye in peace here, or come
ye in war,

Or to dance at our bridal, young
    Lord Lochinvar? "

" I long wooed your daughter, my suit
    you denied;—
Love swells like the Solway, but ebbs
    like its tide—
And now I am come, with this lost
    love of mine,
To lead but one measure, drink one
    cup of wine.
There are maidens in Scotland more
    lovely by far,
That would gladly be bride to the
    young Lochinvar."

The bride kissed the goblet; the
    knight took it up,
He quaffed off the wine, and he
    threw down the cup,
She looked down to blush, and she
    looked up to sigh,
With a smile on her lips and a tear
    in her eye.
He took her soft hand, ere her
    mother could bar,—
"Now tread we a measure!" said
    young Lochinvar.

So stately his form, and so lovely her
    face,
That never a hall such a galliard did
    grace;
While her mother did fret, and her
    father did fume,
And the bridegroom stood dangling
    his bonnet and plume;
And the bride-maidens whispered,
    " 'Twere better by far
To have matched our fair cousin
    with young Lochinvar."

One touch to her hand, and one
    word in her ear,

When they reached the hall door,
    and the charger stood near;
So light to the croupe the fair lady
    he swung,
So light to the saddle before her he
    sprung!
" She is won! we are gone, over bank,
    bush, and scaur;
They'll have fleet steeds that fol-
    low," quoth young Lochinvar.

There was mounting 'mong Græmes
    of the Netherby clan;
Forsters, Fenwicks, and Musgraves,
    they rode and they ran;
There was racing, and chasing, on
    Cannobie Lee,
But the lost bride of Netherby ne'er
    did they see.
So daring in love, and so dauntless
    in war,
Have ye e'er heard of gallant like
    young Lochinvar?

Walter Scott

THE LAY OF THE LAST MINSTREL

The way was long, the wind was cold,
The Minstrel was infirm and old;
His withered cheek and tresses gray
Seemed to have known a better day:
The harp, his sole remaining joy,
Was carried by an orphan boy:
The last of all the Bards was he,
Who sung of Border chivalry.
For, well-a-day! their date was fled,
His tuneful brethren all were dead;
And he, neglected and oppressed,
Wished to be with them, and at rest.
No more, on prancing palfrey borne,
He carolled, light as lark at morn;
No longer courted and caressed,
High-placed in hall, a welcome guest,

He poured, to lord and lady gay,
The unpremeditated lay;
Old times were changed—old manners gone—
A stranger filled the Stuarts' throne.
The bigots of the iron time
Had called his harmless art—a crime.
A wandering harper, scorned and poor,
He begged his bread from door to door;
And tuned, to please a peasant's ear,
The harp, a king had loved to hear.
He passed, where Newark's stately tower
Looks out from Yarrow's birchen bower:
The Minstrel gazed with wishful eye—
No humbler resting-place was nigh.
With hesitating step, at last,
The embattled portal-arch he passed;
Whose ponderous grate and massy bar
Had oft rolled back the tide of war,
But never closed the iron door
Against the desolate and poor.
The Duchess marked his weary pace,
His timid mien and reverend face;
And bade her page the menials tell
That they should tend the old man well;—
For she had known adversity,
Though born in such a high degree;
In pride of power, in beauty's bloom,
Had wept o'er Monmouth's bloody tomb.
When kindness had his wants supplied,
And the old man was gratified,
Began to rise his minstrel pride;
And he began to talk, anon,
Of good Earl Francis, dead and gone;

And of Earl Walter — rest him God!—
A braver ne'er to battle rode:
And how full many a tale he knew
Of the old warriors of Buccelugh;
And, would the noble Duchess deign
To listen to an old man's strain,
Though stiff his hand, his voice though weak,
He thought, even yet,—the sooth to speak,—
That if she loved the harp to hear,
He could make music to her ear.
The humble boon was soon obtained;
The aged Minstrel audience gained;
But when he reached the room of state,
Where she, with all her ladies, sat,
Perchance he wished his boon denied;
For, when to tune his harp he tried,
His trembling heart had lost the ease
Which marks security to please;
And scenes, long past, of joy and pain,
Came wildering o'er his aged brain;—
He tried to tune his harp, in vain.
Amid the strings his fingers strayed,
And an uncertain warbling made;
And oft, he shook his hoary head.
But when he caught the measure wild,
The old man raised his face, and smiled;
And lighted up his faded eye,
With all a poet's ecstasy!
In varying cadence, soft or strong,
He swept the sounding chords along;
The present scene, the future lot,
His toils, his wants, were all forgot;
Cold diffidence, and age's frost,
In the full tide of soul were lost;

Each blank in faithless memory's
    void,
The poet's glowing thought supplied;
And, while his harp responsive rung,
'Twas thus the latest minstrel
    sung:—
"Breathes there the man, with soul
    so dead,—
Who never to himself hath said,
This is my own, my native land!—
Whose heart hath ne'er within him
    burned,
As home his footsteps he hath
    turned
From wandering on a foreign strand?
If such there breathe, go—mark him
    well;
For him, no minstrel raptures swell:
High though his titles, proud his
    name,
Boundless his wealth, as wish can
    claim;
Despite those titles, power and pelf,
The wretch, concentred all in self,
Living, shall forfeit fair renown,
And, doubly dying, shall go down
To the vile dust from whence he
    sprung,
Unwept, unhonoured, and unsung!"

Walter Scott

HERVÉ RIEL

On the sea and at the Hogue, sixteen
    hundred and ninety-two,
Did the English fight the French,—
    woe to France!
And, the thirty-first of May, helter-
    skelter through the blue,
Like a crowd of frightened porpoises
    a shoal of sharks pursue,
Came crowding ship on ship to St.
    Malo on the Rance,
With the English fleet in view.

'Twas the squadron that escaped,
    with the victor in full chase;
First and foremost of the drove, in
    his great ship, Damfreville;
Close on him fled, great and small,
Twenty-two good ships in all;
And they signalled to the place
"Help the winners of a race!
Get us guidance, give us harbor, take
    us quick—or, quicker still,
Here's the English can and will!"

Then the pilots of the place put out
    brisk and leapt on board;
"Why, what hope or chance have
    ships like these to pass?" laughed
    they:
Rocks to starboard, rocks to port, all
    the passage scarred and scored,
Shall the *Formidable* here with her
    twelve and eighty guns
Think to make the river-mouth by
    the single narrow way,
Trust to enter where 'tis ticklish for
    a craft of twenty tons,
And with flow at full beside?
Now, 'tis slackest ebb of tide.
Reach the mooring? Rather say,
While rock stands or water runs,
Not a ship will leave the bay!"

Then was called a council straight.
Brief and bitter the debate:
"Here's the English at our heels;
    would you have them take in tow
All that's left us of the fleet, linked
    together stern and bow,
For a prize to Plymouth Sound?
Better run the ships aground!"
    (Ended Damfreville his speech.)
Not a minute more to wait!
"Let the Captains all and each
Shove ashore, then blow up, burn
    the vessels on the beach!
France must undergo her fate.

"Give the word! " But no such word
Was ever spoke or heard;
For up stood, for out stepped, for in
struck amid all these
—A Captain? A Lieutenant? A
Mate—first, second, third?
No such man of mark, and meet
With his betters to compete!
But a simple Breton sailor pressed
by Tourville for the fleet,
A poor coasting-pilot he, Hervé Riel
the Croisickese.
And, "What mockery or malice
have we here? " cries Hervé Riel:
"Are you mad, you Malouins? Are
you cowards, fools, or rogues?
Talk to me of rocks and shoals, me
who took the soundings, tell
On my fingers every bank, every
shallow, every swell
'Twixt the offing here and Grève
where the river disembogues?
Are you bought by English gold? Is
it love the lying's for?
Morn and eve, night and day,
Have I piloted your bay,
Entered free and anchored fast at
foot of Solidor.

"Burn the fleet and ruin France?
That were worse than fifty
Hogues!
Sirs, they know I speak the truth!
Sirs, believe me there's a way!
Only let me lead the line,
Have the biggest ship to steer,
Get this *Formidable* clear,
Make the others follow mine,
And I lead them, most and least, by
a passage I know well,
Right to Solidor past Grève,
And there lay them safe and sound;
And if one ship misbehave,
—Keel so much as grate the ground,

Why, I've nothing but my life,—
here's my head! " cries Hervé
Riel.

Not a minute more to wait.
"Steer us in, then, small and great!
Take the helm, lead the line, save
the squadron! " cried his chief.
"Captains, give the sailor place!
He is Admiral, in brief."
Still the north-wind, by God's grace.
See the noble fellow's face,
As the big ship with a bound,
Clears the entry like a hound,
Keeps the passage, as its inch of way
were the wide seas profound!
See, safe thro' shoal and rock,
How they flow in a flock,
Not a ship that misbehaves, not a
keel that grates the ground,
Not a spar that comes to grief!
The peril, see, is past,
All are harbored to the last,
And just as Hervé Riel hollas "An-
chor! "—sure as fate
Up the English come, too late!

So, the storm subsides to calm:
They see the green trees wave
On the heights o'erlooking Grève.
Hearts that bled are stanched with
balm.
"Just our rapture to enhance,
Let the English rake the bay,
Gnash their teeth and glare askance,
As they cannonade away!
'Neath rampired Solidor pleasant
riding on the Rance! "
How hope succeeds despair on each
Captain's countenance!
Out burst all with one accord,
"This is Paradise for Hell!
Let France, let France's King
Thank the man that did the thing! "

What a shout, and all one word,
" Hervé Riel! "
As he stepped in front once more,
Not a symptom of surprise
In the frank blue Breton eyes,
Just the same man as before.

Then said Damfreville, " My friend,
I must speak out at the end,
Though I find the speaking hard.
Praise is deeper than the lips:
You have saved the King his ships,
You must name your own reward.
'Faith, our sun was near eclipse!
Demand whate'er you will,
France remains your debtor still.
Ask to heart's content and have! or
     my name's not Damfreville."

Then a beam of fun outbroke
On the bearded mouth that spoke,
As the honest heart laughed through
Those frank eyes of Breton blue:
" Since I needs must say my say,
Since on board the duty's done,
And from Malo Roads to Croisic
     Point, what is it but a run?—
Since 'tis ask and have, I may—
Since the others go ashore—
Come! A good whole holiday!
Leave to go and see my wife, whom
     I call the Belle Aurore! "
That he asked and that he got,—
nothing more.

Name and deed alike are lost:
Not a pillar nor a post
In his Croisic keeps alive the feat as
     it befell;
Not a head in white and black
On a single fishing smack,
In memory of the man but for
     whom had gone to wrack

All that France saved from the fight
     whence England bore the bell.
Go to Paris: rank on rank
Search the heroes flung pell-mell
On the Louvre, face and flank!
You shall look long enough ere you
     come to Hervé Riel.
So, for better and for worse,
Hervé Riel, accept my verse!
In my verse, Hervé Riel, do thou
     once more
Save the squadron, honor France,
     love thy wife, the Belle Aurore!

             Robert Browning.

JAFFÀR

Jaffàr, the Barmecide, the good
     Vizier,
The poor man's hope, the friend
     without a peer.
Jaffàr was dead, slain by a doom
     unjust;
And guilty Hàroun, sullen with mis-
     trust
Of what the good, and e'en the bad
     might say,
Ordain'd that no man living from
     that day
Should dare to speak his name on
     pain of death.
All Araby and Persia held their
     breath.

All but the brave Mondeer.—He,
     proud to show
How far for love a grateful soul
     could go,
And facing death for very scorn and
     grief,
(For his great heart wanted a great
     relief,)
Stood forth in Bagdad, daily in the
     square

Where once had stood a happy
    house, and there
Harangued the tremblers at the
    scimitar
On all they owed to the divine Jaffàr.

"Bring me this man," the caliph
    cried: the man
Was brought, was gazed upon. The
    mutes began
To bind his arms. "Welcome,
    brave cords," cried he;
"From bonds far worse Jaffàr de-
    liver'd me;
From wants, from shames, from
    loveless household fears;
Made a man's eyes friends with de-
    licious tears;
Restor'd me, loved me, put me on a
    par
With his great self. How can I pay
    Jaffàr?"

Hàroun, who felt that on a soul like
    this
The mightiest vengeance could but
    fall amiss,
Now deigned to smile, as one great
    lord of fate
Might smile upon another half as
    great.
He said, "Let worth grow frenzied if
    it will;
The caliph's judgment shall be mas-
    ter still.

Go, and since gifts so move thee,
    take this gem,
The richest in the Tartar's diadem,
And hold the giver as thou deemest
    fit."
"Gifts!" cried the friend. He took;
    and holding it

High towards the heaven, as though
    to meet his star,
Exclaimed, "This, too, I owe to
    thee, Jaffàr!"

Leigh Hunt

THE FOUNDING OF BOLTON PRIORY

Young Romilly through Barden
    Woods
    Is ranging high and low,
And holds a greyhound in a leash,
    To let slip on buck or doe.

The pair have reached that fearful
    chasm,
    How tempting to bestride!
For lordly Wharf is there pent in
    With rocks on either side.

This striding place is called "the
    Strid,"
    A name which it took of yore;
A thousand years hath it borne that
    name,
    And shall a thousand more.

And hither is young Romilly come;
    And what may not forbid
That he, perhaps for the hundredth
    time,
    Should bound across the Strid?

He sprang in glee—for what cared he
    That the river was strong, and the
        rocks were steep?
But the greyhound in the leash hung
    back,
    And checked him in his leap!

The boy is in the arms of Wharf!
    And strangled with a merciless
        force—

For never more was young Romilly
  seen
Till he rose a lifeless corse!

Now there is a stillness in the vale,
  And long unspeaking sorrow;
Wharf shall be to pitying hearts
  A name more sad than Yarrow.

If for a lover the lady wept,
  A solace she might borrow
From death, and from the passion of
  death,
Old Wharf might heal her sorrow.

She weeps not for the wedding-day
  Which was to be tomorrow;
Her hope was a further-looking hope,
  And hers is a mother's sorrow.

He was a tree that stood alone,
  And proudly did its branches wave;
And the root of this delightful tree
  Was in her husband's grave.

Long, long in darkness did she sit,
  And her first words were, " Let
  there be
In Bolton, on the field of Wharf,
  A stately Priory! "

The stately Priory was reared,
  And Wharf, as he moved along,
To matins joined a mournful voice,
  Nor failed at even-song.

And the lady prayed in heaviness
  That looked not for relief;
But slowly did her succour come,
  And patience to her grief.

Oh! there is never sorrow of heart
  That shall lack a timely end,
If but to God we turn, and ask
  Of Him to be our Friend.
        William Wordsworth

THE BATTLE OF BLENHEIM

It was a summer evening,
  Old Kaspar's work was done,
And he before his cottage door
  Was sitting in the sun;
And by him sported on the green,
His little grandchild, Wilhelmine.

She saw her brother Peterkin
  Roll something large and round,
That he beside the rivulet
  In playing there had found;
She ran to ask what he had found,
That was so large, and smooth, and
  round.

Old Kaspar took it from the boy,
  Who stood expectant by;
And then the old man shook his
  head,
  And with a natural sigh—
" 'Tis some poor fellow's skull," said
  he,
" Who fell in the great victory.

" I find them in my garden, for
  There's many hereabout;
And often when I go to plough
  The ploughshare turns them out;
For many thousand men," said he,
" Were slain in that great victory."

" Now tell us what 'twas all about,"
  Young Peterkin, he cries,
And little Wilhelmine looks up
  With wonder-waiting eyes,
" Now tell us all about the war,
  And what they killed each other
  for? "

" It was the English," Kaspar cried,
  " Who put the French to rout;
But what they kill'd each other for
  I could not well make out.

But everybody said," quoth he,
" That 'twas a famous victory!

" My father lived at Blenheim then,
    Yon little stream hard by;
They burn'd his dwelling to the
    ground,
    And he was forced to fly;
So with his wife and child he fled,
Nor had he where to rest his head!

" With fire and sword the country
    round
    Was wasted far and wide;
And many a childing mother then
    And new-born baby died!
But things like that, you know, must
    be
At every famous victory.

" They say it was a shocking sight
    After the field was won;
For many thousand bodies here
    Lay rotting in the sun!
But things like that, you know, must
    be
After a famous victory.

" Great praise the Duke of Marlbor-
    ough won,
    And our good Prince Eugene."
" Why, 'twas a very wicked thing! "
    Said little Wilhelmine.
" Nay, nay, my little girl," quoth he,
" It was a famous victory!

" And everybody praised the Duke
    Who this great fight did win."
" But what good came of it at last? "
    Quoth little Peterkin.
" Why, that I cannot tell," said he,
" But 'twas a famous victory."

                    Robert Southey

THE WRECK OF THE HESPERUS

It was the schooner Hesperus,
    That sailed the wintry sea;
And the skipper had taken his little
    daughter,
    To bear him company.

Blue were her eyes, as the fairy-flax,
    Her cheeks like the dawn of day,
And her bosom white as the haw-
    thorn buds,
    That ope in the month of May.

The skipper he stood beside the
    helm,
    His pipe was in his mouth;
And he watched how the veering
    flaw did blow
    The smoke now West, now South.

Then up and spake an old Sailor,
    Had sailed the Spanish Main:
" I pray thee, put into yonder port,
    For I fear a hurricane.

" Last night, the moon had a golden
    ring,
    And tonight no moon we see! "
The skipper, he blew a whiff from
    his pipe,
    And a scornful laugh laughed he.

Colder and louder blew the wind,
    A gale from the North-east;
The snow fell hissing in the brine,
    And the billows frothed like yeast.

Down came the storm, and smote
    amain
    The vessel in its strength;
She shuddered and paused, like a
    frightened steed,
    Then leaped her cable's length.

"Come hither! come hither! my little
    daughter,
    And do not tremble so;
For I can weather the roughest gale,
    That ever wind did blow."

He wrapped her warm in his sea-
    man's coat,
    Against the stinging blast;
He cut a rope from a broken spar
    And bound her to the mast.

"O father! I hear the church-bells
    ring,
    O say, what may it be?"
"'Tis a fog-bell on a rock-bound
    coast!"—
    And he steered for the open sea.

"O father! I hear the sound of guns,
    O say, what may it be?"
"Some ship in distress, that cannot
    live
    In such an angry sea!"

"O father! I see a gleaming light,
    O say, what may it be?"
But the father answered never a
    word,
    A frozen corpse was he.

Lashed to the helm, all stiff and
    stark,
    With his face turned to the skies;
The lantern gleamed through the
    gleaming snow
    On his fixed and glassy eyes.

Then the maiden clasped her hands,
    and prayed
    That savèd she might be;
And she thought of Christ, who
    stilled the waves,
    On the Lake of Galilee.

And fast through the midnight dark
    and drear,
    Through the whistling sleet and
    snow,
Like a sheeted ghost, the vessel
    swept
    Towards the reef of Norman's
    Woe.

And ever the fitful gusts between
    A sound came from the land;
It was the sound of the trampling
    surf,
    On the rocks and the hard sea-
    sand.

The breakers were right beneath her
    bows,
    She drifted a weary wreck,
And a whooping billow swept the
    crew
    Like icicles from her deck.

She struck where the white and
    fleecy waves
    Looked soft as carded wool,
But the cruel rocks, they gored her
    side,
    Like the horns of an angry bull.

Her rattling shrouds, all sheathed in
    ice,
    With the masts, went by the
    board;
Like a vessel of glass, she stove and
    sank,
    Ho! ho! the breakers roared!

At daybreak, on the bleak sea-beach,
    A fisherman stood aghast,
To see the form of a maiden fair,
    Lashed close to a drifting mast.

The salt sea was frozen on her breast,
    The salt tears in her eyes;

And he saw her hair, like the brown
    sea-weed,
    On the billows fall and rise.

Such was the wreck of the Hesperus,
    In the midnight and the snow!
Christ save us all from a death like
    this,
    On the reef of Norman's Woe!
      Henry Wadsworth Longfellow

THE INCHCAPE ROCK

No stir in the air, no stir in the sea,
The ship was as still as she could be;
Her sails from heaven received no
    motion,
Her keel was steady in the ocean.

Without either sign or sound of
    their shock,
The waves flow'd over the Inchcape
    Rock;
So little they rose, so little they fell,
They did not move the Inchcape
    bell.

The good Abbot of Aberbrothok
Had placed that bell on the Inch-
    cape Rock;
On a buoy in the storm it floated
    and swung,
And over the waves its warning rung.

When the rock was hid by the
    surge's swell,
The mariners heard the warning bell:
And then they knew the perilous
    rock,
And blest the Abbot of Aberbrothok.

The sun in heaven was shining gay,
All things were joyful on that day;

The sea-birds scream'd as they
    wheel'd around,
And there was joyance in their sound.

The buoy of the Inchcape bell was
    seen,
A darker speck on the ocean green;
Sir Ralph the Rover walk'd his deck,
And he fixed his eye on the darker
    speck.

He felt the cheering power of spring,
It made him whistle, it made him
    sing;
His heart was mirthful to excess—
But the Rover's mirth was wicked-
    ness.

His eyes were on the Inchcape float:
Quoth he, "My men, put out the
    boat,
And row me to the Inchcape Rock,
And I'll plague the Abbot of Aber-
    brothok."

The boat is lower'd, the boatmen
    row,
And to the Inchcape Rock they go;
Sir Ralph bent over from the boat,
And he cut the bell from the Inch-
    cape float.

Down sank the bell with a gurgling
    sound—
The bubbles rose and burst around;
Quoth Sir Ralph, "The next who
    comes to the Rock
Won't bless the Abbot of Aber-
    brothok."

Sir Ralph the Rover sail'd away;
He scoured the seas for many a day;
And, now grown rich with plunder'd
    store,

He steers his course for Scotland's
    shore.

So thick a haze o'erspreads the sky,
They cannot see the sun on high;
The wind hath blown a gale all day,
At evening it hath died away.

On the deck the Rover takes his
    stand,
So dark it is they see no land.
Quoth Sir Ralph, " It will be lighter
    soon,
For there is the dawn of the rising
    moon."

" Canst hear," said one, " the breakers
    roar?
For methinks we should be near the
    shore.
Now where we are I cannot tell,
But I wish I could hear the Inchcape
    bell."

They hear no sound—the swell is
    strong;
Though the wind hath fallen they
    drift along
Till the vessel strikes with a shiver-
    ing shock—
" Mercy! it is the Inchcape Rock! "

Sir Ralph the Rover tore his hair,
And beat his breast in his despair:
The waves rush in on every side,
And the ship sinks down beneath
    the tide.

                        Robert Southey

THE WATERFALL AND THE
        EGLANTINE

" Begone, thou fond presumptuous
    Elf,"

Exclaimed an angry voice,
" Nor dare to thrust thy foolish self
    Between me and my choice! "
A small Cascade fresh swoln with
    snows
Thus threatened a poor Briar-rose,
That, all bespattered with his foam,
And dancing high and dancing low,
Was living, as a child might know,
    In an unhappy home.

" Dost thou presume my course to
    block?
    Off, off! or, puny Thing!
I'll hurl thee headlong with the rock
    To which thy fibres cling."
The Flood was tyrannous and strong,
The patient Briar suffered long,
Nor did he utter groan or sigh,
Hoping the danger would be past;
But, seeing no relief, at last,
    He ventured to reply.

" Ah! " said the Briar, " blame me
    not:
    Why should we dwell in strife?
We who in this sequestered spot
    Once lived a happy life!
You stirred me on my rocky bed—
What pleasure through my veins
    you spread!
The summer long, from day to day,
My leaves you freshened and be-
    dewed:
Nor was it common gratitude
    That did your cares repay.

" When spring came on with bud and
    bell,
    Among the rocks did I,
Before you hang my wreaths to tell
    That gentle days were nigh!
And in the sultry summer hours,
I sheltered you with leaves and flow-
    ers;

And in my leaves—now shed and
    gone—
The linnet lodged, and for us two
Chanted his pretty songs, when you
    Had little voice or none.

" But now proud thoughts are in your
    breast—
    What grief is mine you see,
Ah! would you think, even yet how
    blest
    Together we might be!
Though of both leaf and flower
    bereft,
Some ornaments to me are left—
Rich store of scarlet hips is mine,
With which I, in my humble way,
Would deck you many a winter day;
    A happy Eglantine! "

What more he said I cannot tell,
The stream came thundering down
    the dell,
    With aggravated haste:
I listened, nor aught else could hear;
The Briar quaked—and much I fear
    Those accents were his last.

          William Wordsworth

FATHER WILLIAM

" You are old, Father William," the
    young man cried;
    " The few locks that are left you
    are gray:
You are hale, Father William, a
    hearty old man;
    Now tell me the reason, I pray."

" In the days of my youth," Father
    William replied,
    " I remembered that youth would
    fly fast;

And abused not my health and my
    vigour at first,
    That I never might need them at
    last."

" You are old, Father William," the
    young man cried,
    " And pleasures with youth pass
    away;
And yet you lament not the days
    that are gone;
    Now tell me the reason, I pray."

" In the days of my youth," Father
    William replied,
    " I remembered that youth could
    not last;
I thought of the future, whatever I
    did,
    That I never might grieve for the
    past."

" You are old, Father William," the
    young man cried,
    " And life must be hastening away;
You are cheerful, and love to con-
    verse upon death;
    Now tell me the reason, I pray."

" I am cheerful, young man," Father
    William replied;
    " Let the cause thy attention en-
    gage;
In the days of my youth I remem-
    bered my God,
    And He hath not forgotten my
    age! "

          Robert Southey

THE CASTLE BUILDER

It happened on a summer's day,
A country lass as fresh as May,
Decked in a wholesome russet gown,

Was going to the market town;
So blithe her looks, so simply clean,
You'd take her for a May-day queen;
Though for her garland, says the tale,
Her head sustained a loaded pail.
As on her way she passed along,
She hummed the fragments of a song;
She did not hum for want of thought—
Quite pleased with what to sale she
    brought,
She reckoned by her own account,
When all was sold, the whole amount.
Thus she—" In time this little ware
May turn to great account, with care:
My milk being sold for—so and so,
I'll buy some eggs as markets go,
And set them;—at the time I fix,
These eggs will bring as many chicks;
I'll spare no pains to feed them well;
They'll bring vast profit when they
    sell.
With this, I'll buy a little pig,
And when 'tis grown up fat and big,
I'll sell it, whether boar or sow,
And with the money buy a cow:
This cow will surely have a calf,
And there the profit's half in half;
Besides there's butter, milk, and
    cheese,
To keep the market when I please:
All which I'll sell, and buy a farm,
Then shall of sweethearts have a
    swarm.
Oh! then for ribands, gloves, and
    rings!
Ay! more than twenty pretty things—
One brings me this, another that,
And I shall have—I know not what! "

Fired with the thought—the sanguine
    lass!—
Of what was thus to come to pass,
Her heart beat strong; she gave a
    bound,

And down came milk-pail on the
    ground:
Eggs, fowls, pig, hog (ah, well-a-day!)
Cow, calf, and farm—all swam away!
                    Jean de La Fontaine

SOLOMON AND THE BEES

When Solomon was reigning in his
    glory,
    Unto his throne the Queen of
        Sheba came—
(So in the Talmud you may read the
    story)—
    Drawn by the magic of the mon-
        arch's fame,
To see the splendors of his court,
    and bring
Some fitting tribute to the mighty
    King.

Not this alone: much had her high-
    ness heard
    What flowers of learning graced
        the royal speech;
What gems of wisdom dropped with
    every word;
    What wholesome lessons he was
        wont to teach
In pleasing proverbs; and she wished,
    in sooth,
To know if Rumor spoke the simple
    truth.

Besides, the Queen had heard
    (which piqued her most)
    How through the deepest riddles
        he could spy;
How all the curious arts that women
    boast
    Were quite transparent to his
        piercing eye;
And so the Queen had come—a royal
    guest—
To put the sage's cunning to the test.

And straight she held before the
    monarch's view,
      In either hand, a radiant wreath of
      flowers;
The one bedecked with every charm-
    ing hue,
      Was newly culled from Nature's
      choicest bowers;
The other, no less fair in every part,
Was the rare product of divinest Art.

"Which is the true, and which the
    false?" she said.
      Great Solomon was silent. All
      amazed,
Each wondering courtier shook his
    puzzled head;
      While at the garlands long the
      monarch gazed,
As one who sees a miracle, and fain
For very rapture, ne'er would speak
    again.

"Which is the true?" once more the
    woman asked,
Pleased at the fond amazement of
    the King;
"So wise a head should not be hardly
    tasked,
      Most learned Liege, with such a
      trivial thing!"
But still the sage was silent; it was
    plain
A deepening doubt perplexed the
    royal brain.

While thus he pondered, presently
    he sees,
      Hard by the casement—so the
      story goes—
A little band of busy bustling bees,
      Hunting for honey in a withered
      rose.

The monarch smiled, and raised his
    royal head;
"Open the window!"—that was all
    he said.

The window opened at the King's
    command;
      Within the rooms the eager in-
      sects flew,
And sought the flowers in Sheba's
    dexter hand!
      And so the King and all the court-
      iers knew
That wreath was Nature's; and the
    baffled Queen
Returned to tell the wonders she
    had seen.

My story teaches (every tale should
    bear
      A fitting moral) that the wise may
      find
In trifles light as atoms of the air
      Some useful lesson to enrich the
      mind—
Some truth designed to profit or to
    please—
As Israel's King learned wisdom
    from the bees.

                  John Godfrey Saxe

THE FORSAKEN MERMAN

Come, dear children, let us away;
Down and away below!
Now my brothers call from the bay,
Now the great winds shoreward blow,
Now the salt tides seaward flow;
Now the wild white horses play,
Champ and chafe and toss in the
    spray.
Children dear, let us away!
This way, this way!
Call her once before you go—

Call once yet!
In a voice that she will know:
" Margaret! Margaret! "
Children's voices should be dear
(Call once more) to a mother's ear;
Children's voices, wild with pain—
Surely she will come again!
Call her once and come away;
This way, this way!
" Mother dear, we cannot stay!
    The wild white horses foam and
      fret."
    Margaret! Margaret!

Come, dear children, come away
    down;
Call no more!
One last look at the white-wall'd
    town,
And the little grey church on the
    windy shore;
Then come down!
She will not come though you call
    all day;
Come away, come away!

Children dear, was it yesterday
We heard the sweet bells over the
    bay?
In the caverns where we lay,
Through the surf and through the
    swell,
The far-off sound of a silver bell?
Sand-strewn caverns, cool and deep,
Where the winds are all asleep;
Where the spent lights quiver and
    gleam,
Where the salt weed sways in the
    stream,
Where the sea-beasts, ranged all
    round,
Feed in the ooze of their pasture-
    ground;
Where the sea-snakes coil and twine,

Dry their mail and bask in the brine;
Where great whales come sailing by,
Sail and sail, with unshut eye,
Round the world for ever and aye?
When did music come this way?
Children dear, was it yesterday?

Children dear, was it yesterday
(Call yet once) that she went away?
Once she sate with you and me,
On a red gold throne in the heart of
    the sea,
And the youngest sate on her knee.
She comb'd its bright hair, and she
    tended it well,
When down swung the sound of a
    far-off bell.
She sigh'd, she look'd up through
    the clear green sea;
She said, " I must go, for my kins-
    folk pray
In the little grey church on the shore
    today.
'Twill be Easter-time in the world—
    ah me!
And I lose my poor soul, Merman!
    here with thee."
I said: " Go up, dear heart, through
    the waves;
Say thy prayer, and come back to
    the kind sea-caves! "
She smiled, she went up through the
    surf in the bay,
Children dear, was it yesterday?

Children dear, were we long alone?
" The sea grows stormy, the little ones
    moan;
Long prayers," I said, " in the world
    they say;
Come! " I said; and we rose through
    the surf in the bay.
We went up the beach, by the sandy
    down

Where the sea-stocks bloom, to the
  white-wall'd town;
Through the narrow paved streets,
  where all was still,
To the little grey church on the
  windy hill.
From the church came a murmur of
  folk at their prayers,
But we stood without in the cold
  blowing airs.
We climb'd on the graves, on the
  stones worn with rains,
And we gazed up the aisle through
  the small leaded panes.
She sate by the pillar; we saw her
  clear:
"Margaret hist! come quick, we are
  here!

"Dear heart," I said, "we are long
  alone;
The sea grows stormy, the little ones
  moan."
But, ah, she gave me never a look,
For her eyes were sealed to the holy
  book!
Loud prays the priest; shut stands
  the door.
Come away, children, call no more!
Come away, come down, call no
  more!
Down, down, down!
Down to the depths of the sea!
She sits at her wheel in the hum-
  ming town,
Singing most joyfully.
Hark what she sings: "O joy, O joy,
For the humming street, and the
  child with its toy!
For the priest, and the bell, and the
  holy well;
For the wheel where I spun,
And the blessed light of the sun!"
And so she sings her fill,

Singing most joyfully,
Till the spindle drops from her hand,
And the whizzing wheel stands still.
She steals to the window, and looks
  at the sand,
And over the sand at the sea;
And her eyes are set in a stare;
And anon there breaks a sigh,
And anon there drops a tear,
From a sorrow-clouded eye,
And a heart sorrow-laden,
A long, long sigh;
For the cold strange eyes of a little
  Mermaiden,
And the gleam of her golden hair.

Come away, away, children;
Come, children, come down!
The hoarse wind blows colder;
Lights shine in the town.
She will start from her slumber
When gusts shake the door;
She will hear the winds howling,
Will hear the waves roar.
We shall see, while above us
The waves roar and whirl,
A ceiling of amber,
A pavement of pearl.
Singing: "Here came a mortal,
But faithless was she!
And alone dwell for ever
The kings of the sea."

But children, at midnight,
When soft the winds blow,
When clear falls the moonlight,
When spring-tides are low;
When sweet airs come seaward
From heaths starr'd with broom,
And high rocks throw mildly
On the blanch'd sands a gloom,
Up the still, glistening beaches
Up the creeks we will hie,
Over banks of bright seaweed

The ebb-tide leaves dry.
We will gaze, from the sand-hills,
At the white, sleeping town,
At the church on the hill-side—
And then come back down.
Singing: "There dwells a loved one,
But cruel is she!
She left lonely for ever
The kings of the sea."

Matthew Arnold

THE PIED PIPER OF HAMELIN

Hamelin Town's in Brunswick
By famous Hanover city;
   The river Weser, deep and wide,
   Washes its wall on the southern
     side;
   A pleasanter spot you never spied;

But, when begins my ditty,
   Almost five hundred years ago,
   To see the townsfolk suffer so
    From vermin was a pity.

                Rats!

They fought the dogs, and killed the
   cats,
   And bit the babies in the cradles,
And ate the cheeses out of the vats,
   And licked the soup from the cook's
    own ladles,
Split open the kegs of salted sprats,
Made nests inside men's Sunday hats,
And even spoiled the women's chats,
   By drowning their speaking
   With shrieking and squeaking
In fifty different sharps and flats.

   At last the people in a body
    To the Town Hall came flocking:
" 'Tis clear," cried they, "our
    Mayor's a noddy;
   And as for our Corporation—
    shocking

To think that we buy gowns lined
   with ermine
For dolts that can't or won't de-
   termine
What's best to rid us of our vermin!
You hope, because you're old and
   obese,
To find in the furry civic robe ease?
Rouse up, sirs! Give your brain a
   racking
To find the remedy we're lacking,
Or, sure as fate, we'll send you pack-
   ing!"
At this the Mayor and Corporation
Quaked with a mighty consternation.

   An hour they sat in council,
    At length the Mayor broke silence:
" For a guilder I'd my ermine gown
    sell;
   I wish I were a mile hence!
It's easy to bid one rack one's
   brain—
I'm sure my poor head aches again
I've scratched it so, and all in vain,
Oh for a trap, a trap, a trap!"
Just as he said this, what should hap
At the chamber door but a gentle tap?
   " Bless us," cried the Mayor, "what's
    that?"

(With the Corporation as he sat,
Looking little though wondrous fat;
Nor brighter was his eye, nor moister,
Than a too-long-opened oyster,
Save when at noon his paunch grew
   mutinous
For a plate of turtle green and
   glutinous),
   " Only a scraping of shoes on the
    mat?
Anything like the sound of a rat
Makes my heart go pit-a-pat!"
   " Come in!"—the Mayor cried,
    looking bigger:

And in did come the strangest figure.

His queer long coat from heel to head
Was half of yellow and half of red;
And he himself was tall and thin,
With sharp blue eyes, each like a pin,
And light loose hair, yet swarthy skin,
No tuft on cheek nor beard on chin,
But lips where smiles went out and in—
There was no guessing his kith and kin!
And nobody could enough admire
The tall man and his quaint attire.
Quoth one: " It's as my great grand-sire,
Starting up at the Trump of Doom's tone,
Had walked this way from his painted tombstone."

He advanced to the council-table.
And, " Please, your honours," said he, " I'm able,
By means of a secret charm, to draw
All creatures living beneath the sun,
That creep, or swim, or fly, or run,
After me so as you never saw!
And I chiefly use my charm
On creatures that do people harm,
The mole, and toad, and newt, and viper;
And people call me the Pied Piper."
(And here they noticed round his neck
A scarf of red and yellow stripe,
To match with his coat of the selfsame cheque;
And at the scarf's end hung a pipe;
And his fingers, they noticed, were ever straying

As if impatient to be playing
Upon this pipe, as low it dangled
Over his vesture so old-fangled.)
" Yet," said he, " poor piper as I am,
In Tartary I freed the Cham,
Last June, from his huge swarms of gnats;
I eased in Asia the Nizam
Of a monstrous brood of vampire bats:
And, as for what your brain be-wilders,
If I can rid your town of rats
Will you give me a thousand guilders? "
" One? fifty thousand! "—was the exclamation
Of the astonished Mayor and Corpora-tion.

Into the street the Piper stept,
Smiling first a little smile,
As if he knew what magic slept
In his quiet pipe the while;
Then, like a musical adept,
To blow the pipe his lips he wrinkled,
And green and blue his sharp eyes twinkled
Like a candle-flame where salt is sprinkled;
And ere three shrill notes the pipe uttered,
You heard as if an army muttered;
And the muttering grew to a grum-bling;
And the grumbling grew to a mighty rumbling;
And out of the house the rats came tumbling.
Great rats, small rats, lean rats, brawny rats,

Brown rats, black rats, gray rats,
tawny rats,
Grave old plodders, gay young
friskers,
  Fathers, mothers, uncles, cousins,
Cocking tails and pricking whiskers,
  Families by tens and dozens,
Brothers, sisters, husbands, wives—
Followed the Piper for their lives.
From street to street he piped ad-
vancing,
And step by step they followed
dancing,
Until they came to the river Weser
Wherein all plunged and perished
—Save one, who, stout as Julius
Cæsar,
Swam across and lived to carry
(As he the manuscript he cherished)
To Rat-land home his commentary,
Which was, " At the first shrill notes
of the pipe,
I heard a sound as of scraping tripe,
And putting apples, wondrous ripe,
Into a cider press's gripe;
And a moving away of pickle-tub-
boards,
And a leaving ajar of conserve cup-
boards,
And a drawing the corks of train-
oil-flasks,
And a breaking the hoops of butter
casks;
And it seemed as if a voice
(Sweeter far than by harp or by
psaltery
Is breathed) called out, Oh, rats!
rejoice!
The world is grown to one vast dry-
saltery!
To munch on, crunch on, take your
nuncheon,
Breakfast, supper, dinner, luncheon!
And just as a bulky sugar puncheon,

All ready staved, like a great sun
shone
Glorious scarce an inch before me,
Just as methought it said, come, bore
me!
—I found the Weser rolling o'er
me."

You should have heard the Hamelin
people
Ringing the bells till they rocked the
steeple.
  " Go," cried the Mayor, "and get
long poles!
Poke out the nests and block up the
holes!
Consult with carpenters and build-
ers,
And leave in our town not even a
trace
Of the rats! "—when suddenly up
the face
Of the Piper perked in the market-
place,
With a, " First, if you please, my
thousand guilders! "

A thousand guilders! The Mayor
looked blue;
So did the Corporation too.
For council dinners made rare havoc
With Claret, Moselle, Vin-de-Grave,
Hock;
And half the money would replenish
Their cellar's biggest butt with Rhen-
ish.
To pay this sum to a wandering fellow
With a gipsy coat of red and yellow!
  " Beside," quoth the Mayor, with a
knowing wink,
  " Our business was done at the
river's brink;
  We saw with our eyes the vermin
sink,

And what's dead can't come to life,
I think.
So, friend, we're not the folks to
shrink
From the duty of giving you some-
thing to drink,
And a matter of money to put in
your poke,
But, as for the guilders, what we
spoke
Of them, as you very well know, was
in joke.
Besides, our losses have made us
thrifty;
A thousand guilders! Come, take
fifty!"

The piper's face fell, and he cried,
"No trifling! I can't wait, beside!
I've promised to visit by dinnertime
Bagdad, and accepted the prime
Of the Head Cook's pottage, all he's
rich in,
For having left the Caliph's kitchen,
Of a nest of scorpions no survivor—
With him I proved no bargain-
driver,
With you, don't think I'll bate a
stiver!
And folks who put me in a passion
May find me pipe to another fash-
ion."
"How?" cried the Mayor, "d'ye
think I'll brook
Being worse treated than a Cook?
Insulted by a lazy ribald
With idle pipe and vesture piebald?
You threaten us, fellow? Do your
worst,
Blow your pipe there till you burst!"

Once more he stept into the street;
And to his lips again
Laid his long pipe of smooth straight
cane;

And ere he blew three notes (such
sweet
Soft notes as yet musicians cunning
Never gave the enraptured air),
There was a rustling, that seemed like
a bustling
Of merry crowds justling, at pitching
and hustling,
Small feet were pattering, wooden
shoes clattering,
Little hands clapping, and little
tongues chattering,
And, like fowls in a farmyard when
barley is scattering,
Out came the children running.
All the little boys and girls,
With rosy cheeks and flaxen curls,
And sparkling eyes and teeth like
pearls,
Tripping and skipping, ran merrily
after
The wonderful music with shouting
and laughter.
The Mayor was dumb, and the Coun-
cil stood
As if they were changed into blocks of
wood,
Unable to move a step, or cry
To the children merrily skipping by—
And could only follow with the eye
That joyous crowd at the Piper's back.
But how the Mayor was on the rack,
And the wretched Council's bosoms
beat,
As the piper turned from the High
Street
To where the Weser rolled its waters
Right in the way of their sons and
daughters!
However, he turned from South to
West,
And to Koppelberg Hill his steps ad-
dressed,
And after him the children pressed;

Great was the joy in every breast.
  "He never can cross that mighty
    top!
  He's forced to let the piping drop
  And we shall see our children stop! "
When lo! as they reached the moun-
    tain's side,
A wondrous portal opened wide,
As if a cavern was suddenly hollowed;
And the Piper advanced and the chil-
  dren followed,
And when all were in to the very last,
The door in the mountain-side shut
  fast.
Did I say all? No! one was lame,
And could not dance the whole of the
  way;
And in after years, if you would blame
His sadness, he was used to say:
  " It's dull in our town since my play-
    mates left;
  I can't forget that I'm bereft
  Of all the pleasant sights they see,
  Which the Piper also promised me;
  For he led us, he said, to a joyous
    land,
  Joining the town and just at hand,
  Where waters gushed and fruit trees
    grew,
  And flowers put forth a fairer hue,
  And everything was strange and new.
  The sparrows were brighter than pea-
    cocks here,
  And their dogs outran our fallow deer,
  And honey-bees had lost their stings;
  And horses were born with eagle's
    wings;
  And just as I became assured
  My lame foot would be speedily cured,
  The music stopped, and I stood still,
  And found myself outside the Hill,
  Left alone against my will,
  To go now limping as before,
  And never hear of that country more! "

Alas, alas for Hamelin!
  There came into many a burgher's
    pate
  A text which says, that Heaven's
    Gate
  Opes to the Rich at as easy rate
  As the needle's eye takes a camel in!

The Mayor sent East, West, North
    and South,
To offer the Piper by word of mouth,
  Wherever it was men's lot to find
    him,
Silver and gold to his heart's content,
If he'd only return the way he went,
  And bring the children all behind
    him.
But when they saw 'twas a lost en-
    deavour,
And Piper and dancers were gone for-
    ever
They made a decree that lawyers never
  Should think their records dated
    duly
If, after the day of the month and
    year,
These words did not as well appear,
  " And so long after what happened
    here
  On the twenty-second of July,
  Thirteen hundred and seventy-six: "
And the better in memory to fix
The place of the Children's last retreat,
They called it, the Pied Piper's street—
Where any one playing on pipe or
    tabor,
Was sure for the future to lose his
    labour.
Nor suffered they hostelry or tavern
  To shock with mirth a street so
    solemn;
But opposite the place of the cavern
  They wrote the story on a column,

And on the great church window
  painted
The same, to make the world ac-
  quainted
How their children were stolen away;
And there it stands to this very day.
And I must not omit to say
That in Transylvania there's a tribe
Of alien people that ascribe
The outlandish ways and dress,
On which their neighbours lay such
  stress,
To their fathers and mothers having
  risen
Out of some subterraneous prison,
Into which they were trepanned
Long time ago in a mighty band
Out of Hamelin town in Brunswick
  land,
But how or why they don't under-
  stand.

So, Willy, let you and me be wipers
Of scores out with all men—especially
  pipers;
And, whether they pipe us free from
  rats or from mice,
If we've promised them aught, let us
  keep our promise.

Robert Browning

APPLE-SEED JOHN

Poor Johnny was bended well nigh
  double
With years of toil, and care, and
  trouble;
But his large old heart still felt the
  need
Of doing for others some kindly
  deed.

" But what can I do," old Johnny
  said:

" I who work so hard for daily bread?
It takes heaps of money to do much
  good;
I am far too poor to do as I would."

The old man sat thinking deeply a
  while,
Then over his features gleamed a
  smile,
And he clapped his hands with a
  boyish glee,
And said to himself: " There's a way
  for me! "

He worked, and he worked with
  might and main,
But no one knew the plan in his
  brain.
He took ripe apples in pay for
  chores,
And carefully cut from them all the
  cores.

He filled a bag full, then wandered
  away,
And no man saw him for many a
  day.
With knapsack over his shoulder
  slung,
He marched along, and whistled or
  sung.

He seemed to roam with no object
  in view,
Like one who had nothing on earth
  to do;
But, journeying thus o'er the prairies
  wide,
He paused now and then, and his
  bag untied.

With pointed cane deep holes he
  bore,
And in every hole he placed a core;

Then covered them well, and left
  them there
In keeping of sunshine, rain, and air.

Sometimes for days he waded
  through grass,
And saw not a living creature pass,
But often, when sinking to sleep in
  the dark,
He heard the owls hoot and the
  prairie-dogs bark.

Sometimes an Indian of sturdy limb
Came striding along and walked
  with him;
And he who had food shared with
  the other,
As if he had met a hungry brother.

When the Indian saw how the bag
  was filled,
And looked at the holes that the
  white man drilled,
He thought to himself 'twas a silly
  plan
To be planting seed for some future
  man.

Sometimes a log cabin came in view,
Where Johnny was sure to find jobs
  to do,
By which he gained stores of bread
  and meat,
And welcome rest for his weary feet.

He had full many a story to tell,
And goodly hymns that he sung
  right well;
He tossed up the babes, and joined
  the boys
In many a game full of fun and
  noise.

And he seemed so hearty, in work or
  play,

Men, women, and boys all urged him
  to stay;
But he always said: "I have something to do,
And I must go on to carry it
  through."

The boys who were sure to follow
  him round,
Soon found what it was he put in
  the ground;
And so, as time passed and he trav-
  elled on,
Ev'ryone called him " Old Apple-
  Seed John."

Whenever he'd used the whole of
  his store,
He went into cities and worked for
  more;
Then he marched back to the wilds
  again,
And planted seed on hillside and
  plain.

In cities, some said the old man was
  crazy;
While others said he was only lazy;
But he took no notice of jibes and
  jeers,
He knew he was working for future
  years.

He knew that trees would soon
  abound
Where once a tree could not have
  been found;
That a flick'ring play of light and
  shade
Would dance and glimmer along the
  glade;

That blossoming sprays would form
  fair bowers,

And sprinkle the grass with rosy
  showers;
And the little seeds his hands had
  spread,
Would become ripe apples when he
  was dead.

So he kept on travelling far and
  wide,
Till his old limbs failed him, and he
  died.
He said at the last: " 'Tis a comfort
  to feel
I've done good in the world, though
  not a great deal."

Weary travellers, journeying west,
In the shade of his trees find pleasant rest;
And they often start, with glad surprise,
At the rosy fruit that round them
  lies.

And if they inquire whence came
  such trees,
Where not a bough once swayed in
  the breeze,
The answer still comes, as they travel
  on:
" These trees were planted by Apple-
  Seed John."

Lydia Maria Child

OLD GRIMES

Old Grimes is dead; that good old man
  We never shall see more:
He used to wear a long black coat,
  All buttoned down before.

His heart was open as the day,
  His feelings all were true;
His hair was some inclined to gray—
  He wore it in a queue.

Whene'er he heard the voice of pain,
  His breast with pity burned;
The large, round head upon his cane
  From ivory was turned.

Kind words he ever had for all;
  He knew no base design:
His eyes were dark and rather small,
  His nose was aquiline.

He lived at peace with all mankind,
  In friendship he was true;
His coat had pocket-holes behind,
  His pantaloons were blue.

Unharmed, the sin which earth pol-
  lutes
  He passed securely o'er,
And never wore a pair of boots
  For thirty years or more.

But good old Grimes is now at rest,
  Nor fears misfortune's frown:
He wore a double-breasted vest—
  The stripes ran up and down.

He modest merit sought to find,
  And pay it its dessert:
He had no malice in his mind,
  No ruffles on his shirt.

His neighbors he did not abuse—
  Was sociable and gay:
He wore large buckles on his shoes,
  And changed them every day.

His knowledge, hid from public gaze,
  He did not bring to view,
Nor made a noise, town-meeting days,
  As many people do.

His worldly goods he never threw
  In trust to fortune's chances,
But lived (as all his brothers do)
  In easy cricumstances.

Thus undisturbed by anxious cares,
  His peaceful moments ran;
And everybody said he was
  A fine old gentleman.

              Albert Gorton Greene

THE RAVEN

Once upon a midnight dreary, while
  I pondered, weak and weary,
Over many a quaint and curious vol-
  ume of forgotten lore—
While I nodded, nearly napping,
  suddenly there came a tapping,
As of someone gently rapping, rap-
  ping at my chamber door—
" 'Tis some visitor," I muttered, " tap-
  ping at my chamber door—
Only this, and nothing more."

Ah! distinctly I remember, it was in
  the bleak December,
And each separate dying ember
  wrought its ghost upon the
  floor;
Eagerly I wished the morrow; vainly
  I had sought to borrow
From my books surcease of sorrow—
  sorrow for the lost Lenore—
For the rare and radiant maiden
  whom the angels named Lenore—
Nameless here for evermore.

And the silken, sad, uncertain rustling of each purple curtain
Thrilled me—filled me with fantastic
  terrors never felt before;
So that now, to still the beating of
  my heart, I stood repeating,
" 'Tis some visitor entreating entrance
  at my chamber door—
Some late visitor entreating entrance
  at my chamber door:
This it is, and nothing more."

Presently my soul grew stronger;
  hesitating then no longer,
" Sir," said I, " or madam, truly your
  forgiveness I implore;
But the fact is, I was napping, and so
  gently you came rapping,
And so faintly you came tapping,
  tapping at my chamber door,
That I scarce was sure I heard you."
  Here I opened wide the door:
Darkness there, and nothing more.

Deep into that darkness peering,
  long I stood there, wondering,
  fearing,
Doubting, dreaming dreams no mortal ever dared to dream before;
But the silence was unbroken, and
  the stillness gave no token,
And the only word there spoken was
  the whispered word, " Lenore! "
This I whispered, and an echo murmured back the word, " Lenore! "
Merely this, and nothing more.

Back into my chamber turning, all
  my soul within me burning,
Soon again I heard a rapping, something louder than before:
" Surely," said I, " surely that is something at my window lattice;
Let me see then, what thereat is, and
  this mystery explore—
Let my heart be still a moment, and
  this mystery explore.
'Tis the wind, and nothing more."

Open here I flung the shutter, when,
  with many a flirt and flutter,
In there stepped a stately Raven, of
  the saintly days of yore;
Not the least obeisance made he, not
  a minute stopped or stayed he;

But with mien of lord or lady,
    perched above my chamber
    door—
Perched above a bust of Pallas, just
    above my chamber door—
    Perched, and sat, and nothing
    more.

Then this ebony bird beguiling my
    sad fancy into smiling,
By the grave and stern decorum of
    the countenance it wore:
"Though thy crest be shorn and
    shaven, thou," I said, "art sure
    no craven;
Ghastly, grim, and ancient Raven,
    wandering from the nightly
    shore:
Tell me what thy lordly name is on
    the night's Plutonian shore!"
    Quoth the Raven, "Nevermore."

Much I marvelled this ungainly fowl
    to hear discourse so plainly,
Though its answer little meaning,
    little relevancy bore;
For we cannot help agreeing that no
    living human being
Ever yet was blessed with seeing bird
    above his chamber door—
Bird or beast upon the sculptured
    bust above his chamber door
    With such name as "Nevermore."

But the Raven, sitting lonely on that
    placid bust, spoke only
That one word, as if his soul in that
    one word he did outpour:
Nothing further then he uttered, not
    a feather then he fluttered,
Till I scarcely more than muttered—
    "Other friends have flown be-
    fore,

On the morrow *he* will leave me, as
    my hopes have flown before."
    Then the bird said, "Nevermore."

Startled by the stillness broken by
    reply so aptly spoken,
"Doubtless," said I, "what it utters
    is its only stock and store,
Caught from some unhappy master,
    whom unmerciful disaster
Followed fast and followed faster, till
    his songs one burden bore—
Till the dirges of his hope this
    melancholy burden bore—
    Of 'Never, nevermore.'"

But the Raven still beguiling all my
    sad soul into smiling,
Straight I wheeled a cushioned seat
    in front of bird, and bust, and
    door;
Then upon the velvet sinking, I be-
    took myself to linking
Fancy into fancy, thinking what this
    ominous bird of yore—
What this grim, ungainly, ghastly,
    gaunt, and ominous bird of yore
    Meant in croaking "Nevermore."

Thus I sat engaged in guessing, but
    no syllable expressing
To the fowl whose fiery eyes now
    burned into my bosom's core;
This and more I sat divining, with
    my head at ease reclining
On the cushion's velvet lining, that
    the lamp-light gloated o'er,
But whose velvet violet lining, with
    the lamp-light gloating o'er,
    She shall press, ah, nevermore!

Then methought the air grew denser,
    perfumed from an unseen censer
Swung by seraphim, whose footfalls
    tinkled on the tufted floor.

"Wretch," I cried, "thy God hath
    lent thee—by these angels he
    hath sent thee
Respite—respite and nepenthe from
    my memories of Lenore!
Quaff, oh quaff this kind nepenthe,
    and forget this lost Lenore!"
Quoth the Raven, "Nevermore."

"Prophet," said I, "thing of evil—
    prophet still, if bird or devil!
Whether tempter sent, or whether
    tempest tossed thee here ashore
Desolate, yet all undaunted, on this
    desert land enchanted,
On this home by horror haunted—
    tell me truly, I implore,
Is there—is there balm in Gilead?—
    tell me, tell me, I implore!"
Quoth the Raven, "Nevermore."

"Prophet," said I, "thing of evil!—
    prophet still, if bird or devil!
By that heaven that bends above us
    —by that God we both adore—
Tell this soul, with sorrow laden, if,
    within the distant Aiden,
It shall clasp a sainted maiden,whom
    the angels name Lenore:
Clasp a rare and radiant maiden,
    whom the angels name Lenore!"
Quoth the Raven, "Nevermore."

"Be that word our sign of parting,
    bird or fiend," I shrieked up-
    starting—
"Get thee back into the tempest and
    the night's Plutonian shore;
Leave no black plume as a token of
    that lie thy soul hath spoken,
Leave my loneliness unbroken—quit
    the bust above my door,
Take thy beak from out my heart,
    and take thy form from off my
    door!"
Quoth the Raven, "Nevermore."

And the Raven, never flitting, still is
    sitting, still is sitting,
On the pallid bust of Pallas, just
    above my chamber door;
And his eyes have all the seeming of
    a demon's that is dreaming,
And the lamp-light o'er him stream-
    ing, throws his shadow on the
    floor;
And my soul from out that shadow,
    that lies floating on the floor,
Shall be lifted—nevermore!

Edgar Allan Poe

THE LOTOS-EATERS

"Courage!" he said, and pointed to-
    ward the land,
"This mounting wave will roll us
    shoreward soon."
In the afternoon they came unto a
    land
In which it seemed always afternoon.
All round the coast the languid air
    did swoon,
Breathing like one that hath a weary
    dream.
Full-faced above the valley stood the
    moon;
And, like a downward smoke, the
    slender stream
Along the cliff to fall and pause and
    fall did seem.

A land of streams! some, like a
    downward smoke,
Slow-dropping veils of thinnest
    lawn, did go;
And some through wavering lights
    and shadows broke,
Rolling a slumberous sheet of foam
    below.
They saw the gleaming river seaward
    flow

From the inner land: far off, three
    mountain-tops,
Three silent pinnacles of agèd snow,
Stood sun-set flushed; and, dewed
    with showery drops,
Up-clomb the shadowy pine above
    the woven copse.

The charmèd sunset lingered low
    adown
In the red West: through mountain
    clefts the dale
Was seen far inland, and the yellow
    down
Bordered with palm, and many a
    winding vale
And meadow, set with slender gal-
    ingale;
A land where all things always
    seemed the same!
And round about the keel with faces
    pale,
Dark faces pale against that rosy
    flame,
The mild-eyed melancholy Lotos-
    eaters came.

Branches they bore of that en-
    chanted stem,
Laden with flower and fruit, whereof
    they gave
To each, but whoso did receive of
    them
And taste, to him the gushing of the
    wave
Far, far away did seem to mourn and
    rave
On alien shores; and if his fellow
    spake,
His voice was thin, as voices from
    the grave;
And deep-asleep he seemed, yet all
    awake,

And music in his ears his beating
    heart did make.

They sat them down upon the yel-
    low sand,
Between the sun and moon upon
    the shore;
And sweet it was to dream of Father-
    land,
Of child, and wife, and slave; but
    evermore
Most weary seemed the sea, weary
    the oar,
Weary the wandering fields of barren
    foam.
Then someone said, "We will return
    no more;"
And all at once they sang, "Our
    island home
Is far beyond the wave; we will no
    longer roam."

Alfred Tennyson

THE RIME OF THE ANCIENT MARINER

It is an ancient Mariner,
    And he stoppeth one of three.
"By thy long grey beard and glitter-
    ing eye,
    Now wherefore stopp'st thou me?

"The Bridegroom's doors are opened
    wide,
    And I am next of kin;
The guests are met, the feast is set:
    May'st hear the merry din."

He holds him with his skinny hand,
"There was a ship," quoth he.
"Hold off! unhand me, grey-beard
    loon!"
    Eftstoons his hand dropt he.

He holds him with his glittering
  eye—
The Wedding-Guest stood still,
And listens like a three years child:
The Mariner hath his will.

The Wedding-Guest sat on a stone;
He cannot choose but hear;
And thus spake on that ancient man,
The bright-eyed Mariner.

The ship was cheered, the harbor
  cleared,
Merrily did we drop
Below the kirk, below the hill,
Below the lighthouse top.

The Sun came up upon the left,
Out of the sea came he!
And he shone bright, and on the
  right
Went down into the sea.

Higher and higher every day,
Till over the mast at noon—
The Wedding-Guest here beat his
  breast,
For he heard the loud bassoon.

The bride hath paced into the hall,
Red as a rose is she;
Nodding their heads before her goes
The merry minstrelsy.

The Wedding-Guest he beat his
  breast,
Yet he cannot choose but hear;
And thus spake on that ancient man,
The bright-eyed Mariner.

And now the Storm-blast came, and
  he
Was tyrannous and strong:
He struck with his o'ertaking wings,
And chased us south along.

With sloping masts and dipping
  prow,
As who pursued with yell and blow
Still treads the shadow of his foe
And forward bends his head,
The ship drove fast, loud roared the
  blast,
And southward aye we fled.

And now there came both mist and
  snow,
And it grew wondrous cold:
And ice, mast-high, came floating
  by,
As green as emerald.

And through the drifts the snowy
  clift
Did send a dismal sheen:
Nor shapes of men nor beasts we
  ken—
The ice was all between.

The ice was here, the ice was there,
The ice was all around:
It cracked and growled, and roared
  and howled,
Like noises in a swound!

At length did cross an Albatross:
Through the fog it came;
As if it had been a Christian soul,
We hailed it in God's name.

It ate the food it ne'er had eat,
And round and round it flew.
The ice did split with a thunder-fit;
The helmsman steered us through!

And a good south wind sprung up
  behind;
The Albatross did follow,
And every day, for food or play,
Came to the mariners' hollo!

In mist or cloud, on mast or shroud,
It perched for vespers nine;
Whiles all the night, through fog-
smoke white,
Glimmered the white Moon-shine.

" God save thee, ancient Mariner!
From the fiends, that plague thee
thus!—
Why look'st thou so? "—With my
cross-bow
I shot the Albatross.

PART THE SECOND

The Sun now rose upon the right:
Out of the sea came he,
Still hid in mist, and on the left
Went down into the sea.

And the good south wind still blew
behind,
But no sweet bird did follow,
Nor any day, for food or play,
Came to the mariners' hollo!

And I had done an hellish thing,
And it would work 'em woe:
For all averred, I had killed the bird
That made the breeze to blow.
Ah, wretch! said they, the bird to
slay
That made the breeze to blow!

Nor dim nor red, like God's own
head,
The glorious sun uprist:
Then all averred, I had killed the
bird
That brought the fog and mist.
'Twas right, said they, such birds to
slay,
That bring the fog and mist.

The fair breeze blew, the white foam
flew,

The furrow followed free:
We were the first that ever burst
Into that silent sea.

Down dropt the breeze, the sails
dropt down,
'Twas sad as sad could be;
And we did speak only to break
The silence of the sea!

All in a hot and copper sky,
The bloody Sun, at noon,
Right up above the mast did stand,
No bigger than the Moon.

Day after day, day after day,
We stuck, nor breath nor motion,
As idle as a painted ship
Upon a painted ocean.

Water, water, everywhere,
And all the boards did shrink;
Water, water, everywhere,
Nor any drop to drink.

The very deep did rot: O Christ!
That ever this should be!
Yea, slimy things did crawl with legs
Upon the slimy sea.

About, about, in reel and rout
The death-fires danced at night;
The water, like a witch's oils,
Burnt green, and blue, and white.

And some in dreams assurèd were
Of the spirit that plagued us so;
Nine fathom deep he had followed
us
From the land of mist and snow.

And every tongue, through utter
drought,
Was withered at the root;

We could not speak, no more than if
We had been choked with soot.

Ah! well-a-day, what evil looks
Had I from old and young!
Instead of the cross, the Albatross
About my neck was hung.

PART THE THIRD

There passed a weary time. Each
   throat
Was parched, and glazed each eye.
A weary time! a weary time!
How gazed each weary eye,
When looking westward I beheld,
A something in the sky.

At first it seemed a little speck,
And then it seemed a mist:
It moved and moved, and took at
   last
A certain shape, I wist.

A speck, a mist, a shape, I wist!
And still it neared and neared:
As if it dodged a water-sprite,
It plunged and tacked and veered.

With throats unslaked, with black
   lips baked,
We could not laugh nor wail;
Through utter drought all dumb we
   stood!
I bit my arm, I sucked the blood,
And cried, A sail! a sail!

With throats unslaked, with black
   lips baked,
Agape they heard me call:
Gramercy! they for joy did grin,
And all at once their breath drew in,
As they were drinking all.

See! see! (I cried) she tacks no
   more!

Hither to work us weal;
Without a breeze, without a tide,
She steadies with upright keel!

The western wave was all a-flame,
The day was well-nigh done!
Almost upon the western wave
Rested the broad bright Sun;
When that strange shape drove sud-
   denly
Betwixt us and the Sun.

And straight the Sun was decked
   with bars
(Heaven's mother send us grace!)
As if through a dungeon-grate he
   peered,
With broad and burning face.

Alas! (thought I, and my heart beat
   loud,)
How fast she nears and nears!
Are those *her* sails that glance in the
   Sun,
Like restless gossameres?

Are those *her* ribs through which the
   Sun
Did peer, as through a grate?
And is that Woman all her crew?
Is that a Death? and are there two?
Is Death that Woman's mate?

Her lips were red, *her* looks were
   free,
Her locks were yellow as gold;
Her skin was as white as leprosy,
The Night-Mare Life-in-Death was
   she
Who thicks man's blood with cold.

The naked hulk alongside came,
And the twain were casting dice;
"The game is done; I've won! I've
   won!"
Quoth she, and whistles thrice.

The Sun's rim dips; the stars rush
out:
At one stride comes the dark;
With far-heard whisper, o'er the sea,
Off shot the spectre-bark.

We listened and looked sideways up!
Fear at my heart, as at a cup,
My life-blood seemed to sip!
The stars were dim, and thick the
night,
The steersman's face by his lamp
gleamed white;
From the sails the dew did drip—
Till clomb above the eastern bar
The hornèd Moon, with one bright
star
Within the nether tip.

One after one, by the star-dogged
Moon,
Too quick for groan or sigh,
Each turned his face with a ghastly
pang,
And cursed me with his eye.

Four times fifty living men
(And I heard nor sigh nor groan),
With heavy thump, a lifeless lump,
They dropped down one by one.

The souls did from their bodies fly,—
They fled to bliss or woe!
And every soul, it passed me by,
Like the whizz of my cross-bow!

PART THE FOURTH

" I fear thee, ancient Mariner!
I fear thy skinny hand!
And thou art long, and lank, and
brown,
As is the ribbed sea-sand.

" I fear thee, and thy glittering eye,

And thy skinny hand, so brown."—
Fear not, fear not, thou Wedding-
Guest!
This body dropt not down.

Alone, alone, all, all alone,
Alone on a wide, wide sea!
And never a saint took pity on
My soul in agony.

The many men, so beautiful;
And they all dead did lie;
And a thousand thousand slimy
things
Lived on; and so did I.

I looked upon the rotting sea,
And drew my eyes away;
I looked upon the rotting deck,
And there the dead men lay.

I looked to Heaven, and tried to
pray,
But or ever a prayer had gusht,
A wicked whisper came, and made
My heart as dry as dust.

I closed my lids, and kept them close,
And the balls like pulses beat;
For the sky and the sea, and the sea
and the sky,
Lay like a load on my weary eye,
And the dead were at my feet.

The cold sweat melted from their
limbs,
Nor rot nor reek did they:
The look with which they looked on
me
Had never passed away.

An orphan's curse would drag to
Hell
A spirit from on high;

But oh! more horrible than that
Is a curse in a dead man's eye!
Seven days, seven nights, I saw that
   curse,
And yet I could not die.

The moving Moon went up the sky,
And nowhere did abide:
Softly she was going up,
And a star or two beside—

Her beams bemocked the sultry
   main,
Like April hoar-frost spread;
But where the ship's huge shadow
   lay,
The charmèd water burnt alway
A still and awful red.

Beyond the shadow of the ship,
I watched the water-snakes:
They moved in tracks of shining
   white,
And when they reared, the elfish
   light
Fell off in hoary flakes.

Within the shadows of the ship
I watched their rich attire;
Blue, glossy green, and velvet black,
They coiled and swam; and every
   track
Was a flash of golden fire.

O happy living things! no tongue
Their beauty might declare:
A spring of love gushed from my
   heart,
And I blessed them unaware!
Sure my kind saint took pity on me,
And I blessed them unaware.

The self-same moment I could pray;
And from my neck so free

The Albatross fell off, and sank
Like lead into the sea.

PART THE FIFTH

Oh, sleep! it is a gentle thing,
Beloved from pole to pole!
To Mary Queen the praise be given!
She sent the gentle sleep from
   Heaven,
That slid into my soul.

The silly buckets on the deck,
That had so long remained,
I dreamt that they were filled with
   dew;
And when I awoke, it rained.

My lips were wet, my throat was cold,
My garments all were dank;
Sure I had drunken in my dreams,
And still my body drank.

I moved, and could not feel my
   limbs:
I was so light—almost
I thought that I had died in sleep,
And was a blessèd ghost.

And soon I heard a roaring wind:
It did not come anear;
But with its sound it shook the sails,
That were so thin and sere.

The upper air burst into life!
And a hundred fire-flags sheen,
To and fro they were hurried about!
And to and fro, and in and out,
The wan stars danced between.

And the coming wind did roar more
   loud,
And the sails did sigh like sedge;
And the rain poured down from one
   black cloud;
The Moon was at its edge.

The thick black cloud was cleft, and
  still
The Moon was at its side:
Like waters shot from some high crag,
The lightning fell with never a jag
A river steep and wide.

The loud wind never reached the
  ship,
Yet now the ship moved on!
Beneath the lightning and the Moon
The dead men gave a groan.

They groaned, they stirred, they all
  uprose,
Nor spake, nor moved their eyes;
It had been strange, even in a dream,
To have seen those dead men rise.

The helmsman steered, the ship
  moved on;
Yet never a breeze up blew;
The mariners all 'gan work the ropes,
Where they were wont to do;
They raised their limbs like lifeless
  tools—
We were a ghastly crew.

The body of my brother's son
Stood by me, knee to knee!
The body and I pulled at one rope,
But he said nought to me.

" I fear thee, ancient Mariner! "
Be calm, thou Wedding-Guest!
'Twas not those souls that fled in
  pain,
Which to their corses came again,
But a troop of spirits blest:

For when it dawned—they dropped
  their arms,
And clustered round the mast;
Sweet sounds rose slowly through
  their mouths,
And from their bodies passed.

Around, around, flew each sweet
  sound,
Then darted to the Sun;
Slowly the sounds came back again,
Now mixed, now one by one.

Sometimes a-dropping from the sky
I heard the sky-lark sing;
Sometimes all little birds that are,
How they seem to fill the sea and air
With their sweet jargoning!

And now 'twas like all instruments,
Now like a lonely flute;
And now it is an angel's song,
That makes the Heavens be mute.

It ceased; yet still the sails made on
A pleasant noise till noon,
A noise like of a hidden brook
In the leafy month of June,
That to the sleeping woods all night
Singeth a quiet tune.

Till noon we quietly sailed on,
Yet never a breeze did breathe:
Slowly and smoothly went the ship,
Moved onward from beneath.

Under the keel nine fathom deep,
From the land of mist and snow,
The spirit slid: and it was he
That made the ship to go.
The sails at noon left off their tune,
And the ship stood still also.

The Sun, right up above the mast,
Had fixed her to the ocean:
But in a minute she 'gan stir,
With a short uneasy motion—
Backwards and forwards half her
  length
With a short uneasy motion.

Then like a pawing horse let go,
She made a sudden bound;
It flung the blood into my head,
And I fell down in a swound.

How long in that same fit I lay,
I have not to declare;
But ere my living life returned,
I heard and in my soul discerned
Two voices in the air.

" Is it he? " quoth one, " is this the
    man?
By Him who died on cross,
With his cruel bow he laid full low,
The harmless Albatross.

" The spirit who bideth by himself
In the land of mist and snow,
He loved the bird that loved the man
Who shot him with his bow."

The other was a softer voice,
As soft as honey-dew:
Quoth he, " The man hath penance
    done,
And penance more will do."

PART THE SIXTH

FIRST VOICE

But tell me, tell me! speak again,
Thy soft response renewing—
What makes that ship drive on so
    fast?
What is the Ocean doing?

SECOND VOICE

Still as a slave before his lord,
The Ocean hath no blast;
His great bright eye most silently
Up to the Moon is cast—

If he may know which way to go;
For she guides him smooth or grim.

See, brother, see! how graciously
She looketh down on him.

FIRST VOICE

But why drives on that ship so fast,
Without or wave or wind?

SECOND VOICE

The air is cut away before,
And closes from behind.

Fly, brother, fly! more high, more
    high!
Or we shall be belated:
For slow and slow that ship will go,
When the Mariner's trance is abated.

I woke, and we were sailing on
As in a gentle weather:
'Twas night, calm night, the Moon
    was high;
The dead men stood together.

All stood together on the deck,
For a charnel-dungeon fitter:
All fixed on me their stony eyes,
That in the Moon did glitter.

The pang, the curse, with which they
    died,
Had never passed away:
I could not draw my eyes from theirs,
Nor turn them up to pray.

And now this spell was snapt: once
    more
I viewed the ocean green,
And looked far forth, yet little saw
Of what had else been seen—

Like one, that on a lonesome road
Doth walk in fear and dread,
And having once turned round walks
    on,

And turns no more his head;
Because he knows a frightful fiend
Doth close behind him tread.

But soon there breathed a wind on
   me,
Nor sound nor motion made:
Its path was not upon the sea,
In ripple or in shade.

It raised my hair, it fanned my cheek
Like a meadow-gale of spring—
It mingled strangely with my fears,
Yet it felt like a welcoming.

Swiftly, swiftly flew the ship,
Yet she sailed softly too:
Sweetly, sweetly blew the breeze—
On me alone it blew,

Oh! dream of joy! is this indeed
The light-house top I see?
Is this the hill? is this the kirk?
Is this my own countree?

We drifted o'er the harbour-bar,
And I with sobs did pray—
O let me be awake, my God!
Or let me sleep alway.

The harbour-bar was clear as glass,
So smoothly it was strewn!
And on the bay the moonlight lay,
And the shadow of the moon.

The rock shone bright, the kirk no
   less,
That stands above the rock:
The moonlight steeped in silentness
The steady weathercock.

And the bay was white with silent
   light,
Till rising from the same,

Full many shapes, that shadows were,
In crimson colours came.

A little distance from the prow
Those crimson shadows were:
I turned my eyes upon the deck—
Oh, Christ! what saw I there!

Each corse lay flat, lifeless and flat,
And, by the holy rood!
A man all light, a seraph-man,
On every corse there stood.

This seraph-band, each waved his
   hand,
It was a heavenly sight!
They stood as signals to the land,
Each one a lovely light:

This seraph-band, each waved his
   hand,
No voice did they impart—
No voice; but oh! the silence sank
Like music on my heart.

But soon I heard the dash of oars,
I heard the Pilot's cheer;
My head was turned perforce away,
And I saw a boat appear.

The Pilot, and the Pilot's boy,
I heard them coming fast;
Dear Lord in Heaven! it was a joy
The dead men could not blast.

I saw a third—I heard his voice:
It is the Hermit good!
He singeth loud his godly hymns
That he makes in the wood.
He'll shrive my soul, he'll wash away
The Albatross's blood.

PART THE SEVENTH

This Hermit good lives in that wood
Which slopes down to the sea.

How loudly his sweet voice he rears!
He loves to talk with marineres
That come from a far countree.
He kneels at morn, and noon, and
    eve—
He hath a cushion plump;
It is the moss that wholly hides
That rotted old oak stump.

The skiff-boat neared: I heard them
    talk,
" Why, this is strange, I trow!
Where are these lights so many and
    fair,
That signal made but now? "

" Strange, by my faith! " the Hermit
    said—
" And they answered not our cheer!
The planks look warped! and see
    those sails
How thin they are and sere!
I never saw aught like to them,
Unless perchance it were

" Brown skeletons of leaves that lag
My forest-brook along;
When the ivy-tod is heavy with
    snow,
And the owlet whoops to the wolf
    below,
That eats the she-wolf's young."

" Dear Lord! it hath a fiendish look—
    (The Pilot made reply)
I am a-feared "—" Push on, push
    on! "
Said the Hermit cheerily.

The boat came closer to the ship,
But I nor spake nor stirred;
The boat came close beneath the
    ship,
And straight a sound was heard.

Under the water it rumbled on,
Still louder and more dread;
It reached the ship, it split the bay;
The ship went down like lead.

Stunned by that loud and dreadful
    sound,
Which sky and ocean smote,
Like one that hath been seven days
    drowned
My body lay afloat;
But swift as dreams myself I found
Within the Pilot's boat.

Upon the whirl, where sank the ship,
The boat spun round and round;
And all was still, save that the hill
Was telling of the sound.

I moved my lips—the Pilot shrieked
And fell down in a fit;
The holy Hermit raised his eyes,
And prayed where he did sit.

I took the oars; the Pilot's boy,
Who now doth crazy go,
Laughed loud and long, and all the
    while
His eyes went to and fro.
" Ha! ha! " quoth he, " full plain I
    see,
The Devil knows how to row."

And now, all in my own countree
I stood on the firm land!
The Hermit stepped forth from the
    boat
And scarcely he could stand.

" O shrieve me, shrieve me, holy
    man! "
The Hermit crossed his brow,
" Say quick," quoth he, " I bid thee
    say—
What manner of man art thou? "

Forthwith this frame of mine was
    wrenched
With a woeful agony,
Which forced me to begin my tale;
And then it left me free.

Since then, at an uncertain hour,
That agony returns;
And till my ghastly tale is told
This heart within me burns.

I pass, like night, from land to land;
I have strange power of speech;
The moment that his face I see,
I know the man that must hear me:
To him my tale I teach.

What loud uproar bursts from that
    door!
The wedding guests are there:
But in the garden bower the bride
And bride-maids singing are;
And hark the little vesper bell,
Which biddeth me to prayer!

O Wedding-Guest! this soul hath
    been
Alone on a wide, wide sea;
So lonely 'twas that God Himself
Scarce seemed there to be.

O sweeter than the marriage-feast,
'Tis sweeter far to me,
To walk together to the kirk,
With a goodly company!—

To walk together to the kirk,
And all together pray,
While each to his great Father
    bends,
Old men and babes and loving
    friends,
And youths and maidens gay!

Farewell, farewell! but this I tell
To thee, thou Wedding-Guest!
He prayeth well, who loveth well
Both man and bird and beast.

He prayeth best, who loveth best
All things both great and small:
For the dear God who loveth us,
He made and loveth all.

The Mariner whose eye is bright,
Whose beard with age is hoar,
Is gone: and now the Wedding-
    Guest
Turned from the bridegroom's door.

He went like one that hath been
    stunned,
And is of sense forlorn;
A sadder and a wiser man,
He rose the morrow morn.
        Samuel Taylor Coleridge

KUBLA KHAN

In Xanadu did Kubla Khan
A stately pleasure-dome decree:
Where Alph, the sacred river, ran
Through caverns measureless to man
    Down to a sunless sea.
So twice five miles of fertile ground
With walls and towers were girdled
    round:
And there were gardens bright with
    sinuous rills
Where blossomed many an incense-
    bearing tree;
And here were forests ancient as the
    hills,
Enfolding sunny spots of greenery.

But oh! that deep romantic chasm
    which slanted
Down the green hill athwart a cedarn
    cover!

A savage place! as holy and enchanted
As e'er beneath a waning moon was
    haunted
By woman wailing for her demon-
    lover!
And from this chasm, with ceaseless
    turmoil seething,
As if this earth in fast thick pants were
    breathing,
A mighty fountain momently was
    forced:
Amid whose swift half-intermitted
    burst
Huge fragments vaulted like rebound-
    ing hail,
Or chaffy grain beneath the thresher's
    flail:
And 'mid these dancing rocks at once
    and ever
It flung up momently the sacred river,
Five miles meandering with a mazy
    motion
Through wood and dale the sacred
    river ran,
Then reached the caverns measureless
    to man,
And sank in tumult to a lifeless ocean:
And 'mid this tumult Kubla heard
    from far
Ancestral voices prophesying war!

The shadow of the dome of pleasure
Floated midway on the waves;
Where was heard the mingled
    measure
From the fountain and the caves.
It was a miracle of rare device,
A sunny pleasure-dome with caves of
    ice!
A damsel with a dulcimer
In a vision once I saw:
It was an Abyssinian maid,
And on her dulcimer she played,

Singing of Mount Abora.
Could I revive within me
Her symphony and song,
To such a deep delight 'twould win
    me
That with music loud and long,
I would build that dome in air,
That sunny dome! those caves of ice!
And all who heard should see them
    there,
And all should cry, Beware! Beware!
His flashing eyes, his floating hair!
Weave a circle round him thrice,
And close your eyes with holy dread,
For he on honey-dew hath fed,
And drunk the milk of Paradise.

Samuel Taylor Coleridge

TO SEA! TO SEA!

To sea! to sea! the calm is o'er,
    The wanton water leaps in sport,
And rattles down the pebbly shore,
    The dolphin wheels, the sea cows
        snort;
And unseen mermaid's pearly song
Comes bubbling up, the weeds among.
Fling broad the sail, dip deep the oar:
To sea! to sea! the calm is o'er.

To sea! to sea! our white winged bark
    Shall billowing cleave its watery
        way,
And with its shadow, fleet and dark,
    Break the caved Triton's azure day.

Like mountain eagle soaring light
O'er antelopes on Alpine height.
The anchor heaves! the ship swings
    free!
Our sails swell full! To sea! to sea!

Thomas Lovell Beddoes

THE SEA

The sea! the sea! the open sea!
The blue, the fresh, the ever free!
Without a mark, without a bound,
It runneth the earth's wide regions
round;
It plays with the clouds; it mocks the
skies;
Or like a cradled creature lies.

I'm on the sea! I'm on the sea!
I am where I would ever be;
With the blue above, and the blue
below,
And silence wheresoe'er I go;
If a storm should come and awake the
deep
What matter? I shall ride and sleep.

I love (oh, how I love!) to ride
On the fierce, foaming, bursting tide,
When every mad wave drowns the
moon,
Or whistles aloft his tempest tune,
And tells how goeth the world below,
And why the south-west blasts do
blow.

I never was on the dull, tame shore,
But I loved the great sea more and
more,
And backwards flew to her billowy
breast,
Like a bird that seeketh its mother's
nest:
And a mother she was and is to me;
For I was born on the open sea!

I've lived since then in calm and strife,
Full fifty summers a sailor's life,
With wealth to spend, and a power to
range,
But never have sought nor sighed for
change;
And Death, whenever he comes to me,
Shall come on the wild unbounded
sea!

Barry Cornwall

WINDLASS SONG

Heave at the windlass!—Heave O.
cheerly, men!
Heave all at once, with a will!
The tide quickly making,
Our cordage a-creaking,
The water has put on a frill,
Heave O!

Fare you well, sweethearts!—Heave O,
cheerly, men!
Fare you well, frolic and sport!
The good ship all ready
Each dog-vane is steady,
The wind blowing dead out of port.
Heave O!

Once in blue water—Heave O, cheerly,
men!
Blow it from north or from south;
She'll stand to it tightly,
And curtsey politely,
And carry a bone in her mouth,
Heave O!

Short cruise or long cruise—Heave O,
cheerly, men!
Jolly Jack Tar thinks it one.
No latitude dreads he
Of White, Black, or Red Sea,
Great icebergs, or tropical sun,
Heave O!

One other turn, and Heave O, cheerly,
men!
Heave, and good-bye to the shore!
Our money, how went it?
We shared it and spent it;
Next year we'll come back with some
more,
Heave O!
William Allingham

A WET SHEET AND A
FLOWING SEA

A wet sheet and a flowing sea,
   A wind that follows fast,
And fills the white and rustling sail,
   And bends the gallant mast;
And bends the gallant mast, my boys,
   While, like the eagle free,
Away the good ship flies, and leaves
   Old England on the lee.

O for a soft and gentle wind!
   I heard a fair one cry;
But give to me the snoring breeze
   And white waves heaving high;
And white waves heaving high, my
   boys,
   The good ship tight and free—
The world of waters is our home,
   And merry men are we.

There's tempest in yon hornèd moon,
   And lightning in yon cloud;
And hark the music mariners!
   The wind is piping loud;
The wind is piping loud, my boys,
   The lightning flashing free—
While the hollow oak our palace is,
   Our heritage the sea.

Allan Cunningham

Part Three

POEMS OF PATRIOTISM AND HISTORY

THE SOLDIER

If I should die, think only this of me:
    That there's some corner of a foreign
      field
That is for ever England. There shall
    be
    In that rich earth a richer dust con-
      cealed;
A dust whom England bore, shaped,
    made aware,
    Gave, once, her flowers to love, her
      ways to roam,
A body of England's, breathing Eng-
    lish air,
    Washed by the rivers, blest by suns
      of home.

And think, this heart, all evil shed
    away,
    A pulse in the eternal mind, no less
Gives somewhere back the thoughts by
    England given;
Her sights and sounds; dreams happy
    as her day,
    And laughter, learnt of friends; and
      gentleness,
In hearts at peace, under an English
    heaven.

Rupert Brooke

THE STAR-SPANGLED BANNER

Oh say, can you see by the dawn's
    early light,
    What so proudly we hailed at the
      twilight's last gleaming?
Whose broad stripes and bright stars,
    through the perilous fight
    On the ramparts we watched, were
      so gallantly streaming.
And the rocket's red glare, the bombs
    bursting in air,
Gave proof through the night that our
    flag was still there;
    Oh say, does the star-spangled ban-
      ner yet wave
    O'er the land of the free and the
      home of the brave?

On the shore dimly seen, through the
    mists of the deep,
    Where the foe's haughty host in
      dread silence reposes,
What is that which the breeze o'er
    the towering steep,
    As it fitfully blows, half conceals,
      half discloses?
Now it catches the gleam of the morn-
    ing's first beam:

In full glory reflected, now shines on
    the stream;
    'Tis the star-spangled banner, O long
      may it wave
    O'er the land of the free and the
      home of the brave.

And where is that band who so vaunt-
    ingly swore
    That the havoc of war and the bat-
      tle's confusion
A home and a country should leave us
    no more?
    Their blood has washed out their
      foul footsteps' pollution.
No refuge could save the hireling and
    slave
From the terror of flight, or the gloom
    of the grave:
    And the star-spangled banner in
      triumph doth wave
    O'er the land of the free and the
      home of the brave!

Oh! thus be it ever, when freemen
    shall stand
    Between their loved homes and the
      war's desolation!
Blest with victory and peace, may the
    heaven-rescued land
    Praise the Power that hath made
      and preserved us a nation.
Then conquer we must, for our cause
    it is just,
And this be our motto: "In God is
    our trust."
    And the star-spangled banner in
      triumph shall wave
    O'er the land of the free and the
      home of the brave!
              Francis Scott Key

AMERICA

My country, 'tis of thee,
Sweet land of liberty,

Of thee I sing;
Land where my fathers died,
Land of the pilgrims' pride,
From every mountain-side
    Let Freedom ring.

My native country, thee,
Land of the noble free,—
    Thy name I love;
I love thy rocks and rills,
Thy woods and templed hills;
My heart with rapture thrills
    Like that above.

Let music swell the breeze,
And ring from all the trees
    Sweet Freedom's song;
Let mortal tongues awake,
Let all that breathe partake,
Let rocks their silence break,—
    The sound prolong.

Our fathers' God, to Thee,
Author of liberty,
    To Thee we sing;
Long may our land be bright
With Freedom's holy light;
Protect us by Thy might,
    Great God, our King.
           Samuel Francis Smith

AMERICA THE BEAUTIFUL

O beautiful for spacious skies,
    For amber waves of grain,
For purple mountain majesties
    Above the fruited plain!
      America! America!
    God shed His grace on thee
And crown thy good with brotherhood
    From sea to shining sea!

O beautiful for pilgrim feet,
    Whose stern, impassioned stress

A thoroughfare for freedom beat
   Across the wilderness!
         America! America!
   God mend thine every flaw,
Confirm thy soul in self-control,
   Thy liberty in law!

O beautiful for heroes proved
   In liberating strife,
Who more than self their country
      loved,
   And mercy more than life!
         America! America!
   May God thy gold refine
Till all success be nobleness
   And every gain divine!

O beautiful for patriot dream
   That sees beyond the years
Thine alabaster cities gleam
   Undimmed by human tears!
         America! America!
   God shed His grace on thee
And crown thy good with brotherhood
   From sea to shining sea!

                 Katherine Lee Bates

OLD FLAG

What shall I say to you, Old Flag?
You are so grand in every fold,
So linked with mighty deeds of old,
So steeped in blood where heroes fell,
So torn and pierced by shot and shell,
So calm, so still, so firm, so true,
My throat swells at the sight of you,
         Old Flag.

What of the men who lifted you, Old
      Flag,
Upon the top of Bunker's Hill,
Who crushed the Briton's cruel will,
'Mid shock and roar and crash and
      scream,

Who crossed the Delaware's frozen
      stream,
Who starved, who fought, who bled,
      who died,
That you might float in glorious pride,
         Old Flag?

What of the women brave and true,
      Old Flag,
Who, while the cannon thundered
      wild,
Sent forth a husband, lover, child,
Who labored in the field by day,
Who, all the night long, knelt to pray,
And thought that God great mercy
      gave,
If only freely you might wave,
         Old Flag?

What is your mission now, Old Flag?
What but to set all peoples free,
To rid the world of misery,
To guard the right, avenge the wrong,
And gather in one joyful throng
Beneath your folds in close embrace
All burdened ones of every race,
         Old Flag.

Right nobly do you lead the way, Old
      Flag.
Your stars shine out for liberty,
Your white stripes stand for purity,
Your crimson claims that courage high
For Honor's sake to fight and die.
Lead on against the alien shore!
We'll follow you e'en to Death's door,
         Old Flag!

                 Hubbard Parker

BATTLE HYMN OF THE
REPUBLIC

Mine eyes have seen the glory of the
   coming of the Lord;

He is trampling out the vintage
where the grapes of wrath are
stored;
He hath loosed the fateful lightning
of His terrible swift sword;
His truth is marching on.

I have seen Him in the watch-fires of
a hundred circling camps;
They have builded Him an altar in
the evening dews and damps;
I can read His righteous sentence by
the dim and flaring lamps;
His day is marching on.

I have read a fiery gospel, writ in
burnished rows of steel:
" As ye deal with my contemners, so
with you my grace shall deal;
Let the Hero, born of woman, crush
the serpent with his heel,
Since God is marching on."

He has sounded forth the trumpet
that shall never call retreat;
He is sifting out the hearts of men
before His judgment-seat:
Oh, be swift, my soul, to answer
Him! be jubilant, my feet!
Our God is marching on.

In the beauty of the lilies Christ was
born across the sea,
With a glory in His bosom that
transfigures you and me:
As He died to make men holy, let us
die to make men free,
While God is marching on.

Julia Ward Howe

CONCORD HYMN

By the rude bridge that arched the
flood,

Their flag to April's breeze unfurled,
Here once the embattled farmers
stood,
And fired the shot heard round the
world.

The foe long since in silence slept;
Alike the conqueror silent sleeps;
And Time the ruined bridge has swept
Down the dark stream which sea-
ward creeps.

On this green bank, by this soft
stream,
We set today a votive stone;
That memory may their deed redeem,
When, like our sires, our sons are
gone.

Spirit, that made those heroes dare
To die, and leave their children free,
Bid Time and Nature gently spare
The shaft we raise to them and thee.

Ralph Waldo Emerson

OUR MOTHER TONGUE

Beyond the vague Atlantic deep,
Far as the farthest prairies sweep,
Where forest-glooms the nerve appall,
Where burns the radiant western fall,
One duty lies on old and young,—
With filial piety to guard,
As on its greenest native sward,
The glory of the English tongue.
That ample speech! That subtle
speech!
Apt for the need of all and each,
Strong to endure, yet prompt to bend
Wherever human feelings tend.
Preserve its force—expand its powers;
And through the maze of civic life,
In Letters, Commerce, even in Strife,
Forget not it is yours and ours.

Lord Houghton

INDIAN NAMES

Ye say they all have passed away,
  That noble race and brave;
That their light canoes have vanished
  From off the crested wave;
That, mid the forests where they
    roamed,
  There rings no hunter's shout;
But their name is on your waters,
  Ye may not wash it out.

'Tis where Ontario's billow
  Like ocean's surge is curled,
Where strong Niagara's thunders
    wake
  The echo of the world,
Where red Missouri bringeth
  Rich tribute from the west,
And Rappahannoch sweetly sleeps
  On green Virginia's breast.

Ye say their conelike cabins,
  That clustered o'er the vale,
Have disappeared, as withered leaves
  Before the autumn's gale;
But their memory liveth on your hills,
  Their baptism on your shore,
Your everlasting rivers speak
  Their dialect of yore.

Old Massachusetts wears it
  Within her lordly crown,
And broad Ohio bears it
  Amid his young renown.
Connecticut hath wreathed it
  Where her quiet foliage waves,
And bold Kentucky breathes it hoarse
  Through all her ancient caves.

Wachusett hides its lingering voice
  Within its rocky heart,
And Alleghany graves its tone
  Throughout his lofty chart.

Monadnock, on his forehead hoar,
  Doth seal the sacred trust,
Your mountains build their monu-
    ment,
  Though ye destroy their dust.
    Lydia Huntly Sigourney

THE WORD OF GOD TO LEYDEN CAME

The word of God to Leyden came,
  Dutch town by Zuyder Zee:
Rise up, my children of no name,
  My kings and priests to be.
There is an empire in the West,
  Which I will soon unfold;
A thousand harvests in her breast,
  Rocks ribbed with iron and gold.

Rise up, my children, time is ripe!
  Old things are passed away.
Bishops and kings from earth I wipe;
  Too long they've had their day.
A little ship have I prepared
  To bear you o'er the seas;
And in your souls, my will declared,
  Shall grow by slow degrees.

Beneath my throne the martyrs cry:
  I hear their voice, How long?
It mingles with their praises high,
  And with their victor song.
The thing they longed and waited for,
  But died without the sight;
So, this shall be! I wrong abhor,
  The world I'll now set right.

Leave, then, the hammer and the loom,
  You've other work to do;
For Freedom's commonwealth there's
    room,
  And you shall build it too.
I'm tired of bishops and their pride,
  I'm tired of kings as well;

Henceforth I take the people's side,
  And with the people dwell.

Tear off the mitre from the priest,
  And from the king, his crown;
Let all my captives be released;
  Lift up, whom men cast down.
Their pastors let the people choose,
  And choose their rulers too;
Whom they select, I'll not refuse,
  But bless the work they do.

The Pilgrims rose, at this, God's word,
  And sailed the wintry seas:
With their own flesh nor blood con-
  ferred,
    Nor thought of wealth or ease.
They left the towers of Leyden town,
  They left the Zuyder Zee;
And where they cast their anchor
  down,
    Rose Freedom's realm to be.

         Jeremiah Eames Rankin

THE LANDING OF THE PILGRIM FATHERS

The breaking waves dashed high
  On a stern and rock-bound coast,
And the woods against a stormy sky
  Their giant branches tossed.

And the heavy night hung dark
  The hills and waters o'er,
When a band of exiles moored their
  bark
    On the wild New England shore.

Not as the conqueror comes,
  They, the true-hearted, came,
Not with the roll of stirring drums,
  And the trumpet that sings of fame;

Not as the flying come,
  In silence and in fear,—

They shook the depths of the desert's
  gloom
    With their hymns of lofty cheer.

Amidst the storm they sang,
  And the stars heard and the sea!
And the sounding aisles of the dim
  wood rang
    To the anthems of the free!

The ocean-eagle soared
  From his nest by the white waves'
  foam,
And the rocking pines of the forest
  roared,—
    This was their welcome home!

There were men with hoary hair
  Amidst that pilgrim-band;
Why had they come to wither there,
  Away from their childhood's land?

There was woman's fearless eye,
  Lit by her deep love's truth;
There was manhood's brow serenely
  high,
    And the fiery heart of youth.

What sought they thus afar?
  Bright jewels of the mine?
The wealth of seas, the spoils of war?
  They sought a faith's pure shrine!

Ay, call it holy ground,
  The soil where first they trod!
They have left unstained what there
  they found,—
    Freedom to worship God!

         Felicia Dorothea Hemans

POCAHONTAS

Wearied arm and broken sword
  Wage in vain the desperate fight:
Round him press a countless horde,
  He is but a single knight.

Hark a cry of triumph shrill
  Through the wilderness resounds,
  As with twenty bleeding wounds
Sinks the warrior fighting still.

Now they heap the fatal pyre,
  And the torch of death they light;
Ah! 'tis hard to die of fire!
  Who will shield the captive knight?
Round the stake with fiendish cry
  Wheel and dance the savage crowd,
  Cold the victim's mien and proud,
And his breast is bared to die.

Who will shield the fearless heart?
  Who avert the murderous blade?
From the throng, with sudden start,
  See there springs an Indian maid.
Quick she stands before the knight:
  "Loose the chain, unbind the ring;
  I am daughter of the king,
And I claim the Indian right!"

Dauntlessly aside she flings
  Lifted axe and thirsty knife;
Fondly to his heart she clings,
  And her bosom guards his life!
In the woods of Powhatan,
  Still 'tis told by Indian fires,
  How a daughter of their sires
Saved the captive Englishman.
          William Makepeace Thackeray

RODNEY'S RIDE

In that soft mid-land where the
    breezes bear
The North and the South on the
    genial air,
Through the county of Kent, on af-
    fairs of state,
Rode Cæsar Rodney, the delegate.

Burly and big, and bold and bluff,

In his three-cornered hat and coat of
    snuff,
A foe to King George and the Eng-
    lish State,
Was Cæsar Rodney, the delegate.

Into Dover village he rode apace,
And his kinsfolk knew, from his
    anxious face,
It was matter grave that brought him
    there,
To the counties three on the Dela-
    ware.

"Money and men we must have," he
    said,
"Or the Congress fails and our cause
    is dead;
  Give us both and the King shall not
    work his will.
  We are men, since the blood of
    Bunker Hill!"

Comes a rider swift on a panting
    bay:
"Ho, Rodney, ho! you must save the
    day,
  For the Congress halts at a deed so
    great,
  And your vote alone may decide its
    fate."

Answered Rodney then: "I will ride
    with speed;
It is Liberty's stress; it is Freedom's
    need.
When stands it?" "Tonight. Not
    a moment to spare,
But ride like the wind from the
    Delaware."

"Ho, saddle the black! I've but half a
    day,
  And the Congress sits eighty miles
    away—

And I'll be in time, if God grants me
grace,
To shake my fist in King George's
face."

He is up; he is off! and the black
horse flies
On the northward road ere the
" Godspeed " dies;
It is gallop and spur, as the leagues
they clear,
And the clustering mile-stones move
a-rear.

It is two of the clock; and the fleet
hoofs fling
The Fieldboro's dust with a clang
and a cling;
It is three; and he gallops with slack
rein where
The road winds down to the Delaware.

Four; and he spurs into New Castle
town,
From his panting steed he gets him
down—
" A fresh one, quick! not a moment's
wait! "
And off speeds Rodney, the delegate.

It is five; and the beams of the western sun
Tinge the spires of the Wilmington
gold and dun;
Six; and the dust of Chester Street
Flies back in a cloud from the courser's feet.

It is seven; the horse-boat broad of
beam,
At the Schuylkill ferry crawls over
the stream—
And at seven-fifteen by the Ritten-
house clock,
He flings his reins to the tavern jock.

The Congress is met; the debate's
begun,
And Liberty lags for the vote of
one—
When into the hall, not a moment
late,
Walks Cæsar Rodney, the delegate.

Not a moment late! and that half
day's ride
Forwards the world with a mighty
stride;
For the act was passed; ere the midnight stroke
O'er the Quaker City its echoes
woke.

At Tyranny's feet was the gauntlet
flung;
" We are free! " all the bells through
the colonies rung.
And the sons of the free may recall
with pride
The day of Delegate Rodney's ride.

Elbridge Streeter Brooks

MOLLY PITCHER

'Twas hurry and scurry at Monmouth Town,
For Lee was beating a wild retreat;
The British were riding the Yankees
down,
And panic was pressing on flying
feet.

Galloping down like a hurricane
Washington rode with his sword
hung high,
Mighty as he of the Trojan plain
Fired by a courage from the sky.

" Halt, and stand to your guns! " he
cried.

And a bombardier made swift
reply.
Wheeling his cannon into the tide,
He fell 'neath the shot of a foeman nigh.

Molly Pitcher sprang to his side,
Fired as she saw her husband do;
Telling the king in his stubborn
pride
Women like men to their homes
are true.

Washington rode from the bloody
fray
Up to the gun that a woman
manned.
"Molly Pitcher, you saved the day,"
He said, as he gave her a hero's
hand.

He named her sergeant with manly
praise,
While her war-brown face was wet
with tears—
A woman has ever a woman's ways—
And the army was wild with
cheers.

Kate Brownlee Sherwood

MOLLY MAGUIRE AT MONMOUTH

(Selected Stanzas)

On the bloody field of Monmouth
Flashed the guns of Greene and
Wayne.
Fiercely roared the tide of battle,
Thick the sward was heaped with
slain.
Foremost, facing death and danger,
Hessian, horse, and grenadier,
In the vanguard, fiercely fighting,
Stood an Irish Cannonier.

Loudly roared his iron cannon,
Mingling ever in the strife,
And beside him, firm and daring,
Stood his faithful Irish wife.
Of her bold contempt of danger
Greene and Lee's Brigade could
tell,
Everyone knew "Captain Molly,"
And the army loved her well.

Surged the roar of battle round
them,
Swiftly flew the iron hail,
Forward dashed a thousand bayo-
nets,
That lone battery to assail.
From the foeman's foremost col-
umns
Swept a furious fusillade,
Mowing down the massed battalions
In the ranks of Greene's Brigade.

Fast and faster worked the gunner,
Soiled with powder, blood, and
dust,
English bayonets shone before him,
Shot and shell around him burst;
Still he fought with reckless daring,
Stood and manned her long and
well,
Till at last the gallant fellow
Dead—beside his cannon fell.

With a bitter cry of sorrow,
And a dark and angry frown,
Looked that band of gallant patriots
At their gunner stricken down.
"Fall back, comrades, it is folly
Thus to strive against the foe."
"No! not so," cried Irish Molly;
"We can strike another blow."

Quickly leapt she to the cannon,
In her fallen husband's place,
Sponged and rammed it fast and
steady,

Fired it in the foeman's face.
Flashed another ringing volley,
  Roared another from the gun;
" Boys, hurrah! " cried gallant Molly,
  " For the flag of Washington! "

Greene's brigade, though shorn and
    shattered,
  Slain and bleeding half their men,
When they heard that Irish slogan,
  Turned and charged the foe again.
Knox and Wayne and Morgan rally,
  To the front they forward wheel,
And before their rushing onset
  Clinton's English columns reel.

Still the cannon's voice in anger
  Rolled and rattled o'er the plain,
Till there lay in swarms around it
  Mangled heaps of Hessian slain.
" Forward! charge them with the
    bayonet! "
  'Twas the voice of Washington,
And there burst a fiery greeting
  From the Irish woman's gun.

Monckton falls; against his columns
  Leap the troops of Wayne and
    Lee,
And before their reeking bayonets
  Clinton's red battalions flee.
Morgan's rifles, fiercely flashing,
  Thin the foe's retreating ranks,
And behind them onward dashing
  Ogden hovers on their flanks.

Fast they fly, these boasting Britons,
  Who in all their glory came,
With their brutal Hessian hirelings
  To wipe out our country's name.
Proudly floats the starry banner,
  Monmouth's glorious field is won,
And in triumph Irish Molly
  Stands beside her smoking gun.
                    William Collins

TICONDEROGA

The cold, gray light of the dawning
  On old Carillon falls,
And dim in the mist of the morning
  Stand the grim old fortress walls.
No sound disturbs the stillness
  Save the cataract's mellow roar,
Silent as death is the fortress,
  Silent the misty shore.

But up from the wakening waters
  Comes the cool, fresh morning
    breeze,
Lifting up the banner of Britain,
  And whispering to the trees
Of the swift gliding boats on the
    waters
  That are nearing the fog-shrouded
    land,
With the old Green Mountain Lion,
  And his daring patriot band.

But the sentinel at the postern
  Heard not the whisper low;
He is dreaming of the banks of
    Shannon
  As he walks on his beat to and fro,
Of the starry eyes in Green Erin
  That were dim when he marched
    away,
And a tear down his bronze cheek
    courses,
  'Tis the first for many a day.

A sound breaks the misty stillness,
  And quickly he glances around;
Through the mist, forms like towering
    giants
  Seem rising out of the ground;
A challenge, the firelock flashes,
  A sword cleaves the quivering air,
And the sentry lies dead by the postern,
  Blood staining his bright yellow hair.

Then with a shout that awakens
  All the echoes of the hillside and
    glen,
Through the low, frowning gate of the
    fortress,
  Sword in hand rush the Green
    Mountain men.
The scarce wakened troops of the
    garrison
  Yield up their trust pale with fear;
And down comes the bright British
    banner,
  And out rings a Green Mountain
    cheer.

Flushed with pride, the whole eastern
    heavens
  With crimson and gold are ablaze;
And up springs the sun in his splen-
    dour
  And flings down his arrowy rays,
Bathing in sunlight the fortress,
  Turning to gold the grim walls,
While louder and clearer and higher
  Rings the song of the waterfalls.

Since the taking of Ticonderoga
  A century has rolled away;
But with pride the nation remembers
  That glorious morning in May.
And the cataract's silvery music
  Forever the story tells,
Of the capture of old Carillon,
  The chime of silver bells.
                          V. B. Wilson

ENGLAND AND AMERICA
IN 1782

O thou, that sendest out the man
  To rule by land and sea,
Strong mother of a Lion-line,
Be proud of those strong sons of thine
  Who wrenched their rights from
    thee!

What wonder if in noble heat
  Those men thine arms withstood,
Retaught the lesson thou had'st taught,
And in thy spirit with thee fought—
  Who sprang from English blood!

But thou rejoice with liberal joy,
  Lift up thy rocky face,
And shatter, when the storms are black,
In many a streaming torrent back,
  The seas that shook thy base!

Whatever harmonies of law
  The growing world assume,
Thy work is thine—the single note
From that deep chord which Hampden
    smote
  Will vibrate to the doom.
                          Alfred Tennyson

OLD IRONSIDES

Ay, tear her tattered ensign down!
  Long has it waved on high,
And many an eye has danced to see
  That banner in the sky;
Beneath it rung the battle shout,
  And burst the cannon's roar;—
The meteor of the ocean air
  Shall sweep the clouds no more.

Her deck, once red with heroes' blood,
  Where knelt the vanquished foe,
When winds were hurrying o'er the
    flood,
  And waves were white below,
No more shall feel the victor's tread,
  Or know the conquered knee;—
The harpies of the shore shall pluck
  The eagle of the sea!

Oh, better that her shattered hulk
  Should sink beneath the wave:
Her thunders shook the mighty deep,
  And there should be her grave;

Nail to the mast her holy flag,
  Set every threadbare sail,
And give her to the god of storms,
  The lightning and the gale!
                    Oliver Wendell Holmes

BROWN OF OSSAWATOMIE

John Brown of Ossawatomie spake
  on his dying day:
" I will not have to shrive my soul a
  priest in Slavery's pay.
But let some poor slave-mother
  whom I have striven to free,
With her children, from the gallows-
  stair put up a prayer for me! "

John Brown of Ossawatomie, they
  led him out to die;
And lo! a poor slave-mother with her
  little child pressed nigh.
Then the bold, blue eye grew tender,
  and the old harsh face grew mild,
As he stooped between the jeering
  ranks and kissed the negro's child!

The shadows of his stormy life that
  moment fell apart;
And they who blamed the bloody
  hand forgave the loving heart.
That kiss from all its guilty means
  redeemed the good intent,
And round the grisly fighter's hair
  the martyr's aureole bent!

Perish with him the folly that seeks
  through evil good!
Long live the generous purpose unstained with human blood!
Not the raid of midnight terror, but
  the thought which underlies;
Not the borderer's pride of daring,
  but the Christian's sacrifice.

Nevermore may yon Blue Ridges the
  Northern rifle hear,
Nor see the light of blazing homes
  flash on the negro's spear;
But let the free-winged angel Truth
  their guarded passes scale,
To teach that right is more than
  might, and justice more than mail!

So vainly shall Virginia set her battle
  in array;
In vain her trampling squadrons
  knead the winter snow with clay.
She may strike the pouncing eagle,
  but she dares not harm the dove;
And every gate she bars to Hate,
  shall open wide to Love!
                    John Greenleaf Whittier

THE REVEILLE

Hark! I hear the tramp of thousands,
  And of armèd men the hum;
Lo! a nation's hosts have gathered
  Round the quick alarming drum,—
    Saying, " Come,
    Freemen, come!
Ere your heritage be wasted," said the
    quick alarming drum.

" Let me of my heart take counsel:
  War is not of life the sum;
Who shall stay and reap the harvest
  When the autumn days shall
    come? "
    But the drum
    Echoed, " Come!
Death shall reap the braver harvest,"
    said t h e solemn-sounding
    drum.
" But when won the coming battle,
  What of profit springs therefrom?
What if conquest, subjugation,

Even greater ills become? "
But the drum
Answered, " Come!
You must do the sum to prove it," said
    the Yankee-answering drum.

" What if, 'mid the cannons' thunder,
    Whistling   shot   and   bursting
        bomb,
When my brothers fall around me,
    Should my heart grow cold and
        numb? "
        But the drum
        Answered, " Come!
Better there in death united than in
    life a recreant—Come! "

Thus they answered—hoping, fear-
    ing,
    Some in faith, and doubting some,
Till a trumpet-voice proclaiming,
    Said, " My chosen people, come! "
        Then the drum
        Lo! was dumb,
For the great heart of the nation,
    throbbing, answered, " Lord,
    we come! "

Bret Harte

STONEWALL JACKSON'S WAY

Come, stack arms, men! Pile on the
    rails,
    Stir up the camp-fire bright;
No growling if the canteen fails,
    We'll make a roaring night.
Here Shenandoah brawls along,
There burly Blue Ridge echoes
    strong,
To swell the Brigade's rousing song
    Of " Stonewall Jackson's way."

We see **him** now — the queer
    slouched hat

Cocked o'er his eyes askew;
The shrewd, dry smile; the speech so
    pat,
    So calm, so blunt, so true.
The " Blue-Light Elder " knows 'em
    well;
Says he, " That's Banks—he's fond of
    shell;
Lord save his soul! we'll give him—"
    well!
    That's " Stonewall Jackson's way."

Silence! ground arms! kneel all! caps
    off!
    Old Massa's goin' to pray.
Strangle the fool that dares to scoff!
    Attention! it's his way.
Appealing from his native sod,
In forma pauperis to God:
" Lay bare Thine arm; stretch forth
    Thy rod!
    Amen! " That's " Stonewall Jack-
    son's way."

He's in the saddle now. Fall in!
    Steady! the whole brigade!
Hill's at the ford, cut off; we'll win
    His way out, ball and blade!
What matter if our shoes are worn?
What matter if our feet are torn?
" Quick step! we're with him before
    morn! "
    That's " Stonewall Jackson's way."

The sun's bright lances rout the
    mists
    Of morning, and, by George!
Here's Longstreet, struggling in the
    lists,
    Hemmed in an ugly gorge.
Pope and his Dutchmen, whipped
    before
" Bay'nets and grape! " hear Stonewall
    roar;

" Charge, Stuart! Pay off Ashby's
    score! "
  In " Stonewall Jackson's way."

Ah, Maiden, wait and watch and
    yearn
  For news of Stonewall's band!
Ah! Widow, read, with eyes that
    burn,
  That ring upon thy hand.
Ah! Wife, sew on, pray on, hope on;
Thy life shall not be all forlorn;
The foe had better ne'er been born
  That gets in " Stonewall's way."

        John Williamson Palmer

BARBARA FRIETCHIE

Up from the meadows rich with
    corn,
Clear in the cool September morn,

The clustered spires of Frederick
    stand
Green-walled by the hills of Mary-
    land.

Round about them orchards sweep,
Apple and peach tree fruited deep,

Fair as the garden of the Lord
To the eyes of the famished rebel
    horde,

On that pleasant morn of the early
    fall
When Lee marched over the moun-
    tain-wall;

Over the mountains winding down,
Horse and foot, into Frederick town.

Forty flags with their silver stars,
Forty flags with their crimson bars,

Flapped in the morning wind: the
    sun
Of noon looked down, and saw not
    one.

Up rose old Barbara Frietchie then,
Bowed with her fourscore years and
    ten;

Bravest of all in Frederick town,
She took up the flag the men hauled
    down;

In her attic window the staff she set,
To show that one heart was loyal yet.

Up the street came the rebel tread,
Stonewall Jackson riding ahead.

Under his slouched hat left and right
He glanced; the old flag met his
    sight.

" Halt! "—the dust-brown ranks stood
    fast.
" Fire! "—out blazed the rifle-blast.

It shivered the window, pane and
    sash;
It rent the banner with seam and
    gash.

Quick as it fell, from the broken staff
Dame Barbara snatched the silken
    scarf.

She leaned far out on the window-
    sill,
And shook it forth with a royal will.

" Shoot, if you must, this old gray
    head,
  But spare your country's flag," she
    said.

A shade of sadness, a blush of shame,
Over the face of the leader came;

The nobler nature within him stirred
To life at that woman's deed and
    word;

" Who touches a hair of yon gray
    head
Dies like a dog! March on! " he said.

All day long through the Frederick
    street
Sounded the tread of marching feet:

All day long that free flag tossed
Over the heads of the rebel host.

Ever its torn folds rose and fell
On the loyal winds that loved it
    well;

And through the hill-gaps sunset
    light
Shone over it with a warm good-
    night.

Barbara Frietchie's work is o'er,
And the Rebel rides on his raids no
    more.

Honor to her! and let a tear
Fall, for her sake, on Stonewall's bier.

Over Barbara Frietchie's grave,
Flag of Freedom and Union wave!

Peace and order and beauty draw
Round thy symbol of light and law;

And ever the stars above look down
On thy stars below in Frederick
    town!

                    John Greenleaf Whittier

MARCHING THROUGH GEORGIA

Bring the good old bugle, boys, we'll
    sing another song—
Sing it with a spirit that will start
    the world along—
Sing it as we used to sing it fifty
    thousand strong,
    While we were marching through
    Georgia.

Chorus

" Hurrah! Hurrah! we bring the jubi-
    lee!
Hurrah! Hurrah! the flag that makes
    you free! "
So we sang the chorus from Atlanta
    to the sea,
    While we were marching through
    Georgia.

How the darkeys shouted when they
    heard the joyful sound!
How the turkeys gobbled which our
    commissary found!
How the sweet potatoes even started
    from the ground,
    While we were marching through
    Georgia.

Yes, and there were Union men who
    wept with joyful tears,
When they saw the honored flag
    they had not seen for years;
Hardly could they be restrained from
    breaking forth in cheers
    While we were marching through
    Georgia.

" Sherman's dashing Yankee boys will
    never reach the coast! "
So the saucy rebels said—and 'twas a
    handsome boast,

Had they not forgot, alas! to reckon
   on a host,
    While we were marching through
    Georgia.

So we made a thoroughfare for Freedom and her train,
Sixty miles in latitude—three hundred to the main;
Treason fled before us, for resistance
   was in vain,
    While we were marching through
    Georgia.

        Henry Clay Work

SHERIDAN'S RIDE

Up from the South, at break of day,
Bringing to Winchester fresh dismay,
The affrighted air with a shudder
   bore,
Like a herald in haste, to the chief-
   tain's door,
The terrible grumble, and rumble,
   and roar,
Telling the battle was on once more,
   And Sheridan twenty miles away.

And wider still those billows of war
Thundered along the horizon's bar;
And louder yet into Winchester
   rolled
The roar of that red sea uncontrolled,
Making the blood of the listener
   cold,
As he thought of the stake in that
   fiery fray,
   And Sheridan twenty miles away.

But there is a road from Winchester
   town,
A good, broad highway leading
   down:
And there, through the flush of the
   morning light,

A steed as black as the steeds of night
Was seen to pass, as with eagle
   flight;
As if he knew the terrible need,
He stretched away with his utmost
   speed;
Hills rose and fell, but his heart was
   gay,
   With Sheridan fifteen miles away.

Still sprang from those swift hoofs,
   thundering south,
The dust, like smoke from the cannon's mouth,
Or the trail of a comet, sweeping
   faster and faster,
Foreboding to traitors the doom of
   disaster.
The heart of the steed and the heart
   of the master
Were beating like prisoners assault-
   ing their walls,
Impatient to be where the battle-
   field calls;
Every nerve of the charger was
   strained to full play,
   With Sheridan only ten miles
   away.

Under his spurning feet, the road
Like an arrowy Alpine river flowed,
And the landscape sped away behind
Like an ocean flying before the wind;
And the steed, like a bark fed with
   furnace ire,
Swept on, with his wild eye full of
   fire;
But, lo! he is nearing his heart's
   desire;
He is snuffing the smoke of the roar-
   ing fray,
   With Sheridan only five miles
   away.

The first that the general saw were
    the groups
Of stragglers, and then the retreat-
    ing troops;
What was done? what to do? a
    glance told him both,
Then, striking his spurs, with a ter-
    rible oath,
He dashed down the line, 'mid a
    storm of huzzas,
And the wave of retreat checked its
    course there, because
The sight of the master compelled it
    to pause.
With foam and with dust the black
    charger was gray;
By the flash of his eye, and the red
    nostril's play,
He seemed to the whole great army
    to say:
" I have brought you Sheridan all the
    way
    From Winchester town to save
    the day! "

Hurrah! hurrah for Sheridan!
Hurrah! hurrah for horse and man!
And when their statues are placed on
    high,
Under the dome of the Union sky,
The American soldier's Temple of
    Fame,
There, with the glorious general's
    name,
Be it said, in letters both bold and
    bright:
" Here is the steed that saved the day
By carrying Sheridan into the fight,
    From Winchester—twenty miles
    away! "

Thomas Buchanan Read

SONG OF SHERMAN'S MARCH TO THE SEA

Our camp-fires shone bright on the
    mountains
    That frowned on the river below,
While we stood by our guns in the
    morning,
    And eagerly watched for the foe;
When a rider came out from the dark-
    ness
    That hung over mountain and tree,
And shouted: " Boys, up and be
    ready,
    For Sherman will march to the
    sea."

Then cheer upon cheer for bold Sher-
    man
    Went up from each valley and glen,
And the bugles reëchoed the music
    That came from the lips of the men:
For we knew that the stars in our
    banner
    More bright in their splendor would
    be,
And that blessings from Northland
    would greet us
    When Sherman marched down to
    the sea.

Then forward, boys, forward to battle!
    We marched on our wearisome way,
And we stormed the wild hills of
    Resaca;
    God bless those who fell on that
    day!
Then Kenesaw, dark in its glory,
    Frowned down on the flag of the
    free,
But the East and the West bore our
    standards,
    And Sherman marched on to the
    sea.

Still onward we pressed, till our ban-
ners
Swept out from Atlanta's grim walls,
And the blood of the patriot damp-
ened
The soil where the traitor flag falls;
Yet we paused not to weep for the
fallen,
Who slept by each river and tree;
We twined them a wreath of the laurel
As Sherman marched down to the
sea.

Oh! proud was our army that morn-
ing,
That stood where the pine darkly
towers,
When Sherman said: " Boys, you are
weary;
This day fair Savannah is ours! "
Then sang we a song for our chieftain,
That echoed o'er river and lea,
And the stars in our banner shone
brighter
When Sherman marched down to
the sea.
Samuel Hawkins Marshall Byers

AMERICA FOR ME

'Tis fine to see the Old World, and
travel up and down
Among the famous palaces and cities
of renown,
To admire the crumbly castles and the
statues of the kings—
But now I think I've had enough of
antiquated things.

So it's home again, and home again,
America for me!
My heart is turning home again, and
there I long to be,
In the land of youth and freedom
beyond the ocean bars,

Where the air is full of sunlight and
the flag is full of stars.

Oh, London is a man's town, there's
power in the air;
And Paris is a woman's town, with
flowers in her hair;
And it's sweet to dream in Venice, and
it's great to study Rome;
But when it comes to living there is
no place like home.

I like the German fir-woods, in green
battalions drilled;
I like the gardens of Versailles with
dashing fountains filled;
But, oh, to take your hand, my dear,
and ramble for a day
In the friendly western woodland
where Nature has her way!

I know that Europe's wonderful, yet
something seems to lack:
The Past is too much with her, and
the people looking back.
But the glory of the Present is to make
the Future free,—
We love our land for what she is and
what she is to be.

Oh, it's home again, and home
again, America for me!
I want a ship that's westward bound
to plough the rolling sea,
To the blessed Land of Room
Enough beyond the ocean bars,
Where the air is full of sunlight and
the flag is full of stars.
Henry Van Dyke

ENGLAND

I

This royal throne of Kings, this
sceptred isle,

This earth of majesty, this seat of
  Mars,
This other Eden, demi-paradise;
This fortress, built by nature for her-
  self,
Against infection and the hand of war;
This happy breed of men, this little
  world;
This precious stone set in the silver
  sea,
Which serves it in the office of a wall,
Or as a moat defensive to a house,
Against the envy of less happier lands,
This blessed plot, this earth, this realm,
  this England.

II

This England never did, nor never
  shall,
Lie at the proud foot of a conqueror
But when it first did help to wound
  itself.
Now these her princes are come home
  again,
Come the three corners of the world
  in arms
And we shall shock them: Naught
  shall make us rue,
If England to itself do rest but true.

William Shakespeare

TO ENGLAND

I

Lear and Cordelia! 'twas an ancient
  tale
  Before thy Shakespeare gave it
    deathless fame;
  The times have changed, the moral
    is the same.
So like an outcast, dowerless and pale,
Thy daughter went; and in a foreign
  gale

Spread her young banner, till its
  sway became
A wonder to the nations. Days of
  shame
Are close upon thee; prophets raise
  their wail.
When the rude Cossack with an out-
  stretched hand
  Points his long spear across the nar-
    row sea,—
  "Lo! there is England!" when thy
    destiny
Storms on thy straw-crowned head,
  and thou dost stand
Weak, helpless, mad, a by-word in the
  land,—
  God grant thy daughter a Cordelia
    be!

II

Stand, thou great bulwark of man's
  liberty!
  Thou rock of shelter, rising from
    the wave,
  Sole refuge to the overwearied brave
Who planned, arose, and battled to be
  free,
Fell, undeterred, then sadly turned to
  thee,—
  Saved the free spirit from their
    country's grave,
  To rise again, and animate the slave,
When God shall ripen all things.
  Britons, ye
Who guard the sacred outpost, not in
  vain
  Hold your proud peril! Freemen
    undefiled,
  Keep watch and ward! Let battle-
    ments be piled
Around your cliffs; fleets marshalled,
  till the main
Sink under them; and if your courage
  wane,

Through force or fraud, look westward to your child!

George Henry Boker

READY, AY, READY!

Old England's sons are English yet,
Old England's hearts are strong;
And still she wears her coronet
Aflame with sword and song.
As in their pride our fathers died,
If need be, so die we;
So wield we still, gainsay who will,
The sceptre of the sea.
England, stand fast; let heart and
hand be steady;
Be thy first word thy last,—Ready, ay,
ready!

We've Raleighs still for Raleigh's
part,
We've Nelsons yet unknown;
The pulses of the Lion Heart
Beat on through Wellington.
Hold, Britain, hold thy creed of old,
Strong foe and steadfast friend,
And, still unto thy motto true,
Defy not, but defend.
England, stand fast; let heart and
hand be steady;
Be thy first word thy last,—Ready, ay,
ready!

Men whispered that our arm was
weak,
Men said our blood was cold,
And that our hearts no longer speak
The clarion-note of old;
But let the spear and sword draw
near
The sleeping lion's den,
His island shore shall start once
more
To life with armèd men.

England, stand fast; let heart and
hand be steady;
Be thy first word thy last,—Ready, ay
ready!

Herman Charles Merivale

IVRY

Now glory to the Lord of Hosts,
from whom all glories are!
And glory to our Sovereign Liege,
King Henry of Navarre!
Now let there be the merry sound of
music and of dance,
Through thy corn-fields green, and
sunny vines, oh pleasant land of
France!
And thou, Rochelle, our own Ro-
chelle, proud city of the waters,
Again let rapture light the eyes of
all thy mourning daughters.
As thou wert constant in our ills, be
joyous in our joy;
For cold, and stiff, and still are they
who wrought thy walls annoy.
Hurrah! hurrah! a single field hath
turned the chance of war.
Hurrah! hurrah! for Ivry, and Henry
of Navarre.

Oh! how our hearts were beating,
when, at the dawn of day,
We saw the army of the League
drawn out in long array;
With all its priest-led citizens, and
all its rebel peers,
And Appenzel's stout infantry, and
Egmont's Flemish spears.
There rode the brood of false Lorraine, the curses of our land;
And dark Mayenne was in the midst,
a truncheon in his hand;
And, as we looked on them, we
thought of Seine's empurpled
flood,

And good Coligni's hoary hair all
dabbled with his blood;
And we cried unto the living God,
who rules the fate of war,
To fight for His own holy name, and
Henry of Navarre.

The King is come to marshal us, in
all his armor dressed;
And he has bound a snow-white
plume upon his gallant crest.
And looked upon his people, and a
tear was in his eye;
He looked upon the traitors, and his
glance was stern and high.
Right graciously he smiled on us, as
rolled from wing to wing,
Down all our line, a deafening
shout: "God save our Lord the
King!"
"And if my standard-bearer fall, as
fall full well he may,
For never saw I promise yet of such
a bloody fray,
Press where ye see my white plume
shine, amidst the ranks of war,
And be your oriflamme today the
helmet of Navarre."

Hurrah! the foes are moving. Hark
to the mingled din,
Of fife, and steed, and trump, and
drum, and roaring culverin.
The fiery Duke is pricking fast across
Saint André's plain,
With all the hireling chivalry of
Guelders and Almayne.
Now by the lips of those ye love, fair
gentlemen of France,
Charge for the Golden Lilies,—upon
them with the lance!
A thousand spurs are striking deep, a
thousand spears in rest,
A thousand knights are pressing close
behind the snow-white crest;

And in they burst, and on they
rushed, while, like a guiding star,
Amidst the thickest carnage blazed
the helmet of Navarre.

Now, God be praised, the day is
ours. Mayenne hath turned his
rein;
D'Aumale hath cried for quarter; the
Flemish count is slain.
Their ranks are breaking like thin
clouds before a Biscay gale;
The field is heaped with bleeding
steeds, and flags, and cloven mail.
And then we thought on vengeance,
and, all along our van,
"Remember Saint Bartholomew!"
was passed from man to man.
But out spake gentle Henry, "No
Frenchman is my foe:
Down, down with every foreigner,
but let your brethren go."
Oh! was there ever such a knight, in
friendship or in war,
As our Sovereign Lord, King Henry,
the soldier of Navarre?

Right well fought all the Frenchmen
who fought for France today;
And many a lordly banner God gave
them for a prey.
But we of the religion have borne us
best in fight;
And the good Lord of Rosny hath
ta'en the cornet white.
Our own true Maximilian the cornet
white hath ta'en,
The cornet white with crosses black,
the flag of false Lorraine.
Up with it high; unfurl it wide; that
all the host may know
How God hath humbled the proud
house which wrought His Church
such woe.

Then on the ground, while trumpets
   sound their loudest point of war,
Fling the red shreds, a footcloth
   meet for Henry of Navarre.

Ho! maidens of Vienna; ho! matrons
   of Lucerne;
Weep, weep, and rend your hair for
   those who never shall return.
Ho! Philip, send, for charity, thy
   Mexican pistoles,
That Antwerp monks may sing a
   mass for thy poor spearmen's souls.
Ho! gallant nobles of the League,
   look that your arms be bright;
Ho! burghers of St. Genevieve, keep
   watch and ward tonight;
For our God hath crushed the ty-
   rant, our God hath raised the
   slave,
And mocked the counsel of the wise,
   and the valor of the brave.
Then glory to His holy name, from
   whom all glories are;
And glory to our Sovereign Lord,
   King Henry of Navarre!

Thomas Babington Macaulay

THE " REVENGE "

At Florés in the Azores Sir Richard
   Grenville lay,
And a pinnace, like a fluttered bird,
   came flying from far away:
" Spanish ships of war at sea! we have
   sighted fifty-three! "
Then sware Lord Thomas Howard:
   " 'Fore God I am no coward;
But I cannot meet them here, for my
   ships are out of gear,
And the half my men are sick. I
   must fly, but follow quick.
We are six ships of the line; can we
   fight with fifty-three? "

Then spake Sir Richard Grenville:
   " I know you are no coward;
You fly them for a moment to fight
   with them again.
But I've ninety men and more that
   are lying sick ashore.
I should count myself the coward if
   I left them, my Lord Howard,
To these Inquisition dogs and the
   devildoms of Spain."

So Lord Howard passed away with
   five ships of war that day,
Till he melted like a cloud in the si-
   lent summer heaven;
But Sir Richard bore in hand all his
   sick men from the land
Very carefully and slow,
Men of Bideford in Devon,
And we laid them on the ballast
   down below;
For we brought them all aboard,
And they blessed him in their pain,
   that they were not left to Spain,
To the thumbscrew and the stake,
   for the glory of the Lord.

He had only a hundred seamen to
   work the ship and to fight,
And he sailed away from Florés till
   the Spaniard came in sight,
With his huge sea-castles heaving
   upon the weather bow.
" Shall we fight or shall we fly?
Good Sir Richard, tell us now,
For to fight is but to die!
There'll be little of us left by the
   time this sun be set."
And Sir Richard said again: " We
   be all good English men.
Let us bang these dogs of Seville, the
   children of the devil,
For I never turned my back upon
   Don or devil yet."

Sir Richard spoke and he laughed,
and we roared a hurrah, and so
The little *Revenge* ran on sheer into
the heart of the foe,
With her hundred fighters on deck,
and her ninety sick below;
For half of their fleet to the right
and half to the left were seen,
And the little *Revenge* ran on
through the long sea-lane between.

Thousands of their soldiers looked
down from their decks and
laughed,
Thousands of their seamen made
mock at the mad little craft
Running on and on, till delayed
By their mountain-like *San Philip*
that, of fifteen hundred tons,
And up-shadowing high above us
with her yawning tier of guns,
Took the breath from our sails, and
we stayed.

And while now the great *San Philip*
hung above us like a cloud
Whence the thunderbolt will fall
long and loud,
Four galleons drew away
From the Spanish fleet that day,
And two upon the larboard and two
upon the starboard lay,
And the battle-thunder broke from
them all.

But anon the great *San Philip*, she
bethought herself and went,
Having that within her womb that
had left her ill content;
And the rest, they came aboard us,
and they fought us hand to hand,
For a dozen times they came with
their pikes and musqueteers,
And a dozen times we shook 'em off
as a dog that shakes his ears

When he leaps from the water to
the land.

And the sun went down, and the
stars came out far over the summer sea,
But never a moment ceased the fight
of the one and the fifty-three,
Ship after ship, the whole night long,
their high-built galleons came,
Ship after ship, the whole night long,
drew back with her dead and her
shame.
For some were sunk and many were
shattered, and so could fight us
no more—
God of battles, was ever a battle like
this in the world before?

For he said, " Fight on! fight on! "
Though his vessel was all but a
wreck;
And it chanced that, when half of
the short summer night was gone,
With a grisly wound to be dressed
he had left the deck,
But a bullet struck him that was
dressing it suddenly dead,
And himself he was wounded again
in the side and the head,
And he said, " Fight on! fight on! "

And the night went down, and the
sun smiled out far over the summer sea,
And the Spanish fleet with broken
sides lay round us all in a ring;
But they dared not touch us again,
for they feared that we still could
sting,
So they watched what the end would
be.
And we had not fought them in vain,
But in perilous plight were we,

Seeing forty of our poor hundred were slain,
And half of the rest of us maimed for life
In the crash of the cannonades and the desperate strife;
And the sick men down in the hold were most of them stark and cold,
And the pikes were all broken or bent, and the powder was all of it spent;
And the masts and the rigging were lying over the side;
But Sir Richard cried in his English pride,
"We have fought such a fight for a day and a night
As may never be fought again!
We have won great glory, my men!
And a day less or more
At sea or ashore,
We die—does it matter when?
Sink me the ship, Master Gunner— sink her, split her in twain!
Fall into the hands of God, not into the hands of Spain!"

And the gunner said, "Ay, ay," but the seamen made reply:
"We have children, we have wives,
And the Lord hath spared our lives.
We will make the Spaniard promise, if we yield, to let us go;
We shall live to fight again and to strike another blow."
And the lion there lay dying, and they yielded to the foe.

And the stately Spanish men to their flagship bore him then,
Where they laid him by the mast, old Sir Richard caught at last,
And they praised him to his face with their courtly foreign grace;

But he rose upon their decks, and he cried:
"I have fought for Queen and Faith like a valiant man and true;
I have only done my duty as a man is bound to do.
With a joyful spirit I Sir Richard Grenville die!"
And he fell upon their decks, and he died.

And they stared at the dead that had been so valiant and true,
And had holden the power and glory of Spain so cheap
That he dared her with one little ship and his English few;
Was he devil or man? He was devil for aught they knew,
But they sank his body with honour down into the deep,
And they manned the *Revenge* with a swarthier alien crew,
And away she sailed with her loss and longed for her own;
When a wind from the lands they had ruined awoke from sleep,
And the water began to heave and the weather to moan,
And or ever that evening ended a great gale blew,
And a wave like the wave that is raised by an earthquake grew,
Till it smote on their hulls and their sails and their masts and their flags,
And the whole sea plunged and fell on the shot-shattered navy of Spain,
And the little *Revenge* herself went down by the island crags
To be lost evermore in the main.

Alfred Tennyson

INCIDENT OF THE FRENCH CAMP

You know, we French stormed
   Ratisbon:
  A mile or so away
On a little mound, Napoleon
  Stood on our storming day;
With neck out-thrust, you fancy
   how,
  Legs wide, arms locked behind,
As if to balance the prone brow
  Oppressive with its mind.

Just as, perhaps, he mused, "My
   plans
  That soar, to earth may fall,
Let once my army-leader Lannes
  Waver at yonder wall,"—
Out 'twixt the battery-smokes there
   flew
  A rider, bound on bound
Full-galloping; nor bridle drew
  Until he reached the mound.

Then off there flung in smiling joy,
  And held himself erect
By just his horse's mane, a boy:
  You hardly could suspect—
(So tight he kept his lips compressed,
  Scarce any blood came through),
You looked twice ere you saw his
   breast
  Was all but shot in two.

"Well," cried he, "Emperor, by
   God's grace
  We've got you Ratisbon!
The Marshal's in the market-place,
  And you'll be there anon
To see your flag-bird flap his vans,
  Where I, to heart's desire,
Perched him!" The Chief's **eye**
  flashed; his plans
  Soared up again like fire.

The Chief's eye flashed; but pres-
   ently
  Softened itself, as sheathes
A film the mother eagle's eye
  When her bruised eaglet breathes:
"You're wounded!" "Nay," his sol-
  dier's pride
  Touched to the quick, he said:
"I'm killed, sire!" And, his Chief be-
  side,
  Smiling the boy fell dead.

Robert Browning

HOW THEY BROUGHT THE GOOD NEWS FROM GHENT TO AIX

I sprang to the stirrup, and Joris, and
  he;
I galloped, Dirck galloped, we galloped all three;
"Good speed!" cried the watch, as
  the gate-bolts undrew;
"Speed!" echoed the wall to us galloping through;
Behind shut the postern, the lights
  sank to rest,
And into the midnight we galloped
  abreast.

Not a word to each other; we kept
  the great pace
Neck by neck, stride by stride, never
  changing our pace;
I turned in my saddle and made its
  girths tight,
Then shortened each stirrup, and set
  the pique right,
Rebuckled the cheek-strap, chained
  slacker the bit,
Nor galloped less steadily Roland a
  whit.

'Twas moonset at starting; but while
  we drew near

Lokeren, the cocks crew, and twilight dawned clear;
At Boom, a great yellow star came
out to see;
At Düffield, 'twas morning as plain
as could be;
And from Mecheln church-steeple
we heard the half chime,
So Joris broke silence with "Yet
there is time!"

At Aerschot, up leaped of a sudden
the sun,
And against him the cattle stood
black every one,
To stare through the mist at us galloping past,
And I saw my stout galloper Roland
at last,
With resolute shoulders, each but-
ting away
The haze, as some bluff river headland its spray:

And his low head and crest, just one
sharp ear bent back
For my voice and the other pricked
out on his track;
And one eye's black intelligence—
ever that glance
O'er its white edge at me, his own
master, askance!
And the thick heavy spume-flakes
which aye and anon
His fierce lips shook upwards in galloping on.

By Hasselt, Dirck groaned; and cried
Joris, "Stay spur!
Your Ross galloped bravely, the
fault's not in her.
We'll remember at Aix"—for one
heard the quick wheeze
Of her chest, saw her stretched neck
and staggering knees,

And sunk tail, and horrible heave of
the flank,
As down on her haunches she shuddered and sank.

So we were left galloping, Joris and I,
Past Looz and past Tongres, no
cloud in the sky;
The broad sun above laughed a piti-
less laugh,
'Neath our feet broke the brittle
bright stubble like chaff;
Till over by Dalhem a dome-spire
sprang white,
And "Gallop," gasped Joris, "for
Aix is in sight!"

"How they'll greet us!" and all in a
moment his roan
Rolled neck and crop over; lay dead
as a stone;
And there was my Roland to bear
the whole weight
Of the news which alone could save
Aix from her fate,
With his nostrils like pits full of
blood to the brim,
And with circles of red for his eye-
socket's rim.

Then I cast loose my buff-coat, each
holster let fall,
Shook off both my jack-boots, let go
belt and all,
Stood up in the stirrup, leaned,
patted his ear,
Called my Roland his pet-name, my
horse without peer;
Clapped my hands, laughed and
sang, any noise, good or bad,
Till at length into Aix Roland galloped and stood.

And all I remember is, friends flocking round

As I sat with his head 'twixt my
knees on the ground,
And no voice but was praising this
Roland of mine,
As I poured down his throat our last
measure of wine,
Which (the burgess voted by com-
mon consent)
Was no more than his due who
brought good news from Ghent.

Robert Browning

THE CAPTAIN STOOD ON THE CARRONADE

The captain stood on the carronade
—" First lieutenant," says he,
" Send all my merry men aft here,
for they must list to me:
I haven't the gift of the gab, my
sons—because I'm bred to the
sea,
That ship there is a Frenchman, who
means to fight with we.
Odds blood, hammer and tongs,
long as I've been to sea,
I've fought 'gainst every odds—
but I've gained the victory.

" That ship there is a Frenchman, and
if we don't take *she*,
'Tis a thousand bullets to one, that
she will capture *we*;
I haven't the gift of the gab, my
boys, so each man to his gun,
If she's not mine in half-an-hour, I'll
flog each mother's son.
Odds bobs, hammer and tongs,
long as I've been to sea,
I've fought 'gainst every odds—
and I've gained the victory."

We fought for twenty minutes,
when t h e Frenchman had
enough,

" I little thought," said he, " that
your men were of such stuff."
The captain took the Frenchman's
sword, a low bow made to he—
" I haven't the gift of the gab, Mon-
sieur, but polite I wish to be.
Odds bobs, hammer and tongs,
long as I've been to sea,
I've fought 'gainst every odds—
and I've gained the victory."

Our captain sent for all of us; " My
merry men," said he,
" I haven't the gift of the gab, my
lads, but yet I thankful be;
You've done your duty handsomely,
each man stood to his gun,
If you hadn't, you villains, as sure
as day, I'd have flogged each
mother's son.
Odds bobs, hammer and tongs, as
long as I'm at sea,
I'll fight 'gainst every odds—and
I'll gain the victory."

Frederick Marryat

THE CHARGE OF THE LIGHT BRIGADE

Half a league, half a league,
Half a league onward,
All in the valley of Death
Rode the six hundred.
" Forward, the Light Brigade!
Charge for the guns! " he said:
Into the valley of Death
Rode the six hundred.

" Forward the Light Bridgade! "
Was there a man dismay'd?
Not tho' the soldier knew
Someone had blunder'd:
Theirs not to make reply,
Theirs not to reason why,

Theirs but to do and die,
Into the valley of Death
　　Rode the six hundred.

Cannon to right of them,
Cannon to left of them,
Cannon in front of them
　　Volley'd and thunder'd;
Storm'd at with shot and shell,
Boldly they rode and well,
Into the jaws of Death,
Into the mouth of Hell
　　Rode the six hundred.

Flash'd all their sabres bare,
Flash'd as they turned in air.
Sabring the gunners there,
Charging an army, while
　　All the world wonder'd;
Plunged in the battery-smoke
Right thro' the line they broke;
Cossack and Russian
Reel'd from the sabre-stroke
Shatter'd and sunder'd.
Then they rode back, but not—
　　Not the six hundred.

Cannon to right of them,
Cannon to left of them,
Cannon behind them
　　Volley'd and thunder'd;
Storm'd at with shot and shell,
While horse and hero fell,
They that had fought so well
Came thro' the jaws of Death
Back from the mouth of Hell,
All that was left of them—
　　Left of six hundred.

When can their glory fade?
O, the wild charge they made!
　　All the world wonder'd.
Honour the charge they made!
Honour the Light Brigade,
　　Noble six hundred!
　　　　　Alfred Tennyson

CASABIANCA

The boy stood on the burning deck,
　　Whence all but him had fled;
The flame that lit the battle's wreck,
　　Shone round him o'er the dead.

Yet beautiful and bright he stood,
　　As born to rule the storm;
A creature of heroic blood,
　　A proud, though childlike form.

The flames roll'd on—he would not go
　　Without his father's word;
That father, faint in death below,
　　His voice no longer heard.

He call'd aloud—" Say, father, say
　　If yet my task be done! "
He knew not that the chieftain lay
　　Unconscious of his son.

" Speak, father! " once again he cried,
　　" If I may yet be gone! "
And but the booming shots replied,
　　And fast the flames roll'd on.

Upon his brow he felt their breath,
　　And in his waving hair;
And look'd from that lone post of
　　death,
　　In still, yet brave despair;

And shouted but once more aloud,
　　" My father! must I stay? "
While o'er him fast, through sail and
　　shroud,
　　The wreathing fires made way.

They wrapt the ship in splendour
　　wild,
　　They caught the flag on high,
And stream'd above the gallant child,
　　Like banners in the sky.

There came a burst of thunder
     sound—
   The boy—oh! where was he?
Ask of the winds that far around
   With fragments strewed the sea,

With mast, and helm, and pennon
     fair,
   That well had borne their part;
But the noblest thing that perished
     there
   Was that young faithful heart.
               Felicia Dorothea Hemans

THE EVE OF THE BATTLE OF WATERLOO

There was a sound of revelry by
     night,
And Belgium's capital had gathered
     then
Her beauty and her chivalry, and
     bright
The lamps shone o'er fair women
     and brave men;
A thousand hearts beat happily, and
     when
Music arose with its voluptuous
     swell,
Soft eyes looked love to eyes which
     spake again,
And all went merry as a marriage
     bell;
But hush! hark! a deep sound strikes
     like a rising knell.

Did ye not hear it? No; 'twas but
     the wind,
Or the car rattling o'er the stony
     street;
On with the dance, let joy be un-
     confined;
No sleep till morn, when youth and
     pleasure meet

To chase the glowing hours with
     flying feet.
But hark! that heavy sound breaks
     in once more,
As if the clouds its echo would re-
     peat;
And nearer, clearer, deadlier than
     before!
Arm! arm! it is—it is—the cannon's
     opening roar!

Within a windowed niche of that
     high wall
Sate Brunswick's fated chieftain; he
     did hear
That sound, the first amidst the
     festival,
And caught its tone with death's
     prophetic ear;
And when they smiled because he
     deemed it near
His heart more truly knew that peal
     too well
Which stretched his father on a
     bloody bier,
And roused the vengeance blood
     alone could quell;
He rushed into the field, and foremost
     fighting fell.

Ah! then and there was hurrying to
     and fro,
And gathering tears, and tremblings
     of distress,
And cheeks all pale, which but an
     hour ago
Blushed at the praise of their own
     loveliness;
And there were sudden partings,
     such as press
The life from out young hearts, and
     choking sighs
Which ne'er might be repeated; who
     might guess

If ever more should meet those
  mutual eyes,
Since upon night so sweet such awful
  morn could rise?

And there was mounting in hot
  haste: the steed,
The mustering squadron, and the
  clattering car,
Went pouring forward with impetuous speed,
And swiftly forming in the ranks of
  war;
And the deep thunder, peal on peal
  afar;
And near, the beat of the alarming
  drum
Roused up the soldier ere the morning star;
While thronged the citizens with
  terror dumb,
Or whispering with white lips—" The
  foe! They come! They come! "

And wild and high the " Cameron's
  gathering " rose,
The war note of Lochiel, which
  Albyn's hills
Have heard, and heard, too, have
  her Saxon foes:
How in the noon of night that
  pibroch thrills
Savage and shrill! But with the
  breath which fills
Their mountain pipe, so fill the
  mountaineers
With the fierce native daring which
  instils
The stirring memory of a thousand
  years
And Evan's, Donald's **fame rings in**
  each clansman's ears!

And Ardennes waves about them
  her green leaves,

Dewy with nature's tear-drops, as
  they pass,
Grieving, if aught inanimate e'er
  grieves,
Over the unreturning brave—alas!
Ere evening to be trodden like the
  grass
Which now beneath them, but
  above shall grow
In its next verdure, when the fiery
  mass
Of living valour, rolling on the foe,
And burning with high hope, shall
  moulder cold and low.

Last noon beheld them full of lusty
  life,
Last eve in Beauty's circle proudly
  gay,
The midnight brought the signal-
  sound of strife,
The morn the marshalling in arms—
  the day
Battle's magnificently stern array!
The thunder clouds close o'er it,
  which when rent
The earth is covered thick with
  other clay,
Which her own clay shall cover,
  heaped and pent,
Rider and horse—friend, foe—in one
  red burial blent!

George Gordon Byron

THE LEAK IN THE DIKE

The good dame looked from her cot-
  tage
At the close of the pleasant day,
And cheerily called to her little son
  Outside the door at play:
" Come, Peter, come! I want you to
  go,
  While there is yet light to see,

To the hut of the blind old man
   who lives
   Across the dike, for me;
And take these cakes I made for
   him—
   They are hot and smoking yet;
You have time enough to go and
   come
   Before the sun is set."

Then the good wife turned to her
   labor,
   Humming a simple song,
And thought of her husband, work-
   ing hard
   At the sluices all day along;
And set the turf a-blazing,
   And brought the coarse, black
   bread,
That he might find a fire at night,
   And see the table spread.

And Peter left the brother
   With whom all day he had played,
And the sister who had watched
   their sports
   In the willow's tender shade;
And told them they'd see him back
   before
   They saw a star in sight—
Though he wouldn't be afraid to go
   In the very darkest night!
For he was a brave, bright fellow,
   With eye and conscience clear;
He could do whatever a boy might
   do,
   And he had not learned to fear.
Why, he wouldn't have robbed a
   bird's nest,
   Nor brought a stork to harm,
Though never a law in Holland
   Had stood to stay his arm!

And now, with his face all glowing,
   And eyes as bright as the day

With the thoughts of his pleasant
   errand,
   He trudged along the way;
And soon his joyous prattle
   Made glad a lonesome place—
Alas! if only the blind old man
   Could have seen that happy face!
Yet he somehow caught the bright-
   ness
   Which his voice and presence lent;
And he felt the sunshine come and
   go
   As Peter came and went.

And now, as the day was sinking,
   And the winds began to rise,
The mother looked from her door
   again,
   Shading her anxious eyes,
And saw the shadows deepen,
   And birds to their homes come
   back,
But never a sign of Peter
   Along the level track.
But she said, " He will come at
   morning,
   So I need not fret or grieve—
Though it isn't like my boy at all
   To stay without my leave."

But where was the child delaying?
   On the homeward way was he,
And across the dike while the sun
   was up
   An hour above the sea.
He was stooping now to gather
   flowers;
   Now listening to the sound,
As the angry waters dashed them-
   selves
   Against their narrow bound.
" Ah! well for us," said Peter,
   " That the gates are good and
   strong,

And my father tends them carefully,
  Or they would not hold you long!
You're a wicked sea," said Peter;
  " I know why you fret and chafe;
You would like to spoil our lands
    and homes;
  But our sluices keep you safe! "

But hark! through the noise of waters
  Comes a low, clear, trickling
    sound;
And the child's face pales with terror,
  As his blossoms drop to the
    ground.
He is up the bank in a moment,
  And, stealing through the sand,
He sees a stream not yet so large
  As his slender, childish hand.
'Tis a leak in the dike! He is but a
    boy,
  Unused to fearful scenes;
But, young as he is, he has learned
    to know
  The dreadful thing that means.
A leak in the dike! The stoutest
    heart
  Grows faint that cry to hear,
And the bravest man in all the land
  Turns white with mortal fear.
For he knows the smallest leak may
    grow
  To a flood in a single night;
And he knows the strength of the
    cruel sea
  When loosed in its angry might.

And the boy! He has seen the
    danger,
  And, shouting a wild alarm,
He forces back the weight of the sea
  With the strength of his single
    arm!
He listens for the joyful sound
  Of a footstep passing nigh;

And lays his ear to the ground,
    to catch
  The answer to his cry,—
And he hears the rough winds blow-
    ing,
  And the waters rise and fall,
But never an answer comes to him
  Save the echo of his call.

He sees no hope, no succor,
  His feeble voice is lost;
Yet what shall he do but watch and
    wait,
  Though he perish at his post!
So, faintly calling and crying
  Till the sun is under the sea;
Crying and moaning till the stars
  Come out for company;
He thinks of his brother and sister,
  Asleep in their safe, warm bed;
He thinks of dear father and mother;
  Of himself as dying, and dead;
And of how, when the night is over,
  They must come and find him at
    last;
But he never thinks he can leave the
    place
  Where duty holds him fast.

The good dame in the cottage
  Is up and astir with the light,
For the thought of her little Peter
  Has been with her all the night.
And now she watches the pathway,
  As yester-eve she had done;
But what does she see so strange and
    black
  Against the rising sun?
Her neighbors are bearing between
    them
  Something straight to her door;
Her child is coming home, but not
  As he ever came before!

"He is dead!" she cries; "my dar-
　ling!"
And the startled father hears,
And comes and looks the way she
　looks,
And fears the thing she fears;
Till a glad shout from the bearers
Thrills the stricken man and wife—
"Give thanks, for your son has saved
　our land,
And God has saved his life!"
So, there in the morning sunshine
　They knelt about the boy;
And every head was bared and bent
In tearful, reverent joy.

'Tis many a year since then; but still,
　When the sea roars like a flood,
Their boys are taught what a boy can
　do
Who is brave and true and good.
For every man in that country
　Takes his son by the hand,
And tells him of little Peter,
　Whose courage saved the land.

They have many a valiant hero,
　Remembered through the years;
But never one whose name so oft
　Is named with loving tears.
And his deed shall be sung by the
　cradle,
　And told to the child on the knee,
So long as the dikes of Holland
　Divide the land from the sea!

Phoebe Cary

THE DESTRUCTION OF
SENNACHERIB

The Assyrian came down like the wolf
　on the fold,
And his cohorts were gleaming in
　purple and gold;

And the sheen of their spears was like
　stars on the sea,
When the blue wave rolls nightly on
　deep Galilee.

Like the leaves of the forest when
　Summer is green,
That host with their banners at sun-
　set were seen:
Like the leaves of the forest when
　Autumn hath flown,
That host on the morrow lay withered
　and strown.

For the Angel of Death spread his
　wings on the blast,
And breathed in the face of the foe as
　he passed;
And the eyes of the sleepers waxed
　deadly and chill,
And their hearts but once heaved, and
　forever grew still.

And there lay the steed with his nos-
　tril all wide,
But through it there rolled not the
　breath of his pride;
And the foam of his gasping lay white
　on the turf,
And cold as the spray of the rock-
　beating surf.

And there lay the rider distorted and
　pale,
With the dew on his brow, and the
　rust on his mail;
And the tents were all silent, the ban-
　ners alone,
The lances unlifted, the trumpet un-
　blown.

And the widows of Ashur are loud
　in their wail,

And the idols are broke in the temple
of Baal;
And the might of the Gentile, unsmote
by the sword,
Hath melted like snow in the glance of
the Lord!

George Gordon Byron

THE ISLES OF GREECE

(*Selected Stanzas*)

The isles of Greece, the isles of Greece!
  Where burning Sappho loved and
    sung,
Where grew the arts of war and
    peace—
    Where Delos rose, and Phœbus
    sprung!
Eternal summer gilds them yet,
But all except their sun is set.

The Scian and the Teian muse,
  The hero's harp, the lover's lute,
Have found the fame your shores
    refuse;
  Their place of birth alone is mute
To sounds which echo further west
Than your sires' "Islands of the
    Blest."

The mountains look on Marathon—
  And Marathon looks on the sea;
And musing there an hour alone,
  I dreamed that Greece might still be
    free;
For standing on the Persians' grave,
I could not deem myself a slave.

George Gordon Byron

THE BLUEBELLS OF
SCOTLAND

Oh where! and oh where! is your
  Highland laddie gone?

He's gone to fight the French for King
  George upon the throne;
And it's oh! in my heart how I wish
  him safe at home.

Oh where! and oh where! does your
  Highland laddie dwell?
He dwells in merry Scotland at the
  sign of the Bluebell;
And it's oh! in my heart that I love
  my laddie well.

What clothes, in what clothes is your
  Highland laddie clad?
His bonnet's of the Saxon green, his
  waistcoat's of the plaid;
And it's oh! in my heart that I love
  my Highland lad.

Suppose, oh suppose, that your Highland lad should die?
The bagpipes shall play over him, I'll
  lay me down and cry;
And it's oh! in my heart that I wish
  he may not die!

Unknown

MY HEART'S IN THE
HIGHLANDS

My heart's in the Highlands, my heart
  is not here;
My heart's in the Highlands a-chasing
  the deer;
Chasing the wild deer, and following
  the roe,
My heart's in the Highlands wherever
  I go.

Farewell to the Highlands, farewell to
  the North,
The birthplace of valour, the country
  of worth;
Wherever I wander, wherever I rove,

The hills of the Highlands for ever I
love.

Farewell to the mountains high covered with snow;
Farewell to the straths and green valleys below;
Farewell to the forests and wild-hang-
ing woods;
Farewell to the torrents and loud-
pouring floods.

My heart's in the Highlands, my heart
is not here;
My heart's in the Highlands, a-chasing
the deer;
Chasing the wild deer, and following
the roe,
My heart's in the Highlands wherever
I go!

Robert Burns

BRUCE TO HIS ARMY

Scots, wha hae wi' Wallace bled,
Scots, wham Bruce has often led;
Welcome to your gory bed,
 Or to victory!

Now's the day, and now's the hour,
See the front of battle lower;
See approach proud Edward's power,
 Chains and slavery!

Wha will be a traitor knave?
Wha can fill a coward's grave?
Wha sae base as be a slave?
 Let him turn and flee!

Wha for Scotland's king and law,
Freedom's sword would strongly draw,
Freeman stand or freeman fa',
 Let him follow me!

By oppression's woes and pains,
By your sons in servile chains,
We will drain our dearest veins,
 But they shall be free!

Lay the proud usurper low!
Tyrants fall in every foe!
Liberty's in every blow!
 Let us do, or die!

Robert Burns

HAME, HAME, HAME

Hame, hame, hame, O hame fain
 wad I be—
O hame, hame, hame, to my ain
 countree!

When the flower is i' the bud and
 the leaf is on the tree,
The lark shall sing me hame in my
 ain countree;
Hame, hame, hame, O hame fain
 wad I be—
O hame, hame, hame, to my ain
 countree!

The green leaf o' loyaltie's beginning
 for to fa',
The bonnie White Rose it is wither-
 ing an' a';
But I'll water 't wi' the blude of
 usurping tyrannie,
An' green it will graw in my ain
 countree.

O, there's nocht now frae ruin my
 country can save,
But the keys o' kind heaven, to open
 the grave;
That a' the noble martyrs wha died
 for loyaltie
May rise again an' fight for their ain
 countree.

The great now are gane, a' wha ven-
  tured to save,
The new grass is springing on the
  tap o' their grave;
But the sun through the mirk blinks
  blithe in my e'e,
"I'll shine on ye yet in your ain
  countree."

Hame, hame, hame, O hame fain
  wad I be—
O hame, hame, hame, to my ain
  countree!

Allan Cunningham

THE CAVALIER'S SONG

A steed! a steed of matchless speed,
  A sword of metal keen!
All else to noble hearts is dross,
  All else on earth is mean.

The neighing of the war-horse proud,
  The rolling of the drum,
The clangour of the trumpet loud,
  Be sounds from heaven that come.

And oh! the thundering press of
  knights
  Whenas their war cries swell,
May tole from heaven an angel bright,
  And rouse a fiend from hell.

Then mount! then mount, brave gal-
  lants, all,
  And don your helms amain:
Death's couriers, Fame and Honor,
  Call us to the field again.

No shrewish tears shall fill our eye
  When the sword-hilt's in our
  hand,—
Heart-whole we'll part, and no whit
  sigh
  For the fairest of the land!

Let piping swain, and craven wight,
  Thus weep and puling cry,
Our business is like men to fight,
  And hero-like to die!

William Motherwell

THE MINSTREL-BOY

The Minstrel-boy to the war is gone,
  In the ranks of death you'll find
  him;
His father's sword he has girded on,
  And his wild harp slung behind
  him,
"Land of song!" said the warrior-
  bard,
  "Though all the world betrays
  thee,
One sword, at least, thy rights shall
  guard,
  One faithful harp shall praise
  thee!"

The Minstrel fell!—but the foeman's
  chain
  Could not bring his proud soul
  under;
The harp he loved ne'er spoke again,
  For he tore its chords asunder;
And said, "No chains shall sully
  thee,
  Thou soul of love and bravery!
Thy songs were made for the pure
  and free,
  They shall never sound in slav-
  ery!"

Thomas Moore

THE SONG OF THE CAMP

"Give us a song!" the soldiers cried,
  The outer trenches guarding,
When the heated guns of the camps
  allied
  Grew weary of bombarding.

The dark Redan, in silent scoff,
  Lay, grim and threatening, under;
And the tawny mound of the Mala-
    koff
  No longer belched its thunder.

There was a pause. A guardsman
    said,
  "We storm the forts tomorrow;
Sing while we may, another day
  Will bring enough of sorrow."

They lay along the battery's side,
  Below the smoking cannon:
Brave hearts, from Severn and from
    Clyde,
  And from the banks of Shannon.

They sang of love, and not of fame;
  Forgot was Britain's glory:
Each heart recalled a different name,
  But all sang "Annie Laurie."

Voice after voice caught up the song,
  Until its tender passion
Rose like an anthem, rich and
    strong,—
  Their battle-eve confession.

Dear girl, her name he dared not
    speak,
  But, as the song grew louder,
Something upon the soldier's cheek
  Washed off the stains of powder.

Beyond the darkening ocean burned
  The bloody sunset's embers,
While the Crimean valleys learned
  How English love remembers.

And once again a fire of hell
  Rained on the Russian quarters,
With scream of shot and burst of
    shell,
  And bellowing of the mortars!

And Irish Nora's eyes are dim
  For a singer, dumb and gory;
And English Mary mourns for him
  Who sang of "Annie Laurie."

Sleep, soldiers still in honoured rest
  Your truth and valour wearing:
The bravest are the tenderest,—
  The loving are the daring.
                    Bayard Taylor

MY LAND

She is a rich and rare land;
Oh! she's a fresh and fair land,
She is a dear and rare land—
  This native land of mine.

No men than hers are braver—
Her women's hearts ne'er waver;
I'd freely die to save her,
  And think my lot divine.

She's not a dull or cold land;
No! she's a warm and bold land;
Oh! she's a true and old land—
  This native land of mine.

Could beauty ever guard her,
And virtue still reward her,
No foe would cross her border—
  No friend within it pine.

Oh! she's a fresh and fair land,
Oh! she's a true and rare land!
Yes, she's a rare and fair land—
  This native land of mine.
                Thomas Osborne Davis

THE FATHERLAND

Where is the true man's fatherland?
Is it where he by chance is born?
Doth not the yearning spirit scorn

In such scant borders to be spanned?
Oh yes! his fatherland must be
As the blue heaven, wide and free!

Is it alone where freedom is,
    Where God is God and man is man?
    Doth he not claim a broader span
For the soul's love of home than this?
Oh yes! his fatherland must be
As the blue heaven, wide and free!

Where'er a human heart doth wear
    Joy's myrtle-wreath or sorrow's
        gyves,
    Where'er a human spirit strives
After a life more true and fair,
There is the true man's birthplace
        grand,
His is the world-wide fatherland!

Where'er a single slave doth pine,
    Where'er one man may help an-
        other,—
    Thank God for such a birthright,
        brother,—
That spot of earth is thine and mine!
There is the true man's birthplace,
        grand,
His is the world-wide fatherland!

James Russell Lowell

HOME THOUGHTS FROM
ABROAD

Oh! to be in England
    Now that April's there,
And whoever wakes in England
    Sees, some morning, unaware,
That the lowest boughs and the brush-
        wood sheaf
Round the elm-tree bole are in tiny
        leaf,
While the chaffinch sings on the
        orchard bough
In England—now!

And after April, when May follows,
And the whitethroat builds, and all the
        swallows—
Hark! where my blossomed pear-tree
        in the hedge
    Leans to the field and scatters on the
        clover
Blossoms and dew-drops—at the bent
        spray's edge—
    That's the wise thrush; he sings each
        song twice over,
Lest you should think he never could
        recapture
The first fine careless rapture!
And though the fields look rough with
        hoary dew,
All will be gay when noon-tide wakes
        anew
The buttercups, the little children's
        dower,
—Far brighter than this gaudy melon-
        flower.

Robert Browning

IN FLANDERS FIELDS

In Flanders fields the poppies blow
    Between the crosses, row on row,
That mark our place; and in the sky
    The larks, still bravely singing, fly
Scarce heard amid the guns below.

We are the dead. Short days ago
We lived, felt dawn, saw sunset glow,
    Loved and were loved, and now we
        lie
    In Flanders fields.

Take up our quarrel with the foe:
To you from failing hands we throw
    The torch; be yours to hold it high.
    If ye break faith with us who die

We shall not sleep, though poppies
    grow
  In Flanders fields.

John McCrae

HOME THOUGHTS FROM THE SEA

Nobly, nobly Cape Saint Vincent to
  the northwest died away;
Sunset ran, one glorious blood-red,
  reeking into Cadiz Bay;
Bluish mid the burning water, full in
  face Trafalgar lay;
In the dimmest northeast distance,
  dawned Gibraltar grand and gay;
" Here and here did England help
  me—How can I help England? "
  —say,
Whoso turns as I, this evening, turn
  to God to praise and pray,
While Jove's planet rises yonder, silent over Africa.

Robert Browning

THE TRAVELLER'S RETURN

Sweet to the morning traveller
  The song amid the sky,
Where, twinkling in the dewy light,
  The skylark soars on high.

And cheering to the traveller
  The gales that round him play,
When faint and heavily he drags,
  Along his noontide way.

And when beneath th' unclouded sun
  Full wearily toils he,
The flowing water makes to him
  A soothing melody.

And when the evening light decays
  And all is calm around,

There is sweet music to his ear
  In the distant sheep-bell's sound.

But, oh! of all delightful sounds
  Of evening or of morn,
The sweetest is the voice of love
  That welcomes his return.

Robert Southey

THIS MOMENT YEARNING AND THOUGHTFUL

This moment yearning and thoughtful
  sitting alone,
It seems to me there are other men in
  other lands yearning and thoughtful,
It seems to me I can look over and behold them in Germany, Italy,
  France, Spain,
Or far, far away, in China, or in Russia
  or Japan, talking other dialects,
And it seems to me if I could know
  those other men I should become at-
  tached to them as I do to men in my
  own lands.
Oh, I know we should be brethren
  and lovers,—
I know I should be happy with them.

Walt Whitman

BOADICEA

When the British warrior queen,
  Bleeding from the Roman rods,
Sought, with an indignant mien,
  Counsel of her country's gods;

Sage beneath a spreading oak
  Sat the Druid, hoary chief;
Every burning word he spoke
  Full of rage, and full of grief.

Princess! if our aged eyes
  Weep upon thy matchless wrongs,

'Tis because resentment ties
  All the terrors of our tongues.

Rome shall perish—write that word
  In the blood that she has spilt;
Perish, hopeless and abhorr'd,
  Deep in ruin as in guilt.

Rome, for empire far renown'd,
  Tramples on a thousand states;
Soon her pride shall kiss the ground—
  Hark! the Gaul is at her gates!

Other Romans shall arise,
  Heedless of a soldier's name;
Sounds, not arms, shall win the prize,
  Harmony the path to fame.

Then the progeny that springs
  From the forests of our land,
Arm'd with thunder, clad with wings
  Shall a wider world command.

Regions Cæsar never knew
  Thy posterity shall sway;
Where his eagles never flew,
  None invincible as they.

Such the bard's prophetic words,
  Pregnant with celestial fire,
Bending as he swept the chords
  Of his sweet but awful lyre.

She, with all a monarch's pride,
  Felt them in her bosom glow;
Rush'd to battle, fought, and died;
  Dying hurl'd them at the foe;

Ruffians, pitiless and proud,
  Heaven awards the vengeance due;
Empire is on us bestowed,
  Shame and ruin wait on you.

                 William Cowper

Part Four

SONGS OF THE SEASONS

A FROST FANCY

Summer gone,
Winter here;
Ways are white,
Skies are clear.
And the sun
A ruddy boy
All day sliding,
While at night
The stars appear
Like skaters gliding
On a mere.

Richard Le Gallienne

SING A SONG OF SEASONS

Sing a song of seasons!
Something bright in all!
Flowers in the summer,
Fires in the fall!

Robert Louis Stevenson

THE YEAR'S ROUND

The crocus, while the days are dark,
Unfolds its saffron sheen;
At April's touch the crudest bark
Discovers gems of green.

Then sleep the seasons, full of night,
While slowly swells the pod
And round the peach, and in the night
The mushroom bursts the sod.

The winter falls, the frozen rut
Is bound with silver bars;
The snowdrift heaps against the hut,
And night is pierced with stars.

Coventry Patmore

SPRING SONG

Spring comes hither,
Buds the rose;
Roses wither,
Sweet spring goes.

Summer soars—
Wide-winged day;
White light pours,
Flies away.

Soft winds blow,
Westward born;
Onward go,
Toward the morn.

George Eliot

363

THE VOICE OF SPRING

I come! I come! ye have called me
    long;
I come o'er the mountains with light
    and song.
Ye may trace my steps o'er the waking
    earth
By the winds which tell of the violet's
    birth,
By the primrose stars in the shadowy
    grass,
By the green leaves opening as I pass.

I have looked o'er the hills of the
    stormy North,
And the larch has hung all his tassels
    forth;
The fisher is out on the sunny sea
And the reindeer bounds o'er the pas-
    tures free,
And the pine has a fringe of softer
    green,
And the moss looks bright where my
    step has been.

From the streams and founts I have
    loosed the chain;
They are sweeping off to the silvery
    main,
They are flashing down from the
    mountain brows,
They are flinging spray o'er the forest
    boughs,
They are bursting fresh from their
    sparry caves,
And the earth resounds with the joy
    of waves.

Felicia Hemans

AN APPLE ORCHARD IN THE SPRING

Have you seen an apple orchard in the
    spring?
              In the spring?

An English apple orchard in the
    spring?
When the spreading trees are hoary
With their wealth of promised glory,
And the mavis sings its story,
              In the spring.

Have you plucked the apple blossoms
    in the spring?
              In the spring?
And caught their subtle odours in the
    spring?
Pink buds pouting at the light,
Crumpled petals baby white,
Just to touch them a delight—
              In the spring.

Have you walked beneath the blossoms
    in the spring?
              In the spring?
Beneath the apple blossoms in the
    spring?
When the pink cascades are falling,
And the silver brooklets brawling,
And the cuckoo bird soft calling,
              In the spring.

If you have not, then you know not,
    in the spring,
              In the spring,
Half the colour, beauty, wonder of the
    spring,
No sweet sight can I remember
Half so precious, half so tender,
As the apple blossoms render
              In the spring.

William Martin

SONG OF SUMMER

Dis is gospel weathah sho'—
Hills is sawt o' hazy.
Meddahs level ez a flo'
Callin' to de lazy.

Sky all white wit streaks o' blue,
  Sunshine softly gleamin',
D' ain't no wuk hit's right to do,
Nothin's right but dreamin'.

Dreamin' by de rivah side
  Wit de watahs glist'nin',
Feelin' good an' satisfied
  Ez you lay a-list'nin'
To the little nakid boys
  Splashin' in de watah,
Hollerin' fu' to spress deir joys
  Jes' lak youngsters ought to.

Squir'l a-tappin' on his toes,
  So's to hide an' view you;
Whole flocks o' camp-meetin'
    crows
  Shoutin' hallelujah.
Peckahwood erpon de tree
  Tappin' lak a hammah;
Jaybird chattin' wit a bee,
  Tryin' to teach him grammah.

Breeze is blowin' wit perfume,
  Jes' enough to tease you;
Hollyhocks is all in bloom,
  Smellin' fu' to please you.
Go 'way, folks, an' let me 'lone,
  Times is gettin' dearah—
Summah's settin' on de th'one,
  An' I'm a-layin' neah huh!

  Paul Laurence Dunbar

HAPPY WIND

Oh, happy wind, how sweet
  Thy life must be!
The great, proud fields of gold
  Run after thee:
And here are flowers, with heads
  To nod and shake;
And dreaming butterflies
  To tease and wake.

Oh, happy wind, I say,
  To be alive this day.
  W. H. Davies

IS LIFE WORTH LIVING?

Is life worth living? Yes, so long
  As Spring revives the year,
And hails us with the cuckoo's song,
  To show that she is here;
So long as May of April takes,
  In smiles and tears, farewell,
And windflowers dapple all the brakes,
  And primroses the dell;
While children in the woodlands yet
  Adorn their little laps
With ladysmock and violet,
  And daisy-chain their caps;
While over orchard daffodils
  Cloud-shadows float and fleet,
And ousel pipes and laverock trills,
  And young lambs buck and bleat;
So long as that which bursts the bud
  And swells and tunes the rill
Makes springtime in the maiden's
    blood,
  Life is worth living still.

Life not worth living! Come with me,
  Now that, through vanishing veil,
Shimmers the dew on lawn and lea,
  And milk foams in the pail;
Now that June's sweltering sunlight
    bathes
  With sweat the striplings lithe,
As fall the long straight scented
    swathes
  Over the crescent scythe;
Now that the throstle never stops
  His self-sufficing strain,
And woodbine-trails festoon the copse,
  And eglantine the lane;
Now rustic labour seems as sweet
  As leisure, and blithe herds

Wend homeward with unweary feet,
Caroling like the birds;
Now all, except the lover's vow,
And nightingale, is still;
Here, in the twilight hour, allow,
Life is worth living still.

Is life worth living? Yes, so long
As there is wrong to right,
Wail of the weak against the strong,
Or tyranny to fight;
Long as there lingers gloom to chase,
Or streaming tear to dry,
One kindred woe, one sorrowing face
That smiles as we draw nigh;
Long as a tale of anguish swells
The heart, and lids grow wet,
And at the sound of Christmas bells
We pardon and forget;
So long as Faith with Freedom reigns,
And loyal Hope survives,
And gracious Charity remains
To leaven lowly lives;
While there is one untrodden tract
For Intellect or Will,
And men are free to think and act
Life is worth living still.

Not care to live while English homes
Nestle in English trees,
And England's Trident-Sceptre roams
Her territorial seas!
Not live while English songs are sung
Wherever blows the wind,
And England's laws and England's
tongue
Enfranchise half mankind!
So long as in Pacific main,
Or on Atlantic strand,
Our kin transmit the parent strain,
And love the Mother-land;
So long as flashes English steel,
And English trumpets shrill,

He is dead already who doth not feel
Life is worth living still.
Alfred Austin

GREEK CHILDREN'S SONG

The swallow has come again
Across the wide, white sea;
She sits and sings through the falling
rain,
" O March, my beloved March!
And thou, sad February,
Though still you may cover with
snow the plain,
You yet smell sweet of the Spring! "
Unknown

NOW THAT WINTER'S GONE

Now that the winter's gone, the earth
hath lost
Her snow-white robes; and no more
the frost
Candies the grass, or casts an icy cream
Upon the silver lake or crystal stream;
But the warm thaws the benumbed
earth,
And makes it tender; gives a sacred
birth
To the dead swallow; wakes in hollow
tree
The drowsy cuckoo and the humble-
bee.
Now do a choir of chirping minstrels
bring
In triumph to the world, the youthful
Spring:
The valleys, hills, and woods, in rich
array,
Welcome the coming of the long'd-for
May.
Thomas Carew

AUTUMN

The warm sun is failing, the bleak
   wind is wailing,
The bare boughs are sighing, the pale
   flowers are dying;
         And the year
On the earth her death-bed, in a
   shroud of leaves dead,
         Is lying.

Come, Months, come away,
From November to May,
In your saddest array,—
Follow the bier
Of the dead cold year,
And like dim shadows watch by her
   sepulchre.

The chill rain is falling, the nipt worm
   is crawling,
The rivers are swelling, the thunder is
   knelling,
         For the year;
The blithe swallows are flown, and the
   lizards each gone
         To his dwelling.
Come, Months, come away;
Put on white, black, and gray;
Let your light sisters play;
Ye, follow the bier
Of the dead cold year,
And make her grave green with tear
   on tear.

Percy Bysshe Shelley

A VAGABOND SONG

There is something in the autumn that
   is native to my blood—
Touch of manner, hint of mood;
And my heart is like a rhyme,
With the yellow and the purple and
   the crimson keeping time.

The scarlet of the maples can shake me
   like a cry
Of bugles going by.
And my lonely spirit thrills
To see the frosty asters like a smoke
   upon the hills.

There is something in October sets the
   gypsy blood astir;
We must rise and follow her,
When from every hill of flame
She calls and calls each vagabond by
   name.

Bliss Carman

A CHILD'S THOUGHT OF HARVEST

Out in the fields which were green last
   May,
But are rough and stubbled and brown
   today,
They are stacking the sheaves of the
   yellow wheat,
And raking the aftermath dry and
   sweet,
The barley and oats and golden rye
Are safely stored in the granary;
Where the pumpkins border the tall
   corn rows,
The busy reaper comes and goes;
And only the apples set so thick
On the orchard boughs are left to pick.

What a little time it seems since
   May—
Not very much longer than yesterday!
Yet all this growing, which now is done
And finished, was scarcely then begun.
The nodding wheat and high, strong
   screen
Of corn were but little points of green.
The apple blossoms were pink and
   sweet,

But no one could gather them to eat;
And all this food for hungry men
Was but buds or seeds just planted
    then.

Susan Coolidge

FALL, LEAVES, FALL

Fall, leaves, fall; die, flowers, away;
Lengthen night and shorten day;
Every leaf speaks bliss to me,
Fluttering from the autumn tree.

I shall smile when wreaths of snow
Blossom where the rose should grow;
I shall sing when night's decay
Ushers in a drearier day.

Emily Brontë

WINTER

Lastly came Winter clothèd all in
    frize,
Chattering his teeth for cold that did
    him chill;
Whilst on his hoary beard his breath
    did freeze,
And the dull drops that from his pur-
    ple bill
As from a limbeck did adown distill;
In his right hand a tippèd staff he held
With which his feeble steps he stayèd
    still,
For he was faint with cold and weak
    with eld,
That scarce his loosèd limbs he able
    was to weld.

Edmund Spenser

MIDWINTER

The speckled sky is dim with snow,
The light flakes falter and fall slow;
Athwart the hill-top, rapt and pale,
Silently drops a silver veil;
And all the valley is shut in
By flickering curtains gray and thin.

But cheerily the chickadee
Singeth to me on fence and tree;
The snow sails round him as he sings,
White as the down of angels' wings.

I watch the snowflakes as they fall
On bank and brier and broken wall;
Over the orchard, waste and brown,
All noiselessly they settle down,
Tipping the apple-boughs, and each
Light quivering twig of plum and
    peach.

On turf and curb and bower-roof
The snow-storm spreads its ivory woof;
It paves with pearl the garden-walk;
And lovingly round tattered stalk
And shivering stem its magic weaves
A mantle fair as lily-leaves.

The hooded beehive small and low,
Stands like a maiden in the snow;
And the old door-slab is half hid
Under an alabaster lid.

All day it snows: the sheeted post
Gleams in the dimness like a ghost;
All day the blasted oak has stood
A muffled wizard of the wood;
Garland and airy cap adorn
The sumach and the wayside thorn,
And clustering spangles lodge and
    shine
In the dark tresses of the pine.

The ragged bramble, dwarfed and old,
Shrinks like a beggar in the cold;
In surplice white the cedar stands,
And blesses him with priestly hands.

Still cheerily the chickadee
Singeth to me on fence and tree:
But in my inmost ear is heard
The music of a holier bird;
And heavenly thoughts as soft and
    white
As snowflakes on my soul alight,
Clothing with love my lonely heart,
Healing with peace each bruised part,
Till all my being seems to be
Transfigured by their purity.

                John Townsend Trowbridge

THE BROOK IN WINTER

Down swept the chill wind from the
    mountain peak,
    From the snow five thousand sum-
    mers old;
On open wold and hill-top bleak
    It had gathered all the cold,
And whirled it like sleet on the wan-
    derer's cheek;
It carried a shiver everywhere
From the unleafed boughs and pas-
    tures bare;
The little brook heard it and built a
    roof
'Neath which he could house him,
    winter-proof;
All night by the white stars' frosty
    gleams
He groined his arches and matched his
    beams;
Slender and clear were his crystal spars
As the lashes of light that trim the
    stars;
He sculptured every summer delight
In his halls and chambers out of sight;
Sometimes his tinkling waters slipt
Down through a frost-leaved forest
    crypt,
Long, sparkling aisles of steel-stemmed
    trees

Bending to counterfeit a breeze;
Sometimes the roof no fretwork knew
But silvery mosses that downward
    grew;
Sometimes it was carved in sharp relief
With quaint arabesques of ice-fern
    leaf;
Sometimes it was simply smooth and
    clear
For the gladness of heaven to shine
    through, and here
He had caught the nodding bulrush-
    tops
And hung them thickly with diamond
    drops,
That crystalled the beams of moon and
    sun,
And made a star of every one:
No mortal builder's most rare device
Could match this winter palace of ice;
'Twas as if every image that mirrored
    lay
In his depths serene through the sum-
    mer day,
Each flitting shadow of earth and sky,
    Lest the happy model should be lost,
Had been mimicked in fairy masonry
    By the elfin builders of the frost.

                James Russell Lowell

STOPPING BY WOODS ON A
SNOWY EVENING

Whose woods these are I think I know.
His house is in the village though;
He will not see me stopping here
To watch his woods fill up with snow.

My little horse must think it queer
To stop without a farmhouse near
Between the woods and frozen lake
The darkest evening of the year.

He gives his harness bells a shake
To ask if there is some mistake.
The only other sound's the sweep
Of easy wind and downy flake.

The woods are lovely, dark and deep.
But I have promises to keep,
And miles to go before I sleep,
And miles to go before I sleep.

Robert Frost

THE SNOWSTORM

Announced by all the trumpets of the
    sky,
Arrives the snow, and, driving o'er the
    fields,
Seems nowhere to alight; the whited
    air
Hides hills and woods, the river, and
    the heaven,
And veils the farmhouse at the gar-
    den's end.
The sledge and traveller stopped, the
    courier's feet
Delayed, all friends shut out, the
    house-mates sit
Around the radiant fireplace, inclosed
In a tumultuous privacy of storm.

Come, see the north wind's masonry.
Out of an unseen quarry evermore
Furnished with tile, the fierce artificer
Curves his white bastions with pro-
    jected roof
Round every windward stake, or tree,
    or door.
Speeding, the myriad-handed, his wild
    work
So fanciful, so savage, naught cares he
For number or proportion. Mockingly,
On coop or kennel he hangs Parian
    wreaths;

A swan-like form invests the hidden
    thorn;
Fills up the farmer's lane from wall to
    wall,
Maugre the farmer's sighs; and, at the
    gate,
A tapering turret overtops the work:
And when his hours are numbered,
    and the world
Is all his own, retiring, as he were not,
Leaves, when the sun appears, aston-
    ished Art
To mimic in slow structures, stone by
    stone,
Built in an age, the mad wind's night-
    work,
The frolic architecture of the snow.

Ralph Waldo Emerson

VELVET SHOES

Let us walk in the white snow
    In a soundless space;
With footsteps quiet and slow,
    At a tranquil pace,
    Under veils of white lace.

I shall go shod in silk,
    And you in wool,
White as a white cow's milk,
    More beautiful than the breast of
        a gull.

We shall walk through the still town
    In a windless peace;
We shall step upon white down,
    Upon silver fleece,
    Upon softer than these.

We shall walk in velvet shoes:
    Wherever we go
Silence will fall like dews
    On white silence below.
    We shall walk in the snow.

Elinor Wylie

UP IN THE MORNING EARLY

Up in the morning's no for me,
  Up in the morning early;
When a' the hills are cover'd wi' snaw,
  I'm sure it's winter fairly.

Cauld blaws the wind frae east to west,
  The drift is driving sairly;
Sae loud and shrill's I hear the blast,
  I'm sure it's winter fairly.

The birds sit chittering in the thorn,
  A' day they fare but sparely;
And lang's the night frae e'en to morn;
  I'm sure it's winter fairly.

Robert Burns

THE WHIRL-BLAST

A whirl-blast from behind the hill
Rush'd o'er the woods with startling
  sound;
Then—all at once the air was still,
And showers of hailstones patter'd
  round.
Where leafless oaks tower'd high
  above,
I sat within an undergrove
Of tallest hollies, tall and green;
A fairer bower was never seen.
From year to year the spacious floor
With wither'd leaves is cover'd o'er,
And all the year the bower is green;
But see! where'er the hailstones drop
The wither'd leaves all skip and hop;
There's not a breeze—no breath of
  air—
Yet here, and there, and everywhere
Along the floor, beneath the shade
By those embowering hollies made,
The leaves in myriads jump and spring,
As if with pipes and music rare
Some Robin Goodfellow were there,

And all those leaves, in festive glee,
Were dancing to the minstrelsy.

William Wordsworth

WHEN ICICLES HANG BY THE WALL

When icicles hang by the wall,
  And Dick the shepherd blows his
  nail,
And Tom bears logs into the hall,
  And milk comes frozen home in
  pail;
When blood is nipp'd and ways be
  foul,
Then nightly sings the staring owl,
  To-who;
Tu-whit, To-who, a merry note,
While greasy Joan doth keel the pot.

When all around the wind doth blow,
  And coughing drowns the parson's
  saw,
And birds sit brooding in the mow,
  And Marian's nose looks red and
  raw,
When roasted crabs hiss in the bowl,
Then nightly sings the staring owl,
  To-who;
Tu-whit, To-who, a merry note,
While greasy Joan doth keel the pot.

William Shakespeare

A WIDOW BIRD

A widow bird sat mourning for her
  love
  Upon a wintry bough;
The frozen wind crept on above,
  The freezing stream below.

There was no leaf upon the forest bare,
  No flower upon the ground,

And little motion in the air
    Except the mill wheel's sound.
            Percy Bysshe Shelley

THE DEATH OF THE FLOWERS

The melancholy days are come, the
    saddest of the year,
Of wailing winds, and naked woods,
    and meadows brown and sear.
Heaped in the hollows of the grove,
    the withered leaves lie dead;
They rustle to the eddying gust, and
    to the rabbits' tread.
The robin and the wren are flown, and
    from the shrubs the jay,
And from the wood-tops calls the
    crow, through all the gloomy day.

Where are the flowers, the fair young
    flowers that lately sprang and stood
In brighter light and softer airs, a
    beauteous sisterhood?
Alas! they all are in their graves, the
    gentle race of flowers
Are lying in their lowly beds, with the
    fair and good of ours.
The rain is falling where they lie, but
    the cold November rain,
Calls not, from out the gloomy earth,
    the lovely ones again.

The wind-flower and the violet, they
    perished long ago,
And the brier-rose and the orchid died
    amid the summer glow;
But on the hill the golden-rod, and
    the aster in the wood,
And the yellow sunflower by the brook
    in autumn beauty stood,
Till fell the frost from the clear cold
    heaven, as falls the plague on men,

And the brightness of their smile was
    gone, from upland, glade, and glen.

And now when comes the calm mild
    day, as still such days will come,
To call the squirrel and the bee from
    out their winter home;
When the sound of dropping nuts is
    heard, though all the trees are still,
And twinkle in the smoky light the
    waters of the rill,
The south wind searches for the flow-
    ers whose fragrance late he bore,
And sighs to find them in the wood
    and by the stream no more.

And then I think of one who in her
    youthful beauty died,
The fair, meek blossom that grew up
    and faded by my side;
In the cold moist earth we laid her,
    when the forest cast the leaf,
And we wept that one so lovely should
    have a life so brief:
Yet not unmeet it was that one, like
    that young friend of ours,
So gentle and so beautiful, should per-
    ish with the flowers.
            William Cullen Bryant

THE NORTH-EAST WIND

(Selected Stanzas)

Welcome, wild north-easter!
    Shame it is to see
Odes to every zephyr,
    Ne'er a verse to thee.
Welcome, black north-easter!
    O'er the German foam;
O'er the Danish moorlands,
    From thy frozen home.
Tired we are of summer,
    Tired of gaudy glare.

Showers soft and steaming,
 Hot and breathless air.
Tired of listless dreaming,
 Through the lazy day;
Jovial wind of winter,
 Turn us out to play!
Sweep the golden reed-beds;
 Crisp the lazy dyke;
Hunger into madness
 Every plunging pike.
Fill the lake with wild-fowl;
 Fill the marsh with snipe;
While on dreamy moorlands
 Lonely curlew pipe.
Through the black fir forest
 Thunder harsh and dry,
Shattering down the snow flakes,
 Off the curdled sky.

Charles Kingsley

ST. SWITHIN'S DAY

St. Swithin's Day, if thou dost rain,
 For forty days it will remain;
St. Swithin's Day, if thou be fair,
 For forty days 'twill rain na mair.

Unknown

THE SUCCESSION OF THE FOUR SWEET MONTHS

First, *April*, she with mellow show'rs
Opens the way for early flowers;
Then after her comes smiling *May*,
In a more rich and sweet array;
Next enters *June*, and brings us more
Gems, than those two, that went be-
 fore:
Then, lastly, *July* comes, and she
More wealth brings in than all those
 three.

Robert Herrick

SNOWDROP

Many, many welcomes,
February fair-maid,
Ever as of old time,
Solitary firstling,
Coming in the cold time,
Prophet of the gay time,
Prophet of the May time,
Prophet of the roses,
Many, many welcomes,
February fair-made.

Alfred Tennyson

MARCH

March! March! March! They are com-
 ing
In troops to the tune of the wind.
Red-headed woodpeckers drumming,
Gold-crested thrushes behind;
Sparrows in brown jackets hopping,
Past every gateway and door;
Finches, with crimson caps, stopping
Just where they stopped years before.

March! March! March! They are slip-
 ping
Into their places at last—
Little white lily-buds, dripping
Under the showers that fall fast;
Buttercups, violets, roses;
Snowdrop and bluebell and pink,
Throng upon throng of sweet posies,
Bending the dewdrops to drink.

March! March! March! They will
 hurry
Forth at the wild bugle-sound,
Blossoms and birds in a flurry,
Fluttering all over the ground.
Shake out your flags, birch and willow!

Shake out your red tassels, larch!
Grass-blades, up from your earth-pil-
　　low.
Hear who is calling you—March.

Lucy Larcom

MARCH

(Selected Stanzas)

The stormy March is come at last,
　　With wind, and cloud, and chang-
　　　ing skies;
I hear the rushing of the blast
　　That through the snowy valley flies.

Ah, passing few are they who speak,
　　Wild, stormy month, in praise of
　　　thee;
Yet though thy winds are loud and
　　bleak,
　　Thou art a welcome month to me.

For thou to northern lands, again
　　The glad and glorious sun dost
　　　bring;
And thou hast joined the gentle train,
　　And wear'st the gentle name of
　　　Spring.

Then sing aloud the gushing rills
　　In joy that they again are free,
And, brightly leaping down the hills,
　　Renew their journey to the sea.

Thou bring'st the hope of those calm
　　skies,
　　And that soft time of sunny showers,
When the wide bloom, on earth that
　　lies,
　　Seems of a brighter world than ours.

William Cullen Bryant

WRITTEN IN MARCH

The cock is crowing,
The stream is flowing,
The small birds twitter,
The lake doth glitter,
The green field sleeps in the sun:
The oldest and youngest
Are at work with the strongest:
The cattle are grazing,
Their heads never raising,
There are forty feeding like one!

Like an army defeated,
The snow hath retreated,
And now doth fare ill
On the top of the bare hill;
The ploughboy is whooping—anon
　　—anon:
There's joy in the mountains,
There's life in the fountains;
Small clouds are sailing,
Blue sky prevailing,
The rain is over and gone!

William Wordsworth

APRIL

The roofs are shining from the rain,
　　The sparrows twitter as they fly,
And with a windy April grace
　　The little clouds go by.

Yet the back-yards are bare and
　　brown
　　With only one unchanging tree—
I could not be so sure of Spring
　　Save that it sings in me.

Sara Teasdale

IN APRIL

The poplar drops beside the way
Its tasselled plumes of silver-gray;
The chestnut pouts its great brown
buds
Impatient for the laggard May.

The honeysuckles lace the wall,
The hyacinths grow fair and tall;
And mellow sun and pleasant wind
And odorous bees are over all.

Elizabeth Akers

APRIL WEATHER

When April, one day, was asked
    whether
She *could* make reliable weather,
    She laughed till she cried,
    And said, " Bless you, I've tried,
But the things will get mixed up to-
    gether."

Jessie McDermott

MAY

Merry, rollicking, frolicking May
Into the woods came skipping one day;
She teased the brook till he laughed
    outright,
And gurgled and scolded with all his
    might;
She chirped to the birds and bade
    them sing
A chorus of welcome to Lady Spring;
And the bees and butterflies she set
To waking the flowers that were sleep-
    ing yet.
She shook the trees till the buds looked
    out
To see what the trouble was all about,
And nothing in Nature escaped that
    day
The touch of the life-giving bright
    young May.

George MacDonald

GLYCINE'S SONG

A sunny shaft did I behold,
    From sky to earth it slanted:

And poised therein a bird so bold—
    Sweet bird, thou wert enchanted!

He sank, he rose, he twinkled, he
    trolled
    Within that shaft of sunny mist;
His eyes of fire, his beak of gold,
    All else of amethyst!

And thus he sang: " Adieu! Adieu!
Love's dream proves seldom true.
The blossoms, they make no delay;
The sparkling dewdrops will not stay.
    Sweet month of May,
        We must away;
            Far, far away;
                Today! today! "

Samuel Taylor Coleridge

CHLOE

It was the charming month of May,
When all the flowers were fresh and
    gay.
One morning by the break of day,
    The youthful, charming Chloe
From peaceful slumbers she arose,
Girt on her mantle and her hose,
And o'er her flowery mead she goes,
    The youthful, charming Chloe.
    Lovely was she by the dawn,
        Youthful Chloe, charming Chloe,
    Tripping o'er the pearly lawn,
        The youthful, charming Chloe.

The feathered people you might see,
Perch'd all around on every tree,
In notes of sweetest melody
    They hail the charming Chloe;
Till painting gay the eastern skies,
The glorious sun begins to rise,
Outrivall'd by the radiant eyes
    Of youthful, charming Chloe.

Lovely was she by the dawn,
  Youthful Chloe, charming Chloe,
Tripping o'er the pearly lawn,
  The youthful, charming Chloe.
                    Robert Burns

✗ SONG ON A MAY MORNING

Now the bright morning star, Day's
  harbinger,
Comes dancing from the East, and
  leads with her
The flowery May, who from her green
  lap throws
The yellow cowslip and the pale prim-
  rose.
Hail, Bounteous May, that doth in-
  spire
Mirth, and youth, and warm desire;
Woods and groves are of thy dressing,
Hill and dale doth boast thy blessing;
Thus we salute thee with our early
  song,
And welcome thee, and wish thee long.
                    John Milton

JULY

When the scarlet cardinal tells
  Her dream to the dragon fly,
And the lazy breeze makes a nest in
  the trees,
  And murmurs a lullaby,
    It is July.

When the tangled cobweb pulls
  The cornflower's cap awry,
And the lilies tall lean over the wall
  To bow to the butterfly,
    It is July.

When the heat like a mist-veil floats,
  And poppies flame in the rye,

And the silver note in the streamlet's
  throat
  Has softened almost to a sigh,
    It is July.

When the hours are so still that time
  Forgets them, and lets them lie
'Neath petals pink till the night stars
  wink
  At the sunset in the sky,
    It is July.
                    Susan Hartley Swett

OCTOBER'S BRIGHT BLUE
WEATHER

O suns and skies and clouds of June,
  And flowers of June together,
Ye cannot rival for one hour
  October's bright blue weather;

When loud the bumblebee makes
  haste,
  Belated, thriftless vagrant,
And goldenrod is dying fast,
  And lanes with grapes are fragrant;

When gentians roll their fringes tight
  To save them for the morning,
And chestnuts fall from satin burrs
  Without a sound of warning;

When on the ground red applies lie
  In piles like jewels shining,
And redder still on old stone walls
  Are leaves of woodbine twining;

When all the lovely wayside things
  Their white-winged seeds are sowing,
And in the fields, still green and fair,
  Late aftermaths are growing;

When springs run low, and on the
  brooks,

In idle golden freighting,
Bright leaves sink noiseless in the hush
Of woods, for winter waiting;

When comrades seek sweet country
    haunts,
By twos and twos together,
And count like misers, hour by hour,
    October's bright blue weather.

O sun and skies and flowers of June,
    Count all your boasts together,
Love loveth best of all the year
    October's bright blue weather.
            Helen Hunt Jackson

SEPTEMBER

The goldenrod is yellow,
    The corn is turning brown,
The trees in apple orchards
    With fruit are bending down;

The gentian's bluest fringes
    Are curling in the sun;
In dusty pods the milkweed
    Its hidden silk has spun;

The sedges flaunt their harvest
    In every meadow nook,
And asters by the brookside
    Make asters in the brook.

From dewy lanes at morning
    The grapes' sweet odors rise;
At noon the roads all flutter
    With yellow butterflies—

By all these lovely tokens
    September's days are here,
With summer's best of weather
    And autumn's best of cheer.
            Helen Hunt Jackson

NOVEMBER

No sun—no moon—
No morn—no noon—
No dawn—no dusk—no proper time
    of day—
No sky—no earthly view—
No distance looking blue—
No road—no street—no " t'other side
    the way "—
No end to any row—
No indications where the crescents
    go—
No top to any steeple—
No recognitions of familiar people—
No courtesies for showing 'em—
No knowing 'em!
No traveling at all—no locomotion—
No inkling of the way—no notion—
" No go "—by land or ocean—
No mail—no post—
No news from any foreign coast—
No park—no ring—no afternoon gen-
    tility—
No company—no nobility—
No warmth, no cheerfulness, no
    healthful ease,
No comfortable feel in any mem-
    ber—
No shade, no shine, no butterflies,
    no bees—
November!
            Thomas Hood

DECEMBER

In a drear-nighted December,
    Too happy, happy tree,
Thy branches ne'er remember
    Their green felicity.
The north cannot undo them,
With a sleety whistle through them;
Nor frozen thawings glue them
    From budding at the prime.

In a drear-nighted December,
　Too happy, happy brook,
Thy bubblings ne'er remember
　Apollo's summer look;
But with a sweet forgetting,
They stay their crystal fretting
Never, never petting
　About the frozen time.

Ah! would 'twere so with many
　A gentle girl and boy!
But were there ever any
　Writhed not at passèd joy?
To know the change and feel it,
When there is none to heal it,
Nor numbed sense to steal it,
　Was never said in rhyme.

John Keats

Part Five

NATURE IN POETRY

A VIOLET BANK

I know a bank whereon the wild thyme
    blows,
Where oxlips and the nodding violet
    grows:
Quite over-canopied with lush wood-
    bine,
With sweet musk roses and with
    eglantine.

William Shakespeare

PUSSY-WILLOWS

More soft than press of baby lips
They fleck the russet willow-slips
Before the bluebirds hither wing—
These first, faint footfalls of the Spring.

Arthur Guiterman

A ROSEBUD

A rosebud by my early walk,
Adown a corn-enclosed bawk,
Sae gently bent its thorny stalk,
    All on a dewy morning.

Ere twice the shades o' dawn are fled,
In a' its crimson glory spread,
And drooping rich the dewy head,
    It scents the early morning.

Within the bush, her covert nest
A little linnet fondly prest,
The dew sat chilly on her breast
    Sae early in the morning.

So thou, dear bird, young Jenny fair,
On trembling string, or vocal air,
Shall sweetly pay the tender care
    That tents thy early morning.

So thou sweet rosebud, young and gay,
Shalt beauteous blaze upon the day,
And bless the parents' evening ray
    That watch thy early morning.

Robert Burns

THE DAISY'S SONG

(Selected Stanzas)

The sun, with his great eye,
Sees not so much as I;
And the moon, all silver-proud
Might as well be in a cloud.

And O the spring—the spring!
I lead the life of a king!
Couch'd in the teeming grass,
I spy each pretty lass.

I look where no one dares,
And I stare where no one stares,

381

And when the night is nigh
Lambs bleat my lullaby.

           John Keats

ALMOND BLOSSOM

Blossom of the almond trees,
April's gift to April's bees,
Birthday ornament of spring,
Flora's fairest daughterling;
Coming when no flowerets dare
Trust the cruel outer air;
When the royal kingcup bold
Dares not don his coat of gold;
And the sturdy black-thorn spray
Keeps the silver for the May:—
Coming when no flowerets would,
Save thy lowly sisterhood,
Early violets, blue and white,
Dying for their love of light.
Almond blossom, sent to teach us
That the spring days soon will reach
   us,
Lest, with longing over-tried,
We die, as the violets died—
Blossom, clouding all the tree
With thy crimson broidery,
Long before a leaf of green
O'er the bravest bough is seen;
Ah! when winter winds are swinging
All thy red bells into ringing.
With a bee in every bell,
Almond blossoms, we greet thee well.

           Edwin Arnold

I WANDERED LONELY AS A CLOUD

I wandered lonely as a cloud
   That floats on high o'er vales and
   hills,
When all at once I saw a crowd,
   A host of golden daffodils:
Beside the lake, beneath the trees,
Fluttering and dancing in the breeze.

Continuous as the stars that shine
   And twinkle on the milky way,
They stretched in never-ending line
   Along the margin of a bay:
Ten thousand saw I at a glance,
Tossing their heads in sprightly dance.

The waves beside them danced, but
   they
   Out-did the sparkling waves in
   glee:—
A poet could not but be gay,
   In such a jocund company;
I gazed—and gazed—but little thought
What wealth the show to me had
   brought.

For oft, when on my couch I lie
   In vacant or in pensive mood,
They flash upon that inward eye
   Which is the bliss of solitude;
And then my heart with pleasure fills,
And dances with the daffodils.

           William Wordsworth

NARCISSUS

I saw the pride of all the meadows
   At morn, a gay Narcissus, blow
Upon a river's bank, whose shadow
   Bloomed in the silver waves below.
By noontide's heat its youth was
   wasted,
   The waters as they passed com-
   plained;
At eve its glories were all blasted,
   And not one former grace remained.
While the wild rose, more safely grow-
   ing
   Low in the unaspiring vale,
Amidst retirement's shelter blowing,
   Long sheds its sweetness on the gale.

           William Cowper

THE RHODORA

In May, when sea-winds pierced our solitudes,
I found the fresh Rhodora in the woods,
Spreading its leafless blooms in a damp nook,
To please the desert and the sluggish brook:
The purple petals, fallen in the pool,
  Made the black waters with their beauty gay;
Here might the red-bird come his plumes to cool,
  And court the flower that cheapens his array.
Rhodora! if the sages ask thee why
This charm is wasted on the earth and sky,
Dear, tell them, that if eyes were made for seeing,
Then beauty is its own excuse for being.
Why thou were there, O rival of the rose!
I never thought to ask; I never knew,
But in my simple ignorance suppose
  The self-same Power that brought me there, brought you.

Ralph Waldo Emerson

TO THE FRINGED GENTIAN

Thou blossom bright with autumn dew,
And coloured with the heaven's own blue,
That openest, when the quiet light
Succeeds the keen and frosty night.

Thou comest not when violets lean
O'er wandering brooks and springs unseen,
Or columbines in purple dressed,
Nod o'er the ground-bird's hidden nest.

Thou waitest late, and com'st alone,
When woods are bare, and birds are flown,
And frosts and shortening days portend
The aged year is near his end.

Then doth thy sweet and quiet eye
Look through its fringes to the sky,
Blue—blue—as if that sky let fall
A flower from its cerulean wall.

I would that thus, when I shall see
The hour of death draw near to me,
Hope, blossoming within my heart,
May look to Heaven as I depart.

William Cullen Bryant

THE WHITE ANEMONE

(*Selected Stanzas*)

'Tis the white anemone, fashioned so
Like to the stars of the winter snow,
First thinks, " If I come too soon, no doubt
I shall seem but the snow that stayed too long,
So 'tis I that will be Spring's unguessed scout,"
And wide she wanders the woods among.
Then, from out of the mossiest hiding-places,
Smile meek moonlight-colored faces
Of pale primroses puritan,
In maiden sisterhood demure;
Each virgin floweret faint and wan
With the bliss of her own sweet breath so pure.

Owen Meredith

WILD ROSE

Some innocent girlish Kisses by a
    charm
    Changed to a flight of small pink
    Butterflies,
    To waver under June's delicious
    skies
Across   gold-sprinkled   meads — the
    merry swarm
A smiling powerful world did next
    transform
    To little Roses mesh'd in green
    allies
    Of earth and air, and everything we
    prize
For mirthful, gentle, delicate and
    warm.

William Allingham

A SONG OF CLOVER

I wonder what the clover thinks,—
Intimate friend of Bob-o'-links,
Lover of Daisies slim and white,
Waltzer with Buttercups at night;
Keeper of Inn for traveling Bees,
Serving to them wine-dregs and lees
Left by the Royal Humming Birds,
Who sip and pay with fine-spun words;
Fellow with all the lowliest,
Peer of the gayest and the best;
Comrade of winds, beloved of sun,
Kissed by the Dew-drops, one by one;
Prophet of Good-Luck mystery
By sign of four which few may see;
Symbol of Nature's magic zone,
One out of three, and three in one;
Emblem of comfort in the speech
Which poor men's babies early reach;
Sweet by the roadsides, sweet by rills,
Sweet in the meadows, sweet on hills,
Sweet in its white, sweet in its red,—
Oh, half its sweetness cannot be said;—
Sweet in its every living breath,

Sweetest, perhaps, at last, in death!
Oh! who knows what the Clover
    thinks?
No one! unless the Bob-o'-links!

" Saxe Holm "

TO THE SMALL CELANDINE

Pansies, lilies, kingcups, daisies,
Let them live upon their praises;
    Long as there's a sun that sets,
Primroses will have their glory;
    Long as there are violets,
They will have a place in story;
There's a flower that shall be mine,
'Tis the little Celandine.

Eyes of some men travel far
For the finding of a star;
    Up and down the heavens they go,
Men that keep a mighty rout!
    I'm as great as them, I trow,
Since the day I found thee out.
Little Flower! I'll make a stir,
Like a sage astronomer.

Modest, yet withal an elf
Bold, and lavish of thyself;
    Since we needs must first have met,
I have seen thee high and low,
    Thirty years or more, and yet
'Twas a face I did not know;
Thou hast now, go where I may,
Fifty greetings in a day.

Ere a leaf is on a bush,
In a time before the thrush
    Has a thought about her nest,
Thou wilt come with half a call,
    Spreading out thy glossy breast
Like a careless prodigal;
Telling tales about the sun,
When we've little warmth or none.

Poets, vain men in their mood!
Travel with the multitude:

Never heed them; I aver
That they all are wanton wooers;
  But the thrifty cottager,
Who stirs little out of doors,
Joys to spy thee near her home;
Spring is coming, thou art come!

Comfort have thou of thy merit,
Kindly, unassuming spirit!
  Careless of thy neighbourhood,
Thou dost show thy pleasant face
  On the moor, and in the wood,
In the lane—there's not a place
Howsoever mean it be,
But 'tis good enough for thee.

Ill befall the yellow flowers,
Children of the flaring hours!
  Buttercups, that will be seen,
Whether we will see or no;
  Others, too, of lofty mien;
They have done as worldings do,
Taken praise that should be thine,
Little, humble Celandine!

Prophets of delight and mirth,
Ill-requited upon earth;
  Herald of a mighty band,
Of a joyous train ensuing,
  Serving at my heart's command,
Tasks that are no tasks renewing,
I will sing, as dost behove,
Hymns in praise of what I love.
                William Wordsworth

A GARDEN

(*Selected Stanzas*)

A sensitive plant in a garden grew,
And the young winds fed it with silver
  dew,
And it open'd its fan-like leaves to the
  light,
And closed them beneath the kisses of
  night.

And the Spring arose on the garden
  fair,
And the Spirit of Love fell everywhere;
And each flower and herb on Earth's
  dark breast
Rose from the dreams of its wintry
  nest.

The snowdrop, and then the violet,
Arose from the ground with warm rain
  wet,
And their breath was mix'd with fresh
  odour, sent
From the turf, like the voice and the
  instrument.

Then the pied wind-flowers and the
  tulip tall,
And narcissi, the fairest among them
  all,
Who gaze on their eyes in the stream's
  recess,
Till they die of their own dear loveliness.

And the Naiad-like lily of the vale,
Whom youth makes so fair and passion so pale,
That the light of its tremulous bell is
  seen,
Through their pavilions of tender
  green.

And the hyacinth, purple and white
  and blue,
Which flung from its bells a sweet
  peal anew,
Of music so delicate, soft, and intense,
It was felt like an odour within the
  sense.

And the jessamine faint, and the sweet
  tuberose,

The sweetest flower for scent that
  blows;
And all rare blossoms from every clime
Grew in that garden in perfect prime.
          Percy Bysshe Shelley

TIME TO GO

  They know the time to go!
The fairy clocks strike their inaudible
  hour
In field and woodland, and each punc-
  tual flower
Bows at the signal an obedient head
  And hastes to bed.

  The pale Anemone
Glides on her way with scarcely a good
  night;
The Violets tie their purple nightcaps
  tight;
Hand clasped in hand, the dancing
  Columbines,
  In blithesome lines,

  Drop their last courtesies,
Flit from the scene, and couch them
  for their rest;
The Meadow-Lily folds her scarlet vest
And hides it 'neath the Grasses length-
  ening green;
  Fair and serene,

  Her sister Lily floats
On the blue pond, and raises golden
  eyes
To court the golden splendor of the
  skies—
The sudden signal comes, and down
  she goes
  To find repose,

  In the cool depths below.
A little later, and the Asters blue

Depart in crowds, a brave and cheery
  crew;
While Golden-rod, still wide awake
  and gay,
  Turns him away,

  Furls his bright parasol,
And like a little hero, meets his fate.
The Gentians, very proud to sit up
  late,
Next follow. Every Fern is tucked and
  set
  'Neath coverlet,

  Downy and soft and warm.
No little seedling voice is heard to
  grieve
Or make complaints the folding woods
  beneath;
No lingerer dares to stay, for well they
  know
  The time to go.

  Teach us your patience, brave,
Dear flowers, till we shall dare to part
  like you,
Willing God's will, sure that His clock
  strikes true,
  With smiles, not sorrow.
          Susan Coolidge

THE GRASS

The grass so little has to do,—
  A sphere of simple green,
With only butterflies to brood,
  And bees to entertain,

And stir all day to pretty tunes
  The breezes fetch along,
And hold the sunshine in its lap
  And bow to everything;

And thread the dews all night, like
  pearls,

And make itself so fine,—
A duchess were too common
  For such a noticing.

And even when it dies, to pass
  In odours so divine,
As lowly spices gone to sleep,
  Or amulets of pine.

And then to dwell in sovereign barns,
  And dream the days away,—
The grass so little has to do,
  I wish I were the hay!

                    Emily Dickinson

THE IVY GREEN

Oh, a dainty plant is the Ivy green,
That creepeth o'er ruins old!
Of right choice food are his meals, I
    ween,
In his cell so lone and cold.
The wall must be crumbled, the stone
    decayed,
To pleasure his dainty whim:
And the moldering dust that years have
    made
Is a merry meal for him.
  Creeping where no life is seen,
  A rare old plant is the Ivy green.

Fast he stealeth on, though he wears
    no wings,
And a staunch old heart has he.
How closely he twineth, how tight he
    clings
To his friend the huge Oak Tree!
And slyly he traileth along the ground,
And his leaves he gently waves,
And he joyously hugs and crawleth
    round
The rich mold of dead men's graves.
  Creeping where grim death has
    been,
  A rare old plant is the Ivy green.

Whole ages have fled and their works
    decayed,
And nations have scattered been;
But the stout old Ivy shall never fade
From its hale and hearty green.
The brave old plant in its lonely days,
Shall fatten upon the past:
For the stateliest building man can
    raise,
Is the Ivy's food at last.
  Creeping on where time has been,
  A rare old plant is the Ivy green.

                    Charles Dickens

THE CORN SONG

Heap high the farmer's wintry board!
  Heap high the golden corn!
No richer gift has autumn poured
  From out her lavish horn!

Let other lands, exulting, glean
  The apple from the pine,
The orange from its glossy green,
  The cluster from the vine.

We better love the hardy gift
  Our rugged vales bestow,
To cheer us when the storm shall drift
  Our harvest-fields with snow.

Through vales of grass and meads of
    flowers,
  Our plough their furrows made,
While on the hills the sun and showers
  Of changeful April played.

We dropped the seed o'er hill and
    plain
  Beneath the sun of May,
And frightened from our sprouting
    grain
  The robber crows away.

All through the long, bright days of
    June
  Its leaves grew green and fair,
And waved in hot midsummer's noon
  Its soft and yellow hair.

And now with autumn's moonlit eves,
  Its harvest-time has come,
We pluck away the frosted leaves,
  And bear the treasure home.

There richer than the fabled gift
  Apollo showered of old,
Fair hands the broken grain shall sift,
  And knead its meal of gold.

Let vapid idlers loll in silk
  Around their costly board;
Give us the bowl of samp and milk,
  By homespun beauty poured!

Where'er the wide old kitchen hearth
  Sends up its smoky curls,
Who will not thank the kindly earth,
  And bless our farmer girls!

Then shame on all the proud and vain,
  Whose folly laughs to scorn
The blessing of our hardy grain,
  Our wealth of golden corn!

Let earth withhold her goodly root,
  Let mildew blight the rye,
Give to the worm the orchard's fruit,
  The wheat field to the fly:

But let the good old crop adorn
  The hills our fathers trod;
Still let us for His golden corn,
  Send up our thanks to God!
            John Greenleaf Whittier

TREES

I think that I shall never see
A poem lovely as a tree.

A tree whose hungry mouth is prest
Against the sweet earth's flowing
  breast;

A tree that looks at God all day,
And lifts her leafy arms to pray;

A tree that may in summer wear
A nest of robins in her hair;

Upon whose bosom snow has lain;
Who intimately lives with rain.

Poems are made by fools like me,
But only God can make a tree.
            Joyce Kilmer

WHAT DO WE PLANT WHEN WE PLANT THE TREE?

What do we plant when we plant the
  tree?
We plant the ship which will cross the
  sea,
We plant the mast to carry the sails,
We plant the planks to withstand the
  gales—
The keel, the keelson, and beam and
  knee,—
We plant the ship when we plant the
  tree.

What do we plant when we plant the
  tree?
We plant the houses for you and me.
We plant the rafters, the shingles, the
  floors,
We plant the studding, the lath, the
  doors,

The beams and siding, all parts that be,
We plant the house when we plant
   the tree.

What do we plant when we plant the
   tree?
A thousand things that we daily see.
We plant the spire that out-towers the
   crag,
We plant the staff for our country's
   flag,
We plant the shade from the hot sun
   free;
We plant all these when we plant the
   tree.

Henry Abbey

WOODMAN, SPARE THAT TREE

Woodman, spare that tree!
   Touch not a single bough!
In youth it sheltered me,
   And I'll protect it now.
'Twas my forefather's hand
   That placed it near his cot;
There, woodman, let it stand,
   Thy axe shall harm it not!

That old familiar tree,
   Whose glory and renown
Are spread o'er land and sea,—
   And wouldst thou hew it down?
Woodman, forbear thy stroke!
   Cut not its earth-bound ties;
O, spare that agèd oak,
   Now towering to the skies!

When but an idle boy
   I sought its grateful shade;
In all their gushing joy
   Here, too, my sisters played.
My mother kissed me here;
   My father pressed my hand—

Forgive this foolish tear,
   But let that old oak stand!

My heart-strings round thee cling,
   Close as thy bark, old friend!
Here shall the wild-bird sing,
   And still thy branches bend.
Old tree! the storm still brave!
   And, woodman, leave the spot;
While I've a hand to save,
   Thy axe shall harm it not.

George Pope Morris

UNDER THE GREENWOOD TREE

Under the greenwood tree
Who loves to lie with me,
And tune his merry note
Unto the sweet bird's throat,
Come hither, come hither, come hither;
   Here shall he see
   No enemy,
But winter and rough weather.

Who doth ambition shun,
And loves to live i' the sun,
Seeking the food he eats
And pleased with what he gets,
Come hither, come hither, come hither;
   Here shall he see
   No enemy,
But winter and rough weather.

William Shakespeare

MINE HOST OF THE "GOLDEN APPLE"

A goodly host one day was mine,
A Golden Apple his only sign,
That hung from a long branch, ripe
   and fine.

My host was the beautiful Apple-tree;

He gave me shelter and nourished me
With the best of fare, all fresh and
    free.

And light-winged guests came not a
    few,
To his leafy inn, and sipped the dew,
And sang their best songs ere they
    flew.

I slept at night on a downy bed
Of moss, and my Host benignly spread
His own cool shadow over my head.

When I asked what reckoning there
    might be,
He shook his broad boughs cheerily:—
A blessing be thine, green Apple-tree!
           Thomas Westwood

RAIN IN SUMMER

(Selected Stanzas)

How beautiful is the rain!
After the dust and heat,
In the broad and fiery street,
In the narrow lane,
How beautiful is the rain!

How it clatters along the roofs,
Like the tramp of hoofs!
How it gushes and struggles out
From the throat of the overflowing
    spout!

Across the window pane
It pours and pours;
And swift and wide,
With a muddy tide,
Like a river down the gutter roars
The rain, the welcome rain!

The sick man from his chamber looks
At the twisted brooks;

He can feel the cool
Breath of each little pool;
His fevered brain
Grows calm again,
And he breathes a blessing on the rain.

From the neighbouring school
Come the boys,
With more than their wonted noise
And commotion;
And down the wet streets
Sail their mimic fleets,
Till the treacherous pool
Engulfs them in its whirling
And turbulent ocean.

In the country on every side,
Where far and wide,
Like a leopard's tawny and spotted
    hide
Stretches the plain,
To the dry grass and the drier grain
How welcome is the rain!

In the furrowed land
The toilsome and patient oxen stand;
Lifting the yoke-encumbered head,
With their dilated nostrils spread,
They silently inhale
The clover-scented gale,
And the vapours that arise
From the well-watered and smoking
    soil.
For this rest in the furrow after toil
Their large and lustrous eyes
Seem to thank the Lord,
More than man's spoken word.

Near at hand,
From under the sheltering trees,
The farmer sees
His pastures and his fields of grain,
As they bend their tops
To the numberless beating drops

Of the incessant rain,
He counts it as no sin
That he sees therein
Only his own thrift and gain.
Henry Wadsworth Longfellow

SIGNS OF RAIN

The hollow winds begin to blow,
The clouds look black, the glass is low,
The soot falls down, the spaniels sleep,
The spiders from their cobwebs peep;
Last night the sun went pale to bed,
The moon in halos hid her head;
The boding shepherd heaves a sigh,
For, see, a rainbow spans the sky;
The walls are damp, the ditches smell,
Closed is the pink-eyed pimpernel.
Hark how the chairs and tables crack!
Old Betty's joints are on the rack;
Loud quack the ducks, the peacocks
cry,
The distant hills are seeming nigh.
How restless are the snorting swine!
The busy flies disturb the kine;
Low o'er the grass the swallow wings,
The cricket, too, how sharp he sings;
Puss on the hearth, with velvet paws,
Sits wiping o'er her whiskered jaws.
Through the clear stream the fishes
rise,
And nimbly catch the incautious flies.
The glow-worms, numerous and bright,
Illumed the dewy dell last night.
At dusk the squalid toad was seen,
Hopping and crawling o'er the green;
The whirling wind the dust obeys,
And in the rapid eddy plays;
The frog has changed his yellow vest,
And in a russet coat is dressed.
Though June, the air is cold and still,
The mellow blackbird's voice is shrill.
My dog, so altered in his taste,
Quits mutton-bones on grass to feast;

And see yon rooks, how odd their
flight,
They imitate the gliding kite,
And seem precipitate to fall,
As if they felt the piercing ball.
'Twill surely rain I see with sorrow,
Our jaunt must be put off to-morrow.
Edward Jenner

SUNSHINE AFTER A SHOWER

Ever after summer shower,
When the bright sun's returning power
With laughing beam has chased the
storm,
And cheer'd reviving Nature's form,
By sweet-briar hedges bathed in dew,
Let me my wholesome path pursue;
There, issuing forth, the frequent snail
Wears the daub way with slimy trail;
While as I walk from pearlèd bush
The sunny sparkling drop I brush;
And all the landscape fair I view
Clad in robe of fresher hue;
And so loud the blackbird sings,
That far and near the valley rings.
From shelter deep of shaggy rock
The shepherd drives his joyful flock;
From bowering beech the mower
blithe
With new-born vigour grasps the
scythe;
While o'er the smooth unbounded
meads
His last faint gleam the rainbow
spreads.
Thomas Warton

MY HEART LEAPS UP WHEN
I BEHOLD

My heart leaps up when I behold
A rainbow in the sky;
So was it when my life began;

So it is now I am a man;
So be it when I shall grow old,
  Or let me die!
The Child is father of the Man;
And I could wish my days to be
Bound each to each by natural piety.
William Wordsworth

THE CLOUD

I bring fresh showers for the thirsting
  flowers,
  From the seas and the streams;
I bear light shades for the leaves when
  laid
  In their noon-day dreams;
From my wings are shaken the dews
  that waken
  The sweet birds every one,
When rocked to rest on their mother's
  breast,
  As she dances in the sun.
I wield the flail of the lashing hail,
  And whiten the green plains under;
And then again I dissolve it in rain,
  And laugh as I pass in thunder.

I sift the snow on the mountains be-
  low,
  And their great pines groan aghast;
And all the night 'tis my pillow white,
  While I sleep in the arms of the
    blast,
Sublime on the towers of my skyey
  bowers,
  Lightning, my pilot, sits;
In a cavern under is fettered the
  thunder—
  It struggles and howls by fits.
Over earth and ocean, with gentle mo-
  tion,
  This pilot is guiding me,
Lured by the love of the genii that
  move

In the depths of the purple sea;
Over the rills, and the crags, and the
  hills,
  Over the lakes and the plains,
Wherever he dream, under mountain
  or stream,
  The spirit he loves remains;
And I, all the while, bask in heaven's
  blue smile,
  Whilst he is dissolving in rains.

The sanguine sunrise, with his meteor
  eyes,
  And his burning plumes outspread
Leaps on the back of my sailing rack,
  When the morning-star shines dead;
As on the jag of a mountain crag,
  Which an earthquake rocks and
    swings,
An eagle, alit, one moment may sit,
  In the light of its golden wings.
And when sunset may breathe, from
  the lit sea beneath,
  Its ardours of rest and love,
And the crimson pall of eve may fall
  From the depths of heaven above,
With wings folded I rest, on mine airy
  nest,
  And still as a brooding dove.

That orbèd maiden, with white fire
  laden,
  Whom mortals call the moon,
Glides glimmering o'er my fleece-like
  floor,
  By the midnight breezes strewn;
And wherever the beat of her unseen
  feet,
  Which only the angels hear,
May have broken the woof of my tent's
  thin roof,
  The stars peep behind her and peer!
And I laugh to see them whirl and flee,
  Like a swarm of golden bees,

When I widen the rent in my wind-
 built tent,
Till the calm rivers, lakes, and seas,
Like strips of the sky fallen through
 me on high,
 Are each paved with the moon and
 these.

I bind the sun's throne with a burning
 zone,
 And the moon's with a girdle of
 pearl;
The volcanoes are dim, and the stars
 reel and swim,
 When the whirlwinds my banners
 unfurl.
From cape to cape, with a bridge-like
 shape
 Over a torrent sea,
Sunbeam proof, I hang like a roof,
 The mountains its columns be.
The triumphal arch through which I
 march
 With hurricane, fire, and snow,
When the powers of the air are
 chained to my chair,
 Is the million-coloured bow;
The sphere-five above its soft colours
 wove,
 While the moist air was laughing
 below.

I am the daughter of earth and water,
 And the nursling of the sky;
I pass through the pores of the ocean
 and shores;
 I change, but I cannot die:
For, after the rain, when, with never
 a stain,
 The pavilion of heaven is bare,
And the winds and sunbeams, with
 their convex gleams,
 Build up the blue dome of air,
I silently laugh at my own cenotaph,

And out of the caverns of rain,
Like a child from the womb, like a
 ghost from the tomb,
 I arise and unbuild it again.
 Percy Bysshe Shelley

A SUMMER INVOCATION

O, gentle, gentle summer rain,
 Let not the silver lily pine,
The drooping lily pine in vain
 To feel that dewy touch of thine—
To drink thy freshness once again,
O, gentle, gentle summer rain!

In heat the landscape quivering lies;
 The cattle pant beneath the tree;
Through parching air and purple skies
 The earth looks up in vain, for thee;
For thee—for thee, it looks in vain,
O, gentle, gentle summer rain!

Come, thou, and brim the meadow
 streams,
 And soften all the hills with mist,
O falling dew! from burning dreams
 By thee shall herb and flower be
 kissed;
And earth shall bless thee yet again,
O, gentle, gentle summer rain!
 William Cox Bennett

THE WIND

The wind has a language I would I
 could learn;
Sometimes 'tis soothing, and sometimes 'tis stern;
Sometimes it comes like a low, sweet
 song,
And all things grow calm, as the sound
 floats along;
And the forest is lulled by the dreamy
 strain;

And slumber sinks down on the wan-
    dering main;
And its crystal arms are folded in
    rest,
And the tall ship sleeps on its heaving
    breast.

Letitia Elizabeth Landon

THE FOUNTAIN

Into the sunshine,
    Full of the light,
Leaping and flashing
    From morn till night!

Into the moonlight,
    Whiter than snow,
Waving so flower-like
    When the winds blow!

Into the starlight,
    Rushing in spray,
Happy at midnight,
    Happy by day!

Ever in motion,
    Blithesome and cheery,
Still climbing heavenward,
    Never aweary;

Glad of all weathers,
    Still seeming best,
Upward or downward
    Motion thy rest;

Full of a nature
    Nothing can tame,
Changed every moment,
    Ever the same;

Ceaseless aspiring,
    Ceaseless content,
Darkness or sunshine
    Thy element;

Glorious fountain!
    Let my heart be
Fresh, changeful, constant,
    Upward like thee!

James Russell Lowell

THE BROOK

I come from haunts of coot and hern,
    I make a sudden sally,
And sparkle out among the fern,
    To bicker down a valley.

By thirty hills I hurry down,
    Or slip between the ridges,
By twenty thorps, a little town,
    And half a hundred bridges.

Till last by Philip's farm I flow
    To join the brimming river,
For men may come and men may go,
    But I go on for ever.

I chatter over stony ways,
    In little sharps and trebles,
I bubble into eddying bays,
    I babble on the pebbles.

With many a curve my banks I fret
    By many a field and fallow,
And many a fairy foreland set
    With willow-weed and mallow.

I chatter, chatter, as I flow
    To join the brimming river,
For men may come and men may go,
    But I go on for ever.

I wind about, and in and out,
    With here a blossom sailing,
And here and there a lusty trout,
    And here and there a grayling.

And here and there a foamy flake
    Upon me, as I travel

With many a silvery waterbreak
  Above the gravel,

And draw them all along, and flow
  To join the brimming river,
For men may come and men may go,
  But I go on for ever.

I steal by lawns and grassy plots,
  I slide by hazel covers;
I move the sweet forget-me-nots
  That grow for happy lovers.

I slip, I slide, I gloom, I glance,
  Among my skimming swallows;
I make the netted sunbeam dance
  Against my sandy shallows.

I murmur under moon and stars
  In brambly wildernesses;
I linger by my shingly bars;
  I loiter round my cresses;

And out again I curve and flow
  To join the brimming river,
For men may come and men may go,
  But I go on for ever.

Alfred Tennyson

THE WATER! THE WATER

The Water! the Water!
  The joyous brook for me,
That tuneth through the quiet night
  Its ever-living glee.
The Water! the Water!
  That sleepless, merry heart,
Which gurgles on unstintedly,
  And loveth to impart
To all around it, some small measure
Of its own most perfect pleasure.

The Water! the Water!
  The gentle stream for me,

That gushes from the old grey stone
  Beside the alder-tree.
The Water! the Water!
  That ever-bubbling spring
I loved and look'd on while a child,
  In deepest wondering,—
And ask'd it whence it came and went,
And when its treasures would be spent.

The Water! the Water!
  The merry wanton brook
That bent itself to pleasure me,
  Like mine old shepherd crook.
The Water! the Water!
  That sang so sweet at noon,
And sweeter still all night, to win
  Smiles from the pale, proud moon,
And from the little fairy faces
That gleam   in   heaven's   remotest
places.

William Motherwell

A FAREWELL

Flow down, cold rivulet, to the sea,
  Thy tribute wave deliver;
No more by thee my steps shall be,
  For ever and for ever.

Flow, softly flow, by lawn and lea,
  A rivulet then a river;
Nowhere by thee my steps shall be,
  For ever and for ever.

But here will sigh thine alder tree,
  And here thine aspen shiver;
And here by thee will hum the bee
  For ever and for ever.

A thousand suns will stream on thee,
  A thousand moons will quiver;
But not by thee my steps shall be,
  For ever and for ever.

Alfred Tennyson

SONG OF THE CHATTAHOOCHEE

Out of the hills of Habersham,
  Down the valleys of Hall,
I hurry amain to reach the plain,
Run the rapid and leap the fall,
Split at the rock and together again,
Accept my bed, or narrow or wide,
And flee from folly on every side
With a lover's pain to attain the plain
  Far from the hills of Habersham,
  Far from the valleys of Hall.

All down the hills of Habersham,
  All through the valleys of Hall,
The rushes cried *Abide, abide*,
The wilful waterweeds held me thrall,
The laving laurel turned my tide,
The ferns and the fondling grass said
    Stay,
The dewberry dipped for to work de-
    lay,
And the little reeds sighed *Abide,
    abide*,
  Here in the hills of Habersham,
  Here in the valleys of Hall.

High o'er the hills of Habersham,
  Veiling the valleys of Hall,
The hickory told me manifold
Fair tales of shade, the poplar tall
Wrought me her shadowy self to hold,
The chestnut, the oak, the walnut, the
    pine,
Overleaning, with flickering meaning
    and sign,
Said, *Pass not, so cold, these manifold
  Deep shades of the hills of Haber-
    sham*,
  These glades in the valleys of Hall.

And oft in the hills of Habersham,
And oft in the valleys of Hall,

The white quartz shone, and the
    smooth brook-stone
Did bar me of passage with friendly
    brawl,
And many a luminous jewel lone
—Crystals clear or a-cloud with mist,
Ruby, garnet and amethyst—
Made lures with the lights of stream-
    ing stone
  In the clefts of the hills of Haber-
    sham,
  In the beds of the valleys of Hall.

But oh, not the hills of Habersham,
  And oh, not the valleys of Hall
Avail: I am fain for to water the plain.
Downward the voices of Duty call—
Downward, to toil and be mixed with
    the main.
The dry fields burn, and the mills are
    to turn,
And a myriad flowers mortally yearn,
And the lordly main from beyond the
    plain
  Calls o'er the hills of Habersham,
  Calls through the valleys of Hall.

                        Sidney Lanier

THE WATERFALL

Tinkle, tinkle!
Listen well!
Like a fairy silver bell
In the distance ringing,
Lightly swinging
In the air;
'Tis the water in the dell
Where the elfin minstrels dwell,
Falling in a rainbow sprinkle,
Dropping stars that brightly twinkle,
Bright and fair,
On the darkling pool below,
Making music so;
'Tis the water elves who play

On their lutes of spray.
Tinkle, tinkle!
Like a fairy silver bell;
Like a pebble in a shell;
Tinkle, tinkle!
Listen well!

Frank Dempster Sherman

THE HIDDEN MERMAIDS

Sand, sand, hills of sand,
And the wind where nothing is
Green and sweet of the land—
  No grass, no trees,
  No birds, no butterfly,
But hills, hills of sand,
  And a burning sky.

Sea, sea mounds of the sea,
Hollow and dark and blue,
Flashing incessantly
  The whole sea through;
  No flower, no jutting root,
Only the floor of the sea
  With foam afloat.

Blow, blow windy shells!
  And the watery fish,
Deaf to the hidden bells
  In the waters plash:
No streaming gold, no eyes
Watching along the waves,
But far-blown shells, faint bells,
  From the darkling caves.

" Walter Ramal "

MY STAR

All that I know
  Of a certain star
Is, it can throw
  (Like an angled spar)
Now a dart of red,
  Now a dart of blue;

Till my friends have said
  They would fain see, too,
My star that dartles the red and the
  blue!

Then it stops like a bird; like a flower,
  hangs furled:
They must solace themselves with
  the Saturn above it.
What matter to me if their star is a
  world?
  Mine has opened its soul to me;
  therefore I love it.

Robert Browning

THE LIGHT OF STARS

The night is come, but not too soon;
  And sinking silently,
All silently, the little moon
  Drops down behind the sky.

There is no light in earth or heaven,
  But the cold light of stars;
And the first watch of night is given
  To the red planet Mars.

Is it the tender star of love?
  The star of love and dreams?
O no! from that blue tent above,
  A hero's armour gleams.

And earnest thoughts within me rise,
  When I behold afar,
Suspended in the evening skies,
  The shield of that red star.

O star of strength! I see thee stand
  And smile upon my pain;
Thou beckonest with thy mailèd hand,
  And I am strong again.

Within my breast there is no light,
  But the cold light of stars;

I give the first watch of the night
  To the red planet Mars.

The star of the unconquered will,
  He rises in my breast,
Serene, and resolute, and still,
  And calm, and self-possessed.

And thou, too, whosoe'er thou art
  That readest this brief psalm,
As one by one thy hopes depart,
  Be resolute and calm.

O, fear not, in a world like this,
  And thou shalt know ere long,
Know how sublime a thing it is,
  To suffer and be strong.
            Henry Wadsworth Longfellow

HYMN TO THE NIGHT

I heard the trailing garments of the
    Night
  Sweep through her marble halls.
I saw her sable skirts all fringed with
    light
  From the celestial walls!

I felt her presence, by its spell of
    might,
  Stoop o'er me from above;
The calm majestic presence of the
    Night,
  As of the one I love.

I heard the sounds of sorrow and de-
    light,
  The manifold, soft chimes,
That fill the haunted chambers of the
    Night,
  Like some old poet's rhymes.

From the cool cisterns of the midnight
    air
  My spirit drank repose;

The fountain of perpetual peace flows
    there,—
  From those deep cisterns flows.

O holy Night! from thee I learn to
    bear
  What man has borne before!
Thou layest thy finger on the lips of
    Care,
  And they complain no more.

Peace! Peace! Orestes-like I breathe
    this prayer!
  Descend with broad-winged flight,
The welcome, the thrice-prayed for, the
    most fair,
  The best-loved Night!
            Henry Wadsworth Longfellow

THE STARS

They glide upon their endless way,
  For ever calm, for ever bright,
No blind hurry, no delay,
  Mark the Daughters of the Night:
They follow in the track of Day,
  In divine light.

And oh! how still beneath the stars
  The once wild, noisy Earth doth lie;
As though she now forsook her jars,
  And caught the quiet of the sky.
Pride sleeps; and Love (with all his
    scars)
  In smiling dreams doth lie.

Shine on, sweet orbed souls, for aye,
  For ever calm, for ever bright:
We ask not whither lies your way,
  Nor whence ye came, nor what your
    light.
Be, still,—a dream throughout the day,
  A blessing through the night!
            Barry Cornwall

THE MORNING MIST

Look, William, how the morning mists
  Have covered all the scene,
Nor house nor hill canst thou behold
  Grey wood, or meadow green.

The distant spire across the vale
  These floating vapours shroud,
Scarce are the neighbouring poplars
    seen
  Pale shadowed in the cloud.

But seest thou, William, where the
    mists
  Sweep o'er the southern sky,
The dim effulgence of the sun
  That lights them as they fly?

Soon shall that glorious orb of day
  In all his strength arise,
And roll along his azure way,
  Through clear and cloudless skies.

Then shall we see across the vale
  The village spire so white,
And the grey wood and meadows green
  Shall live again in light.

           Robert Southey

THE DYING SWAN

The plain was grassy, wild and bare,
Wide, wild, and open to the air,
Which had built up everywhere
  An under-roof of doleful gray.
With an inner voice the river ran,
Adown it floated a dying swan,
  And loudly did lament.
  It was the middle of the day.
Ever the weary wind went on,
  And took the reed-tops as it went.

Some blue peaks in the distance rose,
And white against the cold-white sky,
Shone out their crowning snows.
  One willow over the river wept,

And shook the wave as the wind did
    sigh;
Above in the wind was the swallow,
  Chasing itself at its own wild will,
  And far thro' the marish green
    and still
The tangled water-courses slept,
Shot over with purple, and green, and
    yellow.

The wild swan's death-hymn took the
    soul
Of that waste place with joy
Hidden in sorrow: at first to the ear
The warble was low, and full and clear:
And floating about the under sky,
Prevailing in weakness, the coronach
    stole
Sometimes afar, and sometimes anear,
But anon her awful jubilant voice.
With a music strange and manifold,
Flow'd forth on a carol free and bold
As when a mighty people rejoice
With shawms, and with cymbals, and
  harps of gold,
And the tumult of their acclaim is
  roll'd
Thro' the open gates of the city afar,
To the shepherd who watcheth the
  evening star.

And the creeping mosses and clamber-
  ing weeds,
And the willow-branches hoar and
  dank,
And the wavy swell of the soughing
  reeds,
And the wave-worn horns of the echo-
  ing bank,
And the silvery marish-flowers that
  throng
The desolate creeks and pools among,
Were flooded over with eddying song.

           Alfred Tennyson

NIGHT IN THE DESERT

How beautiful is night!
A dewy freshness fills the silent air;
No mist obscures, nor cloud, nor speck,
    nor stain,
Breaks the serene of heaven.
In full-orb'd glory yonder moon divine
    Rolls through the dark-blue depths.
    Beneath her steady ray
    The desert-circle spreads,
Like the round ocean, girdled with the
    sky.
    How beautiful is night!

Robert Southey

LINES FROM THE LADY OF
THE LAKE

The western waves of ebbing day
Roll'd o'er the glen their level way;
Each purple peak, each flinty spire,
Was bathed in floods of living fire.
But not a setting beam could glow
Within the dark ravines below,
Where twined the path, in shadow
    hid,
Round many a rocky pyramid.

Boon nature scatter'd, free and wild,
Each plant or flower, the mountain's
    child.
Here eglantine embalm'd the air,
Hawthorn and hazel mingled there;
The primrose pale and violet flower
Found in each cliff a narrow bower;
Fox-glove and night-shade, side by side,
Emblems of punishment and pride,
Group'd their dark hues with every
    stain
The weather-beaten crags retain.
With boughs that quaked at every
    breath,
Gray birch and aspen wept beneath;

Aloft, the ash and warrior oak
Cast anchor in the rifted rock;
And, higher yet, the pine-tree hung
His shatter'd trunk, and frequent flung,
Where seem'd the cliffs to meet on
    high,
His boughs athwart the narrow'd sky.
Highest of all, where white peaks
    glanced,
Where glist'ning streamers waved and
    danced,
The wanderer's eye could barely view
The summer heaven's delicious blue;
So wondrous wild, the whole might
    seem
The scenery of a fairy dream.

Walter Scott

NATURE

O Nature! I do not aspire
To be the highest in thy choir,—
To be a meteor in thy sky,
Or comet that may range on high;
Only a zephyr that may blow
Among the reeds by the river low;
Give me thy most privy place
Where to run my airy race.

In some withdrawn, unpublic mead
Let me sigh upon a reed,
Or in the woods, with leafy din,
Whisper the still evening in:
Some still work give me to do,—
Only—be it near to you!

For I'd rather be thy child
And pupil, in the forest wild,
Than be the king of men elsewhere,
And most sovereign slave of care;
To have one moment of thy dawn,
Than share the city's year forlorn.

Henry David Thoreau

THE EARTH AND MAN

A little sun, a little rain,
    A soft wind blowing from the west—
And woods and fields are sweet again,
    And warmth within the mountain's
        breast.

So simple is the earth we tread,
    So quick with love and life her
        frame:
Ten thousand years have dawned and
    fled,
    And still her magic is the same.

A little love, a little trust,
    A soft impulse, a sudden dream—
And life as dry as desert dust
    Is fresher than a mountain stream.

So simple is the heart of man,
    So ready for new hope and joy:
Ten thousand years since it began
    Have left it younger than a boy.

Stopford Augustus Brooke

THE GLADNESS OF NATURE

Is this a time to be cloudy and sad,
    When our mother Nature laughs
        around,
And even the deep blue heavens look
    glad,
    And gladness breathes from the
        blossoming ground?

There are notes of joy from the hang-
    bird and wren,
    And the gossip of swallows through
        all the sky;
The ground-squirrel gaily chirps by his
    den,
    And the wilding bee hums merrily
        by.

The clouds are at play in the azure
    space,
    And their shadows at play on the
        bright green vale,
And here they stretch to the frolic
    chase,
    And there they roll on the easy gale.

There's a dance of leaves in that aspen
    bower,
    There's a titter of winds in that
        beechen tree,
There's a smile on the fruit, and a
    smile on the flower,
    And a laugh from the brook that
        runs to the sea.

And look at the broad-faced sun, how
    he smiles
    On the dewy earth that smiles in his
        ray,
On the leaping waters and gay young
    isles;
    Ay, look, and he'll smile thy gloom
        away.

William Cullen Bryant

A PSALM OF DAVID

O Lord our Lord, how excellent is
thy name in all the earth! who hast set
thy glory above the heavens.

When I consider thy heavens, the
work of thy fingers, the moon and the
stars, which thou hast ordained;
    What is man, that thou art mindful
of him? and the son of man, that thou
visitest him?
    For thou hast made him a little
lower than the angels, and hast
crowned him with glory and honour.
    Thou madest him to have dominion

over the works of thy hands; thou hast put all things under his feet:

All sheep and oxen, yea, and the beasts of the field;

The fowl of the air, and the fish of the sea, and whatsoever passeth through the paths of the seas.

O Lord our Lord, how excellent is thy name in all the earth!

Psalm 8—The Bible

Part Six

THE ANIMAL KINGDOM

THE LARK

A close gray sky,
And poplars gray and high,
The country-side along;
The steeple hold
Across the acres old—
And then a song!

Oh, far, far, far,
As any spire or star
Beyond the cloistered wall!
Oh, high, high, high,
A heart-throb in the sky—
Then not at all!

Lizette Woodworth Reese

TO A SKYLARK

Hail to thee, blithe spirit!
  Bird thou never wert,
That from heaven, or near it,
  Pourest thy full heart
In profuse strains of unpremeditated
  art.

Higher still and higher
  From the earth thou springest
Like a cloud of fire;
  The blue deep thou wingest
And singing still dost soar, and soar-
  ing ever singest.

In the golden lightning
  Of the sunken sun,
O'er which clouds are brightening,
  Thou dost float and run;
Like an unbodied joy whose race is
  just begun.

The pale purple even
  Melts around thy flight:
Like a star of heaven,
  In the broad daylight
Thou art unseen, but yet I hear thy
  shrill delight.

Keen as are the arrows
  Of that silver sphere
Whose intense lamp narrows
  In the white dawn clear,
Until we hardly see, we feel that it is
  there.

All the earth and air
  With thy voice is loud,
As, when night is bare,
  From one lonely cloud
The moon rains out her beams, and
  heaven is overflowed.

What thou art we know not;
   What is most like thee?
From rainbow clouds there flow not
   Drops so bright to see,
As from thy presence showers a rain of
   melody.

Like a poet hidden
   In the light of thought,
Singing hymns unbidden,
   Till the world is wrought
To sympathy with hopes and fears it
   heeded not:

Like a high-born maiden
   In a palace tower,
Soothing her love-laden
   Soul in secret hour
With music sweet as love, which over-
   flows her bower:

Like a glow-worm golden
   In a dell of dew,
Scattering unbeholden
   Its aërial hue
Among the flowers and grass, which
   screen it from the view:

Like a rose embowered
   In its own green leaves,
By warm winds deflowered,
   Till the scent it gives
Makes faint with too much sweet these
   heavy-winged thieves:

Sound of vernal showers
   On the twinkling grass,
Rain-awakened flowers,
   All that ever was
Joyous and clear, and fresh, thy music
   doth surpass:

Teach us, sprite or bird,
   What sweet thoughts are thine:

I have never heard
   Praise of love or wine
That panted forth a flood of rapture so
   divine.

Chorus Hymenæal,
   Or triumphal chaunt,
Matched with thine would be all
   But an empty vaunt,
A thing wherein we feel there is some
   hidden want.

What objects are the fountains
   Of thy happy strain?
What fields, or waves, or mountains?
   What shapes of sky or plain?
What love of thine own kind? what
   ignorance of pain?

With thy clear keen joyance
   Languor cannot be:
Shadow of annoyance
   Never came near thee:
Thou lovest: but ne'er knew love's sad
   satiety.

Waking or asleep,
   Thou of death must deem
Things more true and deep
   Than we mortals dream,
Or how could thy notes flow in such a
   crystal stream?

We look before and after
   And pine for what is not:
Our sincerest laughter
   With some pain is fraught;
Our sweetest songs are those that tell
   of saddest thought.

Yet if we could scorn
   Hate, and pride, and fear;
If we were things born
   Not to shed a tear,

I know not how thy joy we ever should
come near.

Better than all measures
Of delightful sound,
Better than all treasures
That in books are found,
Thy skill to poet were, thou scorner of
the ground!

Teach me half the gladness
That my brain must know,
Such harmonious madness
From my lips would flow,
The world should listen then, as I am
listening now.

Percy Bysshe Shelley

THE SKYLARK

Bird of the wilderness,
Blithesome and cumberless,
Sweet be thy matin o'er moorland and
lea!
Emblem of happiness,
Blest is thy dwelling-place—
Oh to abide in the desert with thee!

Wild is thy lay and loud,
Far in the downy cloud
Love gives it energy, love gave it birth.
Where, on thy dewy wing,
Where art thou journeying?
Thy lay is in heaven, thy love is on
earth.

O'er fell and fountain sheen,
O'er moor and mountain green,
O'er the red streamer that heralds the
day,
Over the cloudlet dim,
Over the rainbow's rim,
Musical cherub, **soar**, singing, away!

Then, when the gloaming comes,
Low in the heather blooms

Sweet will thy welcome and bed of
love be!
Emblem of happiness,
Blest is thy dwelling-place—
Oh to abide in the desert with thee!

James Hogg

HARK, HARK THE LARK

Hark! hark! the lark at Heaven's gate
sings,
And Phœbus 'gins arise,
His steeds to water at those springs
On chalic'd flowers that lies.

And winking Mary-buds begin
To ope their golden eyes;
With everything that pretty bin:
My lady sweet, arise;
Arise, arise.

William Shakespeare

THE CHICKADEE

Piped a tiny voice hard by,
Gay and polite, a cheerful cry,
"Chic-chicadee-dee!" Saucy note
Out of a sound heart and a merry
throat,
As if it said, "Good day, good sir.
Fine afternoon, old passenger!
Happy to meet you in these places
When January brings new faces!"

Ralph Waldo Emerson

TO THE CUCKOO

O blithe newcomer! I have heard,
I hear thee and rejoice.
O Cuckoo! shall I call thee Bird,
Or but a wandering Voice?

While I am lying on the grass
Thy twofold shout I hear;

From hill to hill it seems to pass,
  At once far off and near.

Though babbling only, to the vale,
  Of sunshine and of flowers,
Thou bringest unto me a tale
  Of visionary hours.

Thrice welcome, darling of the Spring!
  Even yet thou art to me
No Bird, but an invisible Thing,
  A voice, a mystery.

The same whom in my Schoolboy days
  I listened to; that cry
Which made me look a thousand ways,
  In bush, and tree, and sky.

To seek thee did I often rove
  Through woods and on the green,
And thou wert still a hope, a love,
  Still longed for, never seen.

And I can listen to thee yet;
  Can lie upon the plain
And listen till I do beget
  That golden time again.

O blessèd Bird; the earth we pace
  Again appears to be
An unsubstantial, faery place,
  That is fit home for Thee!
            William Wordsworth

ODE TO THE CUCKOO

Hail, beauteous stranger of the grove!
  Thou messenger of spring!
Now Heaven repairs thy rural seat,
  And woods thy welcome sing.

What time the daisy decks the green,
  Thy certain voice we hear;
Hast thou a star to guide thy path,
  Or mark the rolling year?

Delightful visitant, with thee
  I hail the time of flowers,
And hear the sound of music sweet
  From birds among the bowers.

The schoolboy wandering through the
    wood
  To pull the primrose gay,
Starts the new voice of spring to hear,
  And imitates the lay.

What time the pea puts on the bloom
  Thou fliest thy vocal vale
An annual guest in other lands,
  Another spring to hail.

Sweet bird, thy bower is ever green,
  Thy sky is ever clear;
Thou hast no sorrow in thy song,
  No winter in thy year!

O could I fly, I'd fly with thee!
  We'd make with joyous wing,
Our annual visit o'er the globe,
  Companions of the spring.
            Michael Bruce

ROBERT OF LINCOLN

Merrily swinging on brier and weed,
  Near to the nest of his little dame,
Over the mountain-side or mead,
  Robert of Lincoln is telling his
      name;
    Bob-o'-link, bob-o'-link,
    Spink, spank, spink;
Snug and safe is that nest of ours,
Hidden among the summer flowers.
    Chee, chee, chee.

Robert of Lincoln is gayly drest,
  Wearing a bright black wedding-
      coat;
White are his shoulders and white his
    crest,

Hear him call in his merry note:
 Bob-o'-link, bob-o'-link,
 Spink, spank, spink;
Look, what a nice coat is mine,
Sure there was never a bird so fine.
 Chee, chee, chee.

Robert of Lincoln's quaker wife,
 Pretty and quiet, with plain brown
 wings,
Passing at home a patient life,
 Broods in the grass while her hus-
 band sings:
 Bob-o'-link, bob-o'-link,
 Spink, spank, spink;
Brood, kind creature; you need not fear
Thieves and robbers while I am here.
 Chee, chee, chee.

Modest and shy as a nun is she;
 One weak chirp is her only note.
Braggart and prince of braggarts is he,
 Pouring boasts from his little throat:
 Bob-o'-link, bob-o'-link,
 Spink, spank, spink;
Never was I afraid of man;
Catch me, cowardly knaves, if you can!
 Chee, chee, chee.

Six white eggs on a bed of hay,
 Flecked with purple, a pretty sight!
There, as the mother sits all day,
 Robert is singing with all his might:
 Bob-o'-link, bob-o'-link,
 Spink, spank, spink;
Nice good wife that never goes out,
Keeping house while I frolic about.
 Chee, chee, chee.

Soon as the little ones chip the shell,
 Six wide mouths are open for food;
Robert of Lincoln bestirs him well,
 Gathering seeds for the hungry
 brood.

Bob-o'-link, bob-o'-link,
 Spink, spank, spink;
Nobody knows but my mate and I
Where our nest and our nestlings lie.
 Chee, chee, chee.

Summer wanes; the children are grown;
 Fun and frolic no more he knows;
Robert of Lincoln's a humdrum crone;
 Off he flies, and we sing as he goes;
 Bob-o'-link, bob-o'-link,
 Spink, spank, spink;
When you can pipe that merry old
 strain,
Robert of Lincoln, come back again.
 Chee, chee, chee.

William Cullen Bryant

THE O'LINCON FAMILY

A flock of merry singing-birds were
 sporting in the grove;
Some were warbling cheerily, and
 some were making love:
There were Bobolincon, Wadolincon, Winterseeble, Conquedle,—
A livelier set was never led by tabor,
 pipe, or fiddle,—
Crying, " Phew, shew, Wadolincon,
 see, see, Bobolincon,
Down among the tickletops, hiding
 in the buttercups!
I know a saucy chap, I see his shining cap
Bobbing in the clover there—see,
 see, see! "

Up flies Bobolincon, perching on an
 apple-tree,
Startled by his rival's song, quick-
 ened by his raillery,
Soon he spies the rogue afloat, cur-
 veting in the air,

And merrily he turns about, and
    warns him to beware!
" 'Tis you that would a-wooing go,
    down among the rushes O!
But wait a week, till flowers are
    cheery,—wait a week, and, ere you
    marry,
Be sure of a house wherein to tarry!
Wadolink,   Whiskodink,   T o m
    Denny, wait, wait, wait! "

Every one's a funny fellow; every
    one's a little mellow;
Follow, follow, follow, follow, o'er
    the hill and in the hollow!
Merrily, merrily, there they hie; now
    they rise and now they fly;
They cross and turn, and in and out,
    and down in the middle and
    wheel about,—
With a " Phew, shew, Wadolincon!
    listen to me, Bobolincon!—
Happy's the wooing that's speedily
    doing, that's speedily doing,
That's merry and over with the
    bloom of the clover!
Bobolincon, Wadolincon, Winter-
    seeble, follow, follow, follow me! "

Wilson Flagg

THE BOBOLINKS
(Selected Stanzas)

When Nature had made all her birds,
    With no more cares to think on,
She gave a rippling laugh, and out
    There flew a Bobolinkon.

She laughed again; out flew a mate;
    A breeze of Eden bore them
Across the fields of Paradise,
    The sunrise reddening o'er them.
Incarnate sport and holiday,
    They flew and sang forever;

Their souls through June were all in
    tune,
    Their wings were weary never.

Their tribe, still drunk with air and
    light,
    And perfume of the meadow,
Go reeling up and down the sky,
    In sunshine and in shadow.

One springs from out the dew-wet
    grass;
    Another follows after;
The morn is thrilling with their songs
    And peals of fairy laughter.

From out the marshes and the brook,
    They set the tall weeds swinging,
And meet and frolic in the air,
    Half prattling, and half singing.

When far away o'er grassy flats,
    Where the thick wood commences,
The white-sleeved mowers look like
    specks,
    Beyond the zigzag fences,

And noon is hot, and barn-roofs gleam
    White in the pale blue distance,
I hear the saucy minstrels still
    In chattering persistence.

When eve her domes of opal fire
    Piles round the blue horizon,
Or thunder rolls from hill to hill
    A Kyrie Elieson,

Still merriest of the merry birds,
    Your sparkle is unfading,—
Pied harlequins of June,—no end
    Of song and masquerading.

Hope springs with you: I dread no
    more

Despondency and dullness;
For Good Supreme can never fail
  That gives such perfect fulness.

The life that floods the happy fields
  With song and light and color,
Will shape our lives to richer states,
  And heap our measures fuller.
                Christopher Pearse Cranch

THE REDBREAST CHASING A BUTTERFLY

Can this be the bird to man so good,
  That, after their bewildering,
  Covered with leaves the little children
So painfully in the wood?
What ailed thee, Robin, that thou could'st pursue
A beautiful creature
That is gentle by nature?
Beneath the summer sky,
From flower to flower let him fly;
  'Tis all that he wishes to do.

The cheerer thou of our indoor sadness,
He is the friend of our summer gladness;
What hinders then that ye should be
Playmates in the sunny weather,
And fly about in the air together?
His beautiful wings in crimson are drest,
  A crimson as bright as thine own:
If thou wouldst be happy in thy nest,
Love him, or leave him alone!
                William Wordsworth

TO AN ORIOLE

How falls it, Oriole, thou hast come to fly

In tropic splendor through our Northern sky?

At some glad moment was it nature's choice
To dower a scrap of sunset with a voice?

Or did some orange tulip, flaked with black,
In some forgotten garden, ages back,

Yearning toward Heaven until its wish was heard,
Desire unspeakably to be a bird?
                Edgar Fawcett

THE GREEN LINNET

Beneath these fruit-tree boughs, that shed
Their snow-white blossoms on my head,
With brightest sunshine round me spread
  Of Spring's unclouded weather;
In this sequester'd nook how sweet
To sit upon my orchard seat!
And flowers and birds once more to greet,
  My last year's friends together.

One have I mark'd, the happiest guest
In all this corner of the blest,
Hail to thee, far above the rest
  In joy of voice and pinion,
Thou Linnet! in thy green array,
Presiding spirit here today,
Dost lead the revels of the May,
  And this is thy dominion.

While thus before my eyes he gleams,
A brother of the leaves he seems,

When in a moment forth he teems,
  His little song in gushes:
As if it pleas'd him to disdain
And mock the form which he did
    feign,
While he was dancing with the train
  Of leaves among the bushes.

William Wordsworth

THE BLACKBIRD

A Blackbird! sing me something well:
  While all the neighbors shoot thee
    round,
  I keep smooth plats of fruitful
    ground,
Where thou may'st warble, eat, and
    dwell.

The espaliers and the standards all
  Are thine; the range of lawn and
    park.
  The unnetted black-hearts ripen
    dark,
All thine, against the garden wall.

Yet, tho' I spared ye all the spring,
  Thy sole delight is, sitting still,
  With that gold dagger of thy bill
To fret the summer jenneting.

A golden bill! the silver tongue,
  Cold February loved, is dry:
  Plenty corrupts the melody
That made thee famous once, when
    young.

And in the sultry garden-squares,
  Now thy flute-notes are changed to
    coarse,
  I hear thee not at all, or hoarse
As when a hawker hawks his wares.

Take warning! he that will not sing

While yon sun prospers in the blue,
Shall sing for want, ere leaves are
  new,
Caught in the frozen palms of Spring.

Alfred Tennyson

THE NIGHT BIRD

A floating, a floating
  Across the sleeping sea,
All night I heard a singing bird
  Upon the topmost tree.

" Oh, came you off the isles of Greece
  Or off the banks of Seine:
Or off some tree in forests free
  Which fringe the western main? "

" I came not off the old world,
  Nor yet from off the new;
But I am one of the birds of God
  Which sing the whole night
    through."

" Oh sing! and wake the dawning!
  Oh whistle for the wind!
The night is long, the current strong,
  My boat it lags behind."

" The current sweeps the old world,
  The current sweeps the new;
The wind will blow, the dawn will
    glow,
  Ere thou hast sailed them
    through."

Charles Kingsley

THE PEWEE

The listening Dryads hushed the
  woods;
The boughs were thick, and thin
  and few

The golden ribbons fluttering
  through;
Their sun-embroidered, leafy hoods
  The lindens lifted to the blue:
Only a little forest brook
The farthest hem of silence shook:
When in the hollow shades I heard,—
Was it a spirit, or a bird?
Or, strayed from Eden, desolate,
Some Peri calling to her mate,
  Whom nevermore her mate would
    cheer?
    " Pe-ri! pe-ri! peer! "

Through rocky clefts the brooklet fell
  With plashy pour, that scarce was
    sound,
  But only quiet less profound,
A stillness fresh and audible:
  A yellow leaflet to the ground
Whirled noiselessly: with wing of
  gloss
A hovering sunbeam brushed the
  moss,
And, wavering brightly over it,
Sat like a butterfly alit:
The owlet in his open door
Stared roundly: while the breezes
  bore
  The plaint to far-off places drear,—
    " Pe-ree! pe-ree! peer! "

To trace it in its green retreat
  I sought among the boughs in
    vain;
  And followed still the wandering
    strain,
So melancholy and so sweet
  The dim-eyed violets yearned with
    pain.
'Twas now a sorrow in the air,
Some nymph's immortalized despair
Haunting the woods and waterfalls;
And now, at long, sad intervals,

Sitting unseen in dusky shade,
His plaintive pipe some fairy played,
  With long-drawn cadence thin
    and clear,—
    " Pe-wee! pe-wee! peer! "

Long-drawn and clear its closes
  were,—
  As if the hand of Music through
  The sombre robe of Silence drew
A thread of golden gossamer:
  So pure a flute the fairy blew.
Like beggared princes of the wood,
In silver rags the birches stood;
The hemlocks, lordly counselors,
Were dumb; the sturdy servitors,
In beechen jackets patched and gray,
Seemed waiting spellbound all the
  day
  That low, entrancing note to
    hear,—
    "Pe-wee! pe-wee! peer! "

I quit the search, and sat me down
  Beside the brook, irresolute,
  And watched a little bird in suit
Of sober olive, soft and brown,
  Perched in the maple branches,
    mute:
With greenish gold its vest was
  fringed,
Its tiny cap was ebon-tinged,
With ivory pale its wings were
  barred,
And its dark eyes were tender-starred.
" Dear bird," I said, " what is thy
  name? "
And thrice the mournful answer
  came,—
  So faint and far, and yet so near,—
    " Pe-wee! pe-wee! peer! "

For so I found my forest bird,—
  The pewee of the loneliest woods,

Sole singer in these solitudes,
Which never robin's whistle stirred,
  Where never bluebird's plume in-
    trudes.
Quick darting through the dewy
  morn,
The redstart trilled his twittering
  horn,
And vanished in thick boughs: at
  even,
Like liquid pearls fresh showered
  from heaven,
The high notes of the lone wood-
  thrush
Fall on the forest's holy hush:
  But thou all day complainest
    here,—
    " Pe-wee! pe-wee! peer! "

Hast thou, too, in thy little breast,
  Strange longings for a happier
    lot,—
  For love, for life, thou know'st not
    what,—
A yearning, and a vague unrest,
  For something still which thou
    hast not?—
Thou soul of some benighted child
That perished, crying in the wild!
Or lost, forlorn, and wandering maid,
By love allured, by love betrayed,
Whose spirit with her latest sigh
Arose, a little wingèd cry.
  Above her chill and mossy bier!
    " Dear me! dear me! dear! "

Ah, no such piercing sorrow mars
  The pewee's life of cheerful ease!
  He sings, or leaves his song to seize
An insect sporting in the bars
  Of mild bright light that gild the
    trees.
  A very poet he! For him
All pleasant places still and dim:

His heart, a spark of heavenly fire,
Burns with undying, sweet desire:
And so he sings, and so his song,
Though heard not by the hurrying
  throng,
  In solace to the pensive ear:
    " Pewee! pewee! peer! "
      John Townsend Trowbridge

BIRDS IN SUMMER

How pleasant the life of a bird must
  be,
Flitting about in each leafy tree;
In the leafy trees so broad and tall,
Like a green and beautiful palace
  hall,
With its airy chambers, light and
  boon,
That open to sun, and stars, and
  moon;
That open unto the bright blue sky,
And the frolicsome winds as they
  wander by!

They have left their nests in the
  forest bough;
Those homes of delight they need
  not now;
And the young and the old they
  wander out,
And traverse the green world round
  about;
And hark at the top of this leafy
  hall,
How, one to another they lovingly
  call!
" Come up, come up! " they seem to
  say,
" Where the topmost twigs in the
  breezes play! "

" Come up, come up, for the world is
  fair,

Where the merry leaves dance in
the summer air! "
And the birds below give back the
cry,
" We come, we come to the branches
high! "
How pleasant the life of the birds
must be,
Living above in a leafy tree!
And away through the air what joy
to go,
And to look on the green, bright
earth below!

How pleasant the life of a bird must
be,
Skimming about on the breezy sea,
Cresting the billows like silvery
foam,
Then wheeling away to its cliff-built
home!
What joy it must be to sail, up-
borne,
By a strong free wing, through the
rosy morn,
To meet the young sun, face to face,
And pierce, like a shaft, the bound-
less space!

To pass through the bowers of the
silver cloud;
To sing in the thunder halls aloud;
To spread out the wings for a wild,
free flight
With the upper cloud-winds,—oh,
what delight!
Oh, what would I give, like a bird,
to go,
Right on through the arch of the
sun-lit bow,
And see how the water-drops are
kissed
Into green and yellow and amethyst.

How pleasant the life of a bird must
be,
Wherever it listeth, there to flee;
To go, when a joyful fancy calls,
Dashing down 'mong the waterfalls;
Then wheeling about, with its mate
at play,
Above and below, and among the
spray,
Hither and thither, with screams as
wild
As the laughing mirth of a rosy
child!

What joy it must be, like a living
breeze,
To flutter about 'mid the flowering
trees;
Lightly to soar and to see beneath,
The wastes of the blossoming pur-
ple heath,
And the yellow furze, like fields of
gold,
That gladden some fairy region old!
On mountain-tops, on the billowy
sea,
On the leafy stems of the forest-tree,
How pleasant the life of a bird must
be!

Mary Howitt

THE BIRDS OF PASSAGE

Birds, joyous birds of the wandering
wing!
Whence is it ye come with the flow-
ers of spring?
—" We come from the shores of the
green old Nile,
From the land where the roses of
Sharon smile,
From the palms that wave through
the Indian sky,

From the myrrh-trees of glowing
    Araby.

"We have swept o'er cities in song
    renowned,
Silent they lie with the desert round!
We have crossed the proud rivers
    whose tide hath rolled
All dark with the warrior-blood of
    old;
And each worn wing hath regained
    its home
Under peasant's roof or monarch's
    dome."

And what have ye found in the mon-
    arch's dome,
Since last ye traversed the blue sea's
    foam?
—"We have found a change;—we
    have found a pall,
And a gloom o'ershadowing the ban-
    quet hall;
And a mark on the floor as of life-
    drops spilt;—
Nought looks the same save the nest
    we built."

Oh! joyous birds, it hath ever been
    so;
Through the halls of kings doth the
    tempest go,
But the huts of hamlets lie still and
    deep,
And the hills o'er their quiet a vigil
    keep:—
Say, what have ye found in the peas-
    ant's cot
Since last ye parted from that sweet
    spot?

"A change we have found there, and
    many a change,
Faces and footsteps, and all things
    strange;

Gone are the heads of the silvery
    hair,
And the young that were have a
    brow of care;
And the place is hushed where the
    children played;
Nought looks the same save the nest
    we made."

Sad is your tale of the beautiful
    earth,
Birds that o'ersweep it in power and
    mirth;
Yet through the wastes of the track-
    less air
Ye have a guide, and shall we de-
    spair?
Ye over desert and deep have passed,
So may we reach our bright home at
    last.

        Felicia Dorothea Hemans

THE SWALLOW'S NEST

Day after day her nest she moulded,
    Building with magic, love and mud,
A gray cup made by a thousand jour-
    neys,
    And the tiny beak was trowel and
    hod.

        Edwin Arnold

THE HORNED OWL

In the hollow tree in the old grey
    tower,
    The spectral owl doth dwell;
Dull, hated, despised in the sunshine
    hour;
    But at dusk he's abroad and well:
Not a bird of the forest e'er mates with
    him;
    All mock him outright by day;
But at night, when the woods grow
    still and dim,

The boldest will shrink away.
  O, when the night falls, and roosts
    the fowl,
  Then, then is the reign of the
    hornèd owl.

And the owl hath a bride who is fond
    and bold,
  And loveth the wood's deep gloom;
And with eyes like the shine of the
    moonshine cold
She awaiteth her ghastly groom!
Not a feather she moves, not a carol
    she sings,
  As she waits in her tree so still;
But when her heart heareth his flap-
    ping wings,
  She hoots out her welcome shrill!
  O, when the moon shines, and
    dogs do howl,
  Then, then is the joy of the
    hornèd owl.

Mourn not for the owl nor his gloomy
    plight!
  The owl hath his share of good:
If a prisoner he be in the broad day-
    light,
  He is lord in the dark green wood!
Nor lonely the bird, nor his ghastly
    mate;
  They are each unto each a pride—
Thrice fonder, perhaps, since a strange
    dark fate
  Hath rent them from all beside!
So when the night falls, and dogs do
    howl,
  Sing ho! for the reign of the hornèd
    owl!
We know not alway who are kings by
    day,
  But the king of the night is the bold
    brown owl.

Barry Cornwall

THE EAGLE

He clasps the crag with crooked hands;
Close to the sun in lonely lands,
Ringed with the azure world, he
  stands.

The wrinkled sea beneath him crawls;
He watches from his mountain walls,
And like a thunderbolt he falls.

Alfred Tennyson

MY DOVES

My little doves have left a nest
  Upon an Indian tree,
Whose leaves fantastic take their rest
  Or motion from the sea;
For, ever there the sea-winds go
With sunlit paces to and fro.

The tropic flowers looked up to it,
  The tropic stars looked down,
And there my little doves did sit
  With feathers softly brown,
And glittering eyes that showed their
    right
To general Nature's deep delight.

My little doves were ta'en away
  From that glad nest of theirs,
Across an ocean rolling grey,
  And tempest-clouded airs.
My little doves who lately knew
The sky and wave by warmth and blue.

And now, within the city prison
  In mist and chillness pent,
With sudden upward look they listen
  For sounds of past content,
For lapse of water, smell of breeze,
Or nut-fruit falling from the trees.

Elizabeth Barrett Browning

THE SWAN

Under a wall of bronze,
Where beeches dip and trail
Thin branches in the water,
With red-tipped head and wings,
A beaked ship under sail,
There glides a great black swan.

Under the autumn trees
He goes. The branches quiver,
Dance in the wraith-like water,
Which ripples beneath the sedge
With the slackening furrow that
   glides
In his wake when he is gone:
The beeches bow dark heads.

Into the windless dusk,
Where in mist great towers stand
Guarding a lonely strand
That is bodiless and dim,
He speeds with easy stride;
And I would go beside,
Till the low brown hills divide
At last, for me and him.

              John Gould Fletcher

TO A WATER FOWL

Whither, 'midst falling dew,
While blow the heavens with the last
   steps of day,
Far through their rosy depths dost
   thou pursue
   Thy solitary way?

Vainly the fowler's eye
Might mark thy distant flight to do
   thee wrong,
As, darkly painted on the crimson sky,
   Thy figure floats along.

Seek'st thou the plashy brink
Of weedy lake, or marge of river wide,

Or where the rocking billows rise and
   sink
   On the chafed ocean side?

There is a Power whose care
Teaches thy way along that pathless
   coast,
The desert and illimitable air,—
   Lone wandering but not lost.

All day thy wings have fann'd,
At that far height the cold thin atmos-
   phere,
Yet stoop not, weary, to the welcome
   land,
   Though the dark night is near.

And soon that toil shall end;
Soon shalt thou find a summer home,
   and rest
And scream among thy fellows; reeds
   shall bend
   Soon o'er thy shelter'd nest.

Thou'rt gone, the abyss of heaven
Hath swallow'd up thy form: yet on
   my heart
Deeply hath sunk the lesson thou hast
   given,
   And shall not soon depart.

He, who from zone to zone
Guides through the boundless sky thy
   certain flight,
In the long way that I must tread
   alone,
   Will lead my steps aright.

              William Cullen Bryant

THE SEA-MEW

How joyously the young sea-mew
Lay dreaming on the waters blue,
Whereon our little bark had thrown

A little shade, the only one,
But shadows ever man pursue.

Familiar with the waves and free
As if their own white foam were he,
His heart upon the heart of ocean
Lay learning all its mystic motion,
And throbbing to the throbbing sea.

We were not cruel, yet did sunder
His white wing from the blue waves
    under,
And bound it while his fearless eyes
Shone up to ours in calm surprise,
As deeming us some ocean wonder.

We bore our ocean bird unto
A grassy place where he might view
The flowers that curtsey to the bees,
The waving of the tall green trees,
The falling of the silver dew.

But flowers of earth were pale to him
Who had seen the rainbow fishes
    swim;
And when earth's dew around him
    lay,
He thought of ocean's wingèd spray,
And his eye waxed sad and dim.

The green trees round him only made
A prison with their darksome shade,
And drooped his wing, and mournèd
    he
For his own boundless glittering sea—
Albeit he knew not they could fade.

He lay down in his grief to die,
(First looking to the sea-like sky
That hath no waves,) because, alas!
Our human touch did on him pass,
And, with our touch, our agony.

Elizabeth Barrett Browning

THE WATER OUZEL

Little brown surf-bather of the moun-
    tains!
Spirit of foam, lover of cataracts, shak-
    ing your wings in falling waters!
Have you no fear of the roar and rush
    when Nevada plunges—
Nevada, the shapely dancer, feeling her
    way with slim white fingers?
How dare you dash at Yosemite the
    mighty—
Tall, white-limbed Yosemite, leaping
    down, down, over the cliff?
Is it not enough to lean on the blue air
    of mountains?
Is it not enough to rest with your mate
    at timber-line in bushes that hug the
    rocks?
Must you fly through mad waters
    where the heaped-up granite breaks
    them?
Must you batter your wings in the
    torrent?
Must you plunge for life or death
    through the foam?

Harriet Monroe

THE STORMY PETREL

A thousand miles from land are we,
Tossing about on the roaring sea;
From billow to bounding billow cast,
Like fleecy snow on the stormy blast:
The sails are scattered abroad like
    weeds;
The strong masts shake like quivering
    reeds;
The mighty cables, and iron chains,
The hull, which all earthly strength
    disdains,
They strain and they crack, and hearts
    like stone
Their natural proud strength disown.

Up and down! Up and down!
From the base of the wave to the bil-
  low's crown,
And amidst the flashing and feathery
  foam,
The Stormy Petrel finds a home—
A home, if such a place may be,
For her who lives on the wide, wide
  sea,
On the craggy ice, in the frozen air
And only seeketh her rocky lair.
To warm her young, and to teach them
  to spring
At once o'er the waves on their stormy
  wing!

Barry Cornwall

THE PARROT

The deep affections of the breast,
  That Heaven to living things im-
    parts,
Are not exclusively possessed
  By human hearts.

A parrot from the Spanish main,
  Full young, and early caged, came
    o'er
With bright wings, to the bleak do-
  main
  Of Mulla's * shore:

To spicy groves, where he had won
  His plumage of resplendent hue,
His native fruits, and skies, and sun,
  He bade adieu.

For these he changed the smoke of
  turf
  A heathery land and misty sky,
And turned on rocks and raging surf
  His golden eye.

  * *Mulla.*—The island of Mull, one of the
Hebrides.

But petted, in our climate cold
  He lived and chattered many a day;
Until with age, from green and gold
  His wings grew grey.

At last when blind and seeming dumb,
  He scolded, laughed, and spoke no
    more,
A Spanish stranger chanced to come
  To Mulla's shore.

He hailed the bird in Spanish speech,
  The bird in Spanish speech replied,
Flapped round the cage with joyous
    screech,
  Dropped down and died.

Thomas Campbell

CHANTICLEER

Of all the birds from East to West
  That tuneful are and dear,
I love that farmyard bird the best,
  They call him Chanticleer.

Gold plume and copper plume,
  Comb of scarlet gay;
'Tis he that scatters night and gloom,
  And whistles back the day!

He is the sun's brave herald
  That, ringing his blithe horn,
Calls round a world dew-pearled
  The heavenly airs of morn.

O clear gold, shrill and bold!
  He calls through creeping mist
The mountains from the night and
  cold
  To rose and amethyst.

He sets the birds to singing,
  And calls the flowers to rise;
The morning cometh, bringing
  Sweet sleep to heavy eyes.

Gold plume and silver plume,
  Comb of coral gay;
'Tis he packs off the night and gloom,
  And summons home the day!

Black fear he sends it flying,
  Black care he drives afar;
And creeping shadows sighing
  Before the morning star.

The birds of all the forest
  Have dear and pleasant cheer,
But yet I hold the rarest
  The farmyard Chanticleer.

Red cock or black cock,
  Gold cock or white,
The flower of all the feathered flock,
  He whistles back the light!
    Katharine Tynan Hinkson

AT THE AQUARIUM

Serene the silver fishes glide,
Stern-lipped, and pale, and wonder-
  eyed.
As, through the aged deeps of ocean,
They glide with wan and wavy motion.
They have no pathway where they go,
They flow like water to and fro,
They watch, with never-winking eyes,
They watch, with staring, cold surprise,
The level people in the air,
The people peering, peering there:
Who wander also to and fro,
And know not why or where they go,
Yet have a wonder in their eyes,
Sometimes a pale and cold surprise.
    Max Eastman

THE BEE

Like trains of cars on tracks of plush
  I hear the level bee:

A jar across the flowers goes,
  Their velvet masonry

Withstands until the sweet assault
  Their chivalry consumes,
While he, victorious, tilts away
  To vanquish other blooms.

His feet are shod with gauze,
  His helmet is of gold;
His breast, a single onyx
  With chrysoprase, inlaid.

His labor is a chant,
  His idleness a tune;
Oh, for a bee's experience
  Of clovers and of noon!
    Emily Dickinson

THE HUMBLE-BEE

Burly dozing humble-bee,
Where thou art is clime for me.
Let them sail for Porto Rique,
Far-off heats through seas to seek;
I will follow thee alone,
Thou animated torrid zone!
Zigzag steerer, desert cheerer,
Let me chase thy waving lines;
Keep me nearer, me thy hearer,
Singing over shrubs and vines.

Insect lover of the sun,
Joy of thy dominion!
Sailor of the atmosphere;
Swimmer through the waves of air:
Voyager of light and noon;
Epicurean of June;
Wait, I prithee, till I come
Within earshot of thy hum,—
All without is martyrdom.

When the south wind, in May days,
With a net of shining haze

Silvers the horizon wall,
And with softness touching all,
Tints the human countenance
With a color of romance,
And infusing subtle heats,
Turns the sod to violets,
Thou, in sunny solitudes,
Rover of the underwoods,
The green silence dost displace
With thy mellow, breezy bass.

Hot midsummer's petted crone,
Sweet to me thy drowsy tone
Tells of countless sunny hours,
Long days, and solid banks of flowers;
Of gulfs of sweetness without bound
In Indian wildernesses found;
Of Syrian peace, immortal leisure,
Firmest cheer, and birdlike pleasure.

Aught unsavory or unclean
Hath my insect never seen;
But violets and bilberry bells,
Maple-sap and daffodels,
Grass with green flag half-mast high,
Succory to match the sky,
Columbine with horn of honey,
Scented fern, and agrimony,
Clover, catchfly, alder's tongue
And brier-roses, dwelt among;
All beside was unknown waste,
All was picture as he passed.
Wiser far than human seer,
Yellow-breeched philosopher!
Seeing only what is fair,
Slipping only what is sweet,
Thou dost mock at fate and care,
Leave the chaff, and take the wheat.
When the fierce northwestern blast
Cools sea and land so far and fast,
Thou already slumberest deep;
Woe and want thou canst outsleep;
Want and woe, which torture us,
Thy sleep makes ridiculous.

Ralph Waldo Emerson

TO A BEE

Thou wert out betimes, thou busy,
    busy bee!
    As abroad I took my early way,
Before the cow from her resting-place
Had risen up, and left her trace
    On the meadow, with dew so gay,
Saw I thee, thou busy, busy bee!

Thou wert working late, thou busy,
    busy bee!
    After the fall of the cistus flower,
When the primrose of evening was
    ready to burst,
I heard thee last, as I saw thee first;
    In the silence of the evening hour,
Heard I thee, thou busy, busy bee!

Thou art a miser, thou busy, busy bee!
    Late and early at employ;
Still on thy golden stores intent,
Thy summer in keeping and hoarding
    is spent,
What thy winter will never enjoy.
Wise lesson this for me, thou busy,
    busy bee!

Little dost thou think, thou busy, busy
    bee!
    What is the end of thy toil,
When the latest flowers of the ivy are
    gone,
And all thy work for the year is done,
    Thy master comes for the spoil;
Woe then for thee, thou busy, busy
    bee!

Robert Southey

SONG OF THE BEES

We watch for the light of the morn to
    break,
    And colour the eastern sky
With its blended hues of saffron and
    lake;

Then say to each other, "Awake!
  awake!
For our winter's honey is all to make,
  And our bread for a long supply."

And off we hie to the hill and dell,
  To the field, to the meadow and
    bower;
We love in the columbine's horn to
  dwell,
To dip in the lily with snow-white
  bell,
To search for the balm in its fragrant
  cell,
  The mint and the rosemary flower.

We seek the bloom of the eglantine,
  Of the painted thistle and brier;
And follow the steps of the wandering
  vine,
Whether it trail on the earth supine,
Or round the aspiring tree-top twine,
  And aim at a state still higher.

While each, on the good of her sister
  bent,
  Is busy, and cares for all,
We hope for an evening of heart's
  content
In the winter of life, without lament
That summer is gone, or its hours mis-
  spent,
  And the harvest is past recall.
                    Hannah Flagg Gould

TO A BUTTERFLY

I

I've watched you now a full half-hour,
Self-poised upon that yellow flower;
And, little butterfly, indeed,
I know not if you sleep or feed.

How motionless!—not frozen seas
  More motionless; and then,
What joy awaits you when the breeze
Hath found you out among the trees,
  And calls you forth again!

This plot of orchard ground is ours,
My trees they are, my sister's flowers;
Here rest your wings when they are
  weary,
Here lodge as in a sanctuary!

Come to us often, fear no wrong,
  Sit near us on the bough!
We'll talk of sunshine and of song,
And summer days when we were
  young;
Sweet childish days that were as long
  As twenty days are now.

II

Stay near me—do not take thy flight!
A little longer stay in sight!
Much converse do I find in thee,
Historian of my infancy!
Float near me; do not yet depart!
  Dead times revive in thee:
Thou bring'st, gay creature as thou
  art,
A solemn image to my heart,
  My father's family!

Oh! pleasant, pleasant were the days,
The time when, in our childish plays,
My sister Emmeline and I
Together chased the butterfly!
A very hunter did I rush
  Upon the prey—with leaps and
    springs
I followed on from brake to bush,
But she, God love her, feared to brush
  The dust from off its wings.
                    William Wordsworth

THE BUTTERFLY'S BALL

Come, take up your hats, and away let
  us haste
To the Butterfly's ball and the Grasshopper's feast;
The trumpeter Gadfly has summon'd
  the crew,
And the revels are now only waiting
  for you.

On the smooth shaven grass by the
  side of the wood,
Beneath a broad oak that for ages has
  stood,
See the children of earth, and the
  tenants of air,
For an evening's amusement together
  repair.

And there came the Beetle, so blind
  and so black,
Who carried the Emmet, his friend,
  on his back;
And there was the Gnat, and the
  Dragon-fly too,
With all their relations, green, orange,
  and blue.

And there came the Moth in his plumage of down,
And the Hornet in jacket of yellow
  and brown,
Who with him the Wasp his companion did bring,
But they promised that evening to lay
  by their sting.

And the sly little Dormouse crept out
  of his hole,
And led to the feast his blind brother
  the Mole;
And the Snail, with his horns peeping
  out from his shell,
Came from a great distance—the
  length of an ell.

A mushroom their table, and on it was
  laid
A water dock leaf, with a table-cloth
  made;
The viands were various, to each of
  their taste,
And the Bee brought his honey to
  crown the repast.

There close on his haunches, so solemn
  and wise,
The Frog from a corner look'd up to
  the skies;
And the Squirrel well-pleased such diversion to see,
Sat cracking his nuts overhead in a
  tree.

Then out came the spider, with fingers
  so fine,
To show his dexterity on the tight
  line;
From one branch to another his cobwebs he slung,
Then as quick as an arrow he darted
  along.

But just in the middle, oh! shocking
  to tell!
From his rope in an instant poor Har-
  lequin fell;
Yet he touch'd not the ground, but
  with talons outspread,
Hung suspended in air at the end of a
  thread.

Then the Grasshopper came with a
  jerk and a spring,
Very long was his leg, though but
  short was his wing;
He took but three leaps, and was soon
  out of sight,
Then chirp'd his own praises the rest
  of the night.

With step so majestic the Snail did
  advance,
And promised the gazers a minuet to
  dance;
But they all laugh'd so loud that he
  pull'd in his head,
And went in his own little chamber to
  bed.

Then as evening gave way to the
  shadows of night,
The watchman, the Glowworm, came
  out with his light;
Then home let us hasten while yet we
  can see,
For no watchman is waiting for you
  and for me.

  William Roscoe

THE SPIDER

With six small diamonds for his eyes
He walks upon the Summer skies,
Drawing from his silken blouse
The lacework of his dwelling house.

He lays his staircase as he goes
Under his eight thoughtful toes
And grows with the concentric flower
Of his shadowless, thin bower.

His back legs are a pair of hands,
They can spindle out the strands
Of a thread that is so small
It stops the sunlight not at all.

He spins himself to threads of dew
Which will harden soon into
Lines that cut like slender knives
Across the insects' airy lives.

He makes no motion but is right,
He spreads out his appetite
Into a network, twist on twist,
This little ancient scientist.

He does not know he is unkind,
He has a jewel for a mind
And logic deadly as dry bone,
This small son of Euclid's own.

  Robert P. Tristram Coffin

TO AN INSECT

I love to hear thine earnest voice,
  Wherever thou art hid,
Thou testy little dogmatist,
  Thou pretty Katydid!
Thou mindest me of gentlefolks,—
  Old gentlefolks are they,—
Thou say'st an undisputed thing
  In such a solemn way.

Thou art a female, Katydid!
  I know it by the trill
That quivers through thy piercing
  notes,
  So petulant and shrill;
I think there is a knot of you
  Beneath the hollow tree,—
A knot of spinster Katydids,—
  Do Katydids drink tea?

Oh, tell me where did Katy live,
  And what did Katy do?
And was she very fair and young,
  And yet so wicked, too?
Did Katy love a naughty man,
  Or kiss more cheeks than one?
I warrant Katy did no more
  Than many a Kate has done.

Dear me! I'll tell you all about
  My fuss with little Jane,
And Ann, with whom I used to walk
  So often down the lane,
And all that tore their locks of black,
  Or wet their eyes of blue,—
Pray tell me, sweetest Katydid,
  What did poor Katy do?

Ah no! the living oak shall crash,
　That stood for ages still,
The rock shall rend its mossy base
　And thunder down the hill,
Before the little Katydid
　Shall add one word, to tell
The mystic story of the maid
　Whose name she knows so well.

Peace to the ever-murmuring race!
　And when the latest one
Shall fold in death her feeble wings
　Beneath the autumn sun,
Then shall she raise her fainting voice,
　And lift her drooping lid,
And then the child of future years
　Shall hear what Katy did.

　　　　　　Oliver Wendell Holmes

NEAR DUSK

　Gold, red and green flies
　Tease each other in the copse,
　While a tanager takes the air
　In three hops.

　Heavy bees go mumbling,
　Orange, black and brown;
　Little tads go tumbling
　Up and down.

　White moths whirr and flutter
　In the glowworm light,
　Bronze beetles plod and pass
　Out of sight.

　　　　　　Joseph Auslander

THE GRASSHOPPER AND
THE CRICKET

The poetry of earth is never dead:
When all the birds are faint with the
　hot sun,
And hide in cooling trees, a voice will
　run

From hedge to hedge about the **new-**
　mown mead:
That is the grasshopper's—he takes the
　lead
In summer luxury—he has never done
With his delights, for when tired out
　with fun,
He rests at ease beneath some pleasant
　weed.
The poetry of earth is ceasing never:
On a lone winter evening, when the
　frost
Has wrought a silence, from the stove
　there shrills
The Cricket's song, in warmth increas-
　ing ever,
And seems to one in drowsiness half
　lost,
The grasshopper's among the grassy
　hills.

　　　　　　John Keats

TO THE GRASSHOPPER AND
THE CRICKET

Green little vaulter in the sunny grass,
Catching your heart up at the feel of
　June;
Sole voice that's heard amidst the lazy
　noon,
When even the bees lag at the sum-
　moning brass;
And you, warm little housekeeper, who
　class
With those who **think** the candle's
　come too soon,
Loving the fire, and with your trick-
　some tune
Nick the glad silent moments as they
　pass!
O sweet and tiny cousins, that belong
One to the fields, the other to the
　hearth,
Both have your sunshine; both, though
　small, are strong

At your clear hearts; and both seem
  given to earth
To sing in thoughtful ears their natu-
  ral song—
In doors and out, summer and winter,
  Mirth.

Leigh Hunt

TO A CRICKET

Voice of summer, keen and shrill,
  Chirping round my winter fire,
  Of thy song I never tire,
Weary others as they will,
For thy song with summer's filled—
  Filled with sunshine, filled with
  June;
  Firelight echo of that noon
Heard in fields when all is stilled
  In the golden light of May,
  Bringing scents of new-mown hay,
  Bees, and birds, and flowers away,
Prithee, haunt my fireside still,
Voice of summer, keen and shrill.

William Cox Bennett

THE CRICKET

Little inmate, full of mirth,
Chirping on my kitchen hearth,
Wheresoe'er be thy abode
Always harbinger of good:
Pay we for thy warm retreat
With a song more soft and sweet;
In return thou shalt receive
Such a strain as I can give.

Thus thy praise shall be expressed,
Inoffensive, welcome guest!
While the rat is on the scout
And the mouse with curious snout,
With what vermin else infest
Every dish and spoil the best;
Frisking thus before the fire
Thou hast all thy heart's desire.

Though in voice and shape they be
Formed as if akin to thee,
Thou surpassest, happier far,
Happiest grasshoppers that are;
Theirs is but a summer song,
Thine endures the winter long,
Unimpaired, and shrill, and clear,
Melody throughout the year.

Neither night nor dawn of day
Puts a period to thy play:
Sing, then—and extend thy span
Far beyond the date of man.
Wretched man, whose years are spent
In repining discontent,
Lives not, aged though he be,
Half a span, compared with thee.

From the Latin of Vincent Bourne,
by William Cowper

THE HOUSEKEEPER

The frugal snail, with forecast of re-
  pose,
Carries his house with him where'er he
  goes;
Peeps out,—and if there comes a
  shower of rain,
Retreats to his small domicile amain.
Touch but a tip of him, a horn,—'tis
  well,—
He curls up in his sanctuary shell.
He's his own landlord, his own tenant;
  stay
Long as he will, he dreads no Quarter
  Day.
Himself he boards and lodges; both
  invites
And feasts himself; sleeps with himself
  o' nights.
He spares the upholsterer trouble to
  procure
Chattels; himself is his own furniture,

And his sole riches. Whereso'er he
   roam,—
Knock when you will,—he's sure to be
   at home.

From the Latin of Vincent Bourne,
   by Charles Lamb

TO A MOUSE

ON TURNING HER NEST WITH THE PLOW,
NOVEMBER, 1785

Wee, sleekit, cow'rin, tim'rous beastie,
O, what a panic's in thy breastie!
Thou need na start awa' sae hasty,
   Wi' bickering brattle!
I wad be laith to rin an' chase thee,
   Wi' murd'ring prattle!

I'm truly sorry man's dominion
Has broken Nature's social union,
An' justifies that ill opinion,
   Which makes thee startle
At me, thy poor, earth-born com-
   panion,
   An' fellow-mortal!

I doubt na, whiles, but thou may
   thieve;
What then? poor beastie, thou maun
   live!
A daimen icker in a thrave
   'S a sma' request;
I'll get a blessin' wi' the laive,
   And never miss't!

Thy wee bit housie, too, in ruin!
Its silly wa's the win's are strewin'!
An' naething, now, to big a new ane,
   O' foggage green!
An' bleak December's winds ensuin',
   Baith snell an' keen!

Thou saw the fields laid bare an' waste,
An' weary winter comin' fast,

An' cozie here, beneath the blast,
   Thou thought to dwell,—
Till, crash! the cruel coulter passed
   Out through thy cell.

That wee bit heap o' leaves an' stibble
Hast cost thee mony a weary nibble!
Now thou's turned out, for a' thy
   trouble,
   But house or hald,
To thole the winter's sleety dribble,
   An' cranreuch cauld!

But, Mousie, thou art no thy lane,
In proving foresight may be vain:
The best-laid schemes o' mice an' men,
   Gang aft a-gley,
An' lea'e us naught but grief an' pain,
   For promised joy!

Still thou art blest, compared wi' me!
The present only toucheth thee:
But, och! I backward cast my e'e
   On prospects drear!
An' forward, though I canna see,
   I guess an' fear!

            Robert Burns

THE WOODMAN'S DOG

Shaggy, and lean, and shrewd, with
   pointed ears
And tail cropp'd short, half lurcher and
   half cur—
His dog attends him. Close behind his
   heel
Now he creeps slow; and now, with
   many a frisk
Wide-scampering, snatches up the
   drifted snow
With ivory teeth, or ploughs at it with
   his snout;
Then shakes his powder'd coat, and
   barks for joy.

           William Cowper

JOY MEETS BOY

Farm after farm, the schoolbus stops,
And out the proper schoolboy pops,
While his feet are still in air,
Joy flies out and meets him there.

For every ink-scarred, book-worn boy,
A furry bolt of four-foot joy
That darts and hurls him from his feet
And turns him up all shouts and seat.

Collie, scottie, bull, or hound,
Or dog that is all hands around—
It makes no difference to the fun,
Dog meets boy, and they are one.

They unite, none can say which is
Hide and hair or skin and breeches,
No one can tell, for laps and grins,
Where dog leaves off and boy begins.

For every boy, but never, never
For any girl, how nice soever,
Comes the frenzied pounding tail,
This evening song is wholly male.

Dog after dog, the country wakes,
Boy after boy, the country shakes,
Boys cleave to dogs in naked trust,
And all learning falls to dust.

Robert P. Tristram Coffin

THE PET LAMB

The dew was falling fast, the stars
  began to blink;
I heard a voice; it said, "Drink,
  pretty creature, drink!"
And, looking o'er the hedge, before
  me I espied
A snow-white mountain-lamb, with
  a Maiden at its side.

Nor sheep nor kine were near; the
  lamb was all alone,
And by a slender cord was tethered
  to a stone;
With one knee on the grass did the
  little Maiden kneel,
While to that mountain-lamb she
  gave its evening meal.

The lamb, while from her hand he
  thus his supper took,
Seemed to feast with head and ears;
  and his tail with pleasure shook.
"Drink, pretty creature, drink," she
  said in such a tone
That I almost received her heart into
  my own.

'Twas little Barbara Lewthwaite, a
  child of beauty rare!
I watched them with delight, they
  were a lovely pair.
Now with her empty can the maiden
  turned away:
But ere ten yards were gone her
  footsteps did she stay.

Right toward the lamb she looked:
  and from a shady place
I unobserved could see the workings
  of her face;
If Nature to her tongue could measured numbers bring,
Thus, thought I, to her lamb the
  little Maid might sing:

"What ails thee, young One, what?
  Why pull so at thy cord?
Is it not well with thee? well both
  for bed and board?
Thy plot of grass is soft, and green
  as grass can be:
Rest, little young One, rest; what
  is't that aileth thee?

"What is it thou wouldst seek? What
  is wanting to thy heart?

Thy limbs, are they not strong? And
  beautiful thou art:
This grass is tender grass: these
  flowers they have no peers:
And that green corn is all day rustling in thy ears!

"If the sun be shining hot, do but
  stretch thy woollen chain,
This beech is standing by, its covert
  thou canst gain;
For rain and mountain-storms! the
  like thou needst not fear,
The rain and storm are things that
  scarcely can come here.

"Rest, little One, rest; thou hast forgot the day
When my father found thee first, in
  places far away:
Many flocks were on the hills, but
  thou wert owned by none,
And thy mother from thy side for
  evermore was gone.

"He took thee in his arms, and in pity
  brought thee home;
A blessed day for thee! Then
  whither wouldst thou roam?
A faithful nurse thou hast: the dam
  that did thee wean
Upon the mountain-tops no kinder
  could have been.

"Thou know'st that thrice a day I
  have brought thee in this can
Fresh water from the brook, as clear
  as ever ran;
And twice in the day, when the
  ground is wet with dew,
I bring thee draughts of milk—
  warm milk it is and new.

"Thy limbs will shortly be twice as
  stout as they are now,

Then I'll yoke thee to my cart like
  a pony in the plough;
My playmate shalt thou be; and
  when the wind is cold,
Our hearth shall be thy bed, our
  house shall be thy fold.

"It will not, will not rest! Poor creature, can it be
That 'tis thy mother's heart which
  is working so in thee?
Things that I know not of belike to
  thee are dear,
And dreams of things which thou
  canst neither see nor hear.

"Alas! the mountain-tops that look so
  green and fair!
I've heard of fearful winds and darkness that come there;
The little brooks that seem all pastime and all play,
When they are angry, roar like lions
  for their prey.

"Here thou needst not dread the
  raven in the sky;
Night and day thou art safe,—our
  cottage is hard by.
Why bleat so after me? why pull so
  at thy chain?
Sleep—and at break of the day I will
  come to thee again! "

As homeward through the lane I
  went with lazy feet,
This song to myself did I oftentimes
  repeat;
And it seemed, as I retraced the
  ballad line by line,
That but half of it was hers, and
  one half of it was mine.

Again, and once again, did I repeat
  the song,

" Nay," said I, " more than half to the
    damsel must belong,
  For she looked with such a look, and
    she spoke with such a tone,
  That I almost received her heart into
    my own."

            William Wordsworth

HIGHLAND CATTLE
(Selected Stanzas)

Down the wintry mountain
  Like a cloud they come,
Not like a cloud in its silent shroud
    When the sky is leaden and the
    earth all dumb,
But tramp, tramp, tramp,
  With a roar and a shock,
And stamp, stamp, stamp,
  Down the hard granite rock,
With the snow-flakes falling fair
Like an army in the air
Of white-winged angels leaving
Their heavenly homes, half grieving,
And half glad to drop down kindly
    upon earth so bare:
With a snort and a bellow
Tossing manes dun and yellow,
Red and roan, black and gray,
In their fierce merry play,
Though the sky is all leaden and the
    earth all dumb—
Down the noisy cattle come!
Throned on the mountain
  Winter sits at ease:
Hidden under mists are those peaks
    of amethyst
    That rose like hills of heaven above
    the amber seas.
While crash, crash, crash,
  Through frozen heather brown,
And dash, dash, dash,
  Where the ptarmigan drops down

And the curlew stops her cry
And the deer sinks, like to die—
And the waterfall's loud noise
Is the only lifting voice—
With a plunge and a roar
Like mad waves upon the shore,
Or the wind through the pass
Howling o'er the reedy grass—
In a wild battalion pouring from the
    heights unto the plain,
Down the cattle come again!

        Dinah M. Mulock Craik

THE BLOOD HORSE

Gamarra is a dainty steed,
Strong, black, and of a noble breed,
Full of fire, and full of bone,
All his line of fathers known;
Fine his nose, his nostrils thin,
But blown abroad by the pride within!
His mane, a stormy river flowing,
And his eyes like embers glowing
In the darkness of the night,
And his pace as swift as light.

Look—around his straining throat,
Grace and shifting beauty float!
Sinewy strength is in his reins,
And the red blood gallops through his
    veins.
Richer, redder, never ran
Through the boasting heart of man,
He can trace his lineage higher
Than the Bourbon dare aspire,—
Douglas, Guzman, or the Guelph,
Or O'Brien's blood itself!

He, who hath no peer, was born,
Here, upon a red March morn;
But his famous fathers dead
Were Arabs all, and Arab bred,
And the last of that great line
Trod like one of race divine!

And yet—he was but friend to one,
Who fed him at the set of sun,
By some lone fountain fringed with
   green:
With him, a roving Bedouin,
He lived (none else would he obey
Through all the hot Arabian day),—
And died untamed, upon the sands
Where Balkh amidst the desert stands!

Barry Cornwall

THE LION

Lion, thou art girt with might!
King by uncontested right;
Strength, and majesty, and pride,
Are in thee personified!
Slavish doubt, or timid fear,
Never came thy spirit near;
What is it to fly, or bow
To a mightier than thou,
Never has been known to thee,
Creature, terrible and free!

Power the mightiest gave the Lion,
Sinews like to bands of iron;
Gave him force which never failed;
Gave a heart that never quailed.
Triple-mailèd coat of steel,
Plates of brass from head to heel.
Less defensive were in wearing,
Than the Lion's heart of daring;
Nor could towers of strength impart
Trust like that which keeps his heart.

When he sends his roaring forth,
Silence falls upon the earth;
For the creatures, great and small,
Know his terror-breathing call;
And, as if by death pursued,
Leave him to a solitude.

Lion, thou art made to dwell
In hot lands, intractable,

And thyself, the sun, the sand,
Are a tyrannous triple band;
Lion-king and desert throne,
All the region is your own!

Mary Howitt

THE TIGER

Tiger, tiger, burning bright
In the forests in the night,
What immortal hand or eye
Could frame thy fearful symmetry?

In what distant deeps or skies
Burnt the fire of thine eyes?
On what wings dare he aspire?
What the hand dare seize the fire?

And what shoulder and what art,
Could twist the sinews of thy heart?
And when thy heart began to beat,
What dread hand? and what dread
   feet?

What the hammer? what the chain?
In what furnace was thy brain?
What the anvil? what dread grasp
Dares its deadly terrors clasp?

When the stars threw down their
   spears,
And water'd heaven with their tears,
Did He smile his work to see?
Did He who made the lamb make
   thee?

Tiger, tiger, burning bright
In the forests of the night,
What immortal hand or eye
Dare frame thy fearful symmetry?

William Blake

THE BROWN BEAR

Now the wild bees that hive in the
   rocks

Are winding their horns, elfin shrill,
And hark, at the pine tree the wood-
pecker knocks,
And the speckled grouse pipes on
the hill.
Now the adder's dull brood wakes to
run,
Now the sap mounts abundant and
good,
And the brown bear has turned with
his side to the sun
In his lair in the depth of the
wood—
Old Honey-Paw wakes in the wood.

" Oh, a little more slumber," says he,
" And a little more turning to sleep,"
But he feels the spring fervor that
hurries the bee
And the hunger that makes the trout
leap;
So he ambles by thicket and trail,
So he noses the tender young shoots,
In the spring of year at the sign of
the quail
The brown bear goes digging for
roots—
For sappy and succulent roots.

Oh, as still goes the wolf on his
quest
As the spotted snake glides through
the rocks,
And the deer and the sheep count
the lightest foot best,
And slinking and sly trots the fox.
But fleet-foot and light-foot will stay,
And fawns by their mothers will
quail
At the saplings that snap and the
thickets that sway
When Honey-Paw takes to the
trail—
When he shuffles and grunts on the
trail.

He has gathered the ground squir-
rel's hoard,
He has rifled the store of the bees,
He has caught the young trout at the
shoals of the ford
And stripped the wild plums from
the trees;
So robbing and ranging he goes,
And the right to his pillage makes
good
Till he rounds out the year at the
first of the snows
In his lair in the depth of the
wood—
Old Honey-Paw sleeps in the wood.

Mary Austin

THE WOUNDED HARE

Inhuman man! curse on thy barbarous
art,
And blasted be thy murder-aiming
eye;
May never pity soothe thee with a
sigh,
Nor ever pleasure glad thy cruel heart!

Go, live, poor wanderer of the wood
and field,
The bitter little that of life remains;
No more the thickening brakes and
verdant plains
To thee shall home, or food, or pastime yield.

Seek, mangled wretch, some place of
wonted rest.
No more of rest, but now thy dying
bed!
The sheltering rushes whistling o'er
thy head,
The cold earth with thy bloody bosom
prest.

Oft, as by winding Nith, I, musing,
      wait
   The sober eve, or hail the cheerful
      dawn,
   I'll miss thee sporting o'er the dewy
      lawn,
And curse the ruffian's aim, and mourn
      thy hapless fate.

Robert Burns

THE FIRST SWALLOW

The gorse is yellow on the heath;
   The banks with speed-well flowers
      are gay;
The oaks are budding, and beneath,

The hawthorn soon will bear the
      wreath,
   The silver wreath of May.

The welcome guest of settled spring,
   The swallow, too, is come at last;
Just at sunset, when thrushes sing,
I saw her dash with rapid wing,
   And hailed her as she passed.

Come, summer visitant, attach
   To my reed roof your nest of clay,
And let my ear your music catch,
   Low twittering underneath the
      thatch,
   At the grey dawn of day.

Charlotte Smith

Part Seven

HUMOROUS VERSE

LINES FROM L'ALLEGRO

Haste thee, Nymph, and bring with
thee
Jest, and youthful Jollity,
Quips, and Cranks, and wanton Wiles,
Nods, and Becks, and wreathèd Smiles,
Such as hang on Hebe's cheek,
And love to live in dimple sleek;
Sport that wrinkled Care derides,
And Laughter holding both his sides.

John Milton

THE HEIGHT OF THE RIDICULOUS

I wrote some lines once on a time
  In wondrous merry mood,
And thought, as usual, men would
    say
  They were exceeding good.

They were so queer, so very queer,
  I laughed as I would die;
Albeit, in the general way,
  A sober man am I.

I called my servant, and he came;
  How kind it was of him
To mind a slender man like me,
  He of the mighty limb.

"These to the printer," I exclaimed,
  And, in my humorous way,
I added (as a trifling jest),
  "There'll be the devil to pay."

He took the paper, and I watched,
  And saw him peep within;
At the first line he read, his face
  Was all upon the grin.

He read the next; the grin grew
    broad,
  And shot from ear to ear;
He read the third; a chuckling noise
  I now began to hear.

The fourth; he broke into a roar;
  The fifth; his waistband split;
The sixth; he burst five buttons off,
  And tumbled in a fit.

Ten days and nights, with sleepless
    eye,
  I watched that wretched man,
And since, I never dare to write
  As funny as I can.

Oliver Wendell Holmes

THE PLAINT OF THE CAMEL

"Canary-birds feed on sugar and seed,
  Parrots have crackers to crunch;
And as for the poodles, they tell me
    the noodles
  Have chickens and cream for their
    lunch.
    But there's never a question
    About MY digestion—
ANYTHING does for me!

"Cats, you're aware, can repose in a
    chair,
  Chickens can roost upon rails;
Puppies are able to sleep in a stable,
  And oysters can slumber in pails.
    But no one supposes
    A poor Camel dozes—
ANY PLACE does for me!

"Lambs are enclosed where it's never
    exposed,
  Coops are constructed for hens;
Kittens are treated to houses well
    heated,
  And pigs are protected by pens.
    But a Camel comes handy
    Wherever it's sandy—
ANYWHERE does for me!

"People would laugh if you rode a
    giraffe,
  Or mounted the back of an ox;
It's nobody's habit to ride on a rab-
    bit;
  Or try to bestraddle a fox .
    But as for a Camel, he's
    Ridden by families—
ANY LOAD does for me!

"A snake is as round as a hole in the
    ground,
  And weasels are wavy and sleek;

And no alligator could ever be
    straighter
Than lizards that live in a creek,
  But a Camel's all lumpy
  And bumy and humpy—
ANY SHAPE does for me!"

          Charles Edward Carryl

FATHER WILLIAM

"You are old, Father William," the
    young man said,
  "And your hair has become very
    white;
And yet you incessantly stand on
    your head—
  Do you think, at your age, it is
    right?"

"In my youth," Father William re-
    plied to his son,
  "I feared it might injure the
    brain;
But now that I'm perfectly sure I
    have none,
  Why, I do it again and again."

"You are old," said the youth, "as I
    mentioned before,
  And have grown most uncom-
    monly fat;
Yet you turned a back somersault in
    at the door—
  Pray, what is the reason for that?"

"In my youth," said the sage, as he
    shook his gray locks,
  "I kept all my limbs very supple
By the use of this ointment—one
    shilling the box—
  Allow me to sell you a couple."

"You are old," said the youth, "and
    your jaws are too weak

For anything tougher than suet;
Yet you finished the goose, with the
    bones and the beak;
    Pray, how did you manage to do
    it? "

" In my youth," said his father, " I
    took to the law,
    And argued each case with my
    wife;
And the muscular strength which it
    gave to my jaw,
    Has lasted the rest of my life."

" You are old," said the youth; " one
    would hardly suppose
    That your eye was as steady as
    ever;
Yet you balanced an eel on the end
    of your nose—
    What made you so awfully
    clever? "

" I have answered three questions, and
    that is enough,"
    Said his father; " don't give your-
    self airs!
Do you think I can listen all day to
    such stuff?
    Be off, or I'll kick you down-
    stairs! "

Lewis Carroll

THE WALRUS AND THE CARPENTER

The sun was shining on the sea,
    Shining with all his might:
He did his very best to make
    The billows smooth and bright—
And this was odd, because it was
    The middle of the night.

The moon was shining sulkily,
    Because she thought the sun
Had got no business to be there
    After the day was done—
" It's very rude of him," she said,
    " To come and spoil the fun! "

The sea was wet as wet could be,
    The sands were dry as dry.
You could not see a cloud, because
    No cloud was in the sky:
No birds were flying overhead—
    There were no birds to fly.

The Walrus and the Carpenter
    Were walking close at hand:
They wept like anything to see
    Such quantities of sand:
" If this were only cleared away,"
    They said, " it *would* be grand! "

" If seven maids with seven mops
    Swept it for half a year,
Do you suppose," the Walrus said,
    " That they could get it clear? "
" I doubt it," said the Carpenter,
    And shed a bitter tear.

" O, Oysters, come and walk with us! "
    The Walrus did beseech.
" A pleasant talk, a pleasant walk,
    Along the briny beach:
We cannot do with more than four,
    To give a hand to each."

The eldest Oyster looked at him,
    But never a word he said;
The eldest Oyster winked his eye,
    And shook his heavy head—
Meaning to say he did not choose
    To leave the oyster-bed.

But four young Oysters hurried up,
    All eager for the treat:

Their coats were brushed, their faces
    washed,
Their shoes were clean and neat—
And this was odd, because, you
    know,
    They hadn't any feet.

Four other Oysters followed them,
    And yet another four;
And thick and fast they came at last,
    And more, and more, and more—
All hopping through the frothy
    waves,
    And scrambling to the shore.

The Walrus and the Carpenter
    Walked on a mile or so,
And then they rested on a rock
    Conveniently low:
And all the little Oysters stood
    And waited in a row.

" The time has come," the Walrus
    said,
    " To talk of many things:
Of shoes—and ships—and sealing-
    wax—
Of cabbages—and kings—
And why the sea is boiling hot—
    And whether pigs have wings."

" But wait a bit," the Oysters cried,
    " Before we have our chat;
For some of us are out of breath,
    And all of us are fat! "
" No hurry! " said the Carpenter.
    They thanked him much for that.

" A loaf of bread," the Walrus said,
    " Is what we chiefly need:
Pepper and vinegar besides
    Are very good indeed—
Now, if you're ready, Oysters dear,
    We can begin to feed."

" But not on us! " the Oysters cried,
    Turning a little blue.
" After such kindness, that would be
    A dismal thing to do! "
" The night is fine," the Walrus said.
    " Do you admire the view?

" It was so kind of you to come!
    And you are very nice! "
The Carpenter said nothing but
    " Cut us another slice.
I wish you were not quite so deaf—
    I've had to ask you twice! "

" It seems a shame," the Walrus said,
    " To play them such a trick,
After we've brought them out so far,
    And made them trot so quick! "
The Carpenter said nothing but
    " The butter's spread too thick! "

" I weep for you," the Walrus said:
    " I deeply sympathize."
With sobs and tears he sorted out
    Those of the largest size,
Holding his pocket-handkerchief
    Before his streaming eyes.

" O, Oysters," said the Carpenter,
    " You've had a pleasant run!
Shall we be trotting home again? "
    But answer came there none—
And this was scarcely odd, because
    They'd eaten every one.
                   Lewis Carroll

THE COURTSHIP OF THE YONGHY-BONGHY-BO

On the Coast of Coromandel
    Where the early pumpkins blow,
    In the middle of the woods
    Lived the Yonghy-Bonghy-Bo.
Two old chairs, and half a candle,

One old jug without a handle,—
    These were all his worldly
      goods:
    In the middle of the woods,
    These were all the worldly
      goods,
    Of the Yonghy-Bonghy-Bo,
    Of the Yonghy-Bonghy-Bo.

Once, among the Bong-trees walking
    Where the early pumpkins blow,
      To a little heap of stones
Came the Yonghy-Bonghy-Bo.
There he heard a Lady talking
To some milk-white Hens of Dork-
      ing,—
    " 'Tis the Lady Jingly Jones!
    On that little heap of stones
    Sits the Lady Jingly Jones! "
Said the Yonghy-Bonghy-Bo.

" Lady Jingly! Lady Jingly!
    Sitting where the pumpkins blow,
    Will you come and be my
      wife? "
Said the Yonghy-Bonghy-Bo.
" I am tired of living singly,—
On this coast so wild and shingly,—
    I'm a-weary of my life;
    If you'll come and be my wife,
    Quite serene would be my life! "
Said the Yonghy-Bonghy-Bo.

" On this Coast of Coromandel,
    Shrimps and water-cresses grow,
      Prawns are plentiful and cheap,"
Said the Yonghy-Bonghy-Bo.
" You shall have my chairs and candle
And my jug without a handle.
    Gaze upon the rolling deep
    (Fish is plentiful and cheap);
    As the sea, my love is deep! "
Said the Yonghy-Bonghy-Bo.

Lady Jingly answered sadly,
    And her tears began to flow,—
    " Your proposal comes too late,
    Mr. Yonghy-Bonghy-Bo!
I would be your wife most gladly! "
(Here she twirled her fingers madly,)
    " But in England I've a mate!
    Yes! you've asked me far too
      late,
    For in England I've a mate,
    Mr. Yonghy-Bonghy-Bo.

" Mr. Jones—(his name is Handel,—
    Handel Jones, Esquire, & Co.)
      Dorking fowls delights to send,
    Mr. Yonghy-Bonghy-Bo!
Keep, oh! keep your chairs and can-
      dle,
And your jug without a handle,—
    I can merely be your friend!
    —Should my Jones more Dork-
      ings send,
    I will give you three, my friend!
    Mr. Yonghy-Bonghy-Bo.

" Though you've such a tiny body,
    And your head so large doth
      grow,—
    Though your hat may blow
      away,
    Mr. Yonghy-Bonghy-Bo!
Though you're such a Hoddy
      Doddy,—
Yet I wish that I could modi-
    fy the words I needs must say!
    Will you please to go away?
    That is all I have to say,
Mr. Yonghy-Bonghy-Bo! "

Down the slippery slopes of Myrtle,
    Where the early pumpkins blow,
      To the calm and silent sea
Fled the Yonghy-Bonghy-Bo.
There, beyond the Bay of Gurtle,

Lay a large and lively Turtle;—
  "You're the Cove," he said,
    for me;
    On your back beyond the sea,
    Turtle, you shall carry me! "
  Said the Yonghy-Bonghy-Bo.

Through the silent-roaring ocean
  Did the Turtle swiftly go;
    Holding fast upon his shell
  Rode the Yonghy-Bonghy-Bo.
With a sad primeval motion
Toward the sunset isles of Boshen
    Still the Turtle bore him well.
    Holding fast upon his shell,
    " Lady Jingly Jones, farewell! "
  Sang the Yonghy-Bonghy-Bo.

From the Coast of Coromandel,
  Did that Lady never go;
    On that heap of stones she
      moans
  For the Yonghy-Bonghy-Bo.
On the Coast of Coromandel,
In his jug without a handle,
    Still she weeps and daily moans;
    On that little heap of stones
    To her Dorking Hens she moans
  For the Yonghy-Bonghy-Bo,
  For the Yonghy-Bonghy-Bo.
          Edward Lear

JABBERWOCKY

'Twas brillig, and the slithy toves
  Did gyre and gimble in the wabe;
All mimsy were the borogoves,
  And the mome raths outgrabe.

" Beware the Jabberwock, my son!
  The jaws that bite, the claws that
    catch!
  Beware the Jubjub bird, and shun
    The frumious Bandersnatch! "

He took his vorpal sword in hand:
  Long time the manxome foe he
    sought.—
So rested he by the Tumtum tree,
  And stood awhile in thought.

And as in uffish thought he stood,
  The Jabberwock, with eyes of
    flame,
Came whiffling through the tulgey
    wood,
  And burbled as it came!

One, two! One, two! And through
    and through
  The vorpal blade went snicker-
    snack!
He left it dead, and with its head
  He went galumphing back.

" And hast thou slain the Jabberwock?
  Come to my arms, my beamish
    boy!
  O frabjous day! Callooh! Callay! "
  He chortled in his joy.

'Twas brillig, and the slithy toves
  Did gyre and gimble in the wabe;
All mimsy were the borogoves,
  And the mome raths outgrabe.
          Lewis Carroll

THE GARDENER'S SONG

He thought he saw an Elephant,
  That practised on a fife;
He looked again, and found it was
  a letter from his wife.
" At length I realize," he said,
  " The bitterness of life! "

He thought he saw a Buffalo
  Upon the chimney-piece:
He looked again, and found it was

His Sister's Husband's Niece.
" Unless you leave this house," he said,
    " I'll send for the Police! "

He thought he saw a Rattlesnake
    That questioned him in Greek:
He looked again, and found it was
    The Middle of Next Week.
" The one thing I regret," he said,
    " Is that it cannot speak! "

He thought he saw a Banker's Clerk
    Descending from the 'bus:
He looked again, and found it was
    A Hippopotamus.
" If this should stay to dine," he said,
    " There won't be much for us! "

He thought he saw a Kangaroo
    That worked a coffee-mill:
He looked again, and found it was
    A Vegetable-Pill.
" Were I to swallow this," he said,
    " I should be very ill! "

He thought he saw a Coach-and-
        Four
    That stood beside his bed:
He looked again, and found it was
    A Bear without a Head.
" Poor thing," he said, " poor silly
        thing!
    It's waiting to be fed! "

He thought he saw an Albatross
    That fluttered round the lamp:
He looked again, and found it was
    A Penny-Postage-Stamp.
" You'd best be getting home," he
        said:
    " The nights are very damp! "

He thought he saw a Garden Door
    That opened with a key:

He looked again, and found it was
    A Double-Rule-of-Three.
" And all its mystery," he said,
    " Is clear as day to me! "
                        Lewis Carroll

THE ICHTHYOSAURUS

There once was an Ichthyosaurus
Who lived when the earth was all
        porous,
But he fainted with shame
When he first heard his name,
And departed a long time before us.
                        Unknown

THE VULTURE

The Vulture eats between his meals,
    And that's the reason why
He very, very rarely feels
    As well as you or I.
His eye is dull, his head is bald,
    His neck is growing thinner.
Oh, what a lesson for us all
    To only eat at dinner.
                        Hilaire Belloc

FIVE NONSENSE VERSES

There was an Old Man with a beard,
Who said, " It is just as I feared!
    Two Owls and a Hen,
    Four Larks and a Wren,
Have all built their nests in my beard!"

There was an Old Man in a tree,
Who was horribly bored by a bee;
    When they said, " Does it buzz? "
    He replied, " Yes, it does!
It's a regular brute of a bee! "

There was an Old Man in a boat,
Who said, " I'm afloat! I'm afloat! "

When they said, " No, you ain't! "
He was ready to faint,
That unhappy old man in a boat.

There was an Old Man with a poker,
Who painted his face with red ochre;
  When they said, " You're a Guy! "
  He made no reply,
But knocked them all down with his
  poker.

There was an Old Man who said,
  " Hush!
I perceive a young bird in this bush! "
  When they said, " Is it small? "
  He replied, " Not at all!
It is four times as big as the bush! "

Edward Lear

SEEIN' THINGS

I ain't afeard uv snakes, or toads, or
  bugs, or worms, or mice,
An' things 'at girls are skeered uv I
  think are awful nice!
I'm pretty brave, I guess; an' yet I
  hate to go to bed,
For when I'm tucked up warm an'
  snug an' when my prayers are said,
Mother tells me, " Happy Dreams! "
  an' takes away the light,
An' leaves me lyin' all alone an' seein'
  things at night!

Sometimes they're in the corner, sometimes they're by the door,
Sometimes they're all a-standin' in the
  middle uv the floor;
Sometimes they are a-sittin' down,
  sometimes they're walkin' round
So softly and so creepylike they never
  make a sound!
Sometimes they are as black as ink, an'
  other times they're white—

But the color ain't no difference when
  you see things at night!

Once, when I licked a feller 'at had
  just moved on our street,
An' father sent me up to bed without
  a bite to eat,
I woke up in the dark an' saw things
  standin' in a row,
A-lookin' at me cross-eyed an' p'intin'
  at me—so!
Oh, my! I wuz so skeered that time I
  never slep' a mite—
It's almost alluz when I'm bad I see
  things at night!

Lucky thing I ain't a girl, or I'd be
  skeered to death!
Bein' I'm a boy, I duck my head an'
  hold my breath;
An' I am, oh, so sorry I'm a naughty
  boy, an' then
I promise to be better an' I say my
  prayers again!
Gran'ma tells me that's the only way
  to make it right
When a feller has been wicked an'
  sees things at night!

An' so, when other naughty boys
  would coax me into sin,
I try to skwush the Tempter's voice 'at
  urges me within;
An' when they's pie for supper, or
  cakes 'at's big an' nice,
I want to—but I do not pass my plate
  f'r them things twice!
No, ruther let Starvation wipe me
  slowly out o' sight
Than I should keep a-livin' on an'
  seein' things at night!

Eugene Field

LAUGHING SONG

When the green woods laugh with the
  voice of joy,
And the dimpling stream runs laughing by,
When the air does laugh with our
  merry wit,
And the green hill laughs with the
  noise of it;

When the meadows laugh with lively
  green,
And the grasshopper laughs in the
  merry scene,
When Mary and Susan and Emily
With their sweet round mouths sing
  Ha, ha, he!

When the painted birds laugh in the
  shade,
When our table with cherries and nuts
  is spread,
Come live and be happy and join with
  me
To sing the sweet chorus of Ha, ha,
  he!

William Blake

THE COWBOY

" What care I, what cares he,
  What cares the world of the life we
    know?
  Little they reck of the shadowless
    plains,
  The shelterless mesa, the sun and
    the rains,
  The wild, free life, as the winds that
    blow."
    With his broad sombrero,
    His worn chaparajos,
      And clinking spurs,
    Like a Centaur he speeds,
    Where the wild bull feeds;

And he laughs, ha, ha!—who cares,
  who cares!

Ruddy and brown—careless and
  free—
A king in the saddle—he rides at will
O'er the measureless range where
  rarely change
The swart gray plains so weird and
  strange,
Treeless, and streamless, and won-
  drous still!
  With his slouch sombrero,
  His torn chaparajos,
    And clinking spurs,
  Like a Centaur he speeds,
  Where the wild bull feeds;
And he laughs, ha, ha!—who cares,
  who cares!

He of the towns, he of the East,
Has only a vague, dull thought of
  him;
In his far-off dreams the cowboy
  seems
A mythical thing, a thing he deems
A Hun or a Goth as swart and grim!
  With his stained sombrero,
  His rough chaparajos,
    And clinking spurs,
  Like a Centaur he speeds,
  Where the wild bull feeds;
And he laughs, ha, ha!—who cares,
  who cares!

Swift and strong, and ever alert,
Yet sometimes he rests on the dreary
  vast;
And his thoughts, like the thoughts
  of other men
Go back to his childhood days again,
And to many a loved one in the past.
  With his gay sombrero,
  His rude chaparajos,

And clinking spurs,
He rests a while,
With a tear and a smile,
Then he laughs, ha, ha!—who cares,
who cares?

John Antrobus

WHOOPIE TI YI YO, GIT ALONG LITTLE DOGIES

As I walked out one morning for
pleasure,
I spied a cow-puncher all riding
alone;
His hat was throwed back and his
spurs was a-jingling,
As he approached me a-singin' this
song:

Whoopee ti yi yo, git along little
dogies,
It's your misfortune, and none of
my own.
Whoopee ti yi yo, git along little
dogies,
For you know Wyoming will be
your new home.

Early in the spring we round up the
dogies,
Mark and brand and bob off their
tails;
Round up our horses, load up the
chuck-wagon,
Then throw the dogies upon the
trail.

It's whooping and yelling and driving the dogies;
Oh, how I wish you would go on;
It's whooping and punching, go on,
little dogies,
For you know Wyoming will be your
new home.

Some boys goes up the trail for
pleasure,
But that's where you get it most aw-
fully wrong;
For you haven't an idea the trouble
they give us
While we go driving them all along.

When the night comes on and we
hold them on the bedground,
These little dogies that roll on so
slow;
Roll up the herd and cut out the
strays,
And roll the little dogies that never
rolled before.

Your mother she was raised way
down in Texas,
Where the jimson weed and sand-
burrs grow;
Now we'll fill you up on prickly pear
and cholla
Till you are ready for the trail to
Idaho.

Oh, you'll be soup for Uncle Sam's
Injuns;
"It's beef, heap beef," I hear them
cry.
Git along, git along, git along little
dogies
You're going to be beef steers by and
by.

Unknown

OUR HIRED GIRL

Our hired girl, she's 'Lizabuth Ann;
An' she can cook best things to eat!
She ist puts dough in our pie-pan,
An' pours in somepin' 'at's good an'
sweet;
An' nen she salts it all on top

With cinnamon; an' nen she'll stop
 An' stoop an' slide it, ist as slow,
In th' old cook-stove, so's 'twon't slop
 An' git all spilled; nen bakes it, so
 It's custard-pie, first thing you know!
  An' nen she'll say,
 " Clear out o' my way!
They's time fer work, an' time fer play!
 Take yer dough, an' run, child, run!
 Er I can't git no cookin' done! "

When our hired girl 'tends like she's
  mad,
 An' says folks got to walk the chalk
When she's around, er wisht they had!
 I play out on our porch an 'talk
To Th' Raggedy Man 'at mows our
  lawn;
An' he says, " Whew! " an' nen leans
  on
 His old crook-scythe, and blinks his
  eyes,
An' sniffs all 'round an' says, " I
  swawn!
 Ef my old nose don't tell me lies,
 It 'pears like I smell custard-pies! "
  An' nen he'll say,
 " Clear out o' my way!
They's time fer work, an 'time fer
  play!
 Take yer dough, an' run, child, run!
 Er she cain't git no cookin' done! "

Wunst our hired girl, when she
 Got the supper, an' we all et,
An' it wuz night, an' Ma an' me
  An' Pa went wher' the " Social "
  met,—
An' nen when we come home, an' see
A light in the kitchen door, an' we
 Heerd a maccodeun, Pa says,
  " Lan'—
O'—Gracious, who can her beau be? "
 An' I marched in, an' 'Lizabuth Ann

Wuz parchin' corn fer The Raggedy
  Man!
  Better say,
 "Clear out o' the way!
They's time fer work, an' time fer play!
 Take the hint, an' run, child, run!
 Er we cain't git no courtin' done! "

James Whitcomb Riley

WHEN THE FROST IS ON THE PUNKIN *

When the frost is on the punkin and
 the fodder's in the shock,
And you hear the kyouck and gobble
 of the struttin' turkey-cock,
And the clackin' of the guineys, and
 the cluckin' of the hens,
And the rooster's hallylooyer as he
 tiptoes on the fence;
O, it's then's the times a feller is
 a-feelin' at his best,
With the risin' sun to greet him from
 a night of peaceful rest,
As he leaves the house, bareheaded,
 and goes out to feed the stock,
When the frost is on the punkin and
 the fodder's in the shock.

They's something kindo' harty-like
 about the atmusfere
When the heat of summer's over and
 the coolin' fall is here—
Of course we miss the flowers, and the
 blossoms on the trees,
And the mumble of the hummin'-birds
 and buzzin' of the bees;
But the air's so appetizin'; and the
 landscape through the haze
Of a crisp and sunny morning of the
 airly autumn days

* From the Biographical Edition of the complete works of James Whitcomb Riley, copyright 1913, used by special permission of the publishers, The Bobbs-Merrill Company.

Is a pictur' that no painter has the
    colorin' to mock—
When the frost is on the punkin and
    the fodder's in the shock.
The husky, rusty russel of the tossels
    of the corn,
And the raspin' of the tangled leaves,
    as golden as the morn;
The stubble in the furries—kindo'
    lonesome-like, but still
A-preachin' sermuns to us of the barns
    they growed to fill;
The strawstack in the medder, and the
    reaper in the shed;
The hosses in theyr stalls below—the
    clover overhead!—
O, it sets my hart a-clickin' like the
    tickin' of a clock,
When the frost is on the punkin and
    the fodder's in the shock.

Then your apples all is gethered, and
    the ones a feller keeps
Is poured around the celler-floor in
    red and yeller heaps;
And your cider-makin' 's over, and
    your wimmen-folks is through
With their mince and apple-butter,
    and theyr souse and saussage, too!
I don't know how to tell it—but ef sich
    a thing could be
As the Angels wantin' boardin', and
    they'd call around on me—
I'd want to 'commodate 'em—all the
    whole-indurin' flock—
When the frost is on the punkin and
    the fodder's in the shock!

James Whitcomb Riley

LARRIE O'DEE

Now the Widow McGee,
    And Larrie O'Dee,
Had two little cottages out on the
    green,

With just room enough for two pig-
    pens between.
The widow was young and the
    widow was fair,
With the brightest of eyes and the
    brownest of hair,
And it frequently chanced, when she
    came in the morn,
With the swill for her pig, Larrie
    came with the corn,
And some of the ears that he tossed
    from his hand
In the pen of the widow were cer-
    tain to land.

One morning said he:
    " Och! Misthress McGee,
It's a waste of good lumber, this run-
    nin' two rigs,
Wid a fancy purtition betwane our
    two pigs! "
" Indade, sur it is! " answered Widow
    McGee,
With the sweetest of smiles upon
    Larrie O'Dee.
" And thin, it looks kind o' hard-
    hearted and mane,
Kapin' friendly pigs so excaidenly
    near
That whiniver one grunts the other
    can hear,
And yet kape a cruel purtition be-
    twane."

" Shwate Widow McGee,"
    Answered Larrie O'Dee,
" If ye fale in your heart we are mane
    to the pigs,
Ain't we mane to ourselves to be
    runnin' two rigs?
Och! it made me heart ache when I
    paped through the cracks
Of me shanty, lasht March, at yez
    shwingin' yer axe;

An' a-bobbin' yer head an' a-shtomp-
   in' yer fate,
Wid yer purty white hands jisht as
   red as a bate,
A-shplittin' yer kindlin'-wood out in
   the shtorm,
When one little shtove it would
   kape us both warm! "

    " Now, piggy," says she,
    " Larrie's courtin' o' me,
Wid his dilicate tinder allusions to
   you;
So now yez must tell me jisht what
   I must do:
For, if I'm to say yes, shtir the swill
   wid yer snout:
But if I'm to say no, ye must kape
   yer nose out.
Now Larrie, for shame! to be bribin'
   a pig
By a-tossin' a handful of corn in its
   shwig! "
" Me darlint, the piggy says yes,"
   answered he.
And that was the courtship of Larrie
   O'Dee.

          William W. Fink

THE STRANGE MAN

His face was the oddest that ever was
   seen,
His mouth stood across 'twixt his nose
   and his chin;
Whenever he spoke it was then with
   his voice,
And in talking he always made some
   sort of noise.
        Derry down!

He'd an arm on each side to work
   when he pleased,
But he never worked hard when he
   lived at his ease;

Two legs he had got to make him
   complete,
And what is more odd, at each end
   were his feet.

His legs, as folks say, he could move
   at his will,
And when he was walking he never
   stood still.
If you were to see him, you'd laugh till
   you burst,
For one leg or the other would always
   be first.

If this whimsical fellow had a river to
   cross,
If he could not get over, he stayed
   where he was,
He seldom or ever got off the dry
   ground,
So great was his luck that he never
   was drowned.

But the reason he died and the cause
   of his death
Was owing, poor soul, to the want of
   more breath;
And now he is left in the grave for
   to molder,
Had he lived a day longer, he'd have
   been a day older.
        Derry down!
        Unknown

LITTLE BILLEE

There were three sailors of Bristol
   city
Who took a boat and went to sea.
But first with beef and captain's
   biscuits
And pickled pork they loaded she.

There was gorging Jack and guzzling
   Jimmy,

And the youngest he was little
   Billee,
Now when they got so far as the
   Equator
They'd nothing left but one split
   pea.

Says gorging Jack to guzzling Jimmy,
   " I am extremely hungaree."
To gorging Jack says guzzling Jimmy,
   " We've nothing left, us must eat
   we."

Says gorging Jack to guzzling Jimmy,
   " With one another, we shouldn't
   agree!
There's little Bill, he's young and
   tender,
   We're old and tough, so let's eat
   he."

" Oh! Billy, we're going to kill and
   eat you,
   So undo the button of your
   chemie."
When Bill received this information
He used his pocket-handkerchie.

" First let me say my catechism,
   Which my poor mammy taught to
   me."
" Make haste, make haste," says guzzling Jimmy
   While Jack pulled out his snicker-
   snee.

So Billy went up to the main-top
   gallant mast,
   And down he fell on his bended
   knee.
He scarce had come to the twelfth
   commandment
   When up he jumps, " There's land
   I see.

" Jerusalem and Madagascar,
   And North and South Amerikee:
There's the British flag a-riding at
   anchor,
   With Admiral Napier, K. C. B."

So when they got aboard of the
   Admiral's
   He hanged fat Jack and flogged
   Jimmee;
But as for little Bill, he made him
   The Captain of a Seventy-Three.

William Makepeace Thackeray

THE YARN OF THE
" NANCY BELL "

'Twas on the shores that round our
   coast
   From Deal to Ramsgate span,
That I found alone, on a piece of
   stone,
   An elderly naval man.

His hair was weedy, his beard was
   long,
   And weedy and long was he;
And I heard this wight on the shore
   recite,
   In a singular minor key:

" Oh, I am a cook and a captain bold,
   And the mate of the Nancy brig,
And a bo'sun tight, and a midship-
   mite,
   And the crew of the captain's gig."

And he shook his fists and he tore
   his hair,
   Till I really felt afraid,
For I couldn't help thinking the man
   had been drinking,
   And so I simply said:

" Oh, elderly man, it's little I know
 Of the duties of men of the sea,
And I'll eat my hand if I understand
 However you can be

" At once a cook, and a captain bold,
 And the mate of the *Nancy* brig,
And a bo'sun tight, and a midship-
 mite,
And the crew of the captain's gig."

Then he gave a hitch to his trousers,
 which
 Is a trick all seamen larn,
And having got rid of a thumping
 quid,
He spun this painful yarn:

" 'Twas in the good ship *Nancy Bell*
 That we sailed to the Indian Sea,
And there on a reef we come to grief,
 Which has often occurred to me.

" And pretty nigh all o' the crew was
 drowned
 (There was seventy-seven o' soul),
And only ten of the *Nancy's* men
 Said 'Here!' to the muster-roll.

" There was me, and the cook, and the
 captain bold,
And the mate of the Nancy brig,
And the bo'sun tight, and a mid-
 shipmite,
And the crew of the captain's gig.

" For a month we'd neither wittles nor
 drink,
 Till a-hungry we did feel,
So we drawed a lot, and, accordi',
 shot
The captain for our meal.

" The next lot fell to the *Nancy's*
 mate,

And a delicate dish he made;
Then our appetite with the mid-
 shipmite
We seven survivors stayed.

" And then we murdered the bo'sun
 tight,
 And he much resembled pig;
Then we wittled free, did the cook
 and me,
On the crew of the captain's gig.

" Then only the cook and me was left,
 And the delicate question, 'Which
Of us two goes to the kettle?' arose,
 And we argued it out as sich.

" For I loved that cook as a brother,
 I did,
 And the cook he worshipped me;
But we'd both be blowed if we'd
 either be stowed
In the other chap's hold, you see.

" ' I'll be eat if you dines off me,' says
 Tom.
 'Yes, that,' says I, 'you'll be,—
I'm boiled if I die, my friend,' quoth
 I;
And 'Exactly so,' quoth he.

" Says he: 'Dear James, to murder me
 Were a foolish thing to do,
For don't you see that you can't
 cook me,
While I can—and will—cook you!'

" So he boils the water, and takes the
 salt
 And the pepper in portions true
(Which he never forgot), and some
 chopped shalot,
And some sage and parsley too.

" ' Come here,' says he, with a proper
    pride,
  Which his smiling features tell,
' 'Twill soothing be if I let you see
    How extremely nice you'll smell.'

" And he stirred it round and round
    and round,
  And he sniffed at the foaming
    froth;
When I ups with his heels, and
    smothers his squeals
  In the scum of the boiling broth.

" And I eat that cook in a week or less,
  And—as I eating be
The last of his chops, why, I almost
    drops,
  For a wessel in sight I see.

    *   *   *   *   *

" And I never larf, and I never smile,
  And I never lark nor play;
But sit and croak, and a single joke
  I have—which is to say:
" ' Oh, I am a cook and a captain bold
  And the mate of the Nancy brig,
And a bo'sun tight, and a midship-
    mite,
    And the crew of the captain's
    gig!' '"
          William Schwenck Gilbert

THE SAILOR'S CONSOLATION

One night came on a hurricane,
  The sea was mountains rolling
When Barney Buntline turned his
    quid
  And said to Billy Bowling,
" A strong nor-ester's blowing, Bill;
  Hark! don't ye hear it roar, now?
Lord help 'em, how I pities them
  Unhappy folks on shore now!

" Foolhardy chaps who live in towns,
  What danger they are all in,
And now lie quaking in their beds,
  For fear the roof should fall in;
Poor creatures! how they envies us,
  And wishes, I've a notion,
For our good luck, in such a storm,
  To be upon the ocean!

" All as for them who're out all day
  On business from their houses,
And late at night are coming home,
  To cheer their babes and spouses—
While you and I, Bill, on the deck
  Are comfortably lying,
My eyes! what tiles and chimney-
    pots
  About their heads are flying!

" And very often have we heard
  How men are killed and undone
By overturns of carriages,
  By thieves and fires in London;
We know what risks all landsmen
    run,
  From noblemen to tailors;
Then, Bill, let's us thank Providence
  That you and I are sailors."
          Charles Dibdin

ROBINSON CRUSOE'S STORY

The night was thick and hazy
  When the *Piccadilly Daisy*
Carried down the crew and captain in
    the sea;
  And I think the water drowned 'em
  For they never, never found 'em
And I know they didn't come ashore
    with me.

Oh! 'twas very sad and lonely
  When I found myself the only
Population on this cultivated shore;

But I've made a little tavern
In a rocky little cavern,
And I sit and watch for people at the
    door.

I spent no time in looking
For a girl to do my cooking,
As I'm quite a clever hand at making
    stews;
But I had that fellow Friday,
Just to keep the tavern tidy,
And to put a Sunday polish on my
    shoes.

I have a little garden
That I'm cultivating lard in,
As the things I eat are rather tough
    and dry;
For I live on toasted lizards,
Prickly pears, and parrot gizzards,
And I'm really very fond of beetle-pie.

The clothes I had were furry,
And it made me fret and worry
When I found the moths were eating
    off my hair;
And I had to scrape and sand 'em
And I boiled 'em and I tanned 'em,
Till I got the fine morocco suit I wear.

I sometimes seek diversion
In a family excursion
With the few domestic animals you
    see;
And we take along a carrot
As refreshment for the parrot
And a little can of jungleberry tea.

Then we gather as we travel,
Bits of moss and dirty gravel,
And we chip off little specimens of
    stone;
And we carry home as prizes

Funny bugs, of handy sizes,
Just to give the day a scientific tone.

If the roads are wet and muddy
We remain at home and study—
For the Goat is very clever at a sum—
And the Dog, instead of fighting,
Studies ornamental writing,
While the Cat is taking lessons on the
    drum.

We retire at eleven,
And we rise again at seven;
And I wish to call attention, as I close,
To the fact that all the scholars
Are correct about their collars,
And particular in turning out their
    toes.

                    Charles Edward Carryl

A NAUTICAL BALLAD

A capital ship for an ocean trip,
    Was the Walloping Window-Blind;
No gale that blew dismayed her crew,
    Nor troubled the captain's mind.

The man at the wheel was taught to
    feel
    Contempt for the wildest blow;
And it often appeared—when the
    weather had cleared—
    He had been in his bunk below.

The boatswain's mate was very sedate,
    Yet fond of amusement too;
And he played hopscotch with the
    starboard watch,
    While the captain tickled the crew.

And the gunner we had was apparently
    mad,
    For he sat on the after-rail

And fired salutes with the captain's
  boots
In the teeth of the booming gale.

The captain sat on the commodore's
  hat,
And dined, in a royal way,
Off toasted pigs and pickles and figs
  And gummery bread each day.

The cook was Dutch and behaved as
  such,
For the diet he gave the crew,
Was a number of tons of hot-cross
  buns,
  Served up with sugar and glue.

All nautical pride we laid aside,
  And we cast our vessel ashore,
On the Gulliby Isles, where the Poo-
  Poo smiles
  And the Rumpletum-Bunders roar.

We sat on the edge of a sandy ledge,
  And shot at the whistling bee:
And the cinnamon bats wore water-
  proof hats,
  As they danced by the sounding sea.

On Rug-gub bark, from dawn till dark,
  We fed, till we all had grown
Uncommonly shrunk; when a Chinese
  junk
  Came in from the Torriby Zone.

She was stubby and square, but we
  didn't much care,
  So we cheerily put to sea;
And we left the crew of the junk to
  chew
  The bark of the Rug-gub tree.
                    Charles Edward Carryl

A TRAGIC STORY

There lived a sage in days of yore,
And he a handsome pigtail wore;
But wondered much, and sorrowed
  more,
  Because it hung behind him.

He mused upon this curious case,
And swore he'd change the pigtail's
  place,
And have it hanging at his face,
  Not dangling there behind him.

Says he, "The mystery I've found,—
I'll turn me round,"—he turned him
  round;
  But still it hung behind him.

Then round and round, and out and in,
All day the puzzled sage did spin;
In vain—it mattered not a pin—
  The pigtail hung behind him.

And right and left, and round about,
And up and down and in and out
He turned; but still the pigtail stout
  Hung steadily behind him.

And though his efforts never slack,
And though he twist, and twirl, and
  tack,
Alas! still faithful to his back,
  The pigtail hangs behind him.
*From the German of Chamisso, by
    William Makepeace Thackeray*

AN ELEGY ON THE DEATH OF
A MAD DOG

Good people all, of every sort,
  Give ear unto my song,
And if you find it wondrous short,
  It cannot hold you long.

In Islington there was a man
  Of whom the world might say,
That still a godly race he ran,
  Whene'er he went to pray.

A kind and gentle heart he had,
  To comfort friends and foes;
The naked every day he clad,
  When he put on his clothes.

And in that town a dog was found,
  As many dogs there be,
Both mongrel, puppy, whelp and
  hound
  And curs of low degree.

This dog and man at first were friends,
  But when a pique began,
The dog, to gain some private ends,
  Went mad and bit the man.

Around from all the neighboring streets
  The wondering neighbours ran,
And swore the dog had lost his wits,
  To bite so good a man.

The wound it seemed both sore and sad
  To every Christian eye;
And while they swore the dog was mad,
  They swore the man would die.

But soon a wonder came to light,
  That show'd the rogues they lied;
The man recovered of the bite
  The dog it was that died.

Oliver Goldsmith

THE TWINS

In form and feature, face and limb,
  I grew so like my brother,
That folks got taking me for him,
  And each for one another.
It puzzled all our kith and kin,

It reached a fearful pitch;
For one of us was born a twin,
  Yet not a soul knew which.

One day, to make the matter worse,
  Before our names were fixed,
As we were being washed by nurse,
  We got completely mixed;
And thus, you see, by fate's decree,
  Or rather nurse's whim,
My brother John got christened me,
And I got christened him.

This fatal likeness even dogged
  My footsteps when at school,
And I was always getting flogged,
  For John turned out a fool.
I put this question, fruitlessly,
  To everyone I knew,
" What *would* you do, if you were me,
  To prove that you were you? "

Our close resemblance turned the
  tide
  Of my domestic life,
For somehow, my intended bride
  Became my brother's wife.
In fact, year after year the same
  Absurd mistakes went on,
And when I died, the neighbors
  came
  And buried brother John.

Henry S. Leigh

A PLAIN DIRECTION

In London once I lost my way
  In faring to and fro,
And asked a little ragged boy
  The way that I should go;
He gave a nod and then a wink,
  And told me to get there
" Straight down the Crooked Lane,
  And all round the Square."

I boxed his little saucy ears,
And then away I strode;
But since I've found that weary path
Is quite a common road.
Utopia is a pleasant place,
But how shall I get there?
" Straight down the Crooked Lane,
And all round the Square."

I've read about a Fairy Land,
In some romantic tale,
Where dwarfs, if good, are sure to
thrive,
And wicked giants fail.
My wish is great, my shoes are
strong,
But how shall I get there?
" Straight down the Crooked Lane,
And all round the Square."

I've heard about a pleasant land,
Where omelettes grow on trees,
And roasted pigs run, crying out,
" Come eat me, if you please."
My appetite is rather keen,
But how shall I get there?
" Straight down the Crooked Lane,
And all round the Square."

They say there is a golden fair,
That's haunted by the dove,
Where love of gold doth ne'er eclipse
The golden light of love.
The place must be a paradise,
But how shall I get there?
" Straight down the Crooked Lane,
And all round the Square."

Thomas Hood

THE PRIEST AND THE MULBERRY-TREE

Did you hear of the curate who
mounted his mare,

And merrily trotted along to the fair?
Of creature more tractable none ever
heard;
In the height of her speed she would
stop at a word;
But again with a word, when the
curate said " Hey! "
She put forth her mettle and galloped away.

As near to the gates of the city he
rode,
While the sun of September all bril-
liantly glowed,
The good priest discovered, with
eyes of desire,
A mulberry-tree in a hedge of wild
brier;
On boughs long and lofty, in many
a green shoot,
Hung large, black, and glossy, the
beautiful fruit.

The curate was hungry and thirsty
to boot;
He shrunk from the thorns, though
he longed for the fruit;
With a word he arrested his courser's
keen speed,
And he stood up erect on the back
of his steed;
On the saddle he stood while the
creature stood still,
And he gather'd the fruit till he took
his good fill.

" Sure never," he thought, " was a
creature so rare,
So docile, so true, as my excellent
mare;
Lo, here now I stand," and he gazed
all around,
" As safe and as steady as if on the
ground;

Yet how had it been, if some traveller this way
Had, dreaming no mischief, but
chanced to cry 'Hey'?"

He stood with his head in the mul-
berry-tree,
And he spoke out aloud in his fond
reverie.
At the sound of the word the good
mare made a push,
And down went the priest in the
wild-brier bush,
He remember'd too late, on his
thorny green bed,
MUCH THAT WELL MAY BE THOUGHT
CANNOT BE WISELY SAID.

Thomas Love Peacock

DISPUTE BETWEEN NOSE AND EYES

Between Nose and Eyes a strange
contest arose,
The spectacles set them unhappily
wrong;
The point in dispute was, as all the
world knows,
To which the said spectacles ought
to belong.

So Tongue was the lawyer, and argued the cause
With a great deal of skill, and a
wig full of learning,
While chief Baron Ear, sat to balance the laws,
So famed for his talent, in nicely
discerning.

" In behalf of the Nose, it will quickly
appear,
And your lordship," he said, " will
undoubtedly find

That the Nose has had spectacles always in wear,
Which amounts to possession,—
time out of mind."

Then holding the Spectacles up to
the court—
" Your lordship observes they are
made with a straddle,
As wide as the ridge of the Nose is—
in short,
Designed to sit close to it, just like
a saddle.

" Again, would your lordship a moment suppose
('Tis a case that has happened,
and may be again),
That the visage or countenance had
not a nose,
Pray who would, or who could,
wear spectacles then?

" On the whole it appears, and my
argument shows
With a reasoning the court will
never condemn,
That the spectacles plainly were
made for the nose,
And the nose was as plainly intended for them."

Then shifting his side (as a lawyer
knows how)
He pleaded again in behalf of the
Eyes;
But what were his arguments few
people know,
For the court did not think they
were equally wise.

So his lordship decreed with a grave
solemn tone,
Decisive and clear, without one
" if " or " but,"

That, whenever the Nose put his
    spectacles on,
     By day-light or candle-light, Eyes
      should be shut.

              William Cowper

THE LOBSTER AND THE MAID

He was a gentle lobster
  (The boats had just come in),
He did not love the fishermen,
  He could not stand their din;
And so he quietly stole off,
  As if it were no sin.

She was a little maiden,
  He met her on the sand,
" And how d'you do? " the lobster
    said,
  " Why don't you give your
    hand? "
For why she edged away from him
  He *could* not understand.

" Excuse me, sir," the maiden said:
  " Excuse me, if you please,"
And put her hands behind her back,
  And doubled up her knees;
" I always thought that lobsters were
  A little apt to squeeze."

" Your ignorance," the lobster said,
  " Is natural, I fear;
Such scandal is a shame," he sobbed,
  " It is not true, my dear,"
And with his pocket-handkerchief
  He wiped away a tear.

So out she put her little hand,
  As though she feared him not,
When someone grabbed him sud-
    denly
  And put him in a pot,
With water which, I think he found
  Uncomfortably hot.

It may have been the water made
  The blood flow to his head,
It may have been that dreadful fib
  Lay on his soul like lead;
This much is true—he went in grey,
  And came out very red.

        Frederick Edward Weatherly

THE DEACON'S MASTERPIECE, OR THE WONDERFUL " ONE-HOSS SHAY "

Have you heard of the wonderful
  one-hoss shay,
That was built in such a logical way
It ran a hundred years to a day,
And then of a sudden, it—ah, but
  stay,
I'll tell you what happened without
  delay,
Scaring the parson into fits,
Frightening people out of their
  wits,—
Have you heard of that, I say?

Seventeen hundred and fifty-five,
Georgius Secundus was then alive,—
Snuffy old drone from the German
  hive.
That was the year when Lisbon-town
Saw the earth open and gulp her
  down,
And Braddock's army was done so
  brown,
Left without a scalp to its crown.
It was on the terrible Earthquake-day
That the Deacon finished the one-
  hoss shay.

Now in building of chaises, I tell you
  what,
There is always *somewhere* a weakest
  spot,—
In hub, tire, felloe, in spring or thill,

In panel, or crossbar, or floor, or sill,
In screw, bolt, thoroughbrace,—lurking still,
Find it somewhere you must and
  will,—
Above or below, or within or without,—
And that's the reason, beyond a
  doubt,
That a chaise *breaks down,* but
  doesn't *wear out.*

But the Deacon swore (as Deacons
  do,
With an " I dew vum," or an " I tell
  yeou ")
He would build one shay to beat the
  taown
'N' the keounty 'n' all the kentry
  raoun';
It should be so built that it *couldn'*
  break daown:
" Fur," said the Deacon, " 't's mighty
  plain
Thut the weakes' place mus' stan'
  the strain;
'N' the way t' fix it, uz I maintain,
            Is only jest
'T make that place uz strong uz the
  rest."

So the Deacon inquired of the village folk
Where he could find the strongest
  oak,
That couldn't be split nor bent nor
  broke,—
That was for spokes and floor and
  sills;
He sent for lancewood to make the
  thills;
The crossbars were ash, from the
  straightest trees,
The panels of white-wood, that cuts
  like cheese,

But lasts like iron for things like
  these;
The hubs of logs from the " Settler's
  ellum,"—
Last of its timber,—they couldn't sell
  'em,
Never an axe had seen their chips,
And the wedges flew from between
  their lips,
Their blunt ends frizzled like celery-
  tips;
Step and prop-iron, bolt and screw,
Spring, tire, axle, and linchpin too,
Steel of the finest, bright and blue;
Thoroughbrace bison-skin, thick and
  wide;
Boot, top, dasher, from tough old
  hide
Found in the pit when the tanner
  died.
That was the way he " put her
  through."
" There! " said the Deacon, " naow
  she'll dew! "

Do! I tell you, I rather guess
She was a wonder, and nothing less!
Colts grew horses, beards turned
  gray,
Deacon and deaconess dropped
  away,
Children and grandchildren—where
  were they?
But there stood the stout old one-
  hoss shay
As fresh as on Lisbon-earthquake
  day!

EIGHTEEN HUNDRED;—it came and
  found
The Deacon's masterpiece strong
  and sound.
Eighteen hundred increased by ten;
" Hahnsum kerridge " they called it
  then.

Eighteen hundred a n d twenty
  came;—
Running as usual; much the same.
Thirty and Forty at last arrive,
And then come Fifty, and FIFTY-
  FIVE.

Little of all we value here
Wakes on the morn of its hundredth
  year
Without both feeling and looking
  queer.
In fact, there's nothing that keeps its
  youth,
So far as I know, but a tree and
  truth.
(This is a moral that runs at large;
Take it.—You're welcome.—No extra
  charge.)

FIRST OF NOVEMBER,—the Earth-
  quake-day,—
There are traces of age in the one-
  hoss shay.
A general flavor of mild decay,
But nothing local, as one may say.
There couldn't be,—for the Deacon's
  art
Had made it so like in every part
That there wasn't a chance for one
  to start.
For the wheels were just as strong as
  the thills,
And the floor was just as strong as
  the sills,
And the panels just as strong as the
  floor,
And the whipple-tree neither less nor
  more,
And the back-crossbar as strong as
  the fore,
And spring and axle and hub encore.
And yet, as a whole, it is past a
  doubt
In another hour it will be worn out!

First of November, Fifty-five!
This morning the parson takes a
  drive.
Now, small boys, get out of the way!
Here comes the wonderful one-hoss
  shay,
Drawn by a rat-tailed, ewe-necked
  bay.
"Huddup!" said the parson.—Off
  went they.

The parson was working his Sunday's
  text,—
Had got to *fifthly*, and stopped per-
  plexed
At what the—Moses—was coming
  next.
All at once the horse stood still,
Close by the meet'n'-house on the
  hill;
First a shiver, and then a thrill,
Then something decidedly like a
  spill,—
And the parson was sitting upon a
  rock,
At half-past nine by the meet'n'-
  house clock,—
Just the hour of the Earthquake
  shock!
What do you think the parson
  found,
When he got up and stared around?
The poor old chaise in a heap or
  mound,
As if it had been to the mill and
  ground!
You see, of course, if you're not a
  dunce,
How it went to pieces all at once,—
All at once, and nothing first,—
Just as bubbles do when they burst.

End of the wonderful one-hoss shay.
Logic is logic. That's all I say.
                    Oliver Wendell Holmes

Part Eight

HOLIDAY POETRY

EVERYWHERE, EVERYWHERE CHRISTMAS TONIGHT

Christmas in lands of the fir tree and
pine,
Christmas in lands of the palm tree
and vine;
Christmas where snow peaks stand
solemn and white,
Christmas where corn-fields lie sunny
and bright;
Everywhere, everywhere Christmas
tonight!

Christmas where children are hope-
ful and gay,
Christmas where old men are patient
and gray,
Christmas where peace, like a dove
in its flight,
Broods o'er brave men in the thick
of the fight;
Everywhere, everywhere Christmas
tonight!

For the Christ-child who comes is
the Master of all;
No palace too great—no cottage too
small.

The angels who welcome Him sing
from the height,
" In the city of David a King in His
might."
Everywhere, everywhere Christmas
tonight!

Then let every heart keep its Christ-
mas within
Christ's pity for sorrow, Christ's
hatred of sin,
Christ's care for the weakest, Christ's
courage for right,
Christ's dread of the darkness,
Christ's love of the light,
Everywhere, everywhere Christmas
tonight!

So the stars of the midnight which
compass us round,
Shall see a strange glory and hear a
sweet sound,
And cry, " Look! the earth is aflame
with delight,
O sons of the morning rejoice at the
sight."
Everywhere, everywhere Christmas
tonight!

Phillips Brooks

463

BEFORE THE PALING OF THE STARS

Before the paling of the stars,
  Before the winter morn,
Before the earliest cockcrow,
  Jesus Christ was born:
Born in a stable,
Cradled in a manger,
In the world His hands had made
  Born a stranger.

Priest and king lay fast asleep
  In Jerusalem,
Young and old lay fast asleep
  In crowded Bethlehem;
Saint and Angel, ox and ass,
  Kept a watch together
Before the Christmas daybreak
  In the winter weather.

Jesus on His mother's breast
  In the stable cold,
Spotless Lamb of God was He,
  Shepherd of the fold:
Let us kneel with Mary maid,
  With Joseph bent and hoary,
With Saint and Angel, ox and ass,
  To hail the King of Glory.
            Christina Rossetti

THE PEACE-GIVER

Thou whose birth on earth
  Angels sang to men,
While Thy stars made mirth,
Saviour, at Thy birth.
  This day born again;

As this night was bright
  With Thy cradle-ray,
Very Light of Light,
Turn the wild world's night
  To Thy perfect day.

Thou the Word and Lord
  In all time and space
Heard, beheld, adored,
With all ages poured
  Forth before Thy face,

Lord, what worth in earth
  Drew Thee down to die?
What therein was worth,
Lord, Thy death and birth?
  What beneath Thy sky?

Thou whose face gives grace
  As the sun's doth heat,
Let Thy sunbright face
Lighten time and space
  Here beneath Thy feet.

Bid our peace increase,
  Thou that madest morn;
Bid oppression cease;
Bid the night be peace;
  Bid the day be born.
        Algernon Charles Swinburne

LONG, LONG AGO

Winds thro' the olive trees
  Softly did blow,
Round little Bethlehem
  Long, long ago.

Sheep on the hillside lay
  Whiter than snow;
Shepherds were watching them,
  Long, long ago.

Then from the happy sky,
  Angels bent low,
Singing their songs of joy,
  Long, long ago.

For in a manger bed,
  Cradles we know,

Christ came to Bethlehem,
Long, long ago.

Unknown

HYMN FOR CHRISTMAS
(Selected Stanzas)

Oh! lovely voices of the sky
  Which hymned the Saviour's birth,
Are ye not singing still on high,
  Ye that sang, " Peace on earth "?
    To us yet speak the strains
      Wherewith, in time gone by,
    Ye blessed the Syrian swains,
      Oh! voices of the sky!

Oh! clear and shining light, whose
    beams
  That hour Heaven's glory shed,
Around the palms, and o'er the
    streams,
  And on the shepherd's head.
    Be near, through life and death,
      As in that holiest night
    Of hope, and joy, and faith—
      Oh! clear and shining light!

Felicia Hemans

O LITTLE TOWN OF BETHLEHEM

O little town of Bethlehem,
  How still we see thee lie!
Above thy deep and dreamless sleep
  The silent stars go by;
Yet in thy dark streets shineth
  The everlasting Light;
The hopes and fears of all the years
  Are met in thee tonight.

For Christ is born of Mary,
  And, gathered all above,
While mortals sleep, the angels keep
  Their watch of wondering love.

O morning stars, together
  Proclaim the holy birth!
And praises sing to God the King,
  And peace to men on earth.

How silently, how silently,
  The wondrous gift is given!
So God imparts to human hearts
  The blessings of His heaven.
No ear may hear His coming,
  But in this world of sin,
Where meek souls will receive Him
    still,
  The dear Christ enters in.

O holy Child of Bethlehem!
  Descend to us, we pray;
Cast out our sin, and enter in,
  Be born in us today.
We hear the Christmas angels
  The great tidings tell;
Oh, come to us, abide with us,
  Our Lord Emmanuel!

Phillips Brooks

THE FIRST NOWELL

The first Nowell the angel did say,
Was to certain poor shepherds in fields
  as they lay;
In fields where they lay keeping their
  sheep,
On a cold winter's night that was so
  deep.
    Nowell, Nowell, Nowell, Nowell,
    Born is the King of Israel.

They lookèd up and saw a Star
Shining in the East, beyond them far,
And to the earth it gave great light,
And so it continued both day and
  night.
    Nowell, Nowell, Nowell, Nowell,
    Born is the King of Israel.

And by the light of that same Star,
Three Wise Men came from country far;
To seek for a King was their intent,
And to follow the Star wherever it went.
    Nowell, Nowell, Nowell, Nowell,
    Born is the King of Israel.

This Star drew nigh to the northwest,
O'er Bethlehem it took its rest,
And there it did both stop and stay,
Right over the place where Jesus lay.
    Nowell, Nowell, Nowell, Nowell,
    Born is the King of Israel.

Then entered in those Wise Men three,
Full reverently upon their knee,
And offered there, in His presence,
Their gold, and myrrh, and frankincense.
    Nowell, Nowell, Nowell, Nowell,
    Born is the King of Israel.

Then let us all with one accord
Sing praises to our heavenly Lord,
That hath made heaven and earth of nought,
And with His blood mankind hath bought.
    Nowell, Nowell, Nowell, Nowell,
    Born is the King of Israel.

Unknown

IT CAME UPON THE MIDNIGHT CLEAR

It came upon the midnight clear,
    That glorious song of old,
From angels bending near the earth
    To touch their harps of gold;

Peace on earth, good-will to men,
    From heaven's all-gracious King;

The world in solemn stillness lay
    To hear the angels sing.

E. H. Sears

HARK, THE HERALD ANGELS SING

Hark, the herald angels sing,
" Glory to the new-born King;
Peace on earth, and mercy mild,
God and sinners reconciled."

Joyful all ye nations rise,
Join the triumph of the skies;
With the angelic host proclaim,
" Christ is born in Bethlehem! "

Hark, the herald angels sing,
" Glory to the new-born King! "

Charles Wesley

GOD REST YE MERRY, GENTLEMEN

God rest ye merry, gentlemen; let nothing you dismay,
For Jesus Christ, our Saviour, was born on Christmas-day.
The dawn rose red o'er Bethlehem, the stars shone through the gray,
When Jesus Christ, our Saviour, was born on Christmas-day.

God rest ye, little children; let nothing you affright,
For Jesus Christ, your Saviour, was born this happy night;
Along the hills of Galilee the white flocks sleeping lay,
When Christ, the child of Nazareth, was born on Christmas-day.

God rest ye, all good Christians; upon this blessèd morn

The Lord of all good Christians was
of a woman born:
Now all your sorrows He doth heal,
your sins He takes away;
For Jesus Christ, our Saviour, was born
on Christmas-day.

Dinah M. Mulock Craik

CHRISTMAS CAROL

As Joseph was a-walking,
He heard an angel sing,
" This night shall be the birthright
Of Christ our heavenly King.

" His birth-bed shall be neither
In housen nor in hall,
Nor in the place of paradise,
But in the oxen's stall.

" He neither shall be rockèd
In silver nor in gold,
But in the wooden manger
That lieth in the mould.

" He neither shall be washen
With white wine nor with red,
But with the fair spring water
That on you shall be shed.

" He neither shall be clothèd
In purple nor in pall,
But in the fair, white linen
That usen babies all."

As Joseph was a-walking,
Thus did the angel sing,
And Mary's son at midnight
Was born to be our King.

Then be you glad, good people,
At this time of the year;
And light you up your candles,
For His star it shineth clear.

Unknown

WHILE SHEPHERDS WATCHED THEIR FLOCKS BY NIGHT

While shepherds watched their
flocks by night
All seated on the ground,
The angel of the Lord came down,
And glory shone around.

" Fear not," said he; for mighty dread
Had seized their troubled mind:
" Glad tidings of great joy I bring
To you and all mankind.

" To you in David's town this day
Is born of David's line
A Saviour, who is Christ the Lord,
And this shall be the sign.

" The heavenly Babe you there shall
find
To human view displayed,
All meanly wrapped in swathing
bands,
And in a manger laid."

Thus spoke the seraph; and forth-
with
Appeared a shining throng
Of angels, praising God, who thus
Addressed their joyful song:

" All glory be to God on high,
And on the earth be peace;
Good-will henceforth from heaven
to men
Begin and never cease."

Nahum Tate

BRIGHTEST AND BEST OF THE SONS OF THE MORNING

Brightest and best of the sons of the
morning,

Dawn on our darkness, and lend us
　thine aid!
Star of the East, the horizon adorn-
　ing,
　Guide where our infant Redeemer
　is laid!

Cold on His cradle the dewdrops are
　shining,
　Low lies His head with the beasts
　of the stall;
Angels adore Him, in slumber reclin-
　ing,
　Maker, and Monarch, and Saviour
　of all!

Offer Him gifts then, in costly devo-
　tion,
　Odors of Edom and incense divine;
Gems of the mountain, and pearls of
　the ocean,
　Myrrh from the forest, and gold
　from the mine.

Vainly we offer each ample oblation,
　Vainly with gold would His favor
　secure;
Richer by far is the heart's adoration,
　Dearer to God are the prayers of the
　poor.

Reginald Heber

ONCE IN ROYAL DAVID'S CITY

Once in royal David's city
　Stood a lowly cattle shed,
Where a Mother laid her baby
　In a manger for His bed;
Mary was that Mother mild,
Jesus Christ her little child.

He came down to earth from heaven,
　Who is God and Lord of all,

And His shelter was a stable,
　And His cradle was a stall,
With the poor, and mean, and lowly
Lived on earth our Saviour Holy.

And through all His wondrous child-
　hood,
　He would honor and obey,
Love and watch the lowly Maiden,
　In whose gentle arms He lay;
Christian children all must be
Mild, obedient, good as He.

For He is our childhood's pattern,
　Day by day like us He grew,
He was little, weak, and helpless,
　Tears and smiles like us He knew;
And He feeleth for our sadness,
And He shareth in our gladness.

And our eyes at last shall see Him,
　Through His own redeeming love,
For that Child so dear and gentle
　Is our Lord in heaven above;
And He leads His children on
To the place where He has gone.

Not in that poor lowly stable,
　With the oxen standing by,
We shall see Him; but in heaven,
　Set at God's right hand on high,
When like stars His children crowned
All in white shall wait around.

Cecil Frances Alexander

A CHRISTMAS HYMN

It was the calm and silent night!
　Seven hundred years and fifty-three
Had Rome been growing up to might,
　And now was queen of land and sea.
No sound was heard of clashing wars—
　Peace brooded o'er the hushed do-
　main:

Apollo, Pallas, Jove and Mars
 Held undisturbed their ancient
  reign,
   In the solemn midnight,
    Centuries ago.

'Twas in the calm and silent night!
 The senator of haughty Rome,
Impatient, urged his chariot's flight,
 From lordly revel rolling home;
Triumphal arches, gleaming, swell
 His breast with thoughts of bound-
  less sway;
What recked the Romans what befell
 A paltry province far away,
   In the solemn midnight,
    Centuries ago.

Within that province far away
 Went plodding home a weary boor;
A streak of light before him lay,
 Falling through a half-shut stable-
  door
Across his path. He passed—for naught
 Told what was going on within;
How keen the stars, his only thought—
 The air how calm, and cold, and
  thin,
   In the solemn midnight,
    Centuries ago.

Oh, strange indifference! low and high
 Drowsed over common joys and
  cares;
The earth was still—but knew not why,
 The world was listening, unawares.
How calm a moment may precede
 One that shall thrill the world for-
  ever!
To that still moment, none would
  heed,
 Man's doom was linked no more to
  sever—
   In the solemn midnight,
    Centuries ago.

It is the calm and solemn night!
 A thousand bells ring out, and throw
Their joyous peals abroad, and smite
 The darkness—charmed and holy
  now!
The night that erst no name had worn,
 To it a happy name is given;
For in that stable lay, new-born,
 The peaceful prince of earth and
  heaven,
   In the solemn midnight,
    Centuries ago.
     Alfred Domett

CHRISTMAS IN THE OLDEN TIME

Heap on more wood!—the wind is
 chill;
But let it whistle as it will,
We'll keep our Christmas merry still.

 Each age has deem'd the new-born
  year
The fittest time for festal cheer:
And well our Christian sires of old
Loved when the year its course had
 roll'd,
And brought blithe Christmas back
 again,
With all his hospitable train.
Domestic and religious rite
Gave honour to the holy night;
On Christmas Eve the bells were
 rung;
On Christmas Eve the mass was sung:
That only night in all the year,
Saw the stoled priest the chalice rear.
The damsel donn'd her kirtle sheen;
The hall was dress'd with holly green;
Forth to the wood did merry-men go,
To gather in the mistletoe.
Then open'd wide the Baron's hall
To vassal, tenant, serf, and all;

Power laid his rod of rule aside,
And Ceremony doff'd his pride.
The heir, with roses in his shoes,
That night might village partner
    choose;
The lord, underogating, share
The vulgar game of "post and pair."
All hail'd, with uncontroll'd delight
And general voice, the happy night,
That to the cottage, as the Crown,
Brought tidings of salvation down.

    The fire, with well-dried logs sup-
    plied,
Went roaring up the chimney wide;
The huge hall-table's oaken face,
Scrubb'd till it shone, the day to grace,
Bore then upon its massive board
No mark to part the squire and lord.
Then was brought in the lusty brawn,
By old blue-coated serving-man;
Then the grim boar's head frown'd on
    high,
Crested with bays and rosemary.
Well can the green-garb'd ranger tell,
How, when, and where, the monster
    fell;
What dogs before his death he tore,
And all the baiting of the boar.
The wassail round, in good brown
    bowls,
Garnish'd with ribbons, blithely trowls.
There the huge sirloin reek'd; hard by
Plum-porridge stood, and Christmas
    pie;
Nor fail'd old Scotland to produce,
At such high tide, her savoury goose.
Then came the merry maskers in,
And carols roar'd with blithesome din;
If unmelodious was the song,
It was a hearty note, and strong.
Who lists may in their mumming see
Traces of ancient mystery;
White shirts supplied the masquerade,

And smutted cheeks the visors made;—
But, O! what maskers, richly dight,
Can boast of bosoms half so light!
England was merry England, when
Old Christmas brought his sports
    again.
'Twas Christmas broach'd the mighti-
    est ale;
'Twas Christmas told the merriest
    tale;
A Christmas gambol oft could cheer
The poor man's heart through half the
    year.

Walter Scott

GOOD KING WENCESLAS

Good King Wenceslas looked out
    On the Feast of Stephen,
When the snow lay round about,
    Deep, and crisp, and even.
Brightly shone the moon that night,
    Though the frost was cruel,
When a poor man came in sight,
    Gath'ring winter fuel.

" Hither, page, and stand by me,
    If thou know'st it, telling,
Yonder peasant, who is he?
    Where and what his dwelling? "
" Sire, he lives a good league hence,
    Underneath the mountain;
Right against the forest fence,
    By Saint Agnes' fountain."

" Bring me flesh, and bring me wine,
    Bring me pine-logs hither:
Thou and I will see him dine,
    When we bear them thither."
Page and monarch, forth they went,
    Forth they went together;
Through the rude wind's wild lament
    And the bitter weather.

" Sire, the night is darker now,
 And the wind blows stronger;
Fails my heart, I know not how,
 I can go no longer."
" Mark my footsteps, good my page;
 Tread thou in them boldly:
Thou shalt find the winter rage
 Freeze thy blood less coldly."

In his master's steps he trod,
 Where the snow lay dinted;
Heat was in the very sod
 Which the saint had printed.
Therefore, Christian men be sure,
 Wealth or rank possessing,
Ye who now will bless the poor,
 Shall yourselves find blessing.

    John Neal

CHRISTMAS AT SEA

The sheets were frozen hard, and
 they cut the naked hand;
The decks were like a slide, where a
 seaman scarce could stand,
The wind was nor'-wester, blowing
 squally off the sea;
And cliffs and spouting breakers
 were the only things a-lee.

They heard the surf a-roaring before
 the break of day:
But 'twas only with the peep of light
 we saw how ill we lay.
We tumbled every hand on deck in-
 stanter, with a shout,
And we gave her the maintops'l, and
 stood by to go about.

All day we tacked and tacked between the South Head and the
 North;
All day we hauled the frozen sheets,
 and got no further forth;

All day as cold as charity, in bitter
 pain and dread,
For very life and nature we tacked
 from head to head.

We gave the South a wider berth,
 for there the tide-race roared;
But every tack we made we brought
 the North Head close aboard;
So's we saw the cliffs and houses,
 and the breakers running high,
And the coastguard in his garden,
 with his glass against his eye.

The bells upon the church were rung
 with a mighty jovial cheer;
For it's just that I should tell you
 how (of all days in the year)
This day of our adversity was blessèd
 Christmas morn,
And the house above the coastguard's was the house where I was
 born.

O well I saw the pleasant room, the
 pleasant faces there,
My mother's silver spectacles, my
 father's silver hair;
And well I saw the firelight, like a
 flight of homely elves
Go dancing round the china-plates
 that stand upon the shelves!

And well I know the talk they had,
 the talk that was of me,
Of the shadow on the household and
 the sun that went to sea;
And O the wicked fool I seemed, in
 every kind of way,
To be here and hauling frozen rope
 on blessèd Christmas Day.

They lit the high sea-light, and the
 dark began to fall.

"All hands to loose topgallant sails!"
　　I heard the captain call.
"By the Lord, she'll never stand it,"
　　our first mate Jackson cried.
　. . . "It's the one way or the other,
　　Mr. Jackson," he replied.

She staggered to her bearings, but
　　the sails were new and good,
And the ship smelt up to windward
　　just as though she understood.
As the winter's day was ending, in
　　the entry of the night,
We cleared the weary headland, and
　　passed below the light.

And they heaved a mighty breath,
　　every soul on board but me,
And they saw her nose again point-
　　ing handsome out to sea;
But all that I could think of, in the
　　darkness and the cold,
Was just that I was leaving home
　　and my folks were growing old.

　　　　　Robert Louis Stevenson

THE CHRISTMAS HOLLY

The holly! the holly! oh, twine it with
　　bay—
Come give the holly a song;
For it helps to drive stern winter away,
　　With his garment so sombre and
　　long;
It peeps through the trees with its ber-
　　ries of red,
　　And its leaves of burnished green,
When the flowers and fruits have long
　　been dead,
　　And not even the daisy is seen.
Then sing to the holly, the Christmas
　　holly,
　　That hangs over peasant and king;

While we laugh and carouse 'neath its
　　glittering boughs,
　　To the Christmas holly we'll sing.
　　　　　Eliza Cook

JEST 'FORE CHRISTMAS

Father calls me William, sister calls
　　me Will,
Mother calls me Willie, but the fellers
　　call me Bill!
Mighty glad I ain't a girl—ruther be
　　boy,
Without them sashes, curls, an' things
　　what's worn by Fauntleroy!
Love to chawnk green apples an' go
　　swimmin' in the lake—
Hate to take the castor-ile they give
　　for belly-ache!
'Most all the time, the whole year
　　round, there ain't no flies on me,
But jest 'fore Christmas I'm as good as
　　I kin be!

Got a yeller dog named Sport, sick
　　him on the cat;
First thing she knows she doesn't know
　　where she is at;
Got a clipper sled, an' when us kids
　　goes out to slide,
'Long comes the grocery cart, an' we
　　all hook a ride!
But sometimes when the grocery man
　　is worrited an' cross,
He reaches at us with his whip, an'
　　larrups up his hoss,
An' then I laff an' holler, "Oh, ye
　　never teched *me!*"
But jest 'fore Christmas I'm as good
　　as I kin be!

Gran'ma says she hopes that when I
　　git to be a man,

I'll be a missionarer like her oldest
brother, Dan,
As was et up by the cannibuls that
lives in Ceylon's Isle,
Where every prospeck pleases, an' only
man is vile!
But gran'ma she has never been to see
a Wild West show,
Nor read the Life of Daniel Boone, or
else I guess she'd know
That Buff'lo Bill and cowboys is good
enough for me!
Excep' jest 'fore Christmas, when I'm
good as I kin be!

And then old Sport he hangs around,
so solemn-like an' still,
His eyes they keep a-sayin': " What's
the matter, little Bill? "
The old cat sneaks down off her perch
an' wonders what's become
Of them two enemies of hern that
used to make things hum!
But I am so perlite an' 'tend so ear-
nestly to biz,
That mother says to father: " How im-
proved our Willie is! "
But father, havin' been a boy hisself,
suspicions me
When, jest 'fore Christmas, I'm as
good as I kin be!

For Christmas, with its lots an' lots
of candies, cakes, an' toys,
Was made, they say, for proper kids
an' not for naughty boys;
So wash yer face an' bresh yer hair,
an' mind yer p's an' q's,
An' don't bust out yer pantaloons, an'
don't wear out yer shoes;
Say " Yessum " to the ladies, an' " Yes-
sur " to the men,
An' when they's company, don't pass
yer plate for pie again;

But, thinkin' of the things yer'd like to
see upon that tree,
Jest 'fore Christmas be as good as yer
kin be!

Eugene Field

PRAYER

Last night I crept across the snow,
Where only tracking rabbits go,
And then I waited quite alone
Until the Christmas radiance shone!

At midnight twenty angels came,
Each white and shining like a flame.
At midnight twenty angels sang,
The stars swung out like bells and
rang.

They lifted me across the hill,
They bore me in their arms until
A greater glory greeted them.
It was the town of Bethlehem.

And gently, then, they set me down,
All worshipping that holy town,
And gently, then, they bade me raise
My head to worship and to praise.

And gently, then, the Christ smiled
down.
Ah, there was glory in that town!
It was as if the world were free
And glistening with purity.

And in that vault of crystal blue,
It was as if the world were new,
And myriad angels, file on file,
Gloried in the Christ-Child's smile.

It was so beautiful to see
Such glory, for a child like me,
So beautiful, it does not seem
It could have been a Christmas dream.

John Farrar

THE FIRST CHRISTMAS

And there were in the same country shepherds abiding in the field, keeping watch over their flock by night.

And, lo, the angel of the Lord came upon them, and the glory of the Lord shone round about them: and they were sore afraid.

And the angel said unto them, Fear not: for, behold, I bring you good tidings of great joy, which shall be to all people.

For unto you is born this day in the city of David a Saviour, which is Christ the Lord.

And this shall be a sign unto you; Ye shall find the babe wrapped in swaddling clothes, lying in a manger.

And suddenly there was with the angel a multitude of the heavenly host praising God, and saying,

Glory to God in the highest, and on earth peace, good will toward men.

And it came to pass, as the angels were gone away from them into heaven, the shepherds said one to another, Let us now go even unto Bethlehem, and see this thing which is come to pass, which the Lord hath made known unto us.

And they came with haste, and found Mary, and Joseph, and the babe lying in a manger.

St. Luke 2: 8–16—The Bible

THE OXEN

Christmas Eve, and twelve of the clock.
" Now they are all on their knees,"
An elder said as we sat in a flock
By the embers in hearthside ease.

We pictured the meek mild creatures where
They dwelt in their strawy pen,
Nor did it occur to one of us there
To doubt they were kneeling then.

So fair a fancy few would weave
In these years! Yet, I feel,
If someone said on Christmas Eve,
" Come; see the oxen kneel

" In the lonely barton by yonder coomb
Our children used to know,"
I should go with him in the gloom,
Hoping it might be so.

Thomas Hardy

New Year's Day

DEATH OF THE OLD YEAR

Full knee-deep lies the winter snow,
And the winter winds are wearily sighing:
Toll ye the church-bell sad and slow,
And tread softly and speak low,
For the Old Year lies a-dying.

Old Year, you must not die;
You came to us so readily,
You lived with us so steadily,
Old Year, you shall not die.

He lieth still; he doth not move;
He will not see the dawn of day.
He hath no other life above.
He gave me a friend, and a true true-love,
And the New Year will take 'em away.

Old Year, you must not go;
So long as you have been with us,

Such joy as you have seen with us,
Old Year, you shall not go.

He froth'd his bumpers to the brim;
A jollier year we shall not see.
But tho' his eyes are waxing dim,
And tho' his foes speak ill of him,
He was a friend to me.

Old Year, you shall not die;
We did so laugh and cry with you,
I've half a mind to die with you,
Old Year, if you must die.

He was full of joke and jest,
But all his merry quips are o'er.
To see him die, across the waste
His son and heir doth ride post-haste,
But he'll be dead before.

Every one for his own.
The night is starry and cold, my
friend,
And the New Year blithe and bold,
my friend,
Comes up to take his own.

How hard he breathes! over the snow
I heard just now the crowing cock.
The shadows flicker to and fro;
The cricket chirps; the light burns low;
'Tis nearly twelve o'clock.

Shake hands before you die.
Old Year, we'll dearly rue for you;
What is it we can do for you?
Speak out before you die.

His face is growing sharp and thin,
Alack! our friend is gone.
Close up his eyes; tie up his chin;
Step from the corpse, and let him in
That standeth there alone,

And waiteth at the door.
There's a new foot on the floor, my
friend,
And a new face at the door, my
friend,
A new face at the door.

Alfred Tennyson

RING OUT WILD BELLS

Ring out wild bells to the wild sky,
The flying cloud, the frosty light;
The year is dying in the night;
Ring out, wild bells, and let him die.

Ring out the old, ring in the new,
Ring, happy bells, across the snow;
The year is going, let him go;
Ring out the false, ring in the true.

Ring out the grief that saps the mind
For those that here we see no more;
Ring out the feud of rich and poor,
Ring in redress to all mankind.

Ring out a slowly dying cause,
And ancient forms of party strife;
Ring in the nobler modes of life,
With sweeter manners, purer laws.

Ring out the want, the care, the sin,
The faithless coldness of the times;
Ring out, ring out my mournful
rhymes,
But ring the fuller minstrel in.

Ring out false pride in place and blood,
The civic slander and the spite;
Ring in the love of truth and right,
Ring in the common love of good.

Ring out old shapes of foul disease,
Ring out the narrowing lust of gold;
Ring out the thousand wars of old,
Ring in the thousand years of peace.

Ring in the valiant man and free,
The larger heart, the kindlier hand;
Ring out the darkness of the land,
Ring in the Christ that is to be.

Alfred Tennyson

Lincoln's Birthday

ABRAHAM LINCOLN

This man whose homely face you look
upon,
Was one of nature's masterful, great
men;
Born with strong arms, that unfought
battles won;
Direct of speech, and cunning with
the pen.
Chosen for large designs, he had the
art
Of winning with his humor, and he
went
Straight to his mark, which was the
human heart;
Wise, too, for what he could not
break he bent.
Upon his back a more than Atlas-load,
The burden of the Commonwealth,
was laid;
He stooped, and rose up to it, though
the road
Shot suddenly downwards, not a
whit dismayed.
Hold, warriors, councillors, kings! All
now give place
To this dear benefactor of the race.

Richard Henry Stoddard

O CAPTAIN! MY CAPTAIN!

O Captain! my Captain! our fearful
trip is done,
The ship has weather'd every rack, the
prize we sought is won,

The port is near, the bells I hear, the
people all exulting,
While follow eyes the steady keel, the
vessel grim and daring;
But O heart! heart! heart!
O the bleeding drops of red,
Where on the deck my Captain
lies,
Fallen cold and dead.

O Captain! my Captain! rise up and
hear the bells:
Rise up—for you the flag is flung—for
you the bugle trills,
For you bouquets and ribbon'd wreaths
—for you the shores a-crowding,
For you they call, the swaying mass,
their eager faces turning;
Here, Captain! dear father!
This arm beneath your head!
It is some dream that on the deck
You've fallen cold and dead.

My Captain does not answer, his lips
are pale and still,
My father does not feel my arm, he has
no pulse nor will,
The ship is anchor'd safe and sound,
its voyage closed and done,
From fearful trip the victor ship comes
in with object won;
Exult O shores! and ring, O bells!
But I with mournful tread,
Walk the deck my Captain lies,
Fallen cold and dead.

Walt Whitman

THE MASTER *

A flying word from here and there
Had sown the name at which we
sneered,
But soon the name was everywhere,

* Supposed to have been written not long
after the Civil War.

To be reviled and then revered:
A presence to be loved and feared,
We cannot hide it, or deny
That we, the gentlemen who jeered,
May be forgotten by and by.

He came when days were perilous
And hearts of men were sore beguiled;
And having made his note of us,
He pondered and was reconciled.
Was ever master yet so mild
As he, and so untamable?
We doubted, even when he smiled,
Not knowing what he knew so well.

He knew that undeceiving fate
Would shame us whom he served un-
  sought;
He knew that he must wince and
  wait—
The jest of those for whom he fought;
He knew devoutly what he thought
Of us and of our ridicule;
He knew that we must all be taught
Like little children in a school.

We gave a glamour to the task
That he encountered and saw through,
But little of us did he ask,
And little did we ever do.
And what appears if we review
The season when we railed and
  chaffed?
It is the face of one who knew
That we were learning while we
  laughed.

The face that in our vision feels
Again the venom that we flung,
Transfigured to the world reveals
The vigilance to which we clung.
Shrewd, hallowed, harassed, a n d
  among
The mysteries that are untold,

The face we see was never young
Nor could it wholly have been old.

For he, to whom we had applied
Our shopman's test of age and worth,
Was elemental when he died,
As he was ancient at his birth:
The saddest among kings of earth,
Bowed with a galling crown, this man
Met rancor with a cryptic mirth,
Laconic—and Olympian.

The love, the grandeur, and the fame
Are bounded by the world alone;
The calm, the smouldering, and the
  flame
Of awful patience were his own:
With him they are forever flown
Past all our fond self-shadowings,
Wherewith we cumber the Unknown
As with inept, Icarian wings.

For we were not as other men:
'Twas ours to soar and his to see;
But we are coming down again,
And we shall come down pleasantly;
Nor shall we longer disagree
On what it is to be sublime,
But flourish in our perigree
And have one Titan at a time.

Edwin Arlington Robinson

Washington's Birthday

WASHINGTON

Soldier and stateman, rarest unison;
High-poised example of great duties
  done
Simply as breathing, a world's honors
  worn
As life's indifferent gifts to all men
  born;

Dumb for himself, unless it were to
   God,
But for his barefoot soldiers eloquent,
Tramping the snow to corral where
   they trod,
Held by his awe in hollow-eyed con-
   tent;
Modest, yet firm as Nature's self; un-
   blamed
Save by the men his nobler temper
   shamed;
Never seduced through show of pres-
   ent good
By other than unsettling lights to steer
New-trimmed in Heaven, nor than his
   steadfast mood
More steadfast, far from rashness as
   from fear;
Rigid, but with himself first, grasping
   still
In swerveless poise the wave-beat helm
   of will;
Not honored then or now because he
   wooed
The popular voice, but that he still
   withstood;
Broad-minded, higher-souled, there is
   but one
Who was all this and ours, and all
   men's,—WASHINGTON.

James Russell Lowell

INSCRIPTION AT MOUNT VERNON

Washington, the brave, the wise, the
   good,
Supreme in war, in council, and in
   peace,
Valiant without ambition, discreet
   without fear,
Confident without presumption.
In disaster, calm; in success, moderate;
   in all, himself.

The hero, the patriot, the Christian.
The father of nations, the friend of
   mankind,
Who, when he had won all, renounced
   all,
And sought in the bosom of his family
   and of nature, retirement,
And in the hope of religion, immor-
   tality.

THE TWENTY-SECOND OF FEBRUARY

Pale is the February sky,
   And brief the mid-day's sunny hours;
The wind-swept forest seems to sigh
   For the sweet time of leaves and
   flowers.

Yet has no month a prouder day,
   Not even when the summer broods
O'er meadows in their fresh array,
   Or autumn tints the glowing woods.

For this chill season now again
   Brings, in its annual round, the
   morn
When, greatest of the sons of men,
   Our glorious Washington was born.

Lo, where, beneath an icy shield,
   Calmly the mighty Hudson flows!
By snow-clad fell and frozen field,
   Broadening the lordly river goes.

The wildest storm that sweeps through
   space,
   And rends the oak with sudden
   force,
Can raise no ripple on his face,
   Or slacken his majestic course.

Thus, 'mid the wreck of thrones, shall
   live

Unmarred, undimmed, our hero's
fame,
And years succeeding years shall give
Increase of honors to his name.
William Cullen Bryant

LEETLA GIORGIO WASHEENTON

You know w'at for ees school keep
out
Dees holiday, my son?
Wal, den, I gona tal you 'bout
Dees Giorgio Washeenton.

Wal, Giorgio was leetla keed
Ees leeve long time ago,
An' he gon' school for learn to read
An' write hees nam', you know.
He moocha like for gona school
An' learna hard all day,
Baycause he no gat time for fool
Weeth bada keeds an' play.
Wal, wan cold day w'en Giorgio
Ees steel so vera small,
He start from home, but he ees no
Show up een school at all!
Oh, my! hees Pop ees gatta mad
An' so he tal hees wife:
" Som' leetla boy ees gon' feel bad
Today, you bat my life! "
An' den he grab a beega steeck
An' gon' out een da snow
An' lookin' all aroun' for seek
Dat leetla Giorgio.
Ha! w'at you theenk? Firs' theeng he
see
Where leetla boy he stan'
All tangla up een cherry tree,
Weeth hatchet een hees han'.
" Ha! w'at you do? " hees Pop he say,
" W'at for you busta rule
An' stay away like dees for play
Eenstead for gon' to school? "

Da boy ees say, " I no can lie,
An' so I speaka true.
I stay away from school for try
An' gat som' wood for you.
I theenka dees cherry tree
Ees gooda size for chop,
An' so I cut heem down, you see,
For justa help my Pop."
Hees Pop he no can gatta mad,
But looka please' an' say:
" My leetla boy, I am so glad
You taka holiday."
Ees good for leetle boy, you see,
For be so bright an' try
For help hees Pop; so den he be
A granda man bimeby.
So now you gatta holiday
An' eet ees good, you know,
For you gon' do da sama way
Like leetla Giorgio.
Don't play so mooch, but justa stop
Eef you want be som' good,
An' justa help your poor old Pop
By carry home some wood;
An' mebbe so like Giorgio
You grow for be so great
You gona be da Presidant
Of dese Unita State'.
Thomas Augustine Daly

Flag Day

FLAG SONG

Out on the breeze,
O'er land and seas,
A beautiful banner is streaming,
Shining its stars,
Splendid its bars,
Under the sunshine 'tis gleaming.
Hail to the flag,
The dear, bonny flag—
The flag that is red, white, and
blue.

Over the brave
Long may it wave,
Peace to the world ever bringing,
    While to the stars
    Linked with the bars
Hearts will forever be singing:
    Hail to the flag,
    The dear, bonny flag—
    The flag that is red, white, and
    blue.

Lydia Avery Coonley Ward

THE AMERICAN FLAG

(Selected Stanzas)

When freedom, from her mountain
    height
    Unfurl'd her standard to the air,
She tore the azure robe of night,
    And set the stars of glory there.
She mingled with its gorgeous dyes
The milky baldric of the skies,
And striped its pure, celestial white,
With streakings of the morning light;
Then from his mansion in the sun
She call'd her eagle bearer down;
And gave into his mighty hand
The symbol of her chosen land.

Flag of the seas! on ocean wave
Thy stars shall glitter o'er the brave;
When death, careering on the gale,
Sweeps darkly round the bellied sail,
And frighted waves rush wildly back
Before the broadside's reeling rack,
Each dying wanderer of the sea
Shall look at once to heaven and thee,
And smile to see thy splendours fly
In triumph o'er his closing eye.

Flag of the free heart's hope and home!
    By angel hands to valour given;
Thy stars have lit the welkin dome,

And all thy hues were born in
    heaven.
For ever float that standard sheet!
    Where breathes the foe but falls be-
    fore us,
With freedom's soil beneath our feet
And freedom's banner streaming o'er
    us.

Joseph Rodman Drake

Memorial Day

SOLDIER, REST!

Soldier, rest! thy warfare o'er,
    Sleep the sleep that knows not
    breaking;
Dream of battlefields no more,
    Days of danger, nights of waking.
In our isle's enchanted hall,
    Hands unseen thy couch are strew-
    ing,
Fairy strains of music fall,
    Every sense in slumber dewing.
Soldier, rest! thy warfare o'er,
Dream of fighting fields no more:
Sleep the sleep that knows not break-
    ing,
Morn of toil, nor nights of waking.

No rude sound shall reach thine ear,
    Armor's clang, or war-steed clamp-
    ing,
Trump nor pibroch summon here
    Mustering clan, or squadron tramp-
    ing.
Yet the lark's shrill fife may come
    At the daybreak from the fallow,
And the bittern sound his drum,
    Booming from the sedgy shallow.
Ruder sounds shall none be near;
Guards nor warders challenge here;

Here's no war-steeds' neigh and champ-
    ing,
Shouting clans, or squadrons stamping.

Walter Scott

HOW SLEEP THE BRAVE

How sleep the Brave who sink to rest
By all their country's wishes blest!
When Spring, with dewy fingers cold,
Returns to deck their hallowed mould,
She there shall dress a sweeter sod
Than Fancy's feet have ever trod.

By fairy hands their knell is rung;
By forms unseen their dirge is sung;
There Honour comes, a pilgrim gray,
To bless the turf that wraps their clay;
And Freedom shall await repair
To dwell a weeping hermit there.

William Collins

Columbus Day

COLUMBUS

Behind him lay the gray Azores,
    Behind, the Gates of Hercules;
Before him not the ghost of shores;
    Before him only shoreless seas.
The good mate said: " Now must we
    pray,
    For lo! the very stars are gone.
Brave Admiral, speak, what shall I
    say? "
    " Why, say: ' Sail on! sail on! and
    on! ' "

" My men grow mutinous day by day;
    My men grow ghastly, wan and
    weak."
The stout mate thought of home; a
    spray

Of salt wave washed his swarthy
    cheek.
" What shall I say, brave Admiral, say,
    If we sight naught but seas at
    dawn? "
" Why, you shall say at break of day,
    ' Sail on! sail on! and on! ' "

They sailed and sailed, as winds
    might blow,
    Until at last the blanched mate
    said:
" Why, now not even God would
    know
    Should I and all my men fall dead.
These very winds forget their way,
    For God from these dread seas is
    gone.
Now speak, brave Admiral, speak
    and say "—
    He said: " Sail on! sail on! and
    on! "

They sailed. They sailed. Then spake
    the mate:
    " This mad sea shows his teeth
    tonight.
He curls his lip, he lies in wait,
    With lifted teeth, as if to bite!
Brave Admiral, say but one good
    word:
    What shall we do when hope is
    gone? "
The words leapt like a leaping
    sword:
    " Sail on! sail on! sail on! and
    on! "

Then, pale and worn, he kept his
    deck,
    And peered through darkness. Ah,
    that night
Of all dark nights! And then a
    speck—

A light! a light! a light! a light!
It grew, a starlit flag unfurled!
  It grew to be Time's burst of
    dawn.
  He gained a world; he gave that
    world
    Its grandest lesson: "On! sail
    on!"

                    Joaquin Miller

In Fate's unfolding scroll,
Dark woes and ingrate wrongs I read,
  That rack the noble soul.
On! On! Creation's secrets probe,
  Then drink thy cup of scorn,
And wrapped in fallen Cæsar's robe,
Sleep like that master of the globe,
  All glorious,—yet forlorn.

              Lydia Huntly Sigourney

COLUMBUS

St. Stephen's cloistered hall was proud
  In learning's pomp that day,
For there a robed and stately crowd
  Pressed on in long array.
A mariner with simple chart
  Confronts that conclave high,
While strong ambition stirs his heart,
And burning thoughts of wonder part
  From lip and sparkling eye.

What hath he said? With frowning
    face,
  In whispered tones they speak,
And lines upon their tablets trace,
  The Inquisition's mystic doom
  Sits on their brows severe,
And bursting forth in visioned gloom,
Sad heresy from burning tomb
  Groans on the startled ear.

Courage, thou Genoese! Old Time
  Thy splendid dream shall crown;
Yon Western Hemisphere sublime,
  Where unshorn forests frown,
The awful Andes' cloud-wrapped brow,
  The Indian hunter's bow,
Bold streams untamed by helm or
    prow,
And rocks of gold and diamonds, thou
  To thankless Spain shalt show.

Courage, World-finder! Thou hast
    need!

Halloween

HALLOWEEN

Pixie, kobold, elf, and sprite,
All are on their rounds tonight;
In the wan moon's silver ray,
Thrives their helter-skelter play.

Fond of cellar, barn, or stack,
True unto the almanac,
They present to credulous eyes
Strange hobgoblin mysteries.

Cabbage stumps — straws wet with
    dew—
Apple-skins, and chestnuts too,
And a mirror for some lass
Show what wonders come to pass.

Doors they move, and grates they hide;
Mischiefs that on moonbeams ride
Are their deeds—and, by their spells,
Love records its oracles.

Don't we all, of long ago,
By the ruddy fireplace glow,
In the kitchen and the hall,
Those queer, cooflike pranks recall?

Eery shadows were they then—
But tonight they come again;
Were we once more but sixteen,
Precious would be Halloween.

                    Joel Benton

THE HAG

The hag is astride,
This night for a ride,
Her wild steed and she together;
Through thick and through thin,
Now out, and then in,
Though ne'er so foul be the weather.

A thorn or a burr
She takes for a spur;
With a last of a bramble she rides now,
Through brakes and through
briars,
O'er ditches and mires,
She follows the spirit that guides now.

No beast for his food
Dares now range the wood,
But hush'd in his lair he lies lurking;
While mischief by these,
On land and on seas,
At noon of night are found working.

The storm will arise
And trouble the skies,
This night; and, more for the wonder,
The ghost from the tomb
Affrightened shall come,
Called out by the clap of the thunder.

Robert Herrick

LITTLE ORPHANT ANNIE

Little Orphant Annie's come to our
house to stay,
An' wash the cups an' saucers up, an'
brush the crumbs away,
An' shoo the chickens off the porch,
an' dust the hearth, an' sweep,
An' make the fire, an' bake the bread,
an' earn her board-an'-keep;
An' all us other childern, when the
supper-things is done,

We set around the kitchen fire an' has
the mostest fun
A-list'nin' to the witch-tales 'at Annie
tells about,
An' the Gobble-uns 'at gits you
Ef you
Don't
Watch
Out!

Wunst they wuz a little boy wouldn't
say his prayers,—
An' when he went to bed at night,
away upstairs,
His Mammy heerd him holler, an' his
Daddy heerd him bawl,
An' when they turn't the kivvers down,
he wuzn't there at all!
An' they seeked him in the rafter-
room, an' cubby-hole, an' press,
An' seeked him up the chimbly-flue,
an' ever'wheres, I guess;
But all they ever found wuz thist his
pants an' round-about:—
An' the Gobble-uns 'll git you
Ef you
Don't
Watch
Out!

An' one time a little girl 'ud allus laugh
and grin,
An' make fun of ever' one, an' all her
blood-an'-kin;
An' wunst, when they wuz " company," an' ole folks wuz there,
She mocked 'em an' shocked 'em, an'
said she didn't care!
An' thist, as she kicked her heels, an'
turn't to run an' hide,
They wuz two great big Black Things
a-standin' by her side,
An' they snatched her through the
ceilin' 'fore she knowed what she's
about!

An' the Gobble-uns 'll git you
  Ef you
    Don't
      Watch
        Out!

An' little Orphant Annie says, when
  the blaze is blue,
An' the lamp wick sputters, an' the
  wind goes *woo-oo!*
An' you hear the crickets quit, an'
  the moon is gray,
An' the lightnin'-bugs in dew is all
  squenched away,—
You better mind yer parunts, an' yer
  teachers fond an' dear,
An' churish them 'at loves you, an' dry
  the orphant's tear,
An' he'p the pore an' needy ones 'at
  clusters all about,
Er the Gobble-uns 'll git you
  Ef you
    Don't
      Watch
        Out!

          James Whitcomb Riley

Other Days

THE FOURTH OF JULY

Day of glory! Welcome day!
Freedom's banners greet thy ray;
See! how cheerfully they play
  With thy morning breeze,
On the rocks where pilgrims kneeled,
On the heights where squadrons
  wheeled,
When a tyrant's thunder pealed
  O'er the trembling seas.

God of armies! did thy stars
On their courses smite his cars;
Blast his arm, and wrest his bars
  From the heaving tide?
On our standard, lo! they burn,
And, when days like this return,
Sparkle o'er the soldier's urn
  Who for freedom died.

God of peace! whose spirit fills
All the echoes of our hills,
All the murmur of our rills,
  Now the storm is o'er,
O let freemen be our sons,
And let future Washingtons
Rise, to lead their valiant ones
  Till there's war no more!

          John Pierpont

WE PLOUGH THE FIELDS

We plough the fields, and scatter
  The good seed on the land,
But it is fed and watered
  By God's almighty hand;
He sends the snow in winter,
  The warmth to swell the grain,
The breezes and the sunshine,
  And soft refreshing rain.

  All good gifts around us
    Are sent from heaven above;
  Then thank the Lord,
  O thank the Lord,
    For all His love.

He only is the Maker
  Of all things near and far;
He paints the wayside flower,
  He lights the evening star;
The winds and waves obey Him,
  By Him the birds are fed;
Much more to us His children,
  He gives our daily bread.

We thank Thee, then, O Father,

For all things bright and good,
The seed-time and the harvest,
Our life, our health, our food;
Accept the gifts we offer,
For all Thy love imparts,
And, what Thou most desirest,
Our humble, thankful hearts.

Matthius Claudius

SOMEBODY'S MOTHER

The woman was old, and ragged, and gray,
And bent with the chill of the winter's day;

The street was wet with a recent snow,
And the woman's feet were aged and slow.

She stood at the crossing and waited long,
Alone, uncared for, amid the throng

Of human beings who passed her by,
Nor heeded the glance of her anxious eye.

Down the street, with laughter and shout,
Glad in the freedom of " school let out,"

Came the boys like a flock of sheep,
Hailing the snow piled white and deep.

Past the woman so old and gray
Hastened the children on their way,

Nor offered a helping hand to her—
So meek, so timid, afraid to stir

Lest the carriage wheels or the horses' feet
Should crowd her down in the slippery street.

At last came one of the merry troop—
The gayest laddies of all the group;

He paused beside her and whispered low,
" I'll help you across if you wish to go."

Her aged hand on his strong young arm
She placed, and so, without hurt or harm,

He guided the trembling feet along,
Proud that his own were firm and strong.

Then back again to his friends he went,
His young heart happy and well content.

" She's somebody's mother, boys, you know,
For all she's so aged and poor and slow;

" And I hope some fellow will lend a hand
To help my mother, you understand,

" If ever she's poor and old and gray,
When her own dear boy is far away."

And " somebody's mother " bowed low her head
In her home that night and the prayer she said

Was, "God, be kind to the noble
    boy,
Who is somebody's son and pride
    and joy!"

Unknown

THE MAY QUEEN

You must wake and call me early, call
    me early, mother dear;
Tomorrow 'll be the happiest time of
    all the glad New-year;
Of all the glad New-year, mother, the
    maddest merriest day;
For I'm to be Queen o' the May,
    mother, I'm to be Queen o' the
    May.

There's many a black black eye, they
    say, but none so bright as mine;
There's Margaret and Mary, there's
    Kate and Caroline:
But none so fair as little Alice in all the
    land they say,
So I'm to be Queen o' the May
    mother, I'm to be Queen o' the May.

I sleep so sound all night, mother, that
    I shall never wake,
If you do not call me loud when the
    day begins to break:
But I must gather knots of flowers, and
    buds and garlands gay,
For I'm to be Queen o' the May,
    mother, I'm to be Queen o' the
    May.

As I came up the valley whom think
    ye should I see,
But Robin leaning on the bridge be-
    neath the hazel-tree?
He thought of that sharp look, mother,
    I gave him yesterday—
But I'm to be Queen o' the May,
mother, I'm to be Queen o' the
    May.

He thought I was a ghost, mother, for
    I was all in white,
And I ran by him without speaking,
    like a flash of light.
They call me cruel-hearted, but I care
    not what they say,
For I'm to be Queen o' the May,
    mother, I'm to be Queen o' the
    May.

They say he's dying all for love, but
    that can never be:
They say his heart is breaking, mother
    —what is that to me?
There's many a bolder lad 'ill woo me
    any summer day,
And I'm to be Queen o' the May,
    mother, I'm to be Queen o' the
    May.

Little Effie shall go with me tomorrow
    to the green,
And you will be there, too, mother, to
    see me made the Queen;
For the shepherd lads on every side
    will come from far away,
And I'm to be Queen o' the May,
    mother, I'm to be Queen o' the
    May.

The honeysuckle round the porch has
    wov'n its wavy bowers,
And by the meadow-trenches blow the
    faint sweet cuckoo-flowers;
And the wild marsh-marigold shines
    like fire in swamps and hollows gray,
And I'm to be Queen o' the May,
    mother, I'm to be Queen o' the
    May.

The night winds come and go, mother,
    upon the meadow-grass,

And the happy stars above them seem
  to brighten as they pass;
There will not be a drop of rain the
  whole of the live-long day,
And I'm to be Queen o' the May,
  mother, I'm to be Queen o' the
  May.

All the valley, mother, will be fresh
  and green and still,
And the cowslip and the crowfoot are
  over all the hill,
And the rivulet in the flowery dale will
  merrily glance and play,
For I'm to be Queen o' the May,
  mother, I'm to be Queen o' the
  May.

So you must wake and call me early,
  call me early, mother dear,
Tomorrow 'ill be the happiest time of
  all the glad New-year:
Tomorrow 'ill be of all the year the
  maddest merriest day,
For I'm to be Queen o' the May,
  mother, I'm to be Queen o' the
  May.

Alfred Tennyson

A CEREMONY FOR CAN-DLEMAS DAY

Down with the rosemary and so
Down with the bays and mistletoe;
Down with the holly, ivy, all
Wherewith ye dressed the Christmas
  hall;
That so the superstitious find
No one least branch there left behind;
For look, how many leaves then be
Neglected there, maids, trust to me,
So many goblins you shall see.

Robert Herrick

FATHER IS COMING

The clock is on the stroke of six,
  The father's work is done;
Sweep up the hearth, and mend the
  fire,
  And put the kettle on:
The wild night-wind is blowing cold,
'Tis dreary crossing o'er the wold.

He is crossing o'er the wold apace,
  He is stronger than the storm;
He does not feel the cold, not he,
  His heart it is so warm;
For father's heart is stout and true
As ever human bosom knew.

He makes all toil, all hardship light;
  Would all men were the same!
So ready to be pleased, so kind,
  So very slow to blame!
Folks need not be unkind, austere;
For love hath readier will than fear.

Nay, do not close the shutters, child,
  For far along the lane
The little window looks, and he
  Can see it shining plain;
I've heard him say he loves to mark
The cheerful firelight, through the
  dark.

And we'll do all that father likes;
  His wishes are so few;
Would they were more; that every
  hour
  Some wish of his I knew!
I'm sure it makes a happy day,
When I can please him any way.

I know he's coming by this sign,
  That baby's almost wild,
See how he laughs, and crows, and
  stares—
  Heaven bless the merry child!

His father's self in face and limb,
And father's heart is strong in him.

Hark! hark! I hear his footsteps now,
　He's through the garden gate;
Run, little Bess, and ope the door,
　And do not let him wait.
Shout, baby, shout! and clap thy
　hands,
For father on the threshold stands.

Mary Howitt

HOLY THURSDAY

'Twas on a Holy Thursday, their innocent faces clean,
The children walking two and two, in
red and blue and green,
Grey-headed beadles walk'd before
with wands as white as snow,

Till into the high dome of Paul's they
like Thames' waters flow.

Oh, what a multitude they seem'd,
these flowers of London town;
Seated in companies, they sit with
radiance all their own.
The hum of multitudes was there,
but multitudes of lambs,
Thousands of little boys and girls
raising their innocent hands.

Now like a mighty wind they raise to
heaven the voice of song,
Or like harmonious thunderings the
seats of heaven among.
Beneath them sit the aged men, wise
guardians of the poor;
Then cherish pity lest you drive an
angel from your door.

William Blake

Part Nine

POEMS OF REVERENCE

I WILL GIVE YOU

I will give you the end of a golden
    string,
Only wind it into a ball,
It will lead you in at heaven's gate
    Built in Jerusalem's Wall.

William Blake

CHARTLESS

I never saw a moor,
I never saw the sea;
Yet know I how the heather looks,
And what a wave must be.

I never spoke with God,
Nor visited in heaven;
Yet certain am I of the spot
As if the chart were given.

Emily Dickinson

A PRAYER

Teach me, Father, how to go
Softly as the grasses grow;
Hush my soul to meet the shock
Of the wild world as a rock;
But my spirit, propt with power,
Make as simple as a flower.

Let the dry heart fill its cup,
Like a poppy looking up;
Let life lightly wear her crown,
Like a poppy looking down,
When its heart is filled with dew,
And its life begins anew.

Teach me, Father, how to be
Kind and patient as a tree.
Joyfully the crickets croon
Under shady oak at noon;
Beetle, on his mission bent,
Tarries in that cooling tent.
Let me, also, cheer a spot,
Hidden field or garden grot—
Place where passing souls can rest
On the way and be their best.

Edwin Markham

PRAYER FOR A PILOT

Lord of Sea and Earth and Air,
Listen to the Pilot's prayer—
Send him wind that's steady and
    strong,
Grant that his engine sings the song
Of flawless tone, by which he knows
It shall not fail him where he goes;
Landing, gliding, in curve, half-roll—
Grant him, O Lord, a full control,

That he may learn in heights of
Heaven
The rapture altitude has given,
That he shall know the joy they feel
Who ride Thy realms on Birds of
Steel.

Cecil Roberts

WIND IN THE PINE

Oh, I can hear you, God, above the cry
Of the tossing trees—
Rolling your windy tides across the sky,
And splashing your silver seas
Over the pine,
To the water line
Of the moon.
Oh, I can hear you, God,
Above the wail of the lonely loon—
When the pine-tops pitch and nod—
Chanting your melodies
Of ghostly waterfalls and avalanches,
Swashing your wind among the
branches
To make them pure and white.

Wash over me, God, with your piney
breeze,
And your moon's wet silver pool;
Wash over me, God, with your wind
and night,
And leave me clean and cool.

Lew Sarett

A CHILD'S THOUGHT OF
GOD

They say that God lives very high!
But if you look above the pines
You cannot see our God. And why?

And if you dig down in the mines
You never see Him in the gold,

Though from Him all that's glory
shines.

God is so good, He wears a fold
Of heaven and earth across His
face—
Like secrets kept, for love untold.

But still I feel that His embrace
Slides down by thrills, through all
things made,
Through sight and sound of every
place:

As if my tender mother laid
On my shut lids, her kisses' pressure,
Half-waking me at night and said,
"Who kissed you through the dark,
dear guesser?"

Elizabeth Barrett Browning

WHAT CHRIST SAID

I said, "Let me walk in the fields;"
He said, "Nay, walk in the town;"
I said, "There are no flowers there;"
He said, "No flowers, but a crown."

I said, "But the sky is black,
There is nothing but noise and
din;"
But He wept as He sent me back—
"There is more," He said, "there is
sin."

I said, "But the air is thick,
And fogs are veiling the sun;"
He answered, "Yet hearts are sick,
And souls in the dark undone."

I said, "I shall miss the light,
And friends will miss me, they say;"
He answered me, "Choose tonight
If I am to miss you or they."

I pleaded for time to be given;
  He said, " Is it hard to decide?
It will not seem hard in heaven
  To have followed the steps of your
  Guide."

I cast one look at the field,
  Then set my face to the town;
He said, " My child, do you yield?
  Will you leave the flowers for the
  crown? "

Then into His hand went mine.
  And into my heart came He.
And I walk in a light divine
  The path I had feared to see.

George Macdonald

FLOWER IN THE CRANNIED WALL

Flower in the crannied wall,
I pluck you out of the crannies,
I hold you here, root and all, in my
  hand,
Little flower—but if I could under-
  stand
What you are, root and all, and all in
  all,
I should know what God and man is.

Alfred Tennyson

THE COUNTRY FAITH

Here in the country's heart,
Where the grass is green,
Life is the same sweet life
As it e'er hath been.

Trust in a God still lives,
And the bell at morn
Floats with a thought of God
O'er the rising corn.

God comes down in the rain,
And the crop grows tall—
This is the country faith
And best of all!

Norman Gale

OUT IN THE FIELDS WITH GOD

The little cares that fretted me
I lost them yesterday
Among the fields, above the sea,
Among the winds at play,
Among the lowing of the herds,
The rustling of the trees,
Among the singing of the birds,
The humming of the bees.

The foolish fears of what might hap-
  pen,
I cast them all away,
Among the clover-scented grass,
Among the new-mown hay,
Among the husking of the corn,
Where drowsy poppies nod,
Where ill thoughts die and good are
  born—
Out in the fields with God.

Elizabeth Barrett Browning

A STRIP OF BLUE

I do not own an inch of land,
  But all I see is mine,—
The orchards and the mowing-fields,
  The lawns and gardens fine.
The winds my tax-collectors are,
  They bring me tithes divine,—
Wild scents and subtle essences,
  A tribute rare and free;
And, more magnificent than all,
  My window keeps for me
A glimpse of blue immensity,—
  A little strip of sea.

Richer am I than he who owns
  Great fleets and argosies;
I have a share in every ship
  Won by the inland breeze
To loiter on yon airy road
  Above the apple-trees.
I freight them with my untold dreams;
  Each bears my own picked crew;
And nobler cargoes wait for them
  Than ever India knew,—
My ships that sail into the East
  Across that outlet blue.

Sometimes they seem like living
    shapes,—
  The people of the sky,—
Guests in white raiment coming down
  From Heaven, which is close by;
I call them by familiar names,
  As one by one draws nigh,
So white, so light, so spirit-like,
  From violet mists they bloom!
The aching wastes of the unknown
  Are half reclaimed from gloom,
Since on life's hospitable sea
  All souls find sailing-room.

The ocean grows a weariness
  With nothing else in sight;
Its east and west, its north and south,
  Spread out from morn to night;
We miss the warm, caressing shore,
  Its brooding shade and light.
A part is greater than the whole;
  By hints are mysteries told.
The fringes of eternity,—
  God's sweeping garment-fold,
In that bright shred of glittering sea,
  I reach out for, and hold.

The sails, like flakes of roseate pearl,
  Float in upon the mist;
The waves are broken precious
    stones,—

Sapphire and amethyst,
Washed from celestial basement walls
  By suns unsetting kissed.
Out through the utmost gates of space
  Past where the gray stars drift,
To the widening Infinite, my soul
  Glides on, a vessel swift;
Yet loses not her anchorage
  In yonder azure rift.

Here sit I, as a little child:
  The threshold of God's door
Is that clear band of chrysoprase;
  Now the vast temple floor,
The blinding glory of the dome
  I bow my head before:
Thy universe, O God, is home,
  In height or depth, to me;
Yet here upon thy footstool green
  Content am I to be;
Glad, when is opened unto my need
  Some sea-like glimpse of Thee.

Lucy Larcom

SHEEP AND LAMBS

All in the April morning,
  April airs were abroad;
The sheep with their little lambs
  Pass'd me by on the road.

The sheep with their little lambs
  Pass'd me by on the road;
All in an April evening
  I thought on the Lamb of God.

The lambs were weary, and crying
  With a weak human cry,
I thought on the Lamb of God
  Going meekly to die.

Up in the blue, blue mountains
  Dewy pastures are sweet:
Rest for the little bodies,
  Rest for the little feet.

All in the April evening,
  April airs were abroad;
I saw the sheep with their lambs,
  And thought on the Lamb of God.
    Katharine Tynan Hinkson

SHEPHERD BOY'S SONG

He that is down needs fear no fall;
  He that is low no pride;
He that is humble ever shall
  Have God to be his Guide.

I am content with what I have,
  Little be it or much;
And, Lord, contentment still I crave,
  Because thou savest such.

Fulness to such a burden is,
  That go on pilgrimage:
Here little, and hereafter bliss,
  Is best from age to age.
    John Bunyan

CROSSING THE BAR

Sunset and evening star,
  And one clear call for me!
And may there be no moaning of the
    bar,
  When I put out to sea,

But such a tide as moving seems asleep,
  Too full for sound and foam,
When that which drew from out the
    boundless deep
  Turns again home.

Twilight and evening bell,
  And after that the dark!
And may there be no sadness of fare-
    well,
  When I embark;

For tho' from out our bourne of Time
    and Place
  The flood may bear me far,
I hope to see my Pilot face to face,
  When I have crost the bar.
    Alfred Tennyson

MY GARDEN

A garden is a lovesome thing, God wot!
  Rose plot,
  Fringed pool
Fern'd grot—
  The veriest school
  Of peace; and yet the fool
Contends that God is not—
Not God! in gardens! when the eve is
    cool?
  Nay, but I have a sign;
  'Tis very sure God walks in mine.
    Thomas Edward Brown

INVICTUS

Out of the night that covers me,
  Black as the Pit from pole to pole,
I thank whatever gods there be
  For my unconquerable soul.

In the fell clutch of circumstance
  I have not winced nor cried aloud.
Under the bludgeonings of chance
  My head is bloody, but unbowed.

Beyond this space of wrath and tears
  Looms but the horror of the shade,
And yet the menace of the years
  Finds and shall find me unafraid.

It matters not how strait the gate,
  How charged with punishments the
    scroll,
I am the master of my fate:
  I am the captain of my soul.
    William Ernest Henley

UP-HILL

Does the road wind up-hill all the way?
　Yes, to the very end.
Will the day's journey take the whole
　　day long?
　From morn to night, my friend.

But is there for the night a resting-
　　place?
　A roof for when the slow, dark hours
　　begin.
May not the darkness hide it from my
　　face?
　You cannot miss that inn.

Shall I meet other wayfarers at night?
　Those who have gone before.
Then must I knock, or call when just
　　in sight?
　They will not keep you waiting at
　　that door.

Shall I find comfort, travel-sore and
　　weak?
　Of labor you shall find the sum.
Will there be beds for me and all who
　　seek?
　Yea, beds for all who come.
　　　　　　　　Christina Rossetti

NOBILITY

Howe'er it be, it seems to me,
　'Tis only noble to be good.
Kind hearts are more than coronets,
　And simple faith than Norman
　　blood.

　　　　　　　　Alfred Tennyson

WHAT IS GOOD?

" What is the real good? "
　I asked in musing mood.

Order, said the law court;
Knowledge, said the school;
Truth, said the wise man;
Pleasure, said the fool;
Love, said the maiden;
Beauty, said the page;
Freedom, said the dreamer;
Home, said the sage;
Fame, said the soldier;
Equity, the seer;—

Spake my heart full sadly,
" The answer is not here."

Then within my bosom
Softly this I heard:
" Each heart holds the secret;
Kindness is the word."
　　　　　　　　John Boyle O'Reilly

A TURKISH LEGEND

A certain pasha, dead five thousand
　years,
Once from his harem fled in certain
　tears,

And had this sentence on the city's
　gate
Deeply engraven: " Only God is
　great."

So these four words above the city's
　noise
Hung like the accents of an angel's
　voice,

And evermore from the high barbican
Saluted each returning caravan.

Lost is that city's glory. Every gust
Lifts with crisp leaves the unknown
　pasha's dust,

And all is ruin, save one wrinkled gate
Whereon is written, "Only God is
   great."

Thomas Bailey Aldrich

THE OLIVE TREE

Said an ancient hermit, bending
   Half in prayer upon his knee,
" Oil I need for midnight watching,
   I desire an olive tree."

Then he took a tender sapling,
   Planted it before his cave,
Spread his trembling hands above it,
   As his benison he gave.

But he thought, the rain it needeth,
   That the root may drink and
   swell;
" God! I pray Thee send Thy show-
   ers! "
So a gentle shower fell.

" Lord, I ask for beams of summer,
   Cherishing this little child."
Then the dripping clouds divided,
   And the sun looked down and
   smiled.

" Send it frost to brace its tissues,
   O my God! " the hermit cried,
Then the plant was bright and
   hoary,
   But at evensong it died.

Went the hermit to a brother
   Sitting in his rocky cell:
" Thou an olive tree possessest;
   How is this, my brother, tell?

" I have planted one, and prayed,
   Now for sunshine, now for rain;
God hath granted each petition,
   Yet my olive tree hath slain! "

Said the other, " I entrusted
   To its God my little tree;
He who made knew what it needed,
   Better than a man like me.

" Laid I on him no condition,
   Fixed no ways and means; so I
Wonder not my olive thriveth,
   Whilst thy olive tree did die."

Sabine Baring-Gould

ST. FRANCIS' SERMON TO
THE BIRDS
(Selected Stanzas)

Around Assai's convent gate
The birds, God's poor who cannot
   wait,
From moor and mere and darksome
   wood
Come flocking for their dole of food.

" O brother birds," St. Francis said,
" Ye come to me and ask for bread,
   But not with bread alone today
Shall ye be fed and sent away.

" Ye shall be fed, ye happy birds,
   With manna of celestial words;
Not mine, though mine they seem
   to be,
Not mine, though they be spoken
   through me.

" Oh, doubly are ye bound to praise
   The great Creator in your lays;
He giveth you your plumes of down,
Your crimson hoods, your cloaks of
   brown.

" He giveth you your wings to fly
   And breathe a purer air on high,
And careth for you everywhere,
Who for yourselves so little care! "

With flutter of soft wings and songs
Together rose the feathered throngs,
And singing scattered far apart;
Deep peace was in St. Francis' heart.

He knew not if the brotherhood
His homily had understood;
He only knew that to one ear
The meaning of his words was clear.

Henry Wadsworth Longfellow

ABOU BEN ADHEM AND THE ANGEL

Abou Ben Adhem (may his tribe increase)
Awoke one night from a deep dream of peace,
And saw, within the moonlight of the room,
Making it rich, and like a lily in bloom,

An angel writing in a book of gold:—
Exceeding peace had made Ben Adhem bold,
And to the presence in the room he said,
"What writest thou?" The vision rais'd his head,
And with a look made of all sweet accord,
Answer'd, "The names of those who love the Lord."
"And is mine one?" said Abou. "Nay, not so,"
Replied the angel. Abou spoke more low,
But cheerly still; and said: "I pray thee then,
Write me as one that loves his fellow men."

The angel wrote, and vanish'd. The next night

It came again with a great wakening light,
And show'd the names whom love of God had bless'd
And lo! Ben Adhem's name led all the rest.

Leigh Hunt

YUSSOUF

A stranger came one night to Yussouf's tent,
Saying, "Behold, one outcast and in dread,
Against whose life the bow of power is bent,
Who flies, and hath not where to lay his head;
I come to thee for shelter and for food,
To Yussouf, called through all our tribes 'The Good.'"

"This tent is mine," said Yussouf, "but no more
Than it is God's; come in and be at peace;
Freely shalt thou partake of all my store
As I of His who buildeth over these
Our tents His glorious roof of night and day,
And at whose door none ever yet heard Nay."

So Yussouf entertained his guest that night,
And, waking him ere day, said: "Here is gold;
My swiftest horse is saddled for thy flight;
Depart before the prying day grow bold."

As one lamp lights another, nor
  grows less,
So nobleness endkindleth nobleness.

That inward light the stranger's face
  made grand,
Which shines from all self-conquest;
  kneeling low,
He bowed his forehead upon Yussouf's hand,
Sobbing: "O Sheik, I cannot leave
  thee so;
I will repay thee; all this thou hast
  done
Unto that Ibrahim who slew thy
  son!"

"Take thrice the gold," said Yussouf,
  "for with thee
Into the desert, never to return,
My one black thought shall ride
  away from me;
First-born, for whom by day and
  night I yearn,
Balanced and just are all of God's
  decrees;
Thou art avenged, my first-born,
  sleep in peace!"

James Russell Lowell

THE VISION OF BELSHAZZAR

The King was on his throne,
  The Satraps throng'd the hall;
A thousand bright lamps shone
  O'er that high festival.
A thousand cups of gold,
  In Judah deem'd divine—
Jehovah's vessels hold
  The godless Heathen's wine.

In that same hour and hall
  The fingers of a hand

Came forth against the wall,
  And wrote as if on sand:
The fingers of a man:—
  A solitary hand
Along the letters ran,
  And traced them like a wand.

The Monarch saw, and shook,
  And bade no more rejoice;
All bloodless waxed his look,
  And tremulous his voice:—
"Let the men of lore appear,
  The wisest of the earth,
And expound the words of fear,
  Which mar our royal mirth."

Chaldea's seers are good,
  But here they have no skill,
And the unknown letters stood
  Untold and awful still.
And Babel's men of age
  Are wise and deep in lore,
But now they were not sage,
  They saw—but knew no more.

A captive in the land,
  A stranger and a youth,
He heard the King's command,
  He saw that writing's truth;
The lamps around were bright,
  The prophecy in view;
He read it on that night,—
  The morrow proved it true!

"Belshazzar's grave is made,
  His kingdom pass'd away,
He, in the balance weigh'd,
  Is light and worthless clay;
The shroud, his robe of state;
  His canopy, the stone;
The Mede is at his gate!
  The Persian on his throne!"

George Gordon Byron

THE BOY AND THE ANGEL

Morning, evening, noon, and night,
" Praise God," sang Theocrite.

Then to his poor trade he turned,
By which the daily meal was earned.

Hard he laboured, long and well;
Over his work the boy's curls fell:

But ever, at each period,
He stopped and sang, " Praise God."

Then back again his curls he threw,
And cheerful turned to work anew.

Said Blaise, the listening monk,
  " Well done;
I doubt not thou art heard, my son."

" As well as if thy voice today
  Were praising God, the Pope's great
  way.

" This Easter Day the Pope at Rome
Praises God from Peter's dome."

Said Theocrite, " Would God that I
Might praise Him, that great way,
  and die! "

Night passed, day shone
And Theocrite was gone.

With God a day endures alway,
A thousand years are but a day.

God said in Heaven, " Nor day nor
  night
Now brings the voice of my delight."

Then Gabriel, like a rainbow's birth,
Spread his wings and sank to earth;

Entered in flesh, the empty cell,
Lived there and played the craftsman well:

And morning, evening, noon and
  night,
Praised God in place of Theocrite.

And from a boy, to youth he grew;
The man put off the stripling's hue;

The man matured and fell away
Into the season of decay;

And ever o'er the trade he bent,
And ever lived on earth content.

(He did God's will; to him all one
If on the earth or in the sun.)

God said, " A praise is in my ear:
There is no doubt in it, no fear;

" So sing, old worlds, and so
  New worlds that from my footstool
  go.

" Clearer loves sound other ways:
I miss my little human praise."

Then forth sprang Gabriel's wings;
  off fell
The flesh disguise, remained the cell.

'Twas Easter Day; he flew to Rome,
And paused above Saint Peter's
  dome.

In the tiring-room close by
The great outer gallery,

With his holy vestments dight,
Stood the new Pope, Theocrite:

And all his past career
Came back upon him clear,

Since when, a boy, he plied his trade,
Till on his life the sickness weighed;

And in his cell, when death drew
  near,
An angel in a dream brought cheer:

And rising from the sickness drear
He grew a priest, and now stood
  here.

To the East with praise he turned,
And on his right the angel burned.

" I bore thee from thy craftsman's cell
And set thee here; I did not well.

" Vainly I left my angel's sphere,
Vain was thy dream of many a year.

" Thy voice's praise seemed weak; it
  dropped—
Creation's chorus stopped!

" Go back and praise again
The early way—while I remain.

" With that weak voice of our disdain,
Take up Creation's pausing strain.

" Back to the cell and poor employ:
Become the craftsman and the boy! "

Theocrite grew old at home;
A new Pope dwelt in Peter's Dome.

One vanished as the other died:
They sought God side by side.

Robert Browning

THE BURIAL OF MOSES

" And he buried him in a valley in the
land of Moab, over against Beth-peor; but
no man knoweth of his sepulcher unto this
day."—DEUT. 34:6.

By Nebo's lonely mountain,
On this side Jordan's wave,
In a vale in the land of Moab,
There lies a lonely grave;
But no man built that sepulcher,
And no man saw it e'er;
For the angels of God upturned the
  sod
And laid the dead man there.

That was the grandest funeral
That ever passed on earth;
Yet no man heard the trampling,
Or saw the train go forth:

Noiselessly as the daylight
Comes when the night is done,
And the crimson streak on ocean's
  cheek
Grows into the great sun;

Noiselessly as the spring-time
Her crown of verdure weaves,
And all the trees on all the hills
Unfold their thousand leaves:
So without sound of music
Or voice of them that wept,
Silently down from the mountain's
  crown
The great procession swept.

Perchance the bald old eagle
On gray Beth-peor's height
Out of his rocky eyrie
Looked on the wondrous sight;
Perchance the lion stalking
Still shuns that hallowed spot;
For beast and bird have seen and heard
That which man knoweth not.

But, when the warrior dieth,
His comrades of the war,
With arms reversed and muffled
     drums,
Follow the funeral car:
They show the banners taken;
They tell his battles won;
And after him lead his masterless
     steed,
While peals the minute-gun.

Amidst the noblest of the land
Men lay the sage to rest,
And give the bard an honored place
With costly marble dressed,
In the great minster transept
Where lights like glories fall,
And the sweet choir sings, and the
     organ rings
Along the emblazoned wall.

This was the bravest warrior
That ever buckled sword;
This the most gifted poet
That ever breathed a word;
And never earth's philosopher
Traced with his golden pen
On the deathless page truths half so
     sage
As he wrote down for men.

And had he not high honor?—
The hillside for a pall!
To lie in state, while angels wait,
With stars for tapers tall!
And the dark rock-pines, like tossing
     plumes,
Over his bier to wave,
And God's own hand, in that lonely
     land,
To lay him in the grave!—

In that strange grave without a name,
Whence his uncoffined clay

Shall break again — O wondrous
     thought!—
Before the judgment day,
And stand, with glory wrapped
     around,
On the hills he never trod
And speak of the strife that won our
     life
With the incarnate Son of God.

O lonely tomb in Moab's land!
O dark Beth-peor's hill!
Speak to these curious hearts of ours,
And teach them to be still:
God hath His mysteries of grace,
Ways that we cannot tell;
He hides them deep, like the secret
     sleep
Of him He loved so well.

                    Cecil Frances Alexander

CONTENTMENT

My mind to me a kingdom is;
     Such perfect joy therein I find,
As far exceeds all earthly bliss
     That world affords, or grows by kind;
Though much I want what most men
     have,
Yet doth my mind forbid me crave.

Content I live—this is my stay;
     I seek no more than may suffice—
I press to bear no haughty sway;
     Look—what I lack my mind sup-
     plies.
Lo! thus I triumph like a king,
Content with that my mind doth
     bring.

I see how plenty surfeits oft,
     And hasty climbers oft do fall;
I see how those that sit aloft
     Mishap doth threaten most of all;

They get—they toil—they spend with care:
Such cares my mind could never bear.

I laugh not at another's loss,
　I grudge not at another's gain;
No worldly wave my mind can toss;
　I brook that is another's pain.
I fear no foe—I scorn no friend:
I dread no death—I fear no end.

Some have too much, yet still they crave;
　I little have, yet seek no more:
They are but poor, though much they have,
　And I am rich—with little store.
They poor, I rich; they beg, I give:
They lack, I lend: they pine, I live.

I wish not what I have at will:
　I wander not to seek for more:
I like the plain; I climb no hill:
　In greatest storm I sit on shore,
And laugh at those that toil in vain,
To gain what must be lost again.
This is my choice; for why—I find
No wealth is like a quiet mind.

Edward Dyer

FOLLOW THE GLEAM

Not of the sunlight,
Not of the moonlight,
Not of the starlight!
O young Mariner,
Down to the haven,
Call your companions,
Launch your vessel,
And crowd your canvas,
And, ere it vanishes
Over the margin,
After it, follow it,
Follow The Gleam.

Alfred Tennyson

SONNET ON HIS BLINDNESS

When I consider how my life is spent
　Ere half my days, in this dark world and wide,
　And that one talent, which is death to hide,
　Lodged with me useless, though my soul more bent
To serve therewith my Maker, and present
　My true account, lest He, returning, chide;
　" Doth God exact day-labour, light denied? "
　I fondly ask. But Patience, to prevent
That murmur, soon replies: " God doth not need
　Either man's work or his own gifts. Who best
　Bear his mild yoke, they serve Him best. His state
Is kingly. Thousands, at His bidding, speed
　And post o'er land and ocean, without rest;
　They also serve who only stand and wait."

John Milton

THE PILGRIM

Who would true valour see,
　Let him come hither!
One here will constant be,
　Come wind, come weather;
There's no discouragement
Shall make him once relent
His flint-avow'd intent
　To be a Pilgrim.

Whoso beset him round
　With dismal stories,
Do but themselves confound;

His strength the more is.
No lion can him fright;
He'll with a giant fight;
But he will have a right
    To be a Pilgrim.

Nor enemy, nor friend,
    Can daunt his spirit;
He knows he at the end
    Shall Life inherit:—
Then, fancies, fly away;
He'll not fear what men say;
He'll labour, night and day,
    To be a Pilgrim.

John Bunyan

ONWARD, CHRISTIAN SOLDIERS

Onward, Christian soldiers,
    Marching as to war,
With the Cross of Jesus
    Going on before.
Christ the Royal Master
    Leads against the foe;
Forward into battle,
    See, His banners go!
      Onward, Christian soldiers,
        Marching as to war,
      With the Cross of Jesus
        Going on before.

At the sign of triumph
    Satan's host doth flee;
On then, Christian soldiers,
    On to victory.
Hell's foundations quiver
    At the shouts of praise;
Brothers, lift your voices,
    Loud your anthems raise.
      Onward, etc.

Like a mighty army
    Moves the Church of God;

Brothers, we are treading
    Where the Saints have trod;
We are not divided,
    All one body we,
One in hope and doctrine,
    One in charity.
      Onward, etc.

Crowns and thrones may perish,
    Kingdoms rise and wane,
But the Church of Jesus
    Constant will remain;
Gates of hell can never
    'Gainst that Church prevail;
We have Christ's own promise,
    And that cannot fail.
      Onward, etc.

Onward, then, ye people,
    Join our happy throng,
Blend with ours your voices
    In the triumph song;
Glory, laud, and honor
    Unto Christ the King,
This through countless ages
    Men and angels sing.
      Onward, Christian soldiers,
        Marching as to war,
      With the Cross of Jesus
        Going on before.

Sabine Baring-Gould

THE SON OF GOD GOES FORTH TO WAR

The Son of God goes forth to war,
    A kingly crown to gain;
His blood-red banner streams afar!
    Who follows in His train?
Who best can drink his cup of woe,
    Triumphant over pain,
Who patient bears his cross below,
    He follows in His train!

Thy martyr first, whose eagle eye
    Could pierce beyond the grave;
Who saw his Master in the sky,
    And called on Him to save:
Like Him, with pardon on his tongue,
    In midst of mortal pain,
He prayed for them that did the
    wrong!
    Who follows in His train?

A glorious band, the chosen few,
    On whom the Spirit came;
Twelve valiant saints, their hope they
    knew,
    And mocked the cross and flame!
They met the tyrant's brandished steel,
    The lion's gory mane:
They bowed their necks, the death to
    feel!
    Who follows in their train?

A noble army—men and boys,
    The matron and the maid,—
Around the Saviour's throne rejoice
    In robes of light arrayed.
They climbed the steep ascent of
    Heaven,
    Through peril, toil, and pain!
O God! to us may grace be given
    To follow in their train!

Reginald Heber

THE SPACIOUS FIRMAMENT
ON HIGH

The spacious firmament on high,
With all the blue ethereal sky,
And spangled heavens, a shining
    frame,
Their great Original proclaim.
The unwearied sun from day to day
Does his Creator's power display,
And publishes to every land,
The work of an Almighty Hand.

Soon as the evening shades prevail,
The moon takes up the wondrous
    tale,
And nightly to the listening earth
Repeats the story of her birth;
Whilst all the stars that round her
    burn,
And all the planets in their turn,
Confirm the tidings as they roll,
And spread the truth from pole to
    pole.

What though in solemn silence, all
Move round this dark terrestrial ball?
What though nor real voice, nor
    sound
Amidst their radiant orbs be found?
In Reason's ear they all rejoice,
And utter forth a glorious voice,
For ever singing as they shine!
"The hand that made us is divine!"

Joseph Addison

ROCK OF AGES

Rock of Ages, cleft for me,
Let me hide myself in Thee!
Let the water and the blood,
From Thy riven side which flowed,
Be of sin the double cure—
Cleanse me from its guilt and power.

Not the labors of my hands
Can fulfil Thy law's demands;
Could my zeal no respite know,
Could my tears for ever flow,
All for sin could not atone—
Thou must save, and Thou alone.

Nothing in my hand I bring—
Simply to Thy Cross I cling;
Naked come to Thee for dress—
Helpless look to Thee for grace;
Foul, I to the Fountain fly—
Wash me, Saviour, or I die!

While I draw this fleeting breath,
When my eye-strings breathe in
   death;
When I soar to worlds unknown,
See T h e e on Thy judgment
   throne,—
Rock of Ages, cleft for me,
Let me hide myself in Thee.

Augustus Montague Toplady

MORNING HYMN

Awake, my soul, and with the sun
Thy daily stage of duty run;
Shake off dull sloth, and early rise
To pay thy morning sacrifice.

Redeem thy misspent moments past,
And live this day as if thy last;
Thy talents to improve take care;
For the Great Day thyself prepare.

Let all thy converse be sincere,
Thy conscience as the noonday clear;
For God's all-seeing eye surveys
Thy secret thoughts, thy works and
   ways.

Wake, and lift up thyself, my heart,
And with the Angels bear thy part,
Who all night long unwearied sing
High glory to the Eternal King.

Glory to thee! who safe hast kept
And hast refreshed me while I slept;
Grant, Lord, when I from death shall
   wake
I may of endless life partake.

Lord, I my vows to Thee renew!
Scatter my sins as morning dew:
Guard my first spring of thought and
   will,
And with Thyself my spirit fill.

Direct, control, suggest, this day,
All I design, or do or say;
That all my powers, with all their
   might,
In Thy sole glory may unite.

Thomas Ken

FROM GREENLAND'S ICY MOUNTAINS

From Greenland's icy mountains,
   From India's coral strand;
Where Afric's sunny fountains
   Roll down their golden sand:
From many an ancient river,
   From many a palmy plain,
They call us to deliver
   Their land from error's chain.

What though the spicy breezes
   Blow soft o'er Ceylon's isle;
Though every prospect pleases,
   And only man is vile:
In vain with lavish kindness
   The gifts of God are strown;
The heathen, in his blindness,
   Bows down to wood and stone.

Can we, whose souls are lighted
   With wisdom from on high—
Can we, to men benighted,
   The lamp of life deny?
Salvation! oh, salvation!
   The joyful sound proclaim;
Till each remotest nation
   Has learnt Messiah's name.

Waft, waft, ye winds, His story,
   And you, ye waters, roll,
Till, like a sea of glory,
   It spreads from pole to pole;
Till o'er our ransomed nature,
   The Lamb for sinners slain,

Redeemer, King, Creator,
In bliss returns to reign.

Reginald Heber

THE LOST SHEEP

There were ninety and nine that
safely lay
In the shelter of the fold;
But one was out on the hills away,
Far off from the gates of gold.—
Away on the mountains wild and
bare,
Away from the tender Shepherd's
care.

"Lord, Thou hast here Thy ninety
and nine:
Are they not enough for thee?"
But the Shepherd made answer:
" 'Tis of mine
Has wandered away from me;
And although the road be rough and
steep
I go to the desert to find my sheep."

But none of the ransomed ever knew
How deep were the waters crossed,
Nor how dark was the night that the
Lord passed through
Ere He found His sheep that was
lost.
Out in the desert He heard its cry—
Sick and helpless, and ready to die.

"Lord, whence are those blood-drops
all the way,
That mark out the mountain-
track?"
"They were shed for one who had
gone astray
Ere the Shepherd could bring him
back."

"Lord, whence are Thy hands so rent
and torn?"
"They are pierced tonight by many
a thorn."

But all through the mountains, thun-
der-riven,
And up from the rocky steep,
There rose a cry to the gate of
heaven,
"Rejoice! I have found my sheep!"
And the angels echoed around the
throne,
"Rejoice, for the Lord brings back
His own!"

Elizabeth Cecilia Clephane

HOLY, HOLY, HOLY

Holy, holy, holy, Lord God Almighty!
Early in the morning our songs shall
rise to Thee;
Holy, holy, holy! merciful and mighty!
God in Three Persons, Blessed
Trinity!

Holy, holy, holy! all the saints adore
Thee,
Casting down their golden crowns
around the glassy sea,
Cherubim and seraphim falling down
before Thee,
Who wert, and art, and evermore
shalt be!

Holy, holy, holy! though the darkness
hide Thee,
Though the eye of sinful man Thy
glory may not see,
Only Thou art holy, there is none beside Thee,
Perfect in power, in love, and purity!

Holy, holy, holy, Lord God Almighty!
  All Thy works shall praise Thy name
    in earth and sky and sea;
Holy, holy, holy! merciful and mighty!
  God in Three Persons, Blessed
    Trinity!

Reginald Heber

NOW THE DAY IS OVER

Now the day is over,
  Night is drawing nigh,
Shadows of the evening
  Steal across the sky.

Now the darkness gathers,
  Stars begin to peep;
Birds, and beasts, and flowers
  Soon will be asleep.

Jesu, give the weary
  Calm and sweet repose;
With Thy tend'rest blessing
  May mine eyelids close.

Grant to little children
  Visions bright of Thee;
Guard the sailors tossing
  On the deep blue sea.

Comfort every sufferer
  Watching late in pain;
Those who plan some evil,
  From their sin restrain.

Glory to the Father,
  Glory to the Son,
And to Thee, Blest Spirit
  While all ages run.

Sabine Baring-Gould

MORNING HYMN

(Selected Stanzas)

Now the dreary night is done,
Comes again the glorious sun,
Crimson clouds, and silver white,
Wait upon his breaking light.

Glistening in the garden beds,
Flowers lift up their dewy heads,
And the shrill cock claps his wings,
And the merry lark upsprings.

When the eastern sky is red,
I, too, lift my little head.
When the lark sings loud and gay,
I, too, rise to praise and pray.

Saviour, to Thy cottage home
Once the daylight used to come;
Thou hast ofttimes seen it break
Brightly o'er that eastern lake.

With Thee, Lord, I would arise,
To Thee look with opening eyes,
All the day be at my side,
Saviour, Pattern, King, and Guide.

Cecil Frances Alexander

Through the long night watches
  May Thine Angels spread
Their white wings above me,
  Watching round my bed.

When the morning wakens,
  Then may I arise,
Pure and fresh and sinless
  In Thy Holy Eyes.

A PRAYER IN SPRING

Oh, give us pleasure in the flowers to-day;
And give us not to think so far away
As the uncertain harvest; keep us here
All simply in the springing of the year.

Oh, give us pleasure in the orchard white,

Like nothing else by day, like ghosts by
  night;
And make us happy in the happy bees,
The swarm dilating round the perfect
  trees.

And make us happy in the darting bird
That suddenly above the bees is heard,
The meteor that thrusts in with needle
  bill,
And off a blossom in mid air stands
  still.

For this is love and nothing else is love,
The which it is reserved for God above
To sanctify to what far ends He will,
But which it only needs that we fulfil.

Robert Frost

ST. AGNES' EVE

Deep on the convent-roof the snows
  Are sparkling to the moon:
My breath to heaven like vapor goes:
  May my soul follow soon!
The shadows of the convent-towers
  Slant down the snowy sward,
Still creeping with the creeping hours
  That lead me to my Lord:
Make Thou my spirit pure and clear
  As are the frosty skies,
Or this first snowdrop of the year
  That in my bosom lies.

As these white robes are soiled and
  dark,
  To yonder shining ground;
As this pale taper's earthly spark,
  To yonder argent round;
So shows my soul before the Lamb,
  My spirit before Thee;
So in mine earthly house I am,
  To that I hope to be.

Break up the heavens, O Lord! and
  far,
  Through all yon starlight keen,
Draw me, thy bride, a glittering star,
  In raiment white and clean.

He lifts me to the golden doors;
  The flashes come and go;
All heaven bursts her starry floors,
  And strows her lights below,
And deepens on and up! the gates
  Roll back, and far within
For me the Heavenly Bridegroom
  waits,
  To make me pure of sin.
The Sabbaths of Eternity,
  One Sabbath deep and wide—
A light upon the shining sea—
  The Bridegroom with his bride!

Alfred Tennyson

A THANKSGIVING TO GOD
FOR HIS HOUSE

Lord, Thou hast given me a cell,
  Wherein to dwell;
A little house, whose humble roof
  Is weather-proof;
Under the spars of which I lie
  Both soft and dry;
Where thou, my chamber for to ward,
  Hast set a guard
Of harmless thoughts, to watch and
  keep
    Me, while I sleep.
Low is my porch, as is my fate:
  Both void of state;
And yet the threshold of my door
  Is worn by th' poor,
Who thither come, and freely get
  Good words, or meat.
Like as my parlor, so my hall
  And kitchen's small;

A little buttery, and therein
　　A little bin,
Which keeps my little loaf of bread
　　Unchipt, unflead;
Some little sticks of thorn or briar
　　Make me a fire,
Close by whose living coal I sit,
　　And glow like it.
Lord, I confess too, when I dine,
　　The pulse is Thine,
And all those other bits that be
　　There placed by Thee;
The worts, the purslain, and the mess
　　Of water-cress,
Which of Thy kindness Thou hast
　sent;
　　And my content
Makes those, and my beloved beet,
　　To be more sweet.

'Tis Thou that crown'st my glittering
　hearth
　　With guiltless mirth,
And giv'st me wassail-bowls to drink,
　　Spiced to the brink.
Lord, 'tis Thy plenty-drooping hand
　　That soils my land,
And giv'st me, for my bushel sown,
　　Twice ten for one;
Thou mak'st my teeming hen to lay
　　Her egg each day;
Besides my faithful ewes to bear
　　Me twins each year;
The while the conduits of my kine
　　Run cream, for wine—
All these, and better, Thou dost send
　　Me,—to this end,
That I should render, for my part,
　　A thankful heart.

Robert Herrick

Part Ten

OLD FAVORITES

FOUR-LEAF-CLOVER

I know a place where the sun is like
    gold
    And the cherry blooms burst with
      snow,
And down underneath is the loveliest
    nook
    Where the four-leaf clovers grow.

One leaf is for hope, and one is for
    faith,
    And one is for love, you know,
And God put another one in for luck;
    If you search you will find where
      they grow.

But you must have hope, and you must
    have faith,
    You must love and be strong, and so
If you work, if you wait, you will find
    the place
    Where the four-leaf clovers grow.
              Ella Higginson

A FAREWELL

My fairest child, I have no song to give
    you;

No lark could pipe to skies so dull
    and grey:
Yet, ere we part, one lesson I can leave
    you
      For every day.

Be good, sweet maid, and let who will
    be clever,
    Do noble things, not dream them,
      all day long;
And so make life, death, and that vast
    for-ever
      One grand, sweet song.
              Charles Kingsley

THE BAREFOOT BOY

Blessings on thee, little man,
Barefoot boy, with cheek of tan!
With thy turned-up pantaloons,
And thy merry whistled tunes;
With thy red lip, redder still
Kissed by strawberries on the hill;
With the sunshine on thy face,
Through thy torn brim's jaunty grace;
From my heart I give thee joy,—
I was once a barefoot boy!

Prince thou art,—the grown-up man
Only is republican.
Let the million-dollared ride!
Barefoot, trudging at his side,
Thou hast more than he can buy
In the reach of ear and eye,—
Outward sunshine, inward joy:
Blessings on thee, barefoot boy!

Oh, for boyhood's painless play,
Sleep that wakes in laughing day,
Health that mocks the doctor's rules,
Knowledge never learned of schools,
Of the wild bee's morning chase,
Of the wild flower's time and place,
Flight of fowl and habitude
Of the tenants of the wood;
How the tortoise bears his shell,
How the woodchuck digs his cell,
And the ground-mole sinks his well;
How the robin feeds her young,
How the oriole's nest is hung;
Where the whitest lilies blow,
Where the freshest berries grow,
Where the ground-nut trails its vine,
Where the wood-grape's clusters shine;
Of the black wasp's cunning way,
Mason of his walls of clay,
And the architectural plans
Of gray hornet artisans!
For, eschewing books and tasks,
Nature answers all he asks;
Hand in hand with her he walks,
Face to face with her he talks,
Part and parcel of her joy,—
Blessings on the barefoot boy!

Oh, for boyhood's time of June,
Crowding years in one brief moon,
When all things I heard or saw,
Me, their master, waited for.
I was rich in flowers and trees,

Humming-birds and honey-bees;
For my sport the squirrel played,
Plied the snouted mole his spade;
For my taste the blackberry conc
Purpled over hedge and stone;
Laughed the brook for my delight
Through the day and through the
    night,—
Whispering at the garden wall,
Talked with me from fall to fall;
Mine the sand-rimmed pickerel pond,
Mine the walnut slopes beyond,
Mine, on bending orchard trees,
Apples of Hesperides!
Still as my horizon grew,
Larger grew my riches too;
All the world I saw or knew
Seemed a complex Chinese toy,
Fashioned for a barefoot boy!

Oh, for festal dainties spread,
Like my bowl of milk and bread;
Pewter spoon and bowl of wood,
On the door-stone, gray and rude!
O'er me, like a regal tent,
Cloudy-ribbed, the sunset bent,
Purple-curtained, fringed with gold,
Looped in many a wind-swung fold;
While for music came the play
Of the pied frogs' orchestra;
And, to light the noisy choir,
Lit the fly his lamp of fire.
I was monarch: pomp and joy
Waited on the barefoot boy!

Cheerily, then, my little man,
Live and laugh, as boyhood can!
Though the flinty slopes be hard,
Stubble-speared the new-mown sward,
Every morn shall lead thee through
Fresh baptisms of the dew;
Every evening from thy feet

Shall the cool wind kiss the heat:
All too soon these feet must hide
In the prison cells of pride,
Lose the freedom of the sod,
Like a colt's for work be shod,
Made to tread the mills of toil,
Up and down in ceaseless moil:
Happy if their track be found
Never on forbidden ground;
Happy if they sink not in
Quick and treacherous sands of sin.
Ah! that thou couldst know thy joy,
Ere it passes, barefoot boy!

John Greenleaf Whittier

ANNABELLE LEE

(Selected Stanzas)

It was many and many a year ago,
  In a kingdom by the sea,
That a maiden there lived whom you
    may know
  By the name of Annabelle Lee;
And this maiden she lived with no
    other thought,
  Than to love and be loved by me.

I was a child, and she was a child,
  In this kingdom by the sea;
But we loved with a love that was more
    than love,
  I and my Annabelle Lee:
With a love that the wingèd seraphs of
    heaven
  Coveted her and me.

And this was the reason that long ago,
  In this kingdom by the sea,
A wind blew out of a cloud, chilling
  My beautiful Annabelle Lee,
So that her high-born kinsman came,
  And bore her away from me,

To shut her up in a sepulchre,
  In this kingdom by the sea.

But the moon never beams without
    bringing me dreams
  Of the beautiful Annabelle Lee;
And the stars never rise but I feel the
    bright eyes
  Of the beautiful Annabelle Lee;
And so, all the night-tide, I lie down
    by the side
Of my darling—my darling—my life
    and my bride,
  In the sepulchre there by the sea,
  In the tomb by the sounding sea.

Edgar Allan Poe

THE VILLAGE BLACKSMITH

Under a spreading chestnut tree
  The village smithy stands;
The smith, a mighty man is he,
  With large and sinewy hands;
And the muscles of his brawny arms
  Are strong as iron bands.

His hair is crisp, and black, and long,
  His face is like the tan;
His brow is wet with honest sweat,
  He earns whate'er he can,
And looks the whole world in the face,
  For he owes not any man.

Week in, week out, from morn till
    night,
  You can hear his bellows blow;
You can hear him swing his heavy
    sledge,
  With measured beat and slow,
Like a sexton ringing the village bell,
  When the evening sun is low.

And children coming home from
    school

Look in at the open door;
They love to see the flaming forge,
  And hear the bellows roar,
And catch the burning sparks that fly
  Like chaff from a threshing-floor.

He goes on Sunday to the church,
  And sits among his boys;
He hears the parson pray and preach,
  He hears his daughter's voice
Singing in the village choir,
  And it makes his heart rejoice.

It sounds to him like her mother's
  voice,
  Singing in Paradise!
He needs must think of her once more,
  How in the grave she lies;
And with his hard, rough hand he
  wipes
  A tear out of his eyes.

Toiling—rejoicing—sorrowing,
  Onward through life he goes;
Each morning sees some task begun,
  Each evening sees its close;
Something attempted, something done,
  Has earned a night's repose.

Thanks, thanks to thee, my worthy
  friend,
  For the lesson thou hast taught!
Thus at the flaming forge of life
  Our fortunes must be wrought;
Thus on its sounding anvil shaped
  Each burning deed and thought!
      Henry Wadsworth Longfellow

THE CHILDREN'S HOUR

Between the dark and the daylight,
  When the night is beginning to
  lower,

Comes a pause in the day's occupa-
  tions,
That is known as the Children's Hour.

I hear in the chamber above me
  The patter of little feet,
The sound of a door that is opened,
  And voices soft and sweet.

From my study I see in the lamplight,
  Descending the broad hall stair,
Grave Alice, and laughing Allegra,
  And Edith with golden hair.

A whisper, and then a silence:
  Yet I know by their merry eyes
They are plotting and planning to-
  gether
  To take me by surprise.

A sudden rush from the stairway,
  A sudden raid from the hall!
By three doors left unguarded
  They enter my castle wall!

They climb up into my turret
  O'er the arms and back of my chair;
If I try to escape, they surround me;
  They seem to be everywhere.

They almost devour me with kisses,
  Their arms about me entwine,
Till I think of the Bishop of Bingen
  In his Mouse-Tower on the Rhine!

Do you think, O blue-eyed banditti,
  Because you have scaled the wall,
Such an old mustache as I am
  Is not a match for you all!

I have you fast in my fortress,
  And will not let you depart,
But put you down into the dungeon
  In the round-tower of my heart.

And there will I keep you forever,
  Yes, forever and a day,
Till the walls shall crumble to ruin,
  And moulder in dust away.
         Henry Wadsworth Longfellow

THE SHEPHERD

How sweet is the shepherd's sweet lot;
From the morn to the evening he
  strays;
He shall follow his sheep all the day,
And his tongue shall be filled with
  praise.
For he hears the lamb's innocent call,
And he hears the ewe's tender reply;
He is watchful while they are in peace,
For they know when their shepherd is
  nigh.

         William Blake

FULL FATHOM FIVE

Full fathom five thy father lies:
  Of his bones are coral made:
Those are pearls that were his eyes:
  Nothing of him that doth fade,
But doth suffer a sea-change
Into something rich and strange.
Sea-nymphs hourly ring his knell:
  Hark! now I hear them—
    Ding, dong, bell.
         William Shakespeare

THE MILLER OF THE DEE

There dwelt a miller, hale and bold,
  Beside the River Dee;
He wrought and sang from morn till
  night,
  No lark more blithe than he;
And this the burden of his song
  Forever used to be,

"I envy no man, no, not I,
  And no one envies me!"

"Thou'rt wrong, my friend!" said old
  King Hal,
  "As wrong as wrong can be;
For could my heart be light as thine,
  I'd gladly change with thee.
And tell me now what makes thee
  sing
  With voice so loud and free,
While I am sad, though I'm the
  King,
  Beside the River Dee?"

The miller smiled and doffed his
  cap:
  "I earn my bread," quoth he;
"I love my wife, I love my friend,
  I love my children three.
I owe no one I cannot pay,
  I thank the River Dee,
That turns the mill that grinds the
  corn
  To feed my babes and me!"

"Good friend," said Hal, and sighed
  the while,
  "Farewell! and happy be;
But say no more, if thou'dst be true,
  That no one envies thee.
Thy mealy cap is worth my crown;
  Thy mill my kingdom's fee!
Such men as thou are England's
  boast,
  Oh, miller of the Dee!"

         Charles Mackay

THE SANDS OF DEE

"O Mary, go and call the cattle home,
  And call the cattle home,
  And call the cattle home,
  Across the sands of Dee!"

The western wind was wild and dank
    with foam,
    And all alone went she.

The western tide came up along the
    sand,
    And o'er and o'er the sand,
    And round and round the sand,
    As far as eye could see;
The rolling mist came down and hid
    the land,
    And never home came she.

Oh! is it weed, or fish, or floating hair
    A tress of golden hair,
    Of drownèd maiden's hair
    Above the nets at sea?
Was never salmon yet that shone so
    fair
    Among the stakes at Dee!

They rowed her in across the rolling
    foam,
    The cruel, crawling foam,
    The cruel, hungry foam,
    To her grave beside the sea:
But still the boatmen hear her call the
    cattle home
    Across the sands of Dee.
             Charles Kingsley

THE ARROW AND THE SONG

I shot an arrow into the air,
It fell to earth, I knew not where;
For, so swiftly it flew, the sight
Could not follow it in its flight.

I breathed a song into the air,
It fell to earth, I knew not where;
For who has sight so keen and strong,
That it can follow the flight of song?

Long, long afterward, in an oak

I found the arrow, still unbroke;
And the song, from beginning to end,
I found again in the heart of a friend.
        Henry Wadsworth Longfellow

REQUIEM

Under the wide and starry sky
Dig the grave and let me lie.
Glad did I live and gladly die,
    And I laid me down with a will.

This be the verse you grave for me:
Here he lies where he longed to be;
Home is the sailor, home from sea,
    And the hunter home from the
    hill.
        Robert Louis Stevenson

TO CELIA

Drink to me only with thine eyes,
    And I will pledge with mine;
Or leave a kiss but in the cup
    And I'll not look for wine.
The thirst that from the soul doth rise
    Doth ask a drink divine;
But might I of Jove's nectar sup,
    I would not change for thine.

I sent thee late a rosy wreath,
    Not so much honoring thee
As giving it a hope that there
    It could not wither'd be;
But thou thereon didst only breathe
    And sent'st it back to me;
Since when it grows, and smells, I
    swear,
    Not of itself but thee!
        Ben Jonson

THE OLD OAKEN BUCKET

How dear to this heart are the scenes
    of my childhood,

When fond recollection presents
    them to view!
The orchard, the meadow, the deep-
    tangled wild wood,
    And every loved spot which my in-
      fancy knew!
The wide-spreading pond, and the mill
    that stood by it,
    The bridge, and the rock where the
      cataract fell,
The cot of my father, the dairy house
    nigh it,
    And e'en the rude bucket that hung
      in the well—
The old oaken bucket that hung in the
    well.

That moss-covered vessel I hailed as a
    treasure,
    For often at noon, when returned
      from the field,
I found it the source of an exquisite
    pleasure,
    The purest and sweetest that nature
      can yield.
How ardent I seized it, with hands that
    were glowing,
    And quick to the white-pebbled bot-
      tom it fell;
Then soon, with the emblem of truth
    overflowing,
    And dripping with coolness, it rose
      from the well—
The old oaken bucket, the iron-bound
    bucket,
The moss-covered bucket arose from
    the well.

How sweet from the green mossy brim
    to receive it,
    As poised on the curb it inclined to
    my lips!
Not a full blushing goblet could tempt
    me to leave it,

The brightest that beauty or revelry
    sips.
And now, far removed from the loved
    habitation,
    The tear of regret will intrusively
    swell,
As fancy reverts to my father's planta-
    tion,
    And sighs for the bucket that hangs
    in the well—
The old oaken bucket, the iron-bound
    bucket,
The moss-covered bucket that hangs in
    the well!

                Samuel Woodworth

ANNIE LAURIE

Maxwelton braes are bonnie
Where early fa's the dew,
And it's there that Annie Laurie
Gie'd me her promise true—
Gie'd me her promise true,
Which ne'er forgot will be;
And for bonnie Annie Laurie
I'd lay me doune and dee.

Her brow is like the snawdrift,
Her throat is like the swan,
Her face it is the fairest
That e'er the sun shone on—
That e'er the sun shone on:
And dark blue is her e'e;
And for bonnie Annie Laurie
I'd lay me doune and dee.

Like dew on the gowan lying
Is the fa' o' her fairy feet;
Like the winds in summer sighing,
Her voice is low and sweet—
Her voice is low and sweet;
And she's a' the world to me;
And for bonnie Annie Laurie
I'd lay me doune and dee.

                William Douglas

FOR A' THAT, AND A' THAT

Is there, for honest poverty,
  That hangs his head, and a' that?
The coward slave, we pass him by,
  And dare be poor for a' that!
    For a' that, and a' that!
      Our toils obscure, and a' that;
      The rank is but the guinea stamp;
      The man's the gowd for a' that.

What tho' on hamely fare we dine,
  Wear hodden-grey, and a' that;
Gie fools their silks, and knaves their
    wine,
  A man's a man, for a' that.
    For a' that, and a' that!
      Their tinsel show, and a' that,
      The honest man' tho, ne'er sae
        poor,
      Is king o' men for a' that.

You see yon birkie, ca'd a lord,
  Wha struts, and stares and a' that;
Tho' hundreds worship at his word,
  He's but a coof for a' that;
    For a' that, and a' that!
      His riband, star and a' that,
      The man of independent mind
      He looks and laughs at a' that.

A king can make a belted knight,
  A marquis, duke and a' that;
But an honest man's aboon his might,
  Guid faith he maunna fa' that!
    For a' that, and a' that!
      Their dignities, and a' that,
      The pith o' sense, and pride o'
        worth,
      Are higher ranks than a' that.

Then let us pray that come it may,
  As come it will for a' that,
That sense and worth, o'er a' the earth,
  May bear the gree, and a' that;

For a' that, and a' that!
  It's coming yet, for a' that;
That man to man, the warld o'er,
  Shall brothers be for a' that.

                Robert Burns

TODAY

So here hath been dawning
  Another blue day;
Think, wilt thou let it
  Slip useless away?

Out of Eternity
  This new day is born;
Into Eternity
  At night will return.

Behold it aforetime
  No eye ever did;
So soon it forever
  From all eyes is hid.

Here hath been dawning
  Another blue day;
Think, wilt thou let it
  Slip useless away?

              Thomas Carlyle

ELDORADO

Gayly bedight
  A gallant knight
In sunshine and in shadow,
  Had journeyed long,
  Singing a song,
In search of Eldorado.

But he grew old,
  This knight so bold,
And o'er his heart a shadow
  Fell as he found
  No spot of ground
That looked like Eldorado.

And, as his strength
Failed him at length,
He met a pilgrim shadow:
"Shadow," said he,
"Where can it be,
This land of Eldorado?"

"Over the Mountains
Of the Moon,
Down the Valley of the Shadow,
Ride, boldly ride,"
The shade replied,
"If you seek for Eldorado!"

Edgar Allan Poe

WHAT RULES THE WORLD

They say that man is mighty,
He governs land and sea,
He wields a mighty sceptre
O'er lesser powers than he;

But a mighty power and stronger
Man from his throne has hurled,
For the hand that rocks the cradle
Is the hand that rules the world.

W. R. Wallace

MERCY

The quality of mercy is not strained;
It droppeth as the gentle rain from
heaven
Upon the place beneath: it is twice
blessed;
It blesseth him that gives, and him
that takes:
'Tis mightiest in the mightiest; it be-
comes
The throned monarch better than his
crown:
His sceptre shows the force of tem-
poral power,
The attribute to awe and majesty,
Wherein doth sit the dread and fear
of kings;
But mercy is above the sceptred sway,
It is enthroned in the hearts of kings,
It is an attribute to God Himself;
And earthly power doth then show
likest God's,
When mercy seasons justice. There-
fore, Jew,
Though justice be thy plea, consider
this,
That, in the course of justice, none of
us
Should see salvation. We do pray for
mercy;
And that same prayer doth teach us
all to render
The deeds of mercy.

William Shakespeare

LITTLE THINGS

Little drops of water,
Little grains of sand,
Make the mighty ocean
And the pleasant land.

Thus the little minutes,
Humble though they be,
Make the mighty ages
Of eternity.

Thus our little errors
Lead the soul away
From the path of virtue,
Far in sin to stray.

Little deeds of kindness,
Little words of love,
Make our earth an Eden,
Like the heaven above.

Little seeds of mercy,
Sown by youthful hands,

Grow to bless the nations
   Far in heathen lands.
      Ebenezer Cobham Brewer

THE SLUGGARD

'Tis the voice of a sluggard; I heard
   him complain,
"You have waked me too soon; I
   must slumber again ";
  As the door on its hinges, so he on
   his bed
  Turns his sides, and his shoulders,
   and his heavy head.

" A little more sleep and a little more
   slumber ";
  Thus he wastes half his days, and
   his hours without number;
  And when he gets up he sits folding
   his hands
  Or walks about saunt'ring, or trifling
   he stands.

I pass'd by his garden, and saw the
   wild brier
  The thorn and the thistle grow
   broader and higher;
  The clothes that hang on him are
   turning to rags;
  And his money still wastes till he
   starves or he begs.

I made him a visit, still hoping to
   find,
  That he took better care for improv-
   ing his mind;
  He told me his dreams, talk'd of
   eating and drinking:
  But he scarce reads his Bible, and
   never loves thinking.

Said I then to my heart, " Here's a
   lesson for me ";

That man's but a picture of what I
   might be;
  But thanks to my friends for their
   care in my breeding,
  Who taught me betimes to love
   working and reading.
      Isaac Watts

THE HERITAGE

The rich man's son inherits lands,
  And piles of brick, and stones, and
   gold,
And he inherits soft, white hands,
  And tender flesh that fears the cold,
  Nor dares to wear a garment old;
A heritage, it seems to me,
One scarce would wish to hold in fee.

The rich man's son inherits cares:
  The bank may break, the factory
   burn,
A breath may burst his bubble shares,
  And soft white hands could hardly
   earn
  A living that would serve his turn;
A heritage, it seems to me,
One scarce would wish to hold in fee.

The rich man's son inherits wants,
  His stomach craves for dainty fare;
With sated heart, he hears the pants
  Of toiling hinds and brown arms
   bare,
  And wearies in his easy chair!
A heritage, it seems to me,
One scarce would wish to hold in fee.

What doth the poor man's son inherit?
  Stout muscles and a sinewy heart,
A hardy frame, a hardier spirit,
  King of two hands, he does his part
  In every useful toil and art;
A heritage, it seems to me,
A king might wish to hold in fee.

What doth the poor man's son inherit?
  Wishes o'erjoyed with humble
    things,
A rank adjudged by toil-worn merit,
  Content that from employment
    springs,
  A heart that in his labour sings;
A heritage, it seems to me,
A king might wish to hold in fee.

What doth the poor man's son inherit?
  A patience learned of being poor,
Courage, if sorrow come, to bear it,
  A fellow-feeling that is sure
  To make the outcast bless his door;
A heritage, it seems to me,
A king might wish to hold in fee.

O rich man's son! there is a toil
  That with all others level stands;
Large charity doth never soil,
  But only whiten, soft white hands,—
  This is the best crop from thy lands;
A heritage, it seems to me,
Worth being rich to hold in fee.

O poor man's son! scorn not thy state;
  There is worse weariness than thine
In merely being rich and great:
  Toil only gives the soul to shine,
  And makes rest fragrant and benign;
A heritage, it seems to me,
Worth being poor to hold in fee.

Both, heirs to some six feet of sod,
  Are equal in the earth at last;
Both, children of the same dear God,
  Prove title to your heirship vast
  By record of a well-filled past;
A heritage, it seems to me,
Well worth a life to hold in fee.

                    James Russell Lowell

YOUNG AND OLD

When all the world is young, lad,
  And all the trees are green;
And every goose a swan, lad,
  And every lass a queen;
Then hey for boot and horse, lad,
  And round the world away;
Young blood must have its course, lad,
  And every dog his day.

When all the world is old, lad,
  And all the trees are brown;
And all the sport is stale, lad,
  And all the wheels run down:
Creep home, and take your place there,
  The spent and maimed among:
God grant you find one face there
  You loved when all was young.

                    Charles Kingsley

ONE, TWO, THREE

It was an old, old, old, old lady
  And a boy that was half-past three,
And the way that they played to-
    gether
Was beautiful to see.

She couldn't go romping and jump-
    ing,
  And the boy, no more could he;
For he was a thin little fellow,
  With a thin little twisted knee.

They sat in the yellow sunlight,
  Out under the maple tree,
And the game that they played I'll
    tell you,
  Just as it was told to me.

It was hide-and-go-seek they were
    playing,
  Though you'd never have known
    it to be—

With an old, old, old, old lady
And a boy with a twisted knee.

The boy would bend his face down
    On his little sound right knee,
And he guessed where she was hid-
    ing
    In guesses One, Two, Three.

"You are in the china closet!"
    He would cry, and laugh with
    glee—
    It wasn't the china closet,
    But he still has Two and Three.

"You are up in papa's big bedroom,
    In the chest with the queer old
    key,"
And she said: "You are warm and
    warmer;
    But you are not quite right," said
    she.

"It can't be the little cupboard
    Where mamma's things used to
    be—
So it must be in the clothes press,
    Gran'ma,"
    And he found her with his Three.

Then she covered her face with her
    fingers,
    That were wrinkled and white and
    wee,
And she guessed where the boy was
    hiding,
    With a One and a Two and a
    Three.

And they never had stirred from
    their places
    Right under the maple tree—
This old, old, old, old lady

And the boy with the lame little
    knee—
This dear, dear, dear old lady
    And the boy who was half-past
    three.

                              H. C. Bunner

EXCELSIOR

The shades of night were falling fast,
As through an Alpine village passed
A youth, who bore, 'mid snow and
    ice,
A banner, with the strange device,
    Excelsior!

His brow was sad; his eye beneath
Flashed like a faulchion from its
    sheath,
And like a silver clarion rung
The accents of that unknown
    tongue,
    Excelsior!

In happy homes he saw the light
Of household fires gleam warm and
    bright;
Above, the spectral glaciers shone,
And from his lips escaped a groan,
    Excelsior!

"Try not the Pass!" the old man said,
"Dark lowers the tempest overhead,
    The roaring torrent is deep and
    wide!"
And loud that clarion voice replied,
    Excelsior!

"O stay!" the maiden said, "and rest
Thy weary head upon this breast!"
A tear stood in his bright blue eye,
But still he answered, with a sigh,
    Excelsior!

"Beware the pine-tree's withered
branch!
Beware the awful avalanche! "
This was the peasant's last good-
night!
A voice replied, far up the height,
Excelsior!

At break of day, as heavenward
The pious monks of Saint Bernard
Uttered the oft-repeated prayer,
A voice cried through the startled
air,
Excelsior!

A traveler, by the faithful hound,
Half-buried in the snow, was found,
Still grasping in his hand of ice
That banner, with the strange device
Excelsior!

There, in the twilight cold and grey,
Lifeless, but beautiful, he lay,
And from the sky, serene, and far,
A voice fell, like a falling star,
Excelsior!

Henry Wadsworth Longfellow

THANATOPSIS

To him who in the realm of Nature
holds
Communion with her visible forms,
she speaks
A various language; for his gayer hours
She has a voice of gladness, and a
smile,
And eloquence of beauty and she
glides
Into his darker musings with a mild
And healing sympathy that steals away
Their sharpness ere he is aware. When
thoughts
Of the last bitter hour come like a
blight

Over thy spirit, and sad images
Of the stern agony, and shroud, and
pall,
And breathless darkness, and the nar-
row house,
Make thee to shudder, and grow sick
at heart;—
Go forth under the open sky and list
To Nature's teachings, while from all
around—
Earth and her waters, and the depth of
air—
Comes a still voice.—

Yet a few days, and thee
The all-beholding sun shall see no
more
In all his course; nor yet in the cold
ground,
Where thy pale form was laid, with
many tears,
Nor in the embrace of ocean, shall
exist
Thy image. Earth, that nourished thee,
shall claim
Thy growth, to be resolved to earth
again,
And, lost each human trace, surren-
dering up
Thine individual being, shalt thou go
To mix for ever with the elements,
To be a brother to the insensible rock
And to the sluggish clod, which the
rude swain
Turns with his share and treads upon.
The oak
Shall send his roots abroad and pierce
thy mould.

Yet not to thine eternal resting-place
Shalt thou retire alone, nor couldst
thou wish
Couch more magnificent. Thou shalt
lie down

With patriarchs of the infant world—
    with kings,
The powerful of the earth—the wise,
    the good,
Fair forms, and hoary seers of ages past,
All in one mighty sepulchre. The hills
Rock-ribbed and ancient as the sun,—
    the vale
Stretching in pensive quietness be-
    tween;
The venerable woods—rivers that move
In majesty, and the complaining brooks
That make the meadows green; and,
    poured round all,
Old Ocean's gray and melancholy
    waste,—
Are but the solemn decorations all
Of the great tomb of man. The golden
    sun,
The planets, all the infinite host of
    heaven,
Are shining on the sad abodes of
    death,
Through the still lapse of ages. All that
    tread
The globe are but a handful to the
    tribes
That slumber in its bosom.—Take the
    wings
Of morning, pierce the Barcan wilder-
    ness,
Or lose thyself in the continuous
    woods
Where rolls the Oregon, and hears no
    sound,
Save his own dashings—yet the dead
    are there:
And millions in those solitudes, since
    first
The flight of years began, have laid
    them down
In their last sleep—the dead reign there
    alone.

So shalt thou rest, and what if thou
    withdraw
In silence from the living, and no
    friend
Take note of thy departure? All that
    breathe
Will share thy destiny. The gay will
    laugh
When thou art gone, the solemn brood
    of care
Plod on, and each one as before will
    chase
His favorite phantom; yet all these
    shall leave
Their mirth and their employments,
    and shall come
And make their bed with thee. As the
    long train
Of ages glides away, the sons of men,
The youth in life's fresh spring, and
    he who goes
In the full strength of years, matron
    and maid,
The speechless babe, and the gray-
    headed man—
Shall one by one be gathered to thy
    side,
By those who in their turn shall follow
    them.

    So live, that when thy summons
      comes to join
The innumerable caravan which moves
To that mysterious realm where each
    shall take
His chamber in the silent halls of
    death,
Thou go not, like the quarry-slave at
    night,
Scourged to his dungeon, but, sus-
    tained and soothed
By an unfaltering trust, approach thy
    grave

Like one who wraps the drapery of his couch
About him, and lies down to pleasant dreams.

William Cullen Bryant

THE DESERTED VILLAGE

Sweet Auburn! loveliest village of the plain,
Where health and plenty cheered the labouring swain;
Where smiling spring its earliest visits paid,
And parting summer's lingering bloom delayed;
Dear lovely bowers of innocence and ease,
Seats of my youth, when every sport could please!
How often have I loitered o'er thy green,
Where humble happiness endeared each scene;
How often have I paused on every charm—
The sheltered cot, the cultivated farm,
The never-failing brook, the busy mill,
The decent church that topp'd the neighbouring hill,
The hawthorn-bush, with seats beneath the shade,
For talking age and whispering lovers made!
How often have I blessed the coming day,
When toil remitting lent its turn to play,
And all the village train, from labour free,
Led up their sports beneath the spreading tree:
While many a pastime, circled in the shade,
The young contended as the old surveyed;
And many a gambol frolicked o'er the ground,
And sleights of art and feats of strength went round;
And still, as each repeated pleasure tired,
Succeeding sports the mirthful band inspired;
The dancing pair that simply sought renown,
By holding out to tire each other down;
The swain, mistrustless of his smutted face,
While secret laughter titter'd round the place;
The bashful virgin's side-long looks of love,
The matron's glance that would those looks reprove.
These were thy charms, sweet village! sports like these,
With sweet succession, taught e'en toil to please;
These round thy bowers their cheerful influence shed,
These were thy charms—but all these charms are fled.

Oliver Goldsmith

THE CHAMBERED NAUTILUS

This is the ship of pearl, which, poets feign,
Sails the unshadowed main,—
The venturous bark that flings
On the sweet summer wind its purpled wings
In gulfs enchanted, where the Siren sings,
And coral reefs lie bare,

Where the cold sea-maids rise to sun
    their streaming hair.

Its webs of living gauze no more un-
    furl;
    Wrecked is the ship of pearl!
    And every chambered cell,
Where its dim dreaming life was wont
    to dwell,
As the frail tenant shaped his growing
    shell,
    Before thee lies revealed,—
Its irised ceiling rent, its sunless crypt
    unsealed!

Year after year beheld the silent toil
    That spread his lustrous coil;
    Still, as the spiral grew,
He left the past year's dwelling for the
    new,
Stole with soft step its shining arch-
    way through,
    Built up its idle door,
Stretched in his last-found home, and
    knew the old no more.

Thanks for the heavenly message
    brought by thee,
    Child of the wandering sea,
    Cast from her lap, forlorn!
From thy dead lips a clearer note is
    born
Than ever Triton blew from wreathèd
    horn!
    While on mine ear it rings,
Through the deep caves of thought I
    hear a voice that sings—

Build thee more stately mansions, O
    my soul,
    As the swift seasons roll!
    Leave thy low-vaulted past!
Let each new temple, nobler than the
    last,

Shut thee from heaven with a dome
    more vast,
    Till thou at length art free,
Leaving thine outgrown shell by life's
    unresting sea!
                    Oliver Wendell Holmes

ELEGY WRITTEN IN A COUN-
TRY CHURCHYARD

The curfew tolls the knell of parting
    day,
    The lowing herds wind slowly o'er
    the lea,
The ploughman homeward plods his
    weary way,
    And leaves the world to darkness
    and to me.

Now fades the glimmering landscape
    on the sight,
    And all the air a solemn stillness
    holds,
Save where the beetle wheels his
    droning flight,
    And drowsy tinklings lull the dis-
    tant folds.

Save that from yonder ivy-mantled
    tower,
    The moping owl does to the moon
    complain
Of such as, wandering near her se-
    cret bower,
    Molest her ancient solitary reign.

Beneath those rugged elms, that yew
    tree's shade,
    Where heaves the turf in many a
    mouldering heap,
Each in his narrow cell for ever laid,
    The rude forefathers of the ham-
    let sleep.

The breezy call of incense-breathing
morn,
The swallow twittering from the
straw-built shed,
The cock's shrill clarion, or the echoing horn,
No more shall rouse them from
their lowly bed.

For them no more the blazing
hearth shall burn
Or busy housewife ply her evening
care:
No children run to lisp their sire's
return,
Or climb his knees the envied kiss
to share.

Oft did the harvest to their sickle
yield,
Their furrow oft the stubborn
glebe has broke;
How jocund did they drive their
team afield!
How bow'd the woods beneath
their sturdy stroke!

Let not Ambition mock their useful
toil,
Their homely joys, and destiny
obscure;
Nor Grandeur hear with a disdain-
ful smile
The short and simple annals of
the Poor.

The boast of heraldry, the pomp of
power,
And all that beauty, all that
wealth e'er gave
Await alike the inevitable hour:—
The paths of glory lead but to the
grave.

Nor you, ye Proud, impute to these
the fault

If Memory o'er their tomb no
trophies raise,
Where through the long-drawn aisle
and fretted vault
The pealing anthem swells the
note of praise.

Can storied urn or animated bust
Back to its mansion call the fleeting breath?
Can Honour's voice provoke the silent dust,
Or Flattery soothe the dull cold
ear of Death?

Perhaps in this neglected spot is laid
Some heart once pregnant with
celestial fire;
Hands that the rod of empire might
have swayed,
Or waked to ecstasy the living
lyre:

But Knowledge to their eyes her ample page
Rich with the spoils of time did
ne'er unroll;
Chill Penury repressed their noble
rage,
And froze the genial current of
the soul.

Full many a gem, of purest ray
serene,
The dark unfathomed caves of
ocean bear:
Full many a flower is born to blush
unseen,
And waste its sweetness on the
desert air.

Some village Hampden, that with
dauntless breast
The little tyrant of his fields withstood;

Some mute inglorious Milton here
   may rest,
  Some Cromwell guiltless of his
   country's blood.

The applause of listening senates to
   command,
  The threats of pain and ruin to
   despise,
To scatter plenty o'er a smiling land,
  And read their history in a nation's eyes.

Their lot forbade: nor circumscribed
   alone
  Their growing virtues, but their
   crimes confined;
Forbade to wade through slaughter
   to a throne,
  And shut the gates of mercy on
   mankind;

The struggling pangs of conscious
   truth to hide,
  To quench the blushes of ingenu-
   ous shame,
Or heap the shrine of Luxury and
   Pride,
  With incense kindled at the
   Muse's flame.

Far from the madding crowd's ig-
   noble strife
  Their sober wishes never learned
   to stray,
Along the cool sequestered vale of
   life
  They kept the noiseless tenor of
   their way.

Yet even these bones from insult to
   protect,
  Some frail memorial still erected
   nigh,
With uncouth rhymes and shapeless
   sculpture decked

Implores the passing tribute of a
   sigh.

Their name, their years, spelt by the
   unlettered Muse,
  The place of fame and elegy supply:
And many a holy text around she
   strews,
  That teach the rustic moralist to
   die.

For who, to dumb Forgetfulness a
   prey,
  This pleasing anxious being e'er
   resigned,
Left the warm precincts of the cheerful day,
  Nor cast one longing, lingering
   look behind?

On some fond breast the parting
   soul relies,
  Some pious drops the closing eye
   requires;
Even from the tomb the voice of
   nature cries,
  Even in our ashes live their
   wonted fires.

For thee, who, mindful of the unhonoured dead,
  Dost in these lines their artless
   tale relate;
If chance, by lonely Contemplation
   led,
  Some kindred spirit shall inquire
   thy fate;

Haply some hoary-headed swain may
   say,
  " Oft have we seen him at the
   peep of dawn
Brushing with hasty steps the dews
   away,

To meet the sun upon the upland
    lawn.

" There, at the foot of yonder nodding
    beech,
  That wreathes its old fantastic roots
    so high,
His listless length at noontide would
    he stretch,
  And pore upon the brook that bab-
    bles by.

" Hard by yon wood, now smiling as
    in scorn,
  Muttering his wayward fancies he
    would rove;
Now drooping, woeful, wan, like one
    forlorn,
  Or crazed with care, or crossed in
    hopeless love.

" One morn I missed him on the 'cus-
    tomed hill,
  Along the heath and near his fa-
    vourite tree;
Another came; nor yet beside the
    rill,
  Nor up the lawn, nor at the wood
    was he;

" The next, with dirges due in sad
    array
  Slow through the church-way path
    we saw him borne;
Approach and read (for thou canst
    read) the lay
  Graved on the stone beneath yon
    aged thorn."

THE EPITAPH

Here rests his head upon the lap of
    Earth,
  A Youth, to Fortune and to Fame
    unknown;

Fair Science frowned not on his
    humble birth,
  And Mclancholy marked him for
    her own.

Large was his bounty, and his soul
    sincere,
  Heaven did a recompense as
    largely send:
He gave to Misery all he had, a tear,
  He gained from Heaven ('twas all
    he wished) a friend.

No farther seek his merits to dis-
    close,
  Or draw his frailties from their
    dread abode
(There they alike in trembling hope
    repose),
  The bosom of his Father and his
    God.

Thomas Gray

MY LOST YOUTH

Often I think of the beautiful town
  That is seated by the sea;
Often in thought go up and down
The pleasant streets of that dear old
    town,
  And my youth comes back to me.
    And a verse of Lapland song
  Is haunting my memory still:
  " A boy's will is the wind's will,
And the thoughts of youth are long,
    long thoughts."

I can see the shadowy lines of its trees,
  And catch in sudden gleams,
The sheen of the far-surrounding seas,
And islands that were the Hesperides
  Of all my boyish dreams.
    And the burden of that old song,
  It murmurs and whispers still:

" A boy's will is the wind's will,
And the thoughts of youth are long,
     long thoughts."

I remember the black wharves and the
     slips,
  And the sea-tides tossing free;
And Spanish sailors with bearded lips,
And the beauty and mystery of the
     ships,
  And the magic of the sea.
     And the voice of that wayward
       song
     Is singing and saying still:
  " A boy's will is the wind's will,
And the thoughts of youth are long,
     long thoughts."

I remember the bulwarks by the shore,
  And the fort upon the hill:
The sunrise gun, with its hollow roar,
The drum-beat repeated o'er and o'er,
  And the bugle wild and shrill.
     And the music of that old song
     Throbs in my memory still:
  " A boy's will is the wind's will,
And the thoughts of youth are long,
     long thoughts."

I remember the sea-fight far away,
  How it thundered o'er the tide!
And the dead captains, as they lay
In their graves, o'erlooking the tran-
     quil bay,
  Where they in battle died.
     And the sound of that mournful
       song
     Goes through me with a thrill:
  " A boy's will is the wind's will,
And the thoughts of youth are long,
     long thoughts."

I can see the breezy dome of groves,
  The shadows of Deering's Woods;

And the friendships old and the early
     loves
Come back with a Sabbath sound as
     of doves
  In quiet neighborhoods.
     And the verse of that sweet old
       song
     It flutters and murmurs still:
  " A boy's will is the wind's will,
And the thoughts of youth are long,
     long thoughts."

I remember the gleams and glooms
     that dart
  Across the schoolboy's brain:
The song and the silence in the heart,
That in part are prophecies, and in part
  Are longings wild and vain.
     And the voice of that fitful song
     Sings on, and is never still:
  " A boy's will is the wind's will,
And the thoughts of youth are long,
     long thoughts."

There are things of which I may not
     speak;
  There are dreams that cannot die;
There are thoughts that make the
     strong heart weak,
  And bring a pallor into the cheek,
  And a mist before the eye.
     And the words of that fatal song
     Come over me like a chill:
  " A boy's will is the wind's will,
And the thoughts of youth are long,
     long thoughts."

Strange to me now are the forms I
     meet
  When I visit the dear old town:
But the native air is pure and sweet,
And the trees that o'ershadow each
     well-known street,
  As they balance up and down,

Are singing the beautiful song,
Are sighing and whispering still:
" A boy's will is the wind's will,
And the thoughts of youth are long,
  long thoughts."

And Deering's Woods are fresh and
  fair,
And with joy that is almost pain
My heart goes back to wander there,
And among the dreams of the days
  that were,
  I find my lost youth again.
    And the strange and beautiful
    song,
  The groves are repeating it still:
" A boy's will is the wind's will,
And the thoughts of youth are long,
  long thoughts."
    Henry Wadsworth Longfellow

THE OLD CLOCK ON THE STAIRS

(Selected Stanzas)

Somewhat back from the village
  street
Stands the old-fashioned country
  seat.
Across its antique portico
Tall poplar-trees their shadows
  throw;
And from its station in the hall
An ancient time-piece says to all—
    " For ever—never!
    Never—for ever! "

By day its voice is low and light;
But in the silent dead of night,
Distinct as a passing footstep's fall
It echoes along the vacant hall,
Along the ceiling, along the floor,
And seems to say, at each chamber
  door—

" For ever—never!
Never—for ever! "

Through days of sorrow and of
  mirth,
Through days of death and days of
  birth
Through every swift vicissitude
Of changeful time, unchanged it has
  stood,
And as if, like God, it all things saw,
It calmly repeats those words of
  awe—
    " For ever—never!
    Never—for ever! "

In that mansion used to be
Free-hearted Hospitality;
His great fires up the chimney
  roared;
The stranger feasted at his board;
But, like the skeletons at the feast,
That warning time-piece never
  ceased—
    " For ever—never!
    Never—for ever! "

There groups of merry children
  played,
There youths and maidens dreaming
  strayed;
Oh, precious hours! Oh, golden
  prime,
And affluence of love and time!
Even as a miser counts his gold,
Those hours the ancient time-piece
  told—
    " For ever—never!
    Never—for ever! "

From that chamber, clothed in
  white,
The bride came forth on her wedding night;

There, in that silent room below,
The dead lay in his shroud of snow;
And in the hush that followed the
    prayer,
Was heard the old clock on the
    stair—
      " For ever—never!
      Never—for ever! "

All are scattered now and fled,
Some are married, some are dead;
And when I ask, with throbs of pain,
" Ah! when shall they all meet again! "
As in the days long since gone by,
The ancient time-piece makes re-
    ply—
      " For ever—never!
      Never—for ever! "

Never here—for ever there,
Where all parting, pain, and care,
And death, and time shall disap-
    pear,—
For ever there, but never here!
The horologe of Eternity
Sayeth this incessantly—
      " For ever—never!
      Never—for ever! "
      Henry Wadsworth Longfellow

THE CANE-BOTTOMED CHAIR

In tattered old slippers that toast at
    the bars,
And a ragged old jacket perfumed with
    cigars,
Away from the world and its toils and
    its cares,
I've a snug little kingdom up four pairs
    of stairs.

To mount to this realm is a toil, to be
    sure,
But the fire there is bright and the air
    rather pure;

And the view I behold on a sunshiny
    day
Is grand, through the chimney-pots
    over the way.

This snug little chamber is crammed
    in all nooks
With worthless old knickknacks and
    silly old books,
And foolish old odds and foolish old
    ends,
Cracked bargains from brokers, cheap
    keepsakes from friends.

Old armour, prints, pictures, pipes,
    china (all cracked),
Old rickety tables, and chairs broken-
    backed;
A twopenny treasury, wondrous to see;
What matter? 'tis pleasant to you,
    friend, and me.

No better divan need the Sultan re-
    quire,
Than the creaking old sofa that basks
    by the fire,
And 'tis wonderful, surely, what music
    you get
From the rickety, ramshackle, wheezy
    spinet.

That praying-rug came from a Turco-
    man's camp;
By Tiber once twinkled that brazen
    old lamp;
A Mameluke fierce yonder dagger has
    drawn:
'Tis a murderous knife to toast muf-
    fins upon.

Long, long through the hours, and the
    night, and the chimes,
Here we talk of old books, and old
    friends, and old times:

As we sit in a fog made of rich Lata-
kie,
This chamber is pleasant to you,
friend, and me.

But of all the cheap treasures that garnish my nest,
There's one that I love and I cherish
the best;
For the finest of couches that's padded
with hair
I never would change thee, my cane-
bottomed chair.

'Tis a bandy-legged, high-shouldered,
worm-eaten seat,
With a creaking old back, and twisted
old feet;
But since the fair morning when Fanny
sat there,
I bless thee and love thee, old cane-
bottomed chair.

If chairs have but feeling, in holding
such charms,
A thrill must have passed through your
withered old arms!
I looked, and I longed, and I wished
in despair;
I wished myself turned to a cane-bottomed chair.

It was but a moment she sat in this
place,
She'd a scarf on her neck, and a smile
on her face!
A smile on her face, and a rose in her
hair,
And she sat there, and bloomed in my
cane-bottomed chair.

And so I have valued my chair ever
since,

Like the shrine of a saint, or the
throne of a prince;
Saint Fanny, my patroness sweet I
declare,
The queen of my heart and my cane-
bottomed chair.

When the candles burn low, and the
company's gone,
In the silence of nights as I sit here
alone—
I sit here alone, but we yet are a pair—
My Fanny I see in my cane-bottomed
chair.

She comes from the past, and revisits
my room;
She looks as she then did, all beauty
and bloom;
So smiling and tender, so fresh and so
fair,
And yonder she sits in my cane-bottomed chair.

William Makepeace Thackeray

I REMEMBER

I remember, I remember,
 The house where I was born,
The little window, where the sun
 Came peeping in at morn:
He never came a wink too soon,
 Nor brought too long a day,
But now I often wish the night
 Had borne my breath away!

I remember, I remember,
 The roses, red and white,
The violets, and the lily-cups,
 Those flowers made of light!
The lilacs, where the robin built,
 And where my brother set
The laburnum on his birthday:
 The tree is living yet!

I remember, I remember,
   Where I was used to swing,
And thought the air must rush as
   fresh,
   To swallows on the wing.
My spirit flew in feathers then,
   That is so heavy now;
And summer pools could hardly cool
   The fever on my brow!

I remember, I remember,
   The fir-trees, dark and high;
I used to think their slender tops
   Were close against the sky:
It was a childish ignorance:
   But now, 'tis little joy
To know I'm further off from heaven
   Than when I was a boy.

          Thomas Hood

THE SONG OF THE SHIRT

With fingers weary and worn,
   With eyelids heavy and red,
A woman sat, in unwomanly rags,
   Plying her needle and thread.
     Stitch—stitch—stitch!
In poverty, hunger, and dirt;
   And still with a voice of dolorous
     pitch
She sang the "Song of the Shirt!"

" Work—work—work
   While the cock is crowing aloof!
And work—work—work
   Till the stars shine through the
     roof!
It's oh! to be a slave
   Along with the barbarous Turk,
Where woman has never a soul to
   save,
   If this is Christian work!

" Work—work—work
   Till the brain begins to swim!

Work—work—work
   Till the eyes are heavy and dim!
Seam, and gusset, and band,
   Band, and gusset, and seam,
Till over the buttons I fall asleep,
   And sew them on in a dream!

" O men with sisters dear!
   O men with mothers and wives!
It is not linen you're wearing out,
   But human creatures' lives!
     Stitch—stitch—stitch,
In poverty, hunger, and dirt—
Sewing at once, with a double thread
   A shroud as well as a shirt!

" But why do I talk of death,
   That phantom of grisly bone?
I hardly fear his terrible shape,
   It seems so like my own;
It seems so like my own
   Because of the fasts I keep;
O God! that bread should be so dear,
   And flesh and blood so cheap.

" Work—work—work
   From weary chime to chime!
Work—work—work
   As prisoners work for crime!
Band, and gusset, and seam,
   Seam, and gusset, and band,
Till the heart is sick and the brain
     benumbed,
   As well as the weary hand.

" Work—work—work
   In the dull December light!
And work—work—work
   When the weather is warm and
     bright!
While underneath the eaves
   The brooding swallows cling,
As if to show me their sunny backs,
   And twit me with the spring.

" Oh, but to breathe the breath
   Of the cowslip and primrose
      sweet,
With the sky above my head
   And the grass beneath my feet!
For only one short hour
   To feel as I used to feel,
Before I knew the woes of want
   And the walk that costs a meal! "

With fingers weary and worn,
   With eyelids heavy and red,
A woman sat, in unwomanly rags,
   Plying her needle and thread.
      Stitch stitch stitch!
In poverty, hunger, and dirt:
And still with a voice of dolorous
   pitch—
Would that its tone could reach the
   rich!—
   She sang this " Song of the
   Shirt! "

Thomas Hood

IN SCHOOL-DAYS

Still sits the school-house by the
   road,
   A ragged beggar sleeping;
Around it still the sumachs grow,
   And blackberry vines are creeping.

Within, the master's desk is seen,
   Deep scarred by raps official;
The warping floor, the battered
   seats,
   The jack-knife's carved initial;

The charcoal frescoes on its wall;
   Its door's worn sill, betraying
The feet that, creeping slow to
   school,
   Went storming out to playing!

Long years ago a winter sun
   Shone over it at setting;
Lit up its western window-panes,
   And low eaves' icy fretting.

It touched the tangled golden curls
   And brown eyes full of grieving,
Of one who still her steps delayed
   When all the school were leaving.

For near her stood the little boy
   Her childish favor singled:
His cap pulled low upon a face
   Where pride and shame were
   mingled.

Pushing with restless feet the snow
   To right and left, he lingered—
As restlessly her tiny hands
   The blue-checked apron fingered.

He saw her lift her eyes; he felt
   The soft hand's light caressing,
And heard the tremble of her voice,
   As if a fault confessing.

" I'm sorry that I spelt the word:
   I hate to go above you,
Because,"—the brown eyes lower
   fell,—
" Because, you see, I love you! "

Still memory to a gray-haired man
   That sweet child-face is showing.
Dear girl! the grasses on her grave
   Have forty years been growing!

He lives to learn, in life's hard
   school,
   How few who pass above him
Lament their triumph and his loss,
   Like her—because they love him.

John Greenleaf Whittier

THE SCHOOLMASTER

Beside yon straggling fence that skirts
 the way,
With blossomed furze unprofitably
 gay,
There, in his noisy mansion, skilled to
 rule,
The village master taught his little
 school;
A man severe he was, and stern to
 view,
I knew him well, and every truant
 knew;
Well had the boding tremblers learned
 to trace
The day's disasters in his morning face;
Full well they laughed with counter-
 feited glee
At all his jokes, for many a joke had
 he;
Full well the busy whisper circling
 round
Conveyed the dismal tidings when he
 frowned;
Yet he was kind, or, if severe in aught,
The love he bore to learning was in
 fault.
The village all declared how much he
 knew,
'Twas certain he could write, and ci-
 pher too;
Lands he could measure, times and
 tides presage,
And e'en the story ran that he could
 gauge;
In arguing too, the parson owned his
 skill,
For, e'en though vanquished, he could
 argue still,
While words of learned length and
 thundering sound
Amazed the gazing rustics ranged
 around;

And still they gazed, and still the wonder grew
That one small head could carry all he
 knew.

Oliver Goldsmith

JOHN ANDERSON

John Anderson my jo, John,
When we were first acquent
Your locks were like the raven,
Your bonnie brow was brent;
But now your brow is bald, John,
Your locks are like the snaw;
But blessings on your frosty pow,
John Anderson my jo.

John Anderson my jo, John,
We clamb the hill thegither,
And mony a canty day, John,
We've had wi' ane anither:
Now we maun totter down, John,
But hand in hand we'll go,
And sleep thegither at the foot,
John Anderson my jo.

Robert Burns

RUTH

She stood breast-high amid the corn,
Clasp'd by the golden light of morn,
Like the sweetheart of the sun,
Who many a glowing kiss had won.

On her cheek an autumn flush,
Deeply ripen'd: such a blush
In the midst of brown was born,
Like red poppies grown with corn.

Round her eyes her tresses fell,
Which were blackest none could
 tell,
But long lashes veil'd a light
That had else been all too bright.

And her hat, with shady brim,
Made her tressy forehead dim;
Thus she stood amid the stooks,
Praising God with sweetest looks.

" Sure," I said, " Heav'n did not mean
Where I reap thou shouldst but
glean;
Lay thy sheaf adown and come,
Share my harvest and my home."

Thomas Hood

THE BLIND HIGHLAND BOY

He ne'er had seen one earthly sight;
The sun, the day; the stars, the night;
Or tree, or butterfly, or flower,
Or fish in stream, or bird in bower,
Or woman, man, or child.

And yet he neither drooped nor pined,
Nor had a melancholy mind;
For God took pity on the boy,
And was his friend; and gave him joy
Of which we nothing know.

His mother, too, no doubt, above
Her other children him did love!
For, was she here, or was she there,
She thought of him with constant care,
And more than mother's love.

And proud was she of heart, when, clad
In crimson stockings, tartan plaid,
And bonnet with a feather gay,
To Kirk he on the Sabbath day,
Went hand in hand with her.

A dog, too, had he; not for need,
But one to play with and to feed;
Which would have led him, if bereft
Of company or friends, and left
Without a better guide.

And then the bag-pipes he could blow;
And thus from house to house would
go,
And all were pleased to hear and see;
For none made sweeter melody
Than did the poor blind boy.

William Wordsworth

HOME, SWEET HOME!

'Mid pleasures and palaces though we
may roam,
Be it ever so humble, there's no place
like home;
A charm from the sky seems to hallow
us there,
Which, seek through the world, is
ne'er met with elsewhere.
Home, Home, sweet, sweet Home!
There's no place like Home! there's
no place like Home!

An exile from home, splendor dazzles
in vain;
O, give me my lowly thatched cottage
again!
The birds singing gayly, that came at
my call,—
Give me them,—and the peace of
mind, dearer than all!
Home, Home, sweet, sweet Home!
There's no place like Home! there's
no place like Home!

How sweet 'tis to sit 'neath a fond
father's smile,
And the cares of a mother to soothe
and beguile!
Let others delight mid new pleasures
to roam,
But give me, oh, give me, the pleasures
of home!
Home, Home, sweet, sweet Home!
There's no place like Home! there's
no place like Home!

To thee I'll return, overburdened with
care;
The heart's dearest solace will smile
on me there;
No more from that cottage again will
I roam;
Be it ever so humble, there's no place
like home.
Home, Home, sweet, sweet Home!
There's no place like Home! there's
no place like Home!

John Howard Payne

MY OLD KENTUCKY HOME

The sun shines bright in the old Ken-
tucky home;
'Tis summer, the darkeys are gay;
The corn-top's ripe, and the meadow's
in the bloom,
While the birds make music all the
day.
The young folks roll on the little cabin
floor,
All merry, all happy and bright;
By-'n'-by hard times comes a-knock-
ing at the door:—
Then my old Kentucky home, good-
night!

Weep no more, my lady,
O, weep no more today!
We will sing one song for the old
Kentucky home,
For the old Kentucky home, far
away.

They hunt no more for the 'possum
and the coon,
On the meadow, the hill, and the
shore;
They sing no more by the glimmer of
the moon,
On the bench by the old cabin door.

The day goes by like a shadow o'er the
heart,
With sorrow, where all was delight;
The time has come when the darkeys
have to part:—
Then my old Kentucky home, good-
night!

The head must bow, and the back will
have to bend,
Wherever the darkey may go;
A few more days and the troubles all
will end,
In the field where the sugar-canes
grow.
A few more days for to tote the weary
load,—
No matter, 'twill never be light;
A few more days till we totter on the
road:—
Then my old Kentucky home, good-
night!

Weep no more, my lady,
O, weep no more today!
We will sing one song for the
old Kentucky home,
For the old Kentucky home, far
away.

Stephen Collins Foster

HOME SONG

Stay, stay at home, my heart, and rest;
Home-keeping hearts are happiest,
For those that wander they know
not where
Are full of trouble and full of care,
To stay at home is best.

Weary and homesick and distressed,
They wander east, they wander west,
And are baffled, and beaten and
blown about

By the winds of the wilderness of
doubt;
To stay at home is best.

Then stay at home, my heart, and rest;
The bird is safest in its nest:
O'er all that flutter their wings and
fly
A hawk is hovering in the sky;
To stay at home is best.

Henry Wadsworth Longfellow

SWEET AND LOW

Sweet and low, sweet and low,
Wind of the western sea,
Low, low, breathe and blow,
Wind of the western sea!
Over the rolling waters go,
Come from the dropping moon and
blow,
Blow him again to me,
While my little one, while my pretty
one sleeps.

Sleep and rest, sleep and rest,
Father will come to thee soon;
Rest, rest, on mother's breast,
Father will come to thee soon;
Father will come to his babe in the
nest,
Silver sails all out of the west
Under the silver moon:
Sleep, my little one, sleep, my pretty
one, sleep.

Alfred Tennyson

BREAK, BREAK, BREAK

Break, break, break,
On thy cold gray stones, O Sea!
And I would that my tongue could
utter
The thoughts that arise in me.

O well for the fisherman's boy,
That he shouts with his sister at
play!
O well for the sailor lad,
That he sings in his boat on the bay!

And the stately ships go on
To their haven under the hill;
But O for the touch of a vanish'd
hand,
And the sound of a voice that is still.

Break, break, break,
At the foot of thy crags, O Sea!
But the tender grace of a day that is
dead
Will never come back to me.

Alfred Tennyson

BY BENDEMEER'S STREAM

There's a bower of roses by Bendemeer's stream,
And the nightingale sings round it
all the day long;
In the time of my childhood 'twas like
a sweet dream,
To sit in the roses and hear the
bird's song.

That bower and its music I never for-
get,
But oft when alone, in the bloom of
the year,
I think—is the nightingale singing
there yet?
Are the roses still bright by the calm
Bendemeer?

No, the roses soon wither'd that hung
o'er the wave,
But some blossoms were gather'd
while freshly they shone,

And a dew was distill'd from their
    flowers, that gave
    All the fragrance of summer, when
      summer was gone.

Thus memory draws from delight, ere
    it does,
    An essence that breathes of it many
      a year;
Thus bright to my soul, as 'twas then
    to my eyes,
    Is that bower on the banks of the
      calm Bendemeer!

Thomas Moore

FRIENDSHIP

My boat is on the shore,
    And my bark is on the sea;
But, before I go, Tom Moore,
    Here's a double health to thee!

Here's a sigh to those who love me,
    And a smile to those who hate;
And, whatever sky's above me,
    Here's a heart for every fate.

Though the ocean roar around me,
    Yet it still shall bear me on;
Though a desert should surround me,
    It hath springs that may be won.

Were't the last drop in the well,
    As I gasped upon the brink,
Ere my fainting spirit fell,
    'Tis to thee that I would drink.

With that water, as this wine,
    The libation I would pour
Should be, " Peace with thine and
    mine,
    And a health to thee, Tom
    Moore! "

George Gordon Byron

OFT IN THE STILLY NIGHT

Oft in the stilly night,
    Ere Slumber's chain has bound me,
Fond Memory brings the light
    Of other days around me;
      The smiles, the tears,
      Of boyhood's years,
    The words of love then spoken;
      The eyes that shone,
      Now dimmed and gone,
    The cheerful hearts now broken!
Thus, in the stilly night,
    Ere Slumber's chain has bound me,
Sad Memory brings the light
    Of other days around me.

When I remember all
    The friends, so linked together,
I've seen around me fall,
    Like leaves in wintry weather,
      I feel like one
      Who treads alone
    Some banquet-hall deserted,
      Whose lights are fled,
      Whose garlands dead,
    And all but he departed!
Thus, in the stilly night,
    Ere Slumber's chain has bound me,
Sad Memory brings the light
    Of other days around me.

Thomas Moore

IF

If you can keep your head when all
    about you
    Are losing theirs and blaming it on
    you;
If you can trust yourself when all men
    doubt you,
    But make allowance for their doubt-
    ing too:
If you can wait and not be tired by
    waiting,

Or, being lied about, don't deal in
lies,
Or being hated don't give way to hating,
    And yet don't look too good, nor
talk too wise;

If you can dream—and not make
dreams your master;
    If you can think—and not make
thoughts your aim,
If you can meet with Triumph and
Disaster
    And treat those two impostors just
the same;
If you can bear to hear the truth
you've spoken
    Twisted by knaves to make a trap
for fools,
Or watch the things you gave your life
to, broken,
    And stoop and build 'em up with
worn-out tools;

If you can make one heap of all your
winnings
    And risk it on one turn of pitch-and-
toss,

And lose, and start again at your be-
ginnings,
    And never breathe a word about
your loss:
If you can force your heart and nerve
and sinew
    To serve your turn long after they
are gone,
And so hold on when there is nothing
in you
    Except the Will which says to them:
"Hold on!"

If you can talk with crowds and keep
your virtue,
    Or walk with Kings—nor lose the
common touch,
If neither foes nor loving friends can
hurt you,
    If all men count with you, but none
too much:
If you can fill the unforgiving minute
    With sixty seconds' worth of dis-
tance run,
Yours is the Earth and everything
that's in it,
    And—which is more—you'll be a
Man, my son!

Rudyard Kipling

Index of Authors

Index of First Lines

Index of Titles